# Madame Tan's FREAKSHOW

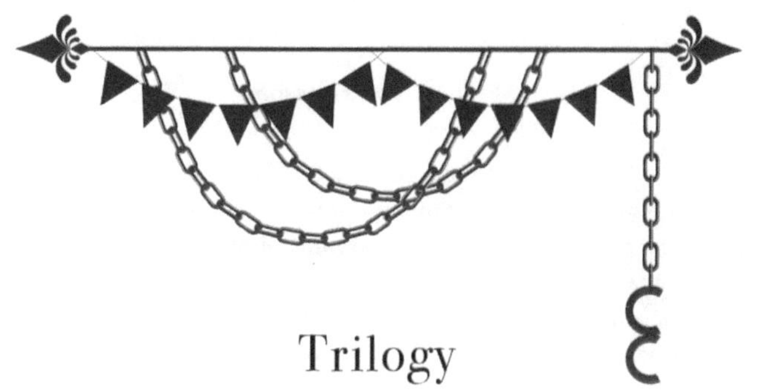

Trilogy

MARINA SIMCOE

THE RIVER OF MISTS

Madame Tan's Freakshow


Marina Simcoe
Marina.Simcoe@Yahoo.com
Facebook/Marina Simcoe Author


Editing by Cissell Ink
Cover image source depositphotos.com

Madame Tan's Freakshow contains graphic descriptions of intimacy and some violence. Intended for mature readers.

# Madame Tan's Freakshow

COMPLETE TRILOGY

MARINA SIMCOE

# Call of Water

Book 1

# Chapter One

IVY

"Voila!" Fleur gestured dramatically at the black door in a yellow stucco building with arched windows.

A glowing red sign above it read *Le Loup Solitaire*/ The Lone Wolf.

"*Cela me paraît petit*/ Seems small," I replied, also in French.

We were in Paris. Fleur was born and raised just outside of the city, and I'd come from Canada for a two-week visit.

According to the rules of our student exchange program back in grade school when in France, we had to speak French, when in Canada, English. Fleur was a university student now, and it'd been at least a couple of years since I earned my college diploma in Graphic Design, but the old habit remained. Whenever I visited her in Paris, we spoke French, and when she came to Toronto, we switched to English.

"Aren't we on the same street where *Moulin Rouge* is? The famous cabaret?" I turned around, the feeling of déjà vu rushing over me. "It's *Boulevard de Clichy?* Isn't it?"

Down the street, was the red façade of the famous burlesque venue.

Its lattice windmill sails stood out among the surrounding beige buildings.

Fleur shook her head, her short, black curls bouncing around her lovely face. "We've been to *Moulin Rouge* already. Twice. But not to *Le Loup Solitaire*. I've heard their show is phenomenal."

She placed her hand on the polished-brass handle and opened the black door under the sign.

*"Bienvenue chez Le Loup Solitaire,"* the hostess in a beige shimmering gown greeted us. "Welcome."

She led us to our table right in front of the stage.

"This is way too close," I half-whispered to Fleur, rubbing my hands down my black velvet shorts.

Unease prickled down my spine as we came closer to the stage, its lights now flooding us. I felt the idle stares of strangers at other tables on my back as Fleur and I took our seats.

"It's not like you're going to be on the stage yourself, scaredy cat," Fleur teased.

"It almost feels like I *am* sitting right on it." I shifted in my seat, casting furtive glances at people around us.

"No one cares about us here." She patted my hand on the table. "Calm down, silly."

I would be so much more comfortable sitting further back in the shadows. Fleur was right, though. We weren't the performers here. No one would pay us any attention once the show started.

Forcing my anxiety down, I glanced around.

The room was tastefully decorated in black and cream with just a touch of red here and there. The faint smell of dust and perfume hung in the air, bringing to mind an antique store.

A pretty brunette in a sparkly red dress approached our table.

"*Bonjour.*" She smiled. "I'm Jaqueline, your waitress. Is it your first visit to *Le Loup Solitaire?*"

"Yes." Fleur grinned back.

I just nodded.

"Ooh, I hope you'll like it here tonight. Zeph is the opening number of the show," Jaqueline added proudly, as if sharing a Chef's special with us.

I leaned across the table toward Fleur after Jaqueline had taken our orders and left. "Who is Zeph?"

"According to their website, Zeph is their in-house singer. He's been here since the place first opened. The house specialty?" She giggled with a shrug, excitement of anticipation bouncing in her dark-brown eyes. "He looked cute in the pictures. You'll see."

Soft music played as Jaqueline brought us drinks and then food. People kept streaming in. The tables had filled up fast. More people sat on the chairs along the back wall, and some even stood on each side of the entrance.

I twisted around, taking in the room. "This place is packed."

"I told you the show must be good." Fleur put a canape in her mouth.

The light in the aged-bronze chandeliers above us dimmed as the music volume increased. The shimmering black curtains opened, revealing a lone figure sitting on a barstool in the center of the stage, a silver microphone in his hand.

I expected an MC to greet the crowd and introduce the first act, but it turned out the singer on stage didn't need an introduction.

"Zeph!" people shouted his name.

Perched casually on the barstool, one foot on the floor, another placed on a higher rung, he lifted a hand in greeting and flashed a smile at the crowd.

Then, he sang.

His strong, hauntingly lyrical voice calmed the crowd. The soft stage light flowed over him in waves of magenta and aquamarine. His voice floated with it, the lyrics weaving a beautiful tale of yearning and love.

He sang "*Ne Me Quitte Pas/* Don't Leave Me" by Jacques Brel, one of the saddest love songs I'd ever heard. It was one of my mom's old favorites. Never before, however, had it had the same effect on me as in Zeph's rendition.

In the song, Zeph was pleading with the woman he loved not to leave him, to give their love another chance. His voice plunged lower, trailing off into a whisper only to surge back up with the music as he sang about all the glorious, wonderful things he would do for his lover if she only stayed with him.

He never made eye contact with me, but it felt as though he sang for me alone. Each note reached through to my very soul. My eyes welled with tears as he repeated the title of the song as the refrain, begging over and over, *"Ne Me Quitte Pas/* Don't leave me..."

My heart twisted with longing for something I couldn't name. A deep, beautiful feeling flooded me, warming me from the inside. I wanted someone to care about me as much as Zeph made me believe he cared about the woman in the song. I wanted to be her, for him to dress me in the gold of light and the pearls of raindrops. I longed to need someone so badly that I, too, had the power to create a kingdom for them and crown them to rule it.

The intensity of longing grew with every word, ebbing and swelling along with the music and the waves of the stage lights.

The crowd seemed to disappear. The awkward feeling from being in a room full of people was gone.

The desire for something grand and wonderful—an amazing adventure or an out-of-this-world love—throbbed in my chest. It called me to move, to strive, to yearn...

As long as he continued to sing, I believed nothing was impossible.

The last note from Zeph's lips faded into the music as the song ended.

The room erupted into applause, brutally yanking me back into reality and shredding the magic he'd created. The elated feeling vanished, and the void it left behind was unbearable. It crushed my chest, making my head spin.

The air grew too thick for me to draw another breath.

I had to get out of there. Away from the singer who teased and tormented people with magical things no one in this world could have.

A side door opened, letting in a waitress with a tray of dishes with food.

"I'll be right back," I whispered to Fleur.

Ignoring her questioning look, I rushed to the door.

"May I help you?" the waitress asked.

"I need to get outside..."

"The main exit is that way." She smiled, gesturing in the direction I had come from.

"That would be too far," I croaked.

She gave me a concerned glance. Blood rushing from my face, I must be looking as if I was about to get sick. "Are you okay?"

"Just need some fresh air," I begged.

Finally, she tipped her head behind her shoulder. "The back entrance is that way."

"Thank you." I hurried down the corridor toward a metal door.

# Chapter Two

IVY

Outside, I drew in the warm summer air. Propping my hands on my thighs, I leaned forward, staring at the toes of my sparkly shoes. A beautiful mix of ache and sweetness swelled in my chest—an echo of what Zeph's singing had made me feel.

I desperately tried to hold on to the magical feeling, but it faded with every passing second, and I hated for it to disappear completely.

"Excuse me," a male voice, rough and deep, sounded from the left of me.

A tall man was leaning against the wall there. He was dressed in a gray, well-made suit, his dark hair neatly cut and styled.

A thin stream of shimmering smoke curled from the end of the long, dark cigarette in his hand.

"Are you going to vomit?" he asked calmly, staring at me with a pair of silvery-gray eyes. "If you do, could you please do it farther away from the door? Maybe move under that tree over there?"

Mortification set my face on fire with a blush.

With another deep breath, I straightened up. "I'm not going to throw up."

This must be one of the most awkward conversations I'd ever had with a stranger. Of course he had to be a young, handsome man, too.

"I'm fine," I said, smoothing my hands down my shorts. "Just needed some air."

He nodded, a flash of understanding crossing his expression. "Is Zeph on stage?"

"Zeph?" I rubbed my face. "Yes. He is...*was* on stage. He's just finished the song."

"His singing tends to have an effect on people." The man took a drag of his cigarette. "It will pass," he added with confidence.

But I didn't want it to pass...

The smoke from his cigarette wafted my way. Fragrant and pleasant, it had an earthy, flowery scent, like moss and lavender, with a hint of sweetness. Oddly, it had no smell of tobacco or of the actual smoke.

"Does *he* know about the 'effect?'" I asked.

"Zeph? Of course he does."

"So, he does it on purpose then?" I blurted out, then bit my tongue, realizing how stupid my question sounded—as if Zeph should be held responsible for what his voice did to me.

The stranger silently regarded me for a moment, making me feel even more foolish.

"Never mind," I mumbled, turning to go back inside.

The door opened before I touched it, letting a person out—Zeph.

"Lero—" he said to the smoking man then cut himself short, spotting me. "I beg your pardon. I didn't realize you had company."

When speaking, his voice sounded pleasant, although not as devastatingly enthralling as when he was singing. I realized I could focus on other things while he spoke, things I had not noticed at all while he was singing.

Like that he was wearing a dark-blue, well-tailored suit, but no tie —the collar of his white shirt open. His hair was so light, it seemed almost white, with a beautiful silvery sheen to it. Cropped short on the sides, it was longer on top, with a few strands falling over his forehead.

His eyes were the most amazing shade of blue—cerulean—like the sea around the beaches in the Caribbean.

Realizing I'd been staring at him for too long, I dropped my gaze. "I was about to leave."

He gave me a close look. "Must you?" He tilted his head in a way I found extremely appealing.

I faltered under his unexpected attention.

"Well, I... My friend..."

He smiled. "I like your hair."

I touched my wavy, shoulder-length tresses, dyed pink and blue.

"Um..." Faced with a compliment, all my words—French or English—deserted me. "Thanks," I finally managed.

"Sea colors."

"See...what?"

"Your hair reminds me of the sunrise in the ocean," he explained. "When the rising sun shines through the water, sometimes it looks just like that under the surface—aquamarine and magenta."

That was romantic. Poetic even. Only how did he know what sunrise looked like from underwater in the ocean?

His eyes twinkled with interest. Was he flirting with me?

Honestly, I couldn't tell. And that wasn't Zeph's fault. As far as interactions with the opposite sex went, I was hopeless.

Since my college graduation, I'd been spending a lot of time alone. Being a graphic designer allowed me to work from home, which nurtured my inner introvert. By now, I'd accumulated a respectable number of clients by creating all kinds of products for them—from company logos, to business cards, to promotional fliers, to book covers. But I never actually had to meet any of my clients face to face.

I loved my work. As a result, however, my already impaired social skills had severely atrophied from the lack of use.

Zeph's expression remained open and friendly, however. I sensed no judgment or mockery from him.

Tension drained from my shoulders. I even ventured a smile in reply. "I love bright colors."

He took in my outfit—a hot-pink off-the-shoulder top, black velvet shorts, violet fishnet stockings, and silver ballet flats.

"I see you do." He grinned.

His down-to-earth manner put me at ease.

"Who was the woman you were singing about?" I blurted out, without thinking, then cringed inside a moment later. This was too personal. I barely met him. Whatever happened to my manners?

"The woman? Are you talking about the song?" He blinked, looking confused. "The lyrics aren't mine."

I should apologize, turn around, and leave.

But I had to know.

"The words may be not yours," I said, "but the passion with which you sing is. It couldn't be faked. It has to be *lived*. There must be a magical love story behind it."

Lero snorted, and Zeph arched an eyebrow, turning his way.

"Lero, Ivan is looking for you, you know? Jaqueline accidentally broke the last bottle of *Guillon*, and Ivan wants to know what to do about it. You should go inside."

"Why did we only have one bottle?" Lero growled. "Tell him to send Jaqueline to the store."

"Why don't you go tell him that yourself?" Zeph opened the door wide. "You're the boss, after all."

Lero shook his head, putting out his cigarette. He paused on his way inside, giving me a stare.

"It was nice meeting you..." He let the end of the sentence hang in the air like a prompt.

"Ivy," I introduced myself. "My name is Ivy. Nice to meet you."

"You should go in with me," he said. "You're missing the show."

"Um..." I glanced at Zeph.

He hadn't answered my question. But even without that, it didn't feel like our conversation was over.

Zeph inserted himself between Lero and me. "She'll be back in a minute."

Lero lingered, obviously reluctant to leave me along with Zeph.

"Go ahead," Zeph nudged. "The customers can't get drunk without *Guillon*, can they?"

"Zeph." Lero pinned him with a stare, a warning ringing in his deep voice.

"I know, I know." Zeph rolled his eyes, dropping his voice down a notch. "I'll be careful. Okay?"

With one last glance my way, Lero went inside, closing the door behind him.

"Careful?" I repeated. "Is he worried I'll hurt you or something?"

Zeph laughed, tossing his head back. His laughter proved as enjoyable as his singing, though more uplifting than heart-wrecking. I smiled in response.

"No." He shook his head. "Lero just generally worries a lot."

"Is he the manager here?" I remembered Zeph calling the other man the boss.

"He's the owner." Zeph ran a hand through his hair. "Listen, can I get you a drink? We're out of *Guillon* for now. But there's plenty of Champagne." He touched the door handle.

"Are you going to sing again?"

"Not until later. Come." In a chivalrous gesture, he offered me his arm.

Inside, Zeph paused to exchange a few phrases with a stocky man who spoke French with a slight Eastern European accent—Ivan, I assumed.

Fleur had been joined by a handsome dark-haired man, who now occupied my seat. The two appeared to be engaged in a lively conversation. She lifted her eyes for a moment, meeting mine, and gave me a smile and a wave of a hand before turning back to her companion.

On the stage, a beautiful dark-skinned woman in a golden gown sang in a strong, vibrant voice while a group of male dancers performed a dynamic choreography around her. Several pairs twirled on the dance floor.

Zeph led me to the bar where he got us two flutes of *Moët & Chandon*.

"Where are you from Ivy?" He pronounced my name slowly, as if tasting it with a sip of his Champagne. "Your French is very good, by the way."

"Thanks. I'm from Canada."

Taking another sip, he peered at me over the rim of his glass.

"Do you live in Paris now or just visiting?" His sunny expression dimmed as he waited for me to reply.

"Visiting. I have a friend in the city. She is, um..." I searched the room for Fleur again. She was no longer at our table. "There." I spotted her on the dance floor with the same man who was talking to her earlier.

"How long are you staying here for?"

"Eight more days."

"Good." My answer seemed to please him. As if released from restraints, his smile beamed bright again.

The Champagne bubbled up to my brain, filling me with sunny effervescence.

I leaned toward Zeph. "You never answered my question."

"About love?" He grinned.

"Yes. Can you tell me about the woman who inspired you to sing like that? Please?"

No one could sing the way he did without having experienced the torment of love and loss. There must be a magnificent love story there, and I yearned to hear it. He had invaded my very soul with his song. It was only fair for me to get a glimpse into his, too.

"Can I tell you a secret, Ivy?" He threw a glance over his shoulder, as if making sure that no one else was listening.

"Um, sure."

"I've never been in love," he said.

"Never?" I breathed out in disbelief.

He smiled unapologetically. "Not even close."

Neither had I. Once, I almost believed I had fallen in love with a guy I dated in college, but it turned out it was just friendship and possibly the sense of camaraderie. The two of us had been the last remaining virgins in our circle of friends, which felt like the last in the whole of Universe. Whatever feelings we'd had for each other quickly faded after an awkward night we spent together, having decided to get rid of our mutual virginity.

But Zeph...

"How can you possibly sing like that, then? Emotions like that... They are too real."

"So, you like my singing?" he asked with a smug expression.

Who wouldn't?

"It's incredible," I confessed. The echo of longing rippled through my chest.

His expression turned thoughtful, the smile retreating to the corners of his mouth.

"I'm not saying it's all an act, Ivy. I love singing. When I'm on stage, it's like the music radiates through me, and I merge with it in a song." His eyebrows moved together, the focus in his eyes sharpened as he explained, "So, I guess, even as the woman is not real, the love is still there. My love for music and the song, that is."

I let his words sink in. It took a true master to convey love without having experienced it.

"Your voice is simply magical, Zeph," I said, in awe of his talent.

"Magic!" He laughed—a deep, cheerful sound. "There you go. Magic explains it all."

With the new act on stage, the music turned slow.

Zeph leaned to my ear.

"Shall we dance?" His warm breath puffed softly against my neck, sending tingles down my skin.

"Oh, no. I don't dance." I shook my head energetically. "I can't..."

"I'll teach you." He took my hand, then maneuvered us between the tables to the dance floor.

"I...I don't believe I'm teachable." I huffed a laugh, nervously glancing around. It felt as if everyone was staring at me right now, judging, ready to laugh.

People waved and smiled at Zeph. He returned their greetings, exchanging a handshake or a few words here and there. I kept half-a-step behind him, hiding from their attention.

"There is nothing to it," he assured me, stopping in the middle of the dance floor.

A spotlight immediately zoomed in on him, illuminating me too. I blinked, blinded by it. The walls seemed to be closing in on me, everyone's attention pressing down on my chest, making it harder to breathe.

"I can't..." I croaked. "It's too much."

"Too much of what?" he asked with confusion.

Zeph obviously had no problem bein the center of attention. He thrived in the spotlight.

How was I supposed to explain this to him? He wouldn't understand.

"Too close to..." I waved my hand around. "Everyone?"

*"Too close?"*

He gave me a penetrating stare. Feeling both hot and cold at once, I had no idea whether I looked pale or flushed. He seemed to notice my distress nevertheless and gestured to the side somewhere. The spotlight slid away from us.

"Is this better?" He asked, leading me to a darker corner of the dance floor and to the fringes of the crowd.

"Yes." I exhaled, feeling like a complete idiot. "Sorry... I'm not good at handling public attention." I huffed a nervous laugh, half-expecting him to leave any minute now. "It's, um, stage fright?"

"Stage fright? I don't know what that is." He chuckled.

"I bet you don't." I giggled, with more mirth than nerves this time.

He placed my hand on his shoulder. Circling my waist with his arm, he leaned in. "Is *this* too close?"

The scent of his cologne, warmed by his body heat, made me a little lightheaded.

"No." My heart thundered wildly in my chest, but I didn't want him to move away from me. "This is just right."

"Good."

A brilliant grin spread on his face. Its radiance seemed to expand like an explosion, sweeping everyone in his vicinity into smiling, too. Of course, I couldn't resist grinning back.

He took my other hand in his. "Now just listen to the music and follow me."

I felt weak in my knees but found it impossible to disobey, swept up by his energy like a strong current.

"Listen carefully," he instructed. "Every second beat, we shift weight..." He leaned slightly side to side, directing me with his hand on my waist.

I followed the movement of his body, side to side, until I no longer had to think about it. After a few moments, it felt as if Zeph, me, and the music—all became one, moving in sync.

"Okay," I said tentatively. "This is just swaying to the music. I can do it."

"Well then. If you have mastered the 'swaying' part, let's add some steps, shall we?" He led me through a few basic steps, probably a waltz if I had to guess.

I watched his feet deftly move along the dance floor and tried to match his steps. The trick was not to plant my ballet flats on top of his polished dress shoes.

"Eyes on me," Zeph commanded. Letting go of my hand for a moment, he lifted my head with his finger under my chin. My eyes met his. "Just like that. Let your feet do the work without your close supervision."

"I don't think I can trust them that much," I laughed.

"Just try."

Miraculously, my feet did end up figuring it out all on their own, with only minor initial tripping over themselves. Which was a good thing, because staring into Zeph's eyes was more enjoyable than watching his feet.

Zeph's long, thick eyelashes were a rich chocolate-brown, considerably darker than his white-blond hair. The combination was unusual but extremely appealing. His eyes seemed to always hide a smile, just like his mouth. The sunny twinkle bounced in his gaze, brightening his entire face.

Staring into his eyes mesmerized me. The wave of their shimmering blue swept me along, carrying me off with the music into the dance.

I blinked, dropping my gaze down to break the spell and catch my breath.

"Up," he commanded, softly but firmly. "Eye contact is part of the dance. A very important part too."

Tentatively, I cast a glance at him from under my eyelashes. "What if I trip and fall?"

"I'll catch you." His voice dipped with the promise, the low vibrating note brushing pleasurably along the bare skin of my arms. "But you won't trip. You're doing great."

I'd never had a chance to learn to dance before. Having Zeph for a partner should've been intimidating. He moved through the music like a fish in water, as if he'd been born to dance. At the same time, somehow, he had managed to put me at ease.

"You're a great student. And I'm an excellent teacher." He flexed his arm around my waist, pulling me closer. "We make a perfect pair."

"Do we now?" I teased, though the thought of us as a pair, even if just a dance pair, pleasantly warmed my heart.

"Are you in a hurry to get to bed after the show tonight?" he asked suddenly, his eyes searching mine.

The "bed" would be my sleeping bag on the floor of Fleur's room in the apartment she shared with two other girls. All of that seemed so far from *Le Loup Solitaire* right now, as if in another dimension.

"I wasn't thinking about that yet."

"Good." He glanced back at the stage where a new act had just begun. "I'll have to go back on stage soon. But can we talk more once I'm done? Maybe I'll take you on a small adventure tonight."

"Adventure?"

"Yes. Isn't that what people all over the world come to Paris for?"

Well, I came to visit a friend, but tonight, it could be all about an adventure with Zeph. Why not?

Maybe it should concern me how easily he got me to agree to everything. But being with Zeph made me feel alive, and I simply wanted more of that feeling.

"What kind of adventure?" I asked.

"Oh, nothing crazy." The playful smile returned to his handsome face. "Maybe we'll get some ice cream?"

I laughed. "Sounds like a wild adventure, indeed."

"Right." He grinned. "I'm taking you on a wild ice-cream-eating trip."

His enthusiasm was just as contagious as his smile. It was impossible to say no to those eyes. Even if I wanted to. But I didn't.

"I'd love that," I agreed once again.

# Chapter Three

IVY

"Is this your first time in Paris?" Zeph asked as we walked along *Boulevard de Clichy*.

He kept the pace slow, and I liked the leisurely stroll. Fleur had told me not to hurry back to her place when she left *Le Loup Solitaire* on the arm of the dark-haired man, who didn't leave her side all evening. I assured her I would take my time, and I was thoroughly enjoying every minute of it.

"No. I've been here a few times before," I replied. "I used to come to France every year, under the language exchange program."

Fleur's family lived in Bourges, south from here. They had taken me to Paris several times over the years. Since Fleur started university, she moved to the city, and I stayed with her whenever I visited.

I didn't get into the details, though. Surely, my mundane, boring life wouldn't be of much interest to someone who had a voice of an angel and sang on stage at a cabaret.

"You must have seen all the touristy things by now, then?" he asked.

I nodded. "Pretty much. I've been exploring this city left, right, and center."

"How about *up* and *down* then?" He tilted his head, gazing at me with those mesmerizing eyes of his.

"Um..." It wasn't easy to focus with his attention directed at me this closely. "What exactly do you mean?"

"Come." He tugged me by my hand to a small door leading to a basement, around the corner off *Boulevard de Clichy*.

"What's here?"

"A wine bar, though not what you may expect. They don't serve Champagne here. Instead, they have sparkling wine infused with strawberries. Lero would call it 'in poor taste'. He doesn't allow such cheesy stuff in his classy establishment. But I think it tastes delicious."

The strawberry-infused sparkling wine indeed was delicious.

"I told you." Zeph beamed at me when I confessed how much I liked it.

"Lero is missing out." I giggled, the effervescence of the fragrant bubbles seemed to have risen from my glass to my brain.

"Lero is an old snob." Zeph huffed a laugh. "He's extremely old-fashioned. To him, things only have value if they have been properly aged. Wine, cheese, liquor, music... Even clothes."

"Well, his clothes seem fashionable." Lero's smart three-piece suit came to mind. Visually, he didn't appear to be much older than Zeph. But there were people born with old souls, weren't there?

"He prefers a classic cut to his clothes." Zeph shrugged. "Which doesn't change much over time."

He had left his own suit jacket back at *Le Loup Solitaire*. The night was too warm for it, anyway.

"Don't get me wrong, I love Lero." Zeph raked his hand through his silky white hair, and I wondered what it would feel like between my fingers if I did the same. "He just makes himself such an easy target for jokes by being an insufferable snob about everything. Just try to call any sparkling wine 'champagne' in his presence, you'll see the face he makes."

"How long have you been working for him?"

"Since I was old enough to sing in a cabaret."

"Are you friends?" The relationship between these two seemed to be closer than that of an employee and a boss.

"More than friends. We're family. Lero raised me since I was six."

"Six?" Surely, I didn't hear him right.

Lero didn't seem to be older than thirty-two or thirty-three. With Zeph being probably in his mid-to-late twenties, Lero couldn't have raised him if he most likely was still a child himself when Zeph was six.

"Isn't he about your age?"

"He's older," Zeph replied vaguely, leaving it at that.

Well, I only ever saw Lero at night, in a poorly lit courtyard. I might've guessed his age incorrectly.

"Where are your parents?" I asked Zeph.

"Dead," he replied, with a somber shadow quickly passing through his expression. "I don't remember them at all."

"What happened? Do you know how they died?"

"There was an accident, but I don't know any details," was all he said, and it did not feel right to ask more after that. "How about *your* parents?" He changed the subject.

"Mine? Oh, they're both alive and well. Both are happily married, although no longer to each other." I smiled, making light out of what was a rather heavy situation for me when I was younger. I spent most of my childhood feeling guilty for spending time with either one of them while they battled each other for a larger share of custody of me. Then, when I was old enough to spend my time any way I pleased, they already had their new families, and I often felt like I was, if not exactly *unwanted* then at least not *missed,* if I didn't show up at family functions and such. "They divorced when I was eight, remarried within a couple of years of each other, and started their new families. They're happy."

I took another sip of my strawberry "Champagne."

"How about you?" he asked. "Are *you* happy, Ivy?"

"Me? Sure I am. I work as a graphic designer. It's always been my dream job."

My mother didn't consider design a serious occupation, more like a hobby. I'd had a long fight with her over my decision to study it in college. She wanted me to become a lawyer, like my stepfather, or an accountant, like herself.

"Anyway," I continued with an awkward one-shouldered shrug. "I've graduated, started my own business, and I'm doing well enough to afford the rent of a basement apartment in Toronto and a trip to Paris every second year." I cheerfully raised my glass to toast to my achievements. "I've got it all."

"I'll drink to that!" Zeph clinked his glass with mine.

It might be the effects of the sparkling wine. Or maybe the heat of the summer night. Or, most likely, Zeph being right next to me, his arm wrapped around my waist, the warmth of his body seeping into me through the thin material of his shirt. But everything inside me floated with happiness as we strolled down a lit street after leaving the wine bar. There was no other place I would rather be at that moment than right there with him.

Zeph steered me into a side street, under an arch between two buildings.

"Shortcut," he replied with a wink to my questioning gaze.

It occurred to me that I had no idea where we were supposed to be going at all.

"A shortcut to where?" I asked.

"You'll see." He gave me a teasing smile. "I promised to take you up and down, didn't I? The wine bar was down, now I'll have to take you—"

He cut himself short. The smile, I was beginning to adore, dimmed as he came to a halt in a dark narrow court between four buildings.

The space appeared deserted. Then I spotted large, tall figures moving towards us from the surrounding shadows.

"Zeph?" I half-whispered, sensing his body tense.

Gently nudging me behind him, he tugged up his sleeves, exposing the long silvery scars on the back of his forearms.

One of the large shapes stepped out of the shadows, emerging as a massive man. He was completely bald with a large, intricate tattoo circling his neck and running down his right arm. The tattoo flashed with streaks of red. They twinkled along the lines of his body art, dove under the short sleeve of his black t-shirt, then skimmed around his neck before disappearing completely.

That must be a trick of the light from the street behind us. I blinked, perplexed and worried at the sight of this silent, ominous shape rising in front of us.

"On another thought, let's forget about the shortcut." Zeph took my arm, stepping back, away from the menacing stranger. "The long way may be more enjoyable tonight."

Shielding me from the scary figures in the courtyard, Zeph quickly retreated into the well-lit street.

"Who were those guys?" I asked when we were back in the relative safety of lights and people once again.

Leading me down the street, Zeph glanced over his shoulder a few times.

"I'm not sure." He tugged his sleeves down again, concealing the pale lines on his arms. "Don't worry. They're gone. All is good." His voice lifted, and he hugged my waist again. "We're going up, remember?"

No one seemed to be following us from the courtyard, and I slowly allowed my body to relax against his again. Since Zeph had dismissed tonight's incident, I decided to do the same.

A block down the street, he maneuvered me between the pedestrians to another basement door. This one was painted with red, white, and blue stripes.

"This is *down*. Not *up*," I pointed out, as we descended the concrete steps. "Down is the opposite of up, Zeph." I giggled, my mood lifting again, along with his.

"Sometimes you need to go down before you can go up." He opened the door to a small ice cream parlor. "What flavor is your favorite?"

Choosing just one flavor of ice cream proved to be impossible. Most of the space was taken up by a long counter flanked by two tall refrigerated display cases, with dozens of different flavors and thousands of possible combinations.

After scouring through them all for a few minutes and tasting nearly half of them, I finally asked for a double scoop of pistachio and lemon ice cream layered with mango sorbet.

"One scoop of strawberry ice cream, please," Zeph ordered, after I'd gotten my combination of flavors tastefully arranged in a tall glass, topped with whipped cream and sprinkled with shredded coconut.

"That's it?" I teased. "Just the good old plain strawberry?"

Zeph took the small waffle cone from the man behind the counter. "Is strawberry not adventurous enough for you?"

"Only *one* scoop? How is that nearly enough?" I shook my head.

"To be honest, I'm counting on stealing a lick or two of yours." Lifting an eyebrow, he stalked my way, pretending to go after my ice cream.

"No way!" I dashed for the door. "I'm not sharing. There are no friends in ice cream."

He caught me by my elbow.

"This way." He opened the door, next to the one we came in. "We need to go up, now. Remember?" He started to ascend the narrow staircase behind the door. "Way, way up."

Holding my ice cream in one hand, I placed the other on the metal railing, following him up, one flight of stairs after another, and another, and another...

After a while, the concrete steps were replaced by a narrower set of wooden ones, then they turned into a metal, spiral staircase.

"Does it ever end?" I panted from the effort of climbing up for what felt like forever.

"Eventually," Zeph replied cheerfully, taking another bite of his ice cream. "Almost there. Trust me, the view is worth it."

I stomped up a few more steps, licking my ice cream above the edge of the glass as it started to melt.

"*Voila!*" Zeph opened the door at the very top of the winding staircase.

A warm summer breeze blew in, playing with my hair, as I followed Zeph onto a tiny outdoor patio.

"The Eiffel Tower is on the other side of the rooftops," he explained. "But I like the view on this side probably even more. It's less tired, you know."

"It's beautiful," I agreed.

The rows of rooftops ascended the hill to the *Sacré-Cœur Basilica*. Backlit by bright lights, its building stood out sharply against the night sky.

Zeph swept his arm in front of us. "Sound travels well over all of this."

"You sing from here?"

"Not as often as I'd like." He laughed. "And definitely not as loud as I would want to. You may be surprised, but there are some people in this world who have no appreciation for music." He shrugged, finishing his ice cream in a few more bites, then stepped closer to the metal railing, facing the city.

His chest rose with a deep breath before he unexpectedly belted out a line of Alfredo from *La Traviata* by Verdi, *"Libiamo, libiamo ne'lieti calici—"*

Immediately, objections came in French and English from quite a few directions.

*"Tais-toi!"*

"Shut the fuck up!"

*"Ta gueule!"*

"See?" He spread his arms wide, grinning at me. "There are no music lovers in this building."

I hid a chuckle behind my hand. "You know, the time of the night might be severely impairing their appreciation of your talent right now."

Something about Zeph singing his heart out from a Parisian rooftop seemed exceptionally hilarious to me. Personally, though, he could sing anything to me anytime. I'd listen to him day and night.

"You have an amazing voice, Zeph. I'm no expert, but your range is impressive. I mean, that was just one line, but opera singing is not an easy feat."

"According to Lero, opera is the most acceptable way of singing. Period."

"Lero? But he owns a cabaret, not an opera theater." I'd heard a wide variety of music performed at *Le Loup Solitaire* that night.

"That is probably the only reason why he suffers through my performing in other music genres. Cabaret crowds love variety."

"What genres do *you* prefer?"

"Honestly? All of them. Why limit yourself? People need all kinds of music. I like to sing what I feel like, depending on the mood I'm in."

"Really?" I narrowed my eyes suspiciously. Surely, someone who could execute an opera aria this well would have a word or two to say about popular music. "Any genre? Rap, techno, pop, Latin? Rock?"

"They all can be fun," Zeph insisted. "All have their purpose."

Tousling his hair in a sexy way, he yanked the collar of his shirt up. With a smoldering look at me, he suddenly broke into the male part of "*Señorita*." The sizzling hot lyrics of that song, combined with the sexy swagger he moved with to me and the sultry note he slipped into his voice, made my breath hitch.

Swallowing a mouthful of ice cream, I parted my lips, suddenly short on oxygen when he came to me and wrapped his arm around my waist.

*"Ooh, la, la..."* I mouthed the end of the last line along with him.

His eyes were a deep turquoise in the night, and I was losing myself in them.

The song lyrics died on his lips as he drew me closer, his gaze sliding down my face. Breathless, I watched his tongue dart out to lick his bottom lip. The sudden desire to taste it burned in my chest.

"Is this *too close*?" he murmured, his lips hovering a hair's breadth away from mine.

"Not close enough," I whispered.

The next moment, his mouth was on mine, tasting, taking, claiming. The strawberry flavor mixed with something hot and spicy—Zeph's taste—an intoxicating combination. I couldn't get enough of it, greedily kissing him back.

Haze swirled through my mind, as if a strong current was dragging me under. But I was unable and unwilling to fight it, hopelessly lost to Zeph's kiss.

Moving my hand with the ice cream out of the way, I pressed my chest to his then slid my free hand up into his hair. The strands caressed between my fingers, soft and silky. The sensation was even better than I'd anticipated.

The glass tilted in my weakened fingers, and I nearly dropped the ice cream. With a noise of surprise against his mouth, I broke the kiss, grabbing the glass firmer. Thankfully, the ice cream was still there.

Zeph didn't release me from his arms, didn't even allow any space between us. His chest rising and falling against mine, I felt his heart thunder under his shirt.

"Do you need my help with this?" he asked, pointing with his chin to the glass with my dessert.

"Yes, please."

"What about that 'no friends in ice cream' statement?" he teased.

"I admit I have overestimated my ice cream eating capacity." Bringing the glass between us, I took a spoonful of my half-melted dessert and fed it to Zeph since both of his arms remained wrapped around my waist.

"Wow." He blinked after tasting it. "This is some crazy combination of flavors."

"Good crazy or bad crazy?"

He tilted his head, considering my question.

"Not sure. I need another taste to decide."

I fed him another spoonful then another, realizing that everything about tonight was kind of crazy. In a good way. In an exceptionally crazy good way.

Our adventure didn't turn out to be wild. By most standards, it could hardly be called an adventure at all. We danced, we went out for drinks, and we ate ice cream—all the things that millions of people our age did on a daily basis.

The craziness, the beautiful wild excitement I felt, from that first dance with him to the very last bit of the ice cream, came from the man I was with.

Being with Zeph was both intense and comfortable. The feelings he stirred inside me flapped like a bunch of disoriented butterflies on steroids in my stomach. Yet I felt no need to pretend to be someone I was not, which was new and unusual for me in the company of a man, or any new person for that matter.

"It was delicious," Zeph murmured after I had fed him the very last spoonful of my ice cream.

"Mhm, it was," I hummed in agreement, licking the spoon after him.

"I don't want this to end," he said. "Spend the rest of the night with me, Ivy."

I dropped the spoon into the glass, and it landed with a loud clank.

"What do you mean?" A new thrill surged through me. I wasn't ready for this night to end, either.

Zeph took the glass from me, setting it on the base of the flower pot by the railing, then slid his hand up my back, cupping my nape, his thumb stroking the side of my neck.

"I want to take you home." His voice rasped, his arms flexing tighter around me. Dark heat flashed in his eyes, letting me know exactly what he had in mind for the rest of the night with me.

Warmth rushed from his hand on my neck down through my chest and...lower.

Giving in to him, I relaxed my spine, and he immediately drew me into his chest. I buried my face in the opening of his shirt, nuzzling the side of his neck and inhaling his scent. Clean, fresh, with a bit of saltiness, like the ocean spray, still with a hint of strawberry sweetness on his breath, he smelled so good.

He *was* good...

"I'll give you my address," he said, raking his fingers through my hair. "Text your friend, tell her where you're going."

...and so very responsible.

# Chapter Four

IVY

"Where do you live?" I asked Zeph.

After finally releasing me from his arms, he'd given me his address, and I'd texted Fleur, but I couldn't tell from the street number alone where his place was in relation to the rooftop patio where we were.

"Just three buildings that way." He gestured left. "On the very top floor."

"So, we'll need to get down then go back up again?" I braced myself for the long climb of the endless stairs.

"Or we could take the shortcut." Zeph tipped his chin up. "The rooftops."

"Are you serious?"

He glanced down at my shoes. "Well, you're not wearing high heels, it should work."

Leaping over the side railing, he landed with both feet on the pitched metal roof next door. Thankfully, the buildings in this part of the city stood flush with each other, with no gaps between them.

"Come." He stretched his arm over the railing to me. "We can see the Eiffel Tower from the ridge of the next roof."

"Is that how high we're going? All the way to the ridge?" I clarified, intrigued but not without some trepidation.

He beamed at me. "I promised you the view."

Taking his hand, I climbed over the railing. Leaning into the pitch of the roof, we climbed up to the ridge. It wasn't as scary as it sounded. There was even a metal railing running along it, although only on one side. Holding on to it, I kept up with Zeph's pace.

He stopped in the middle of the ridge. "How do you like this?"

From this height, the view opened all the way to the horizon. The bright lights of the Eiffel Tower stood out in the sea of the rooftops, along with the rectangular shape of *Arc de Triomphe* and *Sacré-Cœur Basilica* on the other side.

I gasped in amazement. "You can see the entire city from here."

"Yes. The three-hundred-sixty-degree view. Can't be any better."

"And you live up here." I smiled, meeting his eyes once again. "Lucky you."

"Definitely lucky." He stared at me for a moment before getting us back on our way.

At the end of the roof, Zeph jumped onto a built-in patio of the next building.

"The one after this is mine," he explained, gesturing ahead.

"The next one?" I asked as we passed by the dark windows facing the patio. "Then who lives *here*?"

"People." He shrugged, carelessly.

"Do you know them?"

"Nope. We've never met."

"But they don't mind you walking through their property like this?"

"So far, no one's complained." He climbed over the railing onto the ledge of the next building then helped me do the same.

"Well, this is home." Zeph lifted open the frame of a large bay window, positioned right under the roof. "Come in."

I followed him through the window, then stepped around a huge oval bathtub inside.

"Is this your bathroom?"

"No." He turned on the water in the tub then flicked on the light. It illuminated a spacious studio apartment, tastefully decorated in light gray and breezy blue.

A couch stood in the middle with a TV set mounted on the wall in front of it. A few tall bookshelves lined the walls. Partially hidden behind a painted-silk screen, a large bed stood to the side.

"You have a bathtub in your living space," I stated, a bit confused but not overly surprised. With much of the architecture in this city being there for centuries, some of the more modern elements had often been added in unconventional ways over time.

"Yes," he replied simply, as if used to being asked this question, then headed to the kitchenette in a niche to the left. "Are you hungry? I can make you something to eat."

"You can cook?"

"Not as great as Lero, but I can come up with something quick." He opened the small fridge under the kitchen counter.

"No, thank you." I shook my head. "After that ice cream, I don't think I'll get hungry any time soon."

"A glass of Champagne, then?" He took a bottle from the fridge and a couple of champagne flutes from the cabinet above it. "Sorry, this one hasn't been anywhere near strawberries." He glanced at the label. "Just a good, old *Moët*."

"Thank you." I accepted the glass from him.

His fingers brushed mine when he handed me the flute. Anticipation fizzed through me like the bubbles in the glass. It came with a tendril of trepidation.

Without exactly putting it into words, Zeph had made it clear what he wanted from me tonight. I believed I wanted it too. Only...

The one time I'd been with a man hadn't left me with a great opinion about sex. I preferred my own hand to anything my one and only sex partner to date had had to offer.

I set my glass on the window sill, avoiding Zeph's eyes. "I've never had a one-night stand before."

It was best to have it all in the open, wasn't it? If he expected someone skilled and experienced...

Putting his glass next to mine, he wrapped his arms around me. "It doesn't have to be a one-night stand."

I exhaled a short laugh. "I don't have enough time in the city for it to be anything much more than that."

"It doesn't need to be more." He trailed his lips up the side of my neck.

I breathed deeply. His warm scent calmed my nerves. When he was this close, there simply was no place for worries.

"It can be anything you want," he said. "How about a sleepover?"

"A sleepover?" I smiled.

"Mhm," he hummed against my lips. "I'll braid your hair. You'll tell me a scary story."

"That's it?"

He hovered his mouth over mine, his warm breath tickling my skin. "You'll wear my pajamas. We'll spoon. Nothing more."

Oh, I definitely wanted more than that with him.

"Not even a kiss?"

A smile curved his lips. "Only if you want it."

"I do," I confessed.

He looked at me from under the strands of his silvery white hair. His eyes darkened, changing from the serene blue to a stormy turquoise. "So be it."

He took my mouth in a kiss, and I melted into his embrace.

What was it about Zeph that made him so irresistible to me?

Maybe it was that crooked grin of his—teasing, warm, and playful all at once? Or the way he sang? From the moment I heard his voice, I was destined to end this night in his arms.

I wrapped my arms around his neck, returning his kiss. My heart pounded hard against my ribs. The blood in my veins heated. My knees grew weak. I'd never felt like that with anyone before Zeph. The world was spinning around me in a kaleidoscope of smells, sounds, and colors.

Letting go of my mouth, he trailed his kisses down my neck. Warm ripples spread through my body, pooling low in my belly. I swayed in his arms, gripping his shoulders as he kissed along my collar bone. My ragged breathing blended with the sound of water filling the tub.

He slid his hands down my sides then under my top. I moaned as his warm palms connected with my bare skin.

Moving his hands up again, he took my top with it.

"Hands up," he ordered, taking my top off and leaving me in my strapless bra. "Bath time." He kissed the tip of my nose.

I blinked. "Now?"

"Why not?" He opened the button on my shorts. "Is there ever a bad time for a bath?"

I let him slide my shorts down my legs. Kneeling in front of me, he kissed just above the band of my panties. A shiver of pleasure rushed down my thighs.

He must have mistaken it for fear or hesitation because he looked up at me with concern.

"Would it help if I went first?" He opened a button on his shirt.

If Zeph wanted to undress in front of me, I wasn't going to be the one to stop him.

"Please do." I smiled.

He got up from the floor then walked over to the wooden bench on the side of the tub. A stack of blue fluffy towels lay on the bench next to a few toiletries. He took a bottle and poured some pearly blue liquid into the water.

"What's that?" I asked.

"Sea foam." He unbuttoned his shirt, taking it off, then tossed it on the gray rug that covered the pale-wood floor. "At least that's what the label says it's supposed to smell like."

"A bubble bath?" I tried not to stare at his bare torso.

"Right." He unbuckled his belt then slid the zipper open. "Do you like bubble baths?" He shoved his dress pants down, taking his underwear with them.

"Sure." I quickly averted my eyes to the dark window, but my attention did not stay on the window for too long, drawn back to Zeph's tall, muscular body.

He had the figure of a swimmer, with long strong legs. Wide in the shoulders, his torso tapered elegantly to a narrow waist and trim hips.

The lightning speed with which he'd undressed, left me unprepared and slightly anxious. I breathed faster, suddenly finding myself one on one with a completely naked Zeph. The sight of him filled me with lightheaded excitement.

Stepping into the tub, he turned with his back to me. The scars on his arms came into view. A much longer one ran along his spine from his neck down between the two dimples on his lower back. A pair of matching silvery stripes were visible on his calves.

"What happened?" I took a step closer, momentarily forgetting about the anticipation sizzling in the air. "Your scars?" I explained when he glanced at me over his shoulder. "Scars like that, I imagine, would come with a story."

I really wanted to hear it if there was one. In fact, I wished to know everything about him—more than could be possibly learned in just one or two nights.

"There is no story." He stood in the tub. "I just...was born like this."

The pale lines on his body seemed too straight and perfect for birthmarks, as if made by man, not nature.

He stretched out his hand to me. "Come?"

All thoughts scrambled in my head. I wished to be close to him again.

With a brief nod, I took off my bra, feeling Zeph's gaze on my skin. My nipples hardened with the awareness of him staring at me, although I stubbornly kept my eyes focused on the gray rug on the floor.

Next, I shimmied out of my panties, rolled my fishnet stockings down my legs, then stepped out of my crystal-studded flats.

With a deep breath, I raised my eyes to his. My lingering apprehension had nothing to do with doubt—I had none. I wanted to be with Zeph. If his kisses were anything to go by, the night with him promised to be one I would never forget.

What worried me was my own inexperience. I was afraid I'd do or say something that would make it painfully apparent.

"Come on, Ivy." He kept holding out his hand for me. "It's nice in here. Or are you afraid of water?" He gave me an encouraging smile, holding my gaze with his. "Trust me, I'll never let you drown."

The earnestness in his voice was endearing, bringing a smile to my lips.

"I can't swim, Zeph, but I'm certainly not afraid of drowning in a bathtub."

Using his hand for support, I stepped into the tub. The soapy water rose past my ankles, the bubbles caressing my skin.

His hands on the edge of the tub, Zeph lowered himself into the water. I carefully crouched down, too, aiming for the opposite end of the tub, but he caught me around my waist and placed me between his spread legs, my back to his chest.

"This is good, isn't it?" He exhaled a long breath, and I felt his body relax.

The water kept rising, enclosing us in a warm cloud of bubbles.

"During the day," he said above my ear, gesturing at the huge bay window that was now straight ahead of us. "When the sky is blue, with not too many clouds out there, I can imagine I'm looking out to sea."

I leaned my head back on his shoulder. "Do you like big water?"

"It calls to me," he replied enigmatically, wrapping his arms around me. The warmth of the bath and the strength of his body behind me felt comforting. "One day, I want to live on a coast somewhere."

"Why wait? What's holding you in the city?"

"Lero has the cabaret here." He kissed the spot above my right ear. "And I need to work."

"You could work elsewhere, couldn't you? I can't believe some huge record label hasn't discovered you yet. Have you ever been offered a recording contract? With a voice like yours—"

"Oh, I have." He waved me off. "A number of times. I've turned them all down, though."

"Why?"

"Contracts come with too much publicity, which brings a lot of unwanted attention. And Lero says—," he cut himself short. "Well, it doesn't really matter what he says. Once you're in the public's eye, it's impossible to blend in."

"Why would you want to blend in?" I wondered how much control Lero had over Zeph's career. They were a family. Was he also his manager? Either way, why would Lero hold Zeph back? "Doesn't everyone want to stand out from the crowd? Nature made sure you could by giving you a gift."

"So, you like my singing?" He steered the conversation in a slightly different direction. I figured he didn't want to discuss his future with me. Why should he? We were practically strangers.

"I *love* your singing."

"Good." He crossed his arms over my chest, bringing me near.

Starting with a soft hum of the introduction, he crooned the first four lines of "The Way You Look Tonight" in English.

The smooth velvet of his voice curled around my heart. I'd heard this song performed by Frank Sinatra and later, by Michael Bublé. Never had it rung this true to me before. From Zeph's lips, the emotions seemed to seep from his chest straight into mine via the water around us.

The lyrics suited perfectly, as if he were reminding me that tonight was all we had, singing he would keep a warm memory of me.

Lowering his head, he kissed an errant tear off my cheek.

"It's not a sad song, Ivy."

"Maybe," I agreed, rubbing my cheeks dry. "A song is just a song."

It was what it meant to me that made it special. Zeph's singing opened my heart, made me feel vulnerable. At the same time, when he was holding me like this, I felt safe and secure. Unguarded.

"So," I changed the subject this time, needing a moment to get my emotions under control. "You speak English?"

"Fluently," he said in English. His slight accent stroked my ear, resonating through my chest.

I loved the sound of the French language. It was called "the language of love" for a reason. But there was something especially alluring about an attractive Frenchman speaking in my mother tongue to me.

As if I needed Zeph to get any more *alluring*, really.

"How many languages do you speak?" I asked.

"Just two. French and English. But I *sing* many more."

"How does that work?"

"It's easy for me to memorize the lyrics, no matter what language the song was written in."

"Interesting." I recalled reading somewhere about opera singers performing in German, Russian, and Italian, without actually speaking any of those languages. So, it wasn't just Zeph who sang in more languages than he spoke.

Being with Zeph felt like breathing, simple and natural, even as he actually took my breath away. No matter what tomorrow brought, tonight he was mine, fully and completely.

Turning my head, I kissed the corner of his mouth. "I'm glad I discovered *Le Loup Solitaire* today, and...you."

He shifted me in his arms to fully capture my mouth in a kiss.

"Tell me what you like, Ivy?" he whispered against my lips. "What would you like me to do to you?"

I had no answer to give him. The fact that well into my twenties, I still had no idea about my sexual preferences was embarrassing. So far, my experience had only taught me what I *didn't* like about sex.

The fumbling.

The extreme awareness of every clumsy move of mine or my partner's.

The painful awkwardness that intimacy had brought to me.

As Zeph caressed my neck with his lips and stroked my arms with his fingers, I finally realized what I *did* like—the fact that none of the things I disliked happened while I was with him.

When Zeph touched me, I didn't think about the exact position of our bodies or our next move. Instead, I focused on the sensation of his skin gliding against mine, the strength of his arms as he held me, the emotions that churned and grew inside me.

He made me lose myself in the pleasure he created, leaving me only half-aware of the world around us. His touch proved intoxicating.

"*This*, Zeph," I murmured, reaching behind me to sink my fingers into the hair on the back of his head as he kissed my neck. "I like all of this. Your hands on me."

Without skipping a beat, he leaned over to turn the water off. By now, it had reached under my breasts, with the thick layer of foam burying me up to my neck.

Hugging me from behind with one arm around my waist, Zeph moved his other hand in front of me, under the surface of the bubbles.

"I love how responsive you are to me, Ivy." The water swelled in front of me with his gesture, washing over my breasts with a warm caress. "We're on the same wavelength, you and I."

The tub must have had jets I hadn't noticed before, because streams of water sluiced around my body, up my legs, and...between my thighs. I gasped at the stroke of a stream along my folds yet resisted the urge to close my legs as pleasure rolled through me in a thick swell.

"Touching you is like strumming strings of a guitar or stroking piano keys." Zeph's voice sounded low and uncharacteristically raspy. Something hard pressed against my back—his erection, I realized, with a thrill rushing through my body. "My touch creates resonance in you. I can sense it."

He stroked my breasts with his hands, spreading the soapy bubbles along my skin and rubbing my nipples covered with the slippery foam.

"Oh God..." I exhaled sharply, arching my back as another charge of heat shot straight from my chest to my lower belly.

No man had ever come close to making me orgasm, yet I was fairly certain Zeph was about to change that.

The persistent jet of water between my legs grew stronger. The pulsating pressure from it swirled around that one spot where I needed it the most, not quite reaching it.

Pleasure skirted around, building up, ebbing and rising, but not cresting yet.

I reached down with my hand, desperately needing more. Zeph quickly circled my wrist with his fingers, lifting my hand out of the water.

"The song isn't over yet, Ivy," he whispered into my ear, as I arched my back moving my hips in search of more pressure. "The build-up is too beautiful to end it yet."

I rolled my head on his shoulder.

"Zeph...please," was all I could manage through my moans as my breathing shuddered. Both of my hands were now in his grip, preventing me from doing anything about the throbbing need between my legs.

The water churned around me, massaging my body. Need and pleasure rolled through me. I writhed in his lap, gasping and moaning.

He brushed his lips along the side of my neck. "Now," he murmured against my skin. "Crescendo. Come for me, Ivy."

The jet suddenly pulsed higher, the pressure directed exactly where I wanted it, finally releasing the pleasure and setting off a mind-blinding orgasm. I whimpered, nearly doubling in half under the onslaught of ecstasy, my inner muscles pulsing. Bliss I never knew was possible rolled through me.

Releasing my wrists, Zeph hugged me to him with one arm, slipping the other hand where the water jet had just been.

"Just like that," he whispered softly, working me with his fingers to reap every last shudder of the longest climax I'd ever had.

I lay in the soapy water, my head on his shoulder, his arm around my middle anchoring me to him. Covering his hand with mine, I laced my fingers with his.

"I've never thought sex could be like this, Zeph..." I breathed out. "Beautiful and intense. Like music."

Only after Zeph had wrapped me in one of the fluffy blue towels from the bench and carried me to the bed behind the silk screen, did I remember that mine was the only orgasm that had happened that night.

I recalled the sensation of his rock-hard erection pressing urgently against my backside as I writhed in pleasure. Yet he never acted on it, even as we had stayed in the tub, talking until the water started to cool off.

"What do you eat for breakfast?" He tucked the gray-blue comforter around me.

He didn't look like he cared about getting his own pleasure tonight. I had no idea if I should worry about that or approach it in any way. Maybe he did prefer a sleepover to a one-night stand after all?

"For breakfast?" I blinked as sleep started to tug at me. My eyelids felt heavier by the minute. "Coffee and cereal, mostly. A cinnamon bun on special occasions. Why?"

"I just want to know," he said softly, kissing my face. "Sleep, Ivy. I'll be right back."

He went to the bathroom behind the obscure glass door.

The sky outside the window paled with the early sunrise already. After a few days in Paris, I believed I had successfully gotten over the jetlag. What Zeph did to my body tonight, however, drained me of energy. We'd nearly stayed up the entire night, and I felt extremely tired, now.

I didn't remember Zeph returning from the bathroom. By the time he came to bed, I was already asleep, and by the time I woke up, it was bright and sunny.

The sweet scent of cinnamon wafted through the room flooded with sunshine that the silk screen couldn't block.

I stretched in bed. Then my face flushed with heat as the memories of the last night rushed in.

"You up?" Zeph poked his head around the screen, the longer hair on top of his head tousled in a most adorable way.

"Morning." I couldn't hold back a smile at the sight of his wide grin.

"Breakfast?" He placed a tray in my lap, plopping in bed beside me. "I went to two bakeries nearby, they each had a different kind of cinnamon rolls." He pointed at the plate with two pastries—one like a twisty knot with no icing and the other one round, sprinkled with coarse sugar crystals on top. "Which one looks like those you have in Canada?"

Cinnamon rolls?

I recalled the brief conversation we had just before I fell asleep. I'd said I had cinnamon buns for breakfast on special occasions.

Well, Zeph *was* my special occasion.

"Neither." I took a bite of the one closer to me. "But I didn't come to France to eat Canadian cinnamon buns, right? Besides, it's not about the appearance, at all. This one tastes amazing."

"Let me see." He grabbed my wrist, biting a piece of the roll I held. "Hmmm," he hummed, chewing. "You're right, it is pretty good."

"Want more?" I giggled. Sunshine warmed my face, seeping into my chest.

"Nope, thanks, I already ate."

Zeph was fully dressed—a crisp white shirt and black dress pants. Even his shoes were on already.

"What time is it?"

"A little past one in the afternoon."

"What?" I moved to jump out of bed, but he placed his hand on my arm.

"Do you need to be anywhere right now?"

"No, but..." I couldn't believe I'd slept past noon.

"Then there is no rush, Ivy. Have your breakfast. Call your friend if you have to. Take a shower if you want to. Relax."

"Don't *you* need to be somewhere?" I glanced at the polished dress shoes on his feet that he crossed in front of him while reclining in bed with me.

"Just *Le Loup Solitaire*." He shrugged. "Normally, I go there early in the afternoon to help set everything up. But I've already called Lero and told him I'd be late today. Take your time."

Despite his reassurances, I finished the breakfast promptly. Taking my things to the bathroom, I got dressed just as quickly, washed my face and brushed my hair, then put on some lipstick and mascara I had with me.

Zeph offered to get me a taxi, but I declined. Taking the metro to Fleur's apartment would be just as fast if not faster, and much cheaper.

He insisted on walking me to the station. Holding his hand on the way there, I forced myself to let go when we reached the entrance and he had to leave.

"Thank you," I said softly when he turned to face me. "For everything. It was a fun adventure."

*The best in my entire life.*

Zeph was my one and only one-night stand. I had no clue what people normally said in such situations.

How did one say goodbye to someone they really, really didn't want to part with?

"Ivy." He came closer, cupping my face with one hand. I leaned into his touch, closing my eyes.

What did I have to lose at this point?

Just my pride if he said no.

"What are you doing tomorrow?" I blurted out in one breath. Keeping my eyes closed, I waited for his answer.

"I want to see you again." He stroked my cheekbone with his thumb.

"You do?" I opened my eyes wide.

He smiled warmly, his eyes full of sunshine. "Would you like to spend the entire day with me tomorrow?"

*Yes.*

My heart skipped and sang at that.

"Are you off tomorrow?" I asked.

"I will make sure I am. I'll talk to Lero tonight." He wrapped his arms around me, and I linked my hands behind his neck. "I'll meet you at that café over there, at ten." He gestured at the bright red awning over the round tables on the sidewalk. "Then I can show you a few more, non-touristy places I think you'd like."

Everything inside me lifted. I loved spending time with Zeph, and he obviously enjoyed that, too.

What if there was a possibility of something more between us? More than a one-night stand? More than just a vacation fling?

I wanted more of him.

"I'd love that, Zeph." I exhaled a happy sigh just before he kissed me goodbye.

Except that now, "goodbye" did not mean parting forever.

Not yet, anyway.

# Chapter Five

ZEPH

The venue was still closed, but the main room seemed ready to receive the audience when he made it to *Le Loup Solitaire* later that afternoon. The prep work for the food service was in full swing in the kitchen.

"Where is Lero?" he asked Ivan, walking swiftly by the bar counter. "Outside?"

The bar manager nodded.

Asking was hardly necessary. Considering the current phase of the moon, Lero would be spending every spare minute outside for the next couple of days, smoking the fragrant *womora* leaves.

"Lero?" Zeph shoved at the heavy metal door that led to the small courtyard at the back.

As expected, his friend was leaning against the wall, taking long drags from the dark cigarette in his hand.

"You're here?" Lero released two tendrils of the aromatic, silvery smoke through his nostrils, aiming in the direction opposite from Zeph.

Completely harmless to humans, *womora* leaves had a devastating effect on fae magic, stripping Zeph's kind of their abilities. That was the reason Lero chain-smoked *womora* in the first place—to stave off the effects of the approaching full moon.

"I'm here." Zeph leaned against the wall, upwind from Lero. "But I need to take tomorrow off."

"Why?" Lero rolled his head on the wall to face him, his silver-gray eyes focusing on Zeph's face.

"Personal reasons." Zeph glanced away, not ready to talk about Ivy yet.

"Does it have anything to do with that girl you left with last night?" Zeph should have known Lero was perceptive enough to figure things out on his own without being told. And Lero was right, more than he probably realized—it had *everything* to do with Ivy.

Painfully shy at first, she bloomed as he got to know her better. It was exciting to watch her open up to him, like a flower. She delighted in all the things he loved.

The time spent with Ivy was not just fun, it was light and relaxing. He wanted just a little more of that before she left the country and was gone from his life forever.

There was nothing wrong with the way he felt. Yet he sensed Lero would find something unfitting about it—he always did—so Zeph kept quiet, kicking a small rock up the pavement instead of a reply.

"She responded to my singing," he finally said.

"All humans do...to some extent."

They did. Not all humans were the same, though. Their response varied in its intensity. Ivy felt strongly, making him wonder what would happen if he managed to unleash the full potential of her emotions. Her passion.

Part of him wished to be swept away by her feelings and let it all happen, not worrying about consequences for once.

"I like her."

"The better reason to stay away from her," Lero retorted. "For the sake of both of you, Zeph, turn down your charm and let the girl go."

As if it were that simple to "turn the charm down." There was no *off* switch on who he was.

Clenching his jaw so tight it hurt, Zeph kept quiet for a few moments.

Lero grimly took another drag of his cigarette. "We have to be careful."

"You know I am, but Ivy is not a threat," Zeph muttered shaking his head, then remembered the other encounter. "I think I saw *bracks* last night. At least four of them, maybe more."

"Where?" Lero straightened his back, pushing away from the wall.

"Less than a ten-minute walk from here."

His dark, thick eyebrows drawn into a frown, Lero seemed to consider this new information for a moment.

"How do you know they were *bracks?*" he finally asked. "You've never seen one before. Are you sure?"

True, this was Zeph's first encounter, but he'd heard so many warnings from Lero throughout his life, complete with detailed descriptions, that he was certain now. The moment he'd realized that the large figures accosting Ivy and him last night might not be mere humans, he'd thought it was wise to retreat, relieved when they hadn't followed.

"I think that's what they were," he replied. "Bald, huge. I got a good look at one of them. He had a tattoo around his neck and down his arm, just like you've described."

"Still, could be a human." Lero's frown didn't ease.

"The tattoo glowed red in the dark."

Lero's chest rose with a sharp breath. He tossed the butt of his cigarette into a nearby can.

"Ghata's mark," he spat through his teeth.

"What does she want? Why are they here?"

"*That* I wish to know. This city is mine. As long as you and I remain here, we are supposed to stay safe. If things have changed, I was not informed." Lero opened the side of his custom-made suit jacket, getting a new cigarette out from the chest pocket. It trembled slightly in his fingers.

"Well, maybe that's what they came here for?" Zeph offered. "To inform you of some changes?"

"Then why stalk you, instead of coming to me?"

"Maybe that's what they'll do next? Come to you?"

Lero nodded, lighting the cigarette.

"Whatever it is that Ghata wants, her business is with me. She can't touch you." Taking a long pull at the cigarette, he leaned back against the wall, closing his eyes, as if letting the calmness of the *womora* spread through his system while its smoke permeated his lungs. "Still, you need to be careful, Zeph."

"I told you I am." Zeph appreciated Lero's concern for his wellbeing, however the decades of listening to the same old warnings made them sound more like nagging at this point.

"Why do you need a day off tomorrow?" Lero opened his eyes, nailing him to the spot with his questioning gaze once again.

"I said it's personal." Zeph shifted uncomfortably. "Since when do I have to tell you how I'm planning to spend my days off."

"Since you were six years old," Lero deadpanned.

"But I'm no longer six." Zeph huffed, his patience wearing thin. "I'm forty-seven, for fuck's sake, which would be a very mature age for a human, you know."

"For a *human*." Lero's voice hardened. "Not for *us*. I am twice your age, and you act barely half of yours," he pronounced every word slowly, loading it with weight and meaning. "So, when I ask you to listen to me, you do it. Especially now that *bracks* are in the area, for whatever fucking reason!"

A flash of the afternoon sun appeared to reach into the dark courtyard, reflecting blood red in Lero's glare.

"Do you understand, Zeph? Ghata knows I care about you. I don't want anything to happen to you because she may get the idea to use you against me. Is that clear?"

"Yes." Zeph didn't mean for his reply to sound as harsh as it did, but the irritation got the worst of him. "I'll be careful." He made an effort to soften his voice this time.

"Are you planning to spend tomorrow with that girl?"

"Her name is Ivy," Zeph muttered, raking his fingers through his hair. "And yes. I'm meeting her at ten."

"She's a human."

"Of course she is!" The irritation flared up again. "What else could she be? There are no fae girls, are there?"

"Not in this world," Lero conceded. "But a human female would never be a suitable partner for a fae."

"Well..." Zeph let the sarcasm instill his voice, since the pickings are slim in terms of fae partners here—"

"I mean it, Zeph," Lero interrupted gruffly. "Humans live much shorter lives. And they are just," he winced, "much weaker than us, in every sense. Humans aren't capable of dealing with the challenges of spending a lifetime with us."

"I know."

*These* kind of warnings Zeph had been hearing ever since he'd brought home a girl from school and introduced her to Lero as his girlfriend. Impeccably polite while she was there, Lero had nearly lost it once she'd left after dinner.

Humans were weaker, physically and emotionally, Lero had passionately explained to him then. Most did not allow in their minds even for a possibility of sentient beings other than themselves populating their world. And in a way, they were right—Zeph and Lero were not of this world. Technically, they did not belong here at all.

They came when Zeph was six, taking refuge here more than four decades ago. Zeph was an orphan, with nowhere to go, and Lero was on the run from the consequences of a murderous rampage he might've taken part in during a fit of Moon Madness.

Once fae left their world Nerifir, there was no return. They would never make it back to the same time and place. The worlds shifted constantly, finding new touching points and abandoning others, making it impossible for anyone to come back to the same "what" and "when" that they had left from.

Zeph and Lero were stuck on Earth now for the remainder of their five-hundred-year lifespans, with no chance of finding a fae mate. And with humans being as fragile as they were, the hope of any female companion was slim to none. There was just too much risk. Even sex with a fae could be deadly for a human.

Zeph knew that. No matter how close he wished to be with a woman sometimes, he always held back. He'd never spent more than a night with a girl. Every movement during sex was measured and controlled.

"There won't be anything long-term with Ivy," he assured Lero. "She is leaving in a week. It can't last longer than that."

His words pinched his heart with sadness, and he stilled his next breath, lest it hurt more.

"Whatever you do, don't take her out to eat tomorrow," Lero wouldn't quit with his warnings.

"I'm taking her on a date, Lero," he snapped in frustration. "Come on. How am I supposed to stay away from restaurants? In Paris?"

Lero puffed out a stream of smoke over his shoulder before facing him again, his gaze hard and cold as steel. Unyielding.

"Find a way, Zeph. Or I swear, I'll lock you in my cage for a week until she leaves."

"Yeah?" Zeph snapped, losing his patience. "And what are *you* going to do without that cage, two days from now?"

Tossing his barely touched cigarette aside, Lero grabbed Zeph by his shoulders, giving him a shake that would break a human in half.

"Promise me," he gritted through his teeth, the earthy-sweet fragrance of *womora* on his breath, "you will not eat anything outside of *Le Loup Solitaire*. The only food I guarantee is safe is the one prepared here."

Zeph met Lero's glare with one of his own.

"It's nearly opening time." He shrugged a shoulder out of Lero's grip. "I need to go on the stage soon." He turned to leave.

"Zeph," Lero called behind him. "You *know* there are things from Nerifir that would mess you up if you consume them. Not all of the effects are temporary or reversible, either. I honestly have no idea what Ghata has access to."

Hand on the door handle, Zeph threw a glance back over his shoulder, catching the sight of Lero's trembling fingers as he reached for another cigarette. Compassion tugged at his heart. Lero had two more days of this struggle ahead of him. And it would only get worse before it got better.

"All right." His voice softened as the irritation at his friend ebbed. Deep inside, he'd always known Lero pushed because he cared. It just often felt like he still treated Zeph as if he remained that six-year-old boy Lero had found abandoned and alone one cold morning in Nerifir. "Fine. I won't take her out to eat. I'll cook something at home, instead. Happy, now?"

"I'll be much happier, once Ghata gets her goons out of my city," Lero growled. Yet his expression relaxed somewhat at Zeph's words. With another drag at his cigarette, he leaned back against the wall, closing his eyes. "Go now. I'll come back in after this one."

"Stay as long as you need," Zeph said quietly, closing the door behind him.

Staying focused wasn't easy tonight. Even the music didn't merge with him the way it usually did when he sang. Thankfully, songs tended to become an extension of him. The lyrics flowed on their own, and his voice stayed on tune without requiring much mental focus.

Letting his subconscious lead his performance had side effects, he realized, when he found himself singing "The Way You Look Tonight."

Unsurprisingly, his thoughts snapped back to last night for the millionth time since he'd walked Ivy to the metro station earlier today.

He wondered if his sheets would still smell like her when he got home later tonight, and how exciting it would be to have her in them again tomorrow. He moved his gaze along the faces around the tables in the audience, as if she would still be there.

An elderly couple was sitting at the table she had last night. They held hands, their eyes on him, their expressions wistful and tender.

Staring at the couple's linked hands on top of the table cloth, he wondered how long they had been together. Were they from Paris? Or from elsewhere in the world? Were they here on holidays? Celebrating an anniversary, maybe?

What was it like to have someone in life, closer than he could ever be to any woman?

He remembered Amelie, the woman Lero had brought home once. Zeph was eight, maybe nine then, still learning to read in English. Amelie brought him an English children's book as a gift and taught him how to pronounce a few words he didn't know.

He liked her, but even more so he liked the tenderness in Lero's eyes whenever his friend looked at her.

Less than two weeks later though, Lero told him that Amelie wouldn't be coming by anymore. Zeph had never seen another woman with Lero since. Whatever had happened between them, Zeph understood that Lero might be speaking from experience in his warnings.

There were things about fae that could be deadly to a delicate, vulnerable girl like Ivy. Yet he simply didn't have it in him to part with her yet.

*Just for a few more days. She'd be gone soon, anyway.*

He was confident he could control himself around her for a week. Her company was worth the self-restraint.

While finishing the song, he allowed his memory to bring up the images of her. He loved her wavy, pink-blue hair and the two round dimples that popped up high on her cheekbones whenever she was relaxed enough to smile wide and free.

The wonder and adoration had floated in her huge moss-green eyes when she listened to him singing.

He recalled the sensation of her silky skin, lathered with bubble bath, and the way she moaned, arching her back as he played her body like the most exquisite instrument he'd ever held in his hands...

The song ended, allowing Zeph to flee the stage before the memories stretched his pants with an erection too obvious to conceal.

Heading straight to the bar, he poured himself a glass of white wine, feeling parched.

"Zeph." One of the waitresses, Lorraine, tapped his arm. She leaned to his ear as the sound of Selene's luscious voice rose from the stage, her backup dancers burning up the floor behind her. "There is a girl asking for you."

"What girl? Where?"

"Just outside the front door." Lorraine gestured that way. "Medium height, blue-and-pink hair."

"Ivy?" His heart made a leap in his chest.

"She didn't say her name."

"Why wouldn't she come in?"

"She has no ticket." Lorraine shrugged, heading back to the tables, carrying the drink tray above her shoulder.

"Oh, for fuck's sake." Zeph slammed his wine glass on the counter and marched to the main entrance. He had to have a word with Gabriel at the door. For as long as Ivy was in Paris, she would be allowed to come and go as she pleased—no ticket required.

Gabriel was not by the door when he got there. He must have stepped out to chat with the new ticket girl.

A flash of pink-and-blue hair caught Zeph's eye when he exited. A feminine figure descended the basement stairs of the building next door.

"Ivy!" He rushed after her. The initial excitement was suddenly replaced by the worry about what brought her here tonight.

A large van moved in front of the basement entrance, shielding him from the street. The next moment, somebody shoved a bag over his head. It was then yanked all the way down, shrouding his entire body.

The sharp scent of *womora* leaves hit his nostrils, the thick fog of it almost tangible inside the bag.

Instinctively, the spikes on his back, arms, and legs tensed, snapping up from his skin and shredding his clothes to pieces. Fervently, he fought against the rough hands that lifted him and carried him off.

The heavy fabric of the bag held, however. Whoever did this knew exactly what they were doing. The poison from the tips of his spikes dripped uselessly onto his own skin.

The *womora* smoke, mixed with another scent, sharp and unfamiliar, thickened around him, clouding his vision and muffling all his senses.

Until he could no longer feel a thing...

# Chapter Six

IVY

With my fingers wrapped around the mug of my third cappuccino, I stared at the red-and-white checkered tablecloth in front of me.

It was well into the second hour of my sitting here at the table for two in the café where Zeph was supposed to meet me.

Except that he was nowhere in sight.

I'd called his number a couple of times, but he never answered. The cappuccino was cooling in the mug. The warm excitement that had reigned inside me since last night had fizzled out.

I didn't need to sit here for nearly two hours to figure out that he wasn't coming, but I simply couldn't force myself to my feet.

Instead, I was working through all stages of grief right there in the shade of the red awning as people passed me by.

I'd gone from denial.

*He didn't get the day off. His phone got stolen, and he couldn't find another phone in the whole city of Paris to call and let me know...*

To anger.

*Why make promises he didn't intend to keep? He led me on, manipu-*

*lating my feelings. He made me believe he liked me and really wanted to see me again.*

To bargaining, depression, and finally acceptance.

*Maybe I did something wrong, after all? Should I have at least tried to be the sexy siren I never felt I was meant to be? Would that have held his interest?*

*There must be a reason guys didn't flock to my bed. Zeph had figured it out, and now he didn't want me either.*

There was nothing left now but to get over it and move on. With a heavy sigh, I finally pushed to my feet. Leaving the cold cappuccino behind, I paid the bill and left.

The anger did not disappear entirely, though. It seethed in my chest, burning through my bruised heart with searing pain.

Why did it hurt so much? Maybe because I had allowed myself to really care for Zeph? I'd sensed a connection forming between us, and it pained me to see it break before it got a chance to grow.

I'd made the classic mistake that probably every woman made at least once in her lifetime. I trusted too quickly and felt too deeply, falling for a man way too fast.

And now it hurt.

My eyes burned with tears, but I refused to let them flow.

*Get over it and move on.*

Zeph didn't want me. So, what? There were worse things in life. I'd survive this. I'd forget about him.

Thankfully, it was only one night. It was never meant to be much more than that, anyway. No matter how magical or special I thought it was, Zeph obviously didn't think that. For him, it meant nothing, and I had to learn to view it like that, too.

It'd been simply a one-night stand. People had them all the time. Now I'd had one, too.

Passing by *Boulevard de Clichy*, I fought the notion to turn in the direction of *Le Loup Solitaire*. Why would I go there? To stalk the man who stood me up?

The last thing I needed was to see a cold indifference in his eyes or to hear from him something along the lines of "it's not you, it's me." Or even worse, to watch him serenade another tourist from the stage.

*Forget it.*

*Forget it.*

*Forget it.*

The heels of my shoes clicked in rhythm to the thought bouncing in my head as I passed by the turn off to the street with the cabaret.

I fully intended to do just that.

Forget it.

Forget Zeph.

# Chapter Seven

## ONE YEAR AND TWO MONTHS LATER

IVY

"Oh, my God, Ivy. Look at that!" Fleur exclaimed in English. We were in Canada, in Toronto, on the fairgrounds of the Canadian National Exhibition or CNE, the fair that took place by the Toronto waterfront annually. "I didn't think these still existed." She tugged at my loose t-shirt, making me stop near a group of large, red-and-yellow striped tents.

"What's that?" I took another bite of the candy apple on a stick. The red candied sugar cracked under my teeth, filling my mouth with sweetness mixed with the fresh crisp taste of the apple underneath.

"It's a sideshow. A real-life freakshow, right there!" Fleur energetically pointed at the painted sign, *Madame Tan's Menagerie of Oddities*. The group of tents clustered together behind it and appeared to be interconnected.

"That's not what it says." I wiped the sweat beading on my temple with my shoulder. Despite it being the beginning of September, the day was scorching hot. "*Menagerie* is like a collection of something, isn't it? You're French, you should know. This must be a collection of animals. Like a zoo."

"Fine." Fleur tilted her head. "Animals. But with *oddities.* Something unusual. Deformities, maybe?"

"You mean like birth defects?" I cringed. The creepy image of deformed animals preserved in jars or trapped in cages rose to mind. "I'm not sure I'm up for that kind of entertainment."

"Look." Fleur pointed at another sign, right under the first one. This one was written in smaller letters but held more text. "'*Not to be found on Earth,*'" she read out loud. "'*The objects and animals in this exhibit have traveled between dimensions and arrived from a magical kingdom...*' See, it's all make believe, Ivy. Come on, it sounds fun." Sweat also beaded on Fleur's forehead, her dark skin flushed on her high cheekbones. Like me, she must be wishing to get out of the afternoon sun. "I want to see what they have in those tents."

There was some vintage mystery in the setup of the menagerie with its striped tents, painted signs, and the old-fashioned strings of lights. It felt slightly intimidating but enticing.

Not entirely convinced yet, I couldn't deny I was intrigued.

"It's twenty dollars each, just to get in. And there's a line." I gestured at the group of people gathered by the entrance.

"Which means it must be good." Fleur huffed, exasperated by my hesitation. "Lots of people want to see it."

"Fine," I conceded. "After all, you didn't travel all the way from France to miss the *freakshow...*"

She bounced off to the ticket booth nearby. "A freakshow in Toronto sounds even better than the cabaret in Paris."

I paused when she brought that up, then hurried after her, hoping she hadn't noticed that I'd skipped a step. She glanced at me over her shoulder, one dark eyebrow arched up in question.

"Let's hope this one ends better," I muttered.

"Oh, come on." Fleur's shoulders dropped. "Ivy, you couldn't still be that upset about him standing you up. It's been ages!"

I carefully schooled my expression into something hopefully cool and neutral. "I've long since forgotten about that." I waved her off. "Completely."

A lot had happened since. I'd even changed my hair color from the bright blue-and-magenta to a shade much closer to my natural light brown with a touch of red highlights added in for fun.

More than enough time had passed for me to let go of the memory of sitting alone in that café, nursing a cooling cappuccino for nearly two hours, waiting for the man who never bothered to show up or even to call to cancel. I'd made a firm decision to forget him.

Only men like Zeph were not easily forgotten. I never could get his singing out of my mind. I still couldn't take a bath without the phantom sensation of his hands on me whenever the water touched my skin. Every. Freaking. Time.

"You really should get laid again," Fleur said in earnest, staring at me with concern.

"Oh God, Fleur, really? You think sex is the cure to everything?"

"Well, it helps..." She shrugged.

Maybe she was right? Maybe if I found someone I liked enough to sleep with, the memories of Zeph would fade faster or even disappear completely, letting me move on.

Obviously, he and I were never meant to be. Sooner or later, I would get his intense blue eyes and magical voice out of my head.

One day...

Another sigh filled my chest with air as I forced the memories to some more remote parts of my brain.

"Let's go." I grabbed two twenties from the back pocket of my pink denim shorts. "We'll see the freakshow."

"It's a *menagerie*," Fleur corrected, pronouncing the last word with an exaggeratedly annunciated Parisian accent.

"So it says." I smiled at her antics.

"My treat." Fleur elbowed me out of the way, getting to the ticket booth before me. "Two, please." She shoved her bills through the small window to the somber, dark-haired girl behind the plexiglass.

Huddling into a wide black scarf wrapped around her neck despite the afternoon heat, the girl accepted the money, avoiding eye contact.

She handed Fleur our tickets, finally glancing up at us with dark, haunted eyes. Lifting her face out of the scarf, she gave us a practiced smile that never made it to those sorrowful eyes. "Enjoy the exhibit."

"Come." Fleur got hold of my elbow, dragging me to the entrance. "Let's see what wonders these tents hold."

We joined the group of people entering the first tent. Inside, a fragrant, shimmering cloud of silvery smoke enveloped us. The scent triggered a sudden flash of déjà vu—annoying because I couldn't remember where I'd smelled it before.

"Welcome to my little menagerie," a melodious voice greeted us.

A tall woman in a red dress with a mandarin collar stepped out of the semi-darkness. She clapped her hands and a series of multi-colored lights ran up the seams of the tent to the highest point of the ceiling.

"I am Madame Tan," the woman said with a gorgeous smile. "Please follow me." Her fiery red hair was whipped into a high up-do, which then descended down her back in a wide intricate braid.

The striped canvas walls divided the interior of the interconnected tents into sections. We followed a short narrow corridor that opened into a medium size room.

"Here, I keep inanimate objects," Madame Tan explained, making a sweeping gesture. A curl of smoke followed her hand, trailing from a thin cigar in a holder attached to the ring on her finger. "All exhibits in my collection are unique, with no exception. Unless you have visited my menagerie before, I guarantee you haven't seen anything like what you're about to see."

She pointed at the first display, a lit glass container on a small table.

"Here is a dead branch of a *jastira* tree, a predatory plant from Ilimitar Forest."

"Where is that?" Fleur whispered into my ear.

"Not sure." I stared through the glass at the two-foot long stick that somehow reminded me of a human femur with a jaw bone of a wolf-sized animal at one end. "What does it matter? It's not real."

Madame fixed her gaze on me, and I realized she must've heard me.

"Obviously, the branch is dry. It's dead," she said coolly. "If we had a living *jastira* tree in here, none of you would be alive. It's the most bloodthirsty plant across both worlds."

She moved along the canvas wall, fluidly pointing at the shelves, jars, and curio cabinets as she passed them by.

"A shell from Olathana Ocean. It used to house a hermit siren. Most of the merfolk are lively, sociable creatures. Some, however, prefer solitude..."

The shimmering, nearly translucent shell in front of us seemed big enough to encase me and maybe Fleur, too, together.

"This headpiece was made with the feathers from the wings of a griffin." Madame pointed at a gorgeous plumage. It looked more spectacular than anything that could be found at Mardi Gras. "I used to have a griffin in my collection until last year." She sighed. "Unfortunately, he choked on a mouse and died."

"Griffins eat mice?" I tried to recall what I knew about these mythical creatures.

"They don't exist," Fleur whispered back. "It's all a show, remember?"

"Pretty well-done, though," I had to admit.

Fleur reached for the shimmering feathers of the headpiece.

"Please, do not touch the exhibits," Madame warned sternly. Fleur jerked her hand back, and Madame continued, pointing at a row of clear, faceted pieces on display, "*Biqirelle* crystals from the Mountains of Dakath. These have healing powers and are highly treasured by the gargoyles of the mountain peaks..."

Next, she moved on to a square metal object with bizarre gears and bearings visible in the many openings on its surface.

"This here is a communication device, created by the dwellers of the Lorsan Wetlands. They're considered mechanical geniuses, as they're *magical* with their hands."

I lingered by the device for a moment, wondering how all of its moving parts would perform when turned on. Madame's voice, however, redirected my attention to the large curio cabinet, with small, brightly lit sections behind the glass. "This here is my collection of jewelry made from werewolf teeth and claws."

"Wow." Fleur exhaled at my side. The other visitors gathered around as well, admiring the items on display. "I really love that crown." Fleur pointed at a high diadem, made of alternating white and black spikes in an intricate bronze setting.

"That piece is my favorite." Madame smiled, coming closer. "Werewolves have snow-white teeth and graphite-black claws. I find the contrast especially pleasing to the eye." Something sinister flashed through her inky black eyes. "Not all of them were dead when these were extracted."

A chill ran down my spine, even though I knew it was all fake.

"Well." She stood at yet another striped curtain-divider. "The next room holds my exhibit of live creatures. Please keep your voices down so that we don't irritate the animals."

We followed Madame into yet another dark, short corridor of canvas walls. The silver smoke was especially concentrated here. Unlike any other smoke I knew, though, this one wasn't smothering. I could breathe easily through it, with no urge to cough or even to clear my throat.

"What is this one?" Fleur asked, pointing at a large statue of a creature with wings that stood in the shadows. Made of a black, glossy rock, the sculpture depicted a man with leathery wings partially folded behind his back. "Why is it here?"

"Oh, that one..." Madame grimaced, glancing at the statue. "I'm not entirely sure in which section to put him. He is certainly inanimate, but so incredibly lifelike, don't you think?"

The sculpture was very lifelike, I even spotted the stubble of the five o'clock shadow on the chiseled jawline of the man's face.

"So, here he remains. Stuck for now." Madame shrugged, moving along. "Welcome to my very own little zoo," she said in a sing-song voice, entering the next room.

With one last glance at the dragon-man frozen in stone, I hurried after her.

"This is unbelievable, Ivy. Come here." Fleur waved at me, standing at an enclosure by the wall.

"I insist you remain quiet," Madame reminded, puffing a curl of smoke in the direction of my friend. "Loud noises may aggravate the animals."

"Look at this," Fleur hissed in a loud whisper, pointing at the pale pink creature inside the enclosure. From the first glance it appeared to be a small pig—a piglet, rather. Except that it had two heads, one on each side of its long body.

"Where is its bum?" Fleur made big eyes at me.

"The anus is located in the middle of the belly," Madame explained, passing near.

"Is it a real animal?" I frowned, leaning in to stroke the soft velvety skin of the creature—nothing like the coarse-haired pigs I'd seen before.

It snorted at me then snapped its teeth, barely missing my fingers.

"Don't touch the exhibit!" Madame snarled, startling me into obedience. I promptly snatched my hand out of the enclosure.

"Is this some kind of a mutation?" one of the visitors asked. "A birth defect?"

"Maybe due to radiation exposure?" another one ventured a guess.

"Birth defect," Madame confirmed, with another pull at her cigarette. "Normally, this species is born with three heads. This one only had two at birth. So, he is truly unique, in his world and in ours."

"What *is* his world?"

"The Plains of Sarnala, of course, provide the natural habitat of the *virleth* pigs. Unfortunately, this species is nearly extinct. Sarnala is the land of werewolves. They annihilate all living creatures in sight during their Night of Madness. Thankfully, my people managed to rescue Yenric here just in time."

With a smile that was warmer and seemed more genuine than any of those she'd given us, Madame leaned into the enclosure herself, scratching behind the ear of one of the pig's heads. The second head wanted attention too, lurching forward and pivoting the whole animal around to get under her hand.

"He looks so real," Fleur whispered to me.

"No, honestly," a male visitor asked, "where did you get him? And this one here, too?" He pointed at a bright red creature sitting on a tree branch inside another enclosure.

About two to three feet long, its body was narrow and covered in crimson feathers. It had the head of a bird, with three pairs of feet, spread evenly along the length of its snake-like body that curled around the tree branch mounted inside the enclosure.

"Or these?" A woman pointed at the black rocks on the bottom of the snake-bird's enclosure. Every now and then, the "rocks" scurried along the floor, their surface bursting into a kaleidoscope of fluorescent lights. The sign on their enclosure read *"fog turtles."*

At least a dozen more enclosures lined the walls. The creatures in each of them were just as fantastic as the next.

"Well, like the sign at the entrance says," Madame explained, staying in character. "All exhibits are from the magical Kingdom of Nerifir. It is populated by beautiful and mysterious creatures."

"Of course," I muttered with sarcasm. "*The magical kingdom.*"

I had to admit, though, the show was interesting and realistically created, with the exhibits so incredibly lifelike, it boggled my mind. I felt the sense of wonder I used to get while watching a magic show as a kid.

"Humans cannot enter Nerifir," Madame continued. "Not on their own. Luckily, I was able to acquire my collection through means I prefer not to disclose. Thanks to me, you can now view things that were never meant to be seen by a human eye."

"Cool." Fleur nodded, staring intently at the red snake-bird as it cleaned its feathers.

I wondered if she was pondering the mechanics that went into the creation of the exhibit.

"Well." Madame stepped out of the room into another short corridor. "Thank you for your visit. Radax will now show you the way out."

She gestured in the direction of the tall, broad man with a full beard standing nearby. Down the corridor, the open flap of the wall revealed the sunny outdoors.

"Is that it?" I wondered out loud. The group of the tents seemed larger from the outside. "There must be more rooms in here."

A puff of air brushed by my hand from a canvas overlap on my right, and I yanked the fabric to the side. Secured both from the top and the bottom, the canvas stretched tightly in my hand, creating a narrow slit.

Instead of the fresh air, another wave of the fragrant smoke reached me through the gap. The space on the other side was completely dark except for the glowing blue letters *VIP.* They were attached to the thick rope that stretched across what appeared to be the entrance to yet another room.

"Miss?" Madame prompted me impatiently as everyone had already left. Fleur was waiting for me at the exit. "It's time for you to leave."

"But what is in there?" I asked.

"The VIP area," Madame replied curtly, narrowing her eyes at me. "Entrance by invitation only."

"How does one get invited?" I asked, trying hard not to feel intimidated by her tone.

"That would require a certain level of income."

"Like I would need to bring my tax statement or something?"

Fleur was waving at me from the exit, bouncing from foot to foot and gesturing for me to hurry up.

"No," Madame bit off. "But the ticket to that section costs much more."

"Well, I would argue that twenty dollars is high enough already, just to see—"

"To see things not found on Earth?" Madame scoffed. "Hardly."

I decided against pointing out that the show was over, and she could drop her magical kingdom act.

"So, what do you exhibit in that section?" I asked instead. "How much is the VIP ticket?"

"Ten thousand dollars." She crossed her arms over her chest, her mouth pressed into a hard line.

"What?" My face must've displayed my astonishment as satisfaction spread on hers.

"Please follow Radax to the exit," she said calmly. "Or I will be forced to order him to *physically* assist you out."

# Chapter Eight

IVY

"What do you think she is hiding in there?" I kept looking over my shoulder back at the tents after the burly bearded man with a spectacular full-sleeve tattoo had escorted us out.

"Probably another bunch of handmade *oddities*." Fleur shifted her weight to another foot.

"Handmade?"

"What? Do you believe any of those things are real?"

"Of course not," I muttered, thinking back to the exhibits. "The shell must be plastic, and that tree branch looked like no plant life ever would."

"The pig was amazing, though," Fleur gushed. "And the bird."

"Where do you think they came from? They did look rather realistic."

"Not sure. Well, the bird could be a mechanical toy. The rocks, too, could be painted with some wicked glow-in-the-dark paint. The pig looked pretty real, though. I mean you touched it yourself." She scratched her chin. "I don't know. Maybe he's the result of some surgery done by a mad scientist? Do you need to pee?" She asked suddenly, bouncing from foot to foot again.

"Um. No."

"Okay. Wait here then. I'll use the stinky public bathroom, then we'll go get some ice cream. It's so freaking hot today." She waved a hand in front of her face, flushed from heat. "Doesn't even feel like I'm in Canada."

I walked to the side as Fleur sauntered toward the white portable washrooms, taking our backpack with her.

Getting my cell phone out of the back pocket of my shorts, I quickly checked my messages. To get out of the way of the swelling pedestrian traffic of the fairgrounds, I stepped closer to the wall of one of Madame Tan's tents.

"Please, follow me," I suddenly heard her melodious voice, muffled by the fabric of the tent.

Madame must be taking another group on the tour of her "little menagerie."

"For my treasured VIP clients, I have something especially precious to see..." she murmured. Her voice trailed off, lost in the textile bowels of the tents.

There'd better be something "especially precious" for a ten-thousand-dollar ticket. I scoffed to myself, suddenly feeling like a second-class citizen, denied entry into the place reserved for the crème de la crème.

My curiosity made me wish I had x-ray vision to peer through the tent walls. It was just some fabric, after all. Not even that thick or impenetrable.

Squinting over my shoulder, I furtively inspected the weather-proofed canvas, taking a few steps backwards to get closer.

A distant sound of music filtered through, slow and beautiful.

The desire to take a peek, if only for a second, burned through me.

What if I could sneak under the bottom edge?

The lower end of the canvas all around the tent had been weighted down by long bags of sand. Moving them would take the effort and time I was afraid I didn't have. Anyone could peek behind the tent at any moment and find me rearranging sandbags I had no business touching. Someone from Madame's staff could easily see me here as well.

I glanced up at one of the support poles. Moving closer, I lifted the long rubbery flap over it. It protected the seam where two wall panels overlapped. The two sides were clipped together, but the clip proved easy enough to open, creating a gap that I might be able to slide through and into the tent.

*That was it.*

It was simply meant for me to sneak in, wasn't it? In and out before anyone noticed. Just one look, then I'd get out before Fleur was back. There were enough partitions inside the tents to hide me from Madame and her muscle man. I could do it.

With a bracing breath, I squeezed through the gap and into the fragrant semi-darkness of Madame Tan's menagerie. It was dark and stuffy in the narrow corridor that stretched along the outside wall of the tent.

Following the music, I headed right, grateful for the rubber soles of my sandals that allowed me to pad along noiselessly.

The sound of music intensified, then the murmur of voices mingled in. One stood out above the rest—the melodious voice of Madame Tan, who sounded as if she was telling an enchanting tale of old.

"Sirens are known for their enthralling voices and ethereal looks..."

A thick velvet curtain blocked my way. Eerie, blue-green light cut through the darkness in the narrow gaps on each side of it.

"Although their appearance closely resembles humans, Olathana sirens are not sentient," Madame continued with her narration. "They are simply animals, like all other creatures in my menagerie. But aren't they spectacular?"

Something happened behind the curtain, resulting in a series of gasps and murmurs. The light in the gaps intensified.

Unable to stand the suspense of not knowing any longer, I leaned closer, tugging the curtain aside a little, just enough for me to peek through.

A large, tall water tank stood in the middle of the next room. Shimmering green and blue light shone from it, piercing through the waves of the fragrant smoke that curled over the heads of the six people sitting at the bar in front of the tank.

They were enjoying drinks and hors d'oeuvres while watching a figure floating in the water.

Judging by the shape of the body—wide shoulders of a swimmer, well-defined chest, and narrow hips—it was a male, despite the halo of long white hair streaming around his head and the silver skirt with high slits on each side. The skirt was actually a long, loin cloth, I realized, upon a closer look. And it was the only clothing the male was wearing.

The man remained upright in the tank, as if suspended in the glowing water. The glow appeared to be coming from him, his pale skin highlighted by the delicate blues, greens, and pinks. The light shimmered through his long, silvery hair, too.

Madame stood next to the bar.

"Hear the siren sing." She waved her arms in the air dramatically, and a somber, breathtakingly beautiful voice filled the space.

It sliced through me with recognition.

*I knew this voice.*

It had enchanted me back in the cabaret in Paris. I never forgot it, no matter how hard I'd tried. This was the voice of the man with the fascinating blue eyes and a warm smile that hid in the corners of his mouth even when he was singing a song meant to make you cry.

*Zeph.*

I studied the face of the person inside the tank. He seemed paler than I remembered, his hair much longer. There was not a hint of a smile in his features this time. But it was certainly the same man, the one I'd spent a night with and hadn't been able to forget ever since.

My heart thundered so loud, I pressed both hands to my chest, afraid that the people at the bar would hear it.

"He's gorgeous!" a young woman exclaimed, raising a tall glass with luminous liquid to her lips.

A man sitting next to her gave her a side glance. "Looks rather human to me."

Madame leveled him with a stare.

"But he is *not* human." She gestured somewhere behind her.

The dark-haired girl, who had sold us our tickets, entered from the side, carrying a large crystal decanter filled with a shimmering liquid. She refilled the man's glass with it.

"The differences between sirens and humans are not that apparent at a first glance," Madame continued the moment the girl had left.

Radax, the large, bearded man who had escorted me out of the tent earlier, stood in the entrance where the girl with the decanter had departed. Another man, who looked nearly identical to Radax except that this one was clean-shaven, stood on the other side of the entrance. The arms of both were folded across their enormous chests.

"However, there *are* differences." Madame made another theatrical gesture toward the man in the tank—*Zeph*. "Aside from the ability to breathe underwater, sirens swim better than any fish and infinitely better than a human. They can also regulate their body temperature and are not affected by cold."

"Still, looks human to me," the man at the bar retorted gruffly.

"No regular man could be this beautiful," a woman objected.

"So..." The man shrugged dismissively. "A *pretty-boy* human, then."

With another gesture from Madame, a ripple ran through the water, carrying something that made Zeph's body arch. He threw his head back, his features crumbling into a grimace of pain, mouth open in a soundless scream.

This couldn't be right.

Why would Zeph be here? How did he end up in that tank?

Zeph's jaw flexed as he bared his teeth. The singing never stopped, however, making me realize it must be a recording. His arms and legs went rigid and straight.

Two pairs of magnificent fins opened, fanning out from his arms—elbow to wrist—and from the back of his legs—knee to ankle. The multi-colored glow in the water curled into iridescent swirls as Zeph slowly rotated inside the tank.

He turned with his back to the audience, and the people broke into gasps of awe. A large, dorsal fin opened on his back like a shimmering sail of gossamer silk stretched between sharp spikes. It reflected the multicolored lights running through the water.

A few people rose from their seats, leaning forward. "How is this attached?"

"It looks too real," someone said, their voice guarded.

"He doesn't seem to be very comfortable in there." An older woman reached over the counter.

Madame quickly slid between the bar and Zeph's tank.

"Please take your seats, ladies and gentlemen. Remember the rules. You cannot touch the glass," she reprimanded sternly.

With murmurs of awe and bewilderment, the audience settled down.

"Enjoy the refreshments," Madame prompted. Obediently, the six at the bar went back to drinking their cocktails and munching on the food.

Madame's smile returned. "I assure you, like all animals in my menagerie, the siren is kept in the utmost comfort. I make sure to maintain the optimal conditions for the wellbeing of my exhibits. Many would not have survived in the wild for as long as they do in my collection."

I stared at Zeph as he completed his rotation to face the audience once again. His expression was now blank, the clear blue eyes gazing vacantly straight ahead. If I had not seen this face vividly animated when he was singing, talking, laughing a year ago, I would've believed there was no thought, no self-awareness behind those eyes, just as Madame had claimed.

But I *did* know better. I remembered everything from our night together. I knew that Zeph was a real man—smart, fun, and intelligent.

It didn't matter right now how things had ended between us. Locking him in that tank was not right. Keeping him there could not be legal.

Fervently, I tried to decide on the best course of action. I should run back, find Fleur, and call the police.

As the light inside the tank dimmed. Radax and his beardless twin left. The people around the bar continued to eat and drink, with Madame telling them some out-of-this-world trivia about the food on their plates.

I had to get out of here before anyone spotted me. I was not looking forward to facing Madame if I were discovered trespassing on her property. Something about that woman made my skin crawl.

I was about to turn around to go back outside when the sound of footsteps and voices behind me made me freeze.

The noise came from the other end of the corridor, around the curve of the wall. The footsteps were heavy, the conversation stilted, as if the men talking were carrying something heavy. The loud thud of a load being set down on the ground confirmed that.

The footsteps then moved in *my* direction!

I searched for a way out. Yanking at the fabric of the outside wall, I made the tarp on its bottom edge crinkle. The heavy sandbags held it down.

"What's that noise?" Radax's voice asked, so close to me.

"Sounds like someone is trying to sneak under the wall again," another deep male voice replied.

The two were so close, they'd see me any moment now.

"Cheap assholes," Radax grumbled. "No one wants to pay. Everyone wants free entertainment."

Panic spiked in me, making it hard to think clearly. Glancing behind the velvet curtain again, I found the VIP clients had left. Madame was gone, too. The dark-haired girl carried out a pile of dirty dishes from the bar.

With not a second to lose, I slipped behind the curtain and into the empty VIP room. Crouching low to the ground, I scurried behind the bar.

The curtain swished open as the two men entered.

"And?" Radax asked.

"Nope. No breach," the second voice replied. "Someone must be just poking around from the outside."

"Good. Let's help Amira spruce this place up. Madame already went to get the second group of VIP clients. They'll be here any minute."

The sound of chairs being re-arranged around the bar jolted me with a shot of alarm. Someone would certainly come behind the bar next.

Scrambling for a better hiding spot, I padded around the stand with the water tank. The gap between the floor and the tank might be just big enough for me to fit under. Getting down on my belly, I wiggled from the rug behind the bar onto the packed dirt under the water tank. Trying my darndest not to sneeze in the dust, I fit my body between the tubes and hoses running from the bottom of the stand.

"Welcome to my special exhibit," Madame's pleasant voice greeted, followed by shuffling noises of people entering. Another group of VIP clients.

How many did she have scheduled for today?

Listening to her speech about the sirens again, I wondered how *did* Zeph breathe under water? It was impossible for anyone to hold their breath for that long, and I didn't notice any tubes or masks inside the tank.

His fins appeared so incredibly realistic, too, as if they were a natural extension of his body. Were they some ingenious mechanical invention? A sophisticated costume? Or some crazy surgical modification, like Fleur had suggested about the piglet?

The last possibility made my stomach churn.

Watching the reflection of the green-and-blue glow from the water tank on the floor in front of my hiding place, I wished I could see his face. His heart-breaking singing floated through the room once again. The song had no lyrics. The wordless pain and longing of the melody made my heart squeeze in compassion.

If it hadn't been for Radax and his buddy out there, I would've been on my way to get help for Zeph already. Instead, I was lying in dirt while he was being ogled and tortured up there.

Fleur must be losing her mind outside, looking for me. I grabbed my phone from my shorts' pocket, finding no messages from her yet. Could she still be in the bathroom? Then I realized, I had absolutely no signal here.

Disheartened, I shoved the phone back in my pocket and remained still, listening to Madame spinning her tales.

# Chapter Nine

IVY

Madame had two more groups of VIP clients that evening. Unless she'd lied to me about the price of admission, which I didn't see a reason for her to do, she'd made a lot of money that day. If she'd done that every day of the CNE, she'd made a fortune during the fair.

Did I rush to assume that Zeph was forced into that tank? What if he was a business partner of Madame? He certainly could earn enough money to buy that place by the ocean he'd dreamed about.

How well did I know him, anyway? He could be performing willingly.

Getting the police involved would be stupid in that case. If anything, I risked being charged with trespassing.

Another question bugged me while I lay under the water tank. Why would people pay this much money just to see an actor float in the tank, no matter how handsome or talented he was?

*"To see the things not found on Earth."* Madame's words came to mind.

For her words to make sense, though, I'd have to believe that Zeph indeed was not of this world.

My legs started to fall asleep, and my back ached after lying in the same position for nearly two hours. The dust and the smoke that slithered under the tank made me incredibly thirsty, too.

Finally, the last group of VIPs departed. The sounds of dishes being cleared then the broom sweeping the floor meant the place was being cleaned for the night, I hoped.

Someone entered.

"It was a good day, but I'm tired now," Madame's voice announced. "Amira, bring my dinner to my trailer once you're done here. Then start packing up."

No audible reply followed, but I wondered if that was the name of the dark-haired ticket-booth girl. She seemed to do pretty much everything around here, from selling tickets, to waitressing, to cleaning up.

"Radax," Madame ordered to another one of her mostly silent helpers. "You have a few hours. We're leaving at sunrise."

A good few minutes passed in silence after Madame had left. Then I heard the deep voice of Radax, "Go, get her dinner now, Amira, then take a nap before packing. I'll finish here."

As brief as the statement was, I caught a warm note in his voice that I didn't expect from someone like him.

"Thank you," came in a barely audible whisper from the girl, then the soft padding of her shoes sounded as she left.

Radax stomped around the tank for a while as I lay still as a mouse, praying he wouldn't decide to check under it. Once he finally left, I waited, listening for any sound out there. All seemed quiet.

It was time to get out of here.

With a deep breath to calm my nerves, I crawled out onto the rug behind the bar. A faint glow from the streetlights filtered through the roof of the tent above, barely making a dent in the darkness.

Poking my head around the bar, I made sure the room was empty before scurrying to the velvet curtain. Before lifting it, though, I paused, staring back at the water tank.

All the lights inside it were off. The dark water made it impossible to see anything through it. I hadn't heard Zeph getting out of it. Did they leave him inside overnight?

Clutching the curtain in my hand, I recalled Zeph's listless expression and his wordless cry, more harrowing because it was soundless in the water. Was all of that just an act?

What exactly was going on here?

Something didn't feel right about this place.

A noise inside the tents snapped me back to the moment. Madame's people must have started to pack up as she'd ordered. Someone would come here, too, sooner or later.

Drawing back the curtain, I peeked into the corridor behind it to make sure no one was there before starting on my way back to the support pole and the gap in the wall I'd used to sneak in.

Right in front of the pole, though, a massive wooden crate now stood, blocking my way. Frantically patting with my hands around the corner of the crate, I realized there simply was no space for me to squeeze behind it.

Unable to get out the way I'd came in, I searched for the bottom end of the canvas wall. If I yanked at it hard enough, I might be able to free its edge from the sandbags outside and crawl under it.

The tarp on the edge made the crackling noise again when I tugged at it.

"Who's there?" A deep male voice suddenly boomed nearby, startling me into panic.

One of Madame's tattooed men shuffled from around the crate.

Holding my breath, I hid behind the crate, pressing my back to it.

A loud groan, accompanied by rattling metal, suddenly came from right behind me. I jumped forward, with a strangled gasp of alarm. The sounds came from inside the crate, I realized, ducking behind it again.

But it was too late, Madame's man had already seen me.

"Hold there!"

The ray from the flashlight in his hand landed on my face, blinding me for a moment. Breathless from terror, I pivoted on my heel and ran as fast as I could back to the VIP room.

With his heavy steps gaining on me from behind, there was no time to stop and check if the space behind the curtain was still free of

Madame's people. I rushed in at full speed and crashed into the hard-as-rock chest of Radax.

"What's going on?" he roared.

Catching me by the scruff of my t-shirt, he lifted me up as if I were a cat.

"Found her snooping around the gorgonian's crate," the one chasing me replied, catching his breath.

"Who are you?" Radax gave me a shake.

"Nobody," I panted. My heart lodged in my throat, choking me with panic. "Please, let me go."

"What the fuck were you doing by the crate?" the one with the flashlight demanded.

"Just, um..." I remembered Radax complaining about people sneaking in to see the menagerie for free. "Just wanted to see the animals. I'll give you the twenty bucks right now." I patted the back pocket of my shorts. "Just let me go, please."

Radax narrowed his eyes at me. "What *did* you see?"

With my shirt in his firm grip, I barely reached the ground with my toes.

"I saw nothing," I lied, desperately hoping it came out convincingly enough. "Nothing at all."

"Weren't you the one I escorted out of here earlier?"

My heart dropped, he'd recognized me. Denying felt stupid at this point, so I just kept quiet, scrambling for what to do next.

"You wanted to see the VIP exhibit, didn't you?" Radax asked next.

He was too smart for a bouncer of his size.

"No. I have no idea what you're talking about..."

"Well, she's seen it, now." The other one scowled, tipping his head toward the tank.

A pale shape was clearly visible in the water. With both hands pressed against the glass, Zeph appeared to be watching us, although his eyes stared into the void unfocused, his expression remained impassive.

"She didn't have the *camyte* drink." Radax scratched his beard. "She can cause trouble if we let her go."

"I won't," I rushed to assure him. "I want no trouble. Promise. I just want to go home."

Getting the police involved felt absolutely necessary now, but I tried not to even think about that yet, afraid they would read it on my face.

"Trez, go get Madame," Radax ordered the other man.

"Oh God, no please," I whimpered, hating to bring her into this. "Not her. Just let me go, and she would never need to know about any of this. Please."

"This is her property." Radax dragged me to the exit of the room. "Her show and her business. She gets to decide what to do with you."

Yawning, her hair wrapped in a silk turban, Madame arrived. Dressed in a pink kimono painted with golden birds, she tossed but one glance at me.

"Kill her," she ordered curtly, a bored expression on her face.

Kill? Me?

Was she serious?

"Madame?" Something briefly crossed Radax's stern features. Not a shock like I felt, but at least some hesitation.

"You heard me, slave. I don't need any troubles here. Kill her."

Was this woman insane?

"Murder for trespassing?" I desperately thrashed in Radax's grip, dangling inside my oversized t-shirt like a rag doll. "But I didn't do anything!"

"You *saw.*" She glared at me.

"Wouldn't killing her cause more trouble?" Radax asked. "The police—"

"The police have no business snooping around here," she cut him off curtly. "But if this creature gets out there and starts babbling about what she's seen—"

"I won't—" I begged, but she wouldn't let me finish.

"I'm not risking my entire establishment on the word of some girl. The only sure way to keep her quiet is to kill her. The dead can't speak. We're leaving the city in a few hours. If anyone asks during this time, she came to see the exhibit with a group of people. She left. We don't know what happened to her next. That's all." She turned to leave. "Do not disturb me with these things again, Radax. You should be able to make at least some decisions yourself."

The horror of my situation descended on me with bone-chilling terror. Madame really meant what she'd ordered. She left the room, looking convinced that her instructions would be followed.

The two men focused their attention on me, their stares crossing at my face. Nothing in their grim expressions promised any leniency for me.

I had begged, with no results. Now panic spurred me into action.

With a pitiful squeak, I lifted my arms straight up and bent my knees, sliding out of my t-shirt which remained dead-locked in Radax's grip. Left only in my bra and shorts, I scurried to my feet and dashed for the exit.

Radax let out a startled humph, then flung my t-shirt aside, taking off after me. Trez followed. Their heavy footfalls thundered behind me as I ran, desperately searching for the way out of this canvas maze.

The walls disappeared suddenly as I darted into the section of the tent where a group of men, all tattooed, bald, and as large as Radax, were working on tearing the place down. The fabric partitions had been removed and laid in neat rolls on the floor.

Leaping over them, I dashed through the open space.

Burly arms reached for me from every direction. I ducked under them. Darting my gaze around, I frantically searched for any kind of gap or opening—a way out of this nightmare. Not finding one, I tore at the wall in a desperate attempt to yank the bottom edge from under the sand bags weighing it down from the outside.

Unexpectedly, the canvas gave in under my pull—the bags must've been removed already. Dropping down on my hands and knees, I dove under it and crawled.

Freedom was so close. The cooling night air brushed my face outside.

Then someone grabbed my leg, yanking me back inside, hard. I kicked, aiming at the hand holding my ankle.

"Let me go!" I yelled at the top of my lungs, hoping that someone on the fairgrounds would hear me. "Help!"

"Fuck! Get her in here!"

More hands grabbed me, shoving me into the ground. Still, I wouldn't give up, kicking, punching, and thrashing with everything I had. Panic made me stronger, but there were so many of them on me now, holding me down.

When I could no longer move, I still kept screaming.

"Shut up," Radax growled, slapping a hand over my mouth.

With my face down, I couldn't be sure if it was *his* knee shoved between my shoulder blades, pressing me into the dirt.

"Snap her neck," Trez gritted through his teeth. "Make it quick."

Horror sent me into a frenzy. I fought against the hands holding me, even as I could not move an inch in their iron grip.

Struggling, I managed to kick my feet up, smashing my heels into someone on top of me. The person shifted slightly with a grunt. Using the moment, I slipped from under them, almost wiggling free.

A hand grabbed my hair from behind, lifting my head up.

"Stop this," Radax snarled into my ear.

He yanked at my hair, and I bit into his hand covering my mouth.

He cursed under his breath, grabbing me by my throat. "You're *done*, don't you see? Stop fighting."

He pressed the entire bulk of his body onto me, squeezing the air out of my chest.

"I'm not lying here for you to wring my neck," I growled right back at him.

"What else can you do?" he asked, sounding genuinely puzzled.

Barely able to breathe with his weight on top of me, I croaked, "Keep fighting you." Ridiculous claim—since I couldn't even scream for help. Every word came out in a hoarse half-whisper.

His chest pushed against my back with his long inhalation of air. Then I felt him shift off me. One hand still in my hair, the other wrapped around my throat, he yanked me up to my feet, nearly snapping my neck, after all.

Wheezing, I scratched with my fingers against his hand, fighting for air.

He leaned toward my face, staring at me with the most bizarre eyes—red streaks like spokes on a bike pulsed through his brown irises.

"If you scream again, you'll die," he said slowly, his gaze locked with mine, as if he willed me to understand the full meaning of his words. "If you try to run away, you'll die. Do what you're told, promptly and wordlessly, and you may have a chance."

"Just fucking kill her," Trez growled, moving in on us.

Red streaks of light flashed along the lines of the tattoo on Trez's neck and down his right arm, triggering my memory. I remembered where I'd seen that before.

Paris.

The dark courtyard I'd entered with Zeph on the night of our "adventure." These were the people who'd accosted us then.

Now, I knew why the scent of the smoke still clinging to the walls of the tent seemed familiar, too. The cigarettes that Lero had smoked that night smelled exactly like that.

Radax relaxed his grip, letting go of my neck. "She may still be useful. Alive."

I fell to my knees, coughing and gasping for air. He yanked my cell phone out of my back pocket, tossed in onto the ground, and crushed it under his boot.

"Lock her in the griffin's cage and load it into the truck with the animals," Radax ordered.

"But Madame—" Trez glared at me.

"Madame trusts me to make my own decisions," Radax snapped at him. "Hurry, we're leaving at sunset."

# Chapter Ten

IVY

It was a huge bird cage, tall enough for me to stand up at my full height of five feet and a half. The round base allowed me to lay down with my legs bent.

Trez had shoved me inside, glaring silently. He locked the door and threw a large dusty rug over the cage, plunging me into a nearly complete darkness.

The moment I was left alone, I rushed to the door and inspected the lock by touch. The narrow rectangular box was fitted between the bars of the cage. It didn't appear to have any movable parts I could attempt to manipulate in order to unlock it.

Next, I patted the floor of my prison, which was a piece of plywood thrown over a metal grate. There was no getting out that way either. The bars of the cage were as thick as my finger, unyielding when I tried to shake or bend them.

The cage was lifted and carried off, probably to load me onto a truck as per Radax's instructions. I briefly contemplated screaming again, in hopes that someone unrelated to this freakshow would hear me.

*"If you scream again, you'll die."* Radax's warning sounded in my mind.

Chances were, he would get to me before anyone else if I screamed. The memory of his rough fingers gripping my neck made me rub my sore throat. I had every reason to believe he'd kill me if I disobeyed his instructions. Madame wanted him to, after all.

Sooner or later, they would have to let me out of this cage to feed me or at least to let me use the bathroom. There might be an opportunity to escape, then.

Madame had said they were about to leave the country. If so, I had to get the attention of border control.

Sitting on the floor, I kept quiet as they loaded my cage. A short while later, the truck moved, taking me to some unknown place.

I waited for the truck to stop, for any noise outside to let me know we were at the border crossing, but none came. After a while, I must've fallen asleep.

When I woke up, the rhythmic sound of a train on tracks could only mean that they'd loaded my cage into a train car.

I had no idea how much time had passed and how far from Toronto I was. A scary thought that we might've successfully crossed the border by now sank heavily in my stomach.

How could I have fallen asleep?

The late hour of the night, the receding rush of adrenaline after having Radax nearly crush my windpipe, the rocking movement of the vehicle afterwards—all combined proved to be enough to lull me to sleep, even as my life and freedom were at stake. Now, I couldn't shake the heavy feeling that I'd missed a chance to end this nightmare.

On the other hand, staying awake might not have helped me. Radax must've been confident he could smuggle me across the border without an issue. Otherwise, why would he defy Madame's orders, keep me alive, and take me along?

I had no idea to what purpose Radax had spared me. Madame obviously saw no value in my life. What was he planning to do with me behind her back?

Despite the stifling heat inside the train car, shivers ran through my body. I was still wearing only my bra and denim shorts, feeling vulnerable, miserable, and alone.

Fear vibrated inside me. Curling up on the plywood floor of my cage, I let the tears out. Crying for as long as it lasted helped me to calm down somewhat, enough to be able to think again.

With the rug covering my cage, it was almost completely dark inside. Dark and stuffy. Slipping my hand through the bars, I lifted the heavy cover up a little, peeking out.

It was a cargo car. Some light filtered in between the wall boards. In the semi-darkness, I spotted a few crates of various sizes stacked on top of each other. Rolls of the tent fabric were piled up nearby.

A small figure was curled up on top of the pile. Her shoulders covered by her black scarf, Amira appeared to be sleeping among the luggage and equipment of Madame's show.

I wasn't sure what to think of Amira and her role in this place. Could she possibly help me in my situation if I woke her up? Or was she here to keep an eye on me during the trip? In that case, I'd rather she kept sleeping.

Instead, I studied my surroundings in more detail. A large object stood in the corner of the car. Draped in yellow tarp, it seemed big enough to house a couple of my cages. Recognizing the rounded shape of it, I realized it must be Zeph's water tank. It had to be empty now.

They wouldn't transport Zeph inside it, would they?

The tank stood close enough to my cage for me to try to reach it. I spotted a fold where the two ends of the tarp overlapped. Through the gap, obsidian water glistened behind the glass.

Tossing a cautious glance at a sleeping Amira, I reached through the bars and tugged the tarp aside a little, hoping to see more. My fingers brushed by the glass. A charge shot up my arm like electricity, not as painful but even more intense.

*"Help!"*

The plea didn't come as a word but as a feeling, bursting through my chest with a desperation so strong it had the power of a physical punch. I jerked my hand away, falling back on my ass.

What was that?

Whatever it was, it definitely came from the tank.

I pressed my hand to my chest, willing my heart to slow down. Then I examined my fingers that had touched the glass, and found nothing unusual.

What had just happened? And what did it mean?

*"Do not touch the glass,"* Madame's warning to her VIP clients came to mind.

Was this what she'd been afraid of?

Crawling on all fours back to the edge of the cage, I wiggled my arm through the bars again, all the way to my shoulder. With a deep breath, I splayed my hand on the glass, pressing on it firmly.

*"Help!"* came again, with the same power and intensity. Prepared for it now, I didn't remove my hand, allowing the emotions from the message to wash over me.

Sorrow.

Despair.

Fear.

All churned and curled together, filtering through the glass to me. They were the echo of what I was feeling in this place.

I was trapped here, too.

As if the sender of the message had sensed that, the painful desperation eased, giving way to an unexpected warmth of comfort.

Was that Zeph who was trying to console me? Did Madame really leave him in there?

He never left that tank, just like I was afraid I would not be allowed to get out of this cage.

"Zeph," I whispered.

*"Who are you?"* came back, loud and clear.

I glanced back at Amira, afraid the words might wake her up. Then I realized I didn't hear them with my ears. Zeph's voice sounded directly in my mind.

It was raspy, and dull, but it was his voice. I'd recognize it anywhere.

"I'm—" I stopped. Instead of saying it, I *thought* my reply, *"I'm Ivy."*

*"Ivy..."* It sounded like an echo, hollow, without recognition or emotion.

*"You don't remember me?"*

*"No."*

It pinched my pride. I hadn't stopped thinking about Zeph for over a year now. Yet he had no recollection of me at all.

*"Well, I guess I didn't leave a lasting impression."* I scoffed inside.

A warm feeling tingled up my arm. *"Don't be sad."*

The emotion was comforting. He tried to make me feel better, and somehow it worked.

I stroked the glass, warmed by my touch. When I moved my hand aside, a palm came into view. Zeph held his hand pressed to the opposite side of the glass.

I had no idea how this conversation was even possible. Maybe I had simply lost my mind and was now hearing voices in my head. But I didn't really care, as long as it helped me feel less scared and less alone.

*"Zeph, tell me what you know about Madame."*

*"Who?"*

*"You don't remember her, either?"*

*"No."*

*"It's the woman who trapped you in this tank. Do you have any memories of how that happened?"*

*"No."*

I'd hoped to learn more about this place from him, but it appeared I knew more than he did.

*"Well, Madame's men caught me. We ran into them in Paris, remember? Huge guys, bald with tattoos—"*

*"Bracks."* The word came sharp and forceful like a bullet shot from a gun.

*"Bracks? What does it mean?"*

*"Ghata's men. Her monks. Her slaves."*

Madame had called Radax a slave. I'd heard her.

*"Who is Ghata?"*

*"A goddess."*

*"What?"* Was he joking?

Sadly, there was not a hint of humor in his voice.

*"Ghata is a disgraced goddess from Sarnala."*

Madame's words from the show sounded in my mind, *"Sarnala, the land of werewolves."*

Could there be any truth to what she'd said about the magical kingdom? Or was everyone around me delusional, including Zeph?

*"How do you know about Madame...I mean, Ghata?"*

*"She fled Nerifir, banished by the werewolves whom she'd wronged. Lero and I came with her."*

*"You remember Lero?"*

*"Of course I do, he's my one true family."*

Family?

The memory of the scent from Lero's cigarette, the same scent that Madame's cigarette had, tickled my nostrils.

*"How about Ghata? Since you fled together, is she your friend?"*

There was no answer. He either didn't want to tell me or simply no longer knew himself.

*"Who are you, Zeph?"*

This time, the answer came promptly and without hesitation. *"I'm a siren."*

A siren. A being from another world. Someone who swam better than fish, using the fins on his body. Who could breathe underwater. Who sang like an angel and heard the call of the sea.

Could all of that be true?

*"You're confused,"* his voice sounded in my mind.

*"'Confused' is a not strong enough word, I'm afraid."*

*"Lost?"*

That seemed accurate.

*"I'm lost, Zeph. So very lost in here."*

*"Stay with me. Together we're stronger."* Was there a tendril of emotion in his voice this time? Hope, maybe?

*"Are we, Zeph?"* I aligned my palm with his. If it weren't for the glass, we could've laced our fingers together.

*"You distract me from pain, Ivy."*

My chest tightened, and I sucked in a breath. *"Are you hurting?"*

*"I can't breathe."*

*"But don't sirens breathe under water?"*

*"The water is toxic. It's killing me."*

*"Oh, Zeph..."* I flexed my fingers, my nails scraping against the thick glass. *"Tell me how to get you out of there? Is there a way to open the tank?"*

First, I'd have to find a way out of this cage, then—

*"It's inescapable, Ivy. Here, I will die..."*

# Chapter Eleven

IVY

The train came to a stop. Amira stirred, and I quickly pulled my arm back into the cage. Dropping the edge of the rug back in place, I sat in the darkness once again.

*"Here, I will die..."* Zeph's voice sounded in my head. I fought the gloomy feeling that it could also apply to me.

Amira moved around. I heard more people joining her in the car.

No one said a word. The sounds of doors being opened and objects being moved filtered through the rug covering my cage.

Hope stirred in me. Was there a train station? Could I signal for help somehow?

Crawling around the floor of the cage, I anxiously tried to peek under the rug to assess the situation.

The rug was lifted, bringing me face to face with Amira who was holding a bowl with steaming porridge in her hands.

The deep and narrow bowl fit between the bars, and Amira placed it on the floor of the cage in front of me. She then put a bottle of water next to it.

I darted a glance behind her. At least half a dozen men from Madame's staff were unloading the car.

*Bracks*. The slaves of a goddess.

I struggled to wrap my mind around that. They looked like ordinary people, dressed in modern clothes. The men were definitely larger than average. Bald, every single one of them. They had identical tattoos, the lines of each the exact copy of another.

Come to think about it, it was unnatural how similar they looked. Their facial features were different enough for me to tell them apart if I looked closely, but they all had the same color eyes—brown.

One of the men stubbed the toe of his boot on a crate. He cursed under his breath. Red sparks flashed up the lines of his tattoo. Definitely not "ordinary."

The wide sliding door on the side of the train car was open. A truck stood next to the railcar, the back doors of its trailer open. The men loaded the crates, rolls, and containers into it. Other than the *bracks*, there were no people in sight.

My hope of getting help was crushed once again. Even if I managed to get out of this cage somehow and ran, the *bracks* wouldn't let me get far away. Carrying an enormous crate on his shoulder, Radax glanced my way as if to drive that point deeper into my mind.

"I need to use a bathroom," I said to Amira. This wasn't a lie. I had to pee.

Fear flashed in her eyes as I spoke. She cowered as if I'd physically struck her with my words.

"Sorry, but unless you want me to pee on the floor..." I mumbled, confused by her reaction.

She threw a tentative glance at Radax. He was coming back after having loaded the crate into the truck.

"Bathroom." Amira's whisper was barely there. Even this close to her, I could hardly hear her.

Fishing a key out of his pocket, Radax unlocked the door of the cage.

I climbed out, and he gestured for me to follow him, maneuvering between the working men. One of them separated from the group and followed Radax and me.

We squeezed through the side gap between the railcar and the truck's trailer and climbed outside.

It was evening already with the edge of the setting sun barely showing over the horizon.

"Where are we?" I turned around, noting a low, flat-roofed building —possibly a station or a train depot—but no signs of a town or other people around. Even the driver's seat in the truck cab was empty.

"Silence," Radax snarled.

The other man shoved me toward the blue booth of a portable toilet that stood by the rail tracks.

I used it promptly, not wishing to aggravate Radax's temper. When I came outside again, the two men were standing on each side of the toilet door like sentinels to some magical portal. The thought made me snort a laugh, despite my mood being far from merry.

Radax stared at me with a weird expression on his face.

I wrapped my arms around myself, shielding my lacy bra from his stare. "Can I get some clothes?"

Without saying a word, he took his black t-shirt off and handed it to me. Unsure about wearing the shirt of a stranger, still uncomfortably warm with his body heat, I hesitated for a second, then put it on—it was better than being half-naked.

Back in my cage, I greedily drank half of the water from the bottle Amira had left for me, then ate the oatmeal with my hand since she hadn't brought a spoon.

Soon, my cage was loaded into the truck.

When the trailer's doors closed, I lifted the edge of the rug, searching for Zeph's water tank. Its large shape loomed nearby, draped in yellow. I exhaled in relief that he was here. However, the tank stood too far for me to reach it this time.

"Zeph," I whispered.

But there was no answer. I searched my mind, listening for his voice, but it never came. Without the touch, the connection between us was broken.

I assumed we came to another fair. My cage was placed in the bowels of the tents somewhere. The noise of the crowds outside of their fabric walls reached me only as a distant hum.

Radax gave me a warning look, before covering the cage with the rug again.

I knew what that warning meant: I was not to yell for help.

It was tempting to do so, since I knew the menagerie visitors passed through the tents daily. Someone might hear me if I screamed loud enough. But the *bracks* would get to me first before anyone else would. They knew the layout of the tents much better than the outsiders. I wouldn't live long after that, I feared. After all, Radax was hiding me from Madame, who wanted me dead.

The freedom seemed so close, just beyond the striped fabric. Yet as far away as ever.

I didn't see Zeph again. His tank must've been put back into the VIP room, for the rich people to gawk and marvel. He'd asked me to stay with him, and I wish I could. But even just knowing that he was in here somewhere, that I wasn't entirely alone in this place gave me strength.

Amira brought me a bowl of porridge each morning and night, and a sandwich at lunch. I tried to speak with her when no one else was around, but she hid her face in the voluminous scarf around her neck and scurried away as fast as she could. If I hadn't heard her speak before, I would've believed she was mute.

One day, when Amira came to pick up my bowl after dinner, a loud squealing noise pierced the air.

"Oh, you little spawn of Satan!" Madame exclaimed somewhere close. Way too close, as Amira's face paled with horror.

Quickly, she hid the empty bowl between some crates nearby and yanked at the rug to cover my cage. In her haste, she didn't make it come down all the way, leaving a gap for me to peek through.

The squealing intensified. Then a flash of pink dashed into the room.

"You come here." Madame burst in as well, chasing the two-headed piglet. "Oh good, you're here," she exhaled at the sight of Amira.

Winded, Madame tucked a strand of her bright red hair behind her ear and smoothed her hands over her richly embroidered white blouse. "Can you catch him?"

Amira nodded, diving after the pig.

Trez appeared in the doorway. His gaze landed on my cage. I shrank away from the gap.

"Is that where she is?" Madame asked. "In the cage?"

Breath caught in my chest.

Had Trez ratted me out to her?

The rug flew off, and I came face to face with Madame. Her expression left no doubt—she was furious.

"What is she doing here?" She moved on to Amira. "And how, by gods, is she still alive?"

Trembling like a leaf, Amira backed up all the way to the furthest wall in the room.

"It was Radax." Trez smirked. "He disobeyed your order."

"Radax!" Madame yelled, then whipped around to face Amira. "Were you in on this, too?"

Amira just stared at her, pale and still, as if frozen in horror.

"Well, getting rid of two human corpses wouldn't be much more difficult than one," Madame hissed.

Amira looked ready to pass out from fear. I felt sorry for the poor girl. Though, I realized that mine would be one of the corpses Madame was talking about.

"It's not her fault!" I shouted from my cage.

With a flash of panic in her eyes, Amira shot me a warning glance.

The piglet dashed between her feet, nipping at her ankle. She yelped, then bent over quickly, finally catching him. He squealed, fighting against her grip, and bit her hand, but she barely winced at the pain, holding him out to Madame.

Did she hope to pacify her by catching her pet?

If so, it didn't work.

"Radax!" Madame yelled louder, snatching the piglet from Amira. "Where, by the River of Mists, is that slave?"

"I'm here, Madame." Radax rushed in, panting from running

through the textile corridors of the tents. A few more of her men came with him, crowding the small space.

Madame's gaze fell on me and understanding spread on Radax's face. Unlike Amira, he did not cower. His chest rose with a deep breath, his expression resolute.

Madame cradled the pig in her arms. The bizarre animal calmed down in her arms, resting its two heads, one in each of the crooks of her elbows.

"I want you to kill these two females right now, in my presence, then explain to me why I have to give the same order twice." Her voice was cold and sharp like a blade.

I crawled backwards all the way to the back of the cage, my prison suddenly feeling like a safe place.

Radax frowned, darting his gaze from me to Amira.

"Why does Amira need to die?" he asked, not objecting to *my* death.

Madame huffed. "I found her here with the girl she helped you smuggle—"

"She didn't," Radax interrupted. "I made that decision on my own."

"And why would you do that?" Madame's voice dropped in volume, somehow sounding even more menacing that way.

"I figured the girl could be useful."

"How? Pray tell."

He scratched his beard, hesitating.

"She could help Amira take care of things around here."

"Does Amira need help?"

The girl had squeezed herself into a corner, her gaze flickering between Radax and Madame as the attention of both turned to her.

"With the number of new arrivals we're having, Amira could certainly use some help," Radax replied. "There is just too much work for her alone."

"Then maybe she could use her time a little more efficiently?" Madame retorted. "The only interaction I want to have with humans is when they give me their money. It's bad enough you're making me deal with her," she gestured at Amira, who looked like she wished she was dead already. "You dragged that one in here. Now, you decided to keep this one, too?"

"There is no need to kill the new girl," Radax argued. "Make her drink *camyte*, like the others, and let her go—"

"*Camyte* is rare and precious. I'm not wasting it on some commoner off the streets just to keep her quiet. Besides, it's way too late. She should've had it *before* she saw anything here. Tell me..." She paused, giving him a long stare. "You spoke to her, didn't you? That's why you saved her. Out of compassion."

It sounded like an accusation—a grave one at that as Radax flexed his jaw, his rough features hardened. Amira leaned forward, alarm plastered on her terrified face.

"That is what you will be punished for, slave," Madame announced, with an eerie flush of crimson in her dark eyes. "For *talking*, knowing that I forbid it."

Petting one of the pig's heads, she kept her unnervingly intense stare on Radax as everyone in the room stilled.

Radax took a step back, then stopped abruptly as if frozen in place. His tattoos sparked to life. Bright red streaks flashed along the intricate lines. The sparks concentrated around his neck, as if setting it on fire. His hands fisting tight at his sides, his eyes bulging, he seemed to be suffocating, with no one even touching him.

His neck tattoo appeared to be heating and tightening under Madame's glare, squeezing the life out of this huge, strong man.

"No!" Amira's panicky voice cut through the air. Staggering forward, she sank to her knees in front of Madame, pressing her clenched hands to her chest. "Don't hurt him, please," she begged, words rushing out of her like a waterfall. "I kept her, I fed her... It's all my fault. Please, please spare Radax."

Madame diverted her attention to Amira. With her gaze slipping over to the girl, the tattoo on Radax's neck seemed to relax its grip. His massive shoulders dropped, his chest rising and falling rapidly as he panted for air.

"Humans." From Madame's lips, the word sounded like an expletive. "Foolish and ignorant. I know you're lying, girl. You're too meek to act on your own. But I will spare Radax, because he is more useful to me alive than dead, for now. You, however, are replaceable. Keep that in mind. If you wish to live, you can't make any further mistakes." She raised her head, addressing everyone in the room now, "Radax needs to be punished for talking to a human without my permission. Trez, give him as many lashes as he can take."

Trez stepped forward, cracking his knuckles. Another *brack* handed him a coiled, black whip.

"And someone, bring me a chair," Madame demanded. "I'm staying to personally ensure my orders are carried out, this time."

# Chapter Twelve

IVY

The number of lashes Radax could take seemed infinite. I couldn't look away, gripping the bars of the cage so hard my hands hurt.

The whip in Trez's hand hissed through the air, landing with a splatter of blood onto the mutilated back of Radax. The thick red welts of the early blows had split open, his back a mass of torn skin and muscles soaked in blood. Yet he stood tall, his arms held by two other *bracks*.

Whimpering softly, Amira curled up in a corner. Her dark eyes were open wide. Streams of silent tears streaked her pale sunken cheeks. Biting down on her fist, she stared at Radax, unblinking.

Madame sat in a tall-backed chair, the pig nestled in her lap. Her expression remained calm, a bit bored even.

Another swish of the whip cut through the air. Another wet, splattering sound came when it hit the mangled flesh.

*"Just fall already. Give up. Pretend, if you must,"* I mentally begged Radax to end his own torture.

It didn't matter what he did or didn't do. I no longer cared what kind of a man he really was. I simply wanted this cruelty to stop.

Finally, his head lolled to the side. The men holding him let go, and he sank to his knees then toppled over like a cut-down tree.

"Well." Madame rose to her feet. "You'll be rewarded tonight, Trez. Come to my trailer after dinner."

Trez smirked, gathering the whip into blood-soaked coils.

I glared at him. He'd betrayed and then brutally whipped someone he worked with. Maybe they weren't friends, but they were colleagues. Yet Trez displayed no remorse or compassion.

Then I remembered *compassion* was what Radax had been punished for in the first place. What kind of an organization was Madame running here? Ruthless and cruel like herself.

One of the men tipped his chin at Radax spread on the floor. "This needs to be treated," he said impassively. "Or it may start to rot by morning."

Madame shrugged. "He'll heal."

Another *brack* scratched his bald head. "Who's going to do his work while he's healing?"

With an exasperated sigh, Madame conceded, "Fine. You can treat his wounds."

Amira scurried on her hands and knees to Radax.

"Not you!" Madame stopped her. Her gaze then fell on me. "Well. Looks like you may be useful after all." She turned to the *brack* who'd spoken last. "Ulg, let this one out. Lock her back in again once she's done."

On her way to the exit from the room, she tossed a glance at Radax's large, broken body on the floor.

"Let her use the *Biqirelle* crystals on him, so he will return to work sooner."

Madame left, followed by Trez and the rest. Ulg unlocked my cage, letting me out. He waited until Amira brought a dish with warm water and a stack of clean rags. Ulg then left, too, probably to fetch the crystals as he had been ordered to do.

Amira placed everything she'd brought next to Radax, then went to sit on a crate in the shadows a few feet away. Following Madame's orders, she didn't touch Radax, though I could see it on her face how much she wanted to take care of him.

I got down on my knees at his side, wondering where to begin. My medical skills were extremely limited. With any injury too large to be covered by a band-aid, I'd normally just go to the closest emergency room.

This was something I'd never seen before, not even in the movies. Radax's back was just one open wound, blood dripping down his sides and permeating the air with its heavy, metallic smell. I'd never had nausea at the sight of blood before. With this much of it, though, my head swam dizzily, and my stomach roiled.

"That's what she does to her own people." I shook my head.

I dipped a cloth into the water, then carefully wiped the rivulets of coagulating blood off his sides where the skin was not broken.

Radax didn't move, and I prayed he was still alive. Passing out was probably good for him, though. I couldn't even imagine how much pain he'd be in if he were awake.

After a few more dips, the water in the bowl quickly turned red, and Amira replaced it, furtively shoving a small vial into my hand.

"What's this?" I stared at the iridescent liquid inside the small crystal bottle.

She pressed a finger to her lips in a call to be silent. After what we'd just witnessed, I understood her reluctance to speak.

Checking over my shoulder to make sure Ulg wasn't returning yet, I shuffled a little closer to her, leaning in. "Hey, if you want me to give this to him, you'll need to tell me what it is."

She hesitated but only for a second.

"It's *camyte*," she whispered, leaning closer. "He needs to drink it."

"Will it make his pain less?"

"No. But it'll make him care less about it."

Sounded like some kind of anesthetic with a twist.

Radax stirred with a groan, and I uncorked the bottle, then brought it to his lips.

"Drink this," I whispered into his ear, as quietly as possible. "It'll help."

After assisting him to shift to his side, I held the vial at his lips as he drank. I then handed the empty bottle to Amira, and she quickly hid it inside the black oversized hoodie she wore.

Ulg stomped in soon after.

"Crystals." He dropped a small leather trunk on the floor next to me. "Here are the diagrams on how to place them on his back. Use the third one." He shoved a scroll into my hands then left.

Amira took away the bowl with bloody water and returned with a pillow and a blanket for Radax. He lay on his belly, his head turned to the side. I stuffed the pillow under it, covered his legs with the blanket, then placed a clean cloth over his back.

I glanced at the leather chest and the scroll. "Is this really necessary?"

The items appeared as something from a treasure hunt game rather than medical supplies. It didn't seem right to disturb Radax, now that he'd settled down.

Amira nodded eagerly, obviously convinced Radax needed this.

I opened the trunk, finding inside several velvet-lined trays stacked on top of each other. Each tray contained a layer of colorful crystals. Some looked like lens disks with a faceted surface. Others were shaped like elongated diamonds, trapezoids, and pentagons—polished and smooth.

Unrolling the scroll, I found a number of drawings that looked like puzzles made of the crystals from the trunk. I counted the third drawing and set to work, arranging the crystals on top of Radax's back in the pattern of the diagram.

It was hard not to feel silly, putting together a pretty crystal puzzle on the cloth that was soaked with the man's blood.

This place was insane. And I was going crazy with the rest of them, not just because I was doing what they told me to do, but because I genuinely hoped this crystal arrangement would help heal the injured man and ease his suffering.

As soon as I finished the first row of crystals, a light sparked inside each of them. It then grew, reaching from one crystal to another, connecting them.

"Wow," I breathed out in awe, quickly adding more crystals while making sure to follow the pattern precisely. If I misplaced one piece, the whole structure stopped glowing until I got it just right.

Once done, I leaned back, admiring the glow. It blended all the colors of the crystals into magnificent swirls, covering Radax's entire back and illuminating the space around him.

Carefully, I held my hand over the glow, feeling a gentle warming sensation.

"Incredible," I whispered. "What are these things?"

I didn't expect anyone to answer my question, least of all Amira, but she actually replied, "*Biqirelle* crystals from the Dakath Mountains in Nerifir."

Relief was clear on her face, now that Radax had been cared for.

"Have you been to Nerifir?" I asked.

"No." She shook her head. "Only the *bracks* travel between the worlds. Except for Radax. He's lost his ability to cross dimensions." She stared at the sleeping man on the floor. "Thankfully, Madame still finds him useful."

At the sound of approaching footsteps, Amira scurried back into her corner. Ulg returned, making no further conversation possible.

"Time for bed." The *brack* sneered at me, holding the door to the cage wide open.

With a glare at him, I climbed inside again.

Instead of falling asleep that night, I thought about this bizarre world of Madame's menagerie.

Who was this woman? Zeph claimed Madame was a goddess. It couldn't be true, of course, but what other explanation did I have?

Madame had grown men at her beck and call. She ordered them to whip each other to the point of passing out, and they obeyed, with not a word of protest. They seemed to be vying for her attention. That must be at least a part of the reason why Trez betrayed Radax today.

She spoke English without an accent, called herself "Madame" in the French manner, but had an Asian last name and wore colorful traditional Eastern European or oriental style clothing.

Her eyes were black as coal and her hair red as fire. Despite its vivid intensity, her hair color seemed natural, evenly distributed from the tip to the root.

I had a hard time pinpointing her age. Her skin glowed smoothly, fresh like that of a twenty-year-old. However, her facial expressions often made her appear ancient. Her hard confidence and cold-blooded brutality also must have taken years to develop to the level they reached in her.

And all that talk about other worlds and dimensions...

Maybe I was being brainwashed along with the rest of them, but the existence of the magical kingdom of Nerifir no longer seemed that ridiculous.

Lying on the floor in my cage, I glanced at Radax, just a few feet away. The multi-colored glow pulsated softly over his back.

What if all of it was real?

Wouldn't the things I'd seen here and couldn't explain all fall into place, if I just believed that the extraordinary existed?

Crystals that glowed and emitted warmth, without any obvious source of energy.

Pigs with two heads that apparently belonged to a three-headed species.

Tattoos that under the gaze of a woman could strangle a man, possibly to death.

A man, whose voice could bring people to tears of joy. A man, who could breathe underwater for longer than was humanly possible and communicate, using nothing but touch.

How exactly did Zeph fit into all of this?

Madame's menagerie was either one huge deception or a twilight zone between two worlds. Which made Zeph either an actor, pretending to be something he was not, or an actual being from another world, like Madame claimed he was.

Either way, it meant that I knew absolutely nothing about the man I'd spent a night with back in Paris.

Could I trust anything he'd told me?

His wordless plea for help when I'd touched the water tank rippled through me again with the ache of an aftershock. His despair had felt so real. My arm tingled at the memory of the warm feeling he'd sent through the glass afterwards. I had no idea how it had happened, but I craved it again.

Longing stirred in me when I thought about Zeph. I'd wanted to be strong and try to forget him, but I missed him. All these long months since Paris, I'd missed him.

With a soft whimper in her sleep, Amira stirred on a pile of some bags and fabric rolls in the corner. She'd found a pillow and a blanket for Radax, but had settled for the night without either for herself.

In her impeccable obedience to Madame's orders, she'd never once come close enough to Radax to touch him. However, she stayed here for the night.

An important thing happened today—Amira spoke to me. We both witnessed the punishment Madame shelled out for speaking around here. Yet Amira, as timid and terrified of her own shadow as she appeared to be all the time, spoke a few full sentences to me, without being forced to do so.

# Chapter Thirteen

IVY

By the next morning, Radax's wounds had miraculously turned to scars that normally would take weeks to form.

Amira seemed pleased by that, but when I tried to talk to her at breakfast time, she met my attempt with silence, returning to being her usual self, a silent shadow of a person.

Since then, however, my presence in the menagerie was no longer questioned or concealed. Madame let me live, at least for now. I was still locked up, let out only to use the bathroom, but no one bothered covering my cage anymore while we were at the fair.

When the time came for Madame's show to change locations once again, they threw a rug over my cage and loaded it into a truck. The moment it moved, I lifted the rug.

Animal cages surrounded mine, filled with the menagerie's furry and scaly inhabitants. But Zeph's tank was there, too, barely an arm's length from me. Just like before, it was wrapped into a yellow tarp. My heart leaped with hope.

Threading my arm between the bars, I splayed my hand on the tarp.

*"Zeph?"*

There was no answer.

Was he even there?

Worry stirred inside me.

The tarp might be the problem. I needed to touch the glass.

I searched along the side of the water tank, looking for any gap or opening to reach inside. There were none.

Only when I got up to my tiptoes, holding onto the bars of my cage, was I able to feel the end of the tarp on the very top of the tank. Hooking my fingers over it, I grazed the cold, smooth glass.

*"Zeph?"*

*"Who are you?"*

He was there. Alive. Relief flooded me so strongly, it nearly made my knees buckle. I gripped the bars tighter to stay upright.

*"Who are you?"* he repeated.

*"It's me. Ivy. We've spoken before, remember?"* He'd confessed he had no memories of me in Paris, but our last conversation had happened much more recently.

*"I don't remember."*

I had to really focus to "hear" his voice. It sounded faint and low, merely a hoarse whisper. Suddenly, I realized why Madame used a recording of his singing for her VIP shows. Zeph could no longer sing, even if she forced him.

*"It hurts to breathe, Ivy."*

My heart squeezed painfully at the suffering in his voice. This wasn't an act. It couldn't be. I *felt* his pain. It was real.

*"Oh, Zeph... We have to get out of here. We have to get away from Ghata."*

A chill of resentment drifted from the tank up my arm, the moment I thought of her.

*"Don't drink or eat anything she gives you,"* came the warning. *"Don't breathe the smoke."*

The truck jolted on the rough road. I lost my balance, lurching sideways. My cage shifted, sliding along the floor.

*"Zeph!"* I scrambled up, gripping the bars. Clawing at the tarp, I tried to get back to the opening on the top of the tank, but it was out of reach now. *"Zeph..."*

It was a long trip, with only occasional stops for bathroom breaks and for food for me and the animals.

I never saw Amira feeding Zeph. How did he survive at all? Even if he truly was an otherworldly siren, didn't he need some sustenance to live? Or Madame simply didn't care whether he lived or died?

Anger boiled inside me, making sitting idly in the cage even more torturous. I had to do something, only I didn't know how. I was locked in a cage, surrounded by guards twice my size and many times my strength.

The air seemed cooler, making me wonder if we were traveling north. I tried to calculate how long I'd been in this cage. According to my calculations, it was October already. How much longer would I have to spend in this cage?

I had to get Zeph out of that tank. I feared there wasn't much time left for that.

*"Here, I will die..."*

His words worried me. The way he'd sounded the last time we "spoke" only added to my concern. He'd sounded like he was fading away.

At the next stop, Amira brought me a large black hoodie, similar to the one she wore.

She silently shoved it through the bars into the cage, along with a bowl of porridge and a bottle of water, then left, avoiding eye contact.

Stirring my dinner, I noticed a spark of pink in one spot in the porridge. It sparkled subtly in the semi-darkness of the truck, like a sprinkle of pink glitter. I brought the bowl closer to my eyes, but couldn't find the shimmer again.

The scent of the food seemed different today. A pleasant fragrance blended with the smell of watery oatmeal. It made it more appealing, but *different*.

I let go of the spoon.

*"Don't drink or eat anything she gives you,"* Zeph had said.

I'd been eating at Madame's menagerie for weeks now. So far, I didn't think the food had affected me in any negative way, had it? I was still alive. If anything, I could use more to eat. A bowl of porridge twice a day and a sandwich at lunch wasn't much, even if I spent my days sitting in a cage, doing nothing.

But Madame hadn't known I was in the menagerie, until recently.

Could this new "food flavoring" have something to do with her decision to leave me alive?

My stomach growled. I was hungry, but what would happen if I ate this?

I'd seen Madame serve a luminescent drink to her VIP guests, similar to the liquid Amira had asked me to give to Radax. She'd said it would make him care less about the pain.

Now, I wondered if that was exactly what the iridescent drink did to Madame's VIP clients. It made them *care less* about the man trapped in a fish tank for their entertainment.

Zeph had mentioned smoke in his warning, too. The smoke constantly filled the tents. No one bothered to air it out. On the contrary, in addition to the many incense burners placed all over the place, Madame also often carried a cigarette in the holder on her finger, adding the smoke to every room she entered.

I thought of Zeph's vacant stare and Amira's complete and utter obedience. Something definitely wasn't right here.

Maybe it was best to go hungry tonight, after all.

I searched around for a place to dump the tainted porridge. Wherever I'd put it inside the truck, sooner or later someone would find it.

A smaller cage caught my attention. It stood next to mine. Inside it was Yenric, the two-headed pig. One of his heads was eating from a bowl of porridge similar to mine. The other head turned and twisted impatiently in an attempt to get to the food, too.

Sliding my bowl between the bars, I put it in front of the piglet's second head, quickly yanking my hand away from his small but sharp teeth.

"There you go, little guy."

He dove into it eagerly.

If the pink glitter was indeed some kind of a sedative or a substance to improve obedience, it might actually be good for the little brat. The pig gave Amira nasty bites every time she cleaned his cage or brought his food.

As soon as Yenric was done with the porridge, I grabbed the empty bowl and put it back in my cage. When Amira returned to pick up the dishes, she didn't appear to notice a thing.

I had to do without dinner that night. At least the water bottle didn't seem to have been tampered with, and I drank it all, fooling my stomach into feeling full.

The next morning, I felt ravenously hungry. The musty watery smell of the plain oatmeal that Amira brought for breakfast seemed incredibly appetizing. To my relief, there wasn't a hint of the pleasant fragrance this time. Neither could I find any trace of glitter in the dish.

The sandwich I got for lunch also didn't look or smell suspicious. So, I ate it, too.

Upon arriving at the new destination, my cage was brought inside a room, an actual room, not made of the striped canvas walls. It looked like a concrete storage room with no windows. The animals were brought here, too.

I'd expected another fair and wondered why we all had been put in here, instead.

Asking Amira when she brought our food that night didn't get me anything, as expected.

I carefully inspected the porridge again. When I tilted the bowl in the light of the sole lightbulb under the ceiling, tiny sparks flashed pink among the boiled oats. The shimmer was so subtle, I wouldn't have noticed it had I not been looking for it.

As a result, Yenric got the double portion that night again, and I got nothing but water for dinner.

During the day, Amira and a couple of Madame's *bracks* took all the animals away. Later, Amira returned and replaced Yenric's cage with a spacious, open enclosure. She brought the piglet back for the night, and he slept in the pile of fur and suede she'd left for him in the enclosure. The next morning after breakfast, she took him away again.

Wherever we were, Madame must have her menagerie set up and was giving tours again. During the day, Yenric must be doing his job as part of her exhibit.

With Yenric taking his dinner next to me nightly, I continued to feed him my tainted porridge undetected, surviving only on what I got for breakfast and lunch.

For bathroom breaks, I was taken to an actual washroom, just a short walk down the corridor from the storage room where they held me. The entire place appeared to be a basement of an older building.

Still no one had told me anything about where we were or why.

A few days later, Trez and Ulg came in. They escorted me to the bathroom. Then, instead of bringing me back in my cage, they took me up the stairs.

*"Where are we going?"* The question was on the tip of my tongue, but I bit it down.

They had been adding that pink glitter to my dinner for over a week now. I'd noticed that Yenric had stopped biting. When Amira had cleaned his enclosure last, he'd stood quietly nearby, not even snapping his teeth at her.

Since no one knew I hadn't touched the tainted porridge, Madame must've decided I'd eaten enough of it for me to finally be "useful". So, I said nothing, silently following the *bracks* up the concrete stairs while wondering what it was all about.

*"If you do what you're told, you may have a chance."*

Radax's warning came to mind. I was sure he meant I'd have a chance at survival. What I saw here, though, was the opportunity to find a way to get out of here. If I was allowed to move around freely, I should be able to figure out how to escape.

Schooling my features into a neutral expression, I followed my two guides into a large room upstairs.

This must be where the tours took place. The animal enclosures here were intricately constructed and decorated, definitely meant for public view during the day.

The room also had windows, though barred with grates. I hadn't so much as glimpsed a sliver of sky for weeks. Acting as if the view outside didn't affect me now proved nearly impossible. Using a moment when my guards' backs were turned to me, I threw a furtive glance through the windows.

It was a dark night broken by multi-colored street lights, some of which came from carnival rides. We still were at a fair of sorts, only one that appeared to be permanent with attractions housed in buildings rather than tents or trailers. An amusement park, maybe?

Staying in my role of someone drugged into mindless compliance, I tore my attention away from the windows, doing my best to pretend I had no interest in life out there.

Trez handed me a mop and a bucket with cleaning supplies then pointed at one of the animal enclosures.

"Clean this shit, human."

I stepped over the glass barrier carefully, then set my bucket down, and started sweeping the floor with a brush from the bucket.

The space inside the enclosure was littered with large rocks. A pair of yellow eyes watched me from behind a pile of them. My skin crawled with unease. But I kept working, imitating Amira's purposeful way of doing things.

Trez took another bucket out of the broom cabinet in the corner.

"Since we have to keep an eye on her, anyway, may as well change the sand in this one, now." He tipped his chin at another enclosure by the opposite wall.

Ulg got a small shovel and a broom. The two of them shoveled the sand from the floor inside the short fence, then dumped it into the bucket.

"Ugh, this is boring!" Ulg complained. "I'd rather be hunting or trapping in Nerifir."

"Nothing beats that," Trez agreed. "I'd even do another hunt in this shitty world. The one in Paris was fun."

Ulg broke into a laugh. "Trapping men turned out to be not much different than trapping animals, right?"

"Exactly!" Trez snorted. "You just have to figure out what bait to use. A hired chick in a wig was all it took that time."

What were they talking about?

Doing my best to pretend I didn't care about their conversation, I tried to think hard.

The word "Paris" automatically connected with Zeph in my mind. *Bracks* had been there that night. I hadn't seen their faces in the dark. But could Trez or Ulg have been among them?

Was Zeph the one they'd hunted, baited, and trapped? Was that how they got him in the end?

Questions swirled in my brain, making my head spin. Distracted, I forgot all about the creature hiding behind the rocks.

Suddenly, something colorful darted from that direction, bee-lining toward me. I screamed, startled, tripped over a rock and fell on my ass. The dust pan flew out of my hands, spewing the dirt and the creature's poop all over the place.

The animal hissed at my foot. The colorful spikes on its flat, round body rose menacingly, the plume of purple feathers on its head swaying in the air.

Ulg glared my way. Trez rushed to me. Painfully squeezing my arm, he yanked me to my feet.

"Fucking useless, either way," he hissed under his breath.

I blinked rapidly, trying to recover some composure.

"I tripped," I managed to say more or less evenly, determined to keep it cool even if the creature chewed my foot off.

Trez shooed the animal back behind the rocks. "Clean this up. Now."

Picking up the dust pan, I swept again, all the time while feeling the stares of my guards on my back.

How exactly was I expected to behave in this situation? Would Amira freak out?

Despite her wordless obedience, though, Amira didn't appear drugged. She didn't act dazed or confused, just timid and fearful. The men in Madame's service also behaved as efficient employees, rather than mindless automations.

Maybe Madame fed the pink glitter only to me. The others might have their reasons to submit to her willingly.

I decided to observe Yenric more closely, to figure out what exactly the glitter was supposed to have done to me.

Whatever it was, though, my performance that night must've satisfied Madame's people because since then, I was let out of my cage regularly.

After the menagerie closed for the night, I cleaned the animal enclosures, mopped the hallways, and dusted the display cases in the room with the unanimated exhibits, all of that while being watched closely by the *bracks*.

I didn't see Zeph's tank anywhere, and I couldn't stop worrying about him. I hoped Madame wouldn't do anything worse than what she'd already done to him. He was very "useful," after all, considering the crazy amounts of money she made by displaying him in that tank.

I feared, however, that she cared more about his body than his mind. And his mind might be deteriorating.

After another week, the men watching me started to relax their vigilance a little. My ruse must be working, as they would exit the room now and then, leaving me completely alone for a few minutes at a time.

One day, Trez brought me to clean a different room. It was filled with smoke and completely empty except for the dragon-man statue Fleur and I had seen the day we first visited the menagerie.

It seemed so long ago now, as if in another life. I had no doubt that Fleur had made every effort to find me, including calling the police and notifying my parents. The fact that none of that had succeeded at freeing me yet told me that Madame must have her means of avoiding the law. I wondered if she routinely offered glitter-laced tea to officials and law enforcement officers to skirt the rules and avoid detection.

Shrouded in the fragrant smoke, I dusted the dragon-man statue. It was too lifelike for me to stick a feather duster in its face. Instead, I took a clean cloth and gently wiped down the man's features, the way I would clean a face of a real person.

While sweeping the floor after that, I snuck closer to the window. This one was narrow with thick curtains tightly drawn, but it was not barred. As soon as my two guards stepped out of the room, I rushed to the window, getting as close as I dared to see as much as possible.

It resembled an amusement park. The attractions here were permanent, not like those in a traveling show. But it didn't seem to be that big.

Something far in the distance caught my eye—a bright glow over the horizon straight ahead. Another glow of colorful lights rose into the dark night sky, far to my right.

Suddenly, I knew exactly where I was—on the major tourist promenade in Niagara Falls, Canada. The two glowing areas in the sky came from the lights illuminating the Falls—both the American side and the Canadian Horseshoe.

The last time I'd visited here was at least ten years ago. Many buildings had been changed and renamed since. New attractions had been added. What never changed, though, were the Falls. From my vantage point, the Horseshoe was to the right, and the American side was straight ahead, on the other side of the river.

We were back in Canada then.

My heart sped up, and it cost me extra effort to appear unaffected when my two guards returned. Mopping the floor, I kept my eyes down, afraid my face would betray the agitation inside me.

I was so close to home from here. If I found my way out of this building, I could possibly get a ride with someone heading to Toronto. My mind swelled with thoughts and ideas crowding it. The excitement of potential freedom spread through me like fire.

I had to figure out how to escape from this building. And I had to do it soon since Madame didn't seem to stay in any one place for too long.

And Zeph...

I had no idea how he was. Or even where he was now.

But I needed to find him. I couldn't leave him behind.

# Chapter Fourteen

IVY

The *bracks* had grown comfortable enough to leave me one on one with Amira, one day. She washed Yenric the pig in a plastic tub placed on the floor in the basement bathroom. I was tasked with assisting her and learning the process to be able to bathe the pig on my own someday.

The year had moved into November already, but I still only had a vague idea where even the main entrance of the building was located and had no clue if it was locked or guarded.

Without Trez or Ulg around, I saw an opportunity to get Amira to speak. I needed to find out about the exit, the number of *bracks* guarding it, the location of the key. Anything. However, if I started asking about those things, she would get suspicious.

Instead, I asked, "Do you know where Zeph, the siren man is?"

Of course, she didn't reply.

Keeping up with the role of a mindless obedient servant I'd been playing for the past weeks, I asked in a neutral tone, "Who cleans his water tank?"

She glanced up at me, then went back to scrubbing Yenric's tiny hooves. The pig stood calmly, letting her do whatever she pleased. Both his heads were up, the four beady eyes half-closed in his obvious enjoyment of the bath.

The pink glitter had changed his personality. Instead of snapping and biting, Yenric had become a real sweetheart. He liked to cuddle with everyone, not just Madame. He enjoyed belly rubs and would nuzzle Amira's hand for a petting when she brought him food. The bite marks on her hands had healed.

I wondered if she'd noticed the change in him. If she did, she hadn't told Madame yet. Maybe she liked the docile attitude of the pig. It must make her life easier.

"I can clean it. The siren's water tank, I mean," I offered, hoping against all odds for any reply from her.

None came.

Keeping my eyes down, I soaked my sponge in the warm water then brushed it against Yenric's soft side. He leaned into my touch, snorting with pleasure.

He'd been getting chubbier, too, eating double portions for dinner. Whereas I'd been losing weight, going to bed hungry every night.

Not a word came from Amira, and I decided to remind her about the night of Radax's punishment. I hoped it might rekindle that feeling of camaraderie or gratitude or whatever it was that had made her speak to me then.

"I'm glad Radax healed so quickly that time. The crystals turned out to be truly magical." She said nothing, so I continued, "You really care about him, don't you? Is he your boyfriend?"

She shook her head, still without saying a word.

"Would you like him to be?" I asked carefully.

She gave me a cautious look, then glanced over her shoulder at the door that remained closed.

"No," she said softly. "Radax is my family. The only one I have."

"I can tell he cares about you, too." I nodded, excited to hear her speak. "You see, I care about Zeph. It's killing me not knowing how he's doing."

It was a risk to reveal all of that to her. In desperation, I hoped the risk was worth it. My sharing something personal might prompt her to be more open with me, too.

She put her head down again, scrubbing another hoof of Yenric's until it shined.

"It's not the same," she whispered, finally. "The siren is not sentient."

"Is that what you've been told?" Of course. Wasn't Madame spinning tales along those lines to her VIP clients? "Amira, I knew Zeph from before he got here. I talked to him. He is very much a sentient, self-aware, intelligent being. Just like you and I. Trust me, he is not an animal like they say he is. He's my friend."

Zeph might have his reasons not to come for a second date with me, but for one night in my life he made me feel special. With him, I'd touched magic, and it'd stayed with me ever since. He'd made me feel cherished and appreciated. Because of him, I would never settle for anything less.

I couldn't stand thinking he might be dying in that water tank, now.

"Amira, please tell me if he's still alive. Is he here? I *need* to see him. Just for a moment, please."

Silently, Amira rinsed the soap from Yenric then wrapped him in a thick towel. Snorting gratefully, the piglet made himself comfortable in her arms.

"No one can know about this," she said quietly.

About what? Would she take me to Zeph?

My heart stopped then raced, I was afraid to breathe, scared I misunderstood her or that she'd change her mind.

"I swear—"

"Come." She got up to her feet.

Afraid to hope, I promptly emptied the plastic tub into the sink and rushed after her.

My heart sank when Amira turned to the room with my cage.

She placed Yenric back into his enclosure where he energetically nestled into his pile of furs and felt. She then silently gestured for me to follow her out of the room and down one of the basement corridors.

With renewed hope, I turned into a wide hallway with her. The lights here were prettier than everywhere else in the basement. The walls had been painted with glittering murals, and the floor was covered with a purple rug.

This space was clearly meant for visitors. It made sense that Madame would have the VIP room in the windowless basement rather than on the main floor. Was that where Amira was taking me? Was I really going to see Zeph?

"What's that door over there?" I pointed at the metal door at the end of the hallway.

"It leads to the stairs up to the main entrance," Amira whispered, then added hurriedly, "we're not supposed to use it, it's for clients only."

Finally. I found the exit. That could be my way to freedom. Hope grew stronger inside me.

We stopped in front of another door. It was open, but the entrance was roped, with the familiar blue VIP letters on it. Amira stepped over the rope, and I followed, my heart beating faster.

The décor of this room was slightly more extravagant than the tent had been. Shimmering fabrics were draped over the walls, and garlands of fluorescent plants I'd never seen before hung from the ceiling.

Zeph's tank stood at the far wall with the mahogany bar in front of it. At first glance, the tank appeared empty, filled with dark water. Coming closer, however, I made out a pale shape floating inside its depths, like an apparition rising into the night air.

"Zeph," I whispered, placing both hands on the glass.

But I felt nothing in response. Not a word. Not a flicker of an emotion.

"Zeph?"

What was happening?

The pale figure moved closer, Zeph's face emerging from the darkness, framed by the silky halo of his long silver hair.

Breathtakingly beautiful. How did I not realize before that his ethereal beauty simply couldn't be of this world?

Maybe because back in Paris, there had been so much life in his expression. Humor and joy had made him look more human.

Now, with the bluish tint of the water on his pale skin, the long hair floating around his face, he looked more like a vision than a real person.

His expression was unnaturally serene. But his cheeks appeared sunken, as did his eyes, dark shadows gave his beauty a haunting appearance.

He splayed his hands on the glass inside the tank, pressing his palms against mine. Still, I "heard" nothing.

Zeph had lost his voice. Completely. Even his inner voice was now gone.

My chest tightened. I could barely breathe. Tears filled my eyes, choking me. I felt so sorry for everything that had happened to us. To both of us. For all the time he'd lost in that tank. For the many weeks, now going on months, of my life that I'd wasted locked in that cage.

Anger sizzled through me, giving me an odd sense of power.

So much had been taken from us, and much more would be taken if I didn't do something.

"Amira!" A deep male voice called from the main floor somewhere, making both her and me jump.

"Go back to your cage," she whispered hurriedly, rushing out of the room.

I stared into Zeph's eyes and didn't recognize them. Open wide, they appeared to see everywhere and nowhere at once.

Hot angry knot of emotions I'd been concealing from the *bracks* for so long burst out at once.

"Back to my cage, my ass," I muttered under my breath as Amira's footfalls faded down the corridor. "Fuck this tank!"

I grabbed a barstool.

*"Stand back, Zeph,"* I mouthed, then swung the stool, smashing it hard against the side of the tank.

To my disbelief, the glass held. The barstool bounced off it, causing no damage whatsoever. Disheartened, I tossed the stool aside.

"There has to be a way," I whispered, examining the tank.

It appeared to be made from one solid piece of glass, with no lid or door to open anywhere. I'd seen no opening in the bottom of the stand, either, when I'd been hiding under it back at CNE. There was no explanation of how Madame got Zeph inside this thing in the first place. Or how she'd been feeding him ever since.

Keeping any lifeform in a water tank required feeding and cleaning. There had to be a way to provide nourishment and to filter out the waste. If Zeph really was a being from another world, I didn't know much about his kind. Maybe they didn't produce waste, but I knew for a fact that Zeph ate food. I'd seen him eat. I'd fed him ice cream myself.

The nourishment must be added straight to the water somehow. I had a feeling Madame added something else to it, too.

What would be a way to deliver a substance into the tank? Fish would die in a sealed aquarium, unless the water was aerated. Which could be done via tubes. From that night at the CNE, I remembered squeezing between a number of tubes and pipes that were connected to the tank underneath.

Dropping to the floor on my back, I pulled myself under the tank, face up. Several silver wires ran underneath, all connected to the tank in a neat line.

I focused on the ribbed plastic hose, tracing the other end of it to a large canister behind the tank. When I lifted the lid of the canister, it released a thick silver puff of the same fragrant smoke with which Madame constantly fumigated her property.

*"Don't breathe the smoke,"* Zeph had said when he'd warned me against eating Ghata's food.

I'd breathed it for a long time now. There was no getting away from the smoke in the menagerie. It was everywhere. It didn't seem to affect me, though. I didn't feel any different.

But maybe it wasn't the case for Zeph?

Madame was infusing the water in his tank with the smoke. I had no idea why. But I suspected it wasn't good for him. Her motives had never been benevolent.

Zeph had complained that the water was toxic, that he couldn't breathe.

Crawling back to the place where the hose was connected to the bottom of the stand, I unscrewed it from the tank. Smoke puffed from the hose rhythmically. I expected a gush of water from the tank, but none came. Sticking my fingers through the opening, I found a rubber valve blocking it.

I hid the disconnected end of the hose behind the tank, making sure that from the outside it appeared as if the hose was still attached.

For now at least, Zeph was in the water no longer actively contaminated by the smoke.

I got up from the floor when a loud noise from outside the room made me crouch behind the tank. The sound of footsteps moved closer.

Everything inside me dropped with fear. I wasn't supposed to be here. I had no excuse.

"Take it to the second VIP room." I recognized the voice of one of the *bracks*, Nid. "The one after this one."

Another VIP act?

I remembered Radax talking about some new arrivals a while back. Madame was expanding her show, which didn't include just inanimate objects and animals.

When the sound of the footsteps moved on, I tiptoed to the exit.

If discovered missing, I would get both Amira and me in a lot of trouble. But with the *bracks* in the next room, I could possibly sneak back into my cage undetected.

I threw a longing glance at the metal door at the end of the corridor. I wished I could see whether it was locked or not. But with the second VIP room between the door and me, it was too risky to go that way.

Instead, I padded down the hallway, in the direction of my cage.

I glanced over my shoulder behind me, making sure the *bracks* remained in the room. As I turned around the corner, I bumped right into Ulg's broad chest. He was on his way to join his buddies, it seemed.

"Hey!" He grabbed for me.

With a shocked squeak, I twisted away from his hands. Blinded by panic, I dashed back toward Zeph's room.

"Get back here!" Ulg yelled. His heavy footfalls thundered close behind me. "You sneaky fucking human."

"What's going on?" Nid poked his head out of the VIP room down the corridor.

I turned into the one with the water tank again, realizing I was now trapped. There was no way out of here but through the door I'd entered. Two *bracks* stood there now, blocking my way.

"Come here, I said," Ulg growled, grabbing the hood of my sweatshirt and yanking me back.

I choked and coughed as the neckline cut into my throat.

"How did she get here?" Trez entered the room, and my heart sank. Of all the *bracks* in Madame's employ, this one had been the most ruthless and cruel. "She should be in her cage."

"I..." I coughed, squeezing the words through my throat compressed by the hoodie cutting across my neck and by fear. "I was on my way there."

Trez ignored me. "Who was supposed to be watching her?"

Ulg shifted heavily from foot to foot. "I left her with Amira."

"That useless girl!" Trez spat through his teeth. "She's definitely dead, now."

"Amira has nothing to do with this," I croaked. "Just let me go...and I'll go back to the cage. I don't want any trouble."

"Oh, you're not getting out of it that easily this time." Trez smirked.

He grabbed my chin with his meaty fingers, lifting my face to his. His eyes focused on mine, thin streaks of red gleaming menacingly in the brown of his irises.

"You're a clever little bitch, aren't you?" he snarled. With his other hand, he painfully squeezed my hip, then my butt cheek, then the side of my ribcage, making me gasp with each rough grab. "You've been getting way too skinny. On a diet, are you?"

A frost of terror spread down my spine.

"It's not like you're feeding me much in here," I snapped.

"And yet you haven't been eating all you've been given. Did you think you could trick us, huh? Obedience was your last chance to stay alive, and you blew it." He squeezed my throat, a cold resentment in his glare. "There is nothing to stop me from breaking your neck, now."

"No, please," I cried against his thick fingers flexing around my neck.

"That's right. Beg me." He sneered. "It won't help you, but it'll make me enjoy this more."

Nid and Ulg snickered, obviously enjoying my desperation.

Holding me by the throat, Trez lifted me off the floor, crushing my windpipe. I clawed at his hand, trying to reach the ground with my toes. My lungs burned with a desperate need for air.

The world narrowed to a dark tunnel in front of my eyes.

The glow from the tank behind Trez was the light at the end of it.

Z*eph*

The water filtering through his lungs was losing its hostile, menacing quality. It came in clearer with each breath he took.

The headache-inducing hum inside his brain had quieted for once, allowing for some mental clarity. Like a small, tip-of-the-needle peep-hole into reality, it grew wider, as if someone wiped the fog from the window of his awareness.

He breathed deeper, letting the clean water flush the poison out of his system. Each breath he took made him feel more connected with the water around him. It became a part of him—his home, not his prison.

Another breath.

The tingle of this re-established connection spread down his arms and legs in currents. He sensed the water stirring around him. His body shuddered, power coursing through his veins.

He flexed his fingers, willing the water to obey, and it rushed in a glowing twirl around him, following his order.

*"Faster."*

It spun in a twister, twirling the garment he wore around his legs.

Through the shimmer of light, his vision reached into the room beyond the glass, his world expanding past his confinement.

Tall, burly figures stood out there. The sight of their tattooed arms ignited anger.

*Bracks!*

The urge for revenge bubbled hot inside him. Then he spotted the person one of them held in his huge hand. They were about to kill someone. What else could be expected from Ghata's slaves?

Raking his fingers through the water, he tested his returning power. Still weaker than he sensed it should be, it strengthened with his outrage, impossible to contain.

Spreading his arms out, he turned the water into his weapon, sending it outwards in an explosion.

# Chapter Fifteen

IVY

My vision shrank to the size of a keyhole. The glow from the tank turned into a ball of light. It was the last thing I'd see before Trez would snuff the life out of me.

I couldn't pry his hand from my throat. I couldn't even beg.

A loud crash shook the room.

The vise around my neck released, and I dropped to the ground. Clawing at the sweatshirt at my neck, I gasped for air.

A stream of broken glass and water rushed by me, coming out of nowhere.

What was happening?

Instinct sent me back to my feet. Coughing, I staggered into a corner.

Trez lay on the floor on his belly, several long shards of glass spearing his back. Ulg stood on his knees, gripping the piece of glass embedded deep in the side of his neck. Dark blood dripped between his fingers, his tattoo pulsing bright red.

With a deep roar, Nid rushed past me toward the bar, shards of glass sticking out from his arm and shoulder.

The water tank was now gone. Zeph stood on the stand, water sluicing down his hair and body, the long, silver loin cloth plastered to his legs.

He jumped from the stand to the bar counter, blocking Nid's blow with the back of his arm. With a soft snap, the fin on his other arm opened. He swept it in front of Nid, smoothly and gracefully, as if fanning Nid with it.

The *brack* staggered back, as if bitten by a snake. His eyes bulged out of his head. His huge body shuddered before he collapsed to the floor. The long, parallel scratches on Nid's neck and shoulder didn't seem deep, but the blue, fluorescent liquid mixed in with the blood oozing from them bubbled ominously.

Horrified, I stared back at Zeph.

He jumped off the bar counter the moment Trez stirred. Ulg yanked the shard out of his throat. Blood gushed from his severed artery.

My stomach churned. I pressed my back to the wall, wishing I could just disappear. I didn't dare to close my eyes, though.

Ulg rushed Zeph, blood pulsing out of the gaping wound in the *brack's* neck. No man would be able to fight with a wound like that, but these creatures weren't human.

Zeph spun on his heel, his dorsal fin snapping open and closed. The *brack* dropped to the floor like a bag of potatoes, the thin slashes on his chest soaking his t-shirt with dark red and fluorescent blue.

Zeph twisted in the doorway to face me. "Where to?"

For one impossibly long moment, I just stared at him. Words deserted me, and each breath was a struggle.

"Which way is the exit?" he prompted in a rough, hoarse voice.

I willed my feet to move. "Follow me."

Peeling my back off the wall, I waded through the water on the floor. It was full of glass shards. When Zeph stepped in it, however, the glass rolled away from his bare feet and around my sandals.

Stepping around the motionless *bracks*, I made it into the hallway. Here, I was finally able to take a deep breath not tainted by the stench of blood.

The metal door at the end of the hallway blew open, crashing into the wall. Radax barged in, followed by more *bracks*.

"Don't move!" Radax raised a hand in warning.

Back in the room, Trez scrambled to all fours with a groan. The long shards sticking from his back made him look like some grotesque, giant porcupine.

There was but one way to run.

"This way." I yanked at Zeph's arm.

I dashed toward the service staircase that led to the exhibit rooms on the main floor. Zeph ran with me.

"Here." I made a spur-of-the-moment decision, spinning in the direction of the room with the winged dragon-man statue. This was the only room I knew with no bars on the window.

Running past the exhibit of Madame's artifacts from Nerifir, I grabbed the bulky metal object from one of the tables. It was the communication device of some dwellers of some wetlands, as Madame had explained back at the CNE.

Not that it mattered *what* it was. The object was heavy and hard.

I hurled it through the window in the dragon-man's room with all the strength I could muster.

The glass shattered on impact. The alarm blared. The building came to life with screams and hurried footsteps.

With the sleeves of my hoodie pulled over my hands, I smashed out as many shards from the frame as I could, then jumped out of the window.

The night was dark, but the many streetlights on the promenade made everything perfectly visible. Unfortunately, it would also be easy enough for our pursuers to see us.

Zeph stood at my side, his face up, his chest rising as he smelled the air.

"What's that way?"

"The Falls." I spun around, feverishly trying to decide in which direction to run.

With Madame's *bracks* on our heels, I had to come up with something quick.

"The window!" someone shouted from the room behind us.

"Run." I yanked Zeph by his arm, taking off.

I sprinted toward the nearest parking lot. I had no plan, just the urge to put as much distance as possible between us and the *bracks*.

"No. This way." Zeph's voice held much more certainty than I felt.

Grabbing my hand, he ran between two buildings to the promenade.

"Stop!" Trez's voice sounded behind us.

How was he still alive?

A loud popping sound was followed by a bullet hitting the wall of the building on our left, narrowly missing my shoulder.

"Dammit, Zeph!" I yelled, speeding up. "These are real bullets."

Death had threatened me enough times in Madame's menagerie for me to believe they were serious in their intentions to murder me. Yet the fact that we were shot at, with the intent to kill, still shook me to the core.

"Run," he ordered, not looking back.

We reached the promenade. Despite the hour of the night, there were still a lot of people here. The shooting thankfully ceased.

Zeph wouldn't slow down the pace, though. I did my best to keep up.

People stopped and gaped at us. Those who were closer scrambled out of our way under Zeph's warning glare. Some grabbed cell phones, either to snap pictures or possibly to call the police.

I ventured a glance over my shoulder and wished I hadn't. *Bracks*, at least six of them, sprinted after us. Their size didn't affect their speed as they wove through the evening crowds with ease.

Trez, covered in blood, murder on his face, had a gun in his hand. So did a couple of the others, not hiding the weapons from view.

The world around me turned to a blur as we ran past more buildings, shoving people out of the way, then through a park and across a street.

The noise of massive amounts of rushing water grew stronger until the horseshoe of Niagara Falls came into view on our right.

A bolt of panic hit me. Zeph had made a mistake by coming this way. Here, we were in the open, backed up against the river and the Falls, with no options left.

The *bracks* were crossing the street now, weaving between the few cars passing by.

"Come." Zeph ran along the fence that separated the viewing area from the river.

He leaped on top of a short rock pillar of the railing. The water was right below, the enormous horseshoe of the raging Falls just a few feet down the stream.

"Come on." He tugged at my hand, urging me to join him.

"What?" I froze in my spot. "What are you doing?"

"We need to jump."

Jump into Niagara Falls?

My stomach hollowed with dread, and my feet wouldn't move, as if cemented into the pavement.

"You can't be serious." I shook my head. Clearly, his mental abilities had been impaired after too much time in the water tank. "It's suicide."

"Not with me. Trust me."

"Trust you? We'll die!" I wildly gestured at the enormous mass of water crashing over the edge just feet away from us. "It's insane. Don't you understand?"

"I won't let you drown." His words echoed those he'd said in Paris to me. How different both of us were back then. The world was no longer the same, either.

"Stop him!" Someone screamed—not a *brack*, this time. People were rushing our way, ready to pull Zeph back to safety. "Don't do it!"

A bullet chipped a piece of rock next to Zeph's foot.

"Quick!" He grabbed me under my arms, lifting me onto the railing next to him.

Horror engulfed me. I gasped, grasping his arms for balance.

"I can't swim," I whimpered.

It was a stupid thing to say. A swimming ability had nothing to do with surviving the plunge into the massive wall of water that crashed onto the rocks below with incredible power.

"I'll swim for both of us." He wrapped his arms tightly around me. "Just don't touch the spines."

"What spines?" I croaked, terror lodging in my throat along with my heart.

"Get down!" someone yelled, but I could no longer tell if it was a *brack* or a human.

With a hand on the back of my head, Zeph put his mouth over mine and jumped off the railing, taking me with him.

Freezing cold water closed over us, knocking air out of my lungs.

Then the world turned to hell.

# Chapter Sixteen

IVY

A deafening roar thundered in my ears. The sound was everywhere, as if I were inside a raging beast. The world shook and churned. I kept my eyes tightly shut, sensations overwhelming my senses beyond comprehension.

I wasn't even sure whether I was dead or alive.

Through the cacophony of noise and confusion, one thing filtered through—the awareness of someone warm and solid with me here, in this watery chaos.

Zeph.

I clung to his shoulders so hard my fingers turned numb with strain. With my bent legs, I squeezed his hips.

Panic speared through me. We were underwater.

I had to breathe.

I needed to get to the surface. I shoved at his shoulders, in desperation to swim up, even as I had no idea where *up* was.

His arm around my middle flexed, holding tight.

Trapped!

I struggled harder.

*"Calm."* The familiar warm sensation filtered through the water, wrapping around me like a blanket, soothing and comforting. Zeph communicated with me again.

I stopped struggling and tried to understand what was going on.

I wasn't drowning. Somehow, in this hell under water, I kept breathing.

Pinching my nose closed, Zeph had his mouth sealed over mine, sending air to my lungs. Breathable air. I drew some in, the tightness in my chest letting go.

Zeph had the ability to obtain oxygen from water. And he was sharing it with me. Breathing for me.

Instead of pushing him away, I held on tighter, snaking my arms around his shoulders. My fingers brushed against the base of the fin on his back. He had it open wide, hard spines with silky tissue in between.

*"Don't touch the spines."*

His warning made sense now. My mind flashed to the motionless bodies on the floor in the basement room, weird blue liquid oozing from the shallow cuts in their flesh. I quickly withdrew my hands away from his fin.

Still disoriented and confused in the turbulent water, I was getting more aware of our surroundings.

The roaring, churning current of the Falls raged all around us, but we weren't *in* it. The water right next to us was completely still. Zeph and I were suspended in it like in a bubble that carried us down the Falls then through the crushing whirlpool at the bottom. It cushioned our fall, keeping us away from the hard rocks below.

Zeph had asked me to trust him, and I now understood why he had the confidence to demand I jump with him to what I thought would be certain death. He really could swim for both of us, breathe for both of us, and keep me safe in the environment where humans simply were not meant to survive unprotected.

Snuggling closer into the warmth of his body, I let it all happen. Anxiety and some fear still buzzed somewhere deep inside me. Being submerged in the cold water was far from comfortable at this time of the year, but I no longer panicked or dreaded death.

I trusted Zeph to keep me alive.

It was hard to tell exactly how much time had passed. After a while, I sensed the actual movement of the water against my skin, as if the "bubble" protecting us slid away. A moment later, we broke through the surface, and Zeph removed his mouth from mine.

He leaned back, searching my face. "Are you okay?"

Was I?

Still holding on tight to him, I drew in a breath on my own. I felt disoriented, still a little fearful, but unbelievably grateful to be alive.

"I'm good." I nodded. "Thank you."

"Your lips are blue. You're too cold." Zeph frowned. "We need to get out."

The water was painfully freezing. My teeth chattered, and whole-body shakes started to rock through me.

"Where are we?"

"Just down the stream from the Falls." His features tightened in concentration. "Are those Niagara Falls?"

"Yes. Have you been here before?"

"I'm not sure. I don't recall. Maybe I've seen them in a picture somewhere."

His voice was rough and breaking, but he spoke. He looked exhausted and starved, but seemed mentally sound. I heaved a breath in relief. He got out of that tank just in time.

The tall banks on each side of the river suddenly appeared to sink. Then I realized it was us moving up. The water around Zeph and me swelled, raising us higher, its darkness crested with a lacy fringe of foam.

"What's happening?" I gripped his shoulders tighter. "Why is it doing this?"

"Because I'm making it." He remained calm. "The river bank is too steep. It'd be hard to climb."

The swell of water washed up the bank then retreated, gently setting us down.

"Wow..." I exhaled, glad to be on solid ground once again. He didn't want to climb the river bank, so he made the water lift us instead. "It's an unbelievable gift you have, Zeph."

He was a siren from the magical kingdom of Nerifir. With the power to manipulate water.

Unbelievable.

I couldn't wrap my mind around all of this. It didn't help that everything inside me, even my brain cells, it seemed, had shriveled from the cold.

He gave me a distracted nod. "We need to keep moving. The *bracks* will be after us. Are you familiar with this area?"

"A little." I let go of him, turning around.

We stood behind a row of trees on the side of a road with several lanes separated by grassy areas. Across the road, the lights of residential houses.

The sound of the crashing water was still audible.

"If the Falls are that way...it means we're on the American side here, Zeph." I had no ID on me. Zeph certainly couldn't be hiding a valid passport anywhere in his loincloth, either. "We can't stay here. We need to go back."

"Well, the *bracks* are on that side," he pointed out. "They aren't very good swimmers. This side is safer."

"This side is a different country," I explained. "We risk being detained without proper identification. Do you have a valid passport on you?" He shook his head. "Me neither. No ID, no money, and no place to go to get help."

"And there?" He gestured at the opposite bank.

"That's Canada over there. I live in Toronto, just a two-hour drive from here." I wondered if my apartment would still be there for me since I hadn't paid the rent for the past two months. "My mom's house is in Oakville, which is even closer. We can get food, clothes, and some money, then figure out what to do next. Do you have a better plan?"

He glanced up the river hesitantly. "No. No plan. I just want to stay away from *them*."

That was understandable. However, his confused expression worried me. He seemed lost, and not just geographically. I took his hand in mine.

"We'll have to be careful," I said softly. "But we do need to be on that side."

He glanced at me. The night turned the color of his eyes into deep turquoise, bringing Paris to mind. My heart pinched with the memory. I stifled a sigh.

"Trust me," I repeated the words he'd said to me. If I could put my own trust issues aside and jump into the freaking Niagara Falls with him, he should be able to believe me on this one, too.

He peered into my eyes intently, saying with emphasis, "I'm not going back to them."

"Neither am I, believe me." I wrapped my arms around my cold, soggy sweatshirt. "We're in this together, you and I."

He kept staring at me, and it hit me—he didn't recognize me. Zeph had no idea who I was. No wonder he hesitated to put his trust in a stranger.

Not all was well with his mind, after all.

I took his hand in mine. "I'm Ivy."

It seemed like every time I spoke with this man, I had to introduce myself to him, over and over again. My heart squeezed painfully, but I managed a smile. It wasn't his fault. If I had to repeat my name to him a million times, so be it.

"You and I have met before," I said. "But it looks like you don't remember that."

He frowned in concentration for a moment, but then shook his head. "No. I don't."

"It's alright. Maybe it'll come to you—"

He stopped me by lifting his hand.

"I don't recall seeing you, but I remember speaking with you."

"You do?"

He slid his hand up the sleeve of my soggy hoodie. Following his movement, the material dried, the water from it collecting in his palm. He placed his hand on my cheek, with the water from my hoodie between his skin and mine.

A warm sensation tingled along the side of my face.

"You were on the other side of the glass," he said. "You made me feel less alone."

*"Thank you,"* his voice sounded in my head.

I covered his hand with mine. "You can communicate through water?"

He tilted his head. "It's never been as clear as it is with you. Normally, I just feel people's emotions. With you, I can actually speak."

He took his hand away, letting the water drip to the ground.

A gust of wind from the river sent a shudder through me.

"We should go," he said.

I was shaking in my wet clothes. "We have to go back into the water."

The dark, frigid river flowed far below. I braced myself for another plunge into it.

"Just for a little while." Zeph took my hand, heading down the steep riverbank. "We'll need to climb down to the water."

"Can you make it come up here, instead?" Conveniences were hard to give up, even the ones that were hard to believe in, in the first place. As cold as the river was, I'd rather be carried by it then climbing to it.

Sadly, Zeph shook his head. "I need to touch the water, in order to manipulate it. I can't do it from a distance. Do you want me to go down on my own?" he offered. "I can raise the wave to come get you, later."

"No." I followed him down the river bank. Standing alone on the side of the road, while wearing wet clothes in a biting wind appealed even less to me than climbing. "We'll go together."

Holding hands, we descended to the stream.

"Ready?" Zeph wrapped his arms around me.

"As ready as I'll ever be." I shuddered again, glancing at the dark water rushing by in a swift current.

"It'll be quick," he assured me.

"Okay. I'm ready." I tilted my head back, parting my lips for him, as if for a kiss, although it wouldn't be one. The way he'd had his mouth over mine as we'd tumbled down the Niagara Falls had been nothing like his kisses back in Paris. His kisses had been passionate, warm, and magical. This time, his mouth on mine would be simply for survival, like CPR.

Still, I felt a pang of disappointment when he shook his head. "This won't be necessary. We won't go under."

He didn't put his mouth on me, just stepped into the river, holding me in his arms. The water swelled around us once again, reaching higher than my waist.

"Holy cupcake, it's cold!" I gasped loudly, pressing myself to him.

As he'd promised, our heads and shoulders remained above the surface while the swell rolled from one side of the river to the other, at a ninety-degree angle to the natural direction of the current. The freezing water soaked my clothes once again, numbing my body.

Zeph held me close enough for his scent I'd thought long forgotten to reach me. Awareness rushed through me in a wave of shivers that had nothing to do with the cold.

"We're here," he said softly. "No more freezing water."

The wave rolled over the bank on the Canadian side of the river. It set us down on the ground, then retreated into the current. Without releasing me from his arms, Zeph stepped behind a tree quickly, hiding us from the headlights of a car passing by along the two-lane road.

"Here, let me dry you off." He placed his palms on my shoulders, then slid them down my body. Water followed his hands, draining from my clothes and dripping down to the ground.

"It's like...completely dry," I marveled, touching the material.

"And your hair." He took my face between his hands, then raked his fingers through my wet hair.

Water trickled down his arms, dripping down from his elbows. He moved his hands to the back of my head, bringing my head closer to his chest. I leaned my forehead against him, inhaling the warm scent of his skin mixed with the fresh smell of the river.

His hands moved up to the crown of my head, then down to my neck, my shoulders, and down my back. Both my hair and my clothes were dry now, yet he kept touching me, gently rubbing my back.

"Who are you, Ivy?" he rasped. "Where did you come from?" How did you end up next to that water tank?"

"I'm no one special." I exhaled a humorless laugh. "I'm just a victim of my own curiosity. I snuck into the menagerie to see the VIP act and got caught. Madame kept me as a servant." More like a slave, or a wild animal in a cage. I sighed.

"Madame?"

"Ghata." I remembered the name he'd used for that woman.

He stiffened, stilling his hands.

"We need to keep going."

"Right." Reluctantly, I stepped out of his arms.

Across the road was a residential area with one and two-story houses. Several of them had *Bed and Breakfast* signs in the front.

"We may get help there if we ask," I suggested.

Zeph hesitated.

"It's too close to *them*..." He glanced in the direction of the Falls and the menagerie. "I don't want anyone to know where we are."

He was right. Madame must be looking for us. And if she found us, she'd surely get another water tank for Zeph, possibly a much sturdier one, this time. And me...

Well, I'd been kind of on borrowed time with her as it was. I'd survived only because of Radax's unexpected leniency for me that one time. He might be a *brack*, but he saved my life. Madame would never let that happen again.

A car appeared down the road, and Zeph hid behind the tree again, taking me with him.

I wrapped my arms tightly around myself, but it did little to protect me from the cold wind sneaking under my clothes and stealing my body heat. Even with my clothes now dry, I was still shivering violently in the cold November weather.

I leaned against Zeph's half-naked body. Unlike me, he wasn't shivering. His skin looked pale, almost luminous in the golden glow of the streetlights. Water dripped from his long hair. He hadn't bothered drying it.

"You're not cold?" I asked.

"No." He looked at me with concern. "But I need to get you someplace warmer."

I didn't object to that. My feet felt frozen solid, I no longer felt the straps of my sandals. The wind chilled my bare legs. The weather for shorts had passed long ago.

"Come." Taking my hand, Zeph crossed the road when there were no cars in sight.

Instead of going to one of the Bed and Breakfasts, Zeph turned into a side street, taking us away from the road and out of sight of the passing vehicles.

The lights in one of the houses ahead of us, a cute brick bungalow with green window trim, went off all at once.

Zeph stopped, staring at it. "Why do you think that happened?"

"It's late." I shrugged. "People went to bed and turned their lights off."

"In both rooms at once?"

"I don't know. Maybe they have a master switch, like they have in hotels. Or maybe..." I took a few steps toward the house. "The lights may be on a timer. Do you think they're away on vacation?"

Or it could be someone's summer home. They were common in this area. The owners would spend winters somewhere warmer, returning for spring and summer.

Gripping my hand tighter, Zeph headed to the house in long determined strides.

I guessed his intention.

"That would be breaking and entering," I warned. "Which is a real crime, punishable by law."

"I'm willing to take the risk." He slid into the shadows of a cedar hedge around the bungalow. "We need a place to warm you up."

We could also use some clothes for him. The cold might not be affecting Zeph, but the sight of him nearly naked would definitely raise questions if we tried to hitchhike with him dressed the way he was.

Finding a place to rest, some clothes, and maybe even some food would be great. Getting caught while doing that, though, would be a disaster.

I glanced at the mailbox in front of the property. It was stuffed with papers. Sneaking closer, I took a few out, sorting through the papers quickly. No letters or magazines, just flyers, dating back several weeks.

"A summer property, most likely." I rushed back to Zeph, who already was on his way around the corner to the backyard.

I caught up with him at the back door.

"Careful," I pointed at the sticker of an alarm company on the glass as he grabbed the door handle. "They have an alarm system. And it's most likely armed since they're away."

He paused. "I could short-circuit the power to the house by sending water along the line."

"An alarm system may have a backup battery. It'll still work, even during a power outage." Besides, causing serious damages to people's property didn't sit well with me, despite our dire situation.

He let go of the handle, taking a look around the yard. "The garage then?"

I glanced at the small brick building nearby. "It's detached. They might've decided to skip getting the alarm system for it."

We ran to the back door of the garage. "Well, no security company stickers here." I inspected the small window in the door. "That doesn't mean—"

The sound of broken glass stopped me mid-sentence. His hand wrapped in the end of his loincloth, Zeph smashed through the window. I pulled my head into my shoulders, half-expecting the sound of an alarm to blare any moment. Thankfully, nothing happened.

He stuck his hand through the hole and unlocked the deadbolt.

"Come." He opened the door.

# Chapter Seventeen

IVY

"Well, that was lucky," I said quietly.

The small space was unheated, but it already felt warmer simply being out of the wind.

"*Lucky* would've been finding a vehicle, some food, and warm clothes in here," Zeph muttered under his breath. He moved around the place swiftly, searching for the things he'd listed, I assumed.

There were no vehicles parked in the garage. Whoever owned this place must've taken a road trip. Or maybe, they never kept cars at their summer property.

"No food," Zeph concluded, rummaging through the shelves and inside a large metal tool cabinet.

"But there are some clothes." I spotted a few hooks on the wall as my eyes had adjusted to the darkness inside. A hunting jacket and a gray sweatshirt hung on the hooks. A pair of waders, tall rubber boots, and some old running shoes lined up on the floor below. All seemed to belong to a man.

"And shoes, too. Look." I pointed at the pair of runners as Zeph came closer.

Grabbing the sweatshirt off the hook, I slid it over his head. It fit him well with just enough space for his wide shoulders. The sleeves covered the full length of his arms.

"Perfect." I smoothed the material over his chest, then rose on my tiptoes to pull his long hair from the sweatshirt on the back. "Your hair is still wet. Though, I guess it doesn't bother you."

If it did, he would've dealt with it already, in his super effective magical way.

Zeph sure had a way with water. The jets in his tub in Paris came to mind unbidden, making me blush. Now I knew those had been no ordinary jets. Tingles rippled down my skin with the phantom sensation of Zeph's hands on my naked body.

I held a handful of his long hair, turning it in the pale ray of moonlight that shone through the broken door window. The water glistened on the long strands like pearls and silver. Or maybe it was his hair, glowing in the moonlight like magic.

He wrapped his fingers around my hand, warming my skin.

"Ivy, have we met before?" he asked unexpectedly.

Did he remember?

I snapped my gaze to his face.

His brow furrowed in concentration, he focused on me, as if trying to recall something. But there was no recognition in his eyes.

"We have." I dropped my hand, releasing his hair. "Once. Almost a year and a half ago."

"I knew it," he said excitedly.

"Really?" I asked, somewhat confused. He clearly didn't remember me.

"I have the strongest connection with people I'm closest with," he explained. "We must be close."

Hardly.

I couldn't mislead him about that. Absolutely not.

"No, Zeph. It was just, um... a brief encounter." He was my one and only one-night stand. Or maybe not even that. We hadn't even had real sex, in the full sense of that word. "It was nothing important."

"But it had to be," he insisted. "I can feel Lero oceans away. He's in all my earliest memories. The closest family I've ever had. But even with him, the connection has never been as strong as it is with you."

Maybe it was some kind of camaraderie that had formed between us, as partners in misery, the two prisoners in the menagerie.

"Wait a minute." I stirred. He'd said something that caught my attention. "You remember Lero?"

He nodded. "I do."

"How about *Le Loup Solitaire*?"

"Who?" He rubbed his temple, as if trying to jolt his memory.

"It's not a person. It's a place. The cabaret where we met. You worked there."

"In Paris?"

"Yes."

"No. I don't remember it." He raked his fingers through his hair. His expression fell.

Compassion tightened around my heart. It must be hard to lose a part of one's past like that.

"Zeph." I stepped closer. "Madame...the woman you call Ghata. She had the water in the tank infused with smoke. The whole place was constantly filled with it, too. You told me the water was toxic. Could the smoke have affected your memory?"

For a moment, he just stood there in the middle of the empty garage, his hands hanging loosely by his sides, the same lost expression on his face again.

"The water in the tank *was* contaminated," he said slowly. "Hard to breathe. Dead. I couldn't move it. It wouldn't respond to me."

"Then how did you smash the tank today? That glass was very hard to break. I know, I tried."

Hurling the glass shards across the room fast enough to embed into *bracks* required some real power, too.

"The poison had faded, allowing some of my magic to return."

"Magic?" I lifted an eyebrow.

"The power over water," he explained. "I'd lost it while in the tank. Today, it came back."

His power was truly magical, I had to admit.

"There was a hose attached to your tank," I said. "It delivered the smoke inside it. I disconnected it minutes before your tank exploded."

Another memory popped into my brain, nagging at me with concern. "The smell of the smoke was the same like the cigarettes Lero smoked in Paris."

"*Womora* leaves." Zeph nodded. "When inhaled, their smoke neutralizes fae magic."

That explained why it hadn't harmed me. I had no magic to lose in the first place.

Zeph remembered some things, just not all.

"Tell me everything you know. Please. I have to make sense of it all. Tell me about Madame, or Ghata. The *bracks*. Nerifir. Everything."

Zeph rubbed his chest, searching around the garage.

"Let's sit down first. Warm you up." From one of the shelves, he took a blue, quilted blanket, like the one people wrapped around furniture when moving. "I'll try to answer as many questions as I can. Hopefully, you'll be able to fill in some gaps in my memory, too."

"Okay. Maybe, we'll figure out what to do next, then."

He glanced around again. "We may as well stay here for the night."

He spread the blanket by the wall in a corner of the garage while I found a rag and stuffed it into the hole in the glass of the door window. This stopped the wind from blowing in. With the door being in the back of the garage, I hoped, the chance of someone spotting the break-in was low.

"You told me you were a siren." I sat on the blanket. "Did you really come from the magical kingdom of Nerifir?"

"Yes." He wrapped his arm around my shoulders, drawing me into his side. With his other hand, he tucked a corner of the blanket around my bare legs.

"I feel warmer already." I smiled.

"Good." He leaned in and kissed my forehead.

The gesture came so unexpectedly, I shrank back a little.

He looked concerned and slightly confused.

"Was I not supposed to do that?" he asked, studying my face.

"No... I..." I blinked, warm blush flushing my face.

The problem was I liked it. Way too much. His random signs of affection heated my blood faster than any blanket. But this wasn't the kind of a relationship Zeph and I had. We had *no* relationship. We'd spent less than a day together, then parted our ways.

A year and a half ago, he hadn't bothered to come see me again. Now, I didn't want him to think we shared something special when he couldn't remember how he felt about me.

He kept looking at me, clearly waiting for me to clarify this. I didn't want to mislead him. But I most certainly didn't want to push him away, either.

"I don't mind," I said, allowing him to hug my shoulders but keeping my hands to myself. "Tell me more about that magical kingdom, your home."

"I don't remember anything from Nerifir," he said. "And that's not Ghata's fault. I was too young when we left it to come here. My earliest memories are of Lero. We had a townhouse in Paris. I went to school with human children. Lero taught me to never open my fins and not to play with water in public."

"It must've been hard, to suppress what you were."

He shrugged. "I got used to it after a while."

He leaned back against the garage wall, and I snuggled closer into his side. For warmth, of course. Just for warmth, nothing else. The freezing sensation in my legs and feet finally melted under the blanket. I still shivered a little, but without the violent, whole-body shudders.

"It seems that most if not everything Madame has said about Nerifir is true. I didn't believe it." I shook my head in awe. "Who would? By now, I've seen enough miracles with my own eyes, and I still would accept any other 'reasonable' explanation over anything I've seen..."

Zeph shrugged. "Humans tend to be skeptical about such things."

"Can you blame us? You claimed Madame was a *goddess*," I said with sarcasm, then added quickly, "Please don't tell me that's also true. I have my limits, you know. It is just so high and for so long I can suspend my disbelief."

"I'm not sure what Ghata is exactly. Did I call her a goddess?"

"I think that was the word you used. Yes."

That happened back when he was in the tank, submerged in the tainted water. I shouldn't be holding him accountable for anything he'd said while in that tank. His mind had not been his own.

"Maybe she is a goddess," he agreed. "Ghata certainly isn't a fae."

"But she is from Nerifir, isn't she? How else would she know so much about that place?"

"I remember Lero telling me she'd escaped." Zeph's voice was stilted, as if he had to dig deep into his memories before coming up with an answer. "She had a temple in Nerifir."

"A temple? Was she something like a priestess, then? She definitely has some kind of magic, too. Doesn't she?"

"Possibly. I'm not sure." He blew out a breath in frustration. "I don't remember."

"Maybe it'll come to you later. The poison will have to wear out of your system, sooner or later," I tried to console him. "How about the *bracks?* What do you know about them?"

"They're Ghata's servants."

"Right, but she calls them her slaves." The image of the mangled back of Radax rose in my mind. "And she has some real power over them. I saw her punish one of them. His tattoo was glowing and appeared to be strangling him, without her even touching him." A shudder ran across my shoulders.

"Why did she punish him?"

"For talking to me. Radax was supposed to kill me, but he disobeyed her order and let me live."

Suddenly, I was glad Radax hadn't come too close to Zeph during our escape from the basement. I wouldn't want to see him lying on the floor among the dead.

"Madame ordered him whipped until he passed out. Yet he still keeps working for her. They all do."

Hugging my shoulders, Zeph stroked my upper arm soothingly.

"When I was a child, Lero told me that Ghata used to have a whole army of *bracks* in her temple. I don't know what kind of beings they were before she got them under her control, but she changed them somehow to suit her needs. After she escaped from Nerifir, she's been bringing them here. *Bracks* travel between dimensions, fetching things for her from back home."

"Not just things, the animals, and possibly other fae. Some

substances, too. She fed me something that I believe was supposed to turn me into her servant as well."

"She did?" He turned, catching my gaze.

"Yes, but I didn't eat it. I fed it to her pet pig, instead."

He gave me a long stare, either in disbelief or admiration. Finally, a smile moved his lips. "Well done."

Warmth spread through my chest at his praise. He hugged me tighter. Something touched the top of my head. His lips? Did he just place a kiss in my hair?

"Don't ever eat or drink anything in her presence," he said, as if reciting something he'd learned a while ago. "You were smart to figure it out."

"Do you think she is searching for us right now?" I threw a cautious glance at the door window.

"Most definitely," he replied. "But I think we're safe here, for now."

His answer didn't sound convincingly enough for me. I threw a cautious glance at the broken window. There might be a chance Madame would give up looking for me, but she'd certainly want to get Zeph back.

I sighed. She wouldn't give up searching for him.

"You know she charges people an exorbitant amount of money to see you? Even after the expense of running the show, she must have a pretty good sum by now." How could I've ever suspected that Zeph might be in a partnership with Madame? The idea seemed plain stupid, now. "She's expanding the show, too, it seems. There were some new arrivals."

"More fae, you think?"

"I don't know. I never got to see them, but some were meant for new VIP acts. Something or someone worth paying big money to see, I guess."

We sat in silence for a moment. Zeph was probably pondering what I'd told him. And I thought back to our escape.

Zeph had killed two *bracks* in the basement. He was quick and strong and obviously had the skills and tools to defend himself. Catching him couldn't have been easy.

Trez had spoken about trapping men in Paris. Could Zeph be the one he spoke about? The part about the girl in a wig made no sense to me, though.

"How did they take you?" I asked.

"I don't know." He leaned his head back against the wall, his voice sounded sleepy. "I don't remember. There is a gap. I've no memories past my school years. Everything is blank until the time in the water tank."

He fell quiet, and I wondered if he'd fallen asleep. Exhaustion was pulling me under, too, making my eyelids droop.

"You said we've met just briefly," he said, prompting me to open my eyes again. "Why did we part?"

"Well..." There was no other way to put it but to tell the truth, was there? "I came to Paris to visit a friend and met you at the cabaret where you worked. We spent a night together, then agreed to meet in a café the following day. You never showed up..." I bit my lip.

The bitter disappointment of that day echoed through me with ache and regret. It'd never really stopped hurting, no matter how hard I'd tried to force myself to get over it.

Zeph had moved me. He'd made me feel things no one had made me feel before. For the months since, I'd never stopped wondering what could have been.

But I also never forgot sitting in that café alone, trying not to cry into my cold cappuccino.

I cleared my throat and said in a firmer voice, "I left France and hadn't seen you again until two months ago, in Madame's water tank."

"Was I taken the day we'd agreed to meet?" he asked. "Was that why I didn't come?"

He said it as a matter of fact, as if that was the most logical explanation.

Could that be true? Was that what had happened?

"No." I shook my head. "That'd be too much of a coincidence..."

Would it, though?

The *bracks* had been in Paris. They'd shown clear interest in Zeph, stalking us that night.

There was a reason why Zeph's standing me up hurt so much. When we'd parted, I'd had no doubt he wanted to see me again.

By the time we said goodbye at the train station, he'd made me believe that meeting me was important to him, just as it was to me.

I'd spent so much time convincing myself he hadn't shown up because he didn't want to. Could the truth be that he really *couldn't*?

"Zeph." I heaved a long breath. "I know for a fact that Madame's *bracks* were in Paris that day. There is a possibility that you were taken then."

The realization brought a different kind of regret.

"Oh, Zeph..." I exhaled. "I shouldn't have left. I should've gone straight to *Le Loup Solitaire* and talked to Lero. Maybe he could've stopped them? We could've gotten you back before she stuck you in that tank?"

"It could've also put Lero and you in danger."

*Lero.*

Would he have helped me find Zeph?

The image of the lone dark figure by the wall with a cigarette between his fingers rose in my mind.

"How much do you trust Lero?" I asked.

"Implicitly," Zeph replied without hesitation.

"The smoke from Madame's menagerie smells the same like Lero's cigarettes," I pointed out.

"He smokes *womora* leaves." He nodded.

"Where does he get them from?"

A frown settled over his face. He didn't reply.

"*Womora* leaves are from Nerifir, right?" I asked as he kept silent.

He nodded again.

"*Bracks* are the only ones who can cross into Nerifir and back, aren't they?" He said nothing, so I continued, "Why would Madame's men supply Lero with the cigarettes?"

He turned to me. "I don't know."

I let all of that sink into his head for a moment or two. But questions kept multiplying in my mind. I felt like my head was about to explode with all the new information I'd tried to cram into it lately.

"Why does Lero smoke those things?" I asked. "Isn't it harmful for fae?"

"*Womora* strips fae of their power, which can be helpful, too. It calms Lero and prevents him from turning violent."

"Violent?" I sat back, blinking at him. "In what way?"

He shifted uneasily.

"When I was little, we had a cage in the basement of our townhouse. Every now and then, Lero would lock himself in it. I was not allowed to go in the basement on those nights. He locked the basement door, too. But I saw the cage with its door open on the days when he wasn't using it. I even played inside it sometimes."

I gasped. "Just how violent could one turn to need a cage to contain them?"

"I don't know. I've never actually seen him turn into anything. He made sure I didn't. Not as a child, anyway."

"Do you have any memories from being an adult?"

He released a long breath. "Not many. Only those from the tank and of what has happened after I broke free."

His crestfallen expression filled me with compassion. I squeezed his hand, hoping to comfort him.

"Do you think it's the effects of the smoke?"

He nodded. "There were more things in that smoke than just *womora*. I could taste them. Ghata not only wanted me to lose my power, she also numbed my mind in many ways."

"It made it easier for her to control you," I agreed. "But your memories may come back once it all wears off."

His chest rose with another sigh.

"I can't sing, either," he said softly. His jaw muscles flexed.

The despair in his voice nearly broke my heart.

I cupped his face, turning it to me. "Maybe you can? You haven't tried yet."

He shook his head, his throat bobbing with a swallow.

"Not with this voice," he croaked, turning away.

"It'll come back." I wanted to believe it would, with all of my heart. "You've been tortured for months. It'll take time to recover."

He gently lowered me back against his side.

"I hope you're right." He stared straight ahead. "Because what is a siren without his voice?"

# Chapter Eighteen

ZEPH

The sound of someone starting a car woke him up.

He drew in a lungful of air, cool and poison-free. Relief flooded him. He was no longer in a tank. And he was no longer alone. The awareness of the warm body next to him filled his mind with memories of everything that happened last night.

*Ivy*. He remembered.

He felt more like himself this morning, although he still could not recall the *Le Loup Solitaire* Ivy had spoken about. Or how he met her a year and a half ago.

She was curled on her side, her head in his lap. Her light-brown hair with bright red streaks was tangled. Dressed in an oversized black sweatshirt, she seemed so small. Her pale skin, combined with the dark shadows under her eyes and in the hollow of her cheeks, made her look fragile. Unwell.

He had no safe place to take her, not a penny to feed her, and no means to earn any. His throat felt sore, his voice gone...

The feeling of loss overwhelmed him, making him want to scream or punch something. He flexed his jaw, gritting his teeth.

The sky was gray outside the garage door's window. Ivy wanted to catch a ride to Toronto today. Maybe he could try to find one for them while she slept? Maybe by doing something, he'd feel less hopeless, too.

The car drove away, probably on the street along the river, the one with the houses that had *Bed and Breakfast* signs on them. But the sound of another engine starting came right after.

The *bracks* must've been scouring the area down by the river all night. They might be searching up the stream, too. Ghata must know that Zeph would be able to swim upstream, even up the Niagara Falls if he had to, to escape her.

Carefully supporting Ivy's head, he slid from under her, then tucked the blanket around her, cautious not to wake her. She needed the rest.

It amazed him how strong she'd been to survive two months in Ghata's cage. She hadn't just survived, either. She managed to keep her presence of mind and even found the courage to help him break out, too.

He remembered the words Lero had told him when Zeph had brought a girl from school for dinner once, "*Humans are weak.*"

There was definitely more to them than physical strength, he thought, wondering what Lero would say if he could see Ivy now.

He kept on the sweatshirt Ivy had put on him last night. The cold didn't bother him, but he was less likely to attract attention with more clothes on. Before going outside, he also grabbed the old sneakers by the wall, for the same reason. They turned out to be a little small, his toes curled under inside, but they'd do for now. It was better than walking around barefoot.

Leaving the garage, Zeph closed the door quietly and headed in the direction of the river, keeping to the shadows in the weak light of the new sunrise.

As he turned into the street running along the river, a white SUV came into view. The vehicle was parked in front of the nearest Bed and Breakfast. A woman was shuffling a few pieces of luggage inside the trunk area.

"Good Morning." Zeph made an effort to sound friendly and cheerful, forcing a smile. Out of practice, his facial muscles refused to obey smoothly, making him conscious of their every twitch.

Had it always been this difficult for him to smile? He couldn't remember.

"Oh!" The woman jumped, startled. She nearly hit her head on the open back door of the SUV. "Morning."

She glanced at him over her shoulder. Her expression turned guarded as she took in his odd outfit.

He ran his fingers through his long, tangled hair. Had it been this long before he was taken by *bracks?* He wasn't sure he liked it this way.

"So sorry." He turned up his grin. "I didn't mean to startle you."

"It's fine." The woman stepped away from him, glancing back at the door of the Bed and Breakfast. She seemed nervous. Scared? "My husband will be here any minute," she said as if in warning.

Not a very promising start. He obviously didn't leave a good impression.

"Is he? Good." He kept smiling, striving for an open and friendly expression. "I'd love to meet him. My name is Zeph." He refrained from offering her his hand, afraid to freak her out any further by coming closer. "I'm...with a band. We're here from France." He lied on a whim, taking into consideration his outfit. "Alternative and folk music."

That seemed to work. Interest flickered in the woman's dark-brown eyes.

"Oh really?" She appeared to be in her late forties, maybe early fifties. Her dark-brown hair was pulled back into a ponytail. Just a few lines marked her skin, a shade lighter than her hair. "Are you staying here?" She gestured at the Bed and Breakfast behind her.

"No. We're just a few doors down that way." He tipped his thumb in the direction of the street where Ivy slept in the garage. "We're on a tour across Canada."

A tall man with chestnut buzz-cut and neatly trimmed facial hair walked out of the door, carrying a large suitcase. His ruddy complexion still carried traces of the summer tan.

"All done," he said to the woman, shoving the suitcase into the back of the vehicle then tossed an assessing stare at Zeph.

"Morning." Zeph greeted, with a wave of a hand.

"Hi." The man shut the backdoor of the SUV.

"Neal, my husband," the woman introduced. "This is Zeph. He's with a French folk band, traveling through Canada."

Zeph stretched his hand toward Neal. "Nice to meet you."

"Hi," Neal said again, giving his hand a brief shake then started on his way to the driver's door of the SUV.

"Are you going to Toronto, by any chance?" Zeph asked.

"Why?" The husband stared back at him.

"My girlfriend and I are looking for a ride to the city. She's from around here. Her mother lives in..." He strained his memory for the name of the town Ivy had mentioned last night. "In Oakville. She would like to visit her, since we're passing so close by."

The woman nodded energetically. "Oh, she absolutely should visit her mom."

Neal shot her a look.

"Where's the girlfriend?" he asked Zeph.

"She is back at the Bed and Breakfast up that street. I'll get her if you don't mind waiting for just a minute."

"We're not in a hurry." The woman turned to her husband. "We can take them, right, honey? It's on our way, anyway."

Neal rubbed the back of his neck. "It's Monday. We have to leave early to beat the traffic..."

"We won't be long." Not giving him a chance to say no, Zeph dashed down the street and around the corner at full speed.

Back in the garage, he shook Ivy awake as gently as he could. "You'll have to get up. We have a ride to Toronto, but we need to be quick."

"I need some coffee for the road," Neal announced, driving the SUV along a residential road. He glanced in the rear-view mirror at Ivy and Zeph in the back seat. "Does anyone else want anything?"

"I'm good," his wife, who had introduced herself as Mariana, said.

"Me too," Ivy echoed.

Zeph glanced at her.

Ivy's left cheek was still lined with the impression of the blanket, her shoulder-length hair sticking out wildly from sleep. She needed more rest, some good food, and time to recover after the ordeal she'd been through.

"I'd love a chamomile tea and a cinnamon bun, please," he said.

Neal nodded, pulling into a drive-thru of a coffee shop before getting onto the highway to the city.

When Mariana passed the order to Zeph, he carefully opened the flap of the paper cup lid then handed the cup to Ivy. Her mouth dropped open when he gave her the cinnamon bun.

Granted, it wasn't the most nutritious breakfast. He wasn't sure why he chose the pastry over anything else. But it wasn't important at the moment. Ivy hadn't eaten since yesterday. He had to get some food into her. Any food.

Bringing the pastry to her nose, she closed her eyes, her chest expanding with a long breath.

"I love this smell," she murmured, then took a big bite of the cinnamon bun. "Thank you," she said to him, then turned to Neal and Mariana. "Thank you so much."

Smiling, she took another bite. Watching her eat filled him with satisfaction he hadn't remembered getting from food himself.

"Here." Ivy offered the pastry to him. "Have some, too."

He hadn't eaten for ages. But he was a fae, much more resilient than humans. He could wait.

"Please," she insisted, and he felt she'd be disappointed if he refused.

Taking her wrist, he brought her hand with the pastry to his mouth for a bite.

She gave him an odd look, as if waiting for something.

"It's good," he said around the sweet pastry in his mouth.

She placed her other hand on his knee, covered by the silky material of the ridiculous loin cloth that Ghata had made him wear. He had to get rid of this thing at the earliest opportunity.

A song came up on the radio.

Neal perked up, turning up the volume. "I love this one."

"Is that 10cc?" Zeph asked, leaning forward. The very first cords of the music pulled him in.

"Yes," Neal replied. "'I'm Not in Love' by 10cc."

"It's good."

Mariana turned over her shoulder from the front seat. "You're way too young to share Neal's taste in music, Zeph. Neal himself is too young for that, but he loves the ancient songs his parents used to listen to when he was a baby."

Neal sulked. "What are you talking about? This song is timeless. It's on the *Guardians of the Galaxy* soundtrack, too."

Mariana laughed softly, gazing lovingly at her husband.

"I love all music," Zeph said. "New and old."

A rush of excitement flooded his chest. His soul soared, surfing the waves of the music. He opened his mouth, letting a few words of the lyrics escape.

The rough sound of his voice scraped against his nerves. He didn't even try to attempt the higher notes of the chorus, shutting his mouth.

"See?" Neal said to his wife. "It's good music. Makes you want to sing along."

Mariana nodded. Neither of them realized the disaster Zeph was facing.

Singing had been a huge part of his identity. Music flowed through his veins, striving to break through in a song. Without his voice, he couldn't release it. It felt as if it would burst inside him, tearing him apart.

Ivy squeezed his knee gently. She must know what he was going through. She said she'd heard him sing before.

Not that she could help him in any way, of course.

He sighed, staring straight ahead at the gray highway filled with cars.

"I told you my playlist is good," Neal said to his wife, proudly. "Everyone likes it. Right, Zeph?"

"Right." He smiled.

Neal shifted in his seat eagerly, as the next song started playing. "This is another good one. 'Come And Get Your Love' by Redbone."

Ivy leaned forward, then suddenly erupted into the lyrics, singing along with the stereo system.

"Yeah!" Neal beamed at her over his shoulder, enthusiastically joining her in the song.

Zeph stared at Ivy, shocked and slightly shaken. She sang off key, her voice breaking off at times. But her eyes lit up. She looked stunning.

"I'm bad, I know." She shrugged apologetically. "But you don't have to be good to enjoy singing."

He wished he could kiss her.

And why shouldn't he? There was no reason not to.

Catching her chin in his hand, he touched her lips with his in a chase, gentle kiss.

She faltered, skipping a line or two of the lyrics, then stared at him, a blush spreading over her face and neck. His head was spinning at how beautiful she was—mussed hair, weary eyes, and all.

"You *are* bad," he agreed, shaking his head in awe. "Just awful. And I love it."

Mariana looked at him then at Ivy.

"Do either of you sing in your band?" she asked, sounding confused.

"Nope." He grinned. "Ivy plays tambourine, and I'm a groupie, just tagging along."

Ivy laughed, joining Neal again in their impromptu sing-along. Tapping his foot to the rhythm of the music, Zeph hummed along.

Hope rose in his chest, warming him from the inside. He'd lost his voice, his memories, and over a year of his life. But Ivy was still here.

He vowed to do all it took to keep her that way—smiling, singing, and right next to him.

# Chapter Nineteen

IVY

Neal and Mariana dropped us off in front of my mother's house, on the street of nearly identical homes in a subdivision.

Marek, my mom's husband, must've left for work already: his car wasn't in the driveway. I'd also caught a glimpse of the school bus of my half-sisters—both were high-school students—as it was leaving the subdivision when we arrived.

My mother's car was still here, though. She must be home.

As Zeph and I walked up the driveway toward the main entrance, I ran my fingers through my hair, smoothing down my tangled locks. My mother and I rarely saw eye to eye. Apprehension stirred in me when I knocked on her door.

"Marek?" came from inside the house. "Did you forget something? It's not locked."

I shoved at the door with my shoulder, and it opened.

"Mom? It's me," I called down the wide hallway, decorated with art prints and console tables along the walls.

"Ivy?" Mom rushed out of the kitchen at the back of the house, her hands clutched to her chest. "Oh my God..." she exhaled, grabbing me into a hug. I didn't recall her ever giving me one quite as tight before. "You're back." Her voice trembled, making a lump form in my throat, too.

Sadly, it all passed quickly.

"Where the hell have you been?" She shoved at my shoulders, pushing me away from her. "You have no idea what we went through after you took off."

"It wasn't on purpose, Mom..." I trailed off, unsure how to explain or where to even begin.

"It was all my fault," Zeph's upbeat voice sounded right behind me. He stepped forward to face my mother, who stared at him in confusion.

He'd smoothed his long hair into a knot at his nape. In an old hoodie, a silver skirt-like loincloth, and a pair of old sneakers anyone would've looked ridiculous.

Except for Zeph. Somehow, he still managed to remain beautiful. He'd told Neal and Mariana that we were traveling with a music band from France, and he definitely looked the part. I imagined adding a few colorful beads into his hair or around his neck, and he could easily pass for a bohemian flower child, or more accurately in his case—a true water spirit.

Real beauty could not be spoiled by anything, they said. Staring at Zeph, I understood exactly what they meant.

"Who are you?" Mom demanded.

"My name is Zeph." With a charming smile, he offered her his hand. She shook it mechanically.

"What are *you* doing here?" She took in his odd outfit, pointedly pausing on the worn sneakers.

His smile didn't waver.

"Well, Ivy and I met at the CNE where I was working the rides. We had drinks with a few guys I knew. They slipped something in our drinks, packed us up in a truck with some equipment while we were unconscious, and drove us to the next fair."

I gaped at him. The lie slipped from his tongue so easily, so convincingly. Even knowing exactly what actually had happened, I felt inclined to believe him.

"What?" Mom kept staring at him. As he spoke, however, the look in her eyes changed from suspicious to concerned, even friendly. "Why would someone do that?"

"Just a stupid prank." Zeph shrugged. His expression remained open and earnest. "A practical joke gone too far. The next fair happened to be in the United States. With neither Ivy nor I having our passports on us, we couldn't cross the border to get back."

"That's insane." She shook her head, turning to me. "Why didn't you call? Or email? There're ways to prove your identity in these situations."

Zeph shot me a glance.

Was he worried I couldn't lie as well as he did? He was probably right. Only, I didn't have to lie.

"I had nothing on me, Mom. My wallet was in Fleur's backpack. She took it with her when she left for the bathroom. I didn't even have my cell phone."

Radax had crushed my phone under his boot.

"Right. We got your wallet from Fleur, after..." she waved her hand in the air. "After all that mess with the police. Still, if you'd just called, we would've figured something out."

"Ivy was afraid you'd be angry with her," Zeph inserted, blinking innocently. "She didn't want to bother you."

Well, he got *that* right. Typically, my parents were at the bottom on the list of people I'd call for help. The main reason I'd decided to come to Mom's house at all this morning was because of its location—it happened to be the closest.

Zeph's words seemed to calm her a little.

"Well, it's not a bother if you're *really* in trouble, Ivy. Though it was very irresponsible of you. You didn't even tell Fleur where you went." She huffed an exasperated sigh. "Goodness, Ivy." She shook her head again, a way-too-familiar expression of disappointment spreading on her face, her voice rising. "How can someone your age be this foolish and irresponsible? Do you know what we've been through because of you?"

"I'm sorry, Mom." I knew from experience that the most effective way to stop her was not to give her any reason to continue. Eventually, she would run out of steam.

I wished I could just tell her the truth, but I knew better not to. She'd never believe me. And she'd berate me even more.

The fact that Zeph had to witness me being chastised like that was the most embarrassing part of it. I prayed he wouldn't intervene this time, because then she'd never stop.

"'Sorry' is not going to suffice for the police, I'm afraid. You'll have to come with me to the station to close the missing person's case, pull the report, or whatever it is that needs to be done now." She huffed again, very much irritated. "Like I didn't have enough stuff to deal with already."

"I'll go to the station myself to close the case," I said. "You don't have to worry about it."

"Right. Like it's that simple." She rubbed her forehead. "Okay. So... Your things are in the boxes in the basement. The rent for your apartment hasn't been paid for months, your landlord wanted your stuff out. Wait for Marek to come home this afternoon. You can take his car. No —" she cut herself off, her brow furrowing in concentration. "Wait until I come back from work tonight. We'll have to press charges against those criminals who drugged you and smuggled you across the border. They'll have to be held responsible."

I saw the familiar flash of energy in my mother's eyes. The same she used to have before court proceedings during the years-long process of her divorcing my dad. Mom was looking forward to the battle, getting ready for a fight.

"You have a very good case," she continued. "We'll sue the CNE, the fair organizers, and the city. Zeph and Fleur will have to testify as your witnesses. Marek will represent you, I'll call him during my lunch break today."

"We're very tired, Mom. Can we clean up and get some rest first?"

I had a list as long as my arm of things I needed to do. Some of them I couldn't even begin to think about yet. Like what to do with Zeph. He'd need to get back to France somehow.

"Sure," she replied, somewhat distractedly. Her brain must be already busy working on whatever plan she'd started to construct. "I need to leave for work, now. There is no way I could get today off, this close to month-end."

Shoving her feet into her pumps, she grabbed the car keys, then suddenly turned to Zeph.

"Do you have a criminal record?" She pinned him with her penetrating stare.

"No, Ma'am," he replied firmly and without delay. If her question surprised or offended him in any way, he didn't let it show.

"Where is your family?"

"In Paris. France."

She tilted her head, studying him for a second. I could see she *wanted* to be suspicious of him, but she couldn't quite muster enough mistrust or hostility when faced with Zeph's disarming grin.

"Are they looking for you?" she asked rather kindly.

"No. I'm not supposed to be back home until Christmas. They know I work on fairgrounds in North America."

Her chin in her hand, she stared at him a moment longer.

"We will need your full name, home address, and phone number."

"Absolutely." He inclined his head politely.

"Is he your boyfriend?" She turned to me quickly.

"No, Mom." *That* of all things was absolutely true. "Zeph just helped me to catch the ride here."

"Pity. But not surprising. Sadly, nice men don't seem to be your type." She headed to the door.

I fisted my hands tightly, concentrating on the sting of my nails as they dug into my palms to stop myself from snapping back at her. She'd known Zeph for all of two minutes, and she'd already had a much higher opinion of him than she'd ever had about me.

It was hurtful and infuriating.

Zeph's warm hand wrapped around mine. The gesture felt supportive and calming.

The reason for Mom's agreeable attitude toward Zeph was Zeph himself, I realized. He could probably charm a fire-breathing dragon into behaving like a harmless lizard.

"You can stay here," Mom said to me before leaving. "Find him some clothes, will you? Some of Marek's may fit. I'll see you after work."

Only when the door closed behind her, was the tension able to drain from my body. My back to the wall, I slid down to the floor.

"Sorry, she's exhausting." I buried my face in my hands. "Thank you for lying for me. You did it well."

My gratitude was genuine despite some unpleasant feeling that scratched at me from the inside at how masterfully he'd invented and delivered the lies.

He sat on the floor next to me. "You look exhausted. You need some rest."

Unlike Zeph, I knew I couldn't pull off that ragged, shaggy look. Unbrushed hair and wrinkly clothes simply made me appear disheveled and unkempt.

"I need a shower and a hair brush, first and foremost." I got up to my feet.

"A nap and some lunch, too," he added.

"Right, but not here." I had no desire to stay at my mom's house or even to wait for her to come back from work. "Just a quick shower. I'll also have to get some of my stuff from those boxes downstairs, then we'll get out of here."

# Chapter Twenty

IVY

While Zeph was in the shower in the guest room downstairs, I took a quick one upstairs. Cold had seeped through my skin and muscle all the way to the bone for months. If only one warm shower were enough to wash away the time I spent locked in that cage.

Amira had washed my clothes a few times while at the menagerie. Still, I was so glad to be rid of the shorts and hoodie I'd worn for weeks. I changed into a pair of leggings and a long purple sweater. As Mom had offered, I also found a plain white t-shirt and a pair of jeans of Marek's for Zeph. Then, I went through my stuff that was piled up in the boxes in the basement.

My wallet was there. I exhaled with relief, finding my driver's license and credit cards inside. Funny how having those plastic cards back in my possession made me feel like a real person once again. As if I'd just now truly escaped the cage. There even was still some cash left, too, enough for lunch and a cab fare.

Using the phone in the basement, I called to check my bank account. A few payments had come through for the work I'd done before being captured by Madame. Since I hadn't been there to spend it —not even to pay the rent—the money had just been sitting there. It wasn't a lot, but enough to support myself for now until I figured out what to do next.

The sound of the water from the shower stopped. A little while later, Zeph walked out of the basement bathroom. Droplets of water glistened on his wide shoulders. His hair appeared to shimmer, streaming down his back. With just a towel wrapped around his hips, he was breathtaking.

"Hey...um." I hung up the phone, then pointed at the clean clothes on the couch. "These are for you. I hope they'll fit."

He turned with his back to me. The light stripe over his spine came into view. Now I knew it hid his magnificent dorsal fin.

Zeph had fins.

He wasn't human.

That fact still wouldn't settle in my brain. When he stood in my mom's basement, wrapped in a towel and barefoot, instead of slashing the *bracks* or taming the Niagara Falls, he looked so much like an ordinary man.

Gorgeous, but still very much human, like me.

"Pants!" He grabbed the jeans. "Thank you. A loin cloth is so not me. Too drafty." He made a face. "And, generally, not my style."

Despite humor in his voice, sadness pinched my heart. He'd had no choice in anything that had happened to him during the past months, not even in the clothes he wore. Just like me, he'd been a prisoner of an evil entity.

Anger stirred in me.

Was my mom that wrong about wishing to hold someone accountable for my disappearance?

Maybe I should go to the police after all. I did have something to report. A crime had been committed against me. A vindictive part of me longed for some kind of retaliation against Madame and against her *bracks*. Especially Trez.

Resentment burned in my chest. That man had nearly killed me. Twice. I suspected Trez might also be behind Zeph's kidnapping.

Though, I had no proof on that one, just the conversation that I'd overheard.

Zeph dropped his towel, and I quickly turned away to give him some privacy while he got dressed.

"Do you think we should go to the police, like Mom wants us to do?" I asked.

"And tell them we got abducted by an evil goddess? Do you think that'll go well?" There was a smile in his voice.

"We don't need to go into the details of who she is. Madame is evil. And she should be punished for what she did."

"The police won't punish her, Ivy. Ghata clearly has a way of dealing with the law that allows her to get away with things. Besides, she uses *bracks* to do her dirty work. It'd be that much harder to prove any wrongdoing on her part."

"Well, we could start with the *bracks* then." I whipped around to face him.

He'd had the jeans on. They were just the right length, Marek was a tall man, too. Unlike my stepdad, who was rather scrawny, Zeph had more muscle mass. The jeans stretched, tightly hugging his thighs.

"What if we put the *bracks* behind bars, at least," I said. "Madame relies on them."

"Even if we succeeded in jailing them, they wouldn't stay locked up for long. Ghata has the power to pull her *bracks* to her from another world. She surely would find a way to get them back, no matter where they'd be locked up in this one."

I thought about Amira and Radax, still under Madame's full control, and about the new "acquisitions" the *bracks* had been making. There had to be a way to stop them from hurting more people—humans or fae.

"They might've come from the magical kingdom," I protested, "but they live in *this* world, now. They broke our law. There has to be a way to make them pay."

He put on the t-shirt.

"I need to speak to Lero. He knows more about Nerifir. He may know what to do."

Lero. Unease pricked my skin at the sound of that name. The

phantom scent of the fragrant smoke tickled my nostrils, bringing back memories of the menagerie.

Zeph winced, running his fingers through the tangled locks of his long hair.

"Here." I gave him my hair brush. "This works better."

He tried to use the brush, but it got caught on a knot about halfway through.

"Ugh!" He arched his back, trying to get the brush loose. "Did I have this hair before they took me?"

"No." I came closer, taking the brush from him. "When I met you, your hair was short."

"I knew it." He shook his head as I took a handful of his long silky locks. "This doesn't feel natural. And so freaking impractical."

"Shh. Stop jerking around. Let me do this." I ran the brush through his hair, working out the knots. It was still slightly damp after his shower, soft but glossy. Truly luxurious. "You have gorgeous hair, Zeph. It's a shame you don't like it."

"I like it well enough," he grumped. "Just not *this* much of it."

"Does it always grow this fast? I mean it's been only a year and a few months, but it's down past your waist now. When we met..."

I realized he was watching me as I brushed his hair. He'd turned to face me, bringing his hair over his shoulder for me to keep brushing.

I licked my lips. "We should be going, soon. The *bracks* must be still after us."

He looked at the basement window, as if to make sure the *bracks'* boots weren't out there.

"Does Ghata know your name? Or the location of this house?" he asked.

I tried to remember. "I never told my name to anyone. Nothing about my mom or this house, either." No one had ever asked me any of that at the menagerie. In a way, I was now grateful for the no-talking rule Madame imposed on her staff.

"Good."

I thought back to that day at the CNE and talking to Fleur during our tour. "My friend might've said my name the day I got caught. If Madame or Radax heard her, they may still remember it. Oh, and I told

Amira *your* name. I told her I knew you from before and that I cared about you." He glanced at me as I continued, "I needed to convince her to take me to the room with the water tank. I hadn't seen you for weeks. I was so worried..."

No matter how hard or how long I fought against my feelings for Zeph, I always cared for him.

"You were worried?" he echoed. "About me."

He stroked the side of my face with the back of his fingers. I lifted my eyes to his, and he met my gaze with a smile.

I felt exposed and vulnerable when faced with that grin of his. Still unsure about what he wanted with me, I was certain that whatever it was, sooner or later he'd get it.

He traced my jawline with a tip of his finger.

"Tell me about the day we met," he said softly, trailing his caress down my throat. "In that cabaret in Paris."

I swallowed against his fingers on my neck.

"You may remember it yourself one day. When the effects of *womora* have worn off."

"Maybe. But I want to hear it from you. Now."

I couldn't tell him *everything*, could I?

"Well, like I said..." I rushed to get it over with. "Lero owns a cabaret. You were singing there the night my friend and I came to see the show. You asked me to dance..."

"And then?" He moved his hand around my neck, dipping his fingers in the hair on the back of my head.

"We had ice cream..." I closed my eyes. The memories of that night rushed over me, spurred on by the sensation of his touch. "And some strawberry champagne, which is not a real Champagne at all, by the way."

All of that seemed so far away now, even as Zeph stood right next to me. So much had happened since.

"Did I kiss you then?" he asked unexpectedly.

I snapped my eyes open. His gaze hooded, he stared at my mouth. My throat felt suddenly dry, and I licked my lips again.

"Oh Zeph, please. No..." I begged, feeling weak in the knees. "I can't. Not again."

His brows moved closer into a frown. "You didn't like me kissing you?"

I loved his kisses. Every slide of his tongue, every glide of his lips, every nibble of his teeth, the blissful sensation of floating in space as he kissed me—I loved all of that so much, I couldn't forget a thing even after so many months had passed.

The problem with having been touched by Zeph once was that now I knew exactly how wonderful it felt. I loved it, craved it, and didn't know how to fight my need for it.

I also knew exactly how horrible it felt when it all ended...

"I can't do it again, Zeph." I stepped away from his touch, pressing my back to the wall.

"What happened?" His frown deepened as he followed me, stopping but an inch or two from my chest. "Did I hurt you?"

"No, not like that." I shook my head. "You took me home, to your place. You were gentle, loving even..." I blinked, forcing the tears away. I had not cried over Zeph, not for a moment in all of the months that had passed. I was certainly not going to cry now in front of him. "Being with you felt so good. You see, Zeph..." I exhaled a shuddered breath, meeting his questioning gaze. "It would've been so much better if you remembered it yourself, because all I can give you is my own recollection of that night. And for me, it was magical. But I can't tell you what it was for *you*, because I never really knew how you felt about me." I heaved a sigh. "I still don't know." Desperately drawing more air into my chest, I finished in one breath, "The fact is, we only spent one night together. That's it."

"Would you have liked more than one night?"

"Back then I thought I would. You had this effect on me..." I searched for a way to describe the intense attraction I felt for him, the need and the longing, but no word seemed to be exactly right. "Anyway, *not* seeing you the next day affected me more than it probably should have. And... I just don't want to go through that again. It hurt when it ended."

"But what if it didn't end that day? What if it lasted longer? Did you want that?"

*What if...*

It was so very tempting to follow that path, but I couldn't allow myself to do that.

"Zeph," I pleaded. "That night was a wonderful adventure. All I want is to preserve the good memories I have from that."

A twinkle flashed in his eyes, then his mouth curved into a devastatingly handsome grin.

"Since I don't *remember* that adventure, Ivy, would you give me a chance for another one? Just one more night, to create new memories in case the old ones don't come back."

I opened my mouth to reply, but he stopped me.

"You don't have to say yes right now." Concern shadowed his features. Was he worried I'd turn him down? Did it mean that much to him? "Just please don't say no."

The longer I stared into his eyes, the more I wanted to say yes—agree to anything he'd ever ask. I didn't fear for my life around Zeph. But my heart certainly wasn't safe.

"I thought I got to know you a little that night," I said, "but you never even told me you weren't human. One thing is true, you're not a man I can have *just* one night with. I've tried it once, and I can't. You see? Around you, I can't trust my heart."

I was waiting for him to step back, away from me, so I could draw another breath. But he didn't move, trapping me with his closeness.

Every nerve in my body came to life, buzzing with awareness. With the wall at my back, I had nowhere to run, waiting for him to release me from whatever spell he'd put me under.

A fae. A siren. What did he do to me?

"Now that I've been completely honest with you," I said carefully, "could you please stop...whatever it is you're doing?"

"What exactly?" He tilted his head.

"Well, this...magic or power?" I waved my hand between us. "Whatever it is that makes everything inside me flutter when you're around. My heart races, my face gets hot, and I can't even look at you without thinking...things I shouldn't be thinking."

"You want me to *turn it off*?"

"Yes, please. Now more than ever I need to have a clear head, without this...intoxicating haze shrouding my brain. It's distracting. Could you, um, turn it off, please?"

"Sure." He shrugged a shoulder, his tone suspiciously light. "But only if you do the same."

"Do what?"

"You have to stop whatever it is *you're* doing that causes me to feel all the same things you've just mentioned." He propped a hand on the wall above my head, leaning closer. "That would be only fair, don't you think?"

"You're feeling the same things?" I studied his face in disbelief.

He seemed so confident, so in control of the situation both that night and now.

"The same things and *more*." He lowered his head to mine, his breath tangling in my hair. "When I'm this close to you, my pants also get tighter," he chuckled. "But the rest is pretty much what you've described."

I exhaled a nervous laugh, unsure what to do about his confession. Believe it? Agree to have another night with him? Everything inside me longed to do that.

But then what?

"Ivy," Zeph said in a more serious tone. "I've lost my memories, but not my ability to think or to feel, or to tell right from wrong. The events of my life may be wiped from my memory, but I know what kind of person I am. If I ever did you wrong, I could not have done that intentionally. Please, give me a chance to make it up to you."

My head was spinning. Maybe if he could just let me take a breath of air not saturated with his warm, fresh-out-of-the-shower scent, my thoughts would get clearer? Yet he stood so close, his body heat blended with mine.

"I just don't know if I should believe you, Zeph. You lie so easily, so convincingly..."

"Coming up with a lie is easy for me," he admitted. "I rarely have to think long to come up with words. That doesn't mean I lie about everything, Ivy. Or that I do it with malicious intent."

"A lie is a lie," I said softly.

"But is it, really?" He shoved away from the wall, raking his fingers through his hair. "I made up a story for Neal and Mariana to convince them to give us a ride, but it didn't harm them in any way, did it? I came up with another story, to explain your disappearance to your mom. But I didn't do it out of disrespect for her."

A frown of concentration settled over his face.

"Ever since I was a child, Lero has been hammering into my brain to keep secret what we are and where we came from. I don't remember the reasons for it, but I suspect it has to do with the two of us trying to fit in, in this world. I wasn't ready to disclose the truth to your mother when it would make little difference to her but could potentially harm Lero and me. Some decisions we make cannot involve humans."

"Well, I *am* a human, and I'm already very much involved."

Dropping his hands, he stared at me.

"You..." he said slowly. "You amaze me. I remember Lero gave me a speech about the dangers of dating anyone from this world. I brought home a girl from school once. I hoped she could be my girlfriend and wanted Lero to meet her. He got furious. He forbade me to date her or anyone else."

"Why?"

"He said humans are fragile and easily hurt. They couldn't handle our differences or deal with the dangers that could come from being with a fae." He rubbed his forehead. "I believe he tried to become close with a woman once, and it didn't end well. Since there are no female fae in this world, he was determined to spend the rest of his life alone, planning for me to do the same."

"Is that what you want? To be alone?"

His frown deepened. "I don't remember if I've ever been sold on that idea. All I have to go by right now is that speech of his and...you."

"Me?"

He nodded, slowly.

"The two don't add up, Ivy."

"What do you mean?"

"When I look at you, I don't see the weak delicate flower that Lero was convincing me all human women were. You've learned about our world, survived some of the worst parts of it, and only gotten stronger. I don't know why I didn't tell you the truth about myself back in Paris, but I wish I did because I know you *can* handle it."

Back then, I realized, I might not have believed him. Only after spending time in Madame's menagerie had I begun to understand his world enough to accept it as real.

In a way, my experience there, as horrible as it was, brought Zeph and me closer.

He cupped the side of my face. "I'll never lie to you."

I leaned into his touch. "Not even if I ask whether my pants make my butt look big?"

That twinkle in his eye appeared again—warm and humorous.

"I'd never have to lie about that." He grinned. "I love your butt, whatever size or shape it is."

With a half-laugh, I attempted to look away, but he kept my face turned to him, not allowing me to break eye contact.

"You want one more night with me?" I asked.

"One." He nodded. "To start with. We can then have a thousand more. And then ten thousand more after that."

"That's a lot of nights..." I smiled.

"And a lot of new memories to make." His hand curling around my neck, he trailed his thumb along my jawline. "One of the memories I regret losing the most is the one of our first kiss."

There had been many kisses that night, but the first one would always be special, wouldn't it?

He brought his face closer to mine, pausing just a hair's breadth away from my lips. With the wall at my back, I couldn't escape him. But he didn't kiss me, waiting instead for me to close the distance.

"You trusted me enough to jump into the Niagara Falls with me," he whispered, his breath hot on my lips. "Please trust me to keep your heart safe, too, Ivy."

Zeph proved to be a great negotiator, indeed. He'd started by asking for just one night and ended up claiming my heart.

With him, I never stood a chance.

"Let's refresh your memory then." I swayed forward into his arms, as if jumping into an abyss.

He caught my mouth with his, eager and greedy. Running his hands up my back, he fisted one in my sweater, burying the fingers of the other in my hair.

Bruising in its desperation, biting in its reckless passion, the kiss was nothing like the sweet, tender kisses from Paris. Arching backwards in his arms, I gripped his neck, struggling to stay on my feet.

The more he kissed me the more I wanted him, returning every slide of his tongue and each nibble of his teeth. Heat pulsed in my chest, spreading through my body and pooling low in my belly.

It was supposed to be just a kiss. Nothing more for now.

"*You'll* have to stop this..." I panted against his mouth, holding him to me. "Because I don't think I can."

Swaying on his feet, he leaned me back against the wall, propping us against it.

"Just a little longer," he groaned.

I sucked on his bottom lip then grazed my teeth along the edge of his jaw before he nibbled at the skin on the side of my neck. Hooking my leg around his hip, I pressed myself to him. My body melted into his, with a shiver running through us both.

My fingers slipped down the neckline of his t-shirt on his back. His skin moved over a vertebra. Something thin and hard pushed against it from the inside.

The spikes of his dorsal fin strained to get out.

He tore himself from me. "We have to stop. For now."

Breathing hard, he peeled his hands off me, pressing them into the wall over my shoulders.

I kept stroking soothingly over his spine just below his neck, until the pulsing movement under his skin there quieted.

He found my eyes with his. "Was it the same as you remember? The kiss?"

His lips glistening, his expression wild and unguarded, his eyes were searching mine with hope and something else...yearning. Zeph might weave fables with his words, but his kisses didn't lie. They told me the truth I needed to know.

He *felt*, and it was real.

"No. Not exactly the same." I cupped his face, stroking his cheekbones with my thumbs. "This time, it was even better."

# Chapter Twenty-One

IVY

"Ivy, I need to call Lero before we leave," Zeph said, while I was packing my things into a duffel bag in the basement.

I paused with a folded t-shirt in my hands. He crouched in front of me, searching my eyes.

"I know you trust Lero..." I started.

He jerked his head. "I *did* trust him. But I have no recent memories of him." He heaved a sigh, running a hand through his hair. "I don't know what happened, how I got caught. But if I talk to him, it may clear up some things. Besides, we need any information we can get to come up with a plan."

He was right. The more we knew, the easier it may be figuring out what to do next.

"Do you remember Lero's phone number?" I asked.

"Only our home number from a while back. It may no longer be active."

"True," I agreed, then said loudly, "hey, Alexa, what's the phone number of the cabaret *Le Loup Solitaire* in Paris?" I turned to Zeph. "It should be open now."

"Thanks." He grabbed the phone while my mom's Alexa speaker helpfully provided him with the number.

"Zeph..." I said quickly as he brought the phone to his ear. "Be careful. Please."

He nodded before hitting the speaker button for me to hear the conversation, too.

*"Le Loup Solitaire. Bonjour,"* a pleasant female voice sounded on the other end of the line.

"May I speak to Lero?" Zeph asked. He didn't introduce himself, probably being cautious.

"Lero is no longer here. We're operating under new ownership."

"New ownership?" Zeph's eyebrows shot up in surprise. "Has the venue been sold then?"

"Yes."

"When?"

"About a year ago."

Zeph's expression darkened. "Where can I find Lero? Do you know?"

"Would you hold? For just a moment?"

Silence replaced the woman's voice.

Zeph glanced at me, with a puzzled expression on his face. "He sold it. Why?"

"I have no idea." The place seemed to be doing well when I visited. But maybe without Zeph, its main star, things didn't go that well?

"*Allô*," a male voice came on the line this time. "May I ask who is looking for Lero?"

Zeph hesitated, but only for a moment.

"My name is Zeph. I'm a long-time friend of—"

"Zeph? You're back?" The voice rose with excitement. "I didn't recognize you. You don't sound quite the same. Where the hell have you been? Lero was losing his mind here. He left a message for you."

Now, I recognized the man's voice. He spoke fluent French but with a slight Eastern European accent. It was Ivan, the bar manager.

Unfortunately, Zeph didn't remember him. "What message? Um, whom am I talking to?"

"My name is Ivan." The warm excitement in the man's voice disappeared, giving place to suspicion.

"What was the message, Ivan?"

"I'm afraid the instructions were to give it to Zeph only." He spoke in a polite, business-like manner once again, his tone guarded.

"But, I am—"

"In person."

The line went dead.

"Ivan is the bar manager at *Le Loup Solitaire*," I explained. "Or at least he was, back when I visited. I should've told you that before you called. He obviously expected you to remember him."

Zeph hung up the phone.

"It wouldn't have made a difference." He shook his head. "If Lero wanted the message to be given to me in person, I have to go to Paris to pick it up."

"But what if it's a trap?" Dread chilled me from the inside.

He glanced at me, a slight grin playing on his lips. "Then I'll have to be careful."

"It's not a game, Zeph." Sure, he could take care of himself. But *bracks* weren't stupid either. And there were so many of them.

"I know it's not," he said in a more serious voice. "But I'll have to go, Ivy. Lero might've been taken, too. Or maybe he's hiding somewhere, away from Ghata and her *bracks*. In any case, I'll need to find him."

*"Please, be careful,"* flashed through my mind again. Only I didn't say it out loud this time, afraid I'd sound like a broken record.

"How easy is it to kill a fae?" I asked, instead.

He came to me, taking my hand in his. A grim shadow fell over his features, chasing the smile away.

"I have no intention of dying, Ivy. And you've seen for yourself, I'm good at killing."

I nodded, drawing in a shuddered breath.

"I know. It's just that...There are so many of them. And you'll be alone."

He placed his hands on my shoulders, drawing me into his body. "It's not easy to kill a fae, darling. They won't catch me unaware again, either. I'm ready for them. Besides, I'll swim to France. And in the water, I'm invincible."

"You'll swim?" I stared at him. "Across the Atlantic?"

That was insane!

But then again, didn't he bring the mighty Niagara Falls under his control, just last night?

Zeph was so much more than a human. I had to remember that.

"Is it safe to swim that far?" I muttered. "How long does it take to cross the Atlantic? Weeks? Months?"

"For me? Just a few days."

Incredible!

"Have you ever done it before?"

"No."

Well, that was not reassuring. Not at all.

"How about the sharks, whales, and giant squid?" And a whole lot of other dangers I couldn't even think of right now.

A lop-sided grin lit up his face once again.

"I'll swim around them. There is plenty of space in the ocean for all of us."

He was obviously teasing. But I couldn't smile back this time. The idea of Zeph alone deep in the menacing vastness of the ocean was incomprehensible. Terrifying.

"Ivy." He brushed my nose with his. "I'll be fine. Back in Nerifir, sirens live in an Ocean. Water is my home."

I wrapped my arms around his neck, holding him to me. "I'll drive you to the Atlantic coast, then?" I whispered into his ear. "I'll rent a car, whenever you're ready."

"No need," he replied. "I can make it to the ocean from Lake Ontario."

"You can?"

"When we were in Niagara River, I sensed the entire system of the waterways here. It goes all the way to the ocean. I may have to get out of the water to walk past the locks on the river north from here—"

"St. Lawrence River," I said automatically.

"Right. But it's still going to be faster for me to swim than to drive."

If he didn't need me to drive, it meant we would have to part sooner. When I'd just gotten him back...

My time with Zeph had been sprinkled out in tiny, delicious scraps when I didn't think even a full meal would've been enough. He hadn't left yet, and I was already missing him.

"When do you want to leave?"

"Tonight."

So soon. I groaned inside.

He rushed to explain, "With *bracks* looking on our heels, you'll be safer without me. Ghata is likely more focused on getting her money-making exhibit back. She wouldn't spend too much energy on recapturing an escaped human servant. Do you understand? By staying with you, I'm putting you in danger."

In my mind, I understood it all. My heart ached, however.

"Ivy..." He nuzzled my hair.

I let go of him, stopping him from whatever he was about to say...or do. As hard as it was for me to let him go, it would be so much harder if he hugged or kissed me again.

"It's fine." I took a step back. "I understand."

"I won't leave until I'm certain you're safe," he assured me. "You can't stay in Toronto. It's too close to Ghata's lair. Neither Canada nor the States are safe."

"I could fly to Paris, to stay with Fleur for a little while." I'd taken my passport from the things in my mom's basement, and I had enough money for the ticket, but not for much more. Once there, I'd have to start working again to pay for my living expenses.

The good thing was that as a graphic designer I could work from anywhere. But I'd have to see what I could salvage of my clientele. After the months of my unexplained absence, some of my clients might never want to work with me again. Understandably so.

No matter what, I should call Fleur sooner rather than later. She should know I was safe and sound.

Zeph shook his head. "France isn't good, either. Paris would definitely be the place where the *bracks* would look for me."

"What would you suggest?"

He rubbed the back of his neck in thought. "I'm not sure yet. Let me think about it. One thing is certain, the place needs to be on the water. The more of it, the better."

That should give me some time to prepare, mentally.

Why was it always so hard to say goodbye to this man?

"Ivy." He came after me, scooping me into his arms. "This isn't forever. We won't part for long."

That was what I'd thought the last time, too. Back in Paris.

I chased away the buzz of a warning going off in my head. There wasn't much I could do to stop him from leaving. And if he chose not to return to me... I stifled a sigh. There wasn't much I could do about that, either.

"Well, we might as well stop by a bathing suit store. I wouldn't want you crossing the Atlantic in the nude."

He flashed me a teasing grin. "Why not?"

"No need to tempt the fish."

# Chapter Twenty-Two

IVY

I called for a cab, and we left, not lingering in my mom's house a second longer than was necessary.

No one appeared to be following us. It was a relief, though I couldn't quite relax completely.

We stopped at the police station, not to report Madame, but to close my missing person report. It turned out to be easier to do than Mom had made it sound. Once the police officer felt satisfied I was who I said I was, the case was closed. He didn't even bat an eye at the lame excuse I provided for my disappearance: leaving for an adventure to work the fairgrounds with the cute guy I'd met. Running away with the carnival, without letting my family know about my whereabouts might make me look selfish and irresponsible, but it didn't make me a criminal.

After that, Zeph and I took a bus to a shopping mall where we had a quick lunch at the food court.

"Mmm, food." Zeph bit into his roast beef sandwich.

I barely held back a moan myself, wolfing down my pho soup. It was beyond amazing to finally eat a real meal after months of plain oatmeal for breakfast, egg salad sandwiches for lunch, and nothing at all for dinner.

It occurred to me that this might be Zeph's first time in the country.

"Is it your first time in Canada?" I asked.

He nodded. "From what I remember—yes."

"Maybe I should've gotten you a poutine instead, then? Something a little more Canadian."

He smiled. "Well, I've already seen the Niagara Falls, inside and out. How about that for a Canadian experience?"

It'd been a rather harrowing experience, really. But his easy tone made me laugh.

A rush of déjà vu washed over me. It was a different place and time, but the feeling of giddy happiness was very much the same like that night in Paris when I first met Zeph. Affection for him warmed me from the inside.

No. It was a much deeper feeling than affection. I bit my lip at the realization.

I was falling in love with Zeph, head over heels. And there was nothing I could do about that. Nothing I *wanted* to do about that, either.

He looked at me, the sandwich in his hand paused on its way to his mouth.

"I love your laugh," he said. "It's even more wonderful than music."

Coming from him, it was the best compliment a person could get.

After lunch, we stopped at the bank. I took some cash out and exchanged some money for Zeph to take on his trip to France. Then, I got a new cellphone for myself and a pair of swim trunks for him.

"Now what?" I asked when we were done. There was nothing left to do but to wait until Zeph's departure. My chest tightened again at the thought of parting from him soon. "You should rest. Have a nap at least. I don't care how magical you are, it's a freaking long swim."

"A nap sounds great," he agreed. "But we have to decide on a safe place for you, too."

I tried to think. Going back to Mom's house was out of the question.

"We'll get a hotel. I know a cute one, down on the Lakeshore Road. It's closer to the lake too. We can just walk to the water from there."

He grinned, hugging my shoulders, "Lead the way."

"This looks great." Zeph dropped my duffel bag on the floor of the hotel room.

There were two double beds here. I kicked off my shoes, heading to the closest one.

It'd been a crazy couple of days. We'd only gotten a few hours of uncomfortable sleep on the floor in the garage. Exhaustion tugged at me.

"Tired?" Zeph wrapped his arms around me from behind.

I nodded, turning to face him. "You must be, too."

"I'm exhausted," he admitted, walking me backwards toward the bed.

I hooked my arms around his shoulders. The back of my legs hit the edge of the mattress, and Zeph lowered me into bed then climbed over me.

"There are two beds," I pointed out, not releasing him from my arms.

"Each is big enough for two," he retorted, kissing the side of my neck.

I arched my back under him, seeking more contact with his body. He groaned, pressing closer to me.

"Zeph..." I glided my hands down his back.

He rose over me on an elbow. "Sleep or kiss, Ivy? What do you want more right now?"

Was I tired? Not enough to refuse Zeph's kisses. Not when he was leaving me soon.

I moved a long strand of his hair away from his face.

"Kiss me, Zeph."

Sleep could wait.

"Good choice." He smirked, lowering his mouth to mine.

I released a moan against his lips. The weight of all fears or worries was gone with it. Zeph's kisses always made me float, light and free.

Heat rushed me in a swell of desire. My long sweater suddenly felt too hot. All the clothes seemed too stifling.

Zeph slid a hand under my sweater, gripping my hip.

"Tell me, Ivy," he murmured between the kisses. "When I brought you home last time, what did I do to you that night?"

Our one night together.

I melted into his caress. "You got me naked."

He slid my sweater up then off over my head, leaving me in a black tank top and a bra.

"And then?" He kissed down my neck.

Sweet, little ripples of bliss tinged my skin. The sensation proved addictive. I craved more.

"Then... We had a bath."

"Nice," he murmured against my collarbone. "I love baths."

"It was...a nice one," I agreed.

Slipping the bra straps and the shoulder straps of my tank top off my shoulders, he tugged them both down, freeing my breasts.

Breath left my chest in a rush as he dragged his tongue over my hardening nipple. I squirmed, desire throbbing hard between my thighs. He parted my legs with his knee, and I shifted my hips, rubbing myself against his thigh.

"And then?" He grazed my nipple with his teeth.

My hips jerked, pleasure running through me in a shiver of hot tingles.

Did he ask me a question? I couldn't focus on anything but the pressure pulsing low in my belly, craving a release.

His tongue and lips played with my hard, aching nipple as he cupped my other breast with his hand.

"What happened then, Ivy?" he insisted, his words vibrating against my skin. "What happened in the tub?"

A tub?

Oh, right. He was still talking about our first night together.

"You had a huge...tub. Right in the middle of the living space of your apartment..." I groaned, pressing my core to his thigh between my legs.

"Tell me, how did I make you come? Because I did make you come, didn't I?"

"Oh yes... The jets. There were some very naughty water jets."

"Jets?" He chuckled, lifting my tank top up to kiss down my belly. "They sound like fun."

"Lots...lots of fun." Words rushed out of my mouth with another moan.

He shoved down my leggings, taking my underwear with them.

"Oh..." I pressed my knees together, realizing what he was about to do. "Last time, you didn't go...down there, Zeph." No man had done that to me before.

He glanced up at me, parting my legs.

"I didn't? What a shame." He kissed down the inside of my thigh. "A huge oversight on my part."

Pleasure rippled along my sensitive skin. The desire burnt hotter.

"Let me correct that." Zeph slipped his tongue between my folds.

And I forgot...everything. Gripping my thighs with his hands, he gently sucked on the hot throbbing bud at the top of my opening. I gripped his hair, pressing my hips into his mouth. Pleasure cursed through me. My thighs trembled.

More...

I arched my back as he licked, nibbled, and sucked.

The world fell apart. My breath hitched in my throat. Pleasure built up until I couldn't take it anymore.

"Zeph..." His name fluttered from my lips with a moan.

Orgasm burst through me, shuddering my body with bliss. I kept gripping his hair. He nuzzled me gently between my legs, reaping every last ripple of pleasure from me.

I unclenched my fingers, finally releasing his hair. Pure happiness spread through me with languid warmth. My limbs grew heavy and warm.

"This was so...wonderful," I murmured, adjusting my top.

He pulled a blanket over my heated body. Taking off his hoodie and t-shirt, he climbed under the covers with me.

I snuggled into him, his hard length pressing against my thigh. I slid my hand down, searching for it.

Tiredness slipped away, giving way to excitement. I longed to feel Zeph inside me. But he caught my hand before I touched him.

"Nap now." He kissed my palm, shifting slightly away from me.

"But..." It was the second time he'd done that—brought me to a mind shuddering orgasm, never trying to have one himself. "Are you sure?"

"Rest." He kissed the inside of my wrist.

I didn't think I could fall asleep, now. My body was still humming with all the pleasure he'd made me feel. My inner muscles quivered in the aftershock of my climax.

I trailed my fingers down his forearm. The pale stripe of his skin rippled under my touch. He had a fin hidden there.

"How does it work?" I asked. "Your magic? How does water obey you?"

"It becomes a part of me," he replied simply.

"But how? Like an arm or a leg?"

His chuckle sounded over my ear, resonating softly through his chest. "Something like that."

"What happens if there are several sirens in the ocean? Who has the power over the water then?"

"All of them, I guess." His chest moved with a deep breath. "I don't remember ever seeing another siren in my life. But I'd imagine it would be like combining their power. If they worked together, they would accomplish things on a larger scale."

"And if they went against each other?"

"Then there would be a tempest."

I stifled a yawn, sleep pulling me under, aided by his soothing voice. However, the topic proved too intriguing to quit.

"You said Lero didn't allow you to use your power as a kid, but did you ever try?"

"Lero didn't want me to use it in public, out of fear of being discovered. But he didn't stop me from playing with water at home. He actually *asked* me to do it, once."

"He did? Why?"

"Our washing machine broke, flooding the basement. Lero woke me up at four in the morning and brought me downstairs. I was seven. And so sleepy. I remember holding the soapy water in a ball in the middle of the room, trying and failing to understand where he wanted me to dump it."

I imagined a seven-year-old Zeph in his little-boy pajamas, his hair tousled from sleep, wielding his out-of-this-world power to save their basement from a flood.

"I would've loved to see that." I smiled.

"Oh, it was long before you were born."

"Couldn't be that long." I yawned, fighting the sleepy haze settling in. "How old are you?"

"I don't remember exactly, but if I do the math, it should be around mid-to-late forties."

"Forties?" I laughed. Surely, he'd made a mistake. "Your math is terribly wrong, Zeph."

"Not by more than a year or two. The flooding happened in the nineteen eighties. And I know I graduated high school still in the last century."

I turned my face to his. "How long do fae live?"

"At least five hundred years."

"Human years?" I asked stupidly.

The revelation shocked me. The sleep left, blown away.

"Yes. Human years. Is that a problem?"

"Don't you think it is?" I rose on my elbow. "How old is Lero?"

He took a moment, his eyebrows knotting into a frown of concentration. "He would be in his late eighties, early nineties, now."

"No way. Really?" I might not have gotten a good enough look at Lero back in Paris to accurately estimate his age, but he definitely did not have the appearance of an eighty-year-old. "Fae don't age, then?"

"No."

With a groan, I sank back into the pillows.

"What is it that we're doing then, Zeph? I'll never live as long as you will. I'll age. In a few decades, I'll be old and wrinkly."

He gathered me into his arms again.

"I like you, Ivy, and I want a chance for us to see where it goes. I know it's all new to you, but it is for me, too." He rolled me to my back, holding my face between his hands. His expression remained serious, only a tiny smile was hiding deep in the corners of his mouth. "If this works out, I'll stay with you until your dying breath, no matter how old and wrinkly you'll get."

How could he be so sure?

"Careful." I winced. "Don't say things you may regret later. Life is long. *Your* life apparently is even longer."

"I have every intention to stick around, Ivy. For as long as either one of us shall live."

It was more than a simple promise. It sounded more like a vow.

Thrill tingled warmly through my chest. I wanted so much to believe we could have a future together.

*"If it works out,"* he'd said.

It might not, like with any relationship. But what if it did?

"One sure way to gross people out would be to have you on my arm when I'm eighty," I mumbled, settling back into the pillows and into his arms.

"Would you really deny giving us a chance as a couple just because of what strangers may think, sixty years from now?"

Well, when he put it that way...

"Besides, I'll be into my second century by then," he chuckled. "You may end up leaving me for someone younger, anyway."

And just like that, my concerns were gone. He made me laugh once again.

Whatever happened, I just simply wished to have more of this—cuddling and laughing with him.

He kissed the tip of my nose. "Sleep now."

I hid another yawn. "I wish I could. I'm so tired, but somehow not sleepy. How can it be?"

He stroked my arm. A soft hum vibrated deep inside his chest, like a song striving to come out.

"Sing me a lullaby, Zeph," I asked softly. "Please."

"No." He shook his head quickly. "I can't. You know it..."

"It doesn't need to be perfect. You don't have to be good. You just have to try."

He kissed my forehead. "Close your eyes."

I did. Closing my eyes, I snuggled into his warmth.

The hum in his chest grew a little stronger, the sound rolling in his throat. I recognized the melody of *"À la claire fontaine,"* a sweet and a bit melancholy song.

I opened my mouth, murmuring the first line to his humming.

"Shh." He touched my lips with the tip of a finger. "Sleep."

"*You* sing, then..." I kissed his bare chest.

Softy, tentatively, as if ready to die on his lips at any moment, the lyrics of the song left his lips.

"*Il y a longtemps que je t'aime, jamais je ne t'oublierai*/ I've loved you for so long, I will never forget you," Zeph sang.

The melody was simple. He sang softly, carrying the tune easily enough. Once or twice, I stilled my breath as his voice cracked, taking a higher note, but he recovered quickly.

"*Tu as le cœur à rire... moi je l'ai à pleurer*/ Your heart is made for laughing... mine can only cry."

Zeph was singing again...

When I woke up, I found myself practically hanging off the edge of the bed. If it wasn't for Zeph's arm and leg hooked tightly around me, I would've fallen. The rest of his long body was spread out across the entire bed.

"I'm falling here," I muttered sleepily, grabbing him around his neck to hold on.

"Sorry." He rolled to his back, taking me with him, so I ended up on top of his chest. "I'm not used to sharing a bed with anyone."

I didn't remember Zeph sleeping with me the night I'd spent in his apartment. He came to bed after I'd fallen asleep and got up before I awoke.

This felt nice.

The sight of him on the pillow, his silky white hair spread around his beautiful face like a silvery halo, was definitely out-of-this-world.

His hand on my nape, he lowered my head, kissing my lips. It was a light, tender kiss, and he stopped before it had a chance to grow into anything more.

"How are you feeling?" he asked.

"Wonderful." I smiled. "You?"

"Much better."

"Well rested?"

"Well enough to swim the Atlantic." He grinned.

"Right... The swim." Sadness gripped my heart at the reminder.

Outside the window, the sun had dipped towards the horizon already. We must have slept for hours. Not surprising, since we both had been short on sleep.

"We should get going." Zeph untangled himself from me. "Before *bracks* find this place."

Madame's name had the effect of an ice bucket emptied over my head. The remnants of sleep blew away.

I sat up in bed.

Zeph picked up his t-shirt off the floor but didn't put it on. Holding it in his hand he stared straight ahead, as if thinking of something.

"Did you say *bracks* saw you with me in Paris that night?" he asked. "Do they know you knew me from before?"

No one had ever alluded to my previous connection to Zeph back at the menagerie.

"I don't think she or the *bracks* knew. It was dark that night. And I had a different hair color back then."

"You did?" He raised an eyebrow. "What was it?"

"Blue and pink."

"Lovely." He smiled, with a flash of appreciation in his eyes.

I couldn't help grinning back at him. Zeph had the uncanny ability to lighten up even the darkest of situations.

"Unless, Amira told her." I didn't think the quiet girl like Amira would be running around, babbling out my secrets. But if Madame suspected I'd say something to Amira, she might find a way to make her talk.

"Ghata and her *bracks* would most likely search for me between here and Europe," Zeph said. "I think you should go south, out of their travel path completely."

"South?"

"Right. On the water somewhere."

"Like the Caribbean?"

"That'd be nice," he agreed. "Warm and beautiful."

"With lots of water all around." I remembered the island of St. Vincent I'd visited with my parents as a child.

They'd already been going through some troubles in their marriage, and that trip had been one of their many failed attempts to reconnect. But my memories of that vacation were nothing but happy.

Back then, I was eight, on a trip with my still intact family, and the world had seemed wonderful. I'd loved snorkeling with colorful fish and running on the black-sand beaches. The volcanic sand, heated by the sun, burned my bare feet, and I ran to the water as fast as I could, screaming and laughing.

"I went to St. Vincent once," I said to Zeph, smiling at those memories. "It's an island."

"An island is perfect."

"I'll look into renting something there...after you leave here."

He shook his head. "We'll find something now. I need to make sure you have a place to go when I leave."

"Okay, well." I climbed from under the covers. "We may as well go get some dinner in the restaurant across the street first. What do you think?"

I was stalling, trying to postpone his departure for as long as I could. It was obvious to me. Surely. He knew that, too.

He didn't object, though.

"All right," He pulled the t-shirt over his head, then put on his old hoodie. "You can take me out for dinner." He grinned. "It's a date."

# Chapter Twenty-Three

ZEPH

Ivy raked her fork though the spaghetti noodles on her plate, turning them over. Like she'd done with her soup at lunch, she leaned over the plate, carefully inspecting her dinner.

"No glitter?" he asked sympathetically.

Just a few weeks in Madame's "care" were enough to change the way Ivy saw food. It was no longer just pleasure and nourishment to her. It was also a potential threat.

"No." She exhaled a bashful laugh. "Sorry... It's a bad habit."

"Not your fault." He gritted his teeth, wishing he could strangle Ghata with his own hands. The spikes under his skin stirred, begging for action.

He shoved down his anger, wounding some spaghetti on his fork, instead.

"Are you able to obtain nourishment from water, somehow?" Ivy asked, probably thinking about the months he'd spent in a sealed water tank.

"If I have to." Thankfully, he had no clear recollection of his time in the tank. The most vivid memories were that of conversations with Ivy they somehow managed to have telepathically. But the mere fact that he'd been locked like a sardine in a can, helpless and at the mercy of a mad woman, made him wince. "I prefer a proper meal."

He shoved a forkful of spaghetti into his mouth. It wasn't as amazing as Lero could make it, but it was still good. Much better than sucking through his skin particles dissolved in water to survive.

"How is Fleur doing?" he asked to change the subject to something more pleasant.

Before coming in, Ivy had called her friend in Paris.

"Good." She took a sip of her red wine. "I'd told her a slightly modified version of the prank story that you made up for my mom. Then I did my best to dodge her questions."

"Would you've liked to tell her the truth?"

"I couldn't." She shook her head. "Not if you and Lero want to keep your secret. Besides," she smiled, "she wouldn't believe me. From my experience, the stories about fae and magical kingdoms need some sufficient proof to back them up. Anyway." She shrugged. "Fleur is happy that I'm back, safe and sound."

Ivy lingered over her dinner, taking twice as long to finish her food as he did.

The waitress brought them crème brûlée for dessert. Ivy cracked the sugary shell over the custard filling with her spoon, but didn't take a bite.

He sensed the unsettling feeling inside her. She was anxious about his leaving. But there was something else...

She tapped with her spoon at the caramelized crust of her dessert, breaking it into tiny shards.

"Is something wrong, Ivy?"

Her chest rose with a deep breath.

"Can I ask you a question?" She wouldn't look at him. "A *personal* question?"

"Sure." By this point, he didn't think there were any secrets between them. Personal or not.

She drew in another breath, as if getting ready to dive off a cliff.

"Is there a reason why you wouldn't have sex with me?"

He nearly choked on a spoonful of his dessert. Grabbing his glass, he gulped down some water.

"We've had sex, sweetheart. Twice." He cleared his throat. "Sadly, I only remember one time. But I think it was wonderful. You said so yourself."

"For *me*, it was." She nodded, blush brightening the skin on her cheeks. "But what about you?"

"Oh." He leaned toward her across the table. "Believe me, darling, I thoroughly enjoyed every minute."

He licked his lips, making her blush deeper.

"Okay." She glanced aside, then turned back to face him again, meeting his eyes fiercely. "Why wouldn't you fuck me, Zeph?" she blurted out. "For real? Why would you not put your dick inside me?"

"What?" Now it was his turn to blush. "Ivy..." He didn't expect her to be this blunt. She was clearly frustrated.

She leaned closer, lowering her voice.

"Why don't you let me touch you?" The plea in her voice tugged at his heart.

"I..." He took a look around, sensing some uninvited glances on them. "Can we leave? Please."

She dropped her shoulders, took some money from her cross-body purse, and got up.

He followed her out of the restaurant and into the chilly evening. The sun had set. Only the streetlights illuminated the street now.

"Ivy, listen..." He jogged ahead of her, then stood in front of her, making her stop.

She hugged herself against the bitter November wind.

He ran his fingers over his hair tied in the knot low on the back of his head.

"Remember the dead *bracks* in Ghata's basement?" he asked, knowing she would never forget that. "I killed them."

She frowned. "I know."

"I killed them with these." He yanked his sleeve up, then released the spikes in his forearm.

The fin snapped open, the fan of the membrane shimmering with an iridescent glow under the streetlights.

Ivy gasped softly, looking mesmerized.

He turned his arm around, showing her the tiny droplets beading at the end of each spike.

"My body produces poison, Ivy. It's lethal for *bracks* who are just as hard to kill as fae." He stepped over to the closest streetlight and whipped the ends of his spikes at the post. The neon blue liquid streaked the wood. It hissed and charred, with tiny tendrils of smoke. He snapped the fin close, the poison securely hidden inside his body now. "Can you imagine what it would do to *you?*"

"To me?" She looked at him with those summer-green eyes. "Why me?"

"Because there are moments in my life when I can't control them."

"What moments?"

"When I'm angry. *Really* angry. Or scared. Or..." He met her eyes, baring his innermost secret to her, "When I'm fucking someone into oblivion, so hard it feels like my soul left my body and there is nothing but pure pleasure and bliss. Magical, wild, and uncontrollable."

She blinked. "Is that what sex is to you?"

"That's what it'd be like, with *you.*" He sensed it. It would be intense, and he wouldn't be able to control himself. "If I accidentally release the spikes, and you get hurt. Because of me..." He couldn't finish. He refused to even imagine that horror.

"I see." She took his arm and turned it in her hands.

With the tip of a finger, she gently traced the slit over his spikes. Securely sealed, his skin kept the spikes out of reach, and her out of harm.

"Is that the only reason?" She squinted at him.

He frowned. "Is it not enough? It's, literally, a life and death situation, Ivy."

"I think we may be able to do something about it."

"Ivy..." He shook his head in warning. He was not going to risk her life, not for that.

"Come." She took his hand, heading back to their hotel.

"Ivy. Wait." He planted his feet into the pavement of the parking lot, not moving an inch.

She looked at him with a small, wistful smile.

"Obviously, I'm not a siren. My call is not that hard to resist, is it?"

Oh, she had no idea.

Every muscle in his body vibrated with strain. Every fiber of his being wished to intertwine with hers, for them to melt into each other, body and soul. He longed to lose himself inside her.

"It's nearly impossible to resist, Ivy," he pleaded. "Sweetheart, I can't. Please understand—"

"Come, Zeph. Just one night." She batted her eyelashes at him in an adorable way. "Let me seduce you."

*Seduce him?*

She didn't need to try hard.

He couldn't deny her. After all, he was just a fae, not a god.

Weak in his knees, he followed her.

The moment she unlocked the door of the hotel room, he shoved it open, dragging her in.

"Thank you for dinner," he rasped, kicking the door shut.

"It was my pleasure..." She found the edge of his hoodie, then took it off him. The t-shirt followed, and she slid her hands up his chest. Impatiently.

He wanted so much more with her, a night would never be enough. But the thought that this one night was all they had for now added urgency.

"Ivy..." he breathed against the side of her neck, lost in her scent and needing more of her body. Blindly, he walked her backwards to where the bed stood.

He ripped her sweater off before lowering her to the mattress. Cupping her breast, he grazed his teeth against the nipple through the lace of her bra.

Fervently unbuckling his jeans, she yanked the zipper down. Desire raged through him like wildfire, but he caught her hands before she could reach inside his jeans, lifting her arms above her head, instead.

"Zeph, I want you..." Ivy whispered with a sweet whimper as he kissed down her chest.

He peeled off her leggings, and she slid her underwear down for him.

Letting go of her hands, he unhooked her bra behind her back, setting her breasts free, then caught the hard peak of one in his mouth again.

Touching, kissing, tasting...

Every moment with Ivy brought him back to life. He let her take over all of his senses.

"Ivy," he repeated her name, caressing her skin with his lips as he moved down her body.

A shiver ran through her when he stroked the insides of her thighs. He did it again, making sure his touch was slow and deliberate.

He then lowered his mouth to her, gliding his tongue between her slick, heated folds.

"Oh, God, Zeph..." She arched her back, bucking her hips.

Ivy trembled, and he gripped her hips tighter, keeping her in place.

Her moans grew louder. She fisted her hands in his hair, teasing it out of the knot he'd made. Set free, his long hair spilled over her naked thighs.

She tightened her grip on his hair. A shiver of pleasure ran down his body from the sting at the roots. He groaned against her flesh.

She tensed like a string under his caress. He sucked harder, already tasting her impending climax.

"Zeph..." She tugged on his hair, prompting him to glance up. "I want you with me."

The achy pressure in his groin throbbed hot and urgent. A prickling sensation along his spine came with it. The spikes of his fins pushed against his skin from the inside, straining to spring free.

They were filled with poison.

"I'll hurt you," he croaked, pressing the throbbing bulge in his pants into the mattress to alleviate the building pressure. It only made it worse, sending a shudder of need through him.

Wrapping her arms around his neck, she sat up in bed, making him sit up, too. Straddling his thighs, she slid her fingers down his spine, following the curve of each vertebra.

Intense pleasure rippled along his skin in the wake of her touch.

"Ivy, baby, please don't..." he begged, stifling a moan.

"They're hidden." She removed her hands from him.

"For now."

"Have you ever had sex before?" She stared at him.

"I have." He raked his hand through his hair. "Twice. That I remember."

Both times happened after he'd finished school. His memories appeared to be reaching further into his adult life now.

She tilted her head. "How did you do it?"

"Very carefully, holding back, controlling every move." The experience had been more exhausting than enjoyable. Of course, neither of those women knew the truth about him. Releasing his fins in front of them would be unthinkable.

"Can you show them to me again?" she asked. "I haven't seen the dorsal fin up close yet."

"I don't think that's a good idea." The thought of harming her accidentally filled him with paralyzing dread. "Not when we're in bed like this. It's too close."

"Promise I won't touch," she insisted sweetly. "We'll be careful."

Once again, he found it impossible to deny her. But he had to keep her safe.

"Give me your hands." He circled her wrists with his fingers, pressing them to his chest. Bending over, he then placed his chin on her shoulder.

She would be able to see his back over his shoulder, now.

"Watch."

Carefully, he released his dorsal fin. The spikes swished open like a fan from his spine, stretching the tissue that connected them.

"It's beautiful, Zeph," she said softly, nuzzling his hair. "Translucent and iridescent. Like a dragonfly wing."

"But deadly." He sensed the poison swell at the tips, chilling his spine, and he quickly snapped the fin closed, hiding it safely under his skin.

"Only the very tips are poisonous, right?" she asked, and he nodded. "Then I shall stay away from them."

"There is always a chance you'll prick your hand—"

"Like Sleeping Beauty?" she smiled.

For once, he did not share her humor. The poison was potent enough to kill a *brack*. If Ivy so much as pricked her finger, she wouldn't fall asleep like the princess in the fairy tale. She'd die. And *he* would be the one who'd killed her.

"I can still make you feel good..." He placed his hands on her knees, fully intending to finish what he'd started.

Ivy didn't move, though.

"You want hundreds of nights with me, Zeph. They can't all be just about me. I want you to enjoy our time together, too."

He shook his head slowly. "Trust me, darling. I love every single moment with you."

She didn't appear convinced, thinking out loud, "If I'm physically unable to touch your fins, they can't prick me, right?" She yanked his belt out of the loops of his jeans. "Make it so I can't touch you." She offered both her wrists to him. "Tie them up."

He hesitated, afraid to subject her to even a shred of any potential danger.

"Please," she begged. "Let's just try. If you feel it's not working, you can stop."

She might not be a siren, but her call proved impossible to disobey.

"Just to try," he conceded, taking the belt from her. "I won't go all the way. I'll stop."

He tied her wrists together.

"It may turn out safer than you think," she placed a quick kiss on his lips, before turning around in his arms. "We'll do it this way."

Standing on her knees in bed, her back to him, Ivy bent over, propping her bound hands into the mattress. She then stretched her arms in front of her and placed her head on the pillow.

Blood rushed to Zeph's cock so fast, he swayed with a wave of dizziness at the sight of Ivy in this position. With her head down, her hair fanning across the pillow, her back curved gracefully, she presented the unobstructed view of her backside to him.

"Fuck, Ivy..." He groaned. "How is a man supposed to resist this?"

"Then why are you still resisting?" she teased, her voice breathy. Shifting back, she wiggled her ass, rubbing it against his long-suffering, painfully hard cock. "Take me, Zeph. I want you to come for me."

He carefully placed his hands on each side of her hips, then mentally evaluated the direction of the spikes if his fins were to open. Taking her from behind like this would keep all the poisonous tips directed away from her body. She couldn't touch them.

This might work.

Finally, he fully freed his throbbing erection, pressing the tip to her slick opening.

"Oh, yes!" She shifted back, taking him in as he thrust forward.

She was so warm, tight, and slick inside. The intense pleasure nearly doubled him in half, he pressed his face to her back, kissing her skin.

"You're amazing," he muttered, in awe.

There was no way he'd last long this first time. He promptly slid his hand down her belly and found the spot between her thighs that made her moan in ecstasy when he'd kissed it. He rubbed it now while moving slowly inside her. Tenderly at first, he increased the pressure as her moans grew louder and more erratic.

Her breathing hitched. Gripping the sheets, she came hard on his hand, his cock buried deep inside her.

*Beautiful.*

The tremors of her orgasm echoed through his body. He felt *her* pleasure. The spikes stirred under his skin, and he yanked his hand away. Gripping her hips instead, he thrust hard, riding the last waves of her climax while chasing his own.

Then he let go.

His control slipped. For the first time ever, he fully lost himself in a woman.

The release hit him violently. His body shuddered. A pained groan ripped from his throat. He heard the spikes of his fins snap open, but he could no longer stop, even as the ones on his legs threatened to pierce his own ass in this position. Pleasure took over his senses, blinding him to everything else for a moment.

Relief spread thick through his veins, and he crashed, rolling off Ivy's back.

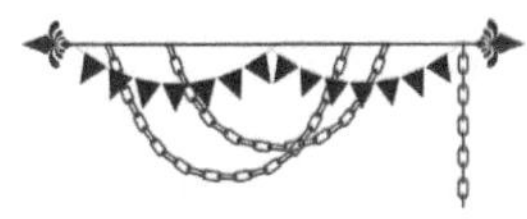

# Ivy

His fins jerked, closing quickly.

I wrapped my arms tightly around him. Our limbs intertwined, we both were slowly coming down from the crest of passion.

"Love me, Ivy," he murmured, hugging me to him. "I *need* you to love me. I don't think I can leave without your love anymore."

Since the moment we met, I'd held so many different feelings for Zeph—fascination, attraction, longing, trust, caring, among many more. All of them had grown so much stronger, the better I got to know him.

"I believe I already do, Zeph." I combed through the luminous silk of his hair with my fingers. "With you, I've never had a choice but to fall in love. The magical man that you are, I fell under your spell the first night we met. You're *my* magical man, now."

"Good." He lifted his head, catching my gaze with his. "Because I love you, too."

The room was dark with only the pale light of the moon casting its glow on us through the window. The moonlight glistened in his cerulean eyes.

"I don't even need to remember the past to love you for all that you are to me *now*, Ivy. I'll spend our entire future together, proving it to you."

# Chapter Twenty-Four

IVY

"Please be careful." I wrapped my arms around myself against the brutal November wind on the shore of Lake Ontario.

It was the morning after our night in the hotel, still early in the day and already very late in the year. The weather was cold and gloomy, and this part of the lakeshore seemed completely deserted.

"Water is my home," Zeph reminded me, taking his clothes off. "I'm safer in the ocean than ashore."

Seeing him disrobe in this weather made me shudder. Despite the freezing wind, however, Zeph wasn't even shivering.

"You don't get cold at all, do you?" I stole a glance at his toned, muscular body.

He grinned, catching me staring. "Does it *look* like I do?"

Of course, my eyes went straight to his crotch at his words. He chuckled, changing into his swim shorts.

"Ivy," he stretched my name on his tongue. "Come here." He wrapped me in his arms, shielding me from the wind. "I hate leaving you."

I pressed my face into his chest, breathing in the fresh, salty scent of his skin. It was impossibly hard to part from him. This time, however, it'd be temporary. He would be coming back.

*Please come back.*

"Be careful," I said, again. "Don't trust anyone. And please, try not to take too long. I'll be waiting."

The inside of my nose prickled, tears welling up in my eyes. I'd never cried for Zeph before, but I didn't bother holding it back, now.

"Ivy, sweetheart." He cradled my head in his hand. "I promise I'll come back as soon as I can." He kissed the tears off my cheeks. "Go straight to the airport from here. And stay safe. Remember, as long as you're in the water, I will find you, no matter where in the world you are."

I nodded, no longer trusting my voice to speak. He kissed me, long and deep, and I wished it would never end. With a soft groan, he pulled away from me, leaning his forehead to mine.

"Straight to the airport from here, promise?"

"Promise," I echoed.

Earlier that morning, we'd booked a plane ticket and a hotel room in St. Vincent, and I'd even sent rental enquiries to a few places around the island.

I dropped my arms as he stepped away from me. Then, I kept my gaze glued to his back as he walked into the lake.

I'd witnessed his incredible powers first hand, but Zeph looked so much like an ordinary man. Strong and handsome, he still seemed vulnerable against the sprawling cold waters of the lake. The thought of him crossing the Atlantic, completely alone and in nothing but swim shorts, terrified me.

He walked farther into the lake, then dove into it, quickly disappearing from sight. A dull ache throbbed in my chest, as if my heart was no longer there because Zeph had taken it with him.

*Please, come back to me.*

Two huge, muscled arms grabbed me from behind, jolting me with panic.

"Got her!"

Alarm ran through me like an electric charge. Horror lodged in my throat at the sight of the familiar tattoos covering one of the arms.

The *bracks* had found us!

A hand came over my mouth. Then the voice of one of them, Nerkan, reached me, "No. Let her scream."

"Right," Trez's familiar growl sounded over my ear. "Go ahead. Scream your head off, human."

He removed his hand from my mouth.

Shaking head to toe with fear and anger, I drew in a lungful of air... then stopped myself, forcing the scream back down.

If I yelled, Zeph might hear me. He'd come back to try to help me. He'd get out of the water where he was safe.

They wanted me to scream to use me as bait, to catch him.

Trez held me from behind with Nerkan standing nearby. At least half a dozen more *bracks* emerged from behind the trees at the end of the beach. Two of them held a large, black net between them. The net crackled with red and scorched the ground whenever it touched it.

Fae could only be killed by means from Nerifir, I remembered. The net definitely didn't look like something from this world. Whether the *bracks* intended to kill or just capture Zeph, that thing would hurt him.

"Come on." Trez shoved a meaty fist into my ribs. "Scream."

I groaned from pain, biting my lip so hard the coppery taste of blood filled my mouth.

"Scream I said!" Trez sounded strangled by rage as he planted another heavy blow into my side.

Nerkan shrugged, striding to the water.

"Does it matter who screams? Hey!" he yelled toward the lake. "Ocean boy! Come get your girl!"

The early morning seemed eerie in its serenity. Not a sound came from the lake.

"Get her in the water." Nerkan gestured to Trez over his shoulder.

Trez dragged me to the water's edge, then waded into the lake with me. The freezing waves sloshed around my ankles.

With a gasp, I drew my legs up as he held me around my middle.

"Get in!" Trez shoved me back into the lake. "You filthy human."

I felt Zeph.

The moment my feet were in the water again, the connection with him snapped into place. It was almost physical, the tug in my chest, as if someone yanked at a string attached straight to my heart.

"Trez..." Nerkan said, his voice much quieter than before. "You need to get out. Now."

Churning water rushed to us from the lake, ominously quiet.

"He is coming," one of the *bracks* rasped.

The group of them holding the net came closer.

Yanking me to him, Trez leaped out of the water, promptly moving away toward the trees.

"Lock her in the truck." He thrust me into Nerkan, then put on a pair of gloves, and rushed toward the *bracks* with the net.

"Let's go." Nerkan grabbed me under his arm, easily lifting me off the ground.

Struggling against his grip, I managed to sneak a peek back at the lake.

The surface bubbled and foamed in a wide path that stretched out from the shore. Zeph's pale figure rose from the water, submerged to his hips.

*"Please don't come here,"* I pleaded in my mind, as if he could hear me without the water connecting us. *"Stay where you are. Safe."*

The *bracks* spread the net wider, casting it along the beach. They were getting ready to catch my man. To hurt him again.

Nerkan dragged me past them.

"No!" Throwing my foot forward, I caught the edge of the net. It crackled with red sparks, scorching my shoe. I kicked my leg back, making the netting whip around Nerkan's ankle.

His massive body jerked, with a strangled gasp from his throat.

The net burnt its way through the pant leg and attached itself to his skin. Tentacles of bright red light snaked up his leg. Shaking, the *brack* collapsed to his knees, dropping me.

I fell on the sandy ground covered with patches of wilted grass.

Nerkan roared in pain, clawing at his leg.

Trez let go of the net.

"Come back here!" He lunged for me. "I swear I'll end you this time!"

I scurried away from him on my hands and knees. Scrambling to my feet, I sprinted toward the place that felt the safest at the moment—the lake. The closer I got, though, the farther it seemed to be. The water retreated as I approached, as if running away from me. Trudging through the wet, mushy sand, I peered into the distance.

Out there, the lake rose higher, pulling away from the shore. A wide swell formed. Its mass glistened with steely gray, blending with the gloomy sky above and obstructing the pale-yellow sun rising over the horizon.

I froze, watching the giant wave approach.

It carried Zeph on the very top of its foaming crest. His arms spread wide, his long hair whipping in the wind behind him, he looked nothing like an ordinary man anymore.

Framed by foam and spray, he was beautifully terrifying. His power over his element was absolute. Led by his will, the massive amounts of water churned, rushing our way.

I stumbled backwards, away from the lake that threatened to swallow the beach.

Trez tripped in the sand, staring at the approaching mass of water.

Someone had managed to tear the net away from Nerkan's leg. He limped toward the trees on his way to the parking lot. His pant leg had completely burnt off below the knee, his skin covered with burns.

The *bracks* on the shore spread out, stretching the net wider. Even from this distance, I saw how pensive their faces had become.

The roar of approaching water filled the air. The swell crashed down, its full impact crushing the *bracks*.

I scrambled backwards, trying to get away from the tsunami. Instead of spreading out to flood the shore, however, a giant whirlpool formed, churning the drowning *bracks* beneath it. It rose in front of me, like a funnel of a hurricane, not touching or harming me.

The black net washed up, getting caught in a tree. Red sparks sizzled and snapped all along its length.

Fighting the currents inside the water twister, Trez swam to the net, grabbing it with his gloved hands.

Higher than all of us, on top of the giant, white-crested wave, Zeph flicked his wrist. Water surged toward Trez, who held onto the net, fighting the pull of the waves.

The sparking from the net ignited a flame that crackled and grew, eating up the leafless tree branches. Trez shrank back from the fire, finally letting go of the net.

The current caught him, bringing him to Zeph.

"I didn't do anything to her," Trez blubbered, his eyes open wide, his arms flailing, fighting the watery madness around him. "I barely even touched her..."

"Then that's what you'll die for." Zeph's voice remained eerily calm. "For daring to touch my woman."

The steel-gray of an ocean storm churned in his blue eyes, making them dark with menace. He slashed through the air with his arm, the spikes on it slicing through the skin on Trez's neck and face. The fluorescent poison glistened in the wounds briefly. Then, it was flushed away by the lake water, along with the *brack's* blood.

His eyes frozen open, Trez tipped backwards and sank. The current spun his dead body into the whirlpool, dragging it down to the ground, as the fire spread through the bare branches of the tree. It stood there, engulfed in flames in the middle of the raging storm.

With a wave of Zeph's hand, the water dropped, receding back into the lake. His fins snapped close as he jogged along the beach toward me.

The *bracks* were scattered all over the beach. Coughing up the water, they rose to their feet, one by one. Being crushed by the tsunami then held under water didn't kill them. They looked worn and beaten. But their appearance proved deceiving.

One of them leaped on Zeph, knocking him off his feet. Zeph rolled on the sand, sliding his deadly spikes out of his arm. Another *brack* caught his wrist, pressing his arm into the ground.

"Zeph! No!" Terrified, I dashed to him.

A *brack* appeared in my path.

"You're coming with us, human." He lunged for me.

I leaped back, evading his hands, then sprinted around him. The *brack* chased me into the lake. Running through the water slowed me down. He was catching up quickly.

I whipped around, searching for a way out.

Cut off from the lake, Zeph fought the *bracks* swarming him. Two already lay in the sand, poison oozing from the cuts on their bodies. But many more surrounded him. One of the *bracks* recovered the net, flicking it Zeph's way. The corner skimmed his leg, searing it with eerie red fire.

"Zeph!" I screamed, my heart jumping high in my throat from terror and pain.

I felt his agony. The most powerful man I knew, the man I loved—was hurting again. And all because of me. He'd come back because of me.

The *brack* grabbed me. "No more running!"

*No more...*

They got us. If they didn't kill us, they'd lock us up again.

Sorrow tightened inside me, bursting into anger.

Not again!

A *brack* waved for the net to be brought closer. They stretched it, aiming to toss it over Zeph.

"No!" The terror, anger, and pain coursed through me in one powerful current.

I trembled so hard, the *brack* holding me was shaking, too. The cold water sloshing around my legs bubbled.

Rage and despair spread through me, reaching out. The water churned around and around. It rose higher, threatening to consume me along with the horror I felt.

"Out!" The *brack* dragged me to shore.

The panic in his voice spurred my newfound strength.

"No." I planted my feet into the sandy bottom.

The water curled around me, coiling up my body like a slithering snake.

"I said out!" The *brack* yanked at my waist.

"No!" I fell to my knees, sliding out of his grip, and threw my arms up.

The watery spiral sprung higher, uncoiling over my head like a spring leaping into the air. The stream shot out in an arch toward Zeph.

Yanking a hand out of a *brack's* grip, he lifted his arm, catching the stream in his palm.

From there, it grew. Thin like a rope at first, the stream bloated to the size of a river in Zeph's hand. He shot it at the *bracks*, blasting them away from him.

The water kept flowing through the air from me to him, in a steady, powerful current. It curved, bending to his will, then blasted at the *brack* next to me, shooting him far into the lake.

I stood on my knees, my arms spread wide for balance. My body shook so hard, I feared I'd tip over with the next gust of wind.

Zeph slaughtered the *bracks* closest to him. The few remaining survivors ran, picking up their dead.

"Ivy!" Zeph rushed to me.

Splashing through the water, he dropped to his knees in front of me.

"Ivy, my love, what happened?" He grabbed my shoulders, then cupped my face, searching my eyes. "Are you okay? Please, please tell me you're okay."

What happened?

I wish I knew.

As the horror receded, the wild power no longer vibrated through me. But I didn't feel quite myself.

My awareness was no longer limited to my body. It spread way beyond that, encompassing Zeph and the lake.

We merged into one entity—Zeph, water, and I.

"I *felt* you," I whispered, struggling to put all of that into words. "I couldn't let them hurt you. I had to stop them from taking you again."

"And you did." He covered my face in hot, desperate kisses. "You stopped them, Ivy."

"But how?"

"I don't know how?" He shook his head. "Magic?"

"I don't have any magic, remember?"

"But I do. Lots of it. Enough for both of us, it seems."

He waved a hand over the water that calmly floated around us now, as if it hadn't been used as a deadly weapon just moments ago. A stream rose to his hand from the surface.

"Catch!" He directed the stream to me.

I splayed my hand. The water hit my palm, then uselessly trickled down between my fingers.

"Not that impressive." I snorted a laugh.

"How about the other way around?" he suggested. "You try."

"Me? But I don't know how."

"How did you do it before?"

Before? I had been so scared for him. So angry at the *bracks* for hunting us.

The memory of those feelings echoed through me. I spread my hand over the surface, letting the emotions take over. My hand moved, as if on its own, circling over the water.

And the water followed.

Slowly, it stirred in a circle, too. I raised my hand, and the spiral rose from the surface, higher and higher.

It funneled up, a few inches into the air, then broke, splashing back into the lake.

"I can't hold it."

A shudder ran through my body.

"Fuck, what am I thinking?" Zeph cursed under his breath. Getting up, he lifted me out of the lake and into his arms. "You're freezing."

The moment he lifted me out of the water, something was lost. The connection wasn't exactly broken, but it had thinned. I felt Zeph, but no longer the lake.

"Wait. Please." I made him set me down on the dry ground, then kneeled at the water's edge.

Cold nipped at me through my soaking wet clothes, but I hardly noticed it. Dipping a hand into the water, I made it churn and stir around my wrist. This time, it seemed easier to do. Practice made perfect, like they said.

"You catch." I flicked my hand at Zeph.

The water slid past my palm, arched through the air in a firm, steady stream. It would have hit him square in the chest, had he not put a hand in front, redirecting the steam over my head and back into the lake behind me.

"It worked." I beamed at him.

I had no power over water on my own. I couldn't have—I wasn't a fae. But somehow, Zeph's magic had expanded to include me. It allowed me to work as a connection between them.

He stared at me, wonder floating in his ocean-blue eyes. "I don't have to touch the water to control it when you're with me."

I nodded. "As long as I am in the water, I can pass it to you."

My teeth chattered with a gust of biting wind.

"Come here." He grabbed my hand, pulling me to shore, then slid his hands down my sides, drying my clothes. "Warmer, now?" He hugged me to his chest.

I shivered in his arms. "A little."

He pressed his lips to my temple.

"Back in Nerifir, magic is often shared between bonded mates. Do you know what that means, Ivy?"

The reverence in his voice made me pause.

"What?" I breathed out.

"You and I share a bond, my darling."

I lifted my face to him. "What does it mean?"

He laughed, shaking his head. "So many wonderful things, Ivy. From what Lero told me, a bond is a rare thing even among the fae. I've never heard of one forming with a human before. I bet Lero hasn't heard of that either."

"Is that why we could 'talk,' back at the menagerie?" Even the glass of the tank hadn't impeded our connection then.

"That's right. I can sense people through water and even send emotions through it when they're strong enough. But you are the only person in the world who managed to have an actual conversation with me like that."

"Because of the bond?"

"Right. You know what else?" he murmured in my ear, drawing me closer. "Bonded mates share a lifespan. If I live to be five hundred years, then so will you."

"Are you sure it's not the other way around? What if it's just under a hundred for both of us?"

He just shrugged. "Either way, we'll grow old and wrinkly *together*. You and I."

*Together.*

My head spun from all of that, my mind reeling.

"Come. I'll get you to the airport myself, now."

"But you have to go to France," I protested.

"I'm not leaving you here alone," he said firmly. "Not with the *bracks* lurking around the city."

He'd killed quite a few of them by now. Sadly, Madame had more, enough to keep hunting us.

Drawing me into his side in a one-armed hug, Zeph walked me up the beach.

"You can't fly with me on the plane, Zeph. You don't have a passport."

"Then, I'll swim to St. Vincent," he replied casually. "Right under your plane—"

The last word cut short, Zeph stopped abruptly.

A *brack* stepped from behind the trees. I recognized Radax by his dark beard covering the lower part of his face.

Zeph raised his arm, placing it in front of us, his fin fanning out.

Radax lifted his hands, both palms facing our way in a calming gesture. "I've come to talk, not to fight."

"I've nothing to tell you, *brack*. Other than if you move any closer, you'll die."

"I don't want any more deaths." Radax stopped a few feet away from us. "I want to make a deal."

Zeph scoffed. "I don't *deal* with the likes of you."

"It'd be to your benefit." Radax's dark eyes flicked my way. "You tried to leave here. But now you're worried about the safety of your woman."

I halted my breath. His words didn't sound like a direct threat, but he was using me as a bargaining chip.

Zeph said nothing, this time. He just drew me closer.

"You can keep your freedom. Both of you." Radax folded his massive arms on his chest. "In exchange for your silence. Yours and hers." He tipped his chin my way.

"Silence?" I asked. "About the menagerie?"

He nodded. "You're not to speak to anyone about Madame Tan's establishment. Or about anything you saw or heard there."

"Is that it?" I narrowed my eyes at him.

Zeph shifted into a little more relaxed pose but kept his arm fin between us and Radax. "Is that the only condition?"

"Yes."

It sounded simple enough.

Speaking to absolutely no one wouldn't work for us, though. Zeph might need to tell Lero what happened, and I wanted a chance to explain some of this to Fleur one day.

On the other hand, we had already decided not to speak of the fae with the authorities.

"I promise not to talk with the police or the media about Madame Tan and her *freakshow*," I said, then added, "in exchange for our freedom. You'll have to stop hunting us."

Radax winced, not looking satisfied by my words at all.

"A human promise means nothing." He moved his stare to Zeph. "Sirens are quick to lie, but they tend to keep their promises. I'll take yours if you make it for both of you."

Zeph widened his stance.

"Fine. I promise on behalf of both of us. We won't speak of Ghata to the authorities."

The *brack* nodded contently. "If your woman breaks your promise, *you* will pay for it."

*That* definitely sounded like a threat.

"Why would Zeph have to pay instead of me?" I demanded from Radax.

"That's how it works," Zeph calmly explained for him. "I made a promise for *both* of us. If either of us speaks, I'll be cursed."

The risk of any harm coming to Zeph bound me more than any promise. Did Radax know that? Was it possible for a *brack* to understand the idea of caring for someone other than himself?

"Zeph," I said somberly. "Radax wouldn't take my promise, but I'll give it to you. I swear I will not break my word."

"I know." He flashed me one of his easy, beautiful smiles, looking more like the Zeph I knew and loved, not the terrifying fae who wielded power over water, using it as a weapon.

Moving his heavy stare from Zeph to me then back to Zeph again, Radax unfolded his arms.

"We're done here, then." He took a step back in the direction of the parking lot. "You're free. My people will not pursue either one of you any longer."

"If I ever see you again," Zeph's tone was light and melodious, which oddly only added gravity to his threat, "I'll kill you and everyone who comes with you."

# Chapter Twenty-Five

ZEPH

It was early morning when he reached the shore of France in Le Havre. He waited until the shops opened, then bought some clothes with the money Ivy had given him.

Back in Canada, he'd walked her to the cab and watched her drive away before leaving for France himself. She was safe now. He'd made a deal with Radax, to make sure Ivy was safe. Yet he still worried about her every moment he was away.

From Le Havre, he took the train to Paris. Ivy had written down the address of *Le Loup Solitaire* for him, but as soon as he turned into *Boulevard de Clichy,* he didn't need to reference it to find the place. As if on their own, his feet carried him to the black door with the red glowing sign above it.

The sight of the entrance also was familiar.

Instead of going to the front door, he walked through the arched entrance into the courtyard. He half-expected to see Lero's tall figure leaning against the wall in his usual place, the shimmering cloud of smoke rising in the air from his cigarette.

Lero of course wasn't there, and the sight of the bare wall was unsettling.

Zeph shoved at the back door, entering the place. Inside, everything was as he remembered.

*Remembered.*

He really did. The dimly lit corridor. The kitchen to his right. The black and beige of the interior. The stage...

He stood in the entrance to the main room, taking it all in as the memories of so many nights spent on this stage rushed over him. Lero would often watch him from this very spot when the full moon was still far away. So many faces in the audience rose in his mind, many of the regulars who knew him personally.

The place was empty, but a few staff members were already bustling around, getting it ready for tonight's show.

"Excuse me," a male voice called from the bar. "We're closed."

"Ivan?" Zeph pivoted on his heel to face the short stocky man in a tailored suit walking toward him.

"Zeph! Is that really you?" The man rushed to him. His slight Russian accent so very familiar, and not just from the last phone conversation they'd had. "Didn't recognize you right away. Your hair is so long!"

"Ivan." He gave him a firm hug. "So glad you're still here."

"Most of us are. Though things haven't quite been the same without you. Where have you been?"

"It's a long story." Zeph frowned in concentration. He recognized the place, but the memories still needed some time to sort themselves out in his head and to settle into a timeline. "I'll need to leave again, soon. I've come for Lero's message."

"Oh, right. It's a good thing you did. Someone had already called here for it. Lero's instructions were clear, though, give it to you personally."

"When did they call?"

"A few days back. A man said he was you, but he didn't recognize me."

"It was me, Ivan. Sorry, I wasn't quite myself back then."

Ivan stared at him closely for a minute or so but didn't demand any further explanation. Lero's staff was well accustomed to the secrecy surrounding the cabaret's previous owner and his family.

"Well, you're here now." Ivan produced a cream-colored envelope from behind the counter. "Like Lero wanted, I'm giving it into your very own hands."

"Thank you." Zeph took the envelope. "How is he, do you know?"

"Lero? No." The bar manager shook his head, regret spreading over his face. "Haven't seen him for over a year now."

"Over a year?" What could be happening to Lero out there all this time?

"Yeah. You were gone in June of last year, and he left at the end of July. So, a year and four months now. Time flies."

*June.*

That was how long Zeph had been gone himself, locked in Ghata's water tank.

"Lero didn't say where he went?" he asked.

"No. Unless he wrote something to you." Ivan pointed with his chin at the sealed envelope in Zeph's hands.

Zeph ripped it open right then and there, taking out a piece of cream paper with *Le Loup Solitaire* letterhead.

*"You know how to find me when the time comes. Stay near the water."*

That was it. Two sentences.

Zeph stared at the paper blankly, as though more would appear if he waited.

"And?" Ivan prompted, visibly fighting the urge to crane his neck to see the note for himself.

"No. He didn't write *where* to find him." Zeph shook his head.

"Do you want to leave a note for him, then? Just in case he shows up again?"

Leaving his and Ivy's new location here would be risky. There was no guarantee where the note would end up and who might see it. That must be the reason why Lero made his own message cryptic as it was.

The deal Zeph had made was with Radax. The *brack* had never mentioned Ghata's name, and Zeph had a feeling it was because Radax had bargained with him behind her back, under his own authority, and possibly even against her orders.

Zeph had gone ahead with the deal anyway because Radax had the means to uphold his end of the bargain. As the head of the *bracks*, Radax could halt or at least sabotage the hunt for Zeph, even if Ghata persisted with it.

Still, Ghata was out there, not bound by any promise, and he had to be cautious.

"No," he told Ivan. "I'll wait for Lero to contact me himself."

"All right. The girls are in the kitchen, do you want to say hi?"

He couldn't leave *Le Loup Solitaire* without seeing the staff he had worked with for years. It took him at least an hour to say hi to everyone and catch up. Then he stopped by his apartment and Lero's townhouse.

Both were locked with the lights off. He had to use a window to get into each.

He found no further messages in Lero's place but was able to recover his own documents and bank cards at his. These he put in the zipped pocket of his swim shorts, intending to take them with him.

After a visit to the bank to organize his finances, he was finally ready to go back.

By the time he returned to Le Havre Beach, it was late evening.

Taking his shoes off, he walked to the water's edge, letting the surf run over his toes. The sea water here was diluted by the stream of the Seine, replacing some of the salty brine with the pungent vibes of the big city.

*"You know how to find me when the time comes."* Lero's words bounced inside his brain with the annoying quality of a puzzle to be solved.

*"Stay near the water."*

Wading deeper into the surf, Zeph closed his eyes, scanning miles and miles of the water in the English Channel and beyond. He tried to detect any trace of his friend anywhere around the coast of this continent and much farther.

There was nothing.

*"...when the time comes."*

This could mean a number of things, neither of which was possible to confirm at the moment. All he could do was wait.

With a deep breath, he reached out again, searching for someone else, now. A faint but alluring tendril of longing filtered through the water to him from far away.

*Ivy.*

She promised to wait, and she was there, swimming in the sea, waiting for him.

The pull of her, delicate and enthralling, drew him in like the moon drew the tides. Subtle but unstoppable.

Stripping down to his shorts, he dove into the surf, merging with water.

# Chapter Twenty-Six

IVY

I washed the dinner plate and placed it into a dish rack to dry. The kitchen was small and cozy, as was the rest of the one-bedroom house I'd rented from the owner of the nearby hotel.

It hadn't taken me long to settle in. The place came furnished, and I hadn't brought much with me.

After I'd said goodbye to Zeph back at Lake Ontario, I went straight to the airport as promised. I called my parents from there. Whether he cared or not, I left a voicemail for my father, letting him know I was okay.

Then I called my mom. I wanted to thank her for taking care of my things, to let her know that the police report had been closed and that I was leaving to start a new life. However, our conversation ended up with her mostly screaming at me. She was disappointed I refused to go ahead with the lawsuit she'd planned. So, I told her I loved her and hung up. After years of trying, I'd learned there was no way to fix the relationship we had, but I could at least maintain whatever little there still remained.

During the past week and a half since I'd arrived on the island, I'd been distracting myself from worrying about Zeph by salvaging what was left from my business.

My two-months absence had cost me a lot of my clients and seriously tarnished my reputation in the industry. It didn't help that I could only provide the vaguest of explanation as to why I was late with all my orders. Despite the high quality of my product, it would take me months if not years to rebuild what I'd lost.

But not all was hopeless. A few people stuck with me. I still had some work from them and a couple potential new clients.

Wiping my hands on the kitchen towel, I walked out into the yard. The house backed onto a small beach with black sand past the concrete breakwater.

*"As long as you are in the water, I will find you."* Zeph's words never left my mind, drawing me to the beach every chance I got, to wade in the sea.

Taking off my sundress, I walked into the warm surf, wearing only my turquoise bikini.

Waves sloshed lazily around my ankles, water caressed my skin, rising higher as I walked deeper. I went as far as I dared, submerged up to my breasts now, and stopped, staring past the small island across from the beach and into the sea stretching all the way to the horizon behind it.

Would he be able to sense me from this far away?

The nature of Zeph's gift remained largely a mystery to me. But his power, no matter how incredible or magical, was not what drew me to him, anyway.

I wanted his smiles and his kisses.

I missed him fiercely.

And I worried about him, no matter what.

Anxiously raking my fingers through the surface, I watched the pale glow follow my hands in their wake. The sea was glowing tonight, streaks of green and blue shimmered in ripples across the waves. Some seemed to gather closer, swirling around me in a slow twirl.

Suddenly, a pair of strong arms caught me around my waist, and I gasped, my heart beating faster.

"Zeph!" I exclaimed as he broke through the water in front of me. His long, wet hair shimmered with silver under the moonlight.

Catching my breath, I pressed my hand to my chest, willing my heart to slow down. I should probably be angry with him for startling me, but I wasn't. His familiar lop-sided grin disarmed me, melting my insides into a warm, fuzzy mess.

"What took you so long?" I breathed out instead, throwing my arms around his neck.

"I rushed as fast as I could." He nuzzled the side of my face. "Not fast enough, it seems. Your anxiety is vibrating like crazy all across the Atlantic. Have you been worrying about me, my Ivy?"

"From the moment you left." I buried my face in the side of his neck.

He smelled like the ocean, cool and salty. His skin still remained warm, somehow, even as he had just swum through the chilly depths of the abyss.

"Are you here to stay?" I asked.

"For as long as you'll have me." He stroked my back.

Relief—warm and fresh like the sea—spread through me at his words. I couldn't wait to wake up next to him tomorrow morning and every day thereafter.

"I'll have you forever. You're not leaving me again." I snuggled closer into his embrace. "Come, I'll show you our house."

"Our?" He kissed the corner of my mouth. "I love the sound of it."

I turned my head, catching his next kiss on my lips. "It's right there, by the beach."

"That's way too far." He shook his head. His voice dipping low. "I need you, now."

The sea water turned in a swirl around us, with a soft caress against my body.

Lifting his hand to my nape, he tugged at the string of my bikini top, untying the knot. The top slid down my front, floating with the waves, and he cupped my naked breast with his hand, kneading it gently.

With a long breath in, I arched my back, pressing closer to him. The warmth of his hand seeped under my skin, setting my desire on fire.

"I've heard sex in the water is not very good," I murmured as he kissed the sensitive skin along my neck. "It gets everywhere, you know..."

"Water gets where I tell it to go," he rasped, flicking his hand in the air.

A wave rose from the surface, following his gesture. It arched over us, creating a water gazebo, with moonlight twinkling in every droplet above.

"So beautiful," I whispered, staring up at the curve of the water arch that concealed us from the view of anyone who happened to be either on the beach or on the island across from it.

Leaving ripples of pleasure in his wake, Zeph kissed down to my breasts then sucked the tip of one into his mouth, cupping the other one with his hand. I moaned into his wet hair.

The strings of my bikini bottom came loose, too. Small, warm streams curled around my thighs in a tantalizing dance, stroking my skin.

Dropping to his knees, Zeph dove under, sliding between my thighs. His tongue glided between my folds. The water sluiced in twirls around my legs, caressing the insides of my thighs and flowing over my breasts.

Tilting my face up, I let myself sink back, and the sea held me. I spread my arms wide as the waves of pleasure rolled through me. Slowly, the current washing over me grew stronger. The stream massaged my body in the same rhythm as Zeph moved his mouth on me—harder and with more urgency.

The achy pressure between my legs intensified, building up. I dug my heels into Zeph's shoulders. My entire body tensed, before the ecstasy burst through me, set off by his mouth, fingers, and tongue.

I splayed my hands wide, raking them through the water, afraid I'd sink, lost in the storm of the mind-blinding orgasm. Yet the sea held me, rocking me softly as I was coming down from the crest of passion.

Zeph tenderly kissed up my body, rising over me. The water rushed off him, streaming down his hair.

"Being with you is truly magical," I panted, clinging to his shoulders as he drew me closer.

"I've *magical* powers." He shrugged with a cocky grin.

I laughed softly into his shoulder. Zeph had more powers than even he knew about—the power to somehow make me adore everything about him, for one.

"Now, where did you say the bed was?" He gathered me into his arms, heading for the beach.

"The house." I pointed at the only lit window at the end of the beach. "Right there. It has a bed, though not a very big one."

"It doesn't need to be big, just has to be sturdy."

"How did it go, in Paris?" I'd finally caught my breath enough to ask.

Zeph hadn't made it all the way to the bed after all, making love to me on the rug in the living room first, hungry and passionate. I took him to bed after that, where we did it all over again, slow and sensual this time.

"Did you get Lero's message?" I slid my finger down his spine as he lay on his stomach next to me. The pale stripe of skin over the folded spikes of his dorsal fin was still quivering, settling down after his most recent orgasm.

"Mhm," he hummed into the pillow, not moving a muscle.

"What was it?"

He shifted to his side, facing me.

"He said I'd know where to find him, but only when the time comes."

"That sounds like a puzzle." Possibly, with a warning.

"He said to stay near the water. I believe he wants me to keep searching the ocean for him."

"How are you going to search?"

"Not by swimming around, of course." He smiled. "I can sense his emotions through the water, the way I sense yours."

"As long as he gets *in* the water, though, right?"

"Right. Which I suspect he'd do when he thinks the time is right."

Something about this was hard for me to understand. "I thought he'd be wanting to see you right away. That he would like to know you're safe."

"Maybe he already does," Zeph dismissed.

"Then why—"

"I don't know." He propped himself with an elbow. "But I trust him to do what's right. Maybe he thinks it's safer to stay away from me for now. For my sake. He's always been protective of me."

"What is his deal with Ghata?" My opinion about Lero had been swinging from respect to suspicion. I remained unsure about what to think about that man.

"Lero and Ghata came to this world together, at the same time. All three of us did, but I was too small to remember how it happened."

"Do you think they were a couple at some point? Lovers?"

Zeph flinched at the idea. "No. Lero would've told me. And Ghata... I don't think she is capable of any tender feelings. According to Lero, she uses sex as a weapon, a currency, and a means to control."

The certainty in his voice prompted me to ask, "When did he tell you that? Do you remember more, now?"

"Yes. When I came to *Le Loup Solitaire*, I recognized the place and remembered working there."

"Do you remember meeting me?" I asked, tentatively.

"Not yet, my sweet Ivy." He tenderly stroked my arm. "But I'm enjoying creating all these new memories with you."

I suppressed a sigh. We'd spent a wonderful night in Paris. I would've liked for Zeph to remember it. But he was right, we had many nights ahead of us now. Every time with him was even better than the one before.

"What else do you recall Lero telling you about Ghata? Is she really a goddess?"

"She is. Ghata is a disgraced goddess."

"For real?" I gaped at him. "How is it even possible?"

"My world works under its own rules, Ivy. It's very different from yours. Magic is real. Some gods walk among the mortals. Their power is amplified by the faith of their worshipers."

I would need to ponder that one for a while.

"It's kind of scary to learn that we've pissed off a real goddess." I huffed a breath, sinking into the pillows.

"Ghata has hardly any power left." Zeph stroked my arm gently in a comforting gesture. "The power of a goddess ebbs and grows. It shifts following the strength of the faith of her followers. Once Ghata broke their trust, their faith in her divinity waned, her power weakened. She committed some grievous crimes. So many that she was supposed to be prosecuted for them. That was when she escaped Nerifir."

"Could we maybe find a way to send her back?"

He shook his head.

"I don't know. Even if we did, what would stop her from coming back?"

"Why are the *bracks* with her? What are they?"

"The *bracks* are her monks."

"Her *monks?*"

He nodded. "Back in Nerifir, they served her in her temple."

"Wow." I rubbed my forehead. "How about Amira?" My heart ached, remembering Amira's dark, somber eyes. "What exactly is her role in Ghata's freakshow? How did she get there, in the first place? And why?"

He heaved a sigh. "I'm not sure. Amira is most definitely a human, though. She has nothing to do with Nerifir."

Yet the menagerie now seemed to be her only home.

"In this world, money is power," Zeph continued. "And Ghata appears determined to make a lot of it. From what you've told me, she must've amassed a large sum just by displaying me to the public."

"And she is obviously not planning to stop. How much does she need? And for what?"

In *bracks*, Madame had her very own army, small but unnaturally strong. They would do anything for her. I'd seen that. If she had the financial means, too, how much could she accomplish, and how much damage could she cause?

"Whatever comes, we're going to stay together Ivy." He wrapped his arms around me. "I'll keep you safe."

I kissed his chest, just because it was the closest part of him to my lips.

"We can do anything we want." He slid his hands down my back, lifting me into his lap. "And you know what I think we both want right now?"

He smiled, winking at me. His erection eagerly bobbed against my inner thigh, as if joining in the fun.

"I love this undying optimism of yours, Zeph. It's one of my favorite things about you, your ability to deal with problems with a wink and a smile." The heavy feeling weighing down on my heart had lifted at the sight of his grin. "You make everything easier to deal with for me, too."

"My sweet Ivy, no need to fret over what you can't change or even predict." He slid his hands up and down my back, soothing the worry in my chest with each glide of his palms along my skin. "We'll stay vigilant, but it doesn't mean I'm letting the evil hang like a shadow over our lives here." Pressing me to him, he kissed my mouth, his hand kneading my breast.

"I wish I could do that." I wrapped my arms around him. "I wish I had your light to shine through any darkness."

"I'll be your light, sweetheart," he murmured, kissing down the side of my neck. "I'll fight the darkness for you."

# Epilogue

IVY

Bright sunlight burst through the window when I woke up. For a moment, I believed I was back in Paris, in Zeph's place. Rubbing my eyes, I sat up in bed. Then I realized what had brought that feeling: the warm smell of cinnamon buns, coming from the kitchen and...Zeph's smooth, rich voice floating through the house with it.

"Zeph?" I called softly.

He poked his head into the bedroom, and my heart stilled with another bout of déjà vu. His long hair was gone. Cropped close to his head above his ears, it was a few inches longer on the top, styled in a tousled wave, similar to the way he'd worn it back in Paris.

He grinned, finishing the song by Elvis Presley, "I can't help falling in love with you..."

"You can sing again?" I exhaled, happiness flooding me in a warm wave. "Your voice is back."

"It is. What do you think?" He drew in a full chest of air, then belted out from Whitney Huston's, "And Iiiiiii Will Always Love Youuuuuu."

The lyrics flowed, rising and dipping in a perfect accord with the melody. His strong voice carried the song in the most perfect way.

"It's wonderful, Zeph," I said sincerely. "Just perfect."

Dressed in a band t-shirt and a pair of shorts, barefoot, with a new haircut and his old smile, he appeared so much like the Zeph I'd met in Paris—so different from the one I'd found locked in a tank filled with toxic water.

And maybe that was the whole point of this. Just like he'd said, we had our lives ahead of us to live however we pleased.

"You cut your hair." I kept smiling.

"Do you like it?" He ran his hand through it.

"I love it, Zeph. I really do." I reached for him.

"Wait." He placed a quick kiss on my lips then rushed out of the room again.

He returned with a tray in his hands.

"Breakfast," he announced proudly, placing the tray in my lap.

"When did you get it all done?" I grabbed the cup with coffee, needing some caffeine in my system to kick my brain into gear. I didn't get much sleep last night. Zeph was to blame for that. Though, I was not going to complain about the night we'd had.

"I made a quick trip to Kingstown while you slept," he said.

"You did? But how?"

"Vasil let me borrow his car. I bought some clothes, got a haircut, and stopped by a grocery store on the way back."

How long *was* I asleep, anyway?

And who was Vasil?

Then I remembered that it was the name of the owner of the hotel nearby and of the house I rented. Vasil was our landlord. Apparently, Zeph had not only managed to meet him while I was sleeping, but he'd also charmed Vasil into letting him use his car.

"Well, I'm glad you've figured out your way around here," I laughed. "Maybe you can show *me* some places." I grabbed the deliciously sticky pastry from the plate on the tray, then froze with my hand half-way up to my mouth. "Cinnamon bun?" I stared at it, then moved my gaze to Zeph, afraid to hope.

"Your favorite breakfast food." He grinned wider. "For special occasions."

I inhaled sharply, covering my mouth with my hand. "You remembered?"

He sat on the bed next to me.

"Everything, Ivy. I finally remembered every single thing."

"Oh God... Zeph." I breathed with relief.

"I remember the first time we met." He leaned in, kissing my face. "The first time we danced. Our first kiss. The very first time I touched you." He kept kissing my nose, my cheeks, my temple. "Now, I have the memories of two first kisses," he chuckled. "And I'm not even sure which one was better."

I caught his next kiss on my lips. "Do you remember how you were taken?"

"Yes. Lero gave me the next day off. I was really looking forward to seeing you again." He took a bite of the cinnamon bun I still held in my hand.

"You were?"

"Mhm." He nodded. "I was going to make you dinner at my place. But the *bracks* took me the night before. They put a bag over my head. It was filled with *womora* smoke and something else that knocked me out."

"Oh, Zeph..." My chest tightened painfully as I listened to him.

"It's all in the past now, Ivy." He shook it off, reaching for another bite of my cinnamon bun. "There was also a girl..."

"A girl?"

He rubbed his forehead.

"Yes. A waitress told me a girl wanted to speak to me. I thought it was you. I remember seeing a flash of pink-and-blue hair before they took me."

"Did you see her face?"

"No. Nothing else but the hair."

*"A hired chick in a wig was all it took."* Trez's bragging came to mind.

"The *bracks* saw me with you the night before," I said. "They obviously didn't get a good enough look at me to remember my face. But the bright hair I had back then would be hard to miss. In the menagerie, I overheard Trez talking about hiring a girl in a wig."

"That was what ruined me," he said with a teasing smile, obviously not at all as upset by his memories as I was. "My fascination with your hair led me to my demise."

"You liked me, and they exploited it."

Zeph's expression grew serious.

"I'll definitely be more careful from now on." He wrapped his arm around my shoulders and leaned back against the headboard with me. "You know, Ivy, there was something good about me not remembering you when we met the second time."

"There was?" I asked, a little confused.

"I had quite a different opinion about you back in Paris."

"In what way?"

"I liked you, very much. The night we spent together was more than just fun for me. I wanted to spend more time with you. But I was fully intending to let you go by the end of your trip."

"Because humans are weak creatures?" I guessed, remembering him telling me about Lero's lessons. "Unsuitable to be fae partners?"

"Right." He kissed my hair. "If it wasn't for the menagerie, you would've been gone from my life forever. Despite everything, I'm glad I got the second chance to get to know you. The day we escaped, I saw the true you, and I had no choice but to fall in love with you. You were magnificent."

*Magnificent?*

I thought back to me shivering in the huge, wet hoodie on the night of our escape. The sight must've been rather pitiful than magnificent.

Deep inside, however, I understood what he meant. When I slammed that barstool into the water tank, I'd never felt stronger in my life. No matter what might come my way in the future, I now knew I had the strength to survive anything.

Carefully setting the tray aside, I kissed him, then whispered against his lips, "I love you, Zeph."

"You're mine, Ivy," he murmured, kissing me back. "Fully and completely. For as long as you'll have me."

"For as long as I shall live."

# MADNESS OF THE MOON

## Book 2

# Chapter One

STELLA

Lero! The impact of recognition came strong and sudden. It hit me like a physical blow in the gut, making me stagger in my high heels.

The man I hadn't seen in fourteen years closed the door of the limo that had brought him to the private dock of the floatplane charter company in Miami. Tall, dark-haired, and even more handsome than I remembered, he headed my way with long, confident strides.

The wild pounding of my heart drowned out the noise of the busy waterfront. My mind spinning, I felt momentarily disoriented. For a few brief moments, I was a fourteen-year-old girl again, lying on the pavement in front of Lero's townhouse, my knee bleeding profusely—the memory so distant, it had largely become a dream over the years.

Until now...

The man of my dreams suddenly barged back into my reality.

Was it really him?

How could it be?

"Are you from the Javier Moreno Agency?" he asked, offering me his hand in greeting.

I took it mechanically. The warmth of his hand pulsed through my veins with the contact.

Dressed in a dark, well-tailored suit, the jacket undone on this sultry August morning, no tie, the top button of his crisp white shirt open, he was a flesh-and-blood version of the vision from my past.

"*Mademoiselle?*" he prompted, tilting his head to the side, a slight concern showing up in his steel-gray eyes.

I blinked, forcing myself to snap out of the stupor.

I was no longer fourteen—I was twice as old—and I had a job to do. By a stroke of fate, he might be the man of my dreams suddenly materializing in front of me, but he was also a client.

I cleared my throat and straightened my back.

"*Oui, je suis avec* Javier Moreno Realty," I said in French. "*Je m'appelle Stella Alarie. Bonjour, Monsieur...*" I feverishly rummaged through my brain for the name Javier had emailed me earlier that morning when he'd asked me to show the island to the potential buyer.

Lero released my hand.

"*...Monsieur Sauveterre.*" I exhaled in relief, finally remembering the name.

The never-forgotten scent reached my nostrils with the breeze from the ocean. Lero's face might've faded in my memory with time, but not his scent—the rich earthy note of moss and expensive wood, with the calming touch of lavender, and just a hint of sweetness.

I could never quite place his scent. If it was a cologne, I had no idea which one it was, and I'd never smelled anything like it either before or after our brief encounter long ago. For me, it had always remained *Lero's scent*. Even if I'd had doubts about who the man standing in front of me was, I could never mistake his scent for anyone else's.

He took a step closer. There was not a hint of recognition in his calm, gray eyes.

I shuffled back, the high heel of my beige sandal nearly catching in the gap between the boards of the dock. His sudden appearance shocked me. His presence proved overwhelming, threatening to take over my senses as I fought to regain control.

"*Enchanté...*" I started, struggling to collect my thoughts.

"If it's the same to you," he said, politely but somewhat detached. "I'm more than happy to speak English."

Dammit.

I must've butchered the grammar or pronunciation in some horrid way. It'd been a while since I'd spoken French. Though, my ability to speak it was one of the reasons I was here this morning. Javier had said the client was from France. Even out of practice, I was confident I could deliver a convincing sales pitch in French if needed. I just didn't expect Javier's client to be...Lero.

"I understand Javier is not joining us this morning?" Lero enquired in English. His own pronunciation was impeccable, the soft purr of his accent smooth like honey.

"No, he isn't." I shook my head. "He had a family emergency but sends his sincere apologies."

That was why I ended up being the one to show one of our agency's most valuable pieces of real estate to *Monsieur Sauveterre*, Javier's newest VIP client. Usually, Javier worked with his top clients himself. He'd wine and dine them, then show them as many exquisite properties as they could handle. Nine times out of ten, he closed the sale, no matter the asking price. The odd time when he didn't, he'd at least charmed the clients into using his agency for a future purchase.

Today, I had to do all the "charming" for him. Except that it was *me* who had fallen under a spell, standing there awkwardly and gawking at the client.

"Shall we, *Mademoiselle* Alarie?" Lero took charge, gesturing at the six-seat floatplane waiting for us by the dock.

"Right, of course," I mumbled, heading to the seaplane. "We're ready, Jose." I nodded to the pilot standing by.

Jose opened the door for us, and Lero promptly grabbed my elbow, helping me climb in. I doubted I could've done it without his help. As per the company's dress code, my clothes were on the dressier side of the business casual—ivory pencil skirt, elegant powder-blue blouse, and high-heeled sandals—not the most practical attire for climbing into a floatplane or visiting an island in the Bahamas with several white-sand beaches as the main selling points.

Thankfully, I'd pulled my hair into a high bun. Otherwise, my thick, auburn mane would be like a wool blanket on my shoulders in the summer heat.

The two seats behind the pilot's and the front passenger's were turned backward, so I promptly took the one in the very last row, as traveling backward would likely make me motion sick.

Instead of sitting next to me, Lero took a seat opposite of mine, facing me.

I was going to spend the next hour in the small cabin of the Cessna 206, face to face with the man I'd thought would forever remain only in my memories.

F*ourteen years ago.*

My aunt's old bike brought me a new level of freedom in Paris. Dad never gave me any spending money when sending me to live with my Aunt Beatrice each summer, not even for public transit.

"That bitch is rolling in money," he'd say. "Trust me, she can afford to buy you anything you want."

Maybe Aunt Beatrice *could* afford to buy me things, but she rarely did. Even when giving me a couple of euros for the metro, she'd never failed to mention that the best lesson to learn in life was that of the value of money.

My father and his sister had gotten equal shares of an inheritance when my grandfather passed away. Dad had gambled his share away quickly, whereas my aunt did well with hers—well enough to open the door to high society, where she met her late husband.

"A man of means," she referred to my late uncle in my presence.

"A filthy-rich, old bastard," my father called him.

I never got to meet my uncle. He was more than twice my aunt's age when she met him, and he died years before my annual visits to Paris started. However, I knew he'd left all his money to Aunt Beatrice, making her one of the richest women in Europe.

She moved to France when I was in grade school. She called the country "the land of our ancestors" because that was where my dad's family moved to New York from in the early twentieth century.

As I got older, I learned my father hoped to get to my aunt's money through me. However, when he'd first arranged for me to stay with her in the summer, I believed it was simply to improve my skills in French.

My skills did improve, though I hardly had anyone to speak with while in Paris. There were no kids my age on the street of luxury townhomes where my aunt lived. And even if any children would've wanted to hang out with me, my aunt would've never allowed it.

Aunt Beatrice kept a strict curfew for me and insisted on knowing my whereabouts at all times.

Finding the old bike in my aunt's cluttered attic made my life so much more exciting. Of course, I still had to tell her where I went and when I'd be back—and God help me if I returned even a minute late—but once out of the house, I could pretty much do whatever I wanted. There was no way for Aunt Beatrice to check on me.

I went anywhere the roads and bike paths would take me, exploring as much of the city as was possible with limited freedom and almost no money.

That evening I was running late, speeding along my aunt's street. If I didn't return precisely on time, I'd be grounded the next day, which meant sitting in my aunt's stuffy living room, listening to the news channel that she perpetually had on, and trying not to lose my mind from her complaints about how the world was ending.

A shiny sports car pulled out in front of me, cutting me off. The driver was speeding, as was I. Neither of us stopped in time. I yanked the handlebars to the side, but it was too late. The collision with the car sent me sliding across the pavement, my right leg and elbow taking the brunt of it.

*"Mademoiselle!"* A strong male voice exclaimed from a distance. Then, the pleasant scent of something that could be a male cologne reached me as I lay on the cobblestone sidewalk.

Someone touched my shoulder.

"I'm okay," I whimpered. The pain of the injuries hadn't fully hit me yet, but tears of fear and self-pity were already burning my eyes.

"Are you American?" the same voice enquired in slightly accented

English. “Where are your parents? Don’t move yet,” he warned, pressing a little harder on my shoulder. “Where does it hurt?”

“My knee...” The burning pain spread along my skin all the way down my leg, now. “My elbow too, but not as much as my knee.”

“Nothing else? How about your head? Your back? Chest?”

“No.” I shook my head, partially to demonstrate that it was okay, then made another attempt to sit up.

The man—a very handsome man I’d never seen before—was crouching by my side. His hand under my arm, he helped me into a sitting position.

I sucked in air through my teeth, bending my leg to take a better look at my wound. The skin on my right leg was shredded from my knee halfway down my shin. Angry red road rash surrounded the bloody mess in the middle.

“Let me, please.” The man produced a crisp white handkerchief from his breast pocket.

Only now, I noticed he was dressed in an elegant evening tuxedo. Clean-shaven, his short, dark hair styled to perfection, the man appeared to be on his way to some formal event.

He pressed his pristine handkerchief below my wound, soaking the blood that trickled down my leg into the starched material.

It didn’t hurt any more than before, but I drew in another deep breath, scared he’d touch too close to the broken skin. Tears rolled out of my eyes. Suddenly, I felt so much younger than my fourteen years.

“Ouch,” I whimpered when he skimmed over the wound, soaking more blood with the ruined piece of cloth.

“Hurts?” He met my gaze.

Through the cloudy film of my tears, I saw the concern in his eyes, soft gray under the streetlights.

“I need a band-aid,” I sobbed in a small voice as my lips quivered.

Sliding his hand under my calf, he leaned over my leg and suddenly dragged his tongue along the entire length of my wound.

I gasped, staring at him in shock.

He licked me!

Who did that? Not grown men, as far as I knew. It couldn’t be right, though I couldn’t exactly explain why it would be wrong, either.

"Lero! What's going on?" a female voice shrilled in English with an American accent. It was followed by the sound of a car door slamming shut.

A tall, slim brunette in a silver evening gown trotted our way from the sports car that had knocked me off my bike, her heels beating a staccato rhythm on the pavement.

"Lero? Are you ready to go?" She stopped abruptly, as if just noticing me. "Did she ram into my car? It'd better not have left a scratch."

Not paying her much attention, Lero dabbed at the corners of his mouth with a clean corner of his handkerchief, wiping a faint smear of my blood off his face as if he'd just had a fine dessert.

"Please forgive my friend's lack of skills behind the wheel, Mademoiselle," he said to me. "She insists on driving when she obviously shouldn't."

"Is she okay?" The brunette stood over us, her hands on her hips.

"She will be," Lero assured her, then turned back to me. "Hold this." He pressed his handkerchief to my knee, and I mechanically held it there as he lifted my bike then walked it over to the entrance of the closest townhouse.

"I'll keep your bike in my house for the night, but I promise to have it delivered first thing tomorrow morning," he assured me upon his return. "Where are you staying in the city?"

"Um, with my aunt, just down this street." I waved along the narrow road lit by the cast-iron lamp posts with lanterns.

"Allow me to help you to the car." He reached for me.

Instead of helping me up as I'd expected he would, he lifted me in his arms. I gasped, grabbing onto his shoulders.

"Shh. I've got you." His voice sounded soothing and confident, making me trust him completely.

He easily carried me to the brunette's sports car.

"We're not taking her anywhere." She hurried after us.

"That's the least we can do." Ignoring her protests, he opened the passenger's door and effortlessly slid me into the cushy, soft-leather seat.

"We're late as it is." She stomped the stiletto of one of her sandals.

He turned to her.

"Then you should've left earlier and driven more carefully, Mara. Keys?" He stretched a hand to her. "I'll drive."

He took the keys out of her hand, not giving her a chance to protest.

"My father is going to be furious, Lero," she warned as he got into the driver's seat.

"He'll wait." He started the engine.

"Hey! How about me?" Mara took a few steps after the car as we drove off.

"I'll come back for you," he promised through the open window.

"Is she your girlfriend?" I asked, watching the glamorous figure of the brunette grow smaller in the car's side mirror.

"No. Mara is the daughter of my current business partner."

The two weren't necessarily mutually exclusive. However, I liked that the bossy, uncaring woman currently had no place in Lero's heart.

"Where does your aunt live?" he asked.

"Right there. The corner townhouse on the right." I pointed at the large, glowing windows up ahead, suddenly sad about having to leave this intimate place filled with the pleasant smells of expensive leather and Lero's cologne.

Aunt Beatrice's mouth dropped wide open when Lero presented me to her a minute later. She didn't even peep a word of rebuke for my showing up late, quickly sending me upstairs to the guest bedroom where I stayed.

Going to bed that night, I recalled over and over the alluring scent of Lero, the way his gray eyes glimmered softly under the street lanterns, and the new-to-me feelings of thrill and safety when he held me in his arms.

N*ow*

Over the years, the memories and feelings had faded. I'd trained myself to think of them as a product of the impressionable mind of a teenager.

I was a late bloomer. Boys paid little attention to me back then. No man had ever carried me in his arms before Lero. I'd never met anyone as elegant and sophisticated as him. For the fourteen-year-old me, he appeared almost like a god. The way he'd treated me—like his equal—raised him even higher in my mind, giving him the starring role in all of my fantasies for years to come.

As he'd promised, he had the bike delivered to my aunt's house the next morning. To my disappointment, Lero didn't bring it over personally, hiring someone to do it for him instead.

I rode my bike past his townhouse every evening after that, hoping to see him again. I'd washed his handkerchief and even mustered the courage to knock on his door once, trying to return it. No one answered the door, and I ended up taking the handkerchief back to New York with me. I still had it tucked in a drawer somewhere in my condo in Miami. Lero's scent had long faded from it, and the silver embroidery of thorn branches surrounding a cursive letter "L" had dulled with time.

Someone else had lived in that townhouse when I'd returned to Paris the next year, and I never saw Lero again.

Until now.

I stared at his shoes as our plane slid along the water's surface before taking off into the air. His brown Italian leather loafers looked expensive, but not nearly as interesting as the man who wore them. Except that I couldn't muster the courage to glance up at him when he was this close.

I needed to get a grip, somehow.

Lero was no longer the man of my teenage dreams. Today, he was the client, the potential buyer of a very expensive property, and I represented Javier's company. This was strictly business, not a trip down memory lane. I had to get my head on straight.

"Would you care for a drink?" I asked over the noise of the plane's engine and opened the cooler placed next to my seat. The charter company stocked it with all kinds of beverages, including alcohol. Some people became more amenable when alcohol was involved, and Javier never failed to have it on hand.

"I can make you a mimosa." I flashed Lero a smile, lifting a small bottle of sparkling wine into his view.

Lero arched an eyebrow at my offer.

"No. Thank you." His deep voice flowed through the cabin like warm butter.

"No *alcohol*? Or no drink at all?"

"Nothing. I'm not thirsty."

"All right."

I stuffed the bottle back into the ice, wishing I could chug it myself. I could definitely use something to calm my nerves around this man. Sadly, as accommodating as Javier was to his clients, he imposed a strict no-drinking-on-the-job rule for his agents. Instead, I got out a fancy glass bottle of water and took a few big gulps.

The small plane had no AC. The two windows the pilot had left open let some fresh air in, but it wasn't enough for me. My face felt hot, and my palms started to sweat.

Lero didn't seem to be affected by the rising late-morning heat as he calmly watched the seascape through the window.

Using the moment, I furtively studied his profile—straight nose, proud chin, the hard edge of his jawline shaded with a five-o'clock shadow despite it being only ten in the morning. I slid my gaze down his throat to the sliver of tanned chest visible in the opening of his shirt.

As if sensing my ogling, he glanced at me. Being caught, I panicked and dropped my stare to his shoes again. The air around us got even hotter. My face must've turned flaming red; it felt as if it had caught on fire.

As much as I'd admired Lero when I was a teenager, my reaction to him now was definitely that of a woman—vivid, more physical, and so much more intense.

It took me a long time to muster the courage to glance up at him. When I finally did, Lero was calmly looking out of the window again. He obviously wasn't sharing my flustered state.

After so many years, Lero had become more of an immaterial idea than an image. Emotions he'd created in me remained strong in my memories even as his features had faded in my mind. When I looked at him now, it all was coming back to me. I remembered the glimmer in his eyes and every line and angle of his face.

Something about his appearance bothered me, now.

Something was...odd.

He looked *exactly* how he did fourteen years ago. The fine lines at the corners of his eyes and mouth had not grown any deeper. The hands he'd rested on his thighs were large and angular—masculine—but not aged. His skin remained just as smooth and youthful as I remembered.

How old was Lero? Right now, he appeared to be around thirty. Which would make him barely sixteen when I first met him.

That was impossible.

He turned abruptly, catching me staring. Again. This time, I was too slow to fake an infatuation with his shoes. He arched a long, dark eyebrow in a silent question, and I scrambled for an answer.

"How old are you, Monsieur Sauveterre?" I blurted out and immediately regretted it.

Smooth, Stella. Very grown-up and professional. I groaned inside.

"Please forgive me." I raised a hand quickly. "It was so rude of me. You really don't need to answer—"

"I'm thirty-one," he replied calmly, then a teasing spark flashed in his eye. "Old enough to own a property in the Bahamas. If that's your concern?"

Maybe he'd sensed my tension after all, and it was his attempt to put me at ease around him. But I couldn't respond.

*Thirty-one?*

That would mean that when I first met him, he would have been... Seventeen? It couldn't be true. The man who carried me in his arms that evening in Paris was considerably older than a teenager.

On the other hand, would anyone older than a kid lick a stranger's leg?

Maybe I'd missed something about his appearance back then? The fourteen-year-old me could've misjudged his age in Paris. Everyone older than me had appeared grown-up and sophisticated when I was younger. His formal clothes then and his more casual attire now could play a role, too. My memories might not be as clear as I believed. It'd been a long time, after all. Finally, Lero could be lying about his current age, too, making himself younger, for whatever reason.

At this point, I was just confusing myself with my own questions, none of which were relevant to my job. The most important part was that I had an island to sell to this man, and I couldn't mess it up for Javier.

I straightened in my seat and beamed a well-practiced smile at Lero.

"Thirty-one is a perfect age to own one of the most magnificent properties in the Bahamas. Blue Cay, the island that we're flying to right now, comprises two islands connected by a bridge over a shallow strait that fills in with water during the high tide. The combined size of the property is almost two hundred acres."

What I was saying couldn't be new to Lero. He must've already read it in the listing and whatever extra information Javier had been feeding him to entice him to come for a viewing, but I didn't care. Reciting the info I'd memorized from the brochure helped me get my emotions under control. The familiar flow of a sales pitch made me feel calm and collected.

"A natural bird sanctuary, lush vegetation covers the islands and offers hidden coves and picturesque reefs to explore along the shore..."

Lero appeared to be listening with enough interest, only glancing out the window occasionally.

By the time I'd covered the main amenities of the two villas of Blue Cay, the pilot was descending.

# Chapter Two

STELLA

Jose docked the floatplane. Lero got out first, while I grabbed a bottle of water from the cooler and stuffed it in my purse, just in case. He'd had no liquids on our way here. The last thing I needed was a dehydrated client passing out during the most important showing of my career to date.

*The client* was now standing on the float, offering me a hand. He ended up using both hands to help me climb out onto the float; balancing in my high heels made the task harder.

He then easily hopped off the float onto the dock.

"Ready?" He stretched both arms out to me.

I nodded, adjusting my shoulder bag. Reaching over, I grabbed his hands and jumped from the float to the dock. Swaying on my heels, I managed not to fall. He steadied me with his hands on my waist.

"I've got you," he said softly.

A sudden wave of déjà vu rushed over me, as if I were fourteen again, and he held me in his arms for comfort.

Even my leg felt tingly again, just like it had after he'd licked my wound. The following morning, it had fully scabbed over and healed completely with no trace of a scar in just a couple of days. The much smaller scratch on my elbow had hurt for much longer and left a faint scar to this day.

He lingered with his hands on me, and I darted a glance up at his face. His expression pensive, he inhaled through his nose. I held my breath, waiting for a spark of recognition in his eyes. Something. Anything.

There was none.

He exhaled slowly then released me from his hold, stepping back.

What did I expect? Him to remember me? Why would he keep a memory of a random teenage girl his friend had knocked off a bike almost a decade and a half ago? Meeting him might've been one of the defining moments of my adolescence, but it'd obviously been hardly a bleep in his past.

"Well, as you see..." I cleared my throat, focusing on the task at hand. "This part of the reef provides a natural harbor for the dock. You could travel here by boat—"

"No. No boat." He looked around the crescent of coral reef and the system of teak docks where the pilot had moored the floatplane. "This would need to go," Lero muttered under his breath.

Did he want to get rid of the docks? I didn't own an island—or a boat—but even I knew demolishing the docks would be stupid.

"Traveling by boat is the most common mode of transportation between the islands in this area. It's also one of the most efficient ways to order supplies and obtain housekeeping help—"

"No. That wouldn't be necessary," he cut me off firmly.

"All right." I conceded with a polite half-nod.

My job was to point out the benefits not to start arguments. If Lero preferred to rough it with no supplies while cleaning and vacuuming both villas on his own, it was his prerogative as the future owner.

"Would you like to see the amenities?" I asked as he surveyed the docks, the reef, and the shore nearby.

"Amenities?"

"The houses," I clarified, gesturing up the path from the beach. "The main villa and what the previous owners called the manager's cottage?"

"Of course." He nodded. "Please."

As soon as we got off the dock and onto the packed sand path that led to the master's house, it became apparent how absolutely wrong my shoes were for this viewing.

I tottered on my tiptoes for a few paces, trying to prevent all three inches of my heels from sinking into the sand. Quickly, however, my calves began to scream in pain from the strain that manner of walking had put on them. As a result, my speed suffered greatly.

Oh, screw it, I decided. Would taking off these stupid shoes really deter Lero from buying the place?

"Would you give me a moment, please?" I took my strappy sandals off, then quickly ran back and tossed them on the dock. "I hope you prefer we do this viewing in a timely manner over my close adherence to the agency's dress code?" I smiled sweetly, returning to him.

A corner of his mouth twitched up in a barely there smile.

"Absolutely. In fact..." he toed off his loafers and casually shoved them aside. "I'll leave mine here, too. I'd love to walk down to one of the beaches after we're done with the main house."

Walking barefoot side by side with Lero felt more casual, even relaxing, as if we'd come here for a retreat, not business. I made a conscious effort not to look at his feet anymore, though. Staring at his shoes had been safe, but there was something much too intimate about bare feet for me to risk ogling them now.

The moment we walked into the house, I was able to shift my focus from the man at my side to the property I'd come here to sell.

Javier had sent someone to get it ready for today. The space had been freshly cleaned and aired. The glass double-doors in the large living area were open, letting the ocean breeze in and making the white gossamer curtains billow like sails. This must be their only purpose here —to billow dramatically. I couldn't imagine any other use for something so sheer.

A wide tray laden with sliced fruit stood in the middle of the large dining room table, next to a pewter bucket with a bottle of Champagne on ice and a jug of orange juice.

"Would you like a glass of Champagne?" I moved to the table.

Lero had refused a mimosa on the plane, so I didn't offer to make him one now. If he took a glass of Champagne, I would pour one for myself too, I decided—the rules be damned. My heart continued to pound heavily in his presence. I really wished I'd at least added some Baileys to my coffee that morning—anything to calm my nerves.

"No. Thank you." He shook his head.

"How about some fruit?" I gestured at the tray to cover my disappointment at not getting a drink.

"I'm not hungry," he replied somewhat distractedly as I took a strawberry off the fruit platter.

The stone patio outside of the glass doors appeared to catch his attention. He stepped out and inspected the door frame, then the doors, sliding his fingers over the locks and wiggling the handles. By focusing on the mundane things like doors, Lero was clearly missing some of the best features of this place.

I needed to rectify that. Tossing the strawberry into my mouth, I hurried after him.

"The pool here is truly unique." I swept my arm across the stone patio that housed a large infinity pool. "It's heated and flows directly into the master bathroom."

A glass wall to the side reached below the water surface, separating the indoor portion of the pool from the outdoor. One had to dive under it to swim in or out.

For a moment, I allowed my imagination to run wild, envisioning myself swimming in the warm, crystal-clear water of the pool. Along with my new husband, maybe? During our honeymoon that we would somehow spend in this "piece of paradise," as Blue Cay was called in the listing.

Of course, both the husband and the honeymoon were completely imaginary. I had no man in my life, and my bank account would never allow me to own anything even close to a property like this.

"Can I see the bedroom?" Lero's voice snapped me out of my inappropriate daydreaming.

"Of course." I gave him a highly professional smile. "This way, please."

I led him to the carved double-doors off the living area and opened them dramatically as if drawing back curtains before a show.

The marble floor was pleasantly cool under my bare feet when we walked in.

"Most materials for the construction and finishes came either from the States or Europe," I continued in my best professional tone. "The bathroom fixtures are from the United States. The marble is imported from Italy."

"I suppose they were delivered by boat?" he asked, walking around the spacious room. It had a glass door to the patio in addition to the large glass wall in the swimming pool in the bathroom that was visible through the arched doorway.

"I believe so, but I can confirm it with the current owner. Some things could have also been shipped by floatplane, within the weight limit, of course."

He nodded, his expression contemplative.

"If you're considering any upgrades or renovations in the future," I suggested, helpfully, "you might want to keep the docks until the construction is complete."

In my opinion, there was no practical sense whatsoever for demolishing the docks when living on an island. I hoped for an explanation from him, but none came—he didn't owe me one.

"Does the furniture come with the house?" he asked instead, tipping his head at the wrought-iron poster bed topped with a pure-white spread edged with lace.

"Um. Yes." I quickly averted my eyes from the bed, resisting yet another fantasy. Daydreaming on the job was unacceptable, especially since my make-believe husband's appearance dangerously closely resembled Lero's.

He sauntered to another set of double doors that separated a huge walk-in closet from the master bedroom. The closet was enormous, bigger than my entire condo in Miami. White built-in shelving units lined the walls. A long oval island with dresser drawers and a quartz countertop stood in the center.

"This room has no outside wall, has it?" Lero enquired.

I brought up the house plan in my mind. "No. There is a guest bathroom here, and another bedroom over there."

He nodded, crossing his arms over his chest. A slight frown appeared on his face as he slowly walked the perimeter of the room.

"Would you like to see the rest of the house?" I asked.

People never usually paid *that* much attention to a closet, even those with a lot of clothes. There were still so many rooms for him to see in this villa alone, not to mention a whole other house across the bridge on the other side of Blue Cay.

"The listing mentioned that there is a basement?"

"A wine cellar." I nodded, leading the way out of the bedroom and over to the door downstairs. "It's temperature controlled, perfect for storing any wine collection."

I flicked on the light before entering the spacious basement at the bottom of the stairs. My feet sank into the soft hand-woven rug on the floor. The air here felt pleasantly cool against my heated skin. The soft lighting showcased floor-to-ceiling shelves of wine racks made from dark wood. The smell of wood blended with the scent of Lero, who followed closely behind me, so close I could feel the warmth of his body on my left arm.

"No windows," he said softly, looking around the dimly lit space. "Is it fully below the grade then?"

"Yes. The elevation in this part of the island is high enough to allow for that."

"How about the other place? What did you call it? The manager's cottage?"

"There is no basement there."

"That's a pity." He rubbed his chin, seemingly lost in thought for a moment.

Did he need a second wine cellar? How much wine did he need to store? This place was big enough to accommodate a small winery, I believed. But then again, what did I know about the whims of the rich?

"The elevation is lower where the manager's cottage is located," I explained. "Which would increase the risk of moisture accumulating or even a flood in the basement. If you need more space for wine storage—"

"I don't," he said dismissively, heading toward the stairs up to the main floor.

All right, then.

"Would you like to see the other bedrooms?" I hurried after him. "Each has an ocean view and features a small patio with a walkout to the yard or to one of the beaches."

"No. I'm done here." At the top of the stairs, Lero turned right, toward the main entrance of the house. "Let's go to the second one. The manager's cottage."

"Right... But are you sure? There is more to see here. The formal area includes a grand room that boasts cathedral ceilings and a spectacular view..."

"I'll take your word for it." He swiftly walked out the front door to the square stone patio, then jogged down the several wide steps to the path that led toward a beach.

He obviously wasn't interested in seeing the formal areas of the house.

Did people really do that? Who would buy a multi-million-dollar property without seeing all of it first? Especially since he'd already gone through the trouble of getting here?

Or maybe he'd seen enough and was no longer interested in buying it at all? My heart sank in disappointment. Losing Lero as a client would most definitely upset Javier. It wouldn't make me look good, either.

Well, Lero still wanted to see the other house. Maybe not all was lost yet. Rich people had their quirks. My job wasn't to question but to humor them.

Without a word, I followed Lero down the sand path, trying to guess his mood. Overall, he hadn't behaved like a typical buyer.

This was the first time I'd shown an island to someone, but I'd been selling homes for years now. My usual clients stayed inland, though. I used to mostly sell condo units and smaller houses. I'd just recently added some larger suburban homes to my portfolio. People normally viewed the place they considered buying from the perspective of living there. Usually, they looked at a property's potential for them to relax, work, and entertain. Many viewed it as a status symbol as well.

In Lero's case, he appeared to be most interested in door locks, the closet, and the basement—a bizarre combination.

Maybe, if I knew more about his reasons for shopping for an island in the first place, I could present Blue Cay in a better light to him?

Reaching a steeper part of the path, he waited until I caught up with him. He then took my elbow, helping me descend to the beach.

"Are you looking for a full-time residence?" I asked, adding, "Because the owners of high-value properties can obtain a permanent residence permit in the Bahamas. Otherwise, there is a limit on how long foreign nationals can stay in the country."

"Maybe," he replied, his tone non-committal. "I haven't decided yet."

So, he'd first buy an island, then decide? Not that it was any of my business how he spent his money, of course, as long as he bought the damn thing from me.

"The water is receding right now," I observed as we neared the pretty arched bridge over the narrow strait between the two halves of Blue Cay. "When it's completely gone, the two islands become one for a little while each day."

I wondered what it would be like to walk through the sand under the bridge, to see what the water had brought and left behind. What neat things could one find?

"The property is unique..." I started, but let my voice trail off without finishing another sentence from the listing brochure.

The selling pitch words fell flat and inadequate to describe this place accurately. Anyone who had eyes could see for themselves the vivid beauty of turquoise water caressing the yellow-white sand. Anyone could hear the soothing sound of waves rolling softly onto the beach and the calling of birds around the reef.

I inhaled deeply the air rich with sun and ocean spray. Anyone who'd been stuck in a city most of their lives would appreciate the peaceful beauty of the two little islands in the sea, connected by the bridge, like a couple holding hands.

"It's... It just feels wonderful here," I exhaled, turning to Lero. "So quiet. Don't you think?"

"Hhm. Quiet," he echoed as we crossed the bridge. "Can we walk along the beach here?"

The wide strip of soft sand curved around the west island on the north side. At the far end of it, a set of stone steps led from the beach up to the manager's cottage in the distance.

"Of course," I agreed.

Lero stepped off the path. Once on the sand, he rolled his pants up to his knees, then waded into the water.

I expected him to keep moving along the shore toward the house, but he just stood there, facing the sea. The breeze teased his short, dark hair. It wasn't entirely black, I noticed—the sun brought out some dark copper highlights. There was something wistful in his expression as he gazed out to the horizon.

I mentally went through what I'd memorized about the caves and the reefs of Blue Cay.

"Do you like swimming?" I asked. "There are some amazing places for snorkeling around here."

He closed his eyes, his wide chest rising with a long breath. It would appear he was simply enjoying the warmth of sunshine on his face, but the deep crease between his long, black eyebrows betrayed his intense concentration.

"No. I don't swim," he replied, without opening his eyes.

"You can't?" I came a little closer, allowing the gentle waves to lick my feet. The reef kept Blue Cay protected from larger swells on this side.

"I *can* swim. I just don't do it."

"You...don't like it?" I prodded, spurred purely by my undying curiosity about him.

Why spend so much money on a piece of land surrounded by water if he didn't even like swimming? He obviously had no plans to do any boating in the future either, since he was ready to rip the docks out.

The more time I spent with this man, the less I understood him.

"You don't like water?"

"Not particularly."

"Then why are you considering buying an island?" I couldn't hold the question back anymore.

He released a breath, turning my way. "Because I should have done it a long time ago. I never even realized the need for it until about two months ago when...someone I cared about was gone."

"Gone?" I gasped, forgetting all about being professional. Compassion swelled thick in my heart. "I'm so sorry, Lero..."

He flinched. His dark eyebrows moved closer to each other, deepening his frown.

"Lero? How do you know this name, Mademoiselle Alarie?" he asked slowly, trapping me in his inquisitive stare.

The file from Javier stated only *L. Sauveterre* as the client's name, I realized belatedly. I'd been calling him Lero in my mind only because that was what Mara, the woman in Paris, had called him.

Unsure how to reply, I kept quiet.

He waded through the water, closing the distance between us. Grabbing my upper arms, he leaned closer, inhaling the air around me.

"We've met before, haven't we?" His voice came out raspy. Sunlight flicked through his eyes with a flash of red.

I kept watching his face for the spark of recognition. I didn't even know why it was so important to me that he'd remember, but it was. I held my breath, feeling the warmth of his skin on mine. And I waited for him to remember...

He didn't.

"When?" he demanded from me, instead. "How?"

"A long time ago," I said softly.

To be fair, it *had* been a very long time ago, too long for anyone to remember the brief meaningless encounter we'd had. Even the fact that I remembered it was odd.

"In Paris. I was fourteen years old. I fell off my bike in front of your house, you drove me home."

He let out a long breath, his posture relaxed as if a weight dropped from his shoulders. "Of course."

The recognition I'd been waiting for spread across his face, softening his sharp features.

"The girl with a scraped knee. I remember the flavor."

"You licked my leg."

He winced, the expression in his eyes turning guarded. "Disgusting, isn't it?"

Oddly, I'd never felt disgusted or appalled by that, only confused and...a little intrigued. What would compel a man to do something like that?

"Why did you do it?"

His gaze lingered on my face for another moment, his expression softening even further in the sunshine. He slid his hands down my arms to cup my elbows.

"How is your wound?" he asked, instead of answering my question.

"The wound? Oh, it's gone. Completely." I lifted the hem of my skirt to display the perfectly healed skin on my knee. "It didn't even leave a scar. Do you know why?" I glanced up at him.

He stared at my leg, then slowly slid his gaze up my body. His attention was almost tangible, like a glide of a hand, learning and exploring on its way.

For the first time ever, I felt like Lero really *saw* me. All of me. My clothes. My body. My gender. That he might finally sense the pull between us, too.

Awareness crackled between us, reaching deep under my skin.

His chest heaved. His gray eyes darkened to the color of the cloudy sky. He bent his head down, bringing his face so close to mine, my breath hitched. His lips parted, and for one heart-stopping moment, I believed he would kiss me.

I wished for the kiss to happen so badly, I ached inside from anticipation.

A spark of red flashed through his eyes again—sudden and unexplained. His hands flexed on my arms, fingers digging into my skin. Inhaling deeply, as if struggling for oxygen, he let go of me and stepped back.

"Would you mind if I smoke?" he asked in a low, raspy voice.

Reeling from what could've happened and crushed that it hadn't, I couldn't summon either words or gestures to answer.

Not waiting for my reply, he reached into the inner pocket of his jacket and produced a long, black cigarette. His fingers trembled slightly as he lit it then took a long, greedy drag.

Tilting his head back, he exhaled slowly. Tension seemed to drain from his body along with the coils of fragrant, silvery smoke. It shimmered in the sunlight, dissipating into the breeze. A tendril of it reached my nostrils, filling them with the fragrance I'd long thought of as "Lero's scent."

Apparently, it wasn't just the cologne he used that made him smell so good, but also the cigarettes he smoked. What were they? I didn't smell a hint of tobacco in the smoke.

"I'm glad to see you've healed well," he said in a much smoother voice. His expression of detached politeness snapped back in place with another drag of his cigarette.

By the calming effect it had on Lero and by the desperation with which he smoked, I wondered if the cigarettes contained some kind of drug—a substance I'd certainly never smelled anywhere but on him.

"Shall we continue, Mademoiselle Alarie?" He offered me his hand to help me up the path to the manager's cottage.

I inhaled a cleansing breath and straightened my spine.

"Certainly, Monsieur Sauveterre." I matched his tone. Calm, detached, professional—it left no doubt what we were to each other, what we ever could be, an agent and a client.

"Thank you, Mademoiselle Alarie. We'll be in touch." Lero shook my hand when we got back to the charter company's dock in Miami.

I kept my hand in his fingers longer than was necessary. Catching myself trying to memorize the sensation of his touch, I quickly let go. With a courteous nod, he headed off to the limo that had come to pick him up.

Would we really "be in touch?"

Even if Lero went ahead with the purchase, he'd deal with Javier directly from now on. I'd just filled in for today because of my boss's family emergency. Chances were, I would never see Lero again.

I watched him get into the vehicle and drive away, out of my life. As quickly as he'd appeared, he was gone.

What did I expect? A warm, friendly smile? A goodbye hug?

Would a smile or even a hug have made this odd feeling of abandonment easier to bear? Why did I feel so empty inside, watching him go? What was there for me to miss?

Lero had never really been a part of my life for me to miss him when he left.

All he'd ever given me was a few minutes of kindness when I was fourteen. Back then, I'd had an aunt who thrived on controlling me, a father who saw me as little more than the means to restoring his wealth, and a mother who had dedicated her life to her husband, caring little about me, her only child. I needed human kindness more than the air I breathed while growing up, yet I got nothing from the adults around me.

The neglect of my family might've amplified the effect Lero's one act of kindness had on me as a teenager, resulting in years of dreaming about him after.

Today hadn't been about kindness, though. His sudden reappearance in my life brought more harm than good, now that I was a grown woman. Seeing him again had added new, vibrant layers to the image of Lero I held in my mind. I worried it would now take even longer to wear off and fade away. How was I supposed to fight them now, when the memories of him were so new and fresh?

And so titillating?

*"This time, you'd better make sure you're gone for good, Lero,"* I thought bitterly.

# Chapter Three

## A MONTH AND TWO DAYS LATER

STELLA

I didn't have an island, but I did own a piece of property—my very own condo the size of a studio apartment. It wasn't on an island either, not even on one of the Venetian Islands in Miami, but it was "in the epicenter of downtown," according to its real estate listing.

Returning to it after a long day of showings truly felt like coming home. There was always a sense of pride, too. I loved my place because I'd bought it entirely with the money I'd earned.

My dad used to think my rich aunt was strict with me because she cared about me. I always believed her behavior toward me simply stemmed from her inherent need for control.

Her death proved me right. Aunt Beatrice died childless, with no heirs but my father and me. She willed all her money to a few carefully selected charities, leaving nothing to either of us.

The only benefit for my future came in the job offer made by Javier Moreno, whom I met at my aunt's funeral. His real estate company had been tasked with selling some properties my aunt owned all over the world. Javier gave me my first office job and encouraged me to get my real estate license.

Javier had also been the one to sell me my condo, after giving me a substantial Christmas bonus that year. The property came from the listings of our agency. He'd negotiated a great price for me and helped me arrange for the mortgage with amazing terms.

Javier, a complete stranger, ended up giving me more support and showing more interest in my future than any of the people related to me by blood.

"If you work for me, we're family, Stella," he'd say every time I would attempt to put into words the deep gratitude I felt for everything he'd done for me.

In another, less law-abiding life, I believed Javier could've headed a cartel in Mexico or a *famiglia* on Corsica. He had that air of power and influence around him, rewarding those loyal to him, despising those who'd ever done him wrong.

The comparison of Javier to a mafia boss made me smile as I pulled into the underground garage of my condo building. My home might be the smallest unit in the building, but it came with the full use of all on-site amenities like the swimming pool, the exercise center, and the spa. I also got a great parking spot in the garage.

As it often happened, the last viewing had ended late. Most people went house hunting after their working hours. To accommodate them, I worked late into the night on most days.

It didn't bother me. I had no one waiting for me at home, not even a pet. For now, my job was my priority. Neither was I worried about walking alone late at night. My building was safe, even the underground garage. Spacious and brightly lit, I was never concerned about being in it on my own.

Tonight, however, the uneasy feeling of being watched nagged at me the moment I climbed out of my car. I locked the car and headed to the elevator, faster than usual.

The clipped staccato of my high heels hitting the concrete floor echoed through the deserted garage. But there was another sound—an indistinct shuffling of someone else's footsteps that seemed to come from the row of cars behind me.

I whipped around, scanning the vehicles and the surrounding space, but saw nothing out of the ordinary.

Another sound, a low rumbling, rolling in from all sides made my insides freeze. Fear brushed against the skin of my arms, pricking it with goosebumps. I darted my gaze between the rows of parked vehicles and the concrete support columns.

No one was there.

Yet when I started walking again—keys clutched in my sweaty hand—the sound of someone following me came again. I slid the narrow blades of the keys between my trembling fingers, fully intending to fight back if attacked.

A distinct sound of breathing behind me spurred my fear into panic.

I ran.

There was no doubt left, someone was after me. And they were running, too. Their labored breathing came closer and closer. Instead of soles of shoes, their footfalls sounded softer, like paws, with the screeching of claws against the concrete floor.

Too terrified to glance back, I slammed into the closed elevator doors at full speed, frantically hitting its call button, again and again. The doors wouldn't open. The elevator was slowly crawling down from the upper floors somewhere. When it'd finally get here, it might be too late...

The hoarse breathing of my pursuer was now right behind me.

Cornered, I had no choice but to fight.

I swiveled on my heels, lashing out with my hand—the keys clutched in my sweaty fist, their sharp ends sticking out between my fingers.

My breath choked me, lodging in my throat, when I came face to face with my pursuer.

It was no human.

Whoever or whatever it was, the creature must've come straight from a nightmare.

It stood on all fours, its great paws spread wide. Lips drawn back, it bared its white teeth—narrow, long, and sharp like rows of slightly curved spikes or needles. Saliva dripped from its mouth. When it hit the floor, it sizzled, sending tendrils of steam up in the air.

The creature's large, red eyes glowed in the artificial light of the garage—wild and unhinged.

And... Oh, my God... Were those horns? Sprouting, straight and spiky, from the side of its head?

What was this monster?

Unable to tear my eyes away from the hellish creature, I kept hitting the elevator's call button mechanically, like a broken robot.

Would the elevator even help me if it came? Now that the beast was barely a leap away from me?

It jerked my way. I jumped, squeezing out a pitiful, choked sound.

Instead of leaping at me, the beast shoved away from the concrete with its front paws, then rose on its hind ones.

It appeared even bigger now, towering over me, seven or eight feet of flesh and thick black fur.

Frozen in terror, I couldn't scream. I could barely breathe. My knees shook, my legs growing too weak to support my weight. I leaned back against the elevator doors. Did I even want them to open now? Even if I made it inside, the doors would never close fast enough to lock the beast out. Then, I'd risk being trapped in the elevator with this murderous monster from hell...

Tipping sideways, I inched to the right, toward the corner of the wall that enclosed the elevator shaft.

The long things I'd mistaken for horns turned out to be the creature's ears. They twitched, then moved back as the monster flattened them against its skull. Tossing its great head back, it roared. So loud, the deafening sound pressed against my chest. The parked vehicles around us appeared to shake.

How did no one hear this? Why was nobody coming to my rescue?

I staggered one more step to the right. The wall behind me ended abruptly, and I tumbled backwards to the ground. My ass painfully hit the concrete floor around the corner of the enclosed elevator shaft.

The ding of the elevator finally announced its arrival, followed by the swishing sound of the doors opening. Scrambling to my hands and knees, I carefully poked my head around the corner.

Was there any chance at all for me to sneak into the elevator and get out of here? The stairs weren't an option—the monster stood right between me and them.

The creature remained on its hind paws. No longer roaring, it was sniffing the air in deep hurried breaths.

Could it smell me?

I ducked back, taking cover behind the wall instead of trying to get into the elevator in plain sight of the monster. Even if the beast couldn't smell me, my heart pounded so hard, I feared it would hear me.

"Get him! Now!" A male voice shouted out of nowhere.

I glanced out again to find a group of men surrounding the beast. Several of them held a black net stretched between them.

The animal must have escaped from the zoo or a circus. Thankfully, the people got here just in time to capture and return it where it belonged. That explained everything.

I slumped against the wall, relief draining the fear and tension out of my body.

The beast must be a bear, a panther, a large wolf or something just as ordinary. Fear had simply made it look "monstrous" to me.

I didn't know exactly what animals were housed in the Miami Zoo. Neither had I heard of any circus coming to town. But I worked a lot and didn't always keep up with the events in the city.

Sitting with my back to the wall, I remained out of sight, waiting for my breathing to return to normal. This had turned out to be quite a night.

The roar of the animal tore through the garage once again. Sharp and loud, it reverberated under the ceiling, bouncing off the surrounding concrete.

I looked out of my hiding place again, to see whether it was safe to come out.

The men threw the net over the animal, wrapping it around. Red sparks flashed along the net where it touched the fur of the animal. It roared again—the sound filled with agony.

The poor thing was clearly in pain.

I gripped the concrete corner with my fingers.

The net obviously hurt the animal that growled and fought desperately against it. The red streaks of light that flashed along the thin black rope of the net left smoldering scorch marks in his fur.

Whether the net had electric current running through it or had been soaked in some kind of harmful chemical, why did these people have to resort to such cruelty? Why not just use a tranquilizer to subdue the animal?

"Steady, *voukalak,*" one of the men gritted through his teeth. "Do what you're told, and you and your sweetheart will live."

*Sweetheart?* What did he mean by that?

What kind of animal control people were these, anyway? I looked for any lettering or insignia on their black t-shirts and found none. They were incredibly similar in their appearance, I noticed. Tall and well-built, all of them were bald and had identical tattoos covering their necks and right arms. Their behavior was closer to that of a gang than to people who worked with animals.

Dread trickled cold down my back. Whatever these men really were, it no longer felt safe for me to come out at all. They didn't appear to have spotted me, and I decided to remain hidden, furtively watching them while being unseen.

One man came closer to their newly captured trophy, securing the net tighter around the tormented beast. The animal struggled against his bonds, then jerked his head, snapping his jaws at his captor. The red sparks appeared to jump off the net, running up the man's arm tattoo.

"Careful, Dez! Watch out for his teeth," another man warned.

Dez shoved the heel of his heavy boot into the animal's snout.

"His teeth will soon be added to Madame's jewelry collection if he doesn't smarten up," he scoffed.

The elevator doors closed at that moment. Someone from the upper floors must've called the elevator up. I jerked back and out of sight once again.

"The girl?" Dez yelled. "Where did she go?"

My heart sped up again. They knew about me. What on earth could they want with me?

The sound of the elevator going up filled the dead silence that followed Dez's questions.

"That must be her," another man suggested. "She escaped in the elevator."

"How much do you think she saw?" someone else asked.

"It doesn't matter." Dez's voice didn't sound too concerned. "Now that we've got him, we don't need her anymore." The sound of another shove of his boot came, followed by a groan of pain from the creature trapped in the net.

*"We don't need her anymore."*

Had they come for me, at first? Why? I didn't even know who these people were. What could they possibly want with me?

"What if she tells someone what she saw?" another man asked.

"Who would believe her?" Dez scoffed. "Come on. Take him to the truck before anyone else sees us. *Two* live witnesses would be a problem."

Afraid to move or even to breathe, I sat on the floor long after the sounds of their heavy footsteps quieted in the distance.

Only when someone else, a young couple, came to the elevator much later, did I venture out of my hiding place and into the elevator with them.

Back in the safety of my condo, I locked the door, turned off the lights, and climbed into bed. Then, I watched the reflection of the city lights on my ceiling until an uneasy sleep finally claimed me.

# Chapter Four

LERO

"So, where is he?" a female voice filtered through the thick fog of pain and rage.

It sounded familiar, but he couldn't place the voice, couldn't focus enough to even comprehend where he was. All-consuming anger dominated his mind. It burned through his brain with the same intensity as the pain that tormented his body.

"Aw, there you are," the woman cooed. "Lero, sweetie, we need to talk."

The familiar scent of *womora* hit him with a puff of air in his face. He drew it into his lungs with hungry, ragged breaths.

Awareness sharpened with each tendril of smoke filling his chest. The rage became manageable, but the pain got more acute. It concentrated around his ankles and wrists where cold metal cuffs held him in place.

His vision cleared as the smoke dissipated, bringing the woman's face in focus. Beautiful, youthful features, framed by vividly red waves of hair. Eyes black as night, with astute, ancient expression in their depths.

She stood in front of him, calm and free, while he was locked in restraints, chained to a concrete wall.

"Ghata..." he exhaled, his tongue and mouth finally able to form words instead of just growls and snarls.

Relief relaxed his muscles, aiding the effects of *womora*. Ghata couldn't be here to harm him. They had a long-standing agreement between them, born from necessity and strengthened by survival.

They both were criminals on the run.

Disgraced and pursued by her former followers, Ghata had helped him escape persecution for crimes he'd committed one grim night during a fit of Moon Madness. She'd shown him how to cross the River of Mists to come from Nerifir to this world.

"Not Ghata, sweetie. It's *Madame Tan*. For now, anyway." She took a long drag from the cigarette clasped in the holder on her finger then released another thick cloud of *womora* smoke in his face.

There were times when his kind had fervently worshiped Ghata. As the werewolves' goddess, she channeled the magic of the Moon. But she had abused her powers, corrupted the magic, and used it for her own gain. Eventually, she'd lost the faith of her followers and triggered their wrath instead.

"Remember how devastated I was, having to run away here?" A fragile note slipped into her voice—intentionally or not, he couldn't tell.

He'd seen Ghata at her most vulnerable when they'd first crossed into this world. Stripped of most of her powers, the little that remained depleted by the crossing, she'd appeared simply as a young woman to him, fragile and unwell.

He had taken care of her and Zeph, the orphaned siren boy who'd come with them from Nerifir. Besides learning how to navigate this new, often confusing world, he'd had two other lives depending on him.

Ghata leaned closer, sliding her finger along his jawline A layer of fur muffled the sensation of her touch. Despite the clearer mind and the ability to speak, he must still physically be a beast, partially at least.

"This world proved to be perfect for my re-birth after all, Lero," she murmured. "Big things are coming, my friend. When I use my old name again, it will be *Goddess* Ghata, as it was meant to be."

Even after Ghata had recovered physically, he had supported her financially. She'd spent their first few years in this world secluded in the small apartment he'd rented for her in Paris. He'd paid the living expenses for the three of them while she'd mourned the loss of her former splendor and the vast armies of followers.

In turn, she had promised him a life-time supply of *womora.* She was able to acquire it from Nerifir though her *bracks*, the werewolves who'd sworn their lives to her and become her slaves in exchange for immortality and the glory of being her priests.

Before the night of the full moon, he needed to smoke the leaves to retain control of his mind for as long as possible. Without *womora*, he wouldn't be able to lead the normal life he'd built for himself and Zeph, whom he'd raised as his own son.

Unlike the fae that Zeph and he were, *bracks* were capable of not only crossing to Nerifir and back, they always returned to the same *when* and *where* Ghata was. Their connection with her pulled them back to her across time and dimensions.

*Bracks!*

The memory of the black net burning his skin through his fur scorched his body with pain again. The *bracks* were the ones who'd caught him. Dez, Lero's own brother, had been the one leading the attack.

The net was gone. He was in a dimly lit room with no windows, his back pressed against the cold wall. The confinement of restraints on his arms and legs speared through him with panic and rage.

"Release me!" He strained his muscles against the hard metal. The restraints burned his wrists and ankles like acid. They must be made from iron brought from Nerifir.

"Hush, sweetie." Ghata puffed out another cloud of the calming smoke, enveloping them both. "You will be released. Soon. All I need is one small promise from you first."

With another deep breath of *womora*, understanding finally crushed him.

"You did this!"

"This, and so many other things." She laughed, a melodious sound like a trill of silver bells. Deceivingly innocent.

"Why?" he bellowed, indignant and enraged.

Ghata laughed again, not at all intimidated by his anger. She actually looked amused by it.

"Because I missed you." She pouted.

The mask of innocence slipped off her face then. A cold, calculating expression took its place.

"Lero." She leaned in so close the strands of her long red hair tickled his fur-covered chest. The hem of her scarlet silk kimono slicked against his knees. "This world is full of opportunities for creatures like us. Humans are weak and pathetic, but they're so easily influenced. They're starving for miracles and longing for a higher power. Born followers, they're eager to serve. And best of all, they're so easy to corrupt using their own greed and thirst for power. Humans are weak, but you're not human. You're fae. You have the strength and magic of your people. Join me, and we'll conquer this world together."

Dread chilled his spine.

"What are you talking about? What have you done?"

"It's not what I've done but what I'm still going to do that's important, my sweet Lero. Will you help me accomplish everything I've planned?"

As a fae, he could not break a promise given. He knew better than to commit to something as vague as "everything." What Ghata demanded sounded very much like slavery. Her plans, whatever they were, worried him.

"Remember why we came to this world, Ghata. Here, we got a chance to earn our redemption through a simple life of peace and restraint. The point was to blend in with humans, not to corrupt and conquer them."

She huffed a laugh, derisive and harsh this time.

"Blend in!" she scoffed, shoving away from him. "With *humans*? I was never meant to be one of them—the pathetic little creatures, with not a spark of magic in them. Their only strength is in their thoughts, their inner world. They don't even realize how much power there is in their beliefs. But they're lost. Can't you see, Lero? Their very nature is that of slaves, searching for a master. They were meant to be subservient. To me."

Ghata was a goddess. Disgraced and powerless at the moment, she would rise if people started believing her a deity again. Instead of learning humility, she'd used her time in this world to plan a return to what she'd been punished for in Nerifir. Except this time, her targets were the defenseless humans, void of any magic to protect themselves.

"You can't," he breathed out, stunned by her revelations.

"Oh yes, I can. And I will. The only question that remains..." She plucked the cigarette out of the holder, tossed it to the floor, and stepped on it, depriving him of the thought-clearing smoke. "Where do *you* want to be, my dear, when it all happens? By my side, as the master of these creatures, or as one of them, serving me?"

Without the *womora*, the power of the Moon began slowly sucking the calm out of his body and the awareness out of his mind.

He blinked, struggling to concentrate.

What did Ghata want from him?

"A promise, Lero," she reminded him, as if sensing his confusion. "I need you to make the *brack's* vow to me."

Her soft lips brushed his. The way his nose touched hers told him his face had its usual shape at the moment, not that of the beast. Or maybe it was something in between as the sensation of the fur on his back, shoulders and arms hadn't left. He was not a man anymore but not quite a beast either—a true monster, frozen mid-shift, his mind suspended between his two forms.

"Swear your life and your loyalty to me," Ghata whispered, her warm, fragrant breath fanning across the side of his face. Then her lips touched his cheek. The sensation of the caress tingled along his skin, spreading down his chest and belly and rushing blood to his groin. "Call me Madame until I am called Goddess Ghata again. Be one of the masters over the humans. Rule this world with me."

She slid her hand down his abs. His cock strained toward her touch, like a marionette puppet on a string. His mind homed in on the downward glide of her hand, his body shaking with anticipation.

"Fuck!" he growled, thrusting his hips forward.

"Yes, sweetie," she cooed ever so tenderly, tickling the tip of his throbbing cock with her fingers. The tease was torture, he needed so much more. "Give me your promise, and I'll let you fuck me. Only you. All night. No one else."

The decades-long practice of fighting his lust helped him wrestle it under control once again.

"Becoming a *brack* wouldn't make me a master, Ghata, but your slave." He attempted a laugh, but it turned into a groan of agony as she squeezed his erection, digging her long nails into his shaft.

"I can wait," she hissed, leaning in. "There is still plenty of time, which will fly fast for me. For you, however..." She dragged her sharp nails up his belly, leaving hot, swelling welts on his skin. "I'll make sure the time goes *torturously* slow. Dez!" she yelled over her shoulder.

Through the thickening fog of madness and pain, he saw a large dark figure step in from the door.

"Yes, Madame," his older brother replied.

"Oh, how often I've wished you were the eldest son in your family, Lero," Ghata lamented. "I would've loved to have you instead of your brother."

This was said intentionally loud for Dez to hear. And judging by the glare his brother hurled his way, he heard her loud and clear.

"You're in charge, Dez," she said. "Keep him in this location, for now. I don't want him at the menagerie just yet. It's best to keep my VIP acts separate, especially since this one can only really perform during the full moon. He can start working from here. I already have some clients who wish to watch him turn next month. That's what I do, *my dear*." She squeezed Lero's cheek painfully. "I make humans pay to see a 'miracle.' They're starving for the *extraordinary* in their mundane world and are willing to pay a lot of money to see someone as special as you or your little siren, who, by the way, turned out to be a gold mine."

*Zeph!*

The sudden realization slammed into him. No longer restrained by *womora*, rage filled him to the brim.

"What have you done to him?" he bellowed, yanking against the iron manacles. "Where is Zeph?"

"Shh." She patted the side of his face soothingly. He snapped his teeth at her hand. "Feisty, are we? Down, boy." She jammed her knee into his crotch.

Sharp pain made him double over as far as the chains would allow.

With his arms spread and his wrists chained to the wall, his shoulders nearly dislocated from their sockets.

He howled in agony.

"That's better." Ghata's voice flowed, thick with satisfaction.

"You swore to me you didn't know where he was!" he growled, furious rage numbing the physical pain and making the agony of loss and fear for Zeph burn that much stronger. "You *promised* to search for him with me!"

"Oh, Lero." She shook her head, her tone mocking. "Unlike your kind, promises do not bind me. I give and break them as easily as humans do, which is the only thing I have in common with these wretched creatures."

"Unlike you, they have honor!"

She chuckled, retreating to the door.

"Thankfully, not all of them."

Her laugh, melodious and so misleadingly sweet, filled the grim space.

"You know it's all your fault, my sweet. You've been searching for the siren so well, I worried you'd find him soon. So, I had to get you, too. You've failed to protect everyone you've ever cared about, Lero. And now, there is no one to protect *you*."

Her laugh stopped abruptly.

"You and the siren are mine," she said firmly. "And I'm not stopping with just the two of you. Gorgonians, gargoyles, maybe even the sky fae themselves. Why not? I can have them all. Whether you want it or not, all of you will help me become what I was always meant to be. A Goddess."

# Chapter Five

LERO

He had only a vague idea how much time had passed. As Ghata had promised, it crawled torturously slow, every moment filled with pain, rage, and lust in any combination of the three.

Sounds and images reached his mind at random, but he lacked the mental power to fully process them. He believed the constant fog hanging over his mind's vision had something to do with the things he ate, but he had no power to refuse food. It was scarce, and he was hungry. So ravenously hungry.

"I've got something for you, *voukalak*."

The voice brought some vivid images to his mind. A memory?

He knew this person. He had spoken to him before, in another world and in what felt like another lifetime.

*A narrow, barely visible path in a forest. Crisp air. Tall pine trees, their needles glistening with early morning frost. The ground dusted with snow.*

*"Come on, Lero!" The older boy laughed. "If you don't improve your aim, the only meat you'll ever eat would be whatever prey you manage to*

*catch in your beast form during the full moon."*

*The boy ran to the tree trunk, yanking Lero's arrow out of the bark. Lero had aimed for a spotted squirrel, but missed. Again.*

*"Here you go." Dez, his older brother, handed the arrow back to Lero, then patted his shoulder. "Maybe we'll get lucky and see another one soon. If it's a rabbit or a virleth pig, though, the shot is mine. No offense, but we're not wasting it on anything bigger than a squirrel just so you can practice. We need to eat, too."*

Memories of emotions flooded in, along with the images.

The desperate desire to impress his brother. The disappointment that he'd missed. The warm gratitude for Dez's kindness and patience.

There was not a hint of kindness in Dez's voice now. Cold and hard, it felt the same as the circle of metal the *brack* put around his neck.

"Here you go. A necklace for you."

Sharp spikes inside the collar pierced Lero's skin, reaping a hiss of pain from his throat.

"You don't like it, do you?" Dez smirked. "Good. I dipped the spikes in *womora*. It'll keep you from shifting unless Madame allows it. After all, she is the goddess, higher than the Moon."

Fog might be clouding Lero's mind, but it was Dez who was delusional. No one was higher than the Moon. *Womora* only lessened the effects before or after the night of the full moon. Nothing ever stopped his transformation the night the full moon rose in the sky.

"Now, eat this, beast. It has some special seasoning, just for you."

Hunger tore at his insides, depriving him of any sense of caution. He swallowed the pieces of raw meat in seconds. Then, the bitter aftertaste in his mouth brought another series of images to mind.

*A puffy yellow mushroom with bright orange dots on its squishy cup. It looked like a toy, fun and whimsical, half-hidden behind the trunk of a tall birch tree where the seven-year-old Lero found it. It felt soft, like a sponge in his hands. The smell of the mushroom reminded him of his mother's warm, freshly baked bread.*

*He licked the mushroom. Its flavor was pleasant, though a hint of bitterness coated his tongue a second later. He opened his mouth wider, ready to bite off a little.*

*"Don't!" Dez ran at him from behind, knocking the mushroom out of*

*his hand. "Kibia mushrooms bring on Moon Madness without the full moon. If you eat them, you won't be able to speak, and your bones will hurt as if you were shifting." He grimaced, watching the discarded mushroom roll into the grass like a squishy ball of rubber. "It also tastes bitter."*

Back then, Dez didn't want Lero to get hurt. Now, he was the one doing the hurting.

"The *kibia* mushrooms will urge you to turn, *voukalak*. The *womora* on the collar spikes will prevent you from turning. You'll get stuck mid-shift, no longer a man but not yet a beast. You know that torturous moment between the two forms? You're going to live that moment forever, for as long as I want. Madame makes money on you every full moon. The rest of the time you're mine to do with as I please. When she finishes with you, she's promised I will be the one to end you."

Dez's voice dripped with hatred, deep and unexplained. Nothing that Lero had done in the short years he and Dez knew each other as children could've caused his brother to hate him this much.

It was Ghata.

She'd changed the boys brought to her temple, making them her *bracks*. She'd altered their emotions and perception of things when she'd turned them into her slaves. The strong affection Dez used to have for his younger brother had been warped and corroded into a hatred even stronger.

*Images of a gray winter's day entered Lero's mind. The day when Dez turned fourteen and left their family home for Ghata's temple. Lero cried, though their father told him it was a joyous day. The goddess had accepted his brother to serve her. In exchange, he would live forever.*

*Once a boy from their village entered her temple, he never returned. Though still young, Lero knew Dez would never come back, either. They'd never go hunting in the woods together again. For him, that day felt like the day he was losing his brother.*

*The next time he saw Dez, it was months later. Lero barely recognized him. His brother's raven-black hair was gone. An elaborate tattoo covered his entire right arm and circled his neck like a collar of servitude. Dressed in the ceremonial clothing in Ghata's colors, red and black, Dez was taking part in a celebration at her temple, along with the other men she'd claimed as boys and turned into bracks over the centuries.*

*The villagers had been invited to the temple to participate in the festivities. Lero stood with his parents, holding his mother's hand. His gaze crossed with Dez's. His brother's eyes were no longer gray but dark brown, almost black. There was not a spark of recognition in them, no life, no kindness, just red streaks of cold fire.*

"Why?" he croaked. His voice sounded more like an animal growl. The ability to speak the *womora* had just given him was already being taken by the *kibia* mushrooms. "Why are you doing this, Dez?"

His brother leaned closer, hissing in his face, "Because if you're not a *brack*, you're a werewolf—one of those who disgraced and banished us. You're an enemy. You deserve to suffer, and I'm here to make sure you do."

Lero closed his eyes, blocking the view of the man who once was his brother and was now his jailer and torturer.

*"You've failed to protect everyone you've ever cared about."*

The memory of Ghata's words brought a bigger agony than anything Dez could ever do to him.

As his voice broke and distorted into a roar and his bones twisted with pain, he thought of the people she'd spoken about. Those few whom he cared for and ruined.

He couldn't stop his father from giving Dez away to Ghata.

He'd failed to protect Amelie.

Now Zeph...

Ghata was right. He'd failed so many.

But he had managed to keep one name off that list—Stella.

He'd learned the *bracks* had spotted him with her the morning she was showing him the island he'd ended up buying. She was only a real estate agent, replacing the man he was supposed to meet that day. But the *bracks* had seen something else between them. The stupid goons imagined he had some special feelings for her. That put her on their radar.

He now knew that when he'd come too close to discovering Zeph's whereabouts, Ghata had ordered her slaves to take Lero. Unable to locate him at that point, the *bracks* had targeted Stella, hoping he would come for her. He took the bait. The moment he'd learned she was in danger, he'd rushed to protect her.

Stella wasn't *his* woman as the *bracks* believed she was, but he couldn't let them have her.

It'd happened right before the full moon. He'd been getting ready to go to the island that night, to prowl and rage in solitude until the sunrise. But he'd found out that *bracks* had come to Miami for Stella, so he had to get to her before they did.

The sun set when he was a few blocks away from her building. He turned into the beast in a dark alley and ran to her place on all fours. In his effort to warn her, he scared her. Despite the lust that consumed him at the mere sight of her, he kept in control, getting ready to fight the *bracks* who were after her.

But then she ran. His control snapped. The predator in him leaped out to chase the prey...

In the end, he had protected her after all. When the *bracks* got him, they lost interest in Stella. She was out there somewhere, free and unaware of the horrible fate she'd so narrowly escaped.

That knowledge was the one ray of light in this mind, now. He'd gladly suffer if it meant no other life was ruined because of him.

The memories of Stella shone through the darkness of pain that racked his body. They kept him sane through the torment. If he were to die here, in this cold concrete room with no windows, he wished he could kiss her first.

He dreamed about that, delusional from pain. Would her kiss have the same flavor as her scent and the taste of her blood?

He knew, in reality, the kiss could never happen. Even if he ever made it out of this basement, the best thing he could do for Stella was to stay as far away from her as possible.

But for as long as he could before his mind blanked out from the agony his body was going through, he held onto the memory of her.

He'd been put into a cage. Bright light shone on him, hot and blinding. He couldn't see them, but he sensed other people in the room, outside the thick, rusty cage he was in.

Someone removed the collar with the in-turned spikes that kept the wounds on his neck permanently raw.

The energy of the Moon flooded him, unimpeded. Despite the torture it brought, he welcomed it—there was an end to the pain now.

The Moon magic coursed through his veins, twisting his bones and re-shaping his muscles. His voice grew stronger, not as a speech but a roar. Loud and liberating, it tore from his chest as he rose to his hind paws.

Every coherent thought moved to the background. The pain disappeared. Only rage and feral lust remained.

He'd *turned*.

For one night, he was fully a beast. Locked in the cage on display for others.

"Aw, it's so nice to see you again, Lero," Ghata purred. "I missed you. Now that you're finally here, in my menagerie, I can come see you whenever I want."

Is that where he was now? He'd fully become part of her freakshow.

Aside from being allowed to shift fully on the nights of the full moon, his body had been kept in the torturous state of mid-shift. It had been so many months, his mental state had suffered. He'd been hardly aware of his surroundings when they'd moved him. Only vague, fragmented memories remained of being loaded into a crate and then transported here.

Instead of the musty air of the concrete basement, the space around him smelled dusty. The sound of Ghata's voice didn't bounce off any hard walls here but was muffled either by rugs or fabric.

He'd learned during his search for Zeph that Ghata had a traveling show. Sometimes, she'd rent a more permanent place for a while. But more often, she operated from large tents set up at fairs and other public events.

Prying his swollen eyelids open, he saw the red-and-yellow canvas that formed the walls of the room where the metal frame stood with the restraints that held him upright.

"Are you ready to give me what I want, Lero?" Ghata's voice slithered like a serpent around him, dangerously seductive. "Just one word, and all of this will end. You'll eat as much meat as you want. No more *kibia* mushrooms, I promise. No cages or chains. You'll sleep in silks, with me." Her hand, warm and soft, slid down his belly. "You want me, don't you?"

He'd want *anyone*. The state of the perpetual arousal with no release had been a torture on its own. Not only had he no control left, but he was barely self-aware, driven to madness by hunger, pain, and lust. By now, he'd fuck anything that moved. The iron restraints were the only things that stopped him from lunging on her.

"Join me," she whispered, sliding her face against the side of his beast snout. "I want your life and your loyalty. Give me your promise, my sweet, and I'll give you the release you crave."

Her cool fingers wrapped around his hot, straining cock. Tenderly, almost lovingly, she slid her hand up and down along his length.

His knees trembling, his insides catching fire, he released a long, tortured groan, frantically pumping his hips into her hand.

"Is this what you want, beast?" she scoffed, flexing her fist around him. Tight. "One word, and you can have it all—"

The pressure spurred his arousal. It shot through him like a lightning, bringing on the long-denied orgasm instantaneously. Relief pumped from him in thick, creamy spurts.

"Ew!" Ghata jumped away from him, shaking her hand out. "Disgusting animal! You have no self-control whatsoever!"

"Madame?" Dez rushed to her from between the fabric partitions. "Did he hurt you?"

Dez slammed a heavy fist into Lero's face. His head rang with a bright flash of pain.

Ghata stopped the next blow with a gesture.

"Guh! I need to go wash my hands." She glared at Lero, her lips curved with disgust. "Apparently, he has even less self-restraint than any of you. Gross and pathetic!"

"I'm leaving tonight to get ready for the exhibition in London." Dez's voice reached him through the fog of the semi-consciousness he'd been suspended in for gods knew how long. By Dez's tone, dismissive but without the usual hatred, Lero assumed Dez wasn't talking to him. "You'll have to take care of this one for me while I'm gone."

A shove of Dez's boot against his shin rattled the chain of the manacle around his ankle.

"W-What is…this?" an unfamiliar female voice whispered shakily, so quietly he barely heard it. The woman sounded as if she hadn't used her voice often.

A female?

The blood in his veins heated anew. A ray of awareness made its way through the dark fog in his mind. His base instincts homed in on her.

With his face swollen from the most recent beating by Dez, he could barely open his eyes. When he managed to peer through the slits between his swollen eyelids, his vision proved too blurry to make out any details. All he could see were two indistinct shapes created by lights and shadows.

"This is one of Madame's VIP exhibits. He's been kept elsewhere. But now that the siren is gone, and the gorgonian is playing hard-to-get, Madame ordered this one to be brought here. Not that you need an explanation." Dez cut himself short. "Just do what I say until all of you have arrived in London, Amira. Then, I'll be taking over his care again. I love looking after him."

Another hard kick in his leg landed. The pain was easier to ignore this time as his awareness was entirely on the girl.

"Is it... Is it an animal?" she asked timidly. "He's standing upright, like a man..."

Apparently, that was all that remained of the man in him—his upright position in the frame, supported by cuffs and chains.

He drew some air through his nostrils, filtering her scent from the smell of metal, dust, and blood.

*A human.*

The female was without a doubt just a human. There was not a hint of magic in her scent. Filled with sweet femininity, it brought another woman to mind. The one whose blood he'd tasted—Stella.

That night in Paris, he had simply wanted to comfort a crying child. So, he'd licked her wound, reducing her pain.

A mating bond was not possible, even between different fae species, and he certainly didn't hope for a bond with a human. Yet meeting Stella as a grown woman proved unforgettable. Somewhere deep on a visceral level, he'd felt a pull toward her. A pull powerful enough to distract him from the scent of the female who was standing in front of him right now.

Instead, he tried to focus on her conversation with Dez.

"Feed him *only* the meat I showed you in the bucket in the kitchen trailer. Once a day, today and tomorrow. No food at all during the flight to London. His crate will be locked, anyway," Dez instructed. "Smear the spikes of his collar in the substance from this jar—thoroughly, you can't miss a single one. Very important. Got it? The full moon is tomorrow. We don't want him to cause any trouble for the rest of the guys who'll be finishing the packing. Do you understand?"

The woman didn't make a sound this time, but the shift of one of the blurry shapes in front of him might have meant she nodded.

"Here," Dez continued, "this is how to take his collar off. Put the noose around his snout first. Stay away from his teeth, they're dripping poison. If it gets on your skin, you'll die."

Dez's voice remained even and business-like as he coolly went over the steps of his cruel daily routine.

The woman's breathing sped up, however. She was frightened.

"Why me?" she whimpered, weakly. "Why don't you ask someone else to do it? Nerkan or Vuk?"

"Because if I ask a *brack* and he messes it up for any reason, Madame will order him whipped. If *you* mess up even a tiny little thing, she'd kill you. You know it as well as I do, Amira. She barely tolerates you lately, waiting for an excuse to end you. That gives you the best motivation to follow my instructions precisely."

# Chapter Six

LERO

A thick leather noose wrapped around his face, but there was no brutal force with which Dez would normally yank at it. Instead, a much gentler touch moved his head aside with a soft tug. The scent of the human woman told him it was she who tended to him today—Amira.

She removed the metal collar from his neck. The spikes tugged painfully at his skin before letting go.

Next came the sound of water before she pressed a cool, wet cloth to his skin, cleaning the puncture wounds around his neck. That was not part of the routine. In Dez's "care," Lero got hosed down only on the nights Ghata put him on display. No one had ever bothered to tend to his wounds before, although quite a few of the *bracks*, not just Dez, had come by to inflict some of them.

With Dez gone, however, there hadn't been any beatings today, allowing for the swelling to come down. He could open his eyes completely.

The woman was young, with pale skin and dark hair. Her lanky body was drowning in an oversized black hoodie and a pair of sweatpants. A wide, black scarf wound around her neck, concealing her chin.

She stared at him with large, haunted eyes, while turning the rusty, iron collar in her hands. A bucket of water, pink from his blood, stood nearby, a piece of cloth floating in it.

The moment their gazes crossed, the woman dropped hers to the floor. Holding his collar in one hand, she produced a plastic-wrapped package of meat from the pocket of her hooded sweatshirt.

He roared through the noose around his snout, lunging for the meat with uncontrollable hunger. The restraints threw him back. Her eyes open wide in fear, the female jerked and dropped the meat into the bucket of water.

"Amira!" Ghata shouted from somewhere outside the canvas walls of the room.

At the sound of her voice, Amira shook so much, she dropped his collar. It followed the meat, splashing into the bucket.

He hadn't eaten since last night. His insides twisted with ravenous hunger. However, with no *kibia* mushrooms for the past twenty-four hours, his mind had started to clear.

"Where is that girl when I need her?" Ghata yelled again.

Amira bent over, snatching his collar from the water, then jerkily yanked a jar with *womora* from her pocket.

Ghata appeared between two partitions of the striped canvas wall.

"How long am I supposed to yell for you? He needs a bath." She thrust a small pink animal toward the startled Amira.

With the jar in one hand and the collar in the other, the poor girl had no way to accept the animal, which was a two-headed *virleth* pig, Lero realized. The creature usually had three heads. He'd hunted plenty of them back in Nerifir. Never did he expect to see one in this world, however.

"Don't just stand there." Ghata stomped her foot. "Take him!"

Amira dropped the collar to the floor and shoved the jar with *womora* back in her pocket.

The pig twisted in Ghata's arms. One of its heads nipped at her elbow, making her yelp in pain and drop the animal.

The pig landed on its side with a piercing squeal. Scrambling to its hooves, it dashed to Amira and hid behind her legs.

"Get him, you useless human!" Ghata screamed. Yanking the beaded leather belt off her waist, she lashed at Amira, who ducked to pick up the pig.

Ghata furiously whipped the girl across her shoulder blades.

Amira only winced with a muffled groan and bit her lip. She took the next hit of the belt just as stoically, not uttering a word of complaint. Holding the pig in her arms, she cowered behind her elbow, protecting the animal and her face from Ghata's belt. It whipped around her elbow, the studded end lashing across her chin. A deep cut bloomed red on her pale skin, the welt quickly filling with blood.

Amira's eyes brimmed with tears, yet she remained quiet, wordlessly taking the abuse.

A *brack* Lero hadn't seen before barged in.

"What's going on here?" he demanded, as if he had any right to demand an explanation from Ghata.

Bald like the rest of them, this *brack* looked slightly different. A full beard covered the bottom part of his face. To Lero's knowledge, *bracks* lost their hair after swearing their lives to Ghata, including all facial and body hair, except for eyelashes and brows. How did this one manage to keep his voluminous, dark-brown beard?

Ghata whipped around to face him. Raising her free hand, she slapped him across his cheek in the same movement.

"This stray runt you've found will not live long enough to die of old age!" she raged. Tossing her belt at Amira, she spun on her heel and stormed out of the room.

Amira crouched on the floor, her arms around the pig, head drawn between her shoulders, and her face hidden in the wide folds of her scarf.

"Amira," the *brack* kneeled at her side. The warm note of concern in his voice caught Lero's ear as extremely unusual to hear from a *brack*. "Let me see."

He gently lifted her face out of her scarf. Blood dripped from the split skin on her chin. Her eyes closed, she sobbed quietly as he leaned in and licked the blood off.

"It'll be okay."

"No..." She shook her head with determination Lero hadn't witnessed in her yet. She freed her face from the *brack's* hands. "It won't be okay, Radax... Not if I stay here."

He caught her by the shoulders. "Amira, what are you saying?"

She cupped his chin with her hands. Her slim fingers disappeared into his beard. The pig squeaked in her lap.

"Tell me how to get to Nerifir, Radax," she said in a soft but resolute voice.

"What?" He shrank back, staring at her—his dark eyes opened as wide as hers.

"How do I open the portal? Please, I need to do it, Radax." Letting go of his face, she wrapped her arms around the *virleth* pig again.

"Why? To save the pig?" he mumbled, looking flabbergasted.

She gently placed her hand on the red spot blooming on the side of Radax's face where Ghata had slapped him.

"To save *you*." She sighed. "And myself. You've been like a family to me, Radax. I love you like a brother. She knows it, and she can't stand it. Can't you see she doesn't miss any opportunity to hurt you for my mistakes. I try so hard to please her, but I just can't do anything right by her. She hates me, and she won't rest until she kills me. She's hurting you too... I need to get away."

Radax slowly moved his head from side to side. When he spoke again, his voice was lower, subdued.

"I can't go to Nerifir, Amira. Even if I could, she'd pull me right back to her. I'm a *brack*. I'm tied to her for eternity."

"I know, Radax." She sighed again, so deeply her breath came out with a soft, sorrowful moan. "I know you can't leave her, but I can." She cautiously glanced over her shoulder at the narrow gap between the partitions, then proceeded in a hushed half-whisper, "If I'm no longer here to mess things up for you, you'll be safer, too. You can finally stop risking your life to protect mine. She nearly choked you to death when the siren escaped because of me. You had to give up your position as leader of the *bracks* to Trez in exchange for Madame keeping me alive. Can't you see? She's been using us against each other, punishing you for my mistakes. She hates you being attached to anyone but her. Neither of us will ever be safe unless I leave."

Had Zeph escaped? Did Lero hear her right?

She'd been speaking so softly, that the acute hearing of the beast was the only reason he'd heard her at all. Now he remembered Dez mentioning that the siren was gone, too.

His heart hammered against his ribs with excitement. If Zeph was free and safely away, he could endure anything Ghata and Dez threw at him.

Radax sat on the packed-dirt floor, dropping his massive shoulders.

"I can't watch over you in Nerifir, Amira. I can't go back and forth like the rest of the *bracks*. And even if I could, the *bracks* land in different times and locations in Nerifir, too. If you leave, I'll never see you again."

He stared at her intensely.

"I love you, Amira, like the daughter I never had or the sister I've lost. You are my only family in this world or any other. Please, let me take care of this. Let me find a safer place for you here, in this world. At least then, I'll be able to check on you now and then and make sure you're safe."

She shifted closer to him. Holding the pig to her with one arm, she took his hand in hers.

"I can't stay in the same world as *her*, Radax. You know she'll search for me, if just out of spite. And eventually, she'll find me."

"I'll divert her efforts. I've been doing it for the siren, too."

"And when she finds out you're hiding me from her, she'll do something even worse than murder. You know what she's capable of. Radax, please. I need to leave this world."

The *brack* stubbornly shook his head, gripping Amira's hand, as if anchoring her to himself.

"You don't know life outside of these tents, girl. Nerifir can be a dangerous place. You won't be safe on your own."

She dropped her gaze to her lap, where the *virleth* pig snuggled peacefully.

"I won't be alone," she said, barely audible.

"What do you mean?" Radax frowned. "*Who* will be with you?"

"The gorgonian. His name is Kyllen. He promised to come with me."

"The gorgonian? Amira!" the *brack* exclaimed, and she hushed him by frantically waving her hands at him. "Have you been talking to him? You know it's strictly forbidden."

"He'll die here, Radax. Madame ordered us to deny him water. He can't survive without it. She is killing him, slowly."

"The gorgonian is a fae. He's much more resilient than you realize. Madame needs him, she won't kill him. Gorgonians are extremely deadly. You can't be around him. I don't trust him to protect your life."

"If I don't leave, there'll soon be no life to protect." Amira exhaled a shuddering breath. The fight appeared to leave her with it. She sat with her shoulders down, looking deflated.

His muscles cramping, Lero shifted involuntarily, rattling his chains. The sounds startled both the *brack* and the woman. They stared at him, both obviously having forgotten about his presence. Or maybe they hadn't paid him much attention because they didn't care about an animal hearing their conversation.

"Are you done with him for tonight?" Radax jerked his chin at Lero.

Amira glanced at the bucket with Lero's dinner on the bottom, concealed by the bloodied water.

"Almost." She pressed her hand against the pocket with the jar of *womora* but didn't take the jar out.

Instead, she grabbed the spiked metal circle off the floor, then approached Lero.

"Are you going to bite me?" she whispered softly, raising the collar to his neck. "Do you want me dead, too?"

The noose remained around his snout, but Amira didn't tighten it and didn't use it to turn his face away. If he wanted to, he could probably shake the leather belt off, free his jaws, and...

The violent beast rose inside him, drawn out by the Moon. This close to the full moon, he needed *womora* to tame the aggression rising to the surface. The beast longed to burst free, to escape the stifling fabric walls and tear to shreds any living creature in his path to freedom.

Whatever was left of the man in him didn't want to see the girl hurt.

He closed his eyes, forcing his rage deeper while her light fingers secured the collar around his neck. Only the threatening rumble of a growl in his chest betrayed the feral bloodthirst that seethed inside him.

"Come." Radax tugged Amira away by her arm. "I'll think of something, but we shouldn't discuss anything with *him* around."

A calculating expression flickered in her dark eyes.

"He is just an animal, isn't he?" she asked, slowly.

"Amira." Radax shook his head. "You of all people should know that in Madame's establishment nothing is what it seems."

# Chapter Seven

LERO

Something sharp poked him in the arm. He opened his eyes to find Amira standing in front of him again.

Hadn't she just left with that *brack*, Radax?

Or had it been hours ago? A day ago? The concept of time had been hard to grasp.

He tried to focus.

It must be the day after she'd had that conversation with Radax. The full moon would be tonight, he could feel it approach. Amira hadn't given him any *womora* last night. Without it, he felt the Moon magic in his bones acutely. It pumped through his veins, making his blood boil. His mind was about to catch the fever of madness.

Soon, he'd have but two urges—kill and fuck. Everything else would move into the background and stay there until the sunrise.

He sucked in the air, rich with feminine scent. Bloodthirst and lust shot through his system like an electric charge, swelling hot between his legs and pounding hard inside his skull.

*Want.*

*Need.*

*Her flesh.*

It had started already.

In addition to the Moon wreaking havoc in his mind, the lingering poison of the *kibia* mushrooms Dez had fed him for too long, weakened and hurt his body.

Oblivious to the storm raging inside him, the girl calmly lifted her hand, holding up a crown—a high diadem. The black and white spikes arranged in the intricate aged-gold setting of the crown must be what she'd poked him with.

"The black thorns in this crown are werewolves' claws," she said, her voice ringing in his ears, echoing inside his head like in a church bell. "The white ones are their teeth. Both are just like yours." She gave him a penetrating stare before leaning just a little closer and lowering her voice to almost a whisper. "You're a werewolf, aren't you? From Nerifir?"

Her image floated in a red haze that clouded his vision. His focus narrowed to the scarf around her neck. The neck he'd bite first...

*Want!*

The word vibrated up his throat and exploded into a roar. He yanked at the restraints lunging at her.

Startled, the woman cowered, jumping away from him.

*No! Closer!*

He roared again. The distance she'd put between them diluted her scent, reducing his madness.

"Can you speak?" she asked softly, desperation shining in the hopeless darkness of her eyes. "Here." She dropped the crown to the dirt floor and yanked two objects from her pockets. One he recognized as the jar of *womora*, the other, a large chunk of meat wrapped in a piece of foil.

"Dez said to give you both daily until we leave tomorrow. I've given you neither because I don't know what they'll do to you. Which one will help you speak, now?"

She held both objects up, one in each hand.

The wild hunger for the bloodied meat made him jerk that way.

"The meat?" She gave it a suspicious look and warned, "Dez laced it with something, a yellow powder. Are you sure that's what you want?"

*Want!*

The beast craved blood. Hunger ravaged his insides. He'd had no food last night. And even when he had been fed here at the freakshow, it had never been enough.

"Will it make you able to talk to me?" she demanded in a quiet but firm voice.

The *kibia* mushroom powder in the meat would deprive him of any coherent thought. Without the *womora* on the collar spikes, the mushrooms would aid the Moon in turning him into the beast faster and completely.

The girl wanted to communicate with him. Maybe she could tell him more about Zeph?

*Zeph!*

He needed to hear what she had to say.

Calling on whatever reason of a man he still possessed, he tore his gaze from the meat and directed it at the jar in her other hand.

"Will this help you speak?" She raised the jar slightly.

He released another roar, making an effort to soften it to a groan.

She nodded, quickly shoving the meat package back into her pocket. When she came closer with the open jar in her hand, his control cracked. The beast lashed out. He growled, snapping his teeth at her.

She jumped back again, clutching the jar in her trembling fingers.

"This needs to get into your bloodstream, under your skin," she muttered. "But I'm not coming anywhere near your teeth again." She slid her gaze down his body. "It should work here, too, right?"

She approached his left hand that was chained to the metal frame. The iron cuffs had rubbed through his skin when he'd thrashed against them during the fits of madness and the beatings by Dez. The Nerifir iron prevented the wounds from healing. The sores remained permanently open under the metal cuffs coated in rusty layers of blood.

Amira dipped a finger into the jar and spread the honey-like substance around his wrist under the iron cuff.

"Sorry if it hurts," she said softly.

The initial contact of the *womora* syrup burned. He jerked against his restraints with a deep snarl. A cooling sensation quickly replaced the burn. It spread from his mangled wrist, up his arm, calm settling in his chest.

He groaned, leaning his head back against the frame that held him prisoner.

"Better?" Amira whispered.

She carefully stepped around him to his right side and spread the *womora* substance in a thin layer around his right wrist, too. Dropping to her knees, she also applied the *womora* to his ankles under the manacles.

He breathed deeply, focusing on the cooling sensation that spread through his body and soothed the heat of Moon Madness.

Amira stepped back, watching him with wide-open eyes.

"You... You're changing," she breathed out in awe.

He must be, as *womora* combated the effects of *kibia* mushrooms. The spikes of his collar slipped out of his flesh as his neck shrank closer to the shape of a man's, losing the bulge of the furry scruff on the back.

"Thank you," he exhaled in a croak.

"You can speak!" Amira hurried closer. "And you look more like a person, now."

Sliding down his body, her gaze reached his crotch. She quickly diverted her eyes, a blush spreading up her pale cheeks. With the fur gone, his private area became exposed. At least he sensed his erection subsiding, now. Her scent no longer drove him crazy.

The generous amount of *womora* she'd spread on his arms and legs made him feel almost himself again. At least until sunset.

Something clanked deep in the tent somewhere, making Amira freeze, horror floating in her dark eyes.

"They're packing up to move," she whispered, her hot breath hitting his bare chest as she leaned closer to him in fear. "They'll be here soon to put you in the crate. We need to hurry. Quick, tell me how to open a portal to Nerifir."

He recalled her conversation with Radax. Despite the *brack's* pleas and assurances, the woman obviously hadn't changed her mind about leaving. After having witnessed the way she'd been treated here, he couldn't blame her.

"You don't *open* a portal," he rasped, clearing his throat. "You *find* one."

The River of Mists flowed between the worlds. Its stream brushed their borders, breaking into the realms and connecting them all.

An expression of deep satisfaction spread across her face.

"I knew you'd know. You weren't abducted straight from Nerifir, were you? How do I find a portal, then?" she demanded.

"The one I came through is near Paris, France. It's the only one I know."

There were more, he just wasn't aware of the exact locations of the others. Scattered throughout the worlds—the innocuous, misty patches of air—the portals tended to show up over a body of water late at night or early in the morning. There was nothing particular or spectacular about their appearance. If spotted, humans wouldn't think twice about them.

"Listen," he said. "I'll tell you everything I know about it, but you'll need to answer some of my questions, too. Deal?"

She chewed on her bottom lip, contemplating his words. Whether she knew anything about the perils of making deals with a fae or not, she proved smart enough to think it through carefully.

He had no plans to trap her, though. All he needed was information and a moment or two of clear mind to process it.

"I'll set you free if you take me to the portal," she counter-offered.

*Free.*

That was so much more than he'd hoped to get out of her tonight. Now that it was on the table, the anticipation of freedom tingled under his skin, lighting a flicker of hope in his chest.

"How would you free me?" He needed to know she could deliver on her promise before he let the hope grow.

"The key that opens your collar is the same that opens the locks on your restraints. I overheard Dez telling the others to shoot you in the head with a human-made gun before moving you into the crate. They worry you'll cause trouble when they try to shove you in. A bullet from this world won't kill you, but it'll make you pass out long enough for them to pack you in. And it'd hurt." She gazed at him, a flash of compassion in her eyes.

Dez had said something about moving. To London?

"Where is Gha...Madame going?"

"To Europe. She has shows booked there. England first, then France. If you say the portal is near Paris, I can pack you into the crate now, with your help of course, so they won't have to shoot you. Dez is in London already. He went ahead with some other *bracks* to get the new venue ready." She rubbed her cheek in thought. "He'll take the key away from me when we get there. I'll have to find a way to release you as soon as we land, while I still have the key."

"No." Now that freedom was so close, he couldn't spend another minute in the restraints—not to mention hours in a crate—and risk getting back into Dez's cruel hands. Besides, Stella was on *this* continent. If he escaped, Ghata would most certainly send the *bracks* after her again. He had to stay here to protect her. "Let me go now. I'll tell you exactly how to find the portal. I'll also tell you the rules of traveling through one."

"There are rules?" She shot him a concerned look.

He nodded.

"Rule number one," he started, impatient to nudge her into action of getting the cuffs off him. "Once you cross over, you will never be able to come back to this world again—not to this time or place, anyway. If you try to cross back to Earth, you may end up a month in the past or a thousand years into the future. There is no way to predict with any certainty."

She drew in a shaking breath. "That's what he said, too."

"Who? Radax?" he asked. "Or the gorgonian?"

He remembered Amira speaking of a captured gorgonian whom Madame tormented by denying him water. Gorgonians lived in the Lorsan Wetlands of Nerifir, far from the werewolves' Plains of Sarnala. Ghata had been expanding her reach, it seemed.

"Never mind *who* said it," Amira dismissed quickly.

"It does matter if you're planning to take him along to Nerifir," he insisted. "Your travel companion has everything to do with rule number two."

"What is rule number two?" She frowned.

"I need you to answer *my* questions first."

Faint sounds of shuffling and packing came through the canvas walls. The *bracks* were nearby. He needed to get more from her since they could be interrupted any minute.

"We don't have much time," he reminded her.

"Fine. What do you want to know?"

"You said something about a siren before?" he started carefully.

"Zeph?"

"Was that his name?"

She shrugged. "That's what the girl who escaped with him called him."

"What girl?"

"She never told me her name. I never asked, either. Names mean friends. It's best not to make friends in Madame Tan's menagerie." She pressed her lips together.

The name didn't matter to him right now, anyway.

"How long was Zeph here?"

Amira cast a sideway glance at him, more curious than suspicious.

"For over a year, I believe. But he is no longer here. He escaped in November."

*Escaped.*

The confirmation flooded him with relief.

"What month is it now?"

"January. The twenty-second," she said, then added the year.

His heart nearly dropped into his stomach when he realized he'd spent sixteen months as Ghata's captive—almost exactly as long as Zeph had. Zeph had been taken about three months before him and escaped two months ago, just before he got this chance to do the same.

He barely remembered anything of the time he'd spent in captivity, and what memories he did have, he wished weren't there.

"Has Madame been searching for Zeph, do you know? Does she want to find him and bring him back?" he asked Amira.

"She tried, but he killed a whole bunch of her *bracks*. Radax is in charge of looking for him now."

*"I'll divert her efforts. I've been doing it for the siren, too."* Radax's words from earlier came to mind.

"And Radax is not that enthusiastic in his efforts, is he?" he guessed.

"No. He made a deal with the siren." Her eyes narrowed, and she brought a finger to his face in warning. "But you cannot say anything about that to the *bracks* or to Madame, do you understand?"

"I'm not exactly on speaking terms with either of them," he deadpanned.

"I mean it." She shook her finger menacingly. "Not a word."

"Promise," he vowed. "I won't say anything to either *bracks* or Madame about Radax's deal with Zeph."

The mere idea of a *brack* making any agreements on his own, behind Ghata's back and against her orders, felt absurd. Radax didn't appear to be an ordinary *brack*, though. Lero wanted to question Amira about that, but time was precious, and he had more pressing matters to resolve. *Womora* had provided only temporary relief. Between the Moon and the leftover mushroom poison in his blood, racking his body with pain, he could barely think straight as it was.

"What other fae does she keep here? Other than the gorgonian?"

"Um... I don't think there are more," she replied uncertainly.

"They may be kept in different forms, but they would be male," he explained.

To his knowledge, there hadn't been any other fae in this world before. With the gorgonian being here now, Ghata must have started kidnapping fae directly from Nerifir. She wouldn't risk returning there herself, which meant she was using *bracks* to do it for her.

*Bracks* always returned to Ghata when crossing the River of Mists. The fae they acquired in Nerifir, however, risked ending up elsewhere unless Ghata used her power to pull them through the mists to her too, helping the *bracks* haul their victims to her. Her female energy would make it much easier to drag male captives through.

Though, that didn't mean that the *bracks* couldn't take human women from this world over to Nerifir. He wouldn't put it past Ghata to resort to trading women from this world for magical goods from Nerifir.

"What do you know about Madame's trade to supply her menagerie, Amira?"

She shook her head.

"Not much. She doesn't talk to me about her business."

He recalled Ghata had mentioned gargoyles and sky fae when he first got into her clutches. "Are there any winged creatures in this establishment?"

Amira nodded. "Many, from the bird-snakes to—"

"Bigger than a bird-snake. My size," he urged.

"Only if you count the statue. The dragon-man..." Her voice trailed off as understanding spread across her face. "He's not just a statue, is he?"

"Nothing is what it seems," he repeated Radax's words.

If Ghata held other fae prisoners, they would have to be released, too. He had to set them free—a rather ambitious idea, since he was still locked in restraints.

"Can you unlock my manacles now, please?" he asked her, keeping his voice low as the noise of the *bracks'* tearing down the tents and packing had moved closer. "I'll have to escape before they get here."

She produced the key from her pocket but held it tightly in her hand, not making a move to unlock anything. "You haven't told me how to get to the portal yet. What is rule number two?"

"Right." His bones ached harder. Sunset must be getting closer. "On your own, you can only cross back to the world where you came from. To travel to Nerifir, you'll need a fae or a *brack* to accompany you, someone native to that world."

She nodded in visible concentration. "I'll have Kyllen with me. I'm not leaving him here."

If Amira freed the gorgonian, it would make his task of liberating the rest that much easier. He'd only have to worry about the gargoyle. Once he was free himself, of course.

"Where does Madame keep the 'dragon-man?'" he asked as she removed his collar.

"He's already been shipped to London, along with other heavy objects. It's just the tents, some equipment, and the live animals here now."

A loud noise of something heavy being dropped startled them both into silence. The noise was followed by *bracks* yelling.

"Amira, please hurry," he pleaded, urgently rattling at his chains. "I'll talk as you unlock."

"Okay," she conceded, dropping to her knees to release his legs.

"Listen carefully," he started. "Once you make it to Paris, take the train to *Parc des Brouillards*, just outside of the city. It's private property, so be careful when getting in." He winced, recalling the guards chasing Ghata, Zeph, and him across the park's lawns when the three of them had first arrived. That had been their first introduction to this world. "The portal only opens for about twenty minutes at three o'clock each morning. It's a small cloud of mist over the water of the pond, at the back of the park."

"Is it there every day?" She unlocked his arms next.

He stumbled away from the frame, the poison of the mushrooms making him dizzy.

"The portal *should* be there every day." He staggered back, grabbing the side rail of the frame to steady himself. "The flow of the River of Mists changes, but very slowly. It's been over forty years since I was last in *Parc des Brouillards*, but it would take centuries if not millennia for the River of Mists to alter its course enough for a portal to disappear."

She paused for a moment, giving him a penetrating look.

"How do you know all of this?"

"Let's just say I spent some time with a goddess when she used to be a more benevolent creature, inclined to share things with me." He sighed in regret. There had been a time when he genuinely cared about Ghata and wished her well. Now, it felt like he'd lost an ally in her for good and gained a foe instead—a cruel and powerful one.

The Moon magic twisted painfully inside him, reminding him who was in charge tonight. He stifled a groan.

"Be careful when crossing to Nerifir, Amira," he warned. "There is danger and hostility in that world, too, maybe even more than in this one."

Her chest rose with a long sigh under the voluminous hoodie.

"I don't really have a choice. I can't stay here. Madame holds my life over Radax's head, forcing him to do things he doesn't always want to do."

It was a statement worth pondering. Amira obviously had no idea how incredible her connection with a *brack* was.

He had no time to linger much longer, but he had to know.

"Why is Radax not like the rest of them?"

She bit her lip, sliding her gaze aside.

"Madame blames me for that. Radax found me when I was little and saved my life. He says I remind him of his sister who died young. Madame says he is...damaged, and she doesn't let him go to Nerifir anymore." Tears glistened in her eyes, and she wiped at them with a sleeve of her hoodie. "Radax's life will be so much easier without me. He can't escape her, but he won't have to worry about me anymore."

His heart ached for this girl who'd been through so much yet still cared for a *brack*—the last person who needed her tears, in his opinion.

"Amira, I wish I could come with you to help you get to the portal, but I can't. The minute my escape is discovered, Madame will send *bracks* to hurt an innocent woman simply because they believe I care about her. I need to make sure she's safe."

He would do nothing more than that, he vowed to himself. Stella needed to get out of Ghata's reach for a few days after the goddess discovered his escape. Once it was safe for Stella to go back, he fully intended to let her be. He would cause no disruption to Stella's peaceful life. He merely wanted to ensure her safety.

"I see." She nodded in understanding, obviously familiar with Ghata's ways. "I'll have to manage on my own, then."

He stepped closer and placed his hands on her shoulders. She flinched but didn't move away.

"Stay with the menagerie until you get to Paris," he instructed, wishing to help this brave, timid woman with all his heart. "I've sold all of my properties there but one."

He gave her the address of the last townhouse he'd lived in before Zeph was taken. He couldn't part with that one. It was his last connection to the city where he'd seen Zeph last.

"In the main bedroom, under a loose floorboard under the bed, I have a safe box with some money. Remember the lock code." He slowly said the string of letters and numbers in the correct order to open the built-in safe, then made her repeat it. "Take as much as you think you'll need—all of it if you have to."

"You keep money under your bed?"

Seeing her innocent confusion made him smile for the first time since the night he was trapped and ended up at Dez's mercy.

"I keep money in a lot of places. In this world, money is more important than magic. But one can never know for sure when and where it may be needed."

"Thank you," she said with genuine gratitude. "You know, I can buy you some time to get to that woman."

"How?"

She ran to one of the canvas walls.

"Come here," she said, swinging a fabric partition aside to reveal a large wooden crate. "Help me load your metal frame in here."

"Why?" he asked, but did as she said.

His knees shook, and his fingers trembled when he lifted the massive frame. Normally, his inhuman strength would make the task easy, but the long captivity and the poison coursing through his body had weakened him. Thankfully, the approaching full moon gave him enough strength to drag the frame to the crate and shove it in.

"I'll throw some of these in here, too." Amira started grabbing the sandbags piled up behind the crate and dragging them into the crate. "To make up for your weight."

When the frame and a few bags were in, she lowered the crate's lid back into place, closing it.

"I'll hammer a few nails in it when you're gone," she explained. "And I'll tell them you've been loaded."

"Will they believe you managed it all on your own?"

If this was discovered, Amira would be punished severely. He hated to think what Ghata would do to her.

"Nerkan is with the group of *bracks* loading the animals in the truck outside of the main tent, and Vuk is with those who are breaking down the tents from the inside." She gestured toward the noise of shuffling feet, rustling of fabric, and clinking of support posts that had been steadily getting closer. "I'll tell Vuk that Nerkan helped me to load you. Then I'll tell Nerkan that Vuk did it. Both are too lazy to break into the crate to check. They'll just be happy to know that it's done, and they won't have to load you themselves."

She appeared to know well those she'd been living with side by side. Both the *bracks* and Madame definitely underestimated this pale, skinny woman.

"Thank you for thinking of that."

"It'll buy you some time." She shrugged awkwardly. "They aren't planning to feed you during the flight. With any luck, no one will know you're gone until the rest of us are in London."

"You'll get in trouble whenever it happens," he warned.

"Well." She heaved a breath. "I may just have to run away before the menagerie moves to Paris. Which wouldn't be that bad, trust me. The sooner I get out of this place, the better."

The sound of voices and feet shuffling appeared to be coming from right behind the next partition, now.

"Come," Amira whispered, creeping away from the noise along the canvas wall. "They'll be coming here next."

She slipped under a fabric flap, gesturing for him to follow. He snuck into the narrow, dusty place after her. The strings of lights high under the ceiling of the massive tent struggled to illuminate the space, separated by several rooms and walls from the center.

He concentrated on not losing sight of the small figure in the baggy sweatshirt as she led the way through the maze of fabric walls and narrow passages.

"Here." She yanked up one of the canvas walls. Fresh air rushed in, chilling his legs and cooling the wounds on his ankles. "There are no *bracks* or people on this side right now. The fair ended today. It wasn't that busy to begin with, I've heard. You'll need to climb over the chain-link fence to get out of the fairgrounds."

"Where are we right now?"

She told him the name of a small town he knew he'd forget soon enough. It didn't matter, anyway. What mattered was that it was only about a hundred miles north of Miami and Stella. In the beast form he was about to take, he'd be able to cover that distance in a single night. Which meant he had just enough time to get to Stella before the crate arrived in London and his escape was discovered.

"Well, goodbye, Amira." He gently touched the hand holding up the canvas for him. "Thank you for everything. Good luck and may you find your happiness in Nerifir."

"Good luck to you too." She hesitated for a fraction of a moment before asking, "What's your name?"

Names meant friends, as she'd said earlier.

"Lero." He smiled.

"Be careful out there, Lero," she said softly.

He crouched by the opening that led outside.

"Um... Do you need any clothes?" she asked tentatively, and he could almost feel her gaze on his bare ass.

"No." He chuckled, slipping under the canvas. "I'll have lots of fur to keep me warm, soon."

The fresh air of freedom licked his skin when he crawled out of the stuffy tent that had been his jail.

It was almost dark already. The muddy yellow of the streetlights along the chain-link fence aided the deep red of the dying sunset. The power of the rising Moon flooded his veins, filling his body with the strength he needed.

He scaled the fence and ran across a dirt road to a field beyond it. The night was fresh. The ground under his feet felt cool. Coarse dry grass cut his feet as he ran across the field, but he hardly noticed.

As every trace of daylight vanished, moonlight illuminated his way. He felt it in his bloodstream, coursing through his veins and pumping his muscles with strength and speed. His bones screamed in pain, twisting out of shape.

He surrendered to the power of the Moon, letting his body take the form it longed to be in.

Rage, lust, bloodthirst, and pain filled him. He used all of them to run faster, heading south. To her.

# Chapter Eight

STELLA

I shut the door of my car but lingered near it. The key fob clutched in my hand, I wasn't pressing the button to lock the doors yet. Sweeping my gaze over the vast space of the underground garage, I didn't know exactly what I searched for when I strained my eyes. A flash of black fur? A red spark of the net? A glimpse of a bald head or a muscled, tattooed arm?

It'd been well over a year since I'd witnessed the wild animal being captured here—sixteen months, to be exact. Nothing scary or unexplained had happened since. Yet every time I parked, the eerie feeling of unease filled me. My skin would prickle with warning, and my breathing would speed up.

A man in a business suit parked in a row ahead of me. I locked my car and hurried to join him on his way to the elevator. He smiled, hitting the button, and I nodded in greeting when getting in the elevator with him, glad not to be alone.

During the months since that night, I'd tried to get an explanation for what had happened. I'd even filed a police report, hoping to get some information that way.

The men who'd captured the beast hadn't wanted to be seen—probably because what they did wasn't legal. If they ran an illegal rare animal trade, they needed to be stopped. The cruel way they'd treated the beast brought tears to my eyes and filled my heart with anger every time I thought about it.

As Dez had predicted, however, no one had believed me. The police officer I'd spoken to had listened with interest at first. When I'd come to the description of the fantastic beast, his expression had grown skeptical. He'd quickly ushered me out of his office and hadn't provided me with any updates since, no matter how many times I'd called.

There was no evidence to back my words. For some unexplained reason, the security cameras in my building had no footage of the incident.

With time, I started believing the whole thing might be a figment of my imagination. The one lasting effect of that night was an uncontrollable fear whenever I was in the garage on my own.

Safely back in my condo, I ate a dinner of cereal and avocado toast, then went to bed. Lying on my back, I watched the lights and shadows dance on the ceiling as the curtains on the open door of my tiny balcony moved in the night breeze.

Over the past year, the memories of the incident in the garage had faded. The nightmares rarely came now. Instead of worrying about the beast while falling asleep, I thought about Lero once again.

The memories of him were always there—sometimes more vivid, other times just a faint echo of themselves. Nothing could get him out of my head for good, though.

I knew he had closed the deal on Blue Cay within days after the viewing. My agency couldn't provide me any updates on him after that, of course. We didn't stalk our clients, no matter how much some of us—me—might wish to do so. Unless Lero decided to buy or sell another property, I wouldn't hear anything about him ever again.

Instead of allowing me to move on, the idea of never seeing Lero again troubled me.

I tossed and turned as the pale disk of the moon gazed at me through the balcony doors, the cool, blue moonlight drowned out by the warm yellow of the streetlights.

After the stress of a busy day, if I allowed myself to revel in the memories of Lero at night, it relaxed me. He'd been my safe place for so long. I loved to recall his image during those few moments of semi-consciousness just before drifting asleep. After our last meeting, I'd had some fresh memories to relive.

Closing my eyes, I remembered the sensation of his strong hands on my waist when he helped me off the plane; the image of his face, breath-takingly handsome but always with a frown; his intense gray eyes offering but a glimpse into his stormy mind.

Thinking about him, I fell asleep smiling.

I wasn't sure if I ended up dreaming about him that night. A loud thud on the balcony snapped me out of sleep just before sunrise.

The sky had brightened along the horizon, with just a sliver of the sun peeking out. It was way too early to get up.

My unit was located on the third floor, high enough from the ground for me to feel safe, even while sleeping with the balcony doors cracked open to let in some fresh air. The sound, however, appeared to have been made by something large enough to be scary.

Sleep flew away.

I grabbed the first thing I could find that would serve as a weapon—a shoe. The convenience of living in a tiny condo unit meant that everything was just a step away, including my closet. The shoe had a stiletto heel—hard and sharp.

Stealing along the wall toward the balcony door, I also grabbed my cell phone off the shelf that served as my night table.

The shoe in my right hand, my left thumb hovering over the emergency call button of the phone, I tiptoed closer to the door.

Something large crouched on the balcony's floor. It growled and grunted as I came closer. Dropping the shoe, I leaped to the door to close it. I'd worry about figuring out what the hell that thing was once I was safely behind the locked door.

"Stella..." came from the balcony in a low, strangled voice.

It knew my name? How did this thing...

A person!

It wasn't a thing, but a man.

He rose to his feet, unsteadily holding on to the door frame. The pale light of the rising sun washed over him in waves of blush and gold. His face came into view, framed by a long, shaggy mane and a full beard. Despite the unkempt appearance, I recognized his silver-gray eyes right away. I could never mistake them for anyone else's.

"Lero?" I exhaled his name, pressing my hands to my chest to calm my thundering heart.

The man of my dreams had literally just dropped onto my balcony. Or was I still dreaming?

"I didn't mean to scare you," he croaked. Swaying in the doorway, he gripped the frame with both hands.

The details of his condition finally registered with me.

Lero was naked. Completely. Not a thread of clothing on his body. His hair was much longer than I'd ever seen on him. Tangled and matted, it fell past his shoulders. He sported a full beard, also wild and unkempt. I'd only ever seen him elegantly dressed and impeccably well-groomed before. It was a miracle I'd recognized him at all.

Deep circular wounds marred his ankles and wrists. Dirt and scratches covered his legs and arms. And... were those half-healed puncture wounds at the base of his neck?

He stumbled on his feet, with a groan and a full-body shudder.

It snapped me out of my shocked stupor.

"God... Lero, are you okay?" I rushed to him and grabbed his arm in an attempt to steady him. "What happened to you?"

I glanced over the railing of the balcony, searching for anything out-of-the-ordinary. All seemed normal for this early in the morning—the courtyard of my building was still deserted.

With another soft groan, Lero let go of the doorframe and dragged a hand over his face, leaning heavily on me.

"You... You can't stay here," he muttered.

"Right. Let's get inside." I led him into my unit.

My bed was directly in front of the balcony entrance. My place wasn't big enough to space the furniture out much.

Lero tripped over his feet, and I let him sink onto my bed. I gave him a long once-over, noting all the wounds and scratches, as well as his pale skin, chapped lips, and the deep shadows under his eyes. My heart ached at the sight of him. Whatever had brought him to this state couldn't have been good.

"You're hurt. I'll call an ambulance." I lifted the phone in my hand.

"No," he rasped, heaving himself up on an elbow. "No ambulance."

He reached for my phone. The wound around his wrist was raw in the middle, its edges ragged and in various stages of healing. An identical wound on his other wrist made me believe he'd had his hands tied long enough to create the wounds and keep them from healing.

"Who did this to you?" I whispered in horror.

"My brother." He winced.

Lero had a brother? What kind of a man was he to treat a person—his own family—like that?

"We need to call the police, not just an ambulance." My voice came out hollow and sharp.

"No phone calls, please." He shook his head resolutely.

"Why not?"

What was he afraid of?

Unless he was a criminal, too. What did I really know about this man? Other than he licked little girls' legs and bought multi-million-dollar islands in the Bahamas? Both of which fell well in line with criminal behavior.

I clutched my phone tighter in my hand, unable to tear my gaze away from the man who was clearly suffering right now. Maybe he was a criminal, but if I had a choice between the police and an ambulance, I'd still go with the ambulance first.

"Lero—" I sat gingerly on the edge of the bed next to him.

"Stella, please listen to me," he rushed out, interrupting me. "It's very important. Someone will be coming for you shortly."

"What?" I either didn't hear him right or he was in so much pain, he was getting delusional.

Why would anyone want anything to do with *me*? However, his solemn expression and the serious voice triggered an alarm in me, raising the fine hairs on my arms.

"Who?" I shot a cautious glance toward the balcony.

"It doesn't matter *who* right now." He swallowed with an effort then licked his dry lips. "What's important is—"

"Is it the same people who did this to you?" I gestured at his wrist. "Your brother?"

Fear vibrated through me, now. Though, I still had no idea why anyone would be after me.

He let his head drop back on my pillow.

"Yes."

I leaned over him, crawling closer. "Why? How do they know about me?"

His chest rose with a sigh. "They've seen you with me. When we went to the island."

"Oh... Lero. That was a long time ago."

He stared at the ceiling. "Time doesn't matter to them."

I ran a hand over my face. Where would I go? What could I do? This couldn't be real.

"What do they want with me?" I asked through the hand over my mouth.

"To get to me," he said, trying to rise on his elbows again to look at me. "They've already come for you once and got me, instead. They'll do it again."

What was he saying? That I'd been hunted, and I didn't even know it?

"Why?"

"Because they think I care about you. That if they take you, I'll come for you."

*They think.*

Didn't mean it was true. Or was it? Did Lero care about me? Well, he did care enough to come here to warn me about the danger, at least. The danger that threatened me because of him. What had I gotten myself into without even realizing it?

And why would they hunt him to begin with?

I rubbed my forehead. All of it was extremely overwhelming.

"I have so many questions," I muttered.

"But there's no time for answers. You need to get to Blue Cay, right now." He closed his eyes tight, frowning in concentration. "In the main house, in the master's closet, there is a security system panel. You'll have to engage it when you get in. Make sure to arm both the house and the island."

"You want me to go to your island? Alone? What about you?"

"I—" He tried to sit up. His arms shook with strain, and he dropped back to the pillow. "I don't think I can manage it right now. The sun is up, and I'm exhausted." He closed his eyes. "Go. I'll be there as soon as I can."

A grimace of pain distorted his handsome features. I couldn't stand watching him suffer. Rushing to the kitchenette, I filled a glass with water.

"Here. Drink this, Lero." I held up his head, helping him drink. "We'll go to the island together. Okay? Once you've rested and recovered. Then, you'll tell me everything that's going on."

"No. You need to go, now." He fell back on the mattress and mumbled, "They're flying to London this morning. By evening, they'll know I'm gone, if they don't know already. There's no time..."

With a long, pained groan, he rolled to his side, clutching his middle with both arms and drawing his legs up to his belly.

"Lero? Please... You're hurting." I grabbed his shoulder. All my questions and doubts moved to the background. Right now, I just wished to ease his suffering in any way he would let me.

"The *kibia* mushrooms..." he gritted through his clenched teeth. "He fed them to me for too long. It'll take a while to wear off..."

What on earth was he talking about?

"I can't leave you here like this."

"Go..." he ordered, not moving.

"Lero," I pleaded, but he no longer responded at all. I shook his shoulder, then shook it again, harder. He remained motionless.

Whatever had been done to him, most certainly had been done over a course of time. The man lying on my bed right now looked nothing like the Lero I knew before. He looked like he'd been kept in a cage for months. Dread chilled my spine at the thought—maybe he had.

If I left him and ran, he'd be completely alone—weak and defenseless in his current state. The cruel people he was talking about would easily get him again.

"I'm not leaving you," I said with determination.

However, I respected his wish not to call the police, not until I learned more about his reasons for avoiding going to the authorities in the first place.

Picking up the phone, I dialed the number of the building's lobby, instead.

"Hello."

Hope filled my heart when I heard the voice of the doorman on shift. Chris and I were on good terms.

"Morning, Chris. It's Stella. Listen, I need a small favor. My, um... cousin had a bit too much to drink last night. If he doesn't make it home right away, his wife will totally kill us both. I'll drive him home, but he is, kind of, a bit...well, passed out." I winced, cursing my inability to come up with a better story on such a short notice. "Would you mind bringing one of the wheelchairs you guys keep on hand for accessibility?"

The building management's memo clearly stated the wheelchairs were provided upon request to assist elderly people and those with health concerns and mobility issues. They were definitely not there to transport passed-out drunk cousins, but Chris was a nice, understanding guy. He and I often chatted outside while he was on a smoke break, and I waited for a friend or a client to take to a viewing.

I released a breath in relief when he cheerfully replied, "Sure. Just give me a minute."

*A minute* suddenly seemed way too short as I dashed around my place, trying to pack. How long was I leaving for? When would I come back, if ever? I was supposed to be at work in a few hours. Should I call Javier? What would I even tell him?

Instead of Javier, I dialed the phone number of the charter company. The mention of Javier's name helped me arrange the flight to Blue Cay on hardly any notice at all.

Lero remained in bed, motionless and uncommunicative. I checked his pulse and breathing to make sure he was still alive. His heart beat wildly, but he didn't speak. He wouldn't even open his eyes anymore.

Yanking off the oversized t-shirt I'd been wearing to bed, I slid it on him. This was probably the only piece of my clothing that'd fit him. Well, maybe also my bathrobe.

I got into a pair of jeans and a long-sleeved shirt. The early-morning weather was chilly this time of year, even for someone like me who was born and raised in New York. Then, I grabbed my white bathrobe from the bathroom.

The doorbell rang as soon as I'd gotten the bathrobe on Lero's uncooperative, limp body.

Chris stood in the doorway when I opened it—a wheelchair in front of him and a bright smile on his well-tanned face.

"Oh, thank you so much!" I gushed, forcing a smile in reply.

"Do you need any help with this?" He gestured at the wheelchair.

My instinct was to decline and send Chris away before he spotted the abused, half-naked man on my bed. Logic told me, however, there was no way I'd be able to lift Lero's tall, muscular body on my own.

"Oh, that would be fantastic, if you don't mind." I opened the door wider, allowing Chris to roll the wheelchair in.

"He's right here," I said cheerfully, trying to act like my biggest worry in the world was getting my drunk cousin home to his wife, not being pursued by someone who were into imprisoning and torturing people.

I quickly threw a sheet over Lero, in addition to the clothes I'd managed to put on him, then drew the hood of the robe over his sunken face smeared with dirt and dried blood.

"Is he okay?" Chris maneuvered the wheelchair to the bed.

"Oh, he's fine!" I waved my hand, with a nervous giggle. "He just can't hold his liquor. He was at some crazy costume party last night." I desperately hoped that would explain Lero's current outfit of a t-shirt, a bathrobe, and a bed sheet. "He stopped by my place for just one more drink this morning. Not that he needed any more, obviously."

Chris looked doubtful, and my heart sank in fear that he might demand further explanation or make me call the police after all.

"I've already called his wife," I added, hurriedly. "She's furious. Poor guy is going to have a hell of a hangover. But first, I need to get him home ASAP. Otherwise, I'm afraid she'll divorce his ass."

I kept blabbering nonsense, hoping that my chattering would distract Chris from any logical thoughts he might be having right now.

“Shall we move him, then?” I grabbed hold of Lero’s legs wrapped in the bed sheet.

“Right...” Hooking his hands under Lero’s arms, Chris tentatively lifted his torso off the bed.

Lero groaned, rolling his head to his shoulder, the bathrobe hood and his beard thankfully concealing most of his face. The groan was a sign of life. It proved to Chris I wasn’t trying to get rid of a dead body, at least. I tried to calm my nerves.

“Dude, are you okay?” Chris asked Lero after we’d placed him in the wheelchair the best we could.

I grabbed the duffel bag with my things.

Lero groaned again.

“Fucking *kibia* mushrooms...” came from under his hood.

“Mushrooms?” Chris gave me a knowing grin. “It’s not just the alcohol problem, then?”

“Yeah, well...” I quickly tucked the sheet around Lero’s feet, then yanked it up his lap too, to better hide the wounds around his ankles and wrists. “I’ll let his wife deal with him.”

“Are you okay to drive?” Chris asked when we’d made it down to the garage and approached my car.

“Sure. I didn’t drink or, you know, do *mushrooms*.” We loaded Lero into the back seat, and I arranged the sheet over his lap. “Just in case he throws up in the car,” I explained to Chris.

“Well,” he said, eyeing the duffel bag I had slung over my shoulder. “Call me if you need anything.”

“Thank you. I’ll be good now.” I threw the bag in the passenger’s seat, relieved he didn’t ask why I was bringing an overnight bag while supposedly driving my cousin home. I’d lied more than enough for one day already, and the day had just begun. “Thank you so much, Chris. Can’t wait to dump his drunk ass into his wife’s lap already.”

Thankfully, the plane was ready when I got to the dock of the charter company. Jose, the pilot, helped me load my “rich, drunk client” into the plane with only a few questions. He’d seen me with Lero on the day of the viewing, and he was obviously aware that Lero was the new owner of Blue Cay.

“You know how it is?” I swept the loose strands of hair from my sweaty forehead after buckling Lero into his seat. Loading and unloading a limp body had proven to be quite a workout. I panted, nearly out of breath. “Once you have enough money, you can buy whatever reputation you want. Then if you let loose and go wild one night, you can hide on your private island until you sober up and are ready to face the world again.”

“Right.” Jose gave me a disapproving look, as if he suspected that I was one of the “rich client’s” vices as well.

I had no energy and no imagination left to defend my reputation. If he thought I fornicated with clients then cleaned up their messes for publicity purposes, then so be it.

The sun was high in the sky when we approached Blue Cay. Lero had barely moved during the flight. Keeping an eye on him, I couldn’t stop myself from comparing this trip to the last one I’d made to this island. My travel companion was the same, however, his state and our circumstances were much different now.

“There’s no dock,” Jose informed me as we got ready to land. “I’ll have to land on the water then beach the plane.”

Lero hadn’t waited long to go ahead with the changes. The docks indeed were gone. Strings of faint blue lights encircled the perimeter of the island.

“What are those?” Jose asked me, descending to the small bay surrounded by the white-sand beach, the closest one to the main house.

“I’m not sure.” I really had no idea.

“Is it even safe to land here, now?” he sounded doubtful.

I remembered Lero’s instructions to “arm the island.” Could the lights be a part of his security system? If so, I hoped it wasn’t armed right now, because the last thing I needed today would be an alarm blaring or something worse.

On the other hand, Lero hadn’t mentioned I’d face any problems getting into the house.

“It’s fine,” I said, injecting more confidence into my voice than I felt. “Go ahead. Land. These are just, um...solar-powered lawn lights.”

After landing on the water, the pilot masterfully backed the plane right onto the beach then tied it to a nearby tree.

Together we dragged Lero—semi-conscious and largely uncooperative—to the house and dropped him on the bed in the main bedroom. I scraped together whatever cash I had left in my wallet after the generous tip I'd given to Chris and handed it all to the pilot.

"Thank you so much, Jose," I said, feeling incredibly grateful for this part to be finally over.

"No problem." He tipped his chin at Lero. "That's going to be a bitch of a hangover later."

"Yeah... He definitely overdid it this time." I rubbed my forehead, thinking about everything else I still had to do.

After Jose left, I walked through the house, making sure all doors were locked. There were so many of them. In addition to the main entrance and several sets of glass double doors in the dining and living areas, each of the six bedrooms had a walkout to a patio with a path to one of the beaches.

Once that was done, I went to the master bedroom closet in search of the security system Lero had talked about.

I opened the closet and stepped back, stunned. Instead of a code panel or a small screen, the entire wall of the spacious room had been converted into a surveillance center.

Flat screens lined the wall. A long panel with hundreds of keys and buttons stretched in front of them. The dresser that'd stood in the middle had been replaced with a computerized workstation.

The lights in the closet lit up the moment I'd opened the doors. That seemed to bring to life the rest of the equipment, too. The screens glowed pale-blue, and some of the buttons on the panel lit up with a rainbow of colors.

I came closer, inspecting the setup that appeared to have come straight from a spy movie or spaceship.

From what I could understand, the entire perimeter of both islands was under surveillance. Judging by some of the labels on the keys and the commands glowing on the screens, I doubted the system would simply blare an alarm when triggered. I wondered if by arming it I'd somehow be loading an actual weapon.

To arm, the system demanded a fingerprint for identification.

Through the open closet doors, I glanced back at Lero on the bed. His arms spread wide, my sheet still swaddling his legs, he seemed to be asleep. His chest rose and fell evenly. His body must've finally conquered the pain enough to allow him some rest. I'd hate to disturb him again to drag him to the closet to obtain the stupid fingerprint.

Then I remembered that he'd wanted me to come to the island on my own. Neither he nor his finger were supposed to be here at all.

How did he mean for me to activate this thing, then?

Tentatively, I pressed my own palm to the screen. Shockingly, it turned green, accepting it.

When did Lero have the time to set this up? How did he know I'd be here? Did he plan it all along? And if so, what had I allowed him to drag me into?

None of these questions could be answered yet. I'd have to wait until he was well, awake, and ready to talk.

Having armed the system, I felt relatively safe, for now anyway. The physical and emotional stress of the past couple of hours had worn me out.

Making it back into the bedroom on shaking legs, I collapsed on the bed next to Lero.

# Chapter Nine

STELLA

The ache in my shoulders woke me up when I turned in bed. I winced, stretching my arms. My muscles throbbed as if I'd been digging in a garden or doing pull-ups.

...or dragging a tall, well-built man to and from planes and automobiles.

I quickly opened my eyes as the memories of that morning rushed in.

Lero lay next to me on his side, his arm thrown over my waist as if in an embrace. His eyes were closed, and his expression was so peaceful.

With the afternoon sun already tipping toward the horizon, I must have slept for hours. The sea, visible through the glass door to the patio, was calm, the sky blue. It wouldn't be much of a stretch of the imagination to believe I really was here on vacation with a man I'd had a crush on since my early teens.

Lero looked much better than he had this morning. Some smudges of dirt remained on his face, but the shadows under his eyes had lightened. His skin tone had improved. And his lips no longer appeared dry or chapped. The beard suited him, as did the longer hair. I doubted anything could ever mar this handsome face.

Unthinking, I reached out and moved a long, wavy strand of hair that had fallen over his forehead.

His thick, black eyelashes fluttered in the warm sunlight that flooded the bedroom. He opened his eyes, meeting mine.

"Stella?" he murmured, his voice soft and dreamy. "This is the most beautiful dream yet..."

He gave me a smile, the first I'd ever seen from him. It was gentle and undisturbed by reality.

"Hi, Lero."

I had so many questions to ask him. All of them could wait a few more moments, though. Lying in bed with Lero like this, side by side, smiling at each other, felt surreal and so peaceful. I wished to enjoy it for a little bit longer.

Lifting his hand, he gently slid his knuckles along my jawline.

"Kiss me," he demanded, suddenly. "There's no harm in kissing in a dream, is there?"

It certainly felt like a dream. After all, I'd spent so much more time with him in dreams than in reality.

Lost in the silver-gray of his eyes, I hardly realized I'd been leaning closer to him. My lips hovered a hairbreadth from his. He rose on an elbow, closing the distance.

His mouth captured mine in a kiss that was so much better than any dream could ever be. Air rushed out of me in a moan, and he swallowed it, sliding his lips along mine.

My heart pounded in my chest, the swishing of blood echoed in my ears, making me blind and deaf to the world around us. There was nothing else but Lero's mouth on mine, his hand in my hair, and his body so close to mine.

I didn't want this to end, pulling away just a little to catch my next breath between his kisses.

"Gods, this is heaven," he exhaled, pressing his forehead to mine. "I don't want to wake up."

*Wake up?*

He still sounded somewhat delusional. Clearly, the effects of what had been done to him hadn't worn off yet.

The realization was as sobering as a bucket of cold water dumped over my head. I'd just kissed a man who hadn't come out of a delirium. He wasn't fully himself yet, couldn't be. I couldn't blame it on anyone or anything but myself. Unlike Lero, I had been awake and fully conscious, taking advantage of him.

"Sorry," I mumbled, awkwardly backing off the bed. "I'll get you some water. You must be thirsty."

I hurried out of the bedroom, found two glasses in a kitchen cabinet, and filled them with water. I emptied one myself, drinking in huge, thirsty gulps. I desperately wished the cool water could drown my mortification and erase the memories of Lero's lips on mine.

After that, I stood over the sink for as long as it took for my heart to calm down and my blood to cool off.

The sensation of his kiss still tingled on my lips, however, buzzing through my body with a thrill I'd never known before. The effect this man had on me was stronger than anyone I'd ever been with. And that was just a kiss, he hadn't even touched me anywhere else...

I closed my eyes for just a moment, breathing in deeply. Then picked up his glass, willing my hand not to shake, and headed back to the bedroom.

"Water," I announced in an upbeat voice, walking through the door.

Lero was sitting in bed, looking rather confused. "What happened?"

He'd gotten out of my bathrobe and was now wearing only my long t-shirt with *I "heart" coffee* written on it in pink and brown letters. It looked so out of place on him, I smiled despite everything.

"What *do* you remember?" I asked.

He winced, spearing his fingers through the tangled mane of his wavy hair.

"I have some memories. But I'm not sure which are real, and which are just echoes of illusions..."

I sat on the bed, handing him the glass. His fingers brushed mine, sending sparks up my arm straight to my heart. He obviously felt nothing like that, calmly taking a drink.

"Okay, so." I swallowed, clasping my hands in my lap and making sure no part of my body touched his. "You showed up on my balcony early this morning, not looking very good. You said your brother did something to you... How are you feeling?"

He put the glass on the nightstand by the bed.

"Good." He rubbed his wrist.

His wounds had healed incredibly well over the last few hours. The scars were still there, but they seemed old, as if at least a week or two had passed between this morning and now—no more fresh blood or open sores.

"You look... better." I frowned, confused while visually assessing his injuries.

I'd had no time to treat his wounds that morning. However, they appeared to not need any treatment at all. The small round scars I'd seen on the side of his neck between his hair and his beard were barely there now. Just this morning, they were clearly visible, even in the muted light of the new sunrise. The scratches that had thickly covered his arms and legs a few hours ago were all but gone now, blending in with his skin.

"Nerifir iron prevents wounds from healing," he murmured distractedly, inspecting his wrists.

I had no idea what he was talking about. I understood most of the words he'd said, but together they made little sense.

"Lero," I said slowly. "We need to talk."

We did. But where would I even start?

"How did I get here?" he asked, glancing around the room.

Physically he had obviously been improving, but his mental processing had not quite caught up yet.

I sighed, thinking back to our physically and emotionally exhausting journey to the island.

"With a lot of muscle power and the kindness of strangers."

"Did you put yourself in danger for me?" he asked sternly.

"Hardly." I shrugged. There was no point going into the details of schlepping his barely conscious self all the way from Miami. "We're both here safe and sound, aren't we? That's what matters."

He stopped his gaze on me, as if really seeing me just now.

"Thank you, Stella."

God, I loved hearing my name from his lips. And now I was

thinking about his lips and what he'd just done with them. Would our kiss remain a dream for him forever?

I cleared my throat, forcing my thoughts in another direction.

"How did you heal so fast?" I pointed at his wrist. "I mean, I'm happy you're feeling better, but I don't understand..."

He inspected his hand again, as if seeing it for the first time. With his skin healed, the dirt stood out more prominently. Sliding his other hand along his jawline, he winced.

"I need a shower and a shave," he said as if he hadn't even heard my question.

"You want to shave it off?" I felt a slight pinch of regret. Lero's disheveled appearance made him a little more approachable in my eyes. Besides, the beard and longer hair suited him.

He scratched his chin, his lips curved with distaste. "It feels too much like fur..."

Tossing the sheet aside, he paused, staring at my t-shirt with the picture of the pink heart and brown letters stretched over his broad chest. The shirt almost reached my knees when I wore it. On him, it barely covered his private area.

I cleared my throat, once again.

"That's my shirt. You, um... You weren't wearing any clothes when you came over this morning."

He arched an eyebrow in a slightly amused expression. "I see. Well, thank you. I'm sorry about showing up naked."

Holding on to the bedpost, he heaved himself out of bed. The metal frame groaned as he leaned heavily against it.

"That's okay." I stepped closer, just in case he needed my help. "You were barely conscious. Lero..." I took a long breath. "Those who did that to you need to be held accountable. I haven't called the police yet, but I think—"

"No police." He shook his head with the same resolution as before.

"Can you explain why? Please?"

He blinked, jerking his gaze aside. "I need to think... I..." He looked straight at me, as if having made a decision. "You must be hungry. I certainly am. There must be some food in the pantry. Help yourself to anything you like, just check the expiration date first. I'll have a shower, then we'll talk."

I nodded reluctantly.

He let go of the post, taking a shaky step toward the bathroom.

I rushed to his side, grabbing his elbow. "Are you sure you can manage? Do you need help?"

"In the shower?"

"Well, um... If-if necessary." I stumbled through my words, feeling my face heat up with a blush. The thought of washing Lero in the shower... Well, it deprived me of any other thoughts.

His smile was a shade too wistful to be considered flirty. "Thanks. I'll be fine."

Taking a deep breath, he carefully moved around the bed on his way to the bathroom. His movements were a little slow but got steadier with each step.

I watched the door close behind him, then listened for any sound of distress or a call for help. When I was satisfied he was indeed fine in there on his own, I took his glass and went back to the kitchen.

Hunger rumbled in my stomach. I hadn't eaten anything since yesterday. The huge double-door fridge in the kitchen was sparkling clean and completely empty. The spacious pantry, however, was fully stocked with non-perishables.

A variety of grains and pasta were displayed in clear, air-tight containers. Rows of canned fruit, meat, and vegetables neatly lined the white shelves. There were also boxes of crackers, spice cookies, and cereal.

I regarded the bounty for a few minutes, then grabbed two cans of chili, a pack of crackers, a can of fruit salad, some cookies, and a box of tea.

After hauling my loot into the kitchen, I found a can opener in a drawer and an electric tea kettle on the counter in the small room behind the kitchen. I vaguely remembered the sales brochure calling that room "the butler's pantry." Small appliances were lined up on the counter there, including a fancy coffee machine I was not even going to attempt to figure out how to use.

So far, the food in the pantry, the state-of-the-art small kitchen appliances, and the security system seemed to be the only things that Lero had added since taking possession of the island. Otherwise, the house looked very much the same as it had during the viewing.

I wondered what that meant about Lero and his priorities. The more time I spent with him, the less I knew him. Right now, he was an even bigger enigma than that night in Paris, now more than fifteen years ago.

I divided the chili from one of the cans into two bowls then warmed them up in the microwave. While waiting for the water to boil for tea, I arranged the crackers on a plate and put fruit salad into two dessert dishes.

It wasn't the greatest dinner, but I worked with what I had. It still turned out better than some of the frozen meals I'd had in my lifetime of living alone and working late.

The tea smelled amazing and tasted delicious. The packaging looked expensive, too. Lero obviously loved living in style.

I took the dishes to the round breakfast table in the casual dining area off the kitchen.

The sound of the bedroom doors opening came soon after I'd set the utensils next to the bowls of chili. Lero walked in, freshly showered and fully dressed. Now, he looked much closer to the elegant man I'd sold this island to over a year ago than the exhausted, delirious person I'd found on my balcony this morning.

Dressed in a white shirt and light-brown pants, his beard completely gone, and his long, damp hair slicked back, he appeared well-rested and refreshed. The last several hours almost felt like nothing more than a nightmare, chased away by the bright afternoon sun. And our kiss seemed even more like just a dream.

"Dinner?" I made an inviting gesture toward the table before taking a seat.

Lero's nostrils flared as he sighted the food. His movements stilted, as if he were forcing himself to hold back, he sat at the table across from me and lifted his spoon.

"It's not fine dining," I said, apologetically.

I'd done my best with the dinner, considering the circumstances. Though, I wouldn't have done much better if I'd had an entire farmer's market of fresh food available. Cooking wasn't exactly my forte. Back in Miami, I didn't eat much better than this—canned foods, cereal, and frozen meals. Fast and easy.

Lero didn't seem to mind the lack of class or flavor in our meal. I'd only taken a few spoonfuls of chili by the time he'd completely emptied his bowl and polished off more than half of the crackers.

"You weren't kidding when you said you were hungry." I took a sip of my tea to hide my astonishment at the speed at which he ate.

"You have no idea," he growled, practically inhaling his fruit salad.

I wondered how long it had been since he'd eaten last. The thought that he might've been starved twisted my insides, driving away my appetite.

Moving aside the empty bowl, Lero regarded it for a moment, looking almost surprised with himself for finishing it. His gaze fell on the second can of chili on the counter over my shoulder. He got out of his chair, heading that way.

"Canned stuff is disgusting." He made a face while eating the cold chili with a spoon straight out of the can. "I'm going to order proper food for us tonight."

Disgusting or not, he ate the entire can of chili before returning to the table to finish the remaining crackers.

With a deep breath, he leaned back in his chair. Taking a small bite of the spice cookie I'd put on the table, he sipped his tea in a slow, dignified manner.

"How long has it been since your last meal?" I asked softly, dreading to hear his answer.

He put down his cup, not meeting my eyes. "Stella—"

"How long have you been gone?" My voice rose, along with my hurt and indignation for him. "How long did they have you, Lero?"

He cleared his throat.

"It doesn't matter."

"It doesn't? How can it possibly not?" I leaned over the table, my heart speeding up as my anger heated. "You said some people—your brother—took you. I can only assume, against your will. They kept you in deplorable conditions, judging by your state this morning. You have wounds, for goodness sake. Did they restrain you? Torture you? And you're going to let them get away with all of that? Why?"

"Because right now, making them pay is not my priority." He leaned in, too, though his voice and expression remained calm.

"What is?"

"Keeping you safe."

"Me?" I stared at him in confusion. "*I'm* the priority? Why?"

"Human lives are short and fragile. I can't concern myself with vengeance or retribution until you're safely back home with no further danger to your life or freedom."

I loved the idea of nothing threatening my life or freedom, of course. But all of it sounded rather vague.

"But, you—"

"I'd like to go down to the beach," he said suddenly, pushing his chair back.

"Wait." I reached over the table for him. "I need you to answer some questions first."

He rubbed the back of his neck uneasily. "Questions are a tricky thing."

"Not if you have honest answers."

He raised an eyebrow, avoiding my eyes. "You see, Stella, I may not have answers, not the ones I can share anyway. And I really don't want to lie to you."

That didn't sound promising.

"Well, tell me what you can at least. Why don't you want to call the police?"

He made a face, shaking his head. "It'd be useless. Human police wouldn't be able to do much, anyway."

*"Human?"*

"*The police*," he corrected himself quickly. "The police won't help here. It'd be a waste of time, in the best-case scenario."

I opened my mouth to argue, then closed it, thinking about my last visit to the police to report the parking garage incident. The visit and the report had been a waste of time. It wasn't the same as what had happened to him, of course, but I understood his mistrust to some degree.

"Just tell me one thing, please," I said. "Do you have something to hide from the police yourself? Have you done anything illegal, Lero?"

He stared straight ahead, not answering. The pause was less than a second, but it proved long enough to scare me.

My mouth felt suddenly dry like sandpaper. I swallowed hard. "Did you… Lero, what have you done?"

His expression remained somber, but he finally moved his gaze to mine. "Ever since I came to this world, Stella, I've been trying to keep those around me safe while leading a peaceful, productive life and obeying all laws of society."

"Trying?" I clarified. "Have you succeeded in living a peaceful, law-abiding life, Lero?"

His chest rose with a sigh as he heaved himself up to his feet. "Keeping others safe is where I've failed."

I got up, too. "What do you mean? Who are the others?"

He held onto the back of his chair, though his stance was much more confident now that he'd eaten.

"*You* are, for one," he said. "I bitterly regret disrupting your life, Stella."

"Well, from what you've told me, it wasn't your fault, right?"

He shook his head, muttering, "I wish Javier had done the showing that morning."

"Would you rather Javier be their target, instead of me?"

The steel-gray of his eyes softened with a barely-there smile.

"The reason you've been targeted is their belief I have a romantic interest in you, Stella. In this case, Javier would've been safe," he added confidently.

"*Do* you have a romantic interest in me?" I blurted out, immediately feeling mortified. Out of everything he'd said, did my mind need to zoom in on *tha*t?

He let his gaze linger on my face for another moment. My skin warmed up under it like under a ray of sun.

"My priority right now, Stella, is to make sure you can go home as soon as possible. Then, I hope for your sake, our paths never cross again."

Rolling his pant legs up to his knees, Lero waded into the sea while I remained on the sand. I'd come with him after our canned chili dinner, worried he might trip and fall on the path, though he was recovering incredibly quickly. In fact, he had even ended up supporting *me* on some steeper parts of the path.

My head was still reeling from the last words he'd said back at the house.

*"I hope our paths never cross again."*

Hearing it from him had been brutal. Though, I realized he'd never promised me anything. Nothing Lero had ever said could be considered "leading me on." My attraction to him had always been one-sided, and I had no one to blame but myself for letting it grow.

The disappointment and rising anger I felt now were directed at myself.

Maybe it was good for me to hear it directly from him like that. That should help me get my head on straight, too. My daydreaming about Lero was not unlike a celebrity crush—I'd never known him as a person. I still didn't know him at all. The reasons I'd found myself on the island with him were shady at best. And so far, he'd refused to clarify anything.

Lero stood ankle-deep in the water, small waves rolling softly around his legs and onto the beach.

"How long do you want me to stay here?" I asked.

He stared out to the horizon.

"I'm not sure yet."

"I'll have to call Javier," I said. "Taking vacation days won't be a problem, but I'll need to give him some kind of an explanation for my absence."

Technically, as a real estate agent I was self-employed with the flexibility to take a vacation whenever I wanted. In reality, I rarely took any at all. I had ongoing listings and showings scheduled year-around, which would now need to be taken care of by someone else while I was gone. Also, since I worked from Javier's office, I had to account to him for my whereabouts. I couldn't drop out of sight with no explanation.

Lero folded his arms across his chest. With the long sleeves of his shirt rolled up, the wound around one of his wrists came into my view. Clean of dirt and blood, it was but a bangle of pale scar, now. I obviously had been mistaken that morning when I'd thought it raw and fresh. It simply couldn't have healed *that* fast.

"Tell Javier you'll be away for a week, maybe two," he finally said. "I'll call him myself if it takes longer than that. I don't want you to have any problems over it."

"How much longer might it be?" I asked.

"I really can't tell yet." He shook his head. "But I will let you know as soon as I figure out more. Did you bring your cellphone?"

"Yes. But it's off." I'd turned it off back in my car, afraid someone might trace where we were going.

"Good." He nodded approvingly. "You can use the phone I have in the surveillance room to call your work and your family. Tell them you're taking a trip. I don't want them to start worrying or report you missing."

"There is no one to worry about me outside of work." That was true. My job had become my entire life, slowly taking over whatever personal life I used to have. I'd let it, because there hadn't been that much personal life to begin with, and I found my advancement at work satisfying enough for now.

"How about your family? Your parents?" Lero asked, regarding me with interest.

I blinked under his stare and glanced down to where the waves churned around his ankles. They rolled back then rushed in again, rising up to his knees and spraying his pants with foam and mist.

"I don't keep in touch with my parents," I said. "Other than a call once a year, at Christmas." Those were very brief strained conversations, too.

Since the death of Aunt Beatrice and the "inheritance disaster," as my father called her omitting us from her will, my parents and I had hardly spoken at all. Mom had finally succeeded in convincing my father to sell their apartment in Manhattan with just enough equity left for them to buy a modest bungalow upstate. They'd been living there ever since. Mom spent most of her time at a quilting club at their church, and Dad sitting in a rocking chair on the porch blaming his sister, me, and everything else under the stars but himself, for depriving him of the money and status he was "meant to have by birthright."

"We've never been close," I replied, sensing Lero's questioning stare. "My father openly disliked me for as long as I can remember. And Mom... Well, she told me that she saw herself as a wife first, not a mother. She never planned to have children. I was an accident..."

She'd said it more than once, enough times for me to believe her words weren't something one would say in the moment of anger while dealing with a moody teenager. Enough times for her confession to lose the sharp quality of a knife stabbing through my heart when I heard it. Enough for me to believe her and accept her words as the truth. Enough time had passed for me to deal with it and move on, becoming my own person, even if she wasn't thrilled to have me as her daughter. Yet saying it out loud, especially to Lero, practically a stranger, felt raw again. As a kid, I'd blamed myself for being unwanted even by my own mother, thinking something must be horribly wrong with me.

Afraid to see his face, lest I find judgment—or even worse, pity—there, I kept staring out to sea.

"Do you have any close friends?" he asked after a little while.

"At work." I nodded, with more enthusiasm.

The lack of a family connection in my life had been easier to deal with thanks to the family-like atmosphere at work. There were plenty of people about my age at the office. We had parties, went out for drinks, and gathered in each other's houses. I did have friends, they just also happened to be my colleagues.

"I'll call them to let them know I'll be away for a while."

"How about—" He stopped in the middle of the next question, and I stared at him expectantly.

His mouth pressed into a firm line. It appeared he didn't want to continue with what he was about to ask.

"Do you have anyone...closer than a friend, Stella?" he said finally. "A man?"

"You mean a boyfriend?"

Over the years, I'd had a number of casual dates. All of them remained just that—casual. Now, I wondered if that was because both my mind and my heart had been occupied by Lero all my adult life. My bed remained the only place free for another man. Maybe that was why none of my relationships had ever moved past the bed…

"No, no one in particular," I said softly.

His chest rose with a long breath, but he said nothing more.

I watched the waves stroking the shore for a few seconds.

"What's going to happen now, Lero?"

He cast a long look out, toward the horizon, as if searching for something out there.

"You'll stay here, safe. You can go swimming any time, just stay close to shore and away from the reef. I may have to leave at some point."

"Leave? Where're you going?"

"Europe. Not yet, though. First, I want to make sure it's safe for me to leave you here by yourself. Then I'll ask you to remain in the house, with the security engaged."

His words spurred another question that had been lodged in my brain since that morning.

"How come my palm print is in your alarm system?" I asked, narrowing my eyes at him.

"Fingerprints," he corrected. "Not the entire palm. Individual fingerprints are easier to obtain. Which we should replace with the full hand scan—now that you're here."

"You've obtained my fingerprints? How?"

He had the decency to look somewhat ashamed. "I got them shortly after the viewing. You touched things around the house."

I glared at him. "Have you planned this? Me being here?"

He winced, rubbing his forehead.

"Not *planned* but got *ready* for it. The system can accept handprints of more than a dozen individuals. I used as many as I could think of—anyone I had around me at the time."

"Anyone? Your friends maybe…" It made no sense to me. I was no one to Lero, a real estate agent who'd showed him a property once. When giving access to a security system, people normally chose close family members or trusted friends.

"I have few friends, Stella. Their palm prints are logged, but so are those of several of my former employees, the hotel manager where I stayed in Miami, Javier's—"

"Javier's? But why? The more people who have access to your security system, the less secure it becomes. Even I know that, and I don't even have one."

"I didn't install it to keep *everyone* off the island, Stella. I just wanted to prevent certain individuals from coming here to harm those I needed to protect. From the very beginning, Blue Cay was supposed to be a safe place for me and whomever I'd bring here. In my case, the more people who had access to the system, the better. Because I couldn't predict with certainty whom I might have to send here."

I needed time to wrap my mind around all of this.

Lero appeared to care about me—about my safety and wellbeing, at least. I believed I could trust him on those accounts, even if I didn't understand his actions and motivations.

The sun crept toward the horizon.

"Shall we go back in the house?" I asked.

"Soon." He nodded, not moving out of the water. "Just another moment."

At our viewing, I'd gotten the impression he didn't like the ocean that much. Yet he'd insisted on wading in the water then, too.

"You said you didn't like swimming."

"Swimming?" He made a face, as if the very notion was absurd. "No. Other than the shower, I detest getting wet."

"You just like getting your feet wet, then?" I glanced down where the receding wave churned the sand around his toes.

"Not really." He followed my gaze. "Baths are especially unsettling," he muttered under his breath, staring at his feet. "I really don't understand humans' desire to submerge themselves in water any chance they get when they can't even breathe in it."

I snorted a laugh. "You sound like an alien from another planet. Like you aren't one of us 'humans' yourself."

He blinked, moving his gaze to my face.

"Do *you* like swimming, Stella?"

"Sure. When the weather is nice, why not? I love going to the beach. Snorkeling should be really fun around here."

"Zeph would be great to snorkel with," he said, glancing out to sea, the same wistful expression I'd seen before crossed his features.

"Who is Zeph?"

He ran his hand over his overgrown hair.

"A friend of mine. A very close friend. Water is his life."

This was the first time Lero had spoken of someone close to him.

"Will he come visit you here some time?"

"Maybe. I hope very much he will."

# Chapter Ten

LERO

It'd been two days since the last full moon. He still had weeks before the next one. But sleep had been escaping him already, leaving him tossing and turning in bed. Without *womora*, calm was a thing of the past, a distant dream. Blood churned in his veins like sea water, rising and ebbing with the call of the Moon. The sensation was gentle for now, like the soothing caress of waves on the beach protected by the reef. In a couple of weeks, however, he knew it would grow into a true tempest.

Hopefully, it would be safe for Stella to return home by then.

Reports from the people he'd hired to keep an eye on Ghata revealed she was too preoccupied with her European tour, and possibly something else, to send anyone to hunt for him. He worried about her true plans, which so far, he'd been unable to decipher.

Giving up on sleep, he climbed out of bed and walked out onto the patio. The large swimming pool had stood empty ever since he'd ordered it drained and the gap into his bathroom boarded up. He had no use for a pool and didn't care to maintain it.

Zeph would've loved having a house with a swimming pool that extended into his bathroom. Lero had bought the place with that at the back of his mind. But Zeph wasn't here, and there hadn't been any news about his whereabouts from the extensive network of humans that Lero had employed to search for him. The more time passed without word about Zeph, the more worry racked him.

Dressed only in the light pair of white lounge pants he wore to bed, he walked down the patio steps then climbed down the slight incline to the beach.

Wading through the water had become his obsession as he anxiously awaited news from Zeph. He had no way of knowing where the siren was, but he knew that as long as he remained in the ocean, Zeph had a way to find him. As a water fae, Zeph could sense people's emotions through the ocean, no matter the distance.

Lero walked to the small beach behind the house then followed the receding wave. The water ebbed then rushed in again, rising to his knees. He forced himself to remain in place, fighting the urge to get out and shake every drop of moisture off his body. The swelling of the waves unsettled him.

Breathing in the fresh night air, he turned his face up to the sky. It was overcast, the moonlight but a puff of silver behind the thick shroud of clouds. He would've found the Moon even if it was completely obscured, though. The awareness of it never left him even on the darkest of nights or the brightest of days.

He had more than three weeks before the effects of the approaching full moon would become unbearable. Without *womora*, they would be much more difficult to resist before the Moon turned him completely. A shudder ran through his body. There were a few brief moments of utter exhilaration right after a shift, then the wild nature of the beast took over, depriving him of control.

Until that night came, however, he had a few important things to do and verify.

He had no way of knowing if Amira had made it to Nerifir, but he'd heard she and the gorgonian had fled Ghata's show shortly after landing at Heathrow in London.

Ghata had fewer and fewer fae to exploit. According to Amira, she still had a gargoyle in her possession. In Nerifir, gargoyles took human form during the day. Here, it appeared she was somehow keeping him in his stone form around the clock. Lero had been working on a plan to free the gargoyle. If it worked, it would leave Ghata with no high-earning exhibits at all.

Logically, it made sense for her to focus on recapturing him and Zeph, as well as on sending her *bracks* to Nerifir in search for more. According to his sources, however, Ghata no longer seemed interested in restocking her menagerie with sentient fae. It should make him happy that he no longer needed to worry about *bracks* coming for him or hunting Zeph. But it worried him instead. Ghata wasn't retiring. She had most likely moved on to the next stage of her plan, and he needed to find out what exactly that was.

Whatever came, having a secure place was more important than ever.

He'd had the idea of a private island for years. He knew Zeph's powers over water would be best utilized here. The two of them would also attract much less attention here compared to densely populated places like Paris. The only reason he'd waited for so long was his desire to raise Zeph as a normal human boy. Lero wanted to give him a real chance at becoming a part of this world. Maybe then the young siren wouldn't feel like an outsider, the way Lero always did.

That decision had backfired, as Zeph ended up wanting everything humans had, including human connections and relationships. Lero desperately wished for Zeph to avoid making the mistakes Lero had made, though he wasn't sure *how* best to stop that.

The cloud cover had thinned, letting moonlight shine through stronger. It reached down to the water, rippling with silver streaks through it, in a magical, shimmering path that stretched from the horizon toward him.

The ripples glowed brighter, no longer fueled by the Moon but by something moving through the water to him. His heart leaped with anticipation even as in his mind, he was still afraid to believe.

The glow brightened and grew, approaching. Impatient, he waded deeper into the water. When it reached his hips, the turquoise glow surrounded him, and the head of the man he'd raised as his son and loved as his only family popped out of the water.

"Zeph!"

The siren grinned at him, blinking droplets of sea water off his long, dark eyelashes. "Found you!"

Not waiting for Zeph to fully emerge from the waves, Lero grabbed him in a big hug, splashing and splattering in the surf.

"I've searched everywhere for you." He squeezed hard, so hard a human would have been screaming for mercy, but Zeph just laughed, hugging him back.

"I've been blending in, Lero, just like you've taught me."

He had taught Zeph many things but assimilating into human society had always been one of the most important lessons. Humans generally didn't respond well to anyone different than themselves. If discovered, Zeph and Lero could have been detained, locked in a lab somewhere, or simply killed.

"I've searched for you, too." Zeph leaned back from the hug but kept holding on to Lero's shoulders. "I went to Paris and got your note from the cabaret. *'You'll know how to find me when the time comes.'* That didn't tell me much."

Lero had kept the message he'd left for Zeph brief and vague for a reason. He didn't want Zeph to stick his head out in search for him and risk putting himself in danger. There had also been the risk of the note landing into the wrong hands.

"I also wrote *'stay near the water.'*"

"Right. That's what I've been doing, swimming every chance I got, scanning the ocean for you. I know you don't like water much, but is it the first time in months that you got your feet wet?"

"I've practically lived in the ocean for the past two days!" He laughed. Happiness spread thick and warm through his chest at finally seeing Zeph, safe and sound. His limbs grew light with relief.

"Well, I work on land—"

"Where? You don't have to work anymore. You know we have enough money to last both of us until the end of our days."

Zeph inhaled deeply. "A job helps us blend in, remember? One needs to have it, like humans do. I sing. It's the most natural thing for me to do. People pay me for it."

As a siren, Zeph's need to sing was more than simply for recreation.

Music was in his blood. He needed to sing as much as he needed to breathe.

"We can find you something in the Bahamas if you want." There were bars and clubs on the islands nearby where Zeph could continue singing for an audience.

Zeph glanced along the beach then up at the house over Lero's shoulder.

"What is this place? Why are you here?"

Lero turned to look at the house, too. From here, it appeared even bigger than from the front—walls of glass and light-gray stucco, with stone on the bottom. The light in Stella's room was off. She must be sleeping. Maybe he'd dream about her tonight. Those always were the best dreams if she was there.

"This is a safe place," he said to Zeph. "I've been trying to make it as safe as possible. Ghata—"

Zeph groaned, his long eyebrows knitting into a grimace of distaste.

"She held you captive," Lero stated.

"You know?" Zeph cut him a glance.

He rubbed the back of his neck, the phantom pain from the collar spikes making him wince. "She got me too."

"When?" Zeph staggered back as if punched in the chest.

"I escaped three days ago."

"Fuuuuck!" Zeph speared his fingers through his white-blond hair, aimlessly wading through the water. "I had no idea you were there! I should've looked for you before taking off myself."

"I wasn't there. Not at the same location as you, anyway." Lero followed him, concerned by his distress. "She kept us separated. I was brought into the menagerie tents only after you'd escaped."

"It wasn't the tents. She was running her show from a building in Niagara Falls, in Canada, when I escaped."

"She went back on the road sometime after that, then." He placed a hand on Zeph's shoulder and squeezed it tightly. "There was nothing you could've done to free me. Getting out of there as quickly as possible was the best thing to do, trust me."

Zeph heaved a sigh.

"Did she exhibit you, too?"

Lero nodded, chasing away the muddy memories of shifting inside a rusty cage.

"With her exhibits escaping, Ghata doesn't have many left," Lero said. "She may still decide to recapture us. We need to be vigilant and prepared. Zeph, I want you here, safe with me."

"I can take care of my own safety, Lero. I'm no longer a kid, you know." The siren pressed his mouth into a hard, stubborn line.

"Together we're stronger, Zeph." He paused, wondering if he should say anything about his fears, as vague as they were. Zeph needed to know, though. He had to warn him. "I'm afraid Ghata is planning something much bigger than anything she's done so far. She was talking about taking over the world."

Zeph lifted an eyebrow, with a hint of amusement—he obviously didn't believe Lero. "And how is she planning to do that? By stealing the moon or firing a giant laser from outer space?"

Lero gave him a look that hopefully conveyed exactly how unimpressed he felt at Zeph's making light of what could be a serious issue soon.

"Through corruption of faith," he said. "Ghata is a disgraced goddess, remember? She longs for power. The power of a deity lies in the faith and number of her followers. She must be secretly recruiting new believers. The more she gets, the more powerful she becomes."

If Ghata succeeded at regaining her former strength, the Earth would suffer the fate of Sarnala, the land of his people.

Zeph was too young to remember Nerifir, but Lero had heard from the elders about how the power of the Moon changed under Ghata. The magical bond that connected his people warped. Instead of freedom and love, the werewolves craved more violence. Aggression had gradually taken over their beasts. Instead of celebrating the full moon by making love and hunting together, they roamed the Plains of Sarnala, craving murder and blood.

Nothing good would come to humans under Ghata's reign, either.

"Whatever comes, we need to stay together."

Zeph studied him closely from under his brow.

"I'm not alone, Lero," he warned.

"What do you mean?" He frowned in confusion, then it dawned on him. "Ah... The girl." Amira had mentioned that the "siren man" had escaped Ghata's menagerie with a girl.

"Her name is Ivy." Zeph's tone hardened.

That sounded familiar.

"Is she the one from Paris?" The vague memory of a shy young woman gasping for air in the back court of the cabaret he used to own came to mind. It was the one and only time Lero had met her. She'd just seen Zeph perform. The experience had proven too intense for her, and she'd come out to the courtyard to get some fresh air, catching Lero smoking *womora* there.

"Yes. We met in Paris first. Later, she saw me at Ghata's."

"How?"

"Coincidence." Zeph shrugged.

"Are you sure?" After Ghata's betrayal, it proved hard to trust anyone.

"Listen..." Zeph sank his fingers into his hair again. Shorn short on the sides, the longer tresses on top draped over his forehead reaching his nose. "Ivy is my everything. I trust her implicitly. If you don't believe me—"

"She is a human, Zeph." He hated to break the boy's bubble but chasing happiness with a human had a price Lero never wanted his friend to pay.

"She is mine." Zeph glared at him, with a hard, silver glimmer in his sea-blue eyes. "We share a bond."

Lero heaved a long breath, calling on his patience. The stubbornness of the younger man had caused him a lot of frustration in the past.

"A true bond is impossible with a human. We've talked about this, Zeph. Humans are much weaker than us. They're not fae, we can't be with them. If you try, you'll end up damaging them. Irreparably so."

The memory of a life he'd ruined painfully clawed at his heart with guilt that never left.

"I don't care about the *fae* bond." Zeph shook his head, sending a spray of droplets from his hair out in a semicircle. "I've never had it or even witnessed it in others. The bond is nothing but an abstract concept to me. Don't you understand? Ivy is real. I love her. What we have is unbreakable. I'm not leaving her."

Lero dug his heels into the soft sand under the water. Both of them had moved a little closer to the shore while talking. The water now barely reached their knees.

"She is just another liability," he said. "In times like these—"

"What are you talking about?" Zeph laughed. "Ivy isn't a liability. She is my strength. My reason to live. My *everything*."

"If you really love her, the right thing to do would be to let her live her life in peace. Being with fae is dangerous for humans. You can kill her just by hugging her. What if she pricks her skin on one of your spikes and dies? Zeph, it's not just selfish and irresponsible on your part. Keeping her around is criminal."

The poison in Zeph's fins was just as potent as that in Lero's teeth. Unlike his long fangs that he only acquired during the full moon, however, Zeph had the ability to open the fins on his back, arms, and legs any time. Sometimes, they'd open spontaneously on their own.

When Zeph was little, he'd come to Lero's bed at night after having a bad dream. After waiting for him to fall asleep again, Lero would quietly go to the boy's bedroom to change the shredded, poison-soaked blankets Zeph had ruined during the nightmare. The fins used to open while he dreamed, spewing the deadly poison. Lero would then move to sleep in the living room for the rest of the night.

"I have much better control now," Zeph replied.

"Are you a hundred percent sure an accident will never happen? Remember Ivy only has one life."

Zeph spun away from him, without a reply. A swirl of water, fanning out around his legs wider than it naturally would, betrayed his agitation. It sprayed high enough to reach the siren's swim shorts.

"Could you live the rest of your life knowing you've killed the one you loved and were meant to protect." Lero couldn't give up now. "Think what you're dragging her into. We don't know exactly what Ghata is up to. There may be a war coming—"

Zeph whipped around to face him again.

"Then we'll fight it together, Ivy and I," he said firmly. "There is no separating us anymore, Lero. She is a part of me. And she is not as fragile as you think. Just because humans aren't as physically strong as us doesn't mean they don't possess a strength in spirit. You said it yourself,

Ghata is planning to use their faith to become a true goddess once again. Human spirit is strong enough to create and topple gods."

"Humans are easy to mislead." He shook his head.

"So are fae, aren't they? If what you've told me about Nerifir and Sarnala is true, then your people were misled by Ghata, too. They're no different than humans. What exactly are your people anyway, Lero? What *are* you? You've been hiding so well, even I don't know who you truly are. Have you been *blending in* so perfectly that you've completely forgotten your true nature?"

Lero's patience worn thin, his temper snapped. His voice thundered over the water, "That's enough, Zeph!"

He'd hidden his beast from everyone, even from those closest to him. Zeph had never seen him on the full moon night, he'd made sure of that. The one time someone had seen his true self, it destroyed them. Poor Amelie and her fragile mind.

"It's better that way," he said, running his hands through his uncomfortably long hair. "My true self is a hideous sight, Zeph. More than that. It's destructive and dangerous."

"Mistrusting," Zeph snapped, his expression grim. "Those who love you would accept you, no matter how hideous you think you look."

Spoken with the true naivety of youth. He sighed.

"Zeph. I want you to stay here. Now."

The younger man crossed his arms over his chest, taking a wide stance.

"Ivy is waiting for me." He backed out into the open sea.

"Zeph!" Lero shouted in desperation, knowing he had no chance of catching the siren in open water once Zeph dove in. "It's not safe out there on your own."

"I'm no longer on my own, Lero. And I'm capable of protecting those I love. I love Ivy, and she loves me. We live together and will fight together if needed. I won't let anyone stand between us, Lero. Not even you."

# Chapter Eleven

STELLA

The sun was already over the horizon when I climbed out of bed. It'd been four days since Lero and I first got to the island. All this time, he'd been distant, as if lost in thought. He would probably say the same about me, as I tried to stay out of his way as much as possible. Lero's gorgeous house didn't exactly feel like a prison, but I certainly wasn't a guest here, either. I harbored no illusions, this wasn't a holiday.

I'd made phone calls and sorted out things in the real world. Javier had no problem with me taking some vacation time. We'd arranged for another agent to take over my viewings in the meanwhile. So, I could relax a little about my job, at least.

Wandering around the island on my own got old fairly quickly. After a day of doing nothing, I ended up working remotely, using one of Lero's computers. The other agent did the viewings, but I did everything else, from updating listings to answering emails. It had kept me busy for a few hours a day since.

This morning, the sun shone bright, and the day promised to be warm. I took off the t-shirt I slept in and shuffled into the bathroom.

After that first day when I had passed out in Lero's bed, I'd moved into a bedroom of my own. There were five rooms to choose from, and I went with the one closest to Lero's. Listening to him move about behind the wall felt comforting while I was falling asleep at night.

Not a sound was coming from his room this morning. He must be up and out of his bedroom already.

I had a shower then put on a pair of denim shorts and a blue flower print blouse. Having brushed my damp hair, I twisted it into a bun.

If I let it loose to dry in the humid ocean air, my hair would spring up and stick out like a wild mane. While living in New York or Paris, I'd occasionally managed to tame it by slicking it down into civilized auburn waves cascading over my shoulders. After moving south, however, fighting the frizz proved to be a losing battle. Eventually, I'd given up and resorted mostly to buns and occasional braids.

"Morning," Lero greeted me in the open-concept breakfast room separated from the kitchen only by the counter.

The back doors were open, the sheer curtains slowly moving in the breeze. The sunlight washed the room in a golden glow. Amazing smells wafted through the air.

"Breakfast?" Lero rose from his chair at the table. Shoving aside his laptop, he moved toward the counter.

Dressed in a white button-down shirt and beige pants—the outfit he seemed to prefer while being on the island—he'd left his dark wavy hair unbound. It lay on his shoulders in thick black locks, with the sun bringing out the streaks of copper highlights.

Smiling, I walked around the table, past the laptop he'd left open. Its screen was still on, and I couldn't help a glance at it.

A message in French lit the screen, next to the picture of a gorgeous flower arrangement in white and purple.

*"Joyeux anniversaire, ma très chère Amélie"*

Which meant *"Happy Birthday, my dearest Amelie."*

The words struck me like an electric shock, rooting me in place. This was a confirmation of a flower delivery. Lero had sent a bouquet to a woman, Amelie, for her birthday.

He'd never said anything about having a woman in his life. But I'd never asked him directly, either.

*"My dearest Amelie..."*

Could it be a sister? An aunt? People sent flowers to relatives all the time.

The problem was the word "my." When it came from Lero, it sounded especially intimate.

Not that it meant anything, of course. It wasn't *supposed* to mean anything. I was leaving here eventually, never to see Lero again. He was perfectly within his right to send women flowers and call them "my." None of it was my business.

Yet I just stood there, frozen in place like having been struck by lightning.

"Would you like some breakfast, now?" Lero's voice sounded right above my ear.

His hand came into view, closing the laptop.

I felt like I'd been caught snooping. It wasn't my fault he'd left it open for me to see, but I knew he hadn't done it on purpose. The way his eyes flicked away from mine and his brows furrowed told me Lero would've preferred to keep the existence of Amelie a secret from me.

I fidgeted with the edge of my blouse.

"Oh. I'll just get some cereal," I mumbled, gesturing at the door to the pantry.

Since our arrival to the island, we'd had groceries delivered by a charter plane. Milk had arrived as well.

"Cereal?" Lero made a face. "That's just for emergencies. I finally got some real food. We now have a good selection of cheeses and fresh cream, too. It's about time we had a decent breakfast."

Personally, I found Lero's obsession with fancy food endearing. Though, I didn't entirely understand it. It was like he created his own problems by stressing out about having an adequate wine selection in the cellar or a certain type of cheese in his fridge.

"Coffee?" he asked, making a move toward the butler's pantry with all the small appliances.

"Yes, please, but... I can get it myself."

It'd taken me a while but with Lero's help, I'd finally figured out how to operate the complex piece of equipment that he called a "coffee machine." Though, it still looked more like a spaceship to me.

"I'll get it." He placed a hand on my shoulder, pressing down gently for me to take my seat on one of the bar stools at the counter.

His frown had smoothed out, which put me more at ease too.

"Here you go." Lero returned to the kitchen a minute later and placed a warm cup of coffee topped with milky foam in front of me. "Just the way you like it."

He'd never asked me how I liked my coffee. It seemed he'd paid attention all along though, for it was exactly how a perfect cup of coffee should be, in my opinion—no sugar and lots of warm milk.

"Thank you." I took a sip. Closing my eyes in pleasure, I savored the rich creamy taste.

Lero's "emergency" supplies tended to be of the highest quality possible. He really knew his stuff when it came to tea, or coffee, or food.

I might have moaned a little, for when I opened my eyes, Lero was staring at me. The gentle half-smile curving his lips reminded me of the one and only time we'd ever woken up in the same bed, just before he'd dreamily asked me to kiss him and I'd so eagerly obliged.

He'd made his intentions clear since then. His goal was to get me off this island as soon as it was safe, and to never see me again. No more kissing. No more daydreaming about it, either. I was at his place out of necessity, not because he enjoyed my company.

"Something smells amazing," I said, dropping my gaze to the coffee cup in my hands. "Like baking?"

"Croissants," he announced, grabbing an oven mitt.

Opening one of the two ovens in the kitchen, he produced a tray full of golden, puffy crescents.

"You baked them?" I gaped at the tray as he set it on the counter.

Even without tasting one, I could tell that these did not come from a pack of frozen dough, either. The mouth-watering smell made my stomach rumble. I reached to grab one of the pastries.

"Too hot." Lero shifted the tray out of my reach. "Let them cool off a little while I make the eggs."

"Eggs?" A tray of freshly-baked croissants was a fine breakfast already, in my opinion.

"Do you like Eggs Benedict?" he asked. "It won't take me long."

Lero obviously wasn't a stranger in the kitchen. His movements were measured, practiced, and confident.

To me, whipping up a Hollandaise sauce from scratch required a level of skill I'd never even dreamed of achieving. But Lero made it look easy as he stirred the egg yolks, butter, and spices in the small pot on the stove.

Watching him, I now understood why he craved the luxuries of life. He'd been starved and tortured. There still was the threat of him being recaptured. Instead of freaking out or crying in the corner like some would in his place, Lero was baking croissants and ordering fine cheeses.

Maybe this was a part of how he was dealing with what had happened to him? By bringing the familiar routine back into his life. By ensuring he had the things he wanted and loved in his life again.

If so, who was I to judge him? Whatever his "normal" was, I wished he would get it back soon. I wished it would comfort him and help him recover from the nightmare he'd been through and from the horrors he wouldn't talk to me about.

"Do you always cook your own food?" I asked softly.

"I try to, yes. I prefer to eat what I make myself or the food prepared in one of my establishments."

"You own a restaurant?" That made perfect sense. "Because if you don't, you totally should."

He tucked a strand of his hair behind his ear.

"I've had restaurants before. But my latest establishment was a cabaret."

"You mean like a *real* cabaret?" I gaped at him.

He glanced my way, a teasing spark lighting his eyes. "Are there any *fake* ones?"

I smiled, too, happy to see him more relaxed this morning.

"I've never been to a cabaret," I said. "Only saw one in a movie. It sounds exciting."

"A cabaret is only as good as its performers. A lot of talented people worked for me. Some were truly magical." His brow twitched with a slight shadow moving over his expression.

"What happened to your place? Where are the performers now?"

"I sold the business, but most of the people who worked for me are still working there now. That was the condition of the sale—the people would keep their jobs," he said, poaching the eggs.

"Why did you sell?"

He glanced aside. "It was time. I'd had it for too long."

"Many people keep their businesses all their lives. There's no time limit on how long you can have it, is there?"

"In my case, there is." He placed a croissant on each of the two plates on the counter between us.

I watched him plate the rest of the food next. "Who taught you how to cook? Your mom?"

He shook his head.

"No, I learned from TV shows and cookbooks. By the time I started really appreciating the benefits of home cooking, my mother was no longer around to teach me."

"I'm sorry." I looked up, finding his eyes with mine. "How did she pass?"

"It's been a long time," he said calmly, not answering my question.

"How about your dad?" I ventured carefully.

He took the cutlery out of the drawer.

"He's passed away, too."

"Is it just you and your brother, then?"

"Yes."

I didn't exactly win a lottery with my own family, but Lero's murderous sibling was truly despicable.

"What happened between you and your brother, Lero?" I blurted out. "Why is he so...brutal to you?"

He stared past me, through the open doors and out to the horizon beyond.

"My brother..." he started slowly. "Dez isn't really himself, not how he used to be. I don't even know how much I can blame him for his actions, which doesn't make them any better of course."

"What happened that made him so?"

"He has been heavily influenced by someone, from a very young age." Lero appeared to be choosing his words carefully. "To the point that his actions or judgements can hardly be considered his own, now."

"Sounds like he's been brainwashed?" I studied his face. There was concern in his expression, even pain, but not as acute as a new hurt would be. Whatever was happening with Lero's brother must've been happening for a while now. "Did he join a gang? Or a cult?"

"Something like that." Lero nodded, heaving a deep breath. A long strand of hair slid down and over his face again. He released a frustrated groan, twisting his hair back.

"Here." I produced a spare hair elastic from the pocket of my shorts. "I have thick hair, too. It can be a real pain."

He glanced at the elastic in my hand. "What exactly do I do with this?"

"A bun. Or a ponytail," I suggested, getting up. "Is this the first time you've ever had long hair?"

"Since I was much younger, yes."

"May I?" I walked behind him and gathered the silky, fragrant mass of his mane in my hands.

He had to bend his knees a little and tilt his head back for me to do it properly. Then I quickly twisted his hair into a fairly neat knot on the back of his head.

"Better?" I stepped back, admiring my handiwork. "It'll be cooler too, now. Long hair can feel like a fur coat on your shoulders in hot weather."

"Fur... Exactly." He gave me a grateful smile over his shoulder. "Thank you. I wish I could order a haircut delivered."

"Well, you could always have a barber shipped over," I quipped. "Or, I could cut your hair, if you absolutely want to chop it off. Though, long hair looks good on you, I have to say."

The long tresses added a romantic, bohemian flair to his appearance, softening the sharp angles of his handsome face.

"You can cut hair?" he asked with a glint of curiosity in his eyes.

"I took a course during Christmas vacation one year," I mumbled, realizing how stupid my offer had been. He'd probably gotten his haircuts from some famous stylist in Paris.

Backing away, I stumbled over to my seat again, clutching my hands into fists to get rid of the lingering sensation of his silky strands sliding between my fingers.

"I'll keep it in mind." He moved back to plating our breakfast but kept looking at me every now and again. My heart skipped a beat every time our gazes crossed, and I wasn't sure whether it was the morning sun heating up the house or...something else.

"Do you like to cook, Stella?" he asked.

"Me? Oh, um... I don't cook much. I live alone, work late... I mostly stick with quick and easy."

Lero topped the eggs with Hollandaise. That stubborn strand had made its way out of the knot I'd made, dropping over his forehead once again. His gray eyes glistened from under it.

"There are few pleasures in life, Stella."

He licked the sauce spoon, sliding his gaze down my body. If I didn't know better, I'd think he might be wondering what it would feel like to lick me, too. The idea of his tongue on my skin made my body feel both uncomfortably hot and pleasantly tingly.

"Why deny yourself the joy of good food?" He cut off a small piece of his creation, speared it on a fork, then offered it to me, not releasing the fork from his fingers. "Try this, but don't just *eat* it. Think about all the flavors, textures, and emotions that fill your senses and your heart while the food is in your mouth."

His voice turned softer and deeper as he spoke, tempting and full of promise.

*"He is just talking about the food, Stella."* I had to remind myself mentally before leaning toward him.

His attention was fully on me as I wrapped my lips around the fork, taking his offering in my mouth. The rich flavors of the sauce hit my senses, with the warm, flaky pastry practically melting on my tongue.

He leaned over the counter, watching me.

"More?" he said softly when I'd swallowed.

"Yes. Please." I licked my lips.

He didn't move, staring at me, his eyes lingering on my mouth.

My heart pounded so hard, I could hear the echo of his words from our first day here *"Kiss me"* in the thundering sound.

"Lero..." I had no idea what to say, but I needed confirmation from him that this almost-palpable tension of attraction that crackled in the air between us right now was not just my imagination. Every nerve in my body stood on end, charging me with energy I thought would rip me apart, unless I… unless *he* did something about it.

He frowned and closed his eyes, leaning back with a long sigh, and my heart dropped into a pit of bitter disappointment.

"Of course you can have more, Stella," he exhaled, sliding the whole plate my way. "I made it all for you."

# Chapter Twelve

STELLA

"Is this the way you usually take?" Lero asked, as we strolled along the path toward the bridge connecting the two halves of Blue Cay.

"Yes. Unless I just go for a walk on a beach."

We'd started our second week on the island. Lero insisted it was safer for me to remain here for now. I hadn't argued too much against staying on the beautiful island instead of returning to the hustle of the city, even though he still hadn't answered many of my questions. Today, he had offered to accompany me on one of my "treasure hunting" outings.

"The tide is low right now." I gestured at the strait under the bridge. "I like coming here to see what the water leaves behind."

"Have you found anything interesting, so far?" he asked.

I nodded.

"A few neat pieces of coral. Oh, and a round piece of glass. The surf has polished it into an almost perfect oval."

Lero spent his mornings either in the closet room or in the spacious office in the front of the house. When I caught glimpses of him there, he'd be on his laptop or on the phone.

I worked the first half of the day, too. The afternoons, we often spent together. Since he took on all the cooking, I did our laundry and vacuumed. Lero would get busy in the kitchen while I read a book on the tablet he'd ordered for me.

It was easy to forget about any danger that might still be out there. I didn't mind staying in this cozy little bubble of the island life we'd created.

"Careful." Lero grabbed my hand, helping me down the slope.

I accepted his help but let go of his hand the moment we reached the wet sand under the bridge. As much as I loved holding hands with Lero, it felt too intimate. He'd voiced his expectations—we were to part for good eventually. Not allowing myself to forget that, I carefully maintained the distance he'd established.

We waded in the ankle-deep water on the very bottom of the straight.

"Look!" I crouched to dig out a dark round object half-covered by the sand.

"What is it?"

"I believe it's a rock." I twisted the flat disk between my fingers. "But it's been polished flat and round, see?"

"Beautiful." He laughed. "Looks like a true treasure."

I tucked the flat rock into the back pocket of my jeans, intending to add it to the collection I'd started to assemble on a shelf in my bathroom.

We approached the south end of the strait. On the right, the beach ended in a rocky cliff that went on, all the way around the western shore of the Blue Cay and behind the manager's cottage.

"You know what a true treasure would be?" I said to Lero as we came closer to the rocky end with surf foaming around it.

He glanced at me. "Tell me."

"I saw a huge shell down there when I went swimming the other day." I gestured at the water beyond the surf. "It must be the queen conch. I don't think it has a mollusk inside. It's enormous, and it appears to be stuck in the rocks. Too deep for me to get it."

"Where exactly was it?" Lero waded into the water closer to me.

"Right there, just about twenty feet from here or so." I gestured with my hand. "Not far from the shore, but there is a drop off. It's deep—"

I turned to face him, only to find him ripping his shirt off over his head.

"Lero? No," I protested, guessing his intentions. "It's really deep there."

But he'd already taken his pants off and tossed them onto the sand, heading into the sea with nothing but a pair of black briefs on.

"Lero!" I hurried through the waves after him, more than a little concerned. "It's too deep."

"I'll be right back." He casually waved me off before diving in.

"But how well can you swim?" I yelled after him, as he disappeared from sight.

He'd said he *could* swim, but he'd also said he disliked water, especially being submerged in it. Which wouldn't be something a good swimmer would say, would it?

I couldn't believe it. Lero wouldn't even take baths or swim in a pool. Now, he dove headfirst into the ocean. Just because I said I wanted a shell from the bottom.

Unlike the northern beaches, the waves on the southern shore of the island were much stronger, unbroken by the reef barrier. They swayed me on my feet, reaching up to my chest, as I peered into the water, anxiously searching for any sign of Lero.

I hadn't thought about starting to count seconds the moment he went in. Now, it felt like an eternity had passed. He'd been down there for ages. Much longer than was humanly possible.

Panic rose in my throat with each passing moment. I wasn't a strong swimmer myself, but dammit I couldn't let him drown.

Taking a step into the waves, I was about to dive in after him when his dark head broke through the water.

"Lero..." I exhaled, pressing my hands to my chest to still my racing heart.

Sea water sluicing down his face, his black hair plastered to his cheeks and forehead, he smiled, holding up the freaking conch shell in his hands.

"Is this the one?" He beamed, coming closer.

Relief made me weak in my knees, the waves nearly knocking me off my feet as he walked me out of the water.

"Don't you ever scare me like that." Placing my hands on the shell, I pressed my forehead to his chest, saying a small prayer in my mind for getting him back alive, safe, and sound.

He let me hold the shell, moving his hands to my waist.

"You were right." His voice sounded soft and low. "*This* is a real treasure."

My heart all but skidded to a stop, then took off in a gallop at his touch. The warmth of his large hands seeped through the wet material of my blouse.

Suddenly, his body stiffened. Like a shield lowered over his features, replacing the warm expression with a deep frown of concern.

"A boat," he said, staring over my shoulder.

The sound of a motor reached me over the noise of the surf. Lero promptly crouched behind a shrub at the edge of the beach, taking me with him.

I peeked through the branches of the shrub. A small, white motorboat was slowly moving parallel with the shore. It kept at a safe distance, however.

"I don't think they're coming this way," I whispered, as if the people on the boat could hear me. Lero's concern had filtered to me, but I tried to calm him. "It's not unusual for watercraft to pass by."

"Have you seen boats pass by before?" he asked.

The location of Blue Cay kept it fairly isolated from the most populated islands and away from the traffic between them.

"No. Not yet, but—"

"I shouldn't have stayed here," he said firmly.

The boat kept gliding past Blue Cay, but I had a feeling it wasn't just this particular watercraft that Lero worried about.

"You said this was a safe place," I reminded him.

"It is, but my being here makes it no longer safe for you. If they come here searching for me..." A shudder rolled across his wide shoulders. "I need to leave."

"Leave me here alone?" I exclaimed. "How would that be safer?"

I didn't share Lero's fears, not to the same degree, anyway. He'd refused to give me any details about the threat. Whatever he was worried about remained very much an abstract concept to me. The idea of him leaving, however, had immediately cast a gloom over the sunny day.

"No one knows Blue Cay is mine, Stella. At least none of the people I don't want to know, and I need to keep it this way. Me being here may compromise that. In my mind, I always knew that. In my heart, however..."

He paused, keeping his eyes on mine. With me crouching sideways in front of him, my knees ended up propped against his naked thigh. His arms remained around me, his large body crowding me. This close to him was both the only place I wanted to be right now, and the one I knew I had to leave as soon as possible.

He cleared his throat, getting up.

"Your clothes are wet. You'll get cold," he said, helping me up, too. "We should go back to the house."

"Where will you go when you leave?" I asked, not worrying about my clothes at all.

"To Europe, as I've planned to do all along. It was selfish and foolish of me to stay here as long as I did." He took a long look out to sea, scanning the horizon, then picked up his clothes from the sand. "I'll go back to Paris, make sure I'm seen in Europe. If they want to hunt me, they can do it there, not here."

"You'll use yourself as bait?"

He shook his head, a corner of his mouth twitching up in a smile.

"Not bait, a lure. The last time they saw me, it was in North America. I'll have to make sure they know I'm no longer even in the same hemisphere. So they'll have no reason to search for me here."

"What if they catch you again?"

"They won't get me that easily this time. I'm much better prepared and far less trusting."

Despite his assurances, the restless worry gnawed at me from inside.

"What do they want from you, Lero?"

My heart squeezed painfully when I thought back to how I'd found him on my balcony—weak and broken. It must've taken hellish torture to break a strong man like Lero.

"Stella," he said as we headed up the path back to the house. "Please, trust me on this. It's best if you don't know any details. None at all."

His plan was to let me go back to my old life after all of this was over. In that he was right, I didn't need to know any of this to live the way I used to before. But could I really go back to the way it was after spending all this time here with him? After having learned even as little as I had?

"Lero, can I come with you?" I hurried up the path next to him.

"No," he said resolutely. "I'll worry less, knowing you're safe and protected here."

"But how would I know if something happened to you? What if I could help you? Maybe we could figure out how to stop your brother for good? Together?"

"Absolutely no—"

"Can you at least tell me who exactly these people are? The name of their gang or their...organization? How would I find you if they take you again?"

He stopped abruptly. Facing me, he took hold of my upper arms.

"Whatever happens, Stella, do not go looking for me. Do you hear me?"

I met his eyes straight on.

"What if you need help breaking free?"

He stroked the bare skin of my arms with his thumbs.

"I won't let them take me. Not again."

"Promise?" I demanded.

His gaze flickered away from mine. For someone who'd made me promise many things to him by now, he wouldn't make promises that easily himself.

The next day, Lero was gone. He calmly shook my hand before climbing into the sea plane cabin, as if I were just his real estate agent, nothing more. As if we hadn't spent nearly two weeks living under the same roof, sharing meals, walks, and conversations. My insides tightened with worry for him the moment he set his foot into the plane to fly away from me.

While he was gone, I did as he'd instructed. I kept the island security system on at all times. In the evening, I locked up the house and armed its system, too. In the morning, I thoroughly checked the feed from all the cameras before disarming the house security to go outside.

Once every few days, a sea plane delivered groceries and other supplies. But Lero had told me to stay in the house while the pilot beached the plane, unloaded the crates, and carried them to the front porch. I was not to talk to or be seen by anyone.

I worked for a few hours every day. In the afternoon, I read to get my mind off things or explored Blue Cay, making sure to stay out of sight of any passing traffic, either in the air or on water. Not that there were many of either.

By now, I'd learned every nook and cranny of the small double-island. Sometimes, I went swimming in the warm lagoon protected by the reef. Lero had sternly instructed me not to swim past the reef, and I wasn't a strong enough swimmer to venture that far, anyway. During low tides, I often went to the bridge, digging pretty shells, intricate pieces of coral, and sometimes polished colored glass out of the wet sand.

A week had passed. And another one was almost through. I hoped things would get better soon, safe enough for Lero to return to me. Though it would also mean that I'd have to leave him then.

At least, he called me almost daily. His calls were brief, and his words few, but I loved hearing his voice. It told me he was safe and free. Talking to him also made me feel connected with the rest of the world. Being all alone here, on the entire island, often felt like being set adrift.

I knew I shouldn't be thinking about him much. I had to use the time away from him to "cleanse" my system from everything Lero. If I had to leave here at some point, I needed to train myself to be without him. But it wasn't easy. The thoughts of him had long been a part of me.

To access the system controls in the closet, I had no choice but to go into his room daily, though I made sure not to linger. He hadn't been smoking lately—at least not in my presence—but the unique fragrance of his cigarettes still clung to his skin when he'd left. It lingered in his room, too, making me feel like he was close.

One morning, he called me while I was in the closet, watching the footage recorded by the cameras overnight. It was the most boring part of my routine—staring at the videos of waves, birds, and tall grass swaying in the breeze. Lero insisted I review them regularly, even if I didn't know exactly what I was looking for other than "anything suspicious."

"How was your night?" he asked, polite but distant.

I released a breath, glad to hear his voice again.

"Quiet."

"Quiet is good. You're not too bored?"

I wasn't bored as much as I was lonely, at times.

"Not really. I have some work to do every day. And I read."

"What are you reading?" He seemed to be in a more talkative mood today.

"A book. It's called *Rein*, by Bex McLynn. It's about wolf shifters."

"Who?" Unexpected interest rang in his voice.

"Wolf shifters. You know, people who sometimes turn into wolves? Kind of like werewolves. It's fiction, of course."

"Oh... And, how do you like the book?" his voice sounded guarded, now.

"I love it. It's..."

The love story was magical, the hero dreamy. And sex... Well, I wasn't going to discuss the amazing sex that took place in *Rein* with Lero.

"It's a very well-done story. It has everything—magic, suspense, mystery... Romance, too."

"Romance? With a werewolf?" A bitter note slipped into his voice. "Well, now I know it's fiction."

"Love knows no boundaries," I said, risking sounding like a hopeless romantic.

But wasn't it true? All of us were a combination of good and bad, weird and normal. The trick was to find a person who'd love the good in us enough to accept the bad, and who would be willing to take our weirdness as normal. At least I firmly believed so.

"And how are you?" I asked since he remained quiet.

"Good. Thank you. Could you please disarm the security at three thirty this afternoon?" he said. "I'm coming back."

My heart had no business jumping as high as it did then racing like crazy at his words.

"You're coming back?" I asked, afraid to believe. "Is everything...well then?"

"Yes. I'll be there in a few hours." Did I hear a smile in his voice, too? "Anything you'd like me to bring for you?"

*Just you.*

My chest swelled with longing. I hadn't even realized how much I wanted to see Lero again. So much for trying to "cleanse my system" of him, I sighed.

"No. Thank you. I have everything I need," I replied, willing my heart to slow down.

As soon as I finished working that afternoon, I hurried to the beach. I stared at the sky for so long, searching for the shape of a plane, that my eyes started to hurt.

When the sound of the plane engine finally reached my ear, I almost jumped up with excitement. Holding my breath, I watched the tiny form of the floatplane grow in the sky as it approached.

The pilot backed it onto the beach as he always did. As soon as he tied the rope to a nearby tree, the passenger's door opened and Lero jumped onto the float and from there to the beach.

Dressed in a light gray-blue suit, a tie, and leather shoes, he was bringing the air of the outside world with him. Somewhere out there, people wore business clothes, had meetings, and traveled, as opposed to wearing flip-flops, shorts, and wading along the same beaches over and over again.

He spotted me, lifted his hand in greeting, and smiled—a wide, happy grin of his I'd never seen before and now didn't want to live without.

Kicking off my flip-flops, I ran to him. The smile lingered on his lips, shining through his eyes. Warm and inviting, it drew me closer. When only a few feet remained between us, I stopped. I'd give anything to feel his arms around me. Despite his smile, however, the usual aura of polite distance hung around him, making even a friendly hug impossible.

"Hi." I peered at him from under a few strands of hair that had made their way out of my bun. My lips spread wide in a smile that couldn't be helped. "Welcome back."

The sea breeze played with his long hair, which gave him an especially romantic flair, as if he'd come from a fantasy world.

"Hi, Stella. It's very good to see you again." He lifted his hand to my face, caught one of the fly-away strands of my hair between his fingers, then gently placed it behind my ear. "I can never tell what color your eyes are," he said unexpectedly. "There is green, and brown, and gray. But right now, they're almost blue."

"Hazel." My face heated under his attention. The warmth of his gaze was spreading to my heart, erupting into a kaleidoscope of butterflies in my stomach. "My aunt used to say hazel is what you call the eyes like mine that have no particular color."

"Or have all colors at once." He let his hand linger just under my ear, the tips of his fingers nearly touching the side of my neck.

The breeze brought a faint whiff of *Lero's scent* my way, and I drew in a long breath, filling my lungs with it. God, how I'd missed him. The day had brightened somehow now that he was here.

If it was wrong for me to want him then why did it feel so right to have him here, with me again?

"Was it a good trip?" I asked, trying hard not to jump into his arms and make a fool out of myself.

"Overall, yes." His grin grew wider. Smiling made him even more handsome if it was at all possible. I loved seeing him happy so much, it could prove addictive.

"How about your brother?" I asked cautiously. "Where is he now?"

He glanced over his shoulder at the pilot who started unloading bags and boxes off the plane.

"All of them are moving East next, farther away from here, which I was glad to learn." He raked a hand through his hair. "I'll have to leave again in four days, Stella. But it'll just be a short, overnight trip."

In four days, I'd probably be leaving myself now that things were starting to look better. I didn't feel like bringing that up right now, though.

Lero turned back to grab one of the boxes.

"I got something for dinner tonight. Do you like lobster?" He lifted the box with a picture of two red lobsters on it.

"Who doesn't?" I smiled.

The breeze blew his hair over his face. My hand jerked to brush it away for him, but he beat me to it, shoving his hair back again.

All this time he'd been away, he never got the haircut he'd so badly wished for before.

"You left your hair long," I said.

He cleared his throat.

"I've decided to take you up on your offer to cut it for me."

"Well, if you trust me—"

"I do."

# Chapter Thirteen

STELLA

"I'm ready whenever you are." Lero placed a pair of barber scissors and a gray box with a picture of hair clippers on it on the table.

It was the day after our lobster dinner, another warm and sunny afternoon. I'd finished work a couple of hours ago, and Lero already had a casserole ready to go in the oven for dinner.

I set aside the tablet with the book I was reading.

"Are you absolutely positive you want to cut off your long hair?"

"It really bothers me." He yanked the hair elastic out of his thick, wavy locks.

Dark as night, they spread over his wide shoulders, sunrays streaking them with burgundy red. It'd be a crime to chop off this beauty. Though, knowing how he got the long hair in the first place, I understood the reasons why he wanted to get rid of it. It was a reminder of his time in captivity.

"And you're sure you want *me* to do it?" I verified.

He could've gotten a haircut during his trip since he'd found the time to get the scissors and the clippers. Instead, he'd been dealing with the long hair he despised, waiting to get home, for me to cut it.

"You offered." He tilted his head, holding my gaze.

"Fine." I smiled, getting up from the couch. "But I need to warn you, the result may not be what you're used to."

He speared his fingers through his mane, shaking it out.

"Will it be shorter?"

"*That* I guarantee!" I laughed.

"Then, I'm all yours."

*I wish.*

I blinked, ducking my head down to hide the sudden blush that warmed my cheeks at that thought.

"Where do you want me?" he asked.

"W-What?"

"Here?" He made a sweeping gesture around the sitting room. "In the bathroom? Or would it be better if we went outside?"

"Oh, outside would be best for cutting hair." Of course, that was what he was talking about—cutting hair. "We can go out on the patio?"

With a nod, he grabbed a chair from the table then walked out through the back doors.

Swiping the scissors and the hair clippers off the table, I ran to my room to grab a comb, then followed Lero to the patio with the drained swimming pool.

Apparently, Lero disliked swimming so much, he didn't even want to bother with the pool maintenance. He hadn't gone down to the beach lately, either. His obsessive wading in the water had stopped abruptly. The last time I saw him in the water was when he dove to get the conch shell for me. I still had it on my shelf with all the ocean treasures I'd collected.

"Here is good?" he asked, gesturing at the chair he'd placed to the right of the empty pool.

"Sure. But we need a towel or a sheet." I took a critical look at his crisp, white shirt. "You'll get covered in hair as I cut."

"Or..." He deftly unbuttoned his shirt then shrugged it off. "Would this work?" He glanced at me innocently, tossing the shirt aside. "I'll just take a shower after."

Cutting his hair while being presented with an unobstructed view of his tanned, muscular torso? He was obviously a brave man, unafraid of losing an ear to my scissors.

"Well..." I swallowed hard. "I need some water, you know...to wet down your hair?"

I ran back to the kitchen, filled a glass with water, and drank half of it. Taking a few deep breaths, I waited until some of my composure returned before going out again.

Lero took a seat in the chair, and I approached him from behind. It felt safer to stay here, out of his sight for now.

"Let's do this." I splashed some water on my hands then ran them through his hair. Silky and soft, with a slight wave, it reached below his shoulders.

"You have beautiful hair," I blurted, enjoying the sensation of it under my fingers. "It's almost a shame to cut it."

"Cut it," he said firmly. "Please. I hate how it feels against my neck." A shudder ran across his shoulders.

"Okay." I snipped a strand off. It fluttered down to the stones of the patio.

Lero remained quiet as I worked. I tried to replicate the stylish haircut he'd had the last time I'd seen him with short hair.

"I'm doing my best, but it won't be perfect." I felt the need to warn him again as I kept snipping at his hair.

"It doesn't need to be perfect," he reassured me.

While working, I tried hard not to pay attention to how smoothly his tanned skin stretched over the dips and valleys of his muscular arms and shoulders or how amazing he smelled this close. Keeping my focus proved incredibly difficult.

Once done, I used the hair clippers to clean up the shape on his nape and temples, then stepped in front of him to assess my handiwork.

Styling his now short hair with my fingers, I made sure I got the shape right. It wasn't just a trim, his hair had been too overgrown for me to follow the previous pattern. Surprisingly, it looked pretty good, better than I thought I could do. But then again, everything looked good on Lero.

I glanced down, and his gaze trapped mine. Gray like a rainy sky, his eyes focused on my face. I froze, staring into them, my fingers tangled in his hair.

My knees buckled, bumping into his. Deep inside, I knew I had to move away from him, but I forgot all the reasons why. More than anything in the world, I just wanted to keep touching him right now.

Instead of taking my hands off him, I flattened them, cupping his face.

Heat flashed in his eyes, reflecting red. His jaw muscles flexed, and his top lip lifted, displaying the tips of his canines. Grabbing me around my waist suddenly, he yanked me into his lap.

Air rushed out of me with a gasp. My hands dropped to his shoulders. The sensation of his bare skin under my palms spread through my body like honey, thick and sweet. Shockingly, the wild expression in his eyes thrilled me instead of terrified.

Silently, he slid his hands under my t-shirt and up my sides, bringing me closer. So close, I felt him grow hard against me through the material of his pants.

*"Kiss me."* His words rushed through my brain, once again.

Had I said it out loud right now, I had no doubt he would kiss me. He'd do more to me than kissing, I sensed. Tingling licks of heat ran up my inner thighs, pooling hot in my lower belly. I longed for his kiss and whatever else he wished to do to me.

His fingers digging into my sides, his body shaking with strain, he did nothing more but hold me.

Something was holding him back.

*Amelie...*

The name rose in my mind unbidden.

Lero had never been the man I wished to have for sex only. For years, I'd held a place reserved for him in my heart. I wanted him to come and claim it, or I didn't want him at all. With Lero, I couldn't do it half-way. It had to be all or nothing.

If there already was another woman, however... None of this would be what I wished to have with him.

"Lero. Who is Amelie?" I asked softly.

My heart sank, as I watched the desire dim in his eyes at the sound of her name. He kept holding me tightly, but his entire body went rigid, as if every muscle in it flexed to the limit.

His eyes were no longer a serene gray. Rings of fire appeared to dance around his pupils. They throbbed and grew, flooding his irises with red.

"Your eyes…" I whispered, unsure about what I was seeing. Did my own eyes deceive me? Was the setting sun playing tricks on me? It looked surreal. Unnatural.

He shut them.

"Get off my lap, Stella," he growled low.

His voice sounded unfamiliar, foreign, and terrifying. But it was his words that hurt me the most.

I realized that was all he'd ever done. He'd lure me in with his kindness, then hold me at arm's length. He'd enthrall me with a smile, then build a wall between us. He'd let me glimpse the genuine attraction I longed for only to slam the door to his soul shut against me.

And like a starving woman, I'd been following the crumbs, unable to stop dreaming of the feast I'd imagine could be there one day.

I took my trembling hands off him.

"You can't do this," I said bitterly. "You can't pull me in, then push me away the very next moment."

Tears burned my eyes, from hurt as much as from the rising anger.

"Talk to me. Lero, I need you to explain—"

"Go! Now!" he roared, lurching up.

Alarm spiked through me at his outburst.

Lifting me by my waist, he deposited me in the chair he'd been sitting in. Without sparing me a glance, he jogged down the stairs to the beach.

Stunned and hurt, I watched as he made his way along the golden sand to the end of the beach then disappeared behind the trees to the right.

How could he make me feel alive with a smile then kill me with one word? Hot, bitter tears rushed out of my eyes. What had I done, for him to treat me that way, to literally toss me aside and run away from me as if I were…a disease?

Pain squeezed my chest like a steel band, making it hard to breathe.

Spinning on my heel, I rushed into the house, then out the front door. Not willing to cross paths with Lero as he'd made it clear he wished to avoid me, I kept to the opposite side of the island.

I wanted to run without stopping, far away from here. But how far could I run on an island?

Soon, I made it to the bridge. Instead of using it, however, I crossed under it, wading barefoot through the water slowly rising with the evening tide. Climbing up a dirt path, I made my way to the second building on Blue Cay, the manager's cottage.

I hadn't been here since the viewing well over a year ago. Lero seemed to have done even fewer updates here. The place looked very much the same as I'd seen it last.

Despite being called "the cottage," it was a full-size house, with four bedrooms and several spacious common areas. It had the same lavish finishes as the main house, too. Marble, expensive wood, and stylish furniture made it just a smaller version of the place where Lero and I stayed.

Well, I couldn't go back to Lero's house, now. Not tonight. I just didn't have it in me to face his usual cool composure when everything inside me bubbled and burned.

Instead, I locked the front door then went to the kitchen to pour myself a glass of water. Like in the main house, the cabinets here were filled with dishes. A number of small appliances graced the granite countertops. The pantry held a selection of non-perishables here, too. Lero obviously had accounted for the possibility of someone staying here. Except that I wasn't hungry at all.

The anger had simmered down somewhat, but the unsettled feeling still weighed heavily on my chest.

Mostly out of habit, I did a full walk-around, just like I'd done every night while at the main house, locking all doors and checking every window.

The backyard here faced west, the shore ended not in a beach but in a drop-off. White-crested waves rolled over it. The rhythmic sound of the surf reached me even with the windows closed, soothing my nerves.

With the glass of water in my hand, I sat on the couch, without turning on the lights, and watched the sky grow darker as the sun sat deeper behind the horizon and my thoughts kept circling around Lero.

Even after all this time, he had largely remained a mystery to me—a man made entirely of questions. The only question I no longer had was "What if?"

For fourteen years, I asked myself, "What if I met him as a grown woman?"

Then, after the viewing of this island, I'd asked, "What if we weren't a client and an agent?"

Now, there were no more "what ifs." I'd met him as a grown woman, I was no longer his agent, and I got my answer.

Nothing.

Absolutely nothing would ever be between us. Lero would never allow for anything at all.

# Chapter Fourteen

STELLA

I fell asleep on the couch. When I woke up, the sun was up already. I didn't remember getting up in the night, but a cozy cotton blanket I'd never seen before covered me to my shoulders.

*Someone had been here.*

The thought jolted me awake. I bolted upright, looking around.

"Who's here?"

All was quiet, the glass back doors closed, windows shut.

My gaze fell on the breakfast tray on the side table next to the couch. The dishes were covered with metal domes. An insulated cup was filled with coffee. I took a sip, it was just the way I liked it.

Lero...

I plopped back on the couch, hugging the mug with both hands and staring at the silver domes arranged on the tray. Among them stood a small, frosted glass vase with a bouquet of local tall grass and flowers.

As the property owner, Lero would obviously have a key to the cottage. He'd come earlier this morning to cover me with the blanket and deliver breakfast. He'd found the time to gather a bouquet for me on the way, it appeared.

I lifted one of the domes, finding a scone with cream and jam under it. When I broke the scone in half, it was still warm in the middle. He'd baked them fresh this morning...

I dropped the pastry back on the plate and buried my face in my hands.

Why would he do this? Why couldn't he just make it easier for me to grow cold with time, instead of warming my heart with any kind of attention.

Why did he need to continue taking care of me if he didn't *care*?

I lifted the other dome, searching the tray for a note, a card, a message, anything. Just a peach yogurt and a bowl of fresh fruit stood there. Not a word written anywhere. What was I supposed to make of this breakfast? And the flowers?

Was it a gesture to apologize? What kind of an apology, though?

*"Sorry, I hope you had a nice stay on Blue Cay. Have a good life."*

Or *"Sorry, let's talk. You mean something to me."*

I couldn't assume anything, definitely couldn't allow myself to read too much into his kind gestures anymore. Lero had always been polite and attentive. It didn't have to mean anything more than that. I was his house guest, and he was a classy host. Nothing more.

He'd told me—straight and clear—he never wanted to have our paths cross again in the future. I'd spent almost four weeks on this island now, and never once had he said anything about having a relationship with me other than that of my protector until it was safe enough for him to take me back home.

I might be angry, and my heart ached as if torn in two, but Lero had never made any romantic promises to me, so I couldn't blame him for breaking any of them.

Sipping the warm, fragrant coffee, I tried to distance myself from longing and heartache and think rationally.

Lero had been taking care of me ever since I got here. He'd cooked for me and made sure I was safe. He'd had fresh groceries delivered for me even while he was away. He dove into the ocean for me, despite his severe dislike of water.

But had he always been just a gracious host? Was I really nothing but a house guest to him? Had I let my imagination run wild, making more of his smiles than they really meant?

Was I the only one to blame?

I recalled the fire in his eyes. It'd been an intense, undiluted desire—for me. I'd never seen such a feral need before, so I couldn't have imagined it to that extent. It had surprised me and excited me, too.

Lero wanted me, without a doubt. I'd felt the physical evidence of that, pressed hard against my core.

But he'd been fighting it. And that was the most important part. He didn't *want* to want me. He'd shoved me away because he *couldn't* want me.

He didn't care to explain his reasons, but I sensed they had everything to do with the woman named Amelie. Hearing her name had acted like the crack of a whip, snapping him out of his desire quicker than a cold shower.

Though, I didn't believe Amelie was the woman he loved. He couldn't love her. For if he truly did, why was he spending any time here with me?

One way or another, however, Lero was obviously unavailable. Which meant I had to get off this island as soon as possible. After yesterday, I no longer trusted him completely. I trusted myself even less around him.

Without even noticing, I finished the scone and yogurt, then started on the fruit, now thinking about the best way to leave.

Lero hadn't told me much about his captors, but after his last trip, I understood the situation must be improving.

He hadn't said anything about me going home, but I hadn't brought it up myself, either. Other than feeling lonely when Lero was gone, I'd been rather comfortable on Blue Cay. He'd made sure of it, by catering to my every wish and more.

A frank conversation on the subject of my departure was long overdue. Maybe I could catch a ride with the next airplane that delivered groceries?

I finished my coffee, gathered the empty dishes, and with a bracing breath, headed back to the main house.

The front door was unlocked when I got there, but I knocked before entering. This was the first time I'd ever knocked when entering Lero's house. This morning was different. I didn't feel I belonged here anymore.

"Lero?" I called, stopping in the hallway.

No one replied to me. I did not hear a sound.

"Thank you for the breakfast," I said in a polite, neutral tone.

Again, no reply.

Maybe he went for a walk?

I made it to the kitchen, put the dishes into the dishwasher, rinsed and dried the serving tray to put it away. Then, I noticed the piece of paper on the kitchen table. The paper was weighted down by the conch shell he'd gotten for me from the ocean. It was a piece of stationery of *Monsieur L. Sauveterre.* On it, in wide, confident cursive stated,

*"Stella, I have to leave earlier than planned. I will be back in three days. Unfortunately, I won't be able to call this time. Please stay safe. Lero.*

*P.S. There's food in the fridge and a bottle of wine."*

I held the paper in my fingers long after I'd finished reading.

He was gone.

My heart pinched painfully, and I let it ache. It was time for my heart to learn how to go on without Lero.

The note was brief and to the point, with no excessive emotions or a hint of sentiment.

I sighed.

This was good. It was how it should be. He set the tone that would make it easier for me to leave him.

Ideally, I would've loved to leave right away. Except that it wasn't that easy to leave an island. I couldn't call the charter company to arrange for a flight using the agency's name again, not without having a very good reason and a detailed explanation for Javier.

Last time I'd done it, almost four weeks ago, it'd been an emergency situation. I *had* to get Lero and myself to Blue Cay. And even then, I'd only avoided having to explain anything to Javier because Lero had called my boss the very next day and settled the matter personally.

Since we'd just received a plane full of supplies yesterday, another grocery delivery probably wouldn't happen in the three days that Lero was gone. Which meant I wouldn't get the ride back to Miami with the pilot either. I was stranded here until Lero came back.

He wasn't even planning to call me this time, which was for the best. Since he wasn't here, I wouldn't have to face him or pretend anything. All I had to do was stay here for three days on my own, I'd been alone for longer than that before. It wasn't a big deal.

Once Lero returned, I would catch the same plane to go back home.

It was time.

The next two days went by, filled with my usual routine. I locked up the house at night, worked from morning until early afternoon, and ate the eggplant casserole Lero had made for dinner the night I'd spent at the cottage.

As he'd informed me in his note, he didn't call me on this trip. Not once. And I couldn't help worrying about him.

I told myself Lero was a grown man who knew what he was doing. He didn't need or want my caring about him. But not knowing how he was doing while away scraped inside me with worry I sensed would never really leave me, no matter how far away I'd be from him in the future or how much time would pass.

To distract myself from thinking about him and fretting over whether he was well and safe out there, I focused on doing things I wouldn't be able to do as easily when I was back in Miami. These were my last days on Blue Cay, after all.

I sunbathed on the patio—naked because who was there to demand I cover up? I took naps, because why not? I went swimming, also naked, because it felt more comfortable without the strings of my bikini digging into my neck and hips. I read to my heart's content.

On my last day alone, I made myself some spaghetti with the pasta sauce from a jar since Lero wasn't here to insist on making one from scratch.

If all went as planned, this would be my last dinner on Blue Cay. I might as well make a celebration out of it, I decided—my way to say goodbye to the island I'd grown quite attached to.

I set the massive dining table in the formal part of the house with a linen placemat and a matching napkin, put my spaghetti on a pretty plate, and even located a chunk of parmesan cheese in the fridge.

Before taking my seat in the chair with a high carved back at the head of the table, I remembered the bottle of wine that Lero had mentioned in his note.

It was white wine, I realized when I got the bottle out of the fridge. Obviously, Lero wouldn't leave a bottle of red in the fridge. According to him, red wine was supposed to remain in the "temperature-controlled environment" of the basement right up until its consumption.

Mostly, I drank white wine while on Blue Cay. I preferred its crisp, cool taste in the heat of the Bahamas. Tonight, however, my spaghetti dinner called to be paired with a glass of red. Spaghetti wasn't seafood. It might only be the premade sauce from a jar, but it was supposed to be my celebration dinner, dammit. I needed a proper wine pairing to go with it.

Maybe I'd have something nice for dessert, too. I'd seen a box of chocolate-dipped macarons in the pantry. Then, I'd take a nice, long walk on the beach to say goodbye to this place.

The perfectly round moon shone bright like a streetlight through the large windows of the house. It illuminated every grain of sand on the beach. I wouldn't even need to bring a flashlight with me.

Leaving the bottle of white wine in the fridge, I headed down to the basement for some red instead.

The massive oak door to the cellar creaked when I shoved it open. Cool air enveloped me, refreshing after the lingering heat upstairs.

I rubbed the goosebumps out of my upper arms while walking along the floor-to-ceiling mahogany shelves that lined the walls of the room. Lero had done a good job stocking on wine. There was still plenty of free space, but dark bottles sealed with red, gold, or black wax glistened on many shelves. Knowing his tastes, some of the wine bottles here might cost as much as my car payment or more.

I grabbed one with a pretty gold label. The writing on it wasn't in a language I could read. Italian, maybe? Spanish? Or Portuguese? I didn't care where the wine came from. The important part was that it looked red, even in the reduced light in the cellar.

Holding the bottle, I turned to leave when a low, rumbling noise reached me. Muffled by the walls, it appeared to be coming from inside the house somewhere.

Dread chilled my chest. The sound reminded me of the growling of a large dog—deep, rolling, threatening sound.

How did an animal get in here?

Where would a dog come from on this island? The biggest creatures I'd seen here that didn't live in the water were birds.

Unless the dog came with someone, on a boat or a plane?

I kept the island security system armed at all times. The house alarm, though, was not set yet because I'd planned to go for a walk later. If some uninvited visitors had made it to the island somehow, bypassing Lero's defense system, they'd have no trouble getting in the house.

My heart beat faster. Pressing the wine bottle to my chest, I stopped to listen for any sounds of footfalls or of moving upstairs. If there indeed were intruders in the house, did they come here for me? And if so, would they think to search the basement?

Staying still as a statue, afraid to move, I heard another long rumble, much clearer this time. It didn't seem to be coming from upstairs but from right here, near me, just behind one of the walls.

Jumping away from the shelves, I spun around, taking in the place. Now, that I thought about it, the cellar looked smaller than I remembered from viewing it with Lero. I didn't recall the exact dimensions from the sales brochure, but it seemed shorter.

Carefully, I crept closer to the wall opposite to the entrance. Had it been here before? Or had it been farther back?

Upon closer inspection, one section of the wall shelving appeared to be set inside a frame that was big enough to be a door. Did Lero have a secret room in his cellar?

He always brought up the wine on the few occasions we'd had some with dinner instead of letting me get it. I'd never questioned it. It was in line with his overall chivalry. Now, I wondered if he'd had a reason to keep me out of the cellar.

I pushed on the shelves, trying to slide the section in, but it wouldn't budge. Setting the bottle down on the floor, I ran my hands along the frame, searching for a lever, a button, or whatever else people usually had to touch to open secret passages in the haunted castles in movies.

I found nothing. If Lero indeed was hiding something here, he'd been smart enough to make it hard to find.

Suddenly, another rumble broke through the dead silence of the basement. It appeared to be coming right from behind the wall with the door frame. I immediately changed my mind about trying to open it. Instead, I bent to pick up my bottle of wine, ready to bolt.

The growl grew louder, turning to a roar.

A crushing noise thundered through the cellar. Bottles crashed to the floor, breaking and spilling the precious wine all over the place.

I jumped back from the wall, tripped on the rug soaked with spilled wine, and fell down on my butt.

The framed section of the shelving was destroyed. Broken boards dangled on nails and brackets, pieces of the wall littering the floor.

Another roar thundered—loud and clear—the sound was no longer obstructed by anything.

Then, I saw *what* had destroyed the shelving.

Two giant hands—or paws? Covered in thick, black-as-night fur, tipped with sharp, curved claws. They tore through the remnants of the wall, ripping the dangling pieces of shelving and wall off and tossing them into the cellar.

I trembled with shock.

"God help me," I whimpered, crab-walking away from the nightmarish thing that was about to tear through the wall separating us.

What on earth could it be?

The creature's face came into view. And suddenly I knew *what* it was.

I'd seen this animal before, almost a year and a half ago, in the underground parking garage of my condo building.

The beast smashed out the remaining pieces of the wall and shelving, but I realized it couldn't make it into the cellar to me. The opening in the wall was barred with thick metal rods, keeping the creature safely away from me.

I drew in a shaky breath. My arms and legs trembled from fear, but I felt a bit safer with the bars between me and the monster. They appeared much stronger than the wall. The beast grabbed on to them, trying to shake or break them, but to no avail.

Its pure rage, however, proved intimidating enough for me to remain on the floor. Deafening roars reverberated through the cellar as the animal thrashed against the metal bars of the cage that enclosed it.

Cinder block walls were visible behind the hulking figure of the beast. Shredded rags littered the floor on his side. I was right, the cellar had been made smaller. A section of it had been barred and walled off to create a holding cell for the animal.

But why? How long had it been there?

There was no stench of filth or excrement coming from the cell. Who fed him and cleaned after him? How did he get here?

The last time I saw the beast, he'd been captured by a group of intimidating bald men.

Was Lero one of them? Did they work for him? Was that where his money came from, the illegal animal trade? The idea made me sick to my stomach.

I'd been on this island for nearly a month now. I'd never seen any cages or crates delivered here. Was this the only animal he kept here?

A feeling of disappointment and betrayal settled heavily in my chest. I trusted Lero with my life. I felt safe coming here with him. I accepted his right to secrecy. And he'd made me believe he led a law-abiding life.

Recognizing the beast as a victim not a monster helped ease my fear. Avoiding any sudden movements, I slowly rose to my feet.

"Why are you here?" I asked softly. I wasn't expecting the animal to answer, of course. I simply tried to calm the creature by using a soothing voice.

The beast must've heard me despite the racket he was creating by roaring and shaking his cage. At the sound of my voice, he quieted, his bright red eyes following my every move.

Slowly, I took a step forward, fascinated by the creature. Separated by the bars, I gave in to my curiosity and inspected it a little closer.

"*What* are you?" I took another step in the direction of the cage.

In the dim lighting of the cellar, the beast's fur appeared black, absolutely void of any color. The flaming red of his eyes stood out on his face like two burning fires in the night. Sharp needle-like teeth filled his mouth. Long, spiky ears rose on each side of his head with a wolf-like snout.

The clawed "paws" he had wrapped around the bars were monstrous, but they had opposable thumbs and looked very much like hands.

"You're like no animal I've ever seen," I said, watching him closely as he stared back at me.

He stood upright, and his hind legs ended in paws, not feet. A long, bushy tail lashed around his legs, menacingly slow. His tense posture made him look ready to pounce. I could only hope the bars would hold if he did.

I came as close as I dared, making sure to stay well out of the reach of his great paws, even if the beast stuck them out between the bars.

Thick fur covered his chest that seemed too wide for a quadrupedal creature. At the same time, it didn't appear like standing upright was entirely natural for the creature. He hunched, towering at least a foot or two over my height. He would be even taller if he fully straightened out, which I didn't believe he could.

"Where on earth did you come from?" I whispered in awe, tilting my head back to take him all in.

The thick bars were positioned too close to each other for him to get his entire arm through, I realized. So I moved just a little closer.

At this distance, a wisp of the familiar scent reached me. Faint and subtle, its impact was like a punch in my stomach.

It was Lero's scent! I could never mistake it for anything else.

"What's going on?" I mumbled, utterly confused.

Why did the beast smell like Lero?

He'd told me there were questions he wasn't able to answer. But the sheer amount of all the unanswered questions I had were now crushing me.

"Why is he holding you here? Why do you smell like him? Why..."

The blazing red in the beast's eyes wavered, drawing back like a curtain of smoke and fire to reveal the serene gray behind it.

"Oh my God..." I clutched my neck with both hands as it suddenly hurt to breathe. "Lero... It can't be."

He closed his eyes, wincing. Despite the fur, the snout, and the grotesque beastly shape of his face, it was *his* expression. I recognized it without a doubt. I'd seen it enough times on his human face.

It was impossible. It simply couldn't be real.

And maybe it wasn't? Maybe all of this was some kind of a delusion, after all? Who on this island would tell me what was real and what wasn't? There was no one here, other than this beast of a man and me.

Forgetting all about keeping a safe distance, I came closer, searching the face of the monster for traces of the familiar features. Now that I knew what I was looking for, there were so many—the way he narrowed his eyes under my scrutiny, the way his lips curved in the corners, the way he jerked his head to toss back a thick clump of fur that hung over his forehead.

"Unbelievable," I breathed out. "Lero? Who did this to you?"

Bits and pieces of information I'd collected like crumbs along the way started to merge into a bigger picture.

Lero had been held captive, with obvious signs of sickness after he'd escaped. He'd been in pain. The glowing red in his irises that I'd spotted after cutting his hair had been the last and most unexplained symptom. Something had been done to him that had eventually transformed him into a beast.

The creature I'd witnessed getting captured in the garage wasn't an animal, either.

*Dez.*

It was the name of one of the men who'd captured the beast in the garage nearly a year and a half ago. Now, I remembered Lero had called his brother Dez, too, when he'd spoken about him earlier. Could it be the same person? It must be.

Lero couldn't be the same animal, of course, since he'd just transformed recently. There must be more like him.

Something evil had been done to Lero. I could only hope there was a cure.

"I'll need to find out who did this to you."

Dez was the only name I had. It wasn't much.

Throwing his head back, the beast released a loud groan, then struck his hand out between the bars and grabbed my upper arm.

"No!" I jerked back.

Lero would never hurt me, not physically anyway. But how much of Lero was left in the beast? Trepidation vibrated through me.

His fingers dug in deeper, holding me in place. With one yank, he brought me closer. Pressed against the bars, I grabbed on to one, straining to push away.

His face hovered next to mine, so close, his breath was moving the hair above my ear.

*"Watch out for his teeth."* The warning of one of Dez's men from long ago rang through my mind.

Those terrifying teeth were less than an inch away from my skin, now.

"Please don't hurt me," I whimpered.

I used to trust Lero, but I'd just learned I knew absolutely nothing about this man. The beast could end me quickly and in many ways.

I heard him breathe in. His lethal teeth snapped next to my neck, making me jump. Fear made me tremble uncontrollably.

"Please..." I struggled against his hold on my arm.

Instead of a bite I felt a gentle touch to my neck—the cool press of his nose, accompanied by the soft tickle of his fur. The hard metal bars between us didn't allow him a real hug, but I believed that was what he was trying to do—not to hurt me but to embrace me.

"Lero?"

Whatever had happened to him, I sensed he was suffering in this form. His reaching out for me suddenly felt like a plea for help. Compassion crushed my heart.

Instead of struggling to get away, I tentatively slid my hand between the bars and touched his arm. My fingers sunk into his fur—long, soft, and luxurious. I couldn't resist stroking up to his shoulder to feel the silky glide of his fur between my fingers.

"What can I do?" I half-whispered, overtaken by concern for him and at the same time, mesmerized by the wonder of this entire experience.

This close, his familiar scent enveloped me, the heat of our bodies warming the metal of the bars trapped between us.

He threaded his other arm through the cage—it fit only up to the elbow between the bars—and grabbed on to my waist. His sharp claws pierced through my shirt and dug into my skin without breaking it.

The surreal sensation of being held by him—half-man, half-beast—made me dizzy. Fog clouded my mind, mixing with his scent. His soft fur brushed against my skin. I was no longer sure whether it was a man or a beast holding me. Somehow it no longer mattered.

Either way, it was Lero.

"Who locked you here? How do I get you out?"

There was no predicting for sure what Lero would do if set free. I had no idea what to expect from him in this form. He clearly couldn't communicate with words. However, I couldn't possibly leave him in the cage now that I'd found him.

Searching around the bars, I noticed they were covered in blood where his hands had just gripped them. Alarm shot through me, my concern rising higher.

"Are you hurt?" I twisted to see the hand gripping my arm.

Smears of blood marred my skin where he held me. The white fabric of my shirt was also stained red by his hand at my waist.

He was bleeding.

I slid my hands up his arms to his shoulders then to his neck, gently feeling for injuries. My arms being thinner than his, I was able to fit them between the bars all the way up to my shoulders.

The hard cords of muscles flexed and bulged under his thick, soft fur. Despite being completely still, he was far from relaxed. A shudder ran through his body. His hands flexed tighter on me. He released a groan filled with pain.

"What is it, Lero? Where are you hurt?"

He pressed harder against the bars, holding on to me like to a life raft. With a sudden loud roar, he thrust his hips against the cage separating us. A hard length—not metal, but just as solid—poked me in my belly.

"Oh God..." I shrank back, with a shocked realization of what it was —his erection.

He yanked me against him with a long growl.

"No!" I fisted my hands in his fur.

He threw his head back, releasing a deafening roar that ended in a blood curdling howl.

Fear chilled my chest. Clamped in his grip, I could barely move. The more I struggled, the firmer he held, his claws scraping against my skin as his hands flexed.

Reaching down, I found his hard-on and squeezed it hard in return.

"Let me go," I threatened in a hiss.

Instead of fighting me, he thrust his hips into my grip with a deep, satisfied rumble.

I leaned back as far as his hold would allow. "Is that what you want?" I relaxed my grip but didn't let go, his shaft hot and pulsing in my hand. It also felt slippery.

Glancing down, I saw where Lero's injuries were. Deep scratches marred the velvety soft skin of his hard length, blood seeping from them and slicking it red.

He'd tried to touch himself, it dawned on me. With those sharp claws on his fingers, he'd only ended up hurting himself.

"What have you done?" I whispered around the hard lump forming in my throat. I relaxed my hand, releasing him.

Letting go of my waist, he quickly grabbed my hand, wrapping my fingers around his erection once again.

The terrifying red glow in his eyes ebbed with the tide of cooling gray again. It appeared like Lero was looking at me from behind the scary face of the beast.

"Lero... Honey, it'll hurt," I whispered, attempting to remove my hand.

With a soft rumble, he pressed my hand in place. Gripping my waist again, he thrust into my hand. Apparently, the pain from his injuries was less than the agony of arousal he was going through.

Tears swelled behind my eyelids. I stopped fighting him. Sliding my free arm between the bars, I snaked it around his neck, keeping my other hand gently wrapped around his straining length.

Resting his nose on my shoulder, he kept pumping his hips with fervent desperation. Holding him to me, I let it happen.

For years, I'd been craving intimacy with this man. Never in my darkest nightmares had I envisioned it would happen this way. The pain in his groans made it feel almost like an act of mercy. My tears dripped, sliding down the metal bars to be soaked up by his fur.

At the same time, there was something thrilling and fulfilling in it, too, despite the sadness. For those few moments, there was no beast, just a man who desperately needed me, and I reveled in being close to him. Right now, the bars between us seemed so much less of a barrier than the distance Lero had maintained before.

Stripped of his human appearance, he seemed to have lost his reasons to keep away from me, and I cherished it for what it was.

His growls grew deeper and stronger. He jerked violently against the bars, then the hot spurts of his release shot to the floor between us. The cage shook. His teeth snapped at my ear again, and he yanked his head back, keeping his mouth away from me.

Something grew beneath my fingers. Glancing down, I saw a thick bulbous swelling form at the base of his shaft.

"What's that?" I jerked my hand away, afraid I'd hurt him.

Lero no longer seemed to be hurting, however. His growls softened to a satisfied purr that vibrated through his chest.

Relieved, I rested my forehead against the cool metal of the cage, a little overwhelmed by it all. The tension and anxiety that had gripped my heart and weighed down my shoulders had drained, leaving just numbness behind.

With a soft snort, Lero fitted his nose between the bars and placed it on my shoulder again. I touched the side of his face, and he snuggled closer—so different from his previous behavior with me, back when he looked like a man and acted like a stranger no matter how much time we'd spend together.

"I need to get you out of here," I said softly. "Then, I'll have to figure out who did this to you and what to do next." I heaved a long, heavy sigh. "I wish you would've told me everything. Back when you still could talk..."

He relaxed his fingers, sliding his hands up and down my sides as far as the bars would let him.

"Is there anything on your computer system about this, Lero?"

The desktop in the closet room was connected to the island security system. Other than the request for a palm print, I hadn't encountered any other password prompts or restrictions. I hadn't snooped, but the current situation might warrant it.

The moment I made a move to leave, however, he wrapped his fingers around my arm again, keeping me in place.

"You want me to stay? But how will I help you from here? I need to go upstairs to search the system."

He stared at me with those clear gray eyes, one of the parts of the old Lero I recognized in the beast. His grip on me remained firm, as if my presence was the only help he needed.

It felt wrong to leave him here alone.

"Show me how to get you out of here." I inspected the metal box fitted between the bars on one side. Flat and solid, it appeared to have an opening on the other side. I couldn't see it, but I felt it with my fingers. If it was indeed a lock, the keyhole was on Lero's side.

"Do you know where the key is?" I asked.

Searching around the remnants of the broken shelves, I tried to locate anything that could hold a key—a box, a hook, anything—and found nothing. Logic told me that since the keyhole was on Lero's side of the bars then the key should be there, too. Though, it made no sense to keep the key in the prisoner's cell.

He didn't appear to be concerned about my efforts to free him. In fact, he seemed tired. His eyelids heavy, he looked like he would crash to the floor, exhausted, had he not held on so tightly to me.

"You look sleepy," I said.

With a long, rumbling exhale, he dropped to his knees, taking me down with him. I grabbed on to the bars, to keep my balance, though he probably wouldn't have let me fall anyway, his grip on my arm and waist as firm as ever.

There was nothing but torn rugs on his side of the bars, with spilled wine, broken glass, and pieces of wood on my side.

"I'll stay," I promised, placing my hand on his at my waist. "Just let me get some blankets and pillows first."

His eyelids flew open. He seemed fully awake once again, giving me a penetrating look as if searching for truth to my promise deep inside my eyes. Finally, he released me, slowly sliding his hands down my sides before letting them drop from me completely.

Carefully stepping over the broken wine bottles on the floor, I made it to the cellar exit.

From there, I glanced back. Standing on his knees, his massive, fur-covered hands gripping the bars of his prison, Lero's intense gaze followed me. There was so much longing in his eyes, my heart squeezed in sorrow for him.

"I'll be back in a minute," I promised, choked with compassion and struggling to hold back a new wave of tears.

I ran up the stairs to the main floor.

There, I grabbed a couple of cushions off the lounge chairs on the patio, then collected some pillows and blankets from my room. Piling it all up on top of the stairs, I rushed to Lero's closet.

No matter how crazy the night had turned out to be, he'd drilled into my head that safety was important. I quickly armed the house alarm system.

On the way through the dining room, I grabbed my untouched plate of "celebratory" spaghetti and shoved it into the fridge in the kitchen. I was no longer hungry, though I wished I'd had some wine—of either color.

When I returned to the cellar, Lero lay on his side, seemingly asleep. His massive body pressed tight against the cage, he had stretched his right arm between the bars as far as he could, almost up to his elbow. My chest tightened with ache and compassion. It looked as if he was waiting for me even as exhaustion had claimed him.

I quickly swept the glass from the floor, then rolled the ruined rug aside. Arranging my loot of cushions and blankets next to the cage, I made a sleeping pallet for myself. I managed to cover Lero with a blanket too, working my hands between the bars.

All this time, he appeared deep asleep, his chest rising and falling rhythmically. His breath came out with a low rumble in his chest, deadly teeth glistening white between his lips.

Even asleep, he was terrifying, but I wasn't frightened of the beast, only of those who'd done this to him.

Lying down on my side of the bars, I took his hand in mine.

"Good night, Lero," I whispered. "Tomorrow is going to be a busy day."

I now had a goal ahead of me—I had to find out what'd happened to Lero and how I could ease his suffering.

# Chapter Fifteen

LERO

Awareness returned to him slowly as the fog of madness cleared. Relief came next. The build-up of the Moon's power had climaxed, releasing him for the next few weeks.

He always felt the energy of the Moon. His people were born with its magic coursing through their veins. Back before Ghata corrupted it in Nerifir, he'd heard that the nights of full moon used to be filled with joy and love.

For him, it had only been pain and madness.

He stretched his legs, sore muscles screaming in protest. His bones ached after the transformation. But his mind cleared, and the pain was quickly receding. All he needed was a hot shower to wash off the blood and soothe his aching body.

The ache seemed to be more pronounced in his right arm, which felt especially stiff. A weight was pressing down on his hand.

He opened his eyes, finding...Stella lying just outside his cage in the cellar. He wondered if he was still asleep and dreaming. Stella had been his constant companion in his dreams. Without ever knowing, she'd been his morning star who led him through darkness. She'd helped him fight the madness and hold on to his sanity through the torture of Ghata's captivity. And now, the dreams of her chased the lingering nightmares away.

Lately, Stella had caused a different kind of insanity in him, however. Over the past weeks, his dreams of her had slowly turned from warm and pleasant to burning hot and filled with things he never could do to her in real life. Desire for her consumed him both while asleep and awake.

Her touch as she'd cut his hair a few days ago ignited an inferno. For a few terrifying moments his control had slipped. She was so soft and delicate, and he burned to ravage her, to fuck her until she screamed his name and prayed to the Moon with him.

Gods, the things he would've done to her had she not run and locked herself in the cottage. A shudder shook his body, jolting his aching muscles.

He'd traced her scent to the front door of the manager's cottage and found it locked. He had the key back at the house. He could have simply broken the door in, too. But the extra effort it would require gave him the moment he needed to regain a modicum of control.

Instead of barging in, which would've surely traumatized and terrified her, he lurked around the building for hours, hoping to catch a glimpse of her through the windows, but she'd never even turned the lights on.

He hadn't gone to bed that night, roaming the island until the bout of madness subsided closer to the morning. Only then had he ventured to unlock the door and check on Stella. She slept on the couch, barefoot, in her shorts and top. Curled up, she looked so small and defenseless.

He'd vowed to protect her. Yet, he had become the biggest threat to her peace and safety. Instead of going down to the basement just for the night of the full moon, he needed to get away from Stella right away. He'd covered her with a blanket and, after making her breakfast, went to his cage, starting his self-confinement early.

The memories of the past three days were a blur of pain and desire —the agony of lust. This had been his first full moon in this world without *womora*, and he'd needed to fuck more than he needed to breathe. But not just anyone. Lately, he'd only wanted Stella, so badly it'd been worse than any torture.

He wanted her still.

Her eyes closed, Stella appeared to be peacefully asleep just outside of his cage. There was so much trust in her placing her head into his hand like that. The heat of her skin warmed his palm. He gently moved his thumb, stroking above the curve of her eyebrow.

Why was she here?

The trashed state of the cellar behind Stella had finally registered with him. The wall that was supposed to conceal the monster the Moon turned him into was gone. The space reeked of spilled wine. The rug shoved aside, Stella slept in a pile of blankets on the floor.

He tried to sift through the fog of his memories from last night. Shattered and distorted like shards of glass, the fragments of what he remembered shifted and aligned enough to form a picture.

Stella had seen his beast!

Fear shot through him, chasing away the post-transformation drowsiness. Worry pulsed in his chest as he slid his gaze down Stella's sleeping form.

Sleeping?

*"Please, gods, let her be asleep, not...dead,"* he fervently prayed in his mind.

He spotted a rusty smidge of dried blood on her temple. There were a few on her arm, too.

The blinding lust had driven him mad as much as the Moon. It'd spurred his rage when he'd caught a tendril of her sweet scent through the wall of his prison.

What had he done?

Gently pulling his hand free, he scrambled up to his feet and opened a compartment in the wall to the right of the barred entrance. The barrel bolt on the compartment's door had been specifically designed to be opened with the fingers of a man, not the claws of a beast. Only when he turned into his usual, less threatening form, could he release himself.

He took out the key that was hanging there and unlocked his cage.

"Stella," he exhaled, struggling against the suffocating panic. He trailed his shaking fingers along her face and neck, begging the stars she was indeed just asleep.

"Mmm?" she murmured. Her eyelids fluttered open.

For one most amazing moment, a gentle warm smile lit up her peaceful expression as she gazed up at him. If it were a dream, he wouldn't want to wake up. Ever.

"Lero?" Her brows drew together, a frown replaced her smile. Her peaceful expression was gone.

Sadly, last night had not been just a dream.

"You're hurt," he rasped.

"What?" She blinked, sitting up, the blanket clutched to her chest.

"The blood." He gestured at her arm. "Where did I scratch you?"

It must have been his claws. Had it been his teeth, she would no longer be alive.

He shuddered at the thought of what could've happened had it not been for the bars of his cage. He shouldn't have stayed on the island during the full moon while Stella was here. He'd been selfish, stealing every last minute he could still spend with her. He should've let her go the moment he'd come back, but he just couldn't...

The room behind the cellar was secure and sound-proof. He'd had it made during the first weeks of taking the possession of Blue Cay, before he was taken by *bracks* just a month later.

The walls were supposed to conceal him in his beast form. Obviously, he'd failed to take into account the effect Stella's scent would have on his lust-crazy beast.

"Where did I hurt you, Stella? You're bleeding."

"Me?" She tugged down the fabric of her shirt, inspecting the long, rust-colored smears on her side. "It's yours, Lero. I'm not hurt."

He cast a glance at his hands, covered in dried blood, too. Suddenly, he knew where it'd come from. He didn't need to see his bare thighs to know there would be blood there, too.

As a beast, he couldn't make himself come, which didn't mean that driven to delirium by unfulfilled desire he hadn't tried. Over and over again. Clawing at his rock-hard, aching cock, drawing blood, and hurting himself, with no release.

Shame chilled his chest and heated his face. Never had he loathed what the Moon forced him to become as much as he did now. His beast state was uncontrollable, dangerously unpredictable, and...mortifying.

"I'm sorry you had to see...that." He winced but forced his gaze to remain on her, studying her face for any signs of trauma.

She looked confused, still adorably sleepy, shaken... But had she been traumatized? Somehow, she was relatively calm after what she'd seen.

How had she survived the night? And managed to fall asleep?

"How are you?" he asked, as gently as he could muster.

"You turned back." She stared at him. "You were... You had fur." She gestured at her shoulders and chest. "You couldn't speak. What happened, Lero?"

He feared the damage she'd suffered might be deeper than he could see. Maybe if he kept things as normal as possible for her now, she'd get over the terrifying experience more smoothly.

"You know what?" he said. "We both need a bath, a decent breakfast, and some fresh air."

With a deep cleansing breath, he scooped her off the floor and lifted her in his arms.

"A bath? What are you talking about? Dammit, Lero, what happened?" A panicky note rang in her voice, making him dread the worst.

"Shh," he whispered soothingly into her hair as he carried her up the stairs and into his bathroom. "The night is over, and so is the nightmare, Stella. You'll leave this place as soon as possible, I swear. Nothing and no one will ever threaten you again. Not even me."

"You want me to leave?" She clung to his shoulders, her entire body trembling. He prayed to every deity in this world and any other that she would survive this unscathed—body and mind.

He turned the tub faucet on, letting the water rush out. The tub was too big and would take forever to fill. He gently sat her down—her bare feet on the tiled floor. She wouldn't let go of his shoulders, though, holding on to him like a drowning woman to a lifesaver.

He was no lifesaver, though. Quite the opposite...

"Lero." She stared into his eyes. "*What* are you?"

He faltered under her question. Simple and direct, it demanded a straightforward answer. Only nothing about his existence was straightforward, not since he'd left his world. And even then...

"Please," he implored. "Please, Stella. Could you think about all of this as a bad dream? Forget last night, forget me. That's your only chance to go on and be happy—"

She let go of him, taking a step back. The disapproval in her stare cut like a knife.

"For half of my life, I tried to forget you, Lero, and failed. It's not going to happen, now, for as long as I live."

# Chapter Sixteen

STELLA

I sat in Lero's massive bathtub, naked. The water swirled around me, rising higher.

Below the tub's marble platform was a rectangular pool that ran along the entire back wall of the bathroom. The glass of the large window separated the indoor portion from the big outdoor pool that took up most of the stone patio at the back of the house.

This was a beautiful water feature that the real estate listing highlighted as one of the property's best selling points.

Only the entire pool was empty, now. Its turquoise and gold mosaic floor and walls remained exposed and dry. The passage to the outdoors had been securely boarded up.

It was so like Lero, to trade joy and beauty for security. I wouldn't be surprised if given enough time, he'd get rid of the island's incredible views by erecting a concrete wall all along its picturesque beaches.

Maybe I failed to fully appreciate his efforts because the threat he worried about had never been fully explained to me. It was hard to feel afraid if I didn't know exactly what the danger was.

The last twelve hours had been an emotional rollercoaster. I'd gone from peace, to terror, to heart-wrenching compassion and anger, to... *"It's all been a dream. Just forget about it."*

His withdrawal this morning hurt more than anything.

Nothing made sense, and I had no one to turn to for explanation. A headache pounded inside my skull the more I tried to make sense of things on my own. Unanswered questions piled up, breeding more questions...

I got out of the soapy water, rinsed off quickly, and drained the tub. Putting on the same shorts and blood-stained top I wore last night, I walked out of Lero's bathroom.

I found him standing at one of the glass doors to the back patio, a closed laptop under his arm. He'd had a shower in one of the guest's bathrooms. His hair still looked damp, though brushed and styled in his usual fashion. Wearing a white shirt with the sleeves rolled up and a pair of light-colored pants, he looked so...normal, as if last night had never happened at all.

He turned to me.

"Are you hungry?" he asked, as calm and distant as ever.

As if I hadn't had my fingers wrapped around his fucking dick just hours ago. As if he hadn't bled in my hand. As if I hadn't wept for him...

I bit my lip and fisted my hands to stop them from trembling.

"So, you can change at will, then?" My voice came out hollow.

His chest rose with a deep breath.

"No. Just during the full moon." His mouth pressed into a stubborn line. "Stella—"

"Do you *remember* things when you're...when you look like you did last night?"

He winced, as if it pained him to remember. And maybe it did. But I needed to know.

"If you're referring to, um..."

He jerked his head aside as if trying to toss away the memories.

"It doesn't matter," he said. "I apologize for *everything* that happened last night. Every single thing that happened from the moment you entered the cellar. You weren't supposed to see any of that."

"I came to get a bottle of red wine," I explained. The evening of my planned spaghetti dinner seemed so far away now, as if it'd been a century ago.

He raked the fingers of his free hand through his hair, glossy from the shower.

"I should've brought some up for you before leaving."

"It's not about the wine," I said, my voice soft but firm.

"It could be!" He snapped, his unshakable composure finally cracking. "It could be all about the damn wine or whatever you want it to be—"

"Just not about the truth, right? As long as I don't ask questions you don't want to answer, isn't it?" I raised my voice, too.

He heaved a breath, the muscles in his jaw flexing as he visibly struggled to compose himself. Sadly, I could almost feel the wall between us grow taller, thicker, and more impenetrable as his composure returned.

Silently, he placed the laptop on the kitchen table and opened it, obviously signaling me the conversation was over.

If I were dirty, he'd run me a bath. If I were hungry, he'd feed me a gourmet meal. If I were cold, he'd bring me a blanket. But if I demanded answers, he wouldn't even spare me a glance.

"You make me miss the beast," I said softly. His shoulders jerked, and he snapped his gaze to mine. "You had no ability to speak last night, yet we understood each other so much better."

His severe expression wavered. His frown softened. The red in his gray eyes remained but a distant echo, glowing faintly like the cooling embers of last night's inferno.

"Tell me, Stella, how were you not repulsed seeing me like that? How were you not terrified of the monster?"

He wouldn't allow me any answers, yet he had his own burning questions.

Unlike him, I wasn't going to deny him the answers. Sliding my gaze aside, I took a moment to collect my thoughts. How could I best explain what I felt?

"I saw the man, silently suffering in the body of the beast, Lero. Not a monster. I knew it was you." I spoke from the heart, "Why do you find it so hard to accept that I care about you, in any shape and form?"

He stared back at me, his expression unreadable. His eyes anxiously flicked between mine, something was happening behind them, but I couldn't say what.

He grabbed my arm.

"Come." He tugged me to his side of the table. "Look."

He ran his fingers over the keyboard of his laptop.

A picture of a smiling young woman came up on the screen. She sat next to a flaxen-blond boy at a table set with dishes. Wearing a pastel-blue dress with a lace collar, she had curly chestnut-colored hair styled into a flirty bob. Her arm was draped around the boy's shoulders.

"You've asked me who Amelie was," Lero said, his voice dark and hollow. "That's her."

"She is...pretty," I said softly, halting my breath. "And happy."

"*Was*," he corrected. "She *was* beautiful, happy, and full of life... until she witnessed me *turn* once."

"Turn?" I kept staring at the smiling woman in the picture.

"She saw me change into the beast one night, and she couldn't handle it." His voice was saturated with pain.

"What happened to her? Where is she now?" I asked, afraid to hear the answer.

He hit a button on the keyboard.

"Here."

A picture of a grave with a white headstone came up. A fresh bouquet of lilacs and dark purple roses lay on it.

"Dead?" I could barely whisper.

"For almost five years now," he confirmed, solemnly. "Dead and buried in the cemetery next to the mental institution where she'd spent the last thirty years of her life."

"A mental institution..." I gasped.

"Well, they call it a *villa*," he said with sarcasm. "Like it's just a relaxing place to spend a summer. In reality, it's a long-term care home where people who can no longer function on their own spend their lives dependent on others."

"Did Amelie's family send her there?"

He raised his darkened gaze at me.

"I did."

My knees gave in, and I let myself drop into one of the chairs at the table.

"You? Why?"

"Because Amelie was—always will be—my shame, my guilt, and my responsibility. My mistake that I never want to repeat."

"What happened?" I asked, begging him to keep talking for once.

Propping his arms onto the table, he hung his head between his shoulders, standing over the laptop with the picture of Amelie's grave.

"I met her in the restaurant I owned at the time. She came with her family, celebrating someone's birthday. I liked her laugh..." He paused, closing his eyes. "We started dating. A true bond isn't possible with a human, but I didn't even hope for one. All I wished for was to have a companion, someone in this world to share my life with, even if for a little while. I liked Amelie, a lot. I brought her home. She got along well with Zeph. I truly believed the three of us could be a happy little family one day." A bitter smile crossed his lips.

"I'd given her the key to my place, for emergencies. She wanted to surprise me one night and came over without letting me know she'd be there."

He stared straight at the picture on the screen, now.

"She found me in the basement. I had my cage there, it wasn't hidden. We'd just moved into that place. I hadn't even put the lock on the door of the room yet. It was my fault. She saw me in the cage, watched me change, and...she couldn't take it."

"What happened?" I breathed out.

"She screamed." He flinched, shutting his eyes tightly. "I'll never get that scream out of my mind. It'll cut through my brain forever. She screamed so much, again and again. Then, she fainted. I don't remember clearly what came next. I see the world differently when I'm in that state. My memories are often choppy and distorted. But when I turned back in the morning, Amelie was still there, in the basement room with me."

"Unconscious?"

"No. She'd come to sometime during the night, but she was no longer herself. She'd been disoriented to the point that she couldn't find the door and leave. Instead, she'd crawled into a corner and spent the night watching me rage in my fucking cage." Balling his hands into fists, he slammed them against the table, making me jump in my seat.

"She lost her mind completely during that night. I took her to the hospital. Her family came. She didn't recognize anyone. They put her in a home. It wasn't a good place..." He shook his head.

"Was that the villa?" I asked.

"No. She got transferred to the villa later. It was much better, in terms of staff, quality of care, location, food—everything."

"Did you pay for it?" I guessed.

He nodded.

"Her family had no proof, but they knew that Amelie's condition had something to do with me. I was the one who got her to the hospital. They would never accept the money from me directly. I had to arrange for payments with the management privately, as an anonymous donor."

"The family never knew?"

"If they did, they never let me know. At the end of the day, Amelie got the best care money could buy. It was the least I could do."

"Did you ever get to see her again?"

He went silent, gazing over the laptop out into the sea.

"Once," he finally said.

"Just once?"

He nodded.

"Amelie didn't recognize anyone. She couldn't take care of herself, but she wasn't violent—until she saw me. She flew into a vicious fit of rage at the sight of me. After that, the staff asked me not to visit anymore."

"So, she recognized you?"

He exhaled a bitter laugh.

"As someone from her nightmares. Apparently, she suffered from night terrors. And I starred in all of them."

I glanced at the exquisite flower arrangement on top of the gravestone in the picture.

"Instead of visiting you sent her flowers?"

"Still do. Every year on her birthday. She loved getting them, I was told. Purple was her favorite color."

He fell silent again, and I kept quiet, too.

*"How were you not terrified of the monster?"* he'd asked me.

The truth was, I had been. I'd just been a little better prepared than Amelie, I believed. I'd seen the same animal before, back in the parking garage. I'd watched him being overpowered, hurt, and restrained. And I felt compassion for him, not just fear.

Unlike Amelie, I hadn't seen Lero actually change. That must have been a traumatic experience on its own.

"Who is the boy in the picture?" I asked.

"Zeph."

"Your friend?" I recognized the name he'd mentioned earlier.

"He is more than a friend. I raised him as my own son, though we're not related by blood."

"How old is Zeph now?"

He lifted his eyes to mine. "He'll be forty-nine, soon."

It shouldn't have made sense, but it did. For the first time ever, things actually started making sense.

"You're not thirty-one like you've said, then." I held his gaze.

"No." He scrubbed his hand over his face. "I turned ninety-six last month."

"Ha!" Air left my lungs with a sharp, nervous laugh.

As incredible as it sounded, the math added up.

I knew the man I met in Paris years ago didn't look like a seventeen-year-old boy he'd claimed he would've been back then.

The picture of Amelie with Zeph as a little boy wasn't taken digitally. It had the quality of an older paper photograph that had been taken decades ago and scanned more recently.

The cut of her dress, Amelie's hair, and makeup were most suitable for the fashion of about four decades ago, when the forty-nine-year-old Zeph would have been a boy.

"I'm not human, Stella." Lero stepped away from the table.

"I gathered that much," I croaked, my mouth turning too dry to speak.

None of this could be real, yet deep in my heart I knew that it was. I could try to come up with a different, maybe a little more believable explanation, but I already knew I'd be wasting my time.

"*What* are you?" I braced myself for his answer.

He crossed his arms over his broad chest, rolling his shoulders back.

"A werewolf." There was a certain pride in his answer. As painful as I understood his existence was at times, he didn't deny his heritage.

And what a heritage that was!

"Like in the movies?" I stared at him. I might have guessed already but hearing him admit it out loud made it sound as extraordinary as it was.

"Movies are based on old legends," he replied. "And no legend is without some truth to it."

I kept staring at him—showered, dressed, well-groomed, and elegant, and so very human, it made me think this whole conversation was an insane dream.

"I don't age," he said. "Not until the very end of my life, which won't be for at least four hundred years. Unless I get killed before that of course."

"Is there still a chance of that?" I asked, thinking about his brother.

"There's always a chance of that as long as the people—the beings—who caught me are alive."

"Are they also..." I paused, before uttering the word out loud, "...werewolves?"

"They're worse." He closed the laptop. "But you don't need to worry about them. The less you know the better. If there is one thing I'll do in this life, it's—"

"To keep me safe by keeping me in the dark," I finished for him. "I know. You've made it abundantly clear by now, Lero. Except that it didn't work. I've been thrust into your world, against your wishes and best intentions. Are there many like you in this world? Where did you come from? Why are you here?"

"Stella." He raised a hand, halting my stream of questions. "No. I've said it before I can't answer everything—"

But I wouldn't give up. I simply couldn't stop, now.

"The least you could do is to explain what I've seen, Lero. You said you change forms on the full moon. Why did you go into the basement for *three* days?"

He nodded, conceding.

"My appearance changes at sunset on the night of the full moon. Inside me, however, the beast starts stirring days before that."

"What do you mean?"

"For days before the full moon, I lose control, little by little. Once I turn, the base instincts take over—the need to hunt, fight, and fuck. Nothing else remains. I lose control." Propping his arms on the table again, he leaned over it, staring at me intently. "Stella, I've killed in that form, and I couldn't help the murders."

"What murders?" Now, he was actively trying to scare me away, I believed. "But last night—"

He didn't let me finish.

"Last night, things could've ended tragically..." He groaned, shaking his head. "Gods, Stella. This is my entire life, right here. That's all there is to it. I'm constantly fighting with the Moon over the control of my mind and body. But like I said, you don't have to worry about any of this. This is not your world and not your problem. It's now safer for you out there than it is here, with me."

He straightened, giving me a calm look.

"The airplane is coming for you later this afternoon. You're finally free to go home, Stella."

Home?

My small, empty apartment didn't feel like home to me, right now. Just hours ago, I was almost ready to *swim* back to Miami. Now that he'd made arrangements for me to leave, it didn't feel right anymore, like I'd be leaving things unfinished.

Lero heaved a breath, picking up his laptop off the table.

"You'll have your old life back."

Did I want it back? Just the way it was? I had my place, my job, things I'd achieved and was proud of. But had I really missed my old life while being here?

"What about you, Lero?" I asked softly. "What kind of life are you planning to have once I'm gone?"

He glanced out the glass doors toward the open sea once again, avoiding my eyes.

"I promised to keep you safe," he growled low, not answering my question. "I *cannot* ruin your life."

With the laptop under his arm, he stormed out the back doors to the patio then jogged down the stone steps toward the beach.

Passing a copse of low trees, he furiously tossed the laptop into the brush under them as I watched speechless.

# Chapter Seventeen

STELLA

My bag had been packed for three days now. It was the same bag I'd come here with. Lero had bought me clothes and toiletries during the month I'd spent on the Blue Cay, but it felt wrong to take anything of that with me—they weren't really mine. The only extra things I was taking with me were a couple of polished rocks and a colored piece of glass I'd found in the strait under the bridge.

With more than an hour left before the airplane was supposed to arrive for me, I waited for it on the beach.

I had cleaned the room where I'd stayed, washed the sheets, and changed the bedding. When Lero had returned to the house, I snuck out, not willing to face him. I knew I'd have to come back to say goodbye before I left. Despite everything, he'd been a generous host. It would be extremely rude of me to leave without at least thanking him for everything he'd done for me.

Except that parting from Lero would hurt, I always knew that. And getting nothing but a cold "goodbye" and a handshake would make it so much worse. I longed to see him again, knowing it'd probably be the last time ever. And I dreaded that moment when I had to look at him for the very last time.

I waded into the warm waves, digging my toes into the soft sand below.

If there was anything I'd learned about my host, it was that his calm façade was forced, carefully practiced, and hard-earned. An inferno raged inside that hard, cold shell of control. Lero had been fighting the storm all his life, alone.

It felt horribly wrong leaving him on his own again. Yet what could I do if he'd been so adamantly shoving me away?

The sun dipped past the summit, its rays twinkling in the waves and forming a shimmering path on the surface of the ocean.

Strangely, the shimmer seemed to be moving, shining brighter the closer it got. I admired the dancing lights for a moment, wondering what would cause the effect since I'd never seen anything like it before.

After a while it became apparent the movement wasn't natural. Something was heading through the water to me.

Lero's warnings rose in my mind. I slowly backed out to the beach as the shimmering glow advanced.

Then, a head popped out of the water. A man emerged from the waves, wading onto the sand to me.

I saw no diving equipment on him, no weapons either, unless he hid any in his rather tight, navy-blue swim shorts. In his hand, he held a small net filled with gray shells.

Just in case, I stepped behind a nearby tree, getting out of view. Too late, it seemed, as he had spotted me already.

"Hi there!" he yelled, waving his free hand at me.

I peeked from around the tree trunk, studying him closely as he approached. He was very handsome, beautiful even. Flashing me a toothy smile, he shook the water out of his white hair, cropped close to his head on the sides and longer on top. Against the afternoon sun, the water droplets broke into an iridescent mist around him, making the newcomer look like a mythical being, not merely a man but a vision, like a water spirit.

"Is Lero in the house?" he asked, cheerfully. "I brought oysters!" He lifted the net filled with shells over his head.

I stepped out from my not-so-secret hiding place. The man's behavior was friendly, not at all threatening. Though, I still had no idea how he got here. There was no plane or boat in sight. Also, the island's security system had been armed ever since Lero got home four days ago. Unless he'd turned it off already, in anticipation of the airplane's arrival?

The man took a few steps closer but not too close, keeping a comfortable distance from me, which I appreciated.

"Lero is here," I said, deciding it was best for him to know I wasn't alone. "Who are you?"

"I'm Zeph. Lero's friend."

"Zeph?"

Of course! Now that he'd introduced himself, I recognized the light-blond hair and the dimpled smile of the boy from the picture with Amelie.

I knew Zeph wouldn't look his forty-nine years when Lero told me his age. But I didn't expect him to appear this youthful. The boyish smile made him seem even younger.

"I'm very glad to meet you." He stretched his hand my way.

I took it.

"I'm Stella." I studied him now with a new curiosity. Was Zeph a werewolf, too? He didn't seem as stiff and tense as Lero. On the contrary, Zeph appeared as relaxed and happy as could be.

"Stella?" His dark eyebrows shot up in delight. "It means 'star,' doesn't it?"

I nodded. My father had big dreams for me when I was born. All of them revolved around riches and stardom. Hence the name he chose for me, Stella—Star.

"How is Lero doing?" Zeph asked. "I thought I'd check on him since it was a full moon last night. He doesn't feel his best around this time."

"Um...Lero is well," I replied carefully, unsure of how much I should say.

He peered at me from under the wet strands of hair falling over his forehead. His eyes, I noted, were of exactly the same color as the sea behind him.

"Are you a friend of his, too?" he asked.

I tried not to flinch.

A friend? Could I call myself that?

"I'm...just a house guest." I blinked, glancing away from his inquisitive stare.

I felt the light touch of his fingers on my hand.

"Lero could really use a friend, Stella," he said softly, then added, "And more."

*More*... More than a friend?

My heart skipped and my face felt hot at the thought of how much I actually wanted to get a chance to have *more* with Lero.

"Zeph!" Lero's sharp voice cut through the air like a whip, from the entrance of the house.

"Oh, and there is the old man himself!" Zeph's smile returned. "It was very nice meeting you, Stella." He tipped his head to me, sun twinkling in his sea-blue eyes, then headed up the slope toward Lero who was rushing our way from the house.

"It was nice to meet you, too." I gave Zeph a friendly wave, catching myself smiling back at him. It was impossible not to, his cheerful mood proved highly contagious.

Watching the two men embrace briefly, I wondered what an easy-going man like Zeph could possibly have in common with someone as distant and withdrawn as Lero.

Wrapping one arm around Zeph's shoulders, Lero led his friend into the house. He threw but a glance my way before going inside and shutting the door.

The airplane would be here to pick me up soon. I had less than an hour left on this island. Then, I'd be back in Miami, just like Lero wanted.

Was that what he truly wanted, though?

*"Lero could really use a friend...and more."*

Lero did want more. I knew it now. He wanted it possibly even more than I did.

I thought back to how desperately he had clung to me through the bars last night. It wasn't just lust, his need had been so much deeper than that.

He'd said he lost control in his beast form. Without the iron grip of his constant composure, his true feelings and emotion got the chance to be seen last night. He'd wanted me and needed me, badly. So much, he'd been reaching for me through the bars even as sleep had claimed him.

He'd held me in his arms, his hands armed with knife-sharp claws. He'd had his teeth near my skin. The violent beast, he thought himself to be, could've torn me to shreds and killed me many times over. Yet he'd never so much as nipped or scratched me.

Lero was not a danger to me as much as his fear made him believe—his fear for me. That was the only thing that stood between us, I realized.

How could I leave here? How could I leave *him*?

I kept pacing the beach, alone, my thoughts barraging my brain. The waves rolled softly over my feet, washing away my footprints in the sand. If only my worries could be washed away like that.

My father had always made me feel like a failure for not delivering on *his* dreams. However, when *I* wanted anything bad enough, I worked hard for it, and I always got it. From that point of view, I was never a failure. I just needed to want something badly enough.

And there was nothing and nobody in this world I'd ever wanted more than Lero.

Because of him, I had now glimpsed into the incredible world I never knew existed. No matter how dangerous Lero said it was, I'd never forget it now. I'd never be able to forget Lero, either. For as long as I lived, he'd be in my mind.

Anger stirred in me, along with hope and desperation. Despite Lero's stubborn insistence that I could simply return to the life he'd plucked me out from, I knew it was no longer possible. I couldn't dismiss my experiences on the island as simply a dream.

I glanced up the path toward the house. There had to be a way for me to make him see it, too. I couldn't leave here without at least trying to make him understand.

Stomping up to the house resolutely, I shoved at the door and barged in.

"Would you stay for dinner?" I heard Lero's voice from the back of the house. "Or for a glass of wine with the oysters?"

If I had to speak to Lero in Zeph's presence, I would. My determination was that strong.

Zeph declined, however, "I need to go. I hate leaving Ivy alone for too long."

I paused in the hallway, unseen by either of the men, waiting for Zeph to leave.

"Bring her over, next time," Lero offered. "Maybe she'll like it here enough to stay."

"To stay?" Zeph exclaimed, with surprise. "Does that mean you're willing to let me keep her?" Even not knowing Zeph well, I could tell he was teasing. He obviously didn't think he needed Lero's permission to "keep" Ivy, whoever she was.

The swishing sound of the back door sliding open came next.

"Ivy is clearly yours already," Lero's voice sounded from a distance now. "All I can do is accept that."

The voices moved away, turning to a distant hum then disappearing completely.

I walked through the formal area into the kitchen. No one was here. Only the net with oysters lay on the counter, dripping sea water on the speckled white granite.

Through the glass of the back doors, I saw Zeph and Lero strolling down toward the water. Both talked animatedly, accompanying their words with hand gestures.

At the water edge, they hugged, then Zeph jogged into the surf. He jumped into the waves, his athletic body arching gracefully. Unless my eyes deceived me, I believed I saw a flash of an iridescent fin open like a fan on his back. The moment I blinked, he was gone.

I watched the surface closely, expecting Zeph's head to bob above the waves any moment, but it didn't. He never came up.

Hands in his pockets, Lero turned back to the house, seemingly unconcerned about his friend's complete disappearance into the waves. Somehow, I knew that Zeph must be fine, too. Whoever Zeph was, he was no ordinary human.

Lero crossed the patio and came into the breakfast room where I stood. He stopped in his tracks, spotting me, then squared his shoulders as if readying himself for disaster to strike.

"Is the plane here?" he asked, his voice low.

He'd thought I'd come to say goodbye.

"Not yet." I cleared my throat. Words that had formed clearly in my mind on the beach scrambled and left me, now. "I...I want to talk first."

"If you have more questions—"

"No. Not those types of questions. Not right now, anyway." I clasped my hands in front of me, gathering my resolve. "What I want to know is... Is it hard for you to let me go?"

He frowned, staring at me for a few moments in complete silence. He obviously hadn't expected that question.

"Because it's impossibly hard for me to leave you," I continued.

"Stella," he breathed out, taking a step my way.

For one incredibly short moment my heart dared hope, then he spoke, crushing it.

"As long as there is a chance for you to have a normal life—"

"What if I didn't want to go back to that life?" I cut him off. "What if I wanted to stay here with you?"

He gripped the back of one of the kitchen chairs, leaning over it and squeezing so hard his knuckles turned white.

"You need to go," he gritted through his teeth.

Lero was worth fighting for, even if *he* was the one I had to fight.

"Is that what you really want?"

"I don't want you involved in this mess!" The back of the chair snapped in his hands like a toothpick, sending splinters of wood all over the floor. He didn't seem to notice, his hands fisted tight. "I'm not human, Stella. My life has been nothing but planning for centuries of survival. I move often, change names, hide. And that was before this new threat appeared. Now, it's a true life and death situation."

His mask of composure cracked and blew away, like last year's leaves. He opened his fists, flexing his hands. His fingers trembled slightly.

"Don't you see?" he said a little softer. "I just want you safe, far away from all of this...and from me. My world is like quicksand, Stella. The more you know, the more you sink in. Until there is no more escape, and you're trapped. I want you to run while you still can."

"I'm not scared." I came closer, and he stepped back, as if I were a plague. "I'm not Amelie, Lero. I proved I can handle it. When I saw you in the cage, fear was not the main emotion I had."

"What did you have? Pity?" he scoffed.

"Compassion!" I raised my voice, allowing the words to come straight from my heart. "I care about you, Lero. I've cared for so long. You can't hide from me. I saw *you* in the beast, not a monster. As long as we're together, I can handle anything. Whatever challenges you face in your life, I can help you deal with them. Just let me in. Please."

"Gods help me..." he groaned, closing his eyes, as if he could banish me and my feelings by simply shutting me from view.

"You're pushing me away, because you care about me, too," I insisted. "You believe you're protecting me. But forcing me to go on without you is sentencing me to a lifetime of misery. I can never be truly happy without you."

"Stella..." His voice was full of sorrow. "If something happens to you because of me, I'd never forgive myself."

"A minute with you is worth a lifetime without you, Lero. Can't you see? I'm in love with you." I opened up my heart, exposing the deepest places of my very soul to let him see all of me. "I've been in love with you for so long, I have no idea how to go on without this feeling. No matter where I am, you're with me, in my heart. And I'm only ever happy when I'm with you. I believe you have feelings for me too, you're just so frustratingly good at hiding them, in *this* form."

He kept backing away from me, shaking his head. Every step he took hurt me, as if he kept stabbing a knife through my chest.

"Prove it," I demanded in desperation. "Kiss me, like you did the day we got here. Then try to tell me it's all just a dream and you'd rather be alone."

"Don't," he croaked, his expression grave, his hands fisted at his side, his eyes of stormy gray. "Please, Stella."

He looked on edge. His control stretched so tight, it'd snap at the slightest provocation. If I touched him, if I kissed him myself, I believed he would let go.

But I couldn't take this last step for him. I needed him to meet me if not half-way than at least one step of the way. One tiny, little step he still wouldn't or couldn't do.

There was nothing else I could do on my own. I'd said everything I'd come here to say and so much more, and still it wasn't enough.

Pain from his continuous rejection suffocated me, making it nearly impossible to breathe. Unshed tears burned my eyes.

"You think you need to protect me from your beast, Lero," I said, willing my voice not to shake. "But you're so much crueler in *this* form. You've hurt me the most when you looked your best."

Pivoting on my heel, I rushed out of the house.

Away from him. Just like he wanted all along.

# Chapter Eighteen

STELLA

I rushed out to the stone patio in front of the main entrance to the house.

The airplane was supposed to arrive any minute now to take me away. But where could I go from here? How far did I have to run to be free from this place and the man who lived here?

He'd rejected me over and over again. I'd tried my best to fight him on it, but maybe I'd made a mistake by believing he could ever let his feelings win.

I tipped my head back, letting the sea breeze cool my face, wishing it could soothe the burning pain in my chest, too.

The door behind me slammed open, the crashing sound startling me.

Two strong arms wrapped around me tightly from behind before I had a chance to look back.

"Don't turn around," Lero rasped in my ear.

One arm just above my breasts, he pressed my shoulders to his chest and leaned the side of his face against mine to stop me from turning to see him.

"Stay just like this." His hot breath fanned across my cheek, sending a flock of goosebumps down my bare arms. "Let me say what I have to say without seeing the hurt in your eyes, or the hope..."

*"God, please, speak, Lero,"* I begged in my mind silently, afraid to say a word out loud. *"Please talk to me."*

"You want to know what my life will be without you? It'll be hell. But I'll endure, knowing that you're happy—"

"I can't *possibly* be happy!"

He covered my mouth with his hand, cutting off my protests.

"Shh." He rubbed the side of his face against mine, his lips almost touching my cheek. "Your words have the power to strip me of my last resolve, and I need you to hear what I have to say first."

I held still, focusing on my breathing and his words.

"I could never forget you, Stella," he said softly, pressing his nose against my skin. "The memories of you kept me sane in the hell I went through for the past year and a half. You're my morning star. Nothing will ever change that. Against my best efforts and best intentions, you've made it so deep under my skin, I'd have to claw out my own heart to get rid of you."

I trembled. It suddenly got even harder to breathe. Maybe because he held me so tight.

"I *know* that being with me would expose you to danger," he continued, his heart thundering wildly against my back. "If any harm came to you, it'd kill me. Yet I selfishly want you, come what may. I want you so much it burns my body and mind, driving me mad without the full moon."

His embrace no longer felt like a restraint but a caress. The heat of his body coursed through mine. Leaning back against him, I felt the fire he was speaking about burn inside me.

"Because of you I've learned what real fear is, Stella." He brought his head lower, growling against the side of my neck. "I'm scared that because of me they may get to you still. I'm terrified that I can hurt you myself. I can't stand the thought of being your ruin. Yet I just don't know how to live without you anymore. I kept you here, for your protection. But I just as much kept you here for me. I don't want you to go home. Ever."

Wrapping my arms around myself, I gripped his hands with mine.

"Lero," I squeezed through my tightened throat. "I only ever feel *home* when I'm with you."

His chest pushed against my back with a long breath.

"I have no means to manage what I am, Stella," he warned. This was said for his sake, not mine—I'd accepted who he was the minute I knew. "I will *turn* every full moon night. I'll rage, and snarl, and rampage for days before that."

"And I'll be there for you, to soothe you." I leaned my head to the side, inviting more of his caresses to my neck. His heated breathing spread ripples of pleasure through my skin.

"What if I hurt you?" He pressed his mouth to my neck, trailing his lips down and breathing me in.

"You won't. Not on *purpose*," I replied confidently. "We'll think about how to prevent anything from happening by *accident*."

"I won't age," he kept going in his desperate attempt to warn me away. "Not during your lifetime."

"It doesn't bother me if it doesn't bother you."

A moment with him was better than a lifetime without.

Raising his mouth to my temple, his lips moved above my ear, as he said the words that felt like a vow, "Once you're mine, you're mine forever. If you're not afraid of me, I'll protect you from any other danger. If you spend the rest of your life with me, I'll live to make you happy. I'll give you my heart, my soul, and my body. All I want is yours in return. Always."

The way he spoke, with reverence and obvious respect for each word, it really sounded like a vow. My skin prickled as I sensed the significance of this moment.

Slowly, he released me, stepping back. I swayed on my feet, feeling bereft of his strength and warmth.

"Your last chance to run, Stella." His voice sounded strained, and I sensed the avalanche of emotions he fought to contain. "Run without looking back, because if you turn around, I *will* kiss you, and I won't stop."

My next step felt more profound than saying "I do" on a wedding day. He demanded a commitment larger than life, one that would ruin us both if broken. Only there was no longer parting from him for me.

I drew in a shaky breath, turning to face him.

He stood but a foot away from me, yet it appeared to cost him a huge effort even keeping that small distance between us. His hands fisted at his sides, his hair messy and wild, his eyes burning with passion.

He may have the appearance of a man right now, but the beast was clearly inside him.

"Kiss me then." I stepped into his arms.

It felt like jumping off a cliff. But he caught me. Gathering me in his arms, he claimed my mouth, claiming me. His kiss was punishing, fervent, and frantic, with bruising passion and scraping of teeth. He parted my lips with his, sliding his tongue in, searching for mine. And I met him, sinking my hands into his thick, silky hair that felt so much like his fur.

He held me so tight, my feet lifted off the patio stones.

"I want you," he growled against my mouth. "Madly."

He slid his hands under my shirt, gripping my sides.

"Take me, Lero," I panted, wrapping my legs around his middle. "Please, please, take me," I begged.

He swung us around, pressing my back to the wall next to the front door of the house.

I frantically tugged at his shirt, ripping the buttons open, needing to feel his skin.

He reached behind me, getting hold of the waistband of my shorts. Holding on to it with both hands, he yanked hard, ripping the shorts in two along the seam and the zipper. The thick material of my denim shorts tore like tissue paper in his fingers.

A frost of trepidation sprinkled through my chest from the demonstration of the inhuman physical strength this man possessed. The feeling quickly turned to tingling anticipation as he promptly tore down the front of my t-shirt and got rid of my bra.

His large, warm hand cupped my breast, leaving me breathless. He groaned, rocking his hips into me. The hard ridge of his erection pressed against my panties through his pants. The layers of fabric now felt like maddening barriers. I fumbled with his belt buckle then tugged his zipper down. He ripped off my panties.

"Stella," he breathed out my name as I slid my hand into his underwear, wrapping my hand around his hard, pulsing length.

"That part of you doesn't change much." I gasped at the familiar sensation of holding him in my hand.

"Gods, I need you." He sounded almost delirious, thrusting into my hand.

I needed him too, so much it hurt.

One arm around my waist, he slid a hand between us, slipping a finger inside me. My inner muscles clenched around his finger, desire spreading through me like wildfire.

With a moan, I arched my back, riding his hand.

"More..." I panted. "More of you, Lero."

*All of you.*

I'd wanted him for so long, his touch still felt like a dream.

In one firm, smooth movement he slid inside me, his length replacing his finger. I sucked in a breath as my body stretched around his sizable girth, my need for him growing stronger.

"Mine," he growled, nuzzling my neck.

I clung to his shoulders as he moved faster, pumping his hips.

For the first time ever, I witnessed Lero lose control completely. Even as the beast, I'd sensed he was holding back. Now, he truly let it go, fucking me ferociously against the wall.

I'd never had anyone take me this passionately and completely before. The world ceased to exist. My entire existence narrowed to where our bodies connected—to that hot, smooth glide of him inside me.

The pressure built between my legs with each fierce thrust of his. I flexed my legs around him, grinding against him in desperate need for release.

"Oh God, yes..." I moaned when it reached me, the white-hot wave of pleasure crested, rolling over me.

My legs trembled, too weak to hold on. I wrapped my arms tighter around Lero's shoulders, holding him close as I rode my orgasm.

Growling against my neck, he came hard, frantically pumping his hips into me. His mouth at my neck opened. Then, I felt a sharp sting of his teeth.

I cried out in pain as he gritted again, "Mine."

My hand pressed to the wound on my neck, I felt the blood trickle warm between my fingers. This wasn't a gentle nibble or a love bite. He'd broken skin.

Jerking my head back, I stared at him in a silent question.

He met my eyes, the red glow in his burning bright. Blood stained his lips—my blood.

His wild expression reminded me of the ferocious beast once again, though he retained the appearance of a man.

The red glow dissipated eventually, giving space to the gray.

I unwrapped my legs from around him.

He took my face between his hands. The wild expression was slowly replaced by the warm affection I'd only ever briefly glimpsed in him before.

"Your blood is in me now. We're one and the same," he said softly. The reverence in his voice made his words sound especially poignant. "Always."

The time seemed to stand still. I felt exceptionally connected to him right now—no longer in body but in spirit and soul.

*"We're one and the same."*

I understood these words with my entire being. I sensed Lero's presence in me. His pain, his sorrow, his loneliness, and his current bliss were now my own. I *felt* what he felt.

"It's the mating vow of my people." He stroked my cheeks with his thumbs, our gazes locked. "I said you'd be mine, now you are."

He gently moved my hand away from the bite wound he'd inflicted.

"For as long as I shall live." He bent his head down and licked the blood off my neck.

The brush of his tongue soothed the sting of the bite. The pain was gone. The tingles that followed felt rather pleasurable.

"For as long as *I* shall live, honey," I corrected him. "Remember, I'll die before you."

"No." He pressed his forehead to mine. "Werewolves mate for life. There'll be no other for me but you, whether you're dead or alive."

Sorrow squeezed my heart. I didn't want to think about death right now. I refused to let anything spoil this moment between us.

"I'm yours, Lero." The words came easily, their meaning clear and true. "And you're mine, now. Always."

The sound of the airplane engine didn't register with me until it was right above us. The pilot was taking the aircraft in for the landing on the water in the lagoon.

From the air, he wouldn't be able to see us on the covered front patio. Once he'd landed, however…

"The plane is here." I tried to wiggle out of Lero's arms. "He's come for me."

"He can fuck right off." Lero grinned, giving me a quick kiss, before finally letting me run inside to hide my bare bottom from the view of the unsuspecting pilot. "You're not going anywhere anymore."

# Chapter Nineteen

STELLA

Lero set a large plate with shucked oysters on a bed of ice in front of me.

"How do you like your oysters?" he asked, arranging an array of small dishes filled with sauces and garnish next to it.

"Oh, I don't eat them nearly often enough to have a preference." I smiled, trying to remember when I'd had oysters at all. Probably at one of Javier's business parties. "I don't even know what half of these are." I gestured at the dishes.

The plane had dropped off some supplies and left without me. My bag was still packed, sitting on the bed in Lero's room. He'd informed me I'd be moving into it with him. I'd be spending every night in his bed from now on.

I had a new pair of shorts on, but my body still hummed faintly with the thrill from Lero's touch. Glass of white wine in hand, I had yet to take a sip from it. However, my head was swimming already, drunk on happiness.

Instead of the nervous energy that had tended to hang in the room when Lero and I had been here before, the atmosphere was warm, tender, and with a new kind of tension gently buzzing between us.

"This is the best hot sauce for these." Lero pointed at a small bottle on the table between us. "And this is Mignonette. Dill and coriander right here. Horseradish and seafood sauce... You know what?" He leaned on one arm at my side, tilting his head to catch my eye. "How about I do one for you to try?"

"That'd be great." I smiled, relieved I didn't have to make any decisions at the moment.

The last decision I'd made had been so overwhelming, it'd drained me. Though, of course I didn't regret it a bit. I'd never traveled anywhere today, yet it felt like I'd finally arrived in my one true home.

Lero gently took a shell off the platter.

"A little of Mignonette.' He scooped some of the finely chopped shallots with red-wine vinegar on top of the contents of the oyster shell. "A drop of the hot sauce, not too spicy. Have you ever tried whiskey on oysters?"

"You mean drinking whiskey with them? How about the wine?" I glanced at my glass. The almost full bottle of chilled wine was sweating with condensation on the table to my right.

"No, you *eat* oysters with whiskey." He raised a shot glass filled with amber liquid. "Would you like to try?"

I nodded. "Why not?"

He drizzled whiskey from the shot glass onto the all-dressed oyster then placed it on a small plate for me.

"Voila!" He grinned. "For you, *mademoiselle.*"

"Thank you."

Our fingers touched when I took the plate from him. He paused before letting go of it. I looked up at him, catching his smile waver and a bright spark flash through his gaze.

The heat in his eyes hadn't been quite extinguished after our sex on the front patio. It seemed more intense now, charged with the knowledge of what we had and what we could have more of.

I lifted the oyster shell off the plate and quickly sucked in its contents. The array of amazing flavors hit my palate. The slight burn of the hot sauce and the whiskey, combined with the crisp texture of shallots made for a delightful combination. I closed my eyes, savoring it.

"And?" Lero's raspy voice reached me. "How do you find it?"

"Simply delicious," I said slowly, opening my eyes.

Sitting in a chair next to me, he watched me closely as I licked my lips, then handed me my glass of wine.

"To us." He lifted his glass.

I clinked against it with mine and echoed, "To us."

I'd never had "us" before. It'd always been just "me." Until Lero. This realization made today feel like a wedding day.

Pleasantly cool, the refreshing taste of wine was welcome after the oyster. I set the glass down, then touched my neck, the spot where he'd bit me, needing a reminder that all of this was actually happening.

The bite mark was no longer detectable by touch. The scar might still be visible, but I couldn't feel it with my fingers.

"You can heal." I'd long suspected it but refused to accept it as a fact even having the evidence since I was fourteen.

"Yes. I can heal if I lick and kill if I bite."

"Well, you've bitten me," I stroked my neck, and he followed my movement with his gaze. "But I'm still alive."

He leaned close, taking my hand in his.

"My teeth only have poison when I'm in my beast form. I would've never bitten you if there was any threat to you, sweetheart." The word of endearment rolled off his tongue, slightly accented and smooth as butter. He brought my hand to his lips, gently kissing my knuckles.

I breathed harder, faced with this new Lero, unrestrained in his tenderness to me. I didn't think I could take it without melting into a puddle at his feet.

"Why bite me at all?" I asked.

"A bite to the neck is a part of the mating ritual of my people, to taste each other's blood."

This wasn't the first time he'd tasted my blood.

"When you licked my leg, back in Paris. I couldn't stop thinking about you ever since. Why? Did it have something to do with my blood, too?"

"No, Stella." He shifted back. "The mating bond is only possible between the same kind—a werewolf with a werewolf. Even then, though, the bond can't form with a child. That night, I simply saw a hurt little girl. You asked for a band-aid, and I happened to have something more effective than that for your pain."

I couldn't blame my early infatuation with him on anything but myself, then. A lonely, socially awkward teenager, I'd responded to the random act of kindness by a stranger. The fact that he also happened to be movie-star gorgeous surely played its role too.

Or maybe, my heart had recognized my soul mate, even then. I didn't care about any magic bonds, but I always felt a connection with Lero—whether it was years ago or now.

"I'd licked plenty of bruises, and scratches for Zeph while he was growing up." Lero chuckled. "The boy was a menace to himself, still is." He shook his head.

"Is Zeph coming back?" I asked, remembering the bit of their conversation I'd overheard.

"I hope so."

"Is he also a werewolf?"

"No. Zeph is a siren, a water fae. Wait until you hear him sing." He smiled. "Humans love Zeph's voice."

*Humans.*

"Where did you and Zeph come from? Are there more like you here? How come no one knows?" I'd been collecting questions for weeks, and the more I learned, the more I wanted to know.

He took a sip of his wine, silently regarding me over the rim of his glass.

"You have me for life, Lero," I reminded. "There can't be any secrets between us now, no half-truths either. You have to tell me everything."

He set his glass down on the table and ran his hand through his hair. After keeping secrets for decades, I imagined it would be hard to put them into words now.

"Zeph and I are fae," he started. "We may look like humans, but unlike them we have access to magic that humans do not."

"How did you...come to be?"

"We were born." He shrugged. "Like humans, fae mate, have babies, and die. Except that we live longer."

"How many of you are there?"

"Millions, but we live in a different world, called Nerifir. It's a beautiful but dangerous place, connected to your world by the River of Mists, a strong current of magic that flows between dimensions and connects realms."

"There're more worlds out there? With sentient beings? How come people, *humans*, don't know about it?" This all sounded like a fairy tale.

"They used to know. Long ago, humans knew about many of these things until they started to explain their knowledge away, using science."

"So, you don't believe in science?" I asked, with a skeptical smile.

"Science is hard facts. It doesn't require belief but understanding. Magic is unexplainable. People believe in it and feel it. Magic and science are two different things, but they aren't mutually exclusive. They can coexist. That's what humans have forgotten. My kind live and breathe magic. We're born with it. It's a big part of our existence, though not all can wield it. For werewolves, Moon magic is a source of power. Other fae have other powers derived from different kinds of magic."

"And does everyone in Nerifir speak French?" I asked with a teasing smile.

"No!" He laughed. "French was the first language I heard when I came to this world."

"Is that how it works?"

"Yes. The first language you hear becomes yours. French is now what you call my *mother tongue*. I had to learn to speak English just like any non-English speaking human would. I can't get rid of the accent, either."

"Well, thank God for that!" I genuinely meant that. I loved his soft, purring accent. It'd be a shame if he'd ever lost it for any reason. "Do you ever go back to Nerifir?"

"No. It's not simple to travel between worlds. If I go back, I won't arrive to the same time and place I've left. And if I try to come back to this world again, I will never come back to *here* exactly." He planted a hand on top of the table as if marking the spot. "I may find myself on another continent, hundreds or thousands of years in the past or in the future. Though, it could be just a day or a month from now. There's no way to predict."

"Does it mean you're staying here forever, then?"

He nodded.

"But do you miss your home at all?" I asked. "How long have you been here?"

"For over forty years now. Enough to get used to this world. I'll always miss some things from back home, but my life is here now. This world is the only home I'll ever have. I'm not going anywhere, especially now that I have you."

I reached out and placed my hand on top of his, vowing in my heart to make this world a happier place for him.

My fingers brushed by his wrist, bringing to mind the wounds he'd had there and how fast they'd healed.

"You can heal yourself, too, can't you?" I gently brushed around his wrist with the tips of my fingers.

"Yes." He smiled. "Only it happens on its own. I don't have to lick myself to heal."

"Well, that's good," I said with a soft giggle. "Some places are hard to reach for licking."

My mind then went to the last time I'd seen him injured. The gruesome memory of his blood-covered hands and blood-soaked fur on his thighs quickly dimmed my merry mood. The wounds had been self-inflicted.

"What is it?" Lero stroked the side of my face with his knuckles. "Where did your smile go? It's the most amazing sight in the world, but it never stays long enough for me to fully enjoy it."

I couldn't deny him, could I? I smiled again, my face heating under his attention.

"I thought about last night," I clarified, sadness gripping my heart despite the smile. "You hurt yourself."

The tanned skin on his cheekbones flushed. He grabbed his glass, taking a large gulp from it.

"I really wish you hadn't seen that." Lero looked uncharacteristically flustered.

"Are you...embarrassed?"

He set his glass down and admitted, "Mortified."

"Why would you be?"

He cleared his throat.

"Well, I don't usually, um...touch myself in front of others." An elbow on the table, he rubbed his eyes with his hand. "On the night of the full moon, the restraints of culture, civilization and any other kind fall off me, Stella. The wild nature takes over. The legend says my people came from animals, *voukalaks,* and back into the animals we turn every full-moon night. The beasts know only hunt, hunger, and lust. Those are the things I feel the most on those nights."

"Lero," I shifted closer to him, taking his hand in mine again. "There is nothing to be ashamed of here. I don't mind your 'wild nature.' I rather enjoy it, actually."

"Enjoy?" Lacing his fingers with mine, he peered at me from under his long eyelashes, studying my face carefully. "To my knowledge, human women like their men to make love to them. What I did to you there..." He tipped his head in the direction of the front door. "Wasn't it."

I leaned even closer.

"I'm afraid your knowledge about human women is severely outdated, *old man,*" I teased, remembering what Zeph had called Lero. I then added quietly, as if sharing a secret, "Making love is lovely of course, but some of us don't mind some good, hard *fucking* once in a while."

I took a drink from my wine glass but kept my gaze on him. The blush thickened on his hard, chiseled cheekbones. With all the men before him, there had been so much unfulfilled desire on my part. I hated for Lero to think he'd been inadequate in any way when in fact, he'd been the best for me.

Heat smoldered in his eyes, and I couldn't resist stoking the flames.

"Do you think I should be embarrassed, too, if I touched myself while you watched?" I asked innocently.

He groaned, then slid off his chair, sinking to his knees in front of me.

"Don't say things like that if you want to have dinner made on time."

I cupped his face with my hands.

"You don't ever have to feel embarrassed about who you are with me. Okay? And I'm not hungry for dinner right now." I slid my hands to the back of his head, threading my fingers into his hair.

"Fuck dinner then," he growled, taking my mouth in a kiss.

I slid forward in my chair, opening my knees wide to let him closer.

He hiked my shirt up to my shoulders, breaking the kiss only to take my top off over my head. His hands then went around me, finding the closure of my bra. Quick and urgent, his movements were more controlled now as compared to the last time. Deftly unclipping the bra, he slid it off my shoulders then leaned back, sliding his gaze down my body.

My chest heaved, my lips hot and tingling after his kiss.

He reached for my left breast with his hand. Cupping it, he gently glided his thumb over my nipple, watching it grow hard under his touch.

"I do both, Stella," he said in a low, rough voice. "Fuck *and* make love. Which one would you prefer right now?"

He gently kneaded my breast, rolling the nipple between his thumb and his finger. I squirmed in the chair, feeling suddenly hot all over.

"I—" I gasped as he put his mouth on my right breast, sucking the tip in.

I wrapped my legs around him. Fisting my hands in his hair, I arched my back, pressing my breast into his caress. Desire throbbed hot between my legs, making me moan in need.

"Both it is," he rasped.

Scooping me out of the chair, he got up and pivoted toward his bedroom, carrying me in his arms.

"Dinner will have to be postponed." He nibbled on my lips in quick, hot kisses while taking me to his room.

Tossing me on his bed, he crawled over me. Air rushed out of my lungs as he leaned closer.

"I don't think I'll ever get used to being able to have you anytime I want," I whispered, wrapping my arms around his neck.

"I don't think you'll ever want me as often as I want *you*," he said before kissing me again.

He slid his hands down my body, and I quickly unbuttoned my shorts.

"Don't ruin this pair." I smiled when he moved his kisses down my neck. "I don't have many more left."

He kissed the spot where he'd bit me earlier.

"I'll buy you more shorts," he groaned into my shoulder when my fingers brushed against the bulge in his pants.

I lifted my hips, and he slid my shorts and underwear off, carefully this time.

"Or maybe you'd like to start wearing more skirts?" He traced a line down my inner thigh with his finger. "And no underwear at all." The tip of his finger touched between my legs.

I exhaled sharply as he lazily circled my most sensitive spot.

Leaning over me, he took my nipple in his mouth again, playing with it with his tongue.

*'Healing unless it's deadly,'* rushed through my brain when I thought about his mouth.

Nothing about Lero was normal. He was further from my world than any person I knew. Yet I felt closer to him than to anyone else.

Arousal coursed through me. Gripping his shoulders with my fingers, I lifted my hips into his touch.

Letting go of my breast, he shifted his body down mine.

"I want to know how you taste," he murmured, kissing a trail down my belly. "Everywhere."

The brush of his tongue between my legs made me whimper with need. I jerked my hips, and he held my thighs to keep me in place.

Moaning, I raked my fingers through his hair. The silk of it tickled the insides of my thighs, spreading hot tingles through my body.

"Oh, it's so good..." I breathed out.

He dipped his tongue inside me then swirled it around, ripping a sharp gasp of pleasure from me.

"Exquisite," he whispered, his breath cool against my heated flesh.

He put his mouth on me again, licking, sucking, and nibbling until I couldn't take it anymore.

"Lero..." I moaned his name before the climax hit me, rendering me speechless.

His touch turned gentle as he helped me ride my pleasure with tender kisses.

The moment I stilled, he pulled himself back up my body.

"You taste delicious," he said with satisfaction, kissing my neck, then my mouth again. "Everywhere."

"You would know about delicious, the gourmet that you are." I smiled, as the post orgasmic warmth lazily took over my body.

He unzipped his pants, fitting himself between my legs.

"Take this off, Lero." I fumbled with the buttons of his shirt. "I need to feel your skin.

Not bothering to open it all the way, he tore his shirt off over his head, tossing it aside.

I splayed my hands along the firm planes of his torso. My fingers slid through the dusting of dark hair on his chest. I cherished the sensations of his bulging muscles underneath, the warmth of his skin, and the weight of his body over mine.

He pushed inside me, slowly, as if savoring every inch. Rising over me on his arms, he gazed at me, his eyes flickering between mine.

With a soft groan, he bent his elbows, lowering over me while moving faster. "Pure pleasure," he breathed out.

At this angle, the pressure of his body on me teased with another orgasm. I quickly reached between us, needing just a little help.

"No. Mine." He swatted my hand away, placing his finger on me instead.

I gasped, tossing my head back, as the tingling pleasure spiked.

"Yesss," he hissed through his teeth, thrusting harder.

"Oh, Lero!" Tossing my head back, I dug my fingers in his shoulders, riding through my climax as he pumped his release into me.

"I've waited decades for this." He buried his face in my shoulder, catching his breath.

"For decades? For me?"

"For someone I'd feel about the way I feel for you." He lifted his head to meet my eyes.

"Decades are an awfully long time, honey." I stroked the side of his face, and he leaned into my touch. There was so much unguarded tenderness in his expression, the question slipped off my tongue, "Do you love me, Lero?"

He drew in a breath, shifting off me. My heart dropped into the hollow of my stomach. He'd pledged a lifetime of loyalty to me but couldn't say he loved me? The longer the pause grew, the more I dreaded his answer.

He rose on his elbow over me and cupped my face with his other hand, turning me to him.

"I enjoy you, Stella. You are my dearest treasure, my heart's deepest desire. Here, on this island, I've been the happiest ever—because of you. I will die to defend you."

I bit my lip. It sounded very much like love. Why wouldn't he say the word then?

"I've lived enough in this world to know how much love means to humans. But I don't know if I can feel it myself. The fae bond takes the guesswork out of that for my people. The physical attraction comes first, then the bond happens."

"What exactly is this bond?"

His gaze slid by me. He stared at the rising disk of the moon outside the glass door. Still perfectly round to the naked eye, the moon shone bright, reflecting with silver in his eyes.

"It's the strongest connection between two beings," he said slowly. "Your blood, your body, and your soul long for that one person in the world. When you find them, the true magic happens. The power of the Moon flows through both of you. You become each other's strengths and each other's weaknesses. When you're together, nothing is impossible. And when you're apart, nothing can stand in your way back to each other."

It did sound like magic, the most wonderful kind.

"Have you ever been mated, Lero?"

"No." He lifted a strand of my hair away from my face then gently placed it behind my ear. "I was just over fifty when I left. A good age to start looking for a mate, but it can take decades to find one."

"Do fae... um, remain celibate while they search?"

"Gods, no!" He laughed. "Why? Sex is too enjoyable. And my people are, well, too virile to stay celibate, anyway."

"But *you* did. For decades you said."

"There are no females of my kind here. And after Amelie... I didn't want to destroy another life."

"Was it easier to stay alone?"

"It was necessary."

We remained silent for a few moments, while I pondered his words.

"Why do you think this connection wouldn't be possible with a human?" I challenged. "We're capable of feelings that even you would call *magical.*"

Propped on an elbow at my side, he trailed his finger down my neck, between my breasts, then cupped the curve of my hip.

"A mating bond doesn't happen between species. A werewolf cannot create one with a water fae, or a sky fae or a gorgonian. Only with another werewolf."

He lowered his head to place a kiss on my temple, then nuzzled my hair.

"I chose to be alone because my being with someone from this world could destroy them." His hand slid from my hip to around my waist. "The poison of a bonded pair of werewolves no longer harms either of them. But a nick of my teeth on a full-moon night would kill you in seconds." He drew me closer to him. "Giving in to keeping you was a weakness, a selfish one, too. But I can't give you up anymore. I'll have to find a way to make sure you're safe while living with someone like me. For one, you'll have to promise me not to go down in the cellar next full moon."

Pain stabbed through my heart when I thought about Lero spending the night alone, locked in his cage. Compassion squeezed my chest.

"There's a few weeks until the next full moon still," I offered, not promising anything. "Maybe we'll come up with a better solution by then?"

"Stella," he warned. "I won't let you play with your life."

I gently stroked his chest, enjoying the soft tickle of hair over his hard muscles.

"I'm not going to take any unnecessary risks." I worded my promise carefully. "Now that I finally have you, I love my life way too much to risk it."

He caught my hand and brought it to his lips for a kiss.

"I don't know how to love without the bond, Stella, but I promise I'll do everything to make you *feel* loved. Whatever it takes."

I'd never been loved, but Lero had already made me feel cherished and cared for.

"You definitely make me feel special," I confessed, then added with a smile, "Of course all those fancy homemade dinners with lobster, oysters, and wine, don't hurt, either."

He shifted, and my fingers slid from his chest to the side of his ribcage.

"Good food is necessary for survival, in my opinion." He squirmed under my touch with a chuckle.

I trailed my fingers along the side of his ribs then over to his belly. The only hair here was the dark trail running from his belly button to the nest of curls that surrounded his renewed erection. It bobbed as I stroked the hard squares of his abs.

"I'm not complaining," I said softly. "If you continue to cook the way you do..."

He huffed a strangled half-laugh, half-moan as I increased the pressure, dragging the tips of my fingers along the hard ridges of his abdominal muscles. He bent his legs, slightly arching his back.

"Don't tell me you like belly rubs!" I exhaled a giggle, scratching his rippling muscles a little harder.

His hard-on jerked higher, a shudder ran down his large body as he groaned.

"You really like that, huh?" I murmured, sliding my hand down, until my fingers sank into the dark hair around his shaft.

"Come here now." He grabbed me under my arms and rolled me over on my back. "I'll show you exactly what I like." He crawled over me and swallowed my laugh with a kiss.

I welcomed him, wrapping my arms around him and opening my legs wider.

*"I love you,"* rushed through my mind, but I didn't let it out, not even when he slid inside me again, whispering how wonderful I felt and how happy I made him.

These three little words required a reply if said out loud. I now knew I wouldn't get one from him.

# Chapter Twenty

STELLA

A phone ringtone shrilled from Lero's closet. It was loud enough to startle me in the lounger on the back patio where I sat, reading.

Could it be Lero again?

He'd been away for the past three days. It wasn't the only time he'd been gone during the three weeks since the last full moon. As much as we loved our quiet life here on the Blue Cay, there were matters on the mainland that required his personal attention.

Lero had already called me this morning to check on me. Our phone calls now were very different from before. No longer holding back his affection, he was so much more generous with words.

"I miss you," he'd added before we'd said our goodbyes. The longing in his voice was so intense, it sent shivers down my arms.

"I miss you, too," I'd barely whispered—the emotions had almost taken my voice away. "Come home soon."

"Tomorrow."

*Home.*

This was what the island had become for both of us. Without Lero, however, our home felt empty.

The phone rang again. Leaving the book on the lounger, I ran into the bedroom through the back doors.

"Hello?" I managed to pick up before the phone stopped ringing.

"Stella?" Zeph's voice sounded excited as if I were his long-lost friend. But maybe this man treated all people like friends. The image of his easy smile rose in my mind, making me grin back even though he couldn't see me.

"Yes, it's me. Lero is not around at the moment," I added carefully.

I knew Lero trusted Zeph. I also knew he'd told me not to discuss his whereabouts with anyone. Always cautious, he didn't want anyone to know when I was left on the island alone.

"I'm calling to invite myself for dinner," Zeph announced cheerfully. "When would be the best time to come over?"

"Dinner?" The prospect of having company on Blue Cay was new and thrilling. We had more than enough space, plenty of food, and fine wine for a real party. "Oh, it'd be fun. Please come. Any time this week would work. How about the day after tomorrow?"

The following week there was a full moon again. I sensed Lero's anxiety increasing with it approaching. Having people over while he had to deal with it would be too difficult for him, I believed. The sooner the dinner happened the better it would be.

"Sounds great!" Zeph replied. "I'll bring a guest if you don't mind."

"A guest?"

"My fiancée. Her name is Ivy. She's a sweetheart. You'll love her," he added with optimistic confidence.

"Is she...a fae?" I asked, intrigued. "Like you?"

"A fae? No." He laughed. "She's human."

He spoke so easily about it. There were none of Lero's reservations. Zeph seemed to enjoy having someone to speak freely about what he was, too.

"I'll talk to Ivy and call back to confirm," he said.

"I'm looking forward to seeing both of you soon," I replied sincerely. Seeing Zeph again presented an exciting opportunity to learn more about the world he and Lero had come from.

During the past weeks, Lero had been telling me more about Nerifir. It indeed sounded like a magical place, where villagers turned into mythical creatures every full moon. He told me about the dangers of his world that had come to ours. He told me about Ghata and her *bracks*, one of whom happened to be his own brother.

His stories often sounded like fantasy tales.

But Zeph was a real person, whom I'd met. He had a fiancée, which meant he was engaged—such a normal, human thing. I was looking forward to meeting Ivy and to see them interact with each other. Would they be like a normal human couple, too?

Or was their relationship more like the sweaty, needy, desperate, undefined mess that Lero and I had? I doubted anyone could have a relationship similar to ours. Somehow our mess seemed to be uniquely us.

He was here!

I'd been straining my hearing all morning, listening for the sound of the sea plane engines, and still somehow, I'd missed it. I saw the plane land in the lagoon visible from the front entrance of the house only when worn out by the anxiety of anticipation, I'd decided to go for a walk.

Lero jumped off a float onto the wet sand and rushed to the house, carrying a crate in his hands.

I met him on the front patio.

"You're here..." was all I managed to say before he dropped the crate at my feet and grabbed me in his arms.

He caught my mouth in a hot, messy kiss while walking me backwards into the house.

"The pilot..." I protested when he broke the kiss for a moment to kick the door closed behind us. "The supplies..."

"They can wait. But I can't," he rasped.

The eerie red flashed bright in his eyes. I noted the perspiration beading on his temples and the way his fingers trembled when he tugged at my clothes.

"Shorts," he muttered, grumpily, tearing the hem of my sleeveless top out from the waistband of my cotton shorts. "I've *got* to buy you some skirts."

Only when his hands finally connected with the bare skin on my back did he relax a little. He slowed my frantic disrobing for a second, pausing like a drowning man who suddenly got a long breath of air.

"I need you, Stella," he groaned, with a shudder across his back. "So badly."

I quickly unbuttoned and unzipped my shorts.

"I missed you," I whispered in his ear.

His need fueled mine. It was thrilling to be wanted this desperately, as if I were the vital part to his very survival.

I shoved my shorts down past my hips, taking the underwear with them.

My gesture seemed to snap the restraints Lero had been trying to hold himself in. He pushed me against the wall right there, next to the front door in the hallway. Hooking his arm under my knee, he lifted my leg, opening me for him. With another biting kiss, he shoved inside me, groaning against my mouth.

I fisted my hand in his hair, halting my breath at the sting of his rough invasion. He growled, moving faster. The sleek heat of my intense desire for him soothed the pressure of his massive girth inside me. The tingling pleasure quickly spread through my belly and along my inner thighs, building up where our bodies connected.

My leg draped over his arm, he grabbed my backside with both hands, shoving my lower body closer to his, as he rutted into me.

Sudden and violent, the orgasm rocked through me in blinding shudders of intense pleasure. I gulped in the air in broken, desperate gasps, my fingers gripping Lero's hair. Still, it wasn't enough. I craved more of him. I needed to become a part of him.

I pressed my mouth to his neck, just above the collar of his shirt. The scent of him was stronger here, and I greedily breathed it in.

Growling through his clenched teeth, he threw his head back, chasing his climax in hard, brutal thrusts. Wild and animalistic, this was not "making love," it was something else. And my body responded to it in an inexplicable but delightful way. Every hard thrust brought on another rocking wave of my never-ending orgasm as he came into me, over and over again.

I flexed my jaw, my teeth piercing his skin. The salty taste of his blood coated my tongue, making me dizzy and drunk with pleasure.

He sank to the floor, sliding my back against the wall, as if his knees suddenly gave out.

Weak and trembling, my muscles quivering, I untangled my fingers from his hair, watching in horror as quite a few strands remained in my hands. The collar of his white shirt was stained with bright red. I wiped my lips with the back of my hand. It came smeared red as well.

"Lero?" I whispered, horrified by what I'd done.

He didn't seem to notice, panting wildly, his head on my shoulder.

"I'm so, so sorry." I hovered my hand over the wound I'd inflicted.

He rubbed his neck, smearing the blood over his skin.

"Did you just mark me?" he glanced up, an amused smile dancing in his eyes.

"I'm sorry?" I repeated, tentatively this time as he seemed rather pleased about having been bitten.

He'd done the same thing to me before, but that was a part of his people's ancient mating tradition, which I understood and accepted. For the life of me, I couldn't explain what had come over me to bite him back, now.

"You're sorry you've claimed me as yours?" he asked, tilting his head.

"Well, if you put it that way..." With my finger, I lightly circled the couple of small puncture wounds my teeth left on his neck. The blood had stopped seeping from them already as the healing process began. "If that's what it means, I'm glad I did it, then. Because you are mine."

He had been mine and only mine from the moment I met him. It just had taken him over fifteen years to figure it out.

I smiled as he kissed me.

"Thank you," he murmured. "Thank you for being there."

His hair was mussed, his skin flushed when he looked at me, but his eyes were back to their normal color—the wild, unhealthy glimmer in them gone.

"Are you feeling better?" I asked, thinking about the feverish state he'd arrived in and the frenzy with which he'd taken me.

He stared at me for a long moment, searching my eyes with his.

"It'll get worse in the next few days, with the last two nights before the full moon being the most excruciating."

I cupped his face with one hand, gently stroking his cheek.

"How does it feel, Lero? Tell me."

He drew in a long, shuddered breath.

"Like slowly losing myself. I'm surrendering my body and mind to another entity, little by little every day."

"To the moon?"

"Yes. I'm losing control, handing it over to it. And there is nothing I can do to stop it."

I couldn't stop it either, but maybe I could slow it down, or at least help him cope.

"You're feeling better right now, aren't you?" I ran my fingers through his hair, smoothing it down.

"I am. As temporary as the relief may be, it feels good."

He caught my hand and placed a tender kiss on the inside of my wrist.

"Can you bear this, Stella? Month after month?" He wouldn't meet my eyes, keeping my wrist pressed to the corner of his mouth.

"Bear what? Being the one you make love to?" I smiled, caressing the back of his neck with the fingers of my other hand.

He huffed a sad laugh.

"This wasn't 'making love,' and you know it."

I shifted in his lap. After the wild sex and the mind-blowing orgasm, I'd just now realized that we both remained mostly clothed. Only my shorts and underwear were off. Lero's pants were undone but he'd somehow managed to keep them on his hips. It all had happened so suddenly.

"Sex with you is no burden, honey. There's nothing wrong with being thoroughly fucked once in a while." I laughed softly, nuzzling his cheek. “Isn’t that how ferocious werewolves do it?” I wiggled my eyebrows, keeping my tone light.

“But you’re not a werewolf.” He glanced at me, still clutching my wrist.

“No. I’m not.” I stifled a sigh.

*I’m just deeply in love with one.*

# Chapter Twenty-One

STELLA

"That was my last trip for a while," Lero told me as we took a leisurely early afternoon stroll the day after his return. We had some time before Zeph and Ivy would arrive for dinner tonight. Excitement bubbled in me at the thought of having company on Blue Cay.

I brushed Lero's fingers with mine, and he quickly caught my hand in his—large and warm. I loved the physical connection with him. No matter how much sex we'd had last night and this morning, I still welcomed every touch of his throughout the day.

"Are you confident Ghata will leave you alone now?"

"It's impossible to be confident in anything as far as Ghata is concerned. I'd trusted her once, I'll never make that mistake again. As long as we share the same world with her, we'll always have to be careful."

He'd been teaching me caution, by fae rules—never make deals with them unless you think through every word very carefully, never eat anything unless you trust where the food came from. Apparently, there were many magical substances in his world that would alter one's perception or even the personality if consumed. Only a few worked on fae, but many were effective on humans. Through *bracks*, Ghata had been able to gain access to some of those substances, and no one knew when and how she might decide to use them.

"I'd love to go back to my job again, at some point," I ventured. "Full-time."

We'd talked about this a little. Despite it being quiet lately, Lero was reluctant to let me go anywhere on my own, and I didn't know if I wanted to do all my viewings accompanied by him as my bodyguard.

"Maybe soon." He heaved a sigh.

I knew he blamed himself for "dragging" me into his life of magic and mayhem, and I didn't want it to make it harder on him. After all, I'd never stopped working. I'd just been sharing my commissions with the agent who did that part of the job that required me to be physically present, which was a lot. But it also allowed me to spend all this time with Lero, which I was grateful for.

"With Ghata moving her show to Asia soon, we'll have less to worry about, right?" I asked.

He nodded, though his expression remained pensive.

"It looks like Ghata is wrapping up her show," he said. "She's not advertising it past the upcoming performance in Singapore."

Lero had put a price on the last sentient fae in Ghata's possession, a gargoyle she'd kept as a statue in her collection. We'd gotten a report recently that the gargoyle had been stolen from her and freed.

"Did the gorgonian and the gargoyle return to Nerifir?"

"Yes."

"So, they're safe, then." Their safety was the most important, though deep inside I wished I'd had a chance to meet them before they left our world.

"As safe as one can hope to be in Nerifir. It can be a dangerous place, no matter what time one lands in there."

"That didn't stop the two from returning," I pointed out. "You said you wouldn't go back, but have you ever considered it?"

He rolled his shoulders uneasily. "Unlike the two fae who went back, the worst for me would be if I returned close to the time and place I left."

"Why?"

His fingers flexed over mine. For a moment, I wondered if he'd brush this question aside.

"No more secrets, right?" he muttered softly as if to himself.

"No more secrets," I echoed.

He drew in a long breath as if about to jump off a cliff.

"I didn't simply cross over to this world one day, Stella. I fled," he finally said.

"You ran away? From whom?"

"Not who, *what*," he corrected. "An arrest and prosecution. A possible execution, too."

"For what?" I gasped in disbelief.

He stopped abruptly, facing me. His gaze, open and imploring, rested on mine, making him look uncharacteristically vulnerable. He cared about what I thought of him, and he knew what he was about to say would test my opinion of him.

"For murder," he confessed grimly. "Multiple murders, possibly."

A chilling sensation trickled through my chest, but I didn't yank my hand from his.

*"Possibly?"* I repeated numbly. "You aren't even sure how many people you've killed?"

He winced, hanging his head between his shoulders. "I... I don't remember."

"How could you forget?"

"It was the night of the full moon."

"You were the beast?"

He nodded.

"You keep some memories in that form, though, right?" I asked.

"Not much. Back in Nerifir, the Moon's magic was under Ghata's power. Full moon nights turned wild, unhinged, and especially violent there. Instead of hunting in couples and making love under the moonlight, my kind turned into a raging army, roaming the Sarnala Plains with our only purpose to fuck and kill."

"So, you killed..."

My fingers trembled, and he squeezed my hand tighter.

"Yes.

"Did you rape, too?"

He sucked in some air through his teeth. A grimace of agony crossed his face.

"I hope not."

"You *hope*?"

"The idea of violating someone like that terrifies and sickens me possibly even more than murder. I desperately hope my inherent aversion to the act of forcing myself on someone kept me from committing it. From the few shreds of distorted memories I retained, there're none of rape."

I exhaled slowly. My heart beat wildly.

"What *is* in those shreds of memories?"

He stared straight ahead, but his gaze turned unseeing. His pupils grew wider, darker, as if the things passing through his mind's eye terrified him anew.

"Blood," he said somberly. "So much blood, I felt drunk on its smell and dizzy with violence. The savage need for more blood... Running so fast, my lungs burned. Hitting, smashing, and ripping apart flesh so ferociously, my muscles hurt..."

He drew in a shaky breath, unsteady on his feet from the weight of the memories he'd carried for decades. He might not remember the details, but he'd obviously never forgotten the horror of that night. He might've escaped the punishment, but he hadn't been spared the torture of guilt.

"It was the Madness," I whispered, frozen in horror with him. "It wasn't you, Lero. That's *not* who you are. It was the madness of that night."

"Moon Madness," he whispered, closing his eyes.

It wasn't the fear of an arrest and prosecution that had tortured him.

"You told me you surrender all control on those nights. To a magical entity. That is what's to blame, Lero." Letting go of his hand, I cupped his face, forcing him to look at me. "Whatever happened that night wasn't your fault. If you had no control over your mind or your body, you cannot hold yourself responsible for what happened."

He stared at me for a long moment. Slowly, I believed, he started seeing *me* again instead of the past.

"It wasn't you," I repeated as he pressed his forehead to mine.

"You are my morning star, Stella," he said softly. "You're the light that always guides me out of my nightmares."

Wrapping his arms around me, he drew me closer for a kiss. Deep and long with a hint of lingering sadness, it was not like any of the kisses we'd shared before.

"I love you, Lero," I murmured.

"Why? How can you love me?"

"You have been a part of me for such a long time." I hugged his neck, running my fingers through the short hair on the back of his head. "I honestly couldn't tell you when exactly I first fell in love. But you've been in my dreams ever since that night in Paris."

"It was so long ago," he said with a hint of a smile. "And all I did was just bring you home that night, not much."

"Maybe, but I didn't get much attention growing up. Finding kindness in a stranger impressed me as a kid." I felt a bit foolish admitting that. But I wanted to be completely honest with him. "When I said I was hurt, you *heard* me and made it better. Of course, helping me didn't mean much to you. But for me, it was special. It didn't hurt that you were...well, still are, drop-dead gorgeous, either." I exhaled a soft laugh. "I'd never seen anyone like you before—or after, for that matter. Your eyes... The memory of them was enough to get my imagination going for years to come."

"My eyes?" He squinted at me, with a curious expression on his face.

"Don't tell me you don't know how good-looking you are." I shook my head.

"Well." He shrugged. "Human women tend to find me attractive."

"Do they, now?" I squinted at him.

"In *this* form only, though. But you..." He stared at me in wonder, as if *I* were a magical being from another world, not he.

My feelings for him went past an adolescent infatuation based on looks long ago. I loved the man he was inside, no matter what he looked like on the outside, whether the handsome fae or the terrifying beast.

"I don't know what lucky star to thank for sending you to me." He hugged me tighter, kissing my hair.

"Despite what you may think, it's not hard to love you," I said, snuggling against his wide chest. "When you're with me, I feel at home. When you're gone, it's like something in the world is missing. No one has ever touched me the way you do. You use me, greedily, like a man dying from thirst would drink water. And at the same time, you give my life a new meaning, filling me to the brim with the love of living. I have something you need, and it thrills me to be needed by you. On the other hand, you fulfill all my desires, even those I wasn't aware of myself." I lifted my face up to his. "I love being with you, talking to you, having sex with you. I love everything about you. I love you, Lero. That's the only way I know how to love—giving my whole to you."

"So much of what you've just said I feel for you, too, Stella." His expression was thoughtful. "Does it mean I love you, too?"

Suddenly, it wasn't that important to hear those three little words from him anymore. What he *did* for me meant so much more.

I smiled wide.

"You most certainly make me feel *loved,* honey."

I held his face in my hands, losing myself in the stormy gray of his eyes. The lightnings of red showed up in them again, but they didn't scare me. They excited me.

"Next full moon, stay with me," I begged. "Don't lock yourself in that basement cell ever again."

His chest rose with a deep breath. "Stella—"

The peaceful afternoon shattered with an explosion.

The island's security system blared an alarm, its splitting sound hurting my ears. The ground shook under my feet. And a humongous cloud of water mist rose in the air, breaking the sunlight into bursts of color.

"Lero!" I dug my fingers onto his biceps. His arms went rigid around me. "What's happening?"

Another explosion thundered through the air. A fountain of sea water blasted up into the sky, flipping a black boat in the distance upside down. Another boat bobbed upturned in the wake of the first explosion. At least three more were sneaking into the lagoon from around the bend in the shore and past the reef. All the boats were laden with men.

It was an invasion!

My head pounded from the noise of the blasts. The echo of them was ringing in my ears.

"Stella!" Lero's voice reached me like through a cotton wall.

He shook me so hard my teeth clanked.

"Run!" he shouted, gripping my shoulders. "Run to the house. Lock the doors. Arm the system. Get in the basement. Lock yourself inside."

He gave me another firm shake, forcing me to meet his eyes.

"Do you hear me?"

His words registered with my brain.

*House...*

*System...*

*Basement...*

I nodded.

The men from the upturned boats waded toward the beach. Some held knives in their hands, swords. One had a bow with a quiver of arrows over his shoulder. I saw no guns.

"Run!" Lero shoved me toward the path to the house.

My feet tripping over themselves, I made it through the sand of the beach to the packed-dirt path, then over to the house, running as fast as I could.

My mind went blank, shock clouding any coherent thought. The racket of the explosions ringing in my head. The noise of new blasts sending violent shudders through my body, again and again.

Lero's orders kept spinning through my mind on a loop, *"House, system, basement..."*

I dashed into the house, shutting the door behind me, then made it to our bedroom and the walk-in closet. My hands hovering over the buttons of the control panel, I paused, not arming the system yet. The fog of shock had finally cleared somewhat, allowing me to think.

If I locked and armed the house, I'd be shutting Lero out along with the men from the boats. He'd ordered me here, trying to save me. But if they harmed him, nothing would stop them from attacking the house and finding me here.

Or maybe they wouldn't come to the house at all. He'd told me before that they would use me to get to him. They didn't need me. They'd come for him. It was Lero who was in danger, not me.

I darted back to the front entrance and peeked out of the main hall window.

Some of the men from the boats had reached Lero. He met them on the beach, two short swords in his hands. Their blades glimmered red as he wielded them. Lunging forward, he stabbed the first man through his chest.

The man threw his head back, falling to his knees. Lero yanked his sword out, sparks of red running along its blade and fanning across the man's chest clad in a black t-shirt. The man dropped to his side and stilled.

Lero got no rest, though, as more invaders emerged from the water, rushing him. All bald-headed, with elaborate tattoos circling their necks and covering their right arms. They looked the same as the men I'd witnessed capturing the beast—who I now knew had been Lero—back in the parking garage.

*Bracks.*

They'd come to get him again.

I couldn't just hide here and let them take him. But how could I possibly stop them?

There were no weapons in the house that I knew of. I had no idea where Lero got the swords he was using now. Maybe he'd kept them hidden on the beach all this time. Or maybe he'd snatched them from a *brack* when I wasn't looking.

Dashing to the kitchen, I grabbed the two biggest knives from the knife block on the counter. If he could stab someone protecting me, so could I, to stop him from being taken.

With a knife in each hand, I ran out the door, heading for the path to the beach.

"Not so fast!" a deep voice snarled behind me. Then, a thick tattooed arm grabbed me across my chest from behind and lifted me off the ground as if I weighed nothing.

The *bracks'* strength was clearly inhuman.

Fear seized my heart, and I fought against it. I couldn't allow fear to paralyze my mind or my body. Twisting in his grip, I stuck one of my knives into his side.

Held from behind, I couldn't see the blade sink into his flesh, but I *felt* it. I sensed through the handle gripped in my hand as the blade cut through the muscle and scraped the bone of his rib on its way in.

The sickening feeling made my stomach roil.

He growled in pain, his grip on me slacking. I twisted out of his hold and jumped away, leaving the knife in his side. Eyes wide open, I stared in shock as he slowly pulled the knife out of the wound.

The *brack* staggered on his feet. Dark blood trickled out of the cut in a steady flow, but he didn't fall. Holding the bloodied knife in his hand, he stomped toward me.

Over his shoulder, I caught the sight of two more *bracks* rushing in our direction from around the house. They must've landed on the beach behind the house or any other small beaches around the island. Blasts of distant explosions, coming from other directions, confirmed my guess. There were so many more of them than when they took Lero the last time.

With a strangled gasp, I pivoted on my heel and ran down the path to Lero.

He'd been busy. Several bodies lay on the sand around him. The slash wounds in them sparkling red.

There must be something in his swords that made the *bracks* go down and stay down for good—something that my knives didn't have. The *brack* I'd wounded was now running after me, as alive and fit as ever.

"Stella!" Lero growled, burying his right sword in the shoulder of one of the *bracks* attacking him while deflecting a blow of a long sword held by another with his left.

Several more *bracks* hurried from the water edge, dragging the dreadfully familiar black net behind them. It crackled and sparked, scorching black the golden sand of the beach.

"Get the net here!" One of them yelled.

*Dez.*

I recognized him.

Despite all *bracks* looking almost identical in their appearance, I could not have mistaken this man for anyone else. The glimmer of intense hate in his gaze directed at Lero set him apart.

"You! Get over here." Another *brack* yanked me by my right arm, dragging me aside. I swung my left hand with the knife his way, stabbing him in the neck.

This time, bringing harm to someone came easier to me. The blade went in smoothly, right under his jaw. Blood gushed out of the wound when I yanked the knife back. The *brack's* eyes opened wide in shock and pain. He obviously hadn't expected me to act. His hand went up to his neck, in a futile attempt to block the blood from leaving his body in a pulsing flow.

With a gurgling sound, he crashed to the ground. Though I had a feeling he wouldn't stay there for long—my knife was not Lero's sword. There were no red sparks from the *brack's* wound, which meant it didn't kill him.

More *bracks* rushed us from all directions. More showed up from behind the house, heading to the beach down the path, too. There were so many...

Lero stabbed, sliced, and cut, the pile of dead bodies growing higher around him. But many more kept coming.

"Get him!" Dez ordered those with the net. "I want him alive. For now, anyway."

The *bracks* tossed the black net over Lero. One of his blades connected with it, setting off an explosion of red sparkling fireworks. Knocked out of his grip, the blade fell to the sand at his feet. The net slid away too, but first it grazed his elbow. He hissed in pain as the sleeve of his shirt smoldered.

I dropped to all fours. Evading the hands of another *brack* grasping for me, I crawled toward Lero.

The *bracks* surrounded him, circling him with the net again.

I climbed over the bodies on the ground, reaching for the sword Lero had dropped. If I got it, I'd be able to fight these men so much more effectively.

A heavy boot stomped on my wrist, stopping me from grabbing the blade.

"Where do you think you're going, human?" A *brack* grabbed me by my ponytail, dragging me away. I screamed in pain, anger, and disappointment.

The net descended on Lero, trapping him. The black ropes of it glowed bright red, burning through his clothes and searing his flesh underneath.

Baring his teeth, he roared in pain.

"Lero!" I screamed, agony wrenching my heart.

"Stella, run!" he yelled.

His eyes glowed red. The veins on his neck bulged. Smoke and red sparks rose from his hands as he gripped the net, straining to rip it apart.

Despite his incredible strength, I knew he wouldn't be able to break free from it. I'd seen it trap him before, hopelessly and securely.

Only this time, I was no mere observer. I *felt* his pain and anguish in my soul and flesh.

The agonizing fire of the net.

The crushing devastation of the impending defeat.

His excruciating worry for me.

His rage.

All of that rushed me, as if they were my own feelings and emotions. As if I were him. I strained my muscles, struggling against the fiery net along with him, even as I was being dragged away from him.

An approaching *brack*, still knee-deep in the sea water, yanked the bow off his shoulder and nocked an arrow. He aimed and shot it in Lero's direction, piercing his upper arm. A bright red spot bloomed on Lero's white shirt that soaked up his blood from the wound. The ominous red lights sparked, running up the arrow embedded in his flesh.

"Lero!" I yelled. My scream mixed with his roar of pain.

I felt his agony, grabbing on to my own arm with my hand. The pain spread through me like a wildfire, melting the chill of fear away and igniting anger. The fury grew, until it was a weapon on its own.

"Get them, Lero!" I screamed at the top of my lungs.

Despite being dragged through the sand, my skull burning from the pull on my hair, I no longer felt weak or powerless. The vicious, unstoppable need to crush, rip, and kill those who wronged us coursed hot through my veins.

"Be the beast that you are. Get them all!" With my entire being, I wished him to be bigger, stronger. Ruthless. I pushed my rage to him, like a blast of power.

His roar grew louder and deeper as his lungs increased in size. He grew taller, his figure hulking, his muscles rippling with strength. His shoulders hunched over, widening and tearing through his shirt.

The shape of his body distorted its outline, turning from that of a man to...something else—unnatural and grotesque.

Black fur burst through the tears in his clothing, immediately smoldering where it touched the net. The sea breeze saturated with the pungent smell of the burnt fur.

With another deafening roar, the beast yanked at the net, knocking the astonished *bracks* who were holding it off their feet.

"Free yourself..." I whispered the command he couldn't possibly hear, but I was certain it reached him somehow.

Shaking the murderous net off his shoulders, he reached for those who kept clinging to it with their glove-protected hands.

My beast growled, closing his needle-sharp teeth over the head of a *brack* and cracking his skull. He bit the other one on his shoulder, ripping his chest open with his long claws. The third one turned to run, and Lero jerked to follow.

Saliva dripped from his fangs and down the back of the escaping *brack*. A thin tendril of smoke rose from the spot where the few drops landed on the *brack's* t-shirt. The material immediately burned through. The poison turned from clear to crimson against the man's bare skin. It glistened, thick like hot lava.

The *brack* howled in agony, arching his back, then crashed to the ground. Dead.

Dez whipped his head my way.

"You!" he gritted through his teeth.

His eyes narrowed to slits, he stomped my way. Grabbing my arm, he yanked me from the hold of the *brack* who'd been dragging me by my hair.

"*You* did this?" Dez growled.

"How?" The other *brack* stared at me in utter bewilderment. "No one can turn a werewolf without the full moon. Not even the most powerful hag. And she doesn't even look like a hag."

Dez brought his face to mine. Red streaks sparked through his dark-brown eyes. The red brought out some eerie similarities, making Dez look momentarily more familiar. The shape of his face, the sharp rise of his cheekbones, and the sensual curve of his mouth, all brought Lero's face to mind.

Even if I didn't know it already, it became obvious Dez was Lero's brother. And his torturer. Despite the physical similarities, however, these two were so different. I couldn't imagine in Lero the pure hatred I saw in Dez's eyes.

"How could you be the sons of the same mother?" I asked in disbelief.

"I have no mother!" Dez snarled. "No family. I belong to the Goddess and her alone. And soon, I'll have no brother, either."

He dragged me back to the part of the beach where Lero fought against the ever-increasing crowd of *bracks*. More of them kept coming from all over the island, swarming the place like rats.

"You started this. You'll end this." Dez spat the words in my face. "Feed the beast!" he yelled, tossing me to Lero.

Propelled by his powerful shove, I fell, hitting the beast's flank with my shoulder. His back to me, Lero turned quickly, snapping his teeth at me.

A spark of recognition flashed in his red eyes, at the last moment. He held back, his teeth clacking shut a hairbreadth away from my bare upper arm. A few drops of poison dripped from them on my skin, burning me like hot lava.

I screamed in pain, rolling on the ground. The poison spread through my body like liquid fire, the burn eating my flesh alive.

The beast's roar shuddered the air, full of anguish. He crouched at my side, turning his back to his enemies.

They used the moment to toss the damn net back on him, yanking him away from me.

I had given him strength. Now, I proved to be his weakness.

*"Lero,"* I wanted to call him, but my mouth wouldn't open to form the word.

My body seemed paralyzed by fire. The muscles felt as if burnt to a crisp, the joints locked up. I lay on the beach, my head propped on a raised tussock of long grass.

Helplessly, I watched the *bracks* wrap the net over Lero as he thrashed against it to get to me. And I was powerless to help him in any way.

Lifting one of Lero's swords off the sand, Dez moved on to the beast.

"Do you know why I'm here, *voukalak?* Because Madame granted me a wish for my service to her. You know what I asked her for? The chance to murder you. That is my only wish, to see you dead. Madame doesn't need you anymore. No one does."

Far in the distance behind him, I saw the sea swell and rise. The water rolled back from the land, as if a sudden low tide had rapidly come in. Or a tsunami was approaching.

Unable to move, I could only watch.

Dez came closer to Lero, lifting the sword ready to strike.

"You should've accepted Madame's offer when she granted you the honor of becoming one of us. She is taking over this world as we speak, and you could be by her side, ruling it with us. Instead, you're going to die here. Useless as you've always been. *Brother*," he spat the last word out like a curse.

The swell behind him rose higher, moving into the lagoon. The sea water crested, foaming white, with...a man on the very top of it, riding the giant wave.

*Zeph!*

I recognized his silvery white hair, but there was no smile on his beautiful face this time. His dark eyebrows furrowed. Steely concentration settled in his blue eyes.

Submerged up to his waist in the foamy water, he remained upright. His arms spread wide, Zeph appeared to direct the water toward the beach with his hands. He wasn't simply carried by the wave. He commanded it.

He wasn't alone. A young woman in a yellow sundress was at his side, her arms wrapped around his bare torso. This must be Ivy.

The wave paused, the movement of the water unnaturally suspended behind the tideline. Zeph slid from the crest, bringing Ivy down with him. He gently set her into the knee-high water at the edge of the beach.

Without saying a word, he moved his hand out toward Dez. A stream of sea water shot from the giant wave, like from a water cannon, knocking Dez off his feet. Unlike a blast from a cannon, the mass of water didn't flow away. Instead, it remained, pressing Dez down with a powerful deluge.

"Fucking *bracks*." Disgust distorted Zeph's handsome features.

With another wave of his hand, the mass of water arched in the air then crashed onto the *bracks* on the beach, washing them away in every direction.

Zeph stepped to me. Lowering himself into a crouch at my side.

"Stella, are you okay? What happened?"

My eyes remained open. I saw everything but could say nothing. It was as if the burn of the poison on my arm pressed me into the ground, sucking the warmth and life out of me.

Or maybe I was dead already? And it was my spirit, watching the devastation on the beach—a silent, passive witness.

With no one holding the net, Lero growled loudly, shrugging the thing off him once again.

Zeph squinted at him, cautiously.

"Is that...Lero? I've never seen him changed..." He rose to his feet slowly, his focus on the massive, black beast who was shedding the last of the net that had burned deep lines in his fur and flesh.

While Zeph's attention focused on his friend, Lero's turned to me. He stumbled my way as fast as his injuries allowed.

Neither of the fae noticed the *bracks* climb out of the shrubs and patches of tall grass around the beach. The massive amount of water hadn't killed them. I believed nothing would, unless it sparked red when it hit them.

A scream of warning bubbled in my chest, growing painfully strong, but nothing came out, no matter how hard I tried to scream to warn them.

Dez gestured to another *brack*, who swung a thin, black rope over his head. Made from the same material as the net, the rope crackled with red sparks when the *brack* threw it at Zeph like a lasso, catching his head in the noose.

Yanked back, Zeph lost his footing, his hands flying up to the rope that burned his neck. The *brack* pulled on the rope, tightening the noose around Zeph's throat, choking him.

"Are you willing to die for the *voukalak*, water man?" Dez taunted. "Will you give your life for the monster who killed your family?"

Lero halted on the way to me, then turned to lunge at Zeph's tormentors. More *bracks* jumped from the hills to the beach. Apparently, not all of them had been washed away, or maybe some had hidden elsewhere on the island before Zeph showed up.

"Drag the siren off the beach!" Dez ordered the two *bracks* who held the rope with the noose around Zeph's neck. "Get him farther away from the water. Then end him. He killed Trez. Madame will be happy to have him dead."

Welding Lero's sword, Dez attacked the beast to keep him from helping Zeph.

"Zeph!" The high-pitched, feminine scream cut through the air like a blade.

Ivy stood in the water where Zeph had left her. Her clear voice rang high above the island and the sea.

Her arms down her sides, she appeared to vibrate with strain. Her fingers curled. The water under her hands bubbled and boiled, churning around her legs in a whirlpool, faster and faster.

The water rose in a spiral, using Ivy's body to climb up like a vine climbed a pillar.

"Zeph!" Ivy screamed again, throwing her arms up toward him.

The waterspout rose over her head, slid up her arms and arched toward Zeph. The stream sparkled in the afternoon sun, stretching and twisting through the air like a brilliant crystal rope—a lifeline.

It showered over Zeph. Uncontrolled at first, but only for a fraction of a second. The moment the stream connected with his skin, it took shape. Instead of sliding off his body, the water gathered over him, then exploded out in a powerful blast that scattered the *bracks* away from Zeph and the rope. Burning his fingers, Zeph ripped the rope off his neck and climbed to his feet.

"That's it!" he growled, his voice low and grave.

Lifting his arms into the air like the wings of an angel bringing justice, he wielded the water like a terrifying weapon.

It slid up and off Ivy's body, forming a massive bridge from her to Zeph. He directed all of its power against the *bracks*.

This time, they didn't simply get washed off. The current spun and turned them like twigs in a drain during a torrential rain. The weapons they'd brought with them were ripped from their hands then plunged into their chests. The rope and the net tangled some of them into a bundle. The flood of seawater then washed over the island, taking them all far into the sea.

"What are you going to do with that one?" Zeph asked Lero, who held Dez down with his knee pressed into the *brack's* chest.

Tossing his great head back, the beast howled to the sky.

Rage vibrated in that sound, devastating and deadly. But I also heard a long sorrowful note woven through. Dez had claimed to have no family, but for Lero it wasn't that simple or straightforward.

"Get your paws off me, you filthy *voukalak.*" Dez struggled against Lero's hold.

The beast pressed Dez's head down with one hand, then leaned over and closed his teeth over the *brack's* neck. Dez's body jerked once as the poison-soaked fangs pierced his skin, then stilled.

My eyes closed, shutting off the death and devastation.

# Chapter Twenty-Two

LERO

From the corner of his eye, he saw Zeph directing the stream of water to sweep Ivy off her feet and carry her into his arms. Once Zeph had her, the water dropped to the ground and flowed back to sea.

"Zeph, baby, how are you?" Ivy hovered her fingers over the red angry scar on Zeph's neck.

His own injuries burned and ached. The one from the arrowhead hurt the most. The iron from Nerifir didn't just stop the wounds from healing, it could kill a fae. Had the arrow pierced any of his vital organs, he'd be dead.

Stella...

He staggered to his feet, leaving the body of his dead brother for Zeph's water power to deal with. It proved easier to walk on all fours after all, as he crawled toward a motionless Stella.

He'd killed her. He had no other entity to blame for this. Unlike any other time he'd been in his beast form, today was no full moon. It wasn't even night yet, the sun hadn't touched the horizon in its descent.

His transformation had been triggered by another power, the one that did not demand the control of his mind. Even as the beast, he retained the clear thinking of a man. And he'd been careless, endangering the only woman in this world who meant the world to him.

With a pained groan, he dropped to his knees at her side.

She remained still, her lovely face pale and cold as the wet sand she lay on. The three drops of poison glistened red on her upper arm.

*His* poison.

He'd been granted the greatest gift by gods when they'd sent her to him. And he'd killed her.

Agony twisted his soul, burning more than any of the wounds on his flesh. He faced the sky and released the pain with a long howl. There was no moon to receive his sorrow. It crashed back down on him, crushing and suffocating.

He gathered her into his arms and pressed his nose to that spot where her neck met her shoulder, nuzzling the tender skin he'd loved to kiss when making love to her.

His tenderness for her, the intense longing, the excruciating pain of loss all rolled into one, growing and encompassing every strong wholesome emotion he'd ever had. The sensation threatened to overwhelm him, yet also strangely uplifted him, making him feel one with her.

"Lero?" Zeph's hand landed heavily on his shoulder. "We should take Stella...her body to the house."

He didn't move. There was no place for death between Stella and him. If she went, he'd be gone too. Why was he still here?

With his nose pressed to the base of her neck, he felt the faintest pulsing sensation. It came again, then again, like a gentle flutter of butterfly wings under her skin.

Stella's pulse!

Her heart kept pumping blood through her body.

He moved his nose to hers, afraid to hope yet desperately wishing to believe. The gentlest puff of breath tickled his sensitive nostrils.

She was breathing!

He grabbed her face in his large, furry hands. His claws pierced through her hair, but he flexed his fingers, keeping his claws away from her skin.

As the beast, he couldn't speak, couldn't even call her name. So, he howled again, softly this time, to coax her awareness to the surface, back to him.

Her eyelids quivered, and he dared to let the hope blossom in his heart, stroking her cheeks with his thumbs.

She opened her most amazing eyes, of no particular color and of all colors at once. Her gaze focused on his scruffy animal face. Instead of fear or repulsion, a brilliant smile curved her lips.

His chest tightened with so much emotion, he wished he could let it all go and cry, but the beast had no tears. He held her instead, rocking on his haunches with her in his arms.

"Lero..." She twined her arms around his neck. The burns left by the nasty iron net from Nerifir protested at her touch, but he didn't care. Her caress soothed his soul.

Zeph and Ivy crowded them.

"She's alive," Zeph said, gaping at Stella in wonder.

"Stella. How are you feeling?" Ivy placed her hand on Lero's woman's shoulder.

He growled softly, the rumble reverberating through his chest. He loved Zeph as his own blood. And lately, he'd been looking forward to seeing Ivy again. But this very moment, he needed Stella all to himself.

"We'd better go," Zeph said, his voice unusually distant.

Dez calling him the monster who killed Zeph's family rose in his mind unbidden. He'd never spoken to Zeph about his true reasons for leaving Nerifir. The conversation was long overdue.

Right now, though, he only wanted Stella.

"We have to make sure they're both all right," Ivy argued with Zeph. "We can't just leave them."

Stella shifted in his lap, her bottom rubbing against his cock hidden in the thick fur between his thighs. She snuggled against his chest.

He released a soft rumble, brushing strands of her hair away from her face. More than anything in the world he wished to keep hearing her voice as the reassurance that she was all right.

"How is she?" Ivy crouched in front of them.

Stella closed her eyes tight then opened them again, moving her gaze from him to Ivy then to Zeph.

"Everyone is safe..." she said softly, the smile lingering on her face.

She was right. For now, all four of them were safe and alive.

Stella rubbed her face with a slight wince.

"I'm fine," she replied to Ivy's question. "My head is a little fuzzy, but it's getting better..."

He tightened his arm around her shoulders, helping her to sit up in his lap. Her bum pressed against his cock again as she adjusted her position. Blood rushed to his groin. She cast him a furtive glance, obviously feeling him grow harder against her.

"Um..." she started, rather breathy, then turned to face Zeph and Ivy. "Glad to see you here, guys."

"Well, if you're feeling better, Zeph is right, we should go," Ivy suggested, a little hesitantly.

"No," Stella protested, rubbing her upper arm, the spot where his poison left three red, tear-shaped scars.

He couldn't explain how she was still alive, he was just insanely grateful that she was.

"Stay, please," Stella said to Ivy. "You've come for dinner. Let's have it."

Ivy glanced at Zeph, who cast Lero a reproachful glance.

"Please." Stella tried to convince them both. "We need to talk."

Ivy wrapped her arms around herself. The breeze must be chilly for her in her wet dress. The sea mist lingered in the air after Zeph's impressive waterworks show.

"We could stay, couldn't we?" she asked the siren. "For a little while?"

Dressed only in swim shorts, Zeph looked as comfortable as ever. He put an arm around Ivy's shoulders, drawing her into his side to shield her from the breeze. Sliding a hand down her dress, he made the water drip out of the material of her dress onto the ground, making her clothes dry in seconds.

"We'll need to warm you up," he said in a clipped voice, avoiding looking at Lero.

"Let's go to the house then. Are you coming?" Ivy asked Stella.

"Um... I'll have to help Lero shift back." She gave him a quick look.

"How?" Ivy asked, gazing at him with curiosity and obvious trepidation.

Stella blew out a breath. Her face momentarily turned a lovely shade of pink, the blush spreading to her neck and shoulders.

"I'm not entirely sure." She rubbed her forehead, hiding her gaze. "But I believe it may need to be something...um, of a sexual nature."

"Oh." Ivy straightened, grabbing Zeph's hand. "We'll wait at the house, then." She tugged the siren toward the path.

"Make yourselves at home," Stella called after them. "Have some tea."

"Thanks! Will do." Ivy waved at her, with Zeph glaring in Lero's direction as both headed up the path.

Lero paid little attention to their departure. His focus had zoomed in on Stella's words "sexual nature" and stayed there. No longer muffled by rage or grief, lust spread through his body, warming his skin under his fur and straining his cock. Pulsing hot, his erection throbbed right beneath Stella's ass. She wiggled it, her eyelids drooping. A wisp of the tantalizing scent of her arousal reached his nostrils, heating his blood.

"Let's hope this works," she said softly, the moment Zeph and Ivy disappeared into the house. "Since I made you shift into the beast, I should be able to reverse it, too, right?"

She turned to face him, spreading her legs wide, one on each side of his hips.

"I'm not even sure if that's what I'm supposed to do." She brushed her hand over the three red marks on her arm again, then slid a strap of her top down her shoulder. "But I want it, so badly." Her breathing turned hot and heavy as her lips parted. "I want you, Lero. So much, I ache..." Slipping her hand inside her bra, she squeezed her breast while grinding against him. "Please... I feel like I'll die again unless you touch me."

His existence narrowed to the present moment. His body vibrated with need. Tossing his head back, he howled with the pain of anticipation.

"No?" She misunderstood him, anxiously searching his eyes.

Yes! He wanted to shout. So much yes! Instead of words, however, only growls came out.

He couldn't speak, but he could *show* her.

Cupping her other breast through her shirt, careful not to pierce her skin with his claws, he circled the hard pebble of her nipple with his thumb. She exhaled a soft moan as he rubbed and pinched it through the thin material.

His cock grew impossibly hard, throbbing with heat. But he shifted away from her, laying her on her back on the warm sand higher up the beach, away from the waves. He slid his fingers along the waistband of her shorts, ready to rip them. He had no patience to deal with buttons and zippers, his claws getting in the way.

"Here." She guessed his intentions, hurriedly unbuttoning her shorts and sliding them down her legs, along with the white lacy underwear underneath.

Her warm scent teased his nostrils, spurring his desire. His mouth watered, craving her taste. Lust blinded his mind, depriving him of reason. She spread her thighs wide in invitation, raising her hips to him. And he dove in, lapping between her legs like the starving beast that he was.

She gasped and hissed, arching her back as his teeth grazed her tender flesh.

A spear of horror chilled his heart. He'd nearly killed her with his poison. And now...

"Oh, it burns... So hot," Stella moaned. Getting hold of his pointy ears, she shoved his head closer to her. "More!" she demanded.

His poison had failed to kill her. Now, it excited her.

Eager to give her everything she desired, he dove in again, lapping along her heated folds, sucking on the hot little bud at their apex, and swirling his long, thick tongue inside her.

Drunk on her taste, he rose to his knees and grabbed her hips. Leaning back, he yanked her to him, impaling her on his cock. He roared from the intense pleasure of sinking into her slick, tight heat.

Her shoulders and head on the sand, her back arched, she threw her arms over her head, moaning loudly.

The lust took over, and the world fell away. Stella and he were all that remained, suspended in the bliss of mating.

He thrust wildly, chasing the climax that teased him with licks of heat running up his inner thighs and pressure squeezing his groin.

Stella released a shuddering groan, her inner muscles spasmed around his cock as her hips jerked, sending him over the edge. He pumped his release into her, tension draining with every drop. His knot grew inside her, anchoring him to her.

Only when the orgasm stopped rocking his body did the cloud of lust finally clear.

Stella lay beneath him, her arms thrown wide, her hair wild, her shirt hiked up to her armpits. A huge, satisfied smile graced her lips. She looked thoroughly ravaged, but...happy.

He released a breath of relief.

# Chapter Twenty-Three

STELLA

The aftershock of the most violent orgasm still quivered through my inner muscles. Now, I understood completely the meaning of "being ravaged by a beast," or by *my* beast, at least.

Heat pulsed in my veins, spreading through my body. The pulsing resonated with the one on my upper arm where the poison from his fangs glistened in three red drops embedded in my skin.

I no longer felt even a hint of weakness. Energy buzzed through me, making me feel stronger and more alive than I'd ever been.

Something had happened between Lero and I, something more than the eye could see.

He let go of my hips, sinking down over me. The warmth of his large, furry body enveloped me like a blanket, so pleasant against my chilled skin. Sliding his arms under me, he rolled onto his back, taking me with him. My body felt boneless, allowing him to move me like a rag doll.

For a moment, I just lay there on top of him. My face pressed to his chest, I listened to his heartbeat slow down and his breathing calm.

Then I rose on my arm over him.

"Do you think it worked?" I watched his face for any signs of Lero's human features. Aside from the calming gray of his eyes, he remained the beast.

"Well, I guess we should wait until the sunrise?" My voice carried the uncertainty I felt. The sunrise was far away. The sun hadn't even set yet, with dinnertime just approaching.

Oddly, the pressure of him inside me didn't ease. I wiggled my hips, trying to make him slide out of me. With a soft, soothing rumble, he placed his large warm hand on my buttocks, keeping me in place.

"What is that?" I asked, as something clearly kept him inside me. Then it dawned on me as the memory of the swelling at the base of the beast's penis I saw in the basement came to me. Swollen inside me, it acted like an anchor, keeping us connected.

"Well, this is...um, new." I relaxed against him again. "How long do you think it will last? We have guests waiting for us in the house." I released a mortified giggle, thinking about Zeph and Ivy.

I knew Lero couldn't answer me. Instead, he stroked my back gently and nuzzled the hair over my temple. I didn't mind staying like that for a while, just cuddling and enjoying his closeness. Wrapped in his arms I felt safe and warm.

"It forces you to cuddle whether you like it or not, doesn't it?" I laughed quietly, raking my fingers through the long, thick fur on his chest. "Good thing I know you like cuddles."

He snorted softly, which I took as him agreeing with me.

Gradually, his fur thinned under my fingers. My hand connected with his skin.

"Lero?" I raised my head again, to see his face.

Unlike his transformation into a beast, which had been brutal and grotesque. Lero's turning back into a man proved to be smooth and gradual.

The fur slowly disappeared, as if melting off his skin. His pointy ears and long snout flattened. His teeth shortened. Within a minute or two, the beast was gone, and I lay on top of the man I knew and loved.

"I love you," he said suddenly.

The shock at finally hearing these words from him dissolved with warmth through my chest.

"You don't have to—" I started, but he wouldn't let me finish.

"I still don't know exactly what love means for others, but I know what it means to me. What *you* mean to me, Stella." He sat upright, sliding me into his lap and finally disconnecting our bodies. "Everything. You mean absolutely everything to me, in this world and any other. I love you."

I blinked at him, happiness spreading through me like sunshine and melting into a wide smile on my face.

"I love you too, my beastly man." I stroked his cheek, the short stubble of his five-o'clock shadow pricking my skin. "Kiss me, Lero," I whispered. "Kiss me like you always do. Like only *you* can do."

# Chapter Twenty-Four

STELLA

"This is a beautiful house," Ivy said politely, both hands tightly wrapped around her cup of tea.

All four of us sat in the family room, having tea after a dinner of pasta with tomato sauce—Lero's homemade tomato sauce, not mine from the jar.

After I'd snuck the naked Lero into the house through the back-patio door to the master bathroom, we'd gotten changed. Then the three of us had helped Lero make dinner and had eaten in relative silence.

I had so many things I wanted to talk about, but the atmosphere was far from easy at the moment. Zeph's friendly disposition would liven up the conversation, I was sure. But even he seemed unusually gloomy and subdued, his contagious smile had yet to make an appearance.

"I hope you don't mind, but we took a little tour of the formal area of the house," Ivy added, sitting next to Zeph on one of the two white couches in the room. Having arrived wearing nothing but his swim shorts, Zeph had reluctantly accepted one of Lero's shirts and a pair of pants before dinner.

Lero and I occupied the couch across from them, with a long magazine table carved from a single piece of wood between us. A tray with a porcelain teapot and a cheese platter stood on the table.

"Oh, I can give you a proper tour of the entire property." I stirred.

"Later," Zeph bit off.

Lero shot a glance his way.

"So," I turned to Ivy, giving up on the men for the time being. "You're human, aren't you?"

"I think so." She didn't sound very convinced.

"Have you always been able to...well, do that thing you did with the water back on the beach?"

"Me? Noooo." She turned her head side to side slowly, her eyes big with wonder at her own abilities. "That has only happened once before. We share a bond. Zeph, what is it exactly?"

He finally smiled, gazing at her.

"You tell me. How do you do it, my love?"

She frowned in visible concentration.

"I-I just get so angry when you're in danger. Angry and scared for you. When someone is hurting them, I want to hurt them back."

*Angry and scared.*

That was exactly how I felt when I ordered Lero to take his beast form—angry at them and scared for him.

"Can you show us, sweetheart?" Zeph asked, pointing at the cup in her hands.

"Sure." Ivy took one hand off the cup and held it over her tea.

She moved her fingers above the cup in a circle, huffing a laugh.

"I still have no idea what I'm doing."

The four of us stared at her tea intently. I even rose in my seat for a better look. The surface of the liquid remained still, with only a subtle ripple from the slight trembling of Ivy's hand holding the cup.

"I may need to touch the liquid," Zeph offered.

"Oh, that's right." Ivy dipped the tip of her pointer finger into her tea, swirling it around.

Without stopping the swirling motion, she lifted her finger out of the cup, and the tea followed.

"Wow!" I breathed out, mesmerized.

A human woman was bending water to her will, right in front of my eyes. Back in the heat of the fight and the dread of mortal danger, I had no chance to fully appreciate the miracle of that.

"It works!" She beamed.

She lifted her hand a few inches higher, and the contact was broken. The spiral of the tea collapsed and fell back into her cup with a splash.

"Well, that's not that impressive." Ivy laughed.

"Hold on." Zeph shifted all the way to the other end of the couch from her. "Toss it to me, now."

Ivy stirred the tea in her cup again. Making the spiral rise a couple of inches over the rim of her cup, she flicked her finger Zeph's way. The tea stretched in a long arc from her cup, forming a bridge between her and Zeph, curved like an amber rainbow.

He met it with his hand open, palm up. The end of the "rainbow" barely touched his skin, then the whole thing looped, landing back into Ivy's cup.

She laughed, and I giggled, too. It turned into a fun show.

Ivy then took a small sip from her cup.

"That's one way to cool off your tea!" She laughed again.

"Fascinating," Lero observed, obviously impressed. "And you're absolutely positive you couldn't do it before you met Zeph?"

"No, I couldn't." She shook her head. "Not that I'd ever tried, of course."

Ivy's abilities had something to do with Zeph's powers.

"Why do you think it happens?" I asked the entire room, inviting any explanation.

Zeph inhaled deeply, but Ivy replied first.

"I *feel* him," she said simply. "The connection between us, I feel it. It's like..." she waved her hand between her and Zeph. "Like that bridge that the tea made. No matter where he is, I'm always..."

"...*aware* of him," I finished for her.

Goosebumps rushed down my arms when she stared at me, the

understanding shining in her eyes. She knew what I knew. I felt the same connection with Lero as she did with Zeph.

Lero gently rubbed the three red drop shapes on the skin of my upper arm.

"That's why my poison didn't kill you," he said softly. "What can't harm me can't hurt you, either. You're a part of me now, Stella."

Ivy's large eyes flew open even wider as she twisted her torso to Zeph. "I bet your spikes wouldn't harm me, either!"

He lifted an eyebrow. "You may be right."

Lero stared straight ahead for a long moment.

"What is it, honey?" I touched his knee.

"The fae mating bond implies shared power. In Nerifir, both partners have similar magic and abilities to begin with, so it's not as apparent. Here..." He moved his gaze to me. "You got access to my magic, and Ivy did to Zeph's. When mated, if the couple live long enough to die of natural causes, they die together, on the same day."

"What are you saying?"

"You'll live as long as me, Stella." He kept his eyes on me. "Five hundred years."

"Are you sure?" I pressed both hands to my chest. My heart beat so fast, I worried it'd jump out. Living for hundreds of years sounded great. Spending all of those years with Lero was truly magical.

"I have no proof, of course," Lero added. "But we'll find out for sure in a decade or so, when you stop aging."

"Tell me, please, how does the siren mating bond happen in Nerifir? Is there a ceremony? A wedding? What traditions do they have?" Ivy asked Lero with eager curiosity. "Zeph was too little when he left your world, he doesn't know."

Lero smiled.

"Sorry, Ivy, but I don't know the details, either. In Nerifir, sirens mate on the bottom of the ocean."

"Oh." Ivy glanced at the cup in her hand. "Well, I've learned to swim pretty good by now, but I still can't breathe under water."

Zeph shifted closer to her, wrapping his arm around her shoulders.

"I'm more than happy to keep mating on the surface with you," he assured her cheerfully.

His words made Ivy blush.

"So, the fae bond you told me about actually happened between us?" I asked Lero, still trying to wrap my mind around all of it.

"The power of human love created it where I didn't think it was possible." He nodded. "Somehow, you managed to harvest the magic of the Moon to *turn* me at will."

I just stared back at him, silently. He already knew all about my feelings, and I had no other explanation to add to that.

"You have power over me now, Stella," he said. "Use it wisely."

"Are you worried?"

"Worried? No." He leaned over, placing a tender kiss on my lips. "Your hold is so much gentler than that of the Moon. It was a pleasure to surrender to you."

Air rushed out of me with a breath of overwhelming relief. I cupped his face. "Are you saying you weren't hurting this time?"

"No, my star. For once, there was no pain and no madness. I changed how I looked but not the way I felt or thought. With you, I remained myself, even in the beast form. Some emotions I felt more strongly, the desire—" he cut himself short, casting a glance in the direction of our guests. Bringing my hand to his mouth, he brushed his lips over my knuckles adding in a softer voice, "The desire is always there, with you around. No matter what form I'm in."

Smiling, I gave him a peck on the tip of his nose.

"I have to say, Lero," Ivy chimed in. "Your other form is amazing. When I first saw you on the beach..." A tremble ran across her shoulders. "It was impressive."

"Um, thank you?" Lero smiled.

"I can't look at you without a certain trepidation, now." She gazed at him with awe. "Though, you've always had that air of intimidation about you, even when we first met."

"You've met before?" I asked.

"Briefly," Lero confirmed. "Outside of my cabaret, back in Paris."

"I had a feeling he didn't like me much," Ivy shared with me, casting a glance Lero's way.

"It wasn't you, personally," Lero said apologetically, looking ashamed as if he'd been called out on lack of good manners. "I worried about the dangers that being with a fae would mean for a human." He squeezed my hand in his, giving me an adorable little smile. "Obviously, I was wrong. There are dangers, but I now believe *some* humans can handle them."

I beamed at him, wishing I could kiss him, thoroughly and completely. But we had company tonight.

"You can stay the night. Or as long as you want, really," I told Ivy. "There's plenty of space. You know it's actually twin islands, with two houses?"

"Well, we..." She glanced at Zeph.

Zeph's expression turned even more serious, his lips pressed together tightly.

Letting go of my hand, Lero drew in a long breath and rose to his feet.

"We need to talk, Zeph. Come with me."

# Chapter Twenty-Five

LERO

He walked through the back door out to the patio. From the corner of his eye, he saw Zeph get up from the couch to follow him out. Lero exhaled in relief. He'd used his authoritative voice of a parent when he'd told Zeph to come with him. However, Zeph hadn't been a child for a long time, now. He was a grown man who very well could tell him go fuck himself. The fact that Zeph actually listened and came out to the patio with him gave him hope.

Zeph didn't go far, however. Closing the door behind him, he silently leaned with his back against it.

"I've never really told you why we left Nerifir," Lero said, wondering where to even begin his explanation. Some things could never be explained. He just hoped that whatever connection he'd managed to build with Zeph over the past decades would hold even after what he had to say.

"You said we came with Ghata," Zepf replied, evenly. "She was escaping prosecution."

"I was escaping, too."

Zeph gave him a heavy look from under his brow.

"After killing my parents?"

Lero'd come out here, ready to talk about that night. However, Zeph's deliberately direct question felt like a punch to his gut. It knocked the air out of him, rendering him speechless.

"That's what that *brack* said," Zeph muttered, obviously expecting an explanation. Or maybe he was hoping for Lero to deny it.

He couldn't deny it, though. He couldn't even keep it a secret anymore.

"The *brack*'s name was Dez. He was my brother."

Zeph paused, staring at him.

"My older brother," Lero explained. "For many generations, Ghata demanded the eldest son from each family be given to her to serve as her priest. The *bracks* are former werewolves that she'd changed into her slaves."

"And the families did that? They gave up their children, willingly?" Zeph stared at him in obvious disbelief.

"It was considered an honor for the boy to be Ghata's priest, to worship her daily, and to live in her grand, luxurious temple. The families were given many blessings in return."

Zeph's gaze turned heavy with accusation.

"You killed your own brother today."

Lero straightened under the siren's judgment. As true as that statement was, Zeph didn't entirely understand what had happened.

"I lost my brother almost nine decades ago," Lero said. "When my parents brought him to Ghata's temple, he stopped resembling my brother in every way. Today, I killed a *brack*, Ghata's slave, who had no will of his own and thrived on murder and torture. Hate was the strongest emotion he'd retained. He hated me because I am what he once was."

"It wasn't easy for you to kill him." A soft note slipped into Zeph's voice. "I could tell."

"Murder is never easy," he agreed. "Unlike *bracks*, neither you nor I seek it or enjoy it."

Zeph dropped his gaze, without arguing. H'd killed his share of *bracks* and knew murder too well.

"Tell me about that night," he demanded, somberly.

Lero drew in a long breath, bracing himself.

"It was a full moon—"

"Of course it was," Zeph scoffed. "Isn't that a great excuse for everything?"

His derisive tone scraped against Lero's nerves with a flare of irritation. He forced it down. Zeph meant too much to him to give up, enough to tell the whole truth and bare himself to his judgment, no matter how condemnatory it might be.

"I'm not using the full moon as an excuse. I'm telling you how it was." He paused for a moment, giving Zeph a chance to reply with anything he had to say.

Zeph remained quiet this time, so he continued.

"As a child, I heard from the elders that the full moon nights used to be spent by couples hunting together and making love. That was not my experience, however. Full moon nights always brought pain, raging lust, and violence. My people call it Moon Madness, and that's exactly how I feel when the Moon takes over—mad. I dread watching the moon grow, every month."

"Smoking *womora* helps?" Zeph asked, with a glint of compassion in his sea-blue eyes.

"It did. But I lost access to *womora* the moment I escaped Ghata's freakshow. It doesn't matter now at all. Having Stella in my life is the best help. Her presence is better than *womora*, better than anything." He smiled, his heart flipping with excitement and tenderness at the thought of her. "But in Nerifir, it was only *womora* that helped manage the signs of the approaching madness. *Womora* has always been scarce, however. It can only be harvested during the full moon, and none of us was ever functioning enough on those nights to do the harvesting. Ghata organized it for us by employing other fae, sirens included. She paid them generously. They would gather *womora* and bring it to her temple 'for safekeeping.' Now I know of course that hoarding it was just another way of her keeping control over us."

His thoughts went back in time, to the place he'd long left, but which would never leave him.

"That night was no different. As the Moon rose, I *turned*, along with all the people in my village. Then, there was nothing but madness and...blood. So much blood. We were supposed to hunt meat for the village for the month ahead, but the Moon deprived us of any reason, leaving only bloodthirst. In that state, I never cared what or *whom* we hunted."

He paused, overwhelmed by the images of bloody carnage attacking his brain once again—torn flesh, broken bones, and blood, so much of it, it flowed in red, glistening rivers.

The pull of the approaching full moon tugged at something deep and carnal inside him, teasing his nostrils with the phantom smell of warm blood. He forced it down. The calming presence of Stella in his heart made it so much easier to control.

"At some point during that night, we came close to the seashore. The water fae had gone deep into the forest to collect *womora* leaves, too far from the water to escape us."

He stopped. The words lodged in his throat, and he could not push them out.

"You attacked them?" Zeph prompted.

"That's what it looked like the next morning. When I woke up... There were dead bodies everywhere. Pieces of sirens, ripped apart by the werewolves' claws, were scattered around. People from my village, no longer in their animal form, were lying dead. Deep, bloodied grooves from the water fae's fin spikes oozed poison on the werewolves' naked bodies. I have no idea how I'd survived. I had scratches all over my body, but none of them came from the poisonous spikes. The true miracle, however, was you."

He lifted his gaze to Zeph, seeing the little boy in the grown man again.

"A little siren boy was sitting in the waves on the beach, playing with seashells among all that death and blood. I don't know if you'd been left on the bottom of the sea while your folks went to the surface, and you came up in the morning looking for them. But there you were—innocent, defenseless, and completely alone."

"So, you took me?"

"I saw no other option." He ran his fingers through his hair. The memories pounded inside his skull with a mounting headache. "Ghata came upon us. The patience of my people for her atrocities had been wearing thin for some time. That morning, overwhelmed by her crimes, the entire kingdom of the Sarnala Plains went to her temple to overthrow and prosecute her. She escaped, but barely. They were on her heels, furious in their search for justice. She knew she wouldn't be safe from their wrath anywhere in Nerifir, but she was scared to flee to another world alone."

"You went with her," Zeph muttered under his breath.

"Yes. I'm not claiming that was the right decision or that it was the only solution at that point. I wasn't much older back then than you are now, Zeph. Faced with the evidence of all the murders I must have committed that night, I believed myself no better than Ghata. She offered me an escape, and I took it. Like me, you had no one left alive from your clan. So, I took you with me. Back then, I truly believed you needed me. Later, I realized how much *I* needed *you*. Ever since, you've been my one true family—"

"Stop it!" Zeph bit out.

Raking his fingers through his silvery hair, Zeph peeled his back from the glass door he'd been leaning against and hurried past him down to the beach.

For a moment, Lero thought he might jump into the waves and be gone, never to return. But Zeph stopped at the water line, pacing the beach instead. Ivy was in the house, Lero realized. As much as Zeph might want to flee Lero with his confessions, he wouldn't leave Ivy behind. Right now, she was his anchor to this place.

Instead, Zeph paced, trapped between water and land, between past and present, between love and hate. The Moon shone down on the beach, her chipped disk bloated but not yet perfectly round.

The moonlight tangled in Zeph's blond hair and bounced off his skin with a shimmer, making him look like the true siren he was— a water spirit, almost an apparition.

When Zeph was growing up, Lero had often been afraid that the little water fae's ethereal appearance would make humans question how the boy came to be. So often he'd worried that someone would recognize a being from another world in his silver-haired child.

It was only the humans' general ignorance and their inability to accept the existence of someone other than themselves that saved the two of them from being discovered.

His heart ached seeing Zeph in pain, now. His confession had just flipped Zeph's entire world upside down. All his life, he'd thought Lero the one person he could trust, and he'd just learned that Lero was the one responsible for him being an orphan in the first place.

Led by compassion, Lero headed down the path to the beach. Zeph might not want to see him right now—or ever—but Lero could never give up on him.

With a glance in his direction, Zeph stopped pacing and slowly lowered himself to the ground. Lero sat on the wet sand next to him.

His knees bent, Zeph placed his elbows on them.

"It's hard to mourn those I never knew," he said, staring straight ahead.

Lero kept silent, letting him speak.

"I don't remember anything. I've tried so many times to remember something from Nerifir, and I can't. I thought you telling me all of this would trigger a memory of that night or the morning after. And I still have nothing..."

"You were so young," Lero offered. "If you witnessed any of the massacre of that night, your mind might've blocked those memories, sparing you any further trauma."

For that he was grateful. He shuddered to think what the boy might've seen that night. The lack of memories would be a blessing in Zeph's case.

"Why did you never tell me before, though?" Zeph frowned.

Because he always dreaded this very moment right now, this accusing, reproachful look in Zeph's eyes.

"You...weren't old enough," he said instead.

"I'm almost forty-nine, Lero. I've been 'old enough' for over three decades, at least."

"Because I didn't want to see you hurt," he confessed. "And I didn't want you to hate me for it."

Zeph shook his head.

"Do you realize you're my only source of information about the place where I come from, Lero? There is no way for me to ask anyone else, no chance for me to ever go back and find out on my own. I need you to talk freely and truthfully to me. There can never be any lies between us."

"I've never lied to you," he objected firmly.

"You can't withhold information from me, either," Zeph replied. "For any reason whatsoever. Not even if you think it's in my best interests not to know. You have no right to make my decisions for me. Only I can make them."

In his heart, Lero screamed, *"It's my job as a parent to protect you!"*

In his mind, however, he understood Zeph perfectly, so he said nothing like that out loud. Whether he liked it or not, his little boy had grown. Lero tended to forget that.

Finally turning to face him fully, Zeph met his gaze. "I can't hate or even resent you. Even if I tried."

Lero drew in a slow breath, not relaxing yet.

"Zeph." He shifted uneasily. "I don't remember much of that night. I have no clear memories of it. I'll never be able to confirm that I was the one who killed your parents. However, I can never say with any certainty that I did not."

"Living with the weight of what you've done—of what you think you might have done—must be a punishment of its own."

Lero just sighed in reply. It had not been easy, but he always believed he deserved the constant feeling of guilt he'd lived with, the guilt that got even more punishing after Amelie.

"I've seen what it did to you," Zeph continued. "I don't recall you ever laughing out loud, while I was growing up, not even once. You barely even smiled."

Lero winced. For so long, his focus had been on keeping Zeph and himself fed and safe. He forgot children paid attention to the state of mind of the adults around them.

Zeph heaved a breath.

"Yet you're the only parent I ever knew. You gave me shit for what I did wrong and praised me for things I got right. When I was hurt, you licked my wounds, often literally." He smiled. "You've been my safe place since I was little. And you're still the only family I have."

"Zeph..." He stirred. Something ached so much in his chest, it rose up to his throat and prickled his eyes behind his eyelids.

He'd felt so many new, strong emotions today, it made him dizzy.

Zeph squeezed his shoulder in a gesture that felt both grounding and supporting.

"You're my only family, too," Lero croaked.

"May not be for long!" Zeph laughed. "I can't believe you found yourself a woman. After trying so hard to talk *me* out of a relationship with one."

"Stella," he whispered her name, loving the way the sound resonated in his heart.

"You really like her, don't you?"

"I love her," he said. The confession came easily. He simply stated the truth.

"Listen..." Zeph rubbed the back of his neck, asking hesitantly, "Do you know anything about fae reproducing with humans?"

He didn't. How could he? To his knowledge, there hadn't been any human-fae couples before them.

"You tell me," he exclaimed. "You're the one with a fiancée."

"Ivy is on a pill, for now anyway. We decided to wait a little before thinking about starting a family. I just hope it'll be possible when we're ready to start."

"I don't see why not. We know now that humans can bond with us." The power of human love proved to be stronger than magic, after all. He now firmly believed it knew no boundaries.

He took a long look at Zeph. His little boy sounded so grown up—he was settling down, making plans. Lero on the other hand hadn't thought about any of that yet. The past weeks had been a mixture of pain and worry, with the blur of pure bliss and pleasure blended in. All he had felt and thought about was Stella.

He made a mental note to talk to her about the practical things, like birth control and if she wanted to use any, or about their future living arrangements, her job, and her condo in Miami.

Dez might be gone, but Ghata remained. He sensed she'd be furious to learn that a huge chunk of her *brack* army had been decimated. To replenish their numbers, she'd have to bring more *bracks* from Nerifir, which would take time.

For now, the four of them were safe. The future, however, remained murky.

"We should go back." Zeph stirred to get up. "I don't like leaving Ivy alone for too long. Even if Stella is there."

"Move here with us," he said and added, not giving Zeph a chance to decline right away, "With Ivy, of course. It'd be easier to keep the women safe if the four of us are together."

Zeph fell quiet, and Lero asked, "What does Ivy do for a living?"

"She is a graphic designer. She works from home."

"She can work from Blue Cay, then?"

"Well, she likes it here. What she's seen anyway." Zeph sounded contemplative.

"Did she like the house? Take it. Stella and I will move to the other one."

"But isn't the other one smaller? That's what Stella said when you were making dinner."

"With four bedrooms, it's still more than enough for the two of us." Even if they had children one day, they'd have enough space for a family, too.

Zeph slid him a glance.

"Where do you keep your cage?"

The cage. He'd been tied to it for decades. When he first arrived in this world, he had one made, refusing to let his beast roam free on the full moon nights and wreak havoc. Since Stella came along, however, things have been changing. Even the past full moon, he realized he'd been able to control himself better. His mind found a way to her calming presence, even in his beast form.

"I may not need a cage anymore, now that Stella is with me. She's been trying to convince me not to use it the next full moon."

"But what do *you* think?"

"I'd love to be free from the fucking cage," he voiced his deepest desire. "For good."

Zeph nodded. Hiding his own true nature his entire life, Zeph knew well enough what restraints meant.

"You can fill in the pool again," Lero suggested, still trying to sell Zeph the idea of moving to the island. It would bring his heart peace, having him here, close by. "You'll love the pool. It goes right into the master bathroom."

Zeph huffed a laugh. "You hate tubs and pools. Did you buy this place with me in mind?"

He didn't deny it—he always made his decisions with Zeph in mind. Lero himself preferred showers to baths. Water running down his body soothed him. Being submerged in it made him uncomfortable. As a siren, Zeph thrived in any pool of water. He even had an enormous tub installed in his small studio apartment in Paris.

"I'll talk to Ivy about moving," Zeph promised.

A weight dropped from Lero's chest at his words. They were a family, after all. Living close by would be the most natural thing to do.

"Let's go back, then." Lero got off the sand and gave Zeph a hand, helping him up as well.

Through the glass of the patio doors, he saw Stella. She was sitting on the couch next to Ivy, talking and laughing. Their expressions were light and carefree.

She turned her head as he stepped into the light on the patio, and their gazes met through the glass.

*'I feel you,'* she'd said.

He felt her, too. Deep, warm, comforting, and thrilling at the same time—he now had the name for this feeling.

*Love.*

# Epilogue

STELLA

The sun, large and rusty-red, was sinking behind the horizon. The crimson ribbon of reflected light stretched from it across the sea, like a river of blood.

I felt Lero's fingers twitch in my hand as we walked along the path to the bridge between the two parts of the island.

"How are you feeling?" I asked, tightening my grip on his hand, as if I could stop him from slipping away from me and into the realm of the full moon.

He drew in a long breath, still looking like the man I loved, despite the already wildly disheveled hair and the steady red glow in his eyes.

"Soon," he said.

We stopped on the bridge. The low tide had drained the water under it.

A magically sensual voice reached us. It was coming from the main house where Ivy and Zeph had moved to a day earlier. The song was in a foreign language I didn't speak. Italian, I believed.

"Beautiful," I whispered, hardly realizing I was taking a few steps into the direction of the voice, led by it to the singer.

Lero laughed softly, tugging me back to him.

"Zeph is serenading Ivy."

"It's so...wonderful," I murmured, mesmerized by the sound which I could only describe as silver and velvet, and pure magic. "Enthralling."

"It's supposed to be," Lero chuckled. "Zeph sings for entertainment, but in Nerifir, a siren's song is often used as a lure during hunting."

"They sing while hunting?"

He nodded. "Sirens sing often. It's one of the ways they express their emotions. But they also sing to attract prey—birds and other animals, mostly. If another sentient being hears it, however, they'd better watch out, too."

"Do water fae hunt and eat other people?" I gasped.

"No, they don't eat them when they catch them. At least I don't think they do." The slight uncertainty in his voice was worrisome. "But they can do a lot of other things just as unpleasant." He shrugged.

The song ended, and a new one started. This one had a popular dance rhythm, which sounded familiar, but I couldn't remember its name.

"A pop song?" Lero winced. "Really. Zeph could do so much better in his choice of music for romance."

"What's wrong with pop music?"

"It's just so..." He waved his hand in the air. "Light and fast. And the lyrics? No substance at all."

"Now you really sound like an *old man!*" I laughed, and he smiled at me.

The angry-red disk of the sun dipped lower, only a narrow sliver of light still peeked over the horizon, awash in the orange and burgundy of the sunset.

"You should go," Lero rasped.

Letting go of my hand, he gripped the railing of the bridge instead. The knuckles on his hands already looked sharper, more prominent than normal.

I had talked Lero into not locking himself in the cage in the cellar tonight. He'd agreed, but I knew he was worried. He always worried about me.

Unlike him, I remained calm. I didn't believe Lero could ever hurt me again, not intentionally, not otherwise. Instead, the anticipation of his letting go sent a shiver of thrill down my bare arms. I *felt* his lust taking over him. It warmed my blood, too.

I took but a tiny step back and tilted my head.

"I won't go, honey, but I will run," I said, teasing. "And when I run, will you chase me?"

"Stella, my star," he growled. His hands flexed on the railing, the angles of his knuckles growing even sharper with a soft cracking noise. "You're playing with fire—"

His voice broke off, ending the sentence in a snarling, animalistic sound.

My body buzzed with excitement. I loved this part of him. I loved all the pieces of this man.

I shook my head, smiling. "I can't wait to play with your beast, my love."

His shoulders widened, bulging out of the ripping shirt. Lero, being Lero, had insisted on getting fully dressed tonight, even knowing perfectly well what would happen to his clean, pressed clothes when he shifted forms. Now, they were ripped to shreds as the bulk of the beast emerged from the body of the man.

Turning his great head my way, he snarled.

Backing away from him, I smoothed my hands down my white cotton sundress.

"I'm wearing a skirt tonight, honey," I challenged, adding. "And *nothing* under it."

His eyes flashed wild.

I whipped around and ran.

Off the bridge. Down the dirt packed path. Then, along the beach.

A long, loud howl cut through the air. It rose to the sky, drowning out Zeph's upbeat singing.

The beast had completely taken over my man.

I ran faster, arms pumping, air rushing through my lungs, burning as if setting them on fire. I was not going to make it easy on him. I wanted to be chased in earnest, and I ran as if my life depended on it.

The sound of his footfalls came from behind me. Not feet. Paws.

They hit the wet sand with thuds that reverberated through the ground, coming closer and closer.

I almost made it to the end of the beach. There'd be another path after that, leading to the back of our house, the manager's cottage, and then another beach on the opposite side of the island.

No matter how fast or how long I ran, there was nowhere for me to hide. Yet I tried to run even faster. My heart thundered in my chest, its sound echoing in my head. Unable to keep up, my feet tripped over themselves. A heavy hand gripped my shoulder, sending me down to the ground.

The beast rolled under me, taking the impact of my fall on his shoulder. Instead of slamming into the wet sand of the beach, my body tangled with his, large and furry.

We rolled once more, together. Then, he gripped my hips, flipping me over on my back. Hiking up my skirt, he shoved his head between my thighs, thrusting his tongue inside me.

I arched my back under the onslaught of pleasure, digging my heels into the sand. The tingle of his poison felt invigorating, not dangerous. It spread through my veins, setting my body on fire with intense desire.

"Oh God, yes...Lero," I moaned his name as he devoured me in the most savage way. His sharp teeth grazed my sensitive flesh. His mouth sucked and nibbled. His fingers dug into my hips, not letting me escape. His claws scraped my skin without breaking it.

My orgasm blinded me, rocking though my body.

He wouldn't wait for the tremors to subside. Flipping me over, he slammed into me from behind. That long, thick cock of his stretched me to the limit. His heat pulsed through me.

He growled, thrusting wildly, and I echoed his sounds with my moans. My inner muscles still trembled with the first climax when the second one started building up.

I clawed at the wet sand as he had his way with me, ravaging me in the most delightful way. A wild growl left my throat when another orgasm hit me. I was no longer sure if the primal passion that coursed through me was even human. It felt base and animalistic—wild and free.

My beast roared to the sky through his release. His frantic thrusts stopped, and he collapsed over me. Connected, we fell to the ground, spooning, side by side—his arms around me, his legs intertwined with mine.

He nuzzled the side of my neck softly, the spot I knew he loved to touch and kiss. I whimpered when I felt a sting of his razor-sharp fangs. He quickly dragged his tongue over the bite, replacing the sting with a tingle of healing.

"That will leave a mark, you know?" I said, remembering the three drop-shaped spots that remained burnt into the skin of my upper arm.

Other than those three spots, his poison left no marks or scars anywhere on me anymore. However, he'd broken my skin this time.

A deep rumble rolled through his chest, and I understood him perfectly.

"That's what you want, isn't it? To mark me?" I stretched in his arms, snuggling deeper into his fur, unable and unwilling to part from him in any way.

The mark from when he bit me in his human form, the first time we had sex, had healed after he'd licked it. He obviously wanted to leave something more permanent.

I raked my fingers through the fur on the side of his neck, over the spot where I had bitten him weeks ago. Unlike every other scar that disappeared within hours from his skin, the two little dots from my teeth had paled but never went away completely. I couldn't see them through the fur, but I knew they were there.

"As if I'm not yours already, silly." I chuckled as he kept nuzzling the spot on my neck he'd just marked.

He held me tightly from behind, and I raked my fingers through the long fur on his forearms.

"I'm yours, Lero. Always will be."

# Power of Rage

## Book 3

# Chapter One

HEIKE

"Ten thousand dollars? Is she insane?" I scoffed, twirling my hand in a circle next to my temple.

"No clue. Maybe." Omkar shrugged, signaling the passing waiter for another round of drinks—whisky on the rocks for him and a mango juice for me.

I didn't come to his bar to get drunk. I'd come to hear what he found out for me about Madame Tan and her show. With that much money for a single ticket, I'd better be completely sober when making my decisions.

"That's crazy!" I shook my head, accidentally sending the end of a long strand of my black-brown hair into my juice glass. "Oops." I fished it out and dried it with a napkin.

The price had been quoted in US dollars, too, not Singapore, which made it even more expensive. No person in their right mind would demand that price for a one-hour show of...something. That was the craziest thing—no one could tell me exactly *what* Madame Tan offered for the money.

I knew a few people who'd seen her show. They'd shelled out ten grand each, some in the United States and a couple in Europe.

*"Out of this world!"*

*"Incredible, magical, and simply fantastic!"*

*"I've never seen anything like it!"*

That was all I'd been able to get from them when I asked them about it.

Omkar took a drink from the glass that the waiter deposited in front of him.

"Apparently, that's the reduced rate." He leaned back, the leather of his trendy jacket creaking against the booth seat. "This being her last show, some tickets went for as high as fifty grand."

"What? You're kidding me, right?"

Not that I didn't have the money to spend. I came from a family who believed in hard work.

My mom was Chinese and my dad German. They met here, in Singapore, when both had been working for the same financial company. Dad's contract ended shortly after they got married, and they moved to Munich, Germany. I was born and grew up there until my parents divorced when I finished the German secondary school. Then, I moved to the States with my dad.

I'd been earning my own money since I was two, first by appearing in commercials, then fashion magazines. My mom signed me up with a modeling agency when I was a baby. By the time I was sixteen, I'd earned enough to pay for any college in Europe or North America. By then, however, I was done with working for others. I'd figured I could do something for myself.

Social media seemed interesting, and I'd tried a few things, some of which stuck. Whatever had worked, I'd expanded and grown, constantly trying new things.

Now, at my current age of twenty-nine, I was running a number of video channels, had a handful of older but still very successful blogs and vlogs, and maintained several websites. I produced podcasts, traded domain names, and managed a number of interest groups. I still did some modeling, but only for my own social media accounts, as well as for my travel and lifestyle channels. My revenue came from selling ads, endorsements, and publicity services, and my expenses were low.

I was also a part of a network of people like myself. We helped boost ratings, expand each other's reach, and maximize exposure.

Omkar was a part of it, too. Originally from India, he owned several businesses in Singapore. The bar where we were sitting was one of them.

I casually swirled the ice cubes in my glass of juice. "Have *you* seen the show?"

"No." He shook his head.

"Are you getting a cut of the ticket price?"

"No. I don't know Madame Tan personally. I've heard about the show from a friend of a friend. It sounded like something you'd like. So, here we are."

"Do you think she'd barter?" I hated spending my hard-earned cash if there were other ways to get what I wanted. Barter was my preferred form of tender most of the time.

"For what?"

I shrugged. "For publicity."

Between all of my accounts, I had tens of millions of followers combined. The power wasn't always in numbers, though. I often had better results with some of the smaller, but highly targeted groups. If Madame Tan let me, I could blow up her show in popularity in no time.

"I could do an interview, record—"

Omkar stopped me with a hand gesture, leaning in across the table. "Absolutely no recordings of any kind. That's the main condition of purchasing the ticket."

I narrowed my eyes at him, as if he were Madame Tan incarnate.

*'We'll see about that,'* flashed through my mind.

"Heike, I mean it." Omkar lifted his hand in warning. "No recording. She doesn't sound like a woman you want to mess with."

I gave him a non-committal shrug and changed the subject, "Would you like to go?"

"Me?" Omkar winced, furrowing his thick, ink-black eyebrows. "I'd rather spend the money on other things."

So would I. Except curiosity nagged at me, now. With it being the last show, I'd never have another chance to find out what this was all about.

"Tell your *friend of a friend* we'll pay fifteen thousand," I offered.

Omkar sputtered his sip of whiskey. "We *what?*"

"We'll pay fifteen for two tickets," I said. "You're coming with me."

I was curious, but not stupid. There were places in this world where a woman shouldn't be going alone, especially to some underground nightclub on the East Side of Singapore, where this show was supposed to be held at midnight.

"Heike..." Omkar raked his hands through the glossy mass of his thick, wavy hair.

He obviously didn't want to come, but couldn't think of a polite way to decline. I fully intended to take advantage of that.

"Come on. This could be phenomenal. Everyone says it is," I pressed.

He blew out a breath. "You need to get yourself a man, Heike. Someone who would take you to all those places you always want to go but shouldn't."

I knew Omkar wasn't hinting in any way for him to be my man. I wasn't his type. Besides, he had a fiancée—a demure girl-next-door from the village where his parents lived in India. It would be an arranged marriage, but Omkar really cared about his future bride.

I found Omkar attractive and intelligent. He'd been a great friend, and were he available, I might possibly consider having something more with him. Though, with my track record, it would be best for him to stay away from me, single or not. My last and only meaningful relationship happened when I was eighteen.

Omkar's leather jacket creaked against the pleather of the bench seat again. "I'm really not that interested in seeing the show," he said.

I leaned over the table toward him. "Don't you want to know what it's all about?"

"I'd love to. But I could just as well live without ever knowing."

"Listen, fifteen thousand for two." I wouldn't give up. "I'll pay ten grand, you'll just have to pay five."

"I don't think she'd sell you two tickets for that price. Besides, I told you there's only one ticket left, anyway. Heike..." He shook his head. "She won't go for it."

"But it's worth a try, isn't it?"

Spending this amount of money had to be an investment. Madame Tan might not be interested in publicity, but a video of her show might end up being very valuable one day, especially if it was indeed the very last show ever.

The two tickets ended up costing me twenty thousand dollars, after all. Madame Tan refused to budge on the price, though she agreed to sell two instead of one. I paid for Omkar's ticket, too, since the poor guy didn't even want to be here.

I was extremely grateful that he came, though. The place was located deep in the basement of a seedy nightclub under the guise of a karaoke bar. There wasn't even a button on the elevator for that floor. We had to take a set of concrete stairs to get there. The noise and the music from the club above barely made their way here, like a distant echo of life above the ground.

A massive bald man with neck and arm tattoos met us as we exited the stairs. Tall and muscular and dressed in a black t-shirt, he could be a bouncer.

"Names?" he asked in perfect English.

"Heike Schneider," I said.

"Heike?" He lifted his thick, dark-brown eyebrows at me. "What kind of name is that?"

"German." I took in the empty hallway—a wide space with concrete walls and a red runner on the floor.

"You don't look German." The man marked something on the tablet in his hands.

I glared at him. With my straight dark hair and my mother's black eyes, I didn't have what some people perceived as "typical German" appearance. If I had a dollar for every time I'd heard a comment like that, I would've possibly made as much money as from any of my other revenue sources by now.

"Sorry. Left my *lederhosen* at home," I quipped, one of the many responses I had ready for this kind of situation.

He smirked, giving me a once-over, then moved on to Omkar, who stood at my side.

"Follow me," the bouncer said after verifying our identities.

I shifted the strap of my purse on my shoulder to make sure the camera in the flower pin on my purple suede jacket wasn't obstructed. Wearing the jacket in today's hot weather was crazy, but I needed layers to hide the camera connected to the phone in my other pocket. I'd turned it on while we walked down the stairs. Madame Tan might have her rules, but I had to get my money's worth, too.

"This way." The bouncer gestured for us to proceed down the corridor.

After a turn, a set of doors came into view. Velvet burgundy curtains opened in front of them, each held back by a twisted, golden rope with tassels.

The bouncer opened the doors, and we were greeted by another man, who looked nearly identical to the first. Of similar build and wearing the same dark clothes, he was also bald and had the same large tattoo on his right arm and neck.

The new man handed each of us a tall glass with shimmering blue-and-pink liquid. "Drink." The way he said it sounded like an order, not a mere offer or invitation.

I sniffed at the liquid as Omkar took a tentative sip. "It's good." He nodded.

It smelled very good, too.

"Does it have alcohol in it?" I asked the man who'd handed the glasses to us.

"Do you want it to?" he replied casually.

That was an odd question.

"No."

"Then it doesn't," he said flatly.

His reply did nothing to assuage my suspicion. I moved my gaze to

Omkar, who kept gulping his drink. He was half-way through his glass already.

"What?" He lifted an eyebrow at my stare, his lips shimmering from the liquid. "It's really good. Try it."

His over-the-top happy expression and the glossy sheen in his eyes made me pause. Omkar could relax and enjoy himself tonight. But I was here to work. With the camera rolling, I was already breaking the rules. I couldn't afford to be inebriated in any way.

We followed the two bouncers to another door. This one was roped off with the glowing *VIP* letters attached to the rope.

"Here." I discreetly traded glasses with Omkar as soon as his was empty. "Have this, I'm not thirsty."

He didn't argue, immediately taking a huge drink from my glass.

"Good evening, my darlings," a melodious feminine voice trilled from inside the room.

The bouncers removed the rope, and a tall, beautiful woman invited us to enter. The room was lavishly decorated with colorful rugs and soft, multi-colored lights. A large round object stood in the middle, covered with silver silk. But it was the woman who attracted my attention the most.

Dressed in a long red garment of an unusual cut, her fiery red hair coiffed into a voluminous up-do with a long, elaborate braid draped over one shoulder, she was a vision of fire and beauty.

"Welcome," she cooed. "My name is Madame Tan. I'm so happy you joined us." She gestured at the long table set next to the round, silk-covered object. Seven people sat in the chairs on one side of the table, the glasses in front of them shimmering pink and blue in the dim lighting of the room.

The long sleeves of Madame's dress draped all the way to the floor, with cut-out slits for her hands. Leaving her shoulders exposed, the robe cascaded in soft folds down her curvy hips and long legs. A wide train of silk trailed behind her as she moved. The gold-embroidered ends of the black sash tied around her waist draped down her skirt at the back.

"Please enjoy the refreshments." She pointedly paused, her gaze on the half-full glass in Omkar's hand, and he hurriedly gulped down the rest of the liquid.

As soon as we took our seats at the table, one of the bouncers appeared with a pitcher to refill our glasses. Another one came, bringing out a tray with small round dishes. He placed a dish in front of each of us.

"That's great!" Omkar happily popped the appetizing roll from the dish into his mouth.

The middle-aged Asian woman on his right smiled at him.

"Simply delightful," she said in a slightly accented English, daintily lifting her roll between her fingers and taking a small bite. "Truly out of this world."

Their eager praise felt a bit off to my ear. Their giddy expressions didn't seem natural. I decided to leave my food on the plate, no matter how "delightful" they claimed it was.

Madame Tan slid her gaze along the table, pausing it on my glass.

I quickly lifted it, as if ready to take a sip. "This is a...um, *delightful* cocktail," I gushed, trying to imitate Omkar's enthusiasm. "What's in it?"

A wide smile spread across Madame Tan's beautiful face, her dark eyes narrowed with cunning glee.

"Magic," she purred.

"Oh, I can't wait to see what's behind the curtain!" The lady next to Omkar clapped her hands, like an excited little girl at a carnival.

Madame glanced back at the silk-covered object, and I quickly traded my plate with Omkar's. He eagerly swiped my roll off the plate and shoved it in his mouth.

Whatever was in the food and drink Madame had been serving to us made him happy. I knew for a fact that spectators of Madame's show didn't get sick or die from her food. Omkar wasn't going to get hurt. If anything, he would have a doubly good time tonight. While I had work to do.

I straightened my back, sticking out my breasts to give the camera in the brooch on my lapel the best angle as it kept rolling.

Madame dramatically waved her hand in the air. Three red spotlights fell on the silver silk, merging into one—crimson bright.

"Ladies and gentlemen! One show only! Behold, the most amazing transformation never before seen by human eyes." She spread her arms, her long sleeves flying through the air like a pair of wings.

I had to give it to her, she was a true show woman, not stingy on dramatics.

The silk flew off the round object, as if with a blast of wind, revealing a large, spherical cage. I'd seen this type before at fairs and carnivals. It was about seventeen feet in diameter, held in place by thick chains attached to the wooden platform it stood on.

At the fairs, there usually was a motorbike inside, and someone would ride it in circles up and down inside the cage. The bars of this cage, however, were too thick and too far apart for a motorbike's wheels.

There was no bike inside the cage. Instead, a man stood in the center of it. Tall and muscular, he had an identical tattoo to the bouncers who'd greeted us and served us drinks. Unlike the bouncers, he sported a full beard and was completely naked.

I didn't know what to think. The man was certainly a sight to behold. He wasn't just well built. He looked like he worked hard on it, too, probably spending his days and nights in the gym and living on a steady diet of protein shakes and steroids.

Was the "amazing" show all about showing off the results of his hard work?

He didn't appear to be here for the attention, though. In fact, he didn't appear to enjoy being here at all. His gaze vacant, he stared over our heads with a blank expression.

Ominous music flowed from the speakers somewhere. At its sinister sound, trepidation scraped unpleasantly in my chest.

Madame sauntered in front of the cage. "Allow me to introduce the species I created myself—a rage shifter. A fine specimen, isn't he?" she cooed. "I'm proud of my creation, rightfully so. Look at him. Handsome, strong, immortal, but most importantly…" she slid a finger up one of the bars, glaring at the man with so much hatred it made my skin crawl with dread.

Could a person be proud of someone and hate them this much?

"Most importantly, my rage shifters are *loyal* to a fault," Madame continued. "They were designed with one purpose—to serve me. Sadly, no design is without its flaws. This one is what one would call 'an older model.'" She sneered, lifting a corner of her mouth to display a sharp white canine.

The man inside the cage kept staring straight ahead over our heads, either not seeing us or purposely ignoring us. He appeared calm. But looking closely, I noticed his chest rise and fall rapidly. His hands were fisted tightly at his sides. The bulky muscles in his arms twitched, flexing.

Did he know what was about to happen? Did he dread it, too?

"Normally," Madame Tan continued, "I don't let my creations reach the level of rage that would trigger their transformation. But this one needs to be punished. Lucky for you, you're the only people on Earth who get to see my creation in all his glory."

She raised her hand, turning her palm to the man in the cage.

His strong features crumbled in a grimace of pain as red sparks ran up the tattoo lines on his arm to his neck. Yet he made no sound. The sparks merged into streaks, lighting up the intricate design of his body art.

He threw his head back, baring his teeth that started to grow, canines lengthening into fangs. His entire body expanded, bulging out of proportion.

The people at the table gasped in awe.

The lines of the man's tattoo swelled and rose like fresh burn scars, changing the color from black to inflamed red.

The man finally released a sound—a blood-curdling roar of agony and rage. His body shook. Much taller and larger than average to begin with, he grew in size, becoming a giant. The cage wasn't tall enough for him anymore. He had to curl his shoulders in and drop his head down to fit inside it.

In addition to the incredible increase in size, his proportions changed, too. His neck grew so thick, it nearly merged with his hulking shoulders. His arms stretched longer as his torso got wider. His beard disappeared, the bald head flattening and widening. The veins on his arms and neck bulged, throbbing along with his tattoo that now looked like one raw inflamed wound.

Monstrous and grotesque, he no longer resembled a man at all.

He roared again, throwing himself against the bars with so much force, I feared it would break the chains and wrench the cage off the platform. Snapping tight, the chains held, however.

Madame laughed. The sound was sweet and melodious, like the trill of silver bells, and I truly hated her at that moment.

"And that's why I call them the rage shifters," she purred. "You can literally watch his temper grow. Isn't he magnificent?"

The people at the table murmured in agreement. Their expressions were those of delight and awe, with not a hint of concern for the tortured man. They certainly seemed like they were getting their money's worth in entertainment.

Omkar winked at me. "Not something you'd see every day, right?" he asked with a happy smile.

"Right..." I moved my gaze back to the cage.

The scarlet spotlights slid down the monstrous man's naked body. The streaks of red light looked like streams of blood.

He growled, twisting his torso in obvious pain. His mangled arm dangled at his side, the tattoo wounds pulsing with light. The wound on his neck seemed just as bad. He avoided moving his head, probably as not to aggravate the pain.

His massive erection appeared to torture him the most. Engorged, it was bluish, pulsing and bobbing in the air while pointing straight up. He hovered his hand over it, his fingers curled and rigid like claws, yet he wouldn't touch himself.

"Turn around, sweetie," Madame ordered. "Let us see more of you."

With a wave of her hand, he jerked as if punched in his tattooed shoulder, then pivoted on his heel. His back came into view. It was covered with long red slashes that had crusted over with dried blood. These must've been inflicted earlier.

What had been done to this man? And for how long had he been enduring the torture?

A deafening roar of pain ripped from his throat. He clawed at his neck with both hands, tearing at his mangled flesh, as if trying to rip the tattoo off his skin.

"Is he okay?" the older lady next to Omkar inquired.

I whipped my head in her direction. Did she share my horror at seeing this?

"Oh no, he isn't okay at all, far from it," Madame replied in a singsong voice, gesturing to the bouncer by the door, who then promptly refilled the lady's drinking glass with the shimmering liquid.

The woman giggled, as if she'd just heard a witty joke.

"Will he turn back?" someone else asked. The question was filled with curiosity, but not the outrage that I felt.

"Maybe," Madame replied with a lazy smile. "*When* and *if* I feel like it."

While the man twisted and rolled in agony inside the cage, Madame spoke. "His name is Radax. He's my first creation. And despite his many misdemeanors, I still have a soft spot for him. Sometimes I think he keeps misbehaving because he craves extra attention from me, like a petulant child. I have so many 'children,' and they all vie for my attention. Well, here you go, Radax, sweetie. This night is all about you. It's your time to shine!"

She snapped her fingers, and Radax's tattoo wounds caught on fire. Real flames burst out from his torn flesh.

His roars of pain twisted my insides, bringing bile to my throat.

"Wow! How did she do it?" Omkar gasped in awe.

His distorted perception of the "show" made the anger flare high inside me, but it wasn't directed at Omkar. I saw him as just another victim of Madame's tricks. Obviously, his feelings and reactions were no longer his own. The Omkar I knew wouldn't be delighted at the suffering of others.

Madame spun back to face her audience, and her gaze crossed with mine.

I couldn't fake the delightful indifference of the others. I couldn't even muster a neutral expression fast enough. She saw it all—my horror at what I was witnessing, my compassion for the tortured man in the cage, and my severe dislike of her.

Her eyes flicked to my still-very-full glass. The cheerful mask of lighthearted fun slipped off her face, revealing a scowl.

"I see you aren't thirsty." She prowled my way menacingly but with eager anticipation, like a cat about to play with a mouse.

I shoved the glass aside. There was no point in pretending to drink it now. Someone had to do something to stop the suffering of the man in the cage. I didn't care about what he'd done to deserve a punishment. This was not a way to treat a living being.

"Let him go," I said softly but firmly.

Fear dampened my anger. The cold menace in Madame's eyes promised no mercy, and I'd seen the level of cruelty she was capable of. But I had to say it, if only to put on the record that she'd been told this was not okay.

"This is not entertainment. It's sick." I fisted my hands on the table, holding her glare.

She tilted her head.

"Sorry, you don't see it my way—*our* way." She gestured at the rest of the spectators at the table. All of them were watching us with the same excited anticipation as they'd watched her torment Radax—as if I were now the second act of the show.

Madame came flush with the table directly opposite from my seat. Every muscle in my body flexed under her stare, getting ready for me to run, but I forced myself to remain seated.

I wasn't some "creation" of hers. I was a free human being. I had rights. She wouldn't dare...

"Bring her over here." She gestured to the two bouncers by the entrance.

They moved my way. The rigid determination on their faces told me they would do anything she told them.

Fear spiked higher.

"No!" I sprang to my feet and dashed for the exit.

Ducking, I tried to evade the hands of the bouncers reaching for me. Unexpectedly agile for his size, one of them launched for me and caught me around my middle.

"The show is over, ladies and gentlemen," Madame cooed in her saccharine-sweet voice she reserved for the public. "Thank you for coming. Nerkan will escort you to the exit, now." She ushered everyone from the table to the door where another burly, tattooed man led them out.

"Omkar!" I yelled in desperation, struggling against the hold of the bouncer.

The serene expression on my friend's face wavered. His brows twitched, moving closer together.

"This way, please." Madame stroked his cheek, bringing his attention to her and renewing his smile.

One by one, everybody left. Omkar did, too. Now, it was but the bouncer holding me, Madame, and the man rolling in rage and agony inside the cage.

I squared my shoulders, getting ready to fight, even as the bouncer's arm around my middle remained unyielding.

"Are you local or a tourist?" Madame asked me sternly, any hint of friendly sweetness gone from her voice and expression.

"She's German, living in the United States," the bouncer reported. "Visiting Singapore for two weeks. Traveling alone."

Somehow, they'd managed to do a background check on me.

Madame squinted at me. "She doesn't look German."

Despite my dire situation, I couldn't help an eye roll at her comment.

"Half-Chinese," the bouncer explained.

"I'm well known in this country," I bit back. It wasn't entirely a lie. Some of my followers did come from Singapore. "If any harm comes to me—"

Madame waved her hand, her expression growing bored.

"You know what? It really doesn't matter who you are or where you come from. No one can stop me from doing whatever I want with you."

"There'll be consequences." I tried to sound strong and threatening.

"None of which I couldn't deal with." She shrugged, glancing back at the cage. "You want me to let Radax go? That'd do more harm than good with him in this state. He needs to be calmed down to shift back before I can release him. The only way to calm a raging *brack* is sex." She settled her heavy stare on me. "I am the only one in this world who can fuck a rage shifter in this form and stay alive. For me, sex with a *brack* gone berserk is fun. For someone like you..."

A playful smile curved her lips, and a spark of amusement flashed in her coal-black eyes.

Her pause was pregnant with meaning that filled me with dread, cold and heavy like lead.

"What? No..." I stared at her, my dread turning to pure horror at the realization of what she implied.

"Did you feel sorry for poor Radax over there?" Madame formed a pout with her full, cherry-red lips. "Then why don't *you* help him instead of me? You see that cock?" She jerked her head at the man's raging erection the size of my freaking thigh and murmured, "I love riding it. But what do you think will happen to *you* when he shoves it in you? Do you think you can take it?" She laughed. The beautiful sound reverberated with sickening panic through me.

"No...please," I begged, clawing at the bouncer's burly arm that held me as tight as a vise.

She smirked, tossing the order to the man holding me.

"Throw her in the cage!"

# Chapter Two

## FIVE MONTHS EARLIER

RADAX

He walked into the tents with a bounce in his step. It was the first day of the new year—a cause of celebration both in this world and in Nerifir, where fae exchanged presents on this day.

Madame didn't allow *bracks* to give anyone presents, not that any of them wanted to, anyway. But he knew Amira would love what he got for her. He gave her the same present every year since the day he found her. He knew she'd smile. It was a rare sight, and he was looking forward to it.

"Where is Amira?" he asked one of the *bracks*, Zuso, who gnawed on a smoked turkey leg on his way out of the tent.

It was late in the evening. All the shows were already done for the day.

Zuso shrugged. "How the fuck am I supposed to know? Probably cleaning something somewhere."

Not possessing any magic, Amira had the uncanny ability to make herself invisible to everyone in Madame's menagerie. She stayed out of the *bracks'* way whenever she could. In the evenings, when the *bracks* who worked in the tents during the day would go outside to get dinner, she would often hide inside the tents.

The entrance to the exhibition area of the menagerie was roped off for the night. Radax stepped over the rope and into the room filled with small cages and enclosures. A faint shuffling reached his ear, and he followed the sound to the corner behind the enclosure of the *virleth* pig.

The piglet was having a nap in a pile of fur and felt. His pink body curled like a donut, his two heads had their noses stuck under the fence around his enclosure and pressed to Amira's running shoe.

She sat on the floor next to the fence with an egg sandwich in her hand. A snake-bird was draped around her neck like a bright red feather boa with its head perched on the girl's shoulder. Ripping off small pieces of her sandwich, Amira fed them to the snake-bird.

The young woman jerked when he came closer, then relaxed, recognizing him. A timid smile curved her pale lips, but she didn't say a word in greeting. Amira usually didn't say much at all.

"Happy birthday." He crouched next to her, holding out his present —a box with the cupcake he'd bought from a food truck outside.

Neither he nor Amira knew when her actual birthday was. So, they decided long ago to celebrate it on the first day of the new year.

Her smile grew wider. It warmed his heart as nothing else ever did.

She shoved her half-eaten sandwich in the front pocket of her hoodie, despite the squawks of protest from the snake-bird. Taking the box from him, she placed it in her lap, then leaned closer and wrapped her arms around his neck.

"Thank you," she whispered, giving him a peck on a cheek.

Her touch was always so different from Madame's. Amira's kiss felt like a clean drink of water or a gulp of fresh air—easy and free. Madame's had an effect like strong liquor combined with a powerful drug—painfully intoxicating.

One made him feel light at heart.

The other gave a momentary oblivion at the price of heavy darkness settling in his soul afterwards.

"Happy Birthday to you, too," Amira said, so softly, only he could hear.

He didn't remember what day he was born, but she refused to let a year go by without wishing him a happy birthday, too. They ended up celebrating their birthdays together, on the day of their own choosing, January the first.

"Thank you." He kissed her hair before she released him from her hug.

"Hey, Radax!" Vuk appeared unexpectedly, yelling from the entrance to the room.

Clutching the box with the cupcake to her chest, Amira scurried deeper into the corner and out of sight. The *brack's* appearance was so sudden, Radax jumped, too, startled.

"What do you want?" he demanded.

"Madame sent me to find you," Vuk informed him.

"What for?"

Vuk smirked. "You know *what*. She wants you." A flush of acute envy flicked in Vuk's eyes before he left.

Madame never *wanted* anyone, but she knew her *bracks* needed her. As former werewolves, they retained the urge to shift. Except that Madame broke their connection to the Moon magic. Now, the monster inside him grew uncontained. The urge to give in built up.

Weeks had passed since he'd been with Madame last. And every day, the pain grew stronger. By now, his muscles ached, his bones felt like being crushed by a hammer, and his cock throbbed with heat so strong, he feared it'd set his pants on fire.

"Don't go," Amira whispered, scooting closer. Touching his hand, she fixed her dark brown, imploring gaze on him.

He never felt well after spending a night with Madame. If he didn't go, however, it'd be worse. Not that he could ever refuse Madame, anyway. He was her slave, in every sense of the word.

Amira knew it. She knew he couldn't refuse if summoned. She just wished he *could* resist.

He wished it, too.

"I have to." He gave her a bright, soothing smile.

"Can't Vuk go instead?" she asked, her fingers nervously crumpling the snake-bird's feathers.

He had no doubt Vuk would've loved to take his place tonight. Any one of the *bracks* would give their left testicle for an extra night with

Madame, but it was never up to any of them. It was always Madame's choice.

Tonight, it was Radax's turn.

Worry floated in Amira's large eyes. The way she looked at him tugged at something deep inside his heart, in that small hidden part of it that Madame's magic hadn't touched—the part that had to do with his little sister.

He'd long forgotten her name, but he knew his sister was younger than him and that she died shortly before Madame had claimed him. He didn't remember how his sister died, but he never forgot the agonizing grief he felt after. The feeling was so strong, it survived even the *brack's* initiation process that Madame took all her newly acquired slaves through.

The vow Madame took from him was meant to erase all feelings and emotions he'd experienced in his life before her. They were supposed to be replaced by a strong, unbreakable loyalty to her.

But something had gone wrong. He remembered nothing from his life before Madame—not who he was, not his childhood home, or his family—but he remembered his sister's eyes.

They were gray, the eye color of most of the werewolves. However, Amira's dark-brown ones often reminded him of his sister's. They held the same innocence, vulnerability, and affection for him. He'd failed to save his sister, but he vowed to protect Amira with all his immortal life.

"I'll be fine." He stroked her cheek tenderly.

"She hurts you," Amira sniffled, diverting her eyes.

He gave her a long look. Amira was no longer a child. Over the years, she had turned into a woman, sometimes a very perceptive one, too. She was old enough to understand what was happening between Madame and the *brack* she brought to her trailer at night.

"It needs to be done. I'll be fine, Amira," he repeated, squeezing her shoulder. "You have a good night." He tipped his chin at the box with the pink-frosted cupcake he'd brought for her. "I hope you'll like it."

He got up and left, not giving her another chance to protest. It would've been useless, anyway. He couldn't refuse Madame. No one and nothing could ever stand between him and his mistress. Not even Amira.

"Oh, there you are." Madame lazily stretched on the richly embroidered silk of her bed spread.

Like everyone at the menagerie, she had to use a travel trailer for accommodation when on the road. Unlike the *bracks'* simple living quarters, however, hers was lavishly furnished and decorated.

A tall candelabrum stood on the carved dresser to the right. Framed pictures of Madame in her Nerifir robes were surrounded by moon crystals and praying beads—her shrine to herself. The tall box with her sacred book locked inside was a part of it, too.

"It's been a long time since I had you here last, hasn't it, my pet?" She waved a hand through the air, and his tattoos heated. Pain engulfed his right arm, spreading to his neck. Heat rushed to his crotch area.

"Six weeks," he croaked.

It'd been six weeks since he stood in front of her like this, racked with pain and burning with need.

"Way too long for my creation to be away from me," she murmured, sitting up. The sides of her red silk kimono fell open, revealing her naked body—visually perfect, as everything about her. "My *favorite* creation."

Madame claimed he was the first *brack* she'd ever created. He didn't know if that was true. Madame lied easily, twisting the truth in any way it pleased her.

He never remembered being the only one. There had always been other *bracks* around. Though, all the ones who'd come before him were now dead. He was, by far, the oldest of those still living. He believed he was about two and a half millennia old. That could be wrong, however. He'd forgotten many things along the way, including his exact age. Some of his earliest memories could also have been just dreams.

Sometimes he wondered if his sister had been a dream, too. He was afraid to lose the memory of her completely. Amira helped him remember. Without ever knowing it, she was his one connection to the boy he once was.

"How are you feeling now?" Madame got off the bed.

He knew she wasn't concerned about his wellbeing. She didn't care for the truth, so he gave her the answer she expected.

"I want you," he said.

She stepped closer, a flash of light turning her black eyes to red. "How much?" she demanded. "Tell me."

The pain grew stronger under her fiery stare. His cock throbbed, swelling so much, the seam of his pants cut into his erection with agony.

"More than life," he groaned.

There wasn't much to love about his life—right now, he'd prefer death—but the answer seemed to please her.

Her full, red lips spread into a satisfied smile. She flicked back her unbound hair. It flew over her shoulder like a long lick of flame.

"Take off your clothes before you rip them," she ordered.

He tore off his plain black t-shirt over his head, then unbuckled and shoved down his pants, all while trying to kick off his boots at the same time. He wished he could disrobe less hurriedly, in some more dignified manner, but it was out of his control. In fact, nothing was in his control from the moment he'd entered her quarters.

The need consumed him like an inferno, burning through his willpower and common sense. He needed to fuck or he'd die, despite being immortal.

His cock sprung free, straining toward her. And like his pathetic member, his entire being, his very soul seemed to reach out for her, too.

Unable to hold back, he shifted forward.

"Tsk, tsk," she clicked her tongue. "So impatient. You know what happens to impatient boys, my pet?"

He knew. She let all his scars fully heal, eventually. If she didn't, his back would have born the marks of her many punishments.

Gathering the last shreds of self-control, he moved his hands back and linked them there.

"That's better," she murmured approvingly, then shrugged the kimono off her shoulders. "Do you want this, Radax?" She slid her hands down the elegant curves of her hips. "How about these?" Hands under her full breasts, she stroked her already erect pink nipples with her thumbs.

He growled, clutching his hands together so hard his fingernails cut through his skin. He had to keep his hands off her. Madame didn't like to be touched. She preferred to do all the touching herself.

"Lean down." She curled her finger, gesturing for him to move closer.

He bent over, and she took his bottom lip between her teeth. This was the only kiss on the lips he'd ever known—a bite, with pierced skin, and spilled blood.

"Oh, I missed you," she moaned, licking off the blood that trickled down his beard.

Another flick of her wrist, and the pain spread through every cell of his body. His bones groaned and cracked, shifting out of proportion as his muscles bulked up.

"Not too big, my pet." She lowered her hand, halting his transformation. He stopped growing. "We don't want you to break my trailer."

He had to keep his head down between his shoulders. The ceiling was no longer high enough to accommodate his increased size and height.

She gripped his cock, her fingers barely coming around half of its girth.

"Now, let's have some fun, monster." She headed toward the bed, tugging him along by his cock.

Her sharp nails dug into his sensitive flesh. He hissed from the added agony, but she only laughed in the melodious sound of clinking crystal.

"Aw," she murmured. "You know I'll make it all better, right after I've had some fun with you. Come, my hideous."

And he did. Like the needy, desperate monster that he was, he followed her to bed, both dreading and craving what he was about to do —fuck a goddess.

# Chapter Three

## ABOUT THREE WEEKS LATER

RADAX

After years of touring North America, Madame had finally wrapped up her operations on that continent and headed to Europe.

Bitter winds of late January greeted them as Madame and her escort exited the terminal of Heathrow Airport in London.

"It's so disgustingly cold in this pathetic human world," Madame complained, huddling into her fur stole.

There were cold parts in Nerifir, too. Snow never melted high in the Mountains of Dakath, for example. Even in the werewolves' Plains of Sarnala, where Madame's temple used to stand, winter came every year. But Madame preferred warmer weather. Ever since the menagerie had left Niagara Falls late last December, they'd been traveling across the southern US. The bitter winter winds of London, England, were a drastic change from that, now.

Madame climbed into the taxi that took her to her hotel, leaving Radax and the rest of the *bracks* to receive the cargo and set up the menagerie in their new location.

Several tractor trailers waited for them at the expo center Madame had rented for her menagerie for a month. Radax was glad it wasn't the tents anymore, considering the weather.

Along with Nerkan, he went over the paperwork, verifying the cargo that came with them as well as the crates that had arrived last week with Dez. All had cleared customs without any delays or issues. The inspection had gone smoothly, after Madame had talked to the officials before leaving. Like always in such cases, Radax suspected she must've fed the humans something the *bracks* had brought for her from Nerifir. There were many plants and substances in Nerifir that could change people's behavior and perception. Humans were so easily susceptible to their effects.

Nerkan was already at the location when Radax arrived.

"Madame wanted the VIP area set up first," Nerkan informed him as they surveyed the section of the expo center that would house Madame's show for the next month. "She wants to exhibit the werewolf as soon as possible tomorrow night. His crate is being unloaded right now."

Dez came from the kitchenette they had in their section for their exclusive use. "Where is Amira?" He had a metal bowl in his hands. The raw meat in it was generously sprinkled with thick yellow powder.

The full moon was last night. They'd missed it while moving. If Madame wanted to exhibit the werewolf, Dez had to feed him some extra *kibia* mushroom powder. It wouldn't fully turn the werewolf, but he'd look hideous enough for Madame's VIP clients to deem him interesting to look at and their money well spent.

"Do you know where she is?" Dez insisted.

"Who?" Nerkan moved past him, examining the nearest wall, possibly searching for an electric outlet they'd need for power tools.

"Amira," Dez snapped impatiently. "I gave her the key to the beast's chains before I left for London last week. I need it back. Have you seen her?"

"Not since we got here." Radax shook his head.

He'd been watching Amira more closely lately. She worried him. Always shy and quiet, she'd seemed exceptionally reserved the past few weeks. Their last conversation troubled him. The day before they'd boarded the flight to London, she'd asked him to open a portal to Nerifir because she wanted to leave here.

Her words still buzzed in his brain, making him anxious. He couldn't "open" a portal. No one could. But there were enough portals between the worlds to find for those who searched hard enough. If she crossed the River of Mists, she would be lost to him forever.

For some time now, he'd been having difficulties crossing the River himself. The last time he'd gone to Nerifir, Madame had a hard time pulling him back into this world to her. Ever since, she stopped sending him, relying on the others to supply her menagerie.

If Amira left, he couldn't go with her. And he'd never know whether she was dead or alive. The world of Nerifir was different. Better in some ways than this one, but also more dangerous, especially for a fragile human girl like Amira. And he wouldn't be there to guide her or protect her from harm.

From their conversation, he'd learned she believed she'd be protecting *him* by leaving the menagerie, which wasn't true at all.

True, Madame found joy in punishing him for Amira's mistakes. And she deemed a mistake any action of Amira's she didn't like, depending on her mood at that moment. What the poor girl didn't realize was that Madame loved punishing. Period. If Amira wasn't around, she'd find other things to whip him for.

Pain had become second nature. He'd had experienced so much of it, he'd almost grown numb to Madame's cruelties. Even if there was a slight chance of easing his pain, it wasn't worth losing Amira.

Zuso ran inside from the parking lot.

"Dez!" He gestured wildly. "Madame sent for you. The car is waiting outside to take you to her hotel. You have to leave, right now."

Dez's face split with a smug smirk.

"Here." He shoved the bowl with meat into Radax's hands. "Feed the werewolf for me, will you? Or don't." He shrugged. "I'll feed him in the morning. He'll wait."

"Hurry!" Zuso yelled. "She's waiting. And you know how much she hates to wait for anything."

"Ha! She misses me." Dez kept grinning, heading for the door with a confident swagger.

They all knew Madame never truly missed anyone. But she would tell Dez that she did, right before she would bite his lips in a kiss. Then, she would ride his cock in her hotel bed, making him come again and again, until all pain drained from his body and his mind sank into oblivion. For a couple of weeks after that, there'd be no pain at all.

The meat bowl in his hands, Radax stretched his shoulders. His muscles ached. Dull pain throbbed in his bones. It'd get increasingly worse over the next weeks, until one day Madame would call him to her hotel room, too.

He shook his head, not willing to dwell on that yet. His attention went to the bowl in his hands. The werewolf hadn't eaten since before they left the US. Fae weren't easy to starve to death. The werewolf would survive until the morning when Dez promised to feed him, but he'd suffer from hunger.

With another roll of his shoulders that did nothing to ease the ache in his muscles, Radax headed to the docking area. The truck with the VIP exhibit crates was unloading here. One of the crates contained the werewolf.

The VIP crates held fae—a gargoyle in his stone form, a gorgonian, and a werewolf. Madame used to have a male siren as well, but he escaped back in November. With the gargoyle and the gorgonian refusing to cooperate so far, the werewolf was the only one Madame currently had to display to her VIP clients.

"Which one has the werewolf?" he asked two *bracks*, Vuk and Leslo. "This one?"

They had just wheeled a dolly with a large wooden crate out of the truck at the loading dock and now were taking it into the hallway leading to the exhibition area.

"Yep," Vuk said, stopping the dolly by the hallway and kicking the crate. "That's him."

"We may need to shoot him first." Leslo pulled a handgun out of the leather holster under his arm. "It'd be easier to get him out of the crate and move him into the cage. He'll fight, otherwise."

A human-made weapon wouldn't kill a fae or a *brack*. A bullet in his head would knock the werewolf out for a while, long enough for them to transport him wherever they wished.

"Let me feed him first." Placing the bowl on top of the crate, Radax grabbed one of the boards hammered across the front of the crate and yanked it off. The long nails bent and snapped under his force. He ripped the rest of the boards off with his bare hands, and the crate opened.

"What the..." He gaped in shock, staring inside.

The metal frame that the werewolf was supposed to be chained to was in there, but the restraints dangled uselessly. Empty. The werewolf was gone. Just a few sandbags that were used to hold down the bottom of the tent's canvas walls back in the US lay on the floor of the crate.

The werewolf had been chained. How did he escape?

There simply wasn't the kind of magic in *this* world that would allow a fae to escape the iron restraints and the locked crate.

Unless he'd had help from someone else.

"Hey!" The two *bracks* stared inside the empty crate over his shoulder. "He isn't here! Where did he go?"

Radax turned to face them. "Who loaded him? Back in the US?"

"Vuk did," Leslo said confidently.

"No," Vuk argued. "Nerkan and his team loaded him."

"Who told you that?" Radax asked with a queasy feeling rising in his stomach.

"I don't remember." Leslo shrugged.

"Amira told me that it was Nerkan," Vuk replied.

*Amira.*

The sickening feeling grew. The pain in his muscles spread to his chest.

*"I gave her the key..."* Dez had said.

She had the means to release the beast.

But why?

Why would she do it? Did the werewolf coerce her? Why wouldn't she say anything to Radax if that were the case?

Madame strictly forbade talking to the captive fae. But Amira had admitted she'd spoken to the gorgonian before.

She had no idea how dangerous fae could be. Fae couldn't break their promises, which didn't mean some of them weren't masters of deceit. Even talking to one could mean grave danger for an unsuspecting human.

Amira didn't know. How could she? He'd warned her, but not enough. He should've made it clearer to her that making deals with a fae had consequences.

Surely, she'd been tricked.

"Where is Amira?" he asked the *bracks*.

Both shook their heads, chattering excitedly.

"If the girl had anything to do with it, she's dead."

"Ha! Madame will surely kill her this time."

Their merry tone grated on his nerves. The pain in his muscles heated, turning to anger.

"Has anyone seen her since we got here?" he raised his voice, trying to keep it together.

Both just shrugged in response. *Bracks* generally paid little attention to the pale human girl who did all the tedious, menial work around the menagerie that no one else wished to do. That was the main reason Amira had been tolerated at Madame's establishment for this long. But it wouldn't help her stay alive if she indeed was the one who'd released the werewolf.

Panic unfurled inside him, spiraling out of control.

He had to find her.

Warn her.

Keep her safe...

A noise came from inside the truck trailer by the dock—a crack of wood, followed by a loud thud.

"What was that?" Leslo whipped around, pointing his gun in that direction. "There wasn't anyone in there."

"There's just the gorgonian's crate left," Vuk mumbled, shifting uneasily.

"I'll go check." Holding his gun in front of him, Leslo disappeared inside the trailer.

"Stand back!" a high girlish voice screamed from that direction.

Amira's voice!

Radax had never heard her scream. She simply never raised her voice. Ever.

Her name was the first word Amira had said to him when he'd found her as a little girl on the street one day, hiding behind a crumbled building. Completely alone.

A memory of his sister had blown over him like a light breeze when he'd looked into the little girl's eyes. It brought back the pain of mourning, but there also was a poignant beauty in that memory that he didn't wish to let go.

So, he took the girl from the street and brought her to the only place where he could watch over her, Madame's menagerie.

For years, Amira had said absolutely nothing, even though he'd talked to her whenever he had a break in his duties and no one else was around to hear them. It took years of gentle coaxing, but eventually she'd begun to speak again—timidly, in half-whispers, sparingly using words as if they were precious gold coins.

But she never screamed.

Until now.

Worry and panic shot through him like iron arrows.

He rushed into the trailer.

The large wooden crate was open. The tall, hooded figure of the gorgonian stood outside of it, facing Leslo, who pointed a gun at him.

The *brack* released but one strangled sound. His hand unclenched, dropping the gun. The next moment, he stilled. His skin fused with his clothes, both turning gray and solid. Like a rock.

"Amira?" Radax spotted her slender figure wearing her usual baggy clothes in the shadow of the crate.

If she so much as looked at the gorgonian, she'd be the next one turned to stone.

"Close your eyes, Amira!" Radax yelled, launching himself on the gorgonian.

The fae made a move to turn his way next.

"Radax, no!" Amira screamed again, her voice full of terror.

Somehow, the gun dropped by Leslo was in Amira's hand now.

"I'm so, so sorry," she whispered, pointing it at Radax.

The last thing he saw was her large, brown eyes, wide open and flooded with tears.

"I'll never forget you," she whispered, pulling the trigger.

# Chapter Four

RADAX

"Time to get up, sleeping beauty!" Madame's sharp voice cut through his brain with a jolt of pain. It really felt like his brain had been cut in two, split in the middle with a burning rod throbbing inside it.

"Get up, I said!" she hissed, jamming the pointy toe of her shoe into his ribs. "It's been more than twenty hours already."

He moaned, rolling to his side. His body didn't obey him well. His movements were jerky and uncoordinated. He managed to brush his arm over his face. It came back speckled with fragments of dried blood.

"I left you in charge for one night." Madame stomped her foot. "And look what happened! My gorgonian is gone, and the werewolf is missing."

He swept the place with his gaze, his vision blurry, red lights flashing in front of his eyes. He lay on the floor inside the truck trailer. The empty crate stood nearby. Pieces of gray stone littered the floor. The trunk with the *biqirelle* crystals was here, too. Madame must've allowed the *bracks* to use the crystals to heal him faster. Though it wasn't fast enough. He wasn't fully healed yet. It felt like a continuous explosion was happening inside his head.

Wincing, he tried to piece together what had happened here, but couldn't. His brain wouldn't function fully yet. It needed time to heal properly. Somehow, he knew he wouldn't get the time to do so.

"The only reason I'm not banishing you for eternity, *slave*," Madame uttered the last word with so much disdain, it hung between them like a putrid cloud, "is because I appreciate the beauty of irony here. The little street rat you rescued repaid you by shooting you in the head!" She tossed her head back with a silvery peal of laughter. "I'd say you should've listened to me when I told you to get rid of her, but now you finally got to see it for yourself. Humans are pathetic, ungrateful creatures."

Amira had shot him. That was the reason for the pounding agony in his head.

"Where..." He swallowed hard, focusing on every syllable leaving his mouth. "...is she?"

Madame waved her hand in a vague gesture.

"Gone. Along with the gorgonian." She crouched by his side because he couldn't get up, despite her orders. The end of her stole made from the jet-black fur of *chimera* brushed by his arm. "With the werewolf missing, too, I lost *two* of my precious fae yesterday."

Someone stepped into the narrow circle of his vision. Another *brack*. Dez.

"Madame, say the word, and I'll get the werewolf back," he said.

"No." Madame sighed. "I've just sent Nerkan with most of my *bracks* to track down the gorgonian. I need you here. At least until more of you arrive from Nerifir in a month or two."

Dez shifted from foot to foot impatiently. "Can I get the werewolf, *then?* After more of us have come to this world?"

Madame straightened, giving Dez a warm gaze.

"What will you do with the werewolf when you find him?" she asked sweetly.

"I'll drag him back into his cage for you," he replied fervently, then added, holding his breath, "unless you let me kill him."

She stroked Dez's beardless chin.

"Is that what you want, sweetie? To kill your brother?"

Dez's chest expanded with a deep breath. "That's my heart's deepest desire, Madame."

"I love that your heart is in the right place, my pet." She smiled. "You were so good last night, you earned a little favor. Wait until more *bracks* are here, then take as many as you want and kill the werewolf in any way you wish. That's my gift to you." She released another sigh and shook her head. "Your brother turned out to be a complete disappointment."

"Lero will die," Dez vowed with a bow of his head to her. "Thank you, Madame."

She shifted her attention back to Radax, who remained lying on the floor motionless because every movement hurt.

"Now *you*." Madame's voice changed drastically, all sweetness gone from it. "You will need to be punished for your negligence." She placed her hands on her hips. "I have shows booked through mid-May, all over Europe and Asia. And all I have left for the VIP exhibit is the useless gargoyle, who's nothing but a pretty piece of rock. The stubborn dragon refuses to work for me, too proud for his own good. He'd rather spend the rest of his life as a statue. Useless fool."

She stepped closer, shoving her foot into his side again.

"*You* are going to take the werewolf's place."

"Me?" Straining his shaking muscles, he managed to get up to his knees.

A wave of dizziness rolled through him, making him sway.

"Yes, my monster." Madame stepped back quickly, out of his reach in case he dared grabbing onto her for support. "You're too pretty for the act right now, but I can change that. For once, I will allow your full transformation to take place. It will be dramatic enough to impress the most pragmatic of minds. With the help of the *camyte* drink to make humans happy, we can have a great show yet. You, my hideous, will be my VIP exhibit from now on. I promise, it'll hurt. A lot."

She leaned closer, grabbing a handful of his beard.

"Let this be your punishment for letting the fae go."

# Chapter Five

## PRESENT TIME

HEIKE

"Radax, sweetie, I have a present for you," Madame cooed, unlocking the cage with her right hand.

Her left arm outstretched, she directed it at the man in the cage. A force seemed to emit from that gesture, flattening the man she'd called "a rage shifter" against the opposite bars of the cage and keeping him there.

"Enjoy!" With the door fully open, she signaled the bouncer to shove me into the cage.

I yelled and clawed at his arm as he carried me over. When he tried to shove me through the door, I grabbed on to anything and everything I could get hold of. When he pried my hand off his arm, I grabbed on to his t-shirt. He worked his shirt out of my fingers, and I clamped on to the bars of the cage, hooking my leg around his for good measure.

"Get her in, Vuk," Madame growled, impatiently.

"No! Let me go!" I yelled.

The bouncer swore under his breath as I fought with the desperation of a cat about to be plunged into a tub of water.

"No!"

I kicked at his shin with my pump's stiletto heel, landing a satisfying blow.

"Fuck." Vuk grabbed my throat, squeezing hard.

Air escaped my lungs in a gasp. I struggled to draw another breath in. The room swayed.

Vuk's angry face faded as darkness moved in from the fringes of my vision. I scratched at the hand choking me, my feet kicking meekly. Fight left me, replaced by the all-consuming need for air.

"That's better," he gritted through his teeth, his voice thick with satisfaction.

My body rigid and stiff, Vuk tossed me into the cage.

I landed on my back, my ass hitting the flat circle of the floor slightly larger than a manhole cover. My shoulder hit Radax's shin, sending a jolt of panic through me.

Gasping for air, I scrambled to get up, losing my shoes in the process. Their heels caught in the bars, which wrenched them off my feet. Coughing, I ignored the pain in my throat, scurrying for the door.

"Don't, please!"

But Madame slammed the door in my face.

"He'll kill you," she said with absolute certainty. "What a way to die! Just look at him. Isn't he simply magnificent?"

I didn't dare to even glance back, but she dropped her left hand, and I knew the monster behind me had been released from her hold that had kept him pressed against the bars and away from me. The growling at my back struck me with terror.

"Have fun." Madame folded her arms across her chest.

My heart beating high in my throat, I forced myself to turn around. Up close, the beast Madame called Radax looked like a real giant. He seemed so much more monstrous, too.

Towering over me, he had his shoulders pressed against the ceiling of the seventeen-foot cage, his head dropped between them. I barely reached past his knee in height.

Nothing about him looked human anymore. Not his distorted face with flattened forehead and beastly fangs. Not the shape of his body, stretched and bulged out of proportions, with the long arms, the hunched back, and the thick neck that merged with his shoulders. Not his flaming red eyes that stared at me with menace and need. Not the huge erection that bobbed right above me, thick like a log.

What kind of creature was he?

This couldn't be real. All of it felt like a nightmare I couldn't wake up from, no matter how hard I tried.

Lowering his head, he roared. The air from his lungs hit my face, blowing back my long, unbound hair.

Then he lunged.

There was nowhere for me to run in the confined space of the cage. I ducked between his legs, getting behind him. He swiped his hand, catching the back of my jacket with his claws. I shrugged out of the garment, leaving it in his hands as I climbed up the bars and away from him.

He tried to twist around. But turning wasn't easy for him, being so incredibly, inhumanly huge.

I used the moment to get around him again, using my much smaller size to my advantage.

With a frustrated growl, he threw my jacket aside before lunging for me again. My phone and camera crunched under his foot when he stomped on my jacket. Both must be now crushed to pieces, but I couldn't bring myself to care.

The door to the room suddenly opened, letting another one of Madame's men in.

"What is it, Nerkan?" she asked, sounding annoyed at the interruption. Watching my wild dash for my life around the cage must be too exciting to look away.

"The human who came with her is refusing to leave," Nerkan informed her.

Omkar! Even drugged out of his mind by this woman, he didn't want to leave me behind. Hope added me speed, as I evaded yet another attempt of Radax to grab me.

"So?" She shrugged. "Make him. And if he still refuses, kill him."

What?

No!

*"Please, don't."* I wanted to yell, but my throat seized. I struggled to breathe while running from the monster chasing me. Not that they

would've listened to me, anyway. For them, I was as good as dead already.

"I would kill him," Nerkan replied, "but he snuck out into the club when I wasn't looking and started asking questions."

"What kind of questions?" Madame frowned.

He tipped his chin my way. "About her."

She inhaled slowly, looking extremely displeased. "Where is he now?"

"Talking to the owner."

"The club owner?" She leveled a glare at Nerkan.

"Right," he said, backing away from her. "The security people are there, too. I'd have to kill a lot of people to hush it up, now."

"Guh!" Madame blew out a frustrated breath and pinched the bridge of her nose with her fingers. "That'd be too much mess to clean up for one evening. I still need to get some sleep. Fine," she concluded with reluctance, then handed the key to the cage to Vuk. "Let Radax out when he's done with her. I will deal with the consequences of Nerkan's incompetence."

Nerkan's shoulders drooped. He looked like a kicked puppy as he followed her out.

I was running out of breath. My feet hurt. My knees and elbows ached—I'd bruised them too many times, bumping into the metal bars of the cage. But I couldn't stop. The only way to stay alive was to keep moving and moving fast.

Radax released a frustrated roar as I ducked under his hand. His finger caught in the neckline of my sequin top. I jerked in desperation. The thin material ripped on the back, choking me.

Losing my balance, I fell to my knees, my foot wedged between the bars, trapping me. Radax stumbled, too. Hovering over me, he scrambled to regain his balance.

Vuk howled with laughter, watching the struggle.

"Please let me out!" I pleaded with him.

But he just kept laughing and shaking his head. He stepped on the platform to get closer, as if afraid to miss any detail of us fumbling in the cage that was too small for Radax and too awkwardly shaped for anyone to run inside it.

Radax suddenly slid his hand out between the bars. He hooked his fingers around Vuk's neck, then slammed the bouncer against the cage, smashing his face in.

Blood burst out of Vuk's crushed skull. He sank to his knees, then dropped to the floor.

A scream stuck in my throat. Choking with horror, I stared at the motionless body.

Vuk's hand dropped under the cage. His fist opened to release the key Madame had just given him—the key to the cage and my freedom.

I reached for it through the bars, but Radax grabbed me. He yanked me up, freeing my foot.

"No..." I whimpered, faced with his flaming red eyes. There was nothing but feral lust in them.

His huge hand completely curled around my waist, his pointer finger overlapping with his thumb. Grunting with satisfaction, he plopped down on his ass, fitting me between his legs. His massive member stood upright in front of me. It was bluish-purple and pulsing like a living, breathing thing on its own.

I shook with terror. The bloodied body of the man Radax had killed without blinking lay still warm nearby. I'd be next. And there was no one to stop this.

He inspected my black dress pants, impatiently poking at the waistband with a finger of his other hand.

I scrambled for a solution, for any way out of this insane situation.

"Listen," I panted, grabbing his finger, which was almost as thick as my wrist.

He growled, throwing my hand off him.

I inhaled sharply and grabbed his dick in desperation instead.

His entire body shook the moment my hands connected with his flesh. He roared, the same pained deafening sound he'd released before when Madame tortured him. But his hand around me suddenly relaxed.

I stood on my own two feet. My hands wrapped around his massive girth, both not nearly enough to circle it completely.

"Does it hurt?" I tilted my head up and squinted at him, trying to read his expression.

His eyelids dropped. His shoulders relaxed against the bars of the cage. He sat back with me between his legs.

At that point, I didn't care if I hurt him as long as he would stop trying to hurt *me*. But he didn't seem to be suffering with my hands on him. On the contrary, my touch appeared to relax him.

"I'll tell you what," I said, my voice shaking so badly, my words came out scrambled.

I didn't believe he'd understand me, anyway. He'd been acting more like a mindless animal than a sentient being. I kept talking just for the sake of hearing my own voice. The sound of it helped me fight the panic.

"I'll make a deal with you." I kept squeezing his hot flesh as it pulsated in my hands. "You want to come?" I spat on my hands, one by one, afraid to let go of him completely. "I'll make you come, like this..." My voice and my hands trembled. Fear shook through me so hard, my teeth clattered. "As long as you don't shove this thing anywhere inside me. Okay?"

I didn't expect him to reply as I slid my hands down his length. He didn't say a word, but a shudder rolled through his massive body, rocking and rattling the cage.

Shaking with terror, I kept working his massive hard-on between my hands. My confidence increased as he remained still. My ability to think returned.

If I was fast enough, I could grab the key and unlock the cage while he was distracted. I just needed to choose the right moment. I glanced up at him.

A pained expression froze on his face, but his odd, distorted features relaxed with every stroke of my hands.

For him, it was more than sexual, I realized. The lust that literally drove him crazy was meant to be a part of his torture. I wondered if the climax then would mean his release in a more literal sense of the word, too.

*"You want me to let Radax go?"* Madame had said.

Did that mean that his release would set him free somehow?

Instead of thinking about the key, I focused on my hands, gliding them over his silky, tightly stretched skin. The veins bulging under it were thicker than my fingers—massive, like everything else about the creature this man had become. I felt the hot blood running through them, pulsing in the same rhythm as the fire glowing in his eyes under the half-dropped eyelids, or the glow of his raw flesh between the split, ragged edges of his skin inside his tattoos.

I moved my hands faster, rubbing and squeezing them together. A pained groan tore from deep inside his chest. His upper lip quivered, curling up and baring his fangs, each longer than my finger and as sharp as an icepick.

Sensing his dick jerk, I threw my hands up in the air and jumped aside a fraction of a moment before the bright red spurts shot out. Red like fire, they hit the metal bottom of the cage with a hiss. Thin, silver tendrils of smoke rose into the air as the metal corroded.

"Holy shit..." I cursed under my breath, staring at the puddle of his release, too close to my bare feet for my liking.

Did he just come with acid or something?

He groaned softly, bringing my attention back to him. The monstrous giant was now shrinking right in front of my eyes. His body grew smaller, regaining the human proportions once again. The wounds on his arm and neck closed and darkened, looking like nothing more than harmless tattoos. Beard sprang on his chin and jawline.

Other than the beard, the eyelashes, and the brows, there was not a single hair visible anywhere else on his body. Even his crotch area remained absolutely hairless, the now flaccid penis hanging peacefully between his muscled thighs.

Back to his previous size, he stepped over the scarlet, fizzling puddle he'd just made, then crouched down and swiped the key off the floor outside the cage.

Dammit. I kicked myself for letting him get to the key first. *He* was supposed to be distracted, not *me*.

"You need to leave," he said in a deep, raspy voice.

He spoke!

Until now, he hadn't said a word. I snapped my gaze to his face—a very human face now, not monstrous at all, maybe even more ruggedly handsome than most. His eyes returned to their dark chocolate brown. With the wild, heated frenzy in them gone, he seemed just tired, now.

He unlocked the cage door, then held it open for me. "Go."

I didn't need him to ask me twice. After wresting my shoes free from between the bars, I hurried past him and out of the cage. Shoving my feet into my pumps, I grabbed my purse, still hanging over the back of the chair at the table, and rushed for the door.

"Not there," Radax called from the cage. "That way." He pointed in the opposite direction, at a metal door with a red silk curtain half-draped over it.

Of course. If I left the way I came, I risked running into Madame and her bouncers. However, I had no idea where the metal door would take me.

"Where does this door lead?" I asked Radax.

"To the stairs that will take you out to the back alley," he said calmly. "It's a fire exit."

"Thanks." I dashed to the metal door, then stopped with my hand on the handle. I felt his stare on my back. Unable to fight the sudden urge, I glanced back over my shoulder.

He remained inside the cage. The door was open for him to flee, but he made no effort to get out.

"Go," he repeated as I lingered. "If she finds you alive, she'll kill you herself."

Madame had been so sure Radax would end me tonight. Yet I was still alive. Because against her orders, he didn't kill me.

"What will she do to you?" I asked.

He just shrugged, staying inside the damn cage.

It was not my business what Madame would do to him when she came back and found me gone. Whatever his dealings with Madame were, I sensed it was better for my health and wellbeing not to know.

What did I know about Radax, anyway? I felt compassion for him when Madame tortured him, but maybe he wasn't much better than she? Didn't he just commit a murder, right in front of my eyes? The body of the man he'd killed was right there, next to the cage, with half of his head missing.

Radax followed my eyes with his.

"Vuk will be fine," he assured me. "But you need to go before he wakes up."

"Wakes up?" I huffed a dry laugh charged with nerves. "He's not sleeping. Half of his head is gone, including his face. There is no *waking up* from that."

Radax stretched his neck, finally stepping out of the cage.

"Vuk is immortal, like me. He isn't easy to kill. He'll heal and regenerate. You need to leave before it happens or before Madame returns. They will kill you, if just because *I* didn't."

I knew he was right. Getting out of here as soon as possible would be the best course of action. And yet, I lingered...

*Immortal?*

What was this place, and who were these people?

Radax could still kill me if he wanted to. Considerably smaller than he was before, he was still far larger than an average man and much bigger than me. He could snap my neck with those huge hands of his. It wouldn't take long.

He made no move toward me, though.

"Why didn't you kill me?" I asked, standing by the door.

"I don't kill if I can help it," he replied simply.

I thought back to him in his monstrous form. Madame had seemed so confident he'd do as she'd said. Remembering his insanely red eyes, I absolutely believed he would've done it too had I not...distracted him.

*"I don't kill if I can help it."*

As the giant monster, he *couldn't* help it, I guessed. Now that he looked and sounded like a human again, he seemed more in control.

*What* was he?

This was by far the most surreal experience of my entire life. Could it have been some kind of hallucination?

The crimson puddle on the floor of the cage glistened like molten lava, proving I didn't dream how it got there.

I hadn't eaten or drunk anything they'd served to us, and yet I couldn't explain what I'd seen with my own eyes. Nothing was "normal" about tonight. If I left now, I'd never find out what this was all about.

"Come with me." I couldn't leave him here, not when I still had so many questions.

Letting go of the door handle, I ran over to the "dead" body on the floor.

"What are you doing?" Radax asked as I started removing Vuk's clothes.

The possibility that Vuk might be not dead but "regenerating" made the process less morbid for me. I moved that much faster, afraid he would "wake up" any minute. With his face gone, it'd be a nightmare I didn't want to add to my horrible experiences here.

"Help me get these off." I unbuckled one boot.

"Why?" Radax crouched next to me. Despite his obvious confusion at my request, he opened the buckles of the second boot.

"You look like you're about the same size," I muttered under my breath, taking the boot off, then moving on to Vuk's belt.

"We're exactly the same size. All of us," Radax said.

"Right." I gave him a long look, then filed that information away for now, along with all the events of this night, to sift through later when I was safe again and far away from this place where nothing made sense.

We pulled Vuk's pants off, and I tossed them to Radax.

"Put these on."

"Why?" He caught the pants in the air but didn't get dressed.

"Because I can't take you through the streets of Singapore naked. You're coming with me." It sounded crazy, but I had more than enough reasons to take him along.

First, I had no doubt Madame would do more nasty things to Radax once she found Vuk passed out and me gone. I couldn't leave him here, knowing well that she would torture him again. His claim of being immortal only made it worse. If he really wasn't easy to kill, she'd only have more possibilities to make his life a living hell.

He'd released me. The least I could do was the same to him.

Second, I had a lot of questions that I could never answer on my own. I'd come here for a discovery, and I believed I'd just stumbled on something beyond my wildest imagination. But first, I needed someone to explain to me exactly what I'd seen.

Radax shook his head.

"I can't leave." He sounded calm, simply stating the fact. He knew what was coming, and he seemed resigned.

I refused to accept that. I couldn't leave him, knowing the horrors he'd face if he stayed.

"Put these on," I insisted, energetically pointing at the pants he held in his hands.

He wouldn't move. "She won't let me go far."

*She?*

Madame.

Resentment and defiance flared inside me at the thought of that woman. She called Radax her pet, her slave.

*"We'll see about that,"* flashed through my mind in challenge.

I absolutely needed to convince him to leave with me.

"I... I can't leave without you, I'll get lost," I said in a pleading "damsel in distress" tone. Not a role I was good at, but desperate times called for desperate measures. "Radax, I need you to show me the way out of here, please." I batted my eyelashes at him, going for an innocent and helpless expression. "What if someone attacks me in the back alley? Can you protect me? Can you take me up to the street, please?"

That seemed to work. He nodded.

"I can." He finally got his legs in the pants, then yanked them up his hips and buckled the belt. "I know the way. We used this door to bring in the equipment." He gestured at the cage.

A shiver ran down my spine from a mere look at that thing. "Equipment" was such an innocuous word for this torture device.

It was hard to believe Radax was the same monster who raged inside it just minutes earlier. Yet had I met him in the street in his current state, I'd probably still be wary. His size alone was intimidating. His bald head, bushy eyebrows, intense eyes, and the tattoos probably wouldn't have done much to put me at ease, either.

After seeing him at his worst, however, I didn't feel intimidated by him at all now.

"Here. Put these on, too." I shoved the boots his way, then headed for the metal door again.

He glanced back at the door to the corridor leading to the club where Madame had left.

"You'll be back soon," I said, hurriedly, eager to leave this place and afraid he'd change his mind about following me.

"Let's hurry, then." He stepped in front of me and opened the metal door.

His back came into my view. The long scars on it didn't disappear after his transformation. They'd gotten worse. Fresh blood oozed from them.

"Wait." I grabbed the red curtain that hang over the door and yanked at it, hard. The silk ripped at the top, leaving the entire curtain in my hands.

Radax gave me a confused look, but didn't ask any questions. Grabbing my hand, he silently led me out of the room and into a concrete corridor. From here, he took me up the stairs and out to the back alley —a dark, narrow space between two windowless walls. I spotted several dumpsters in here. The air stunk of garbage and urine.

The lights of the brightly illuminated street shone in the distance. The sounds of the city filled the air, bringing echoes of life into the tunnel between the walls. The city kept moving ahead as the nightmare of Madame's freakshow unfolded just below the surface.

Radax led us around the dumpsters toward the street.

"It's best for you not to go home tonight." He stopped at the exit from the alley. "Stay with someone, a friend, for a couple of days. Madame is leaving the country soon. She'll call off the search for you, then."

He turned to go back, but I took his hand, stopping him.

"Why did you help me, Radax?" I asked.

Even not knowing much about Madame's people, I was certain Vuk or the other bouncers wouldn't have let me go. There was something different about Radax, something better compared to the rest of them.

He shrugged uneasily. "I don't want you hurt."

I had a feeling Madame would make him pay dearly for his kindness.

It just wasn't right. I squeezed his hand tighter. "Come with me."

He shook his head. "She'll never allow that."

*"I own them,"* Madame had said

The words made my blood boil. Radax wasn't her property. People couldn't be "owned." That shit wasn't legal anywhere in the world.

"We don't need her permission. You're free, Radax," I said with a firm conviction. "*I* released you, remember?"

He gave me a long look. Suddenly, a corner of his mouth twitched up, and I realized he was smiling. It was a lopsided grin, half-hidden by his full beard, but he was smiling. And it was...nice.

Something warm and bright lit up inside me in response.

"You are free, Radax." I smiled back.

A loud slam of the metal door boomed from where we'd just come from. It echoed through the bowels of the alley.

The smile slipped off Radax's face.

Chill rushed down my bare back with goosebumps.

"We need to get out of here." I tossed the red curtain to Radax. "Here, cover your back with it."

He threw the curtain over his shoulders, letting it drape down his back like a cape. Setting my purse down on the floor, I took off my ruined top and put it on again backwards, with the rip to the front.

Glancing up, I caught the stare Radax slid down my chest, now covered only by my black strapless bra. He didn't appear leering, but oddly curious.

Heavy footsteps sounded in the alley behind us. The bouncers must be after us.

I poked my head out around the corner.

"See the taxi right there?" I pointed at one of the several vehicles parked at the curb. The drivers lingered around waiting for the club-goers to exit the building.

I took a critical look at Radax and adjusted the curtain-cape on his wide shoulders. "Let's pretend you're the eccentric, artistic type, ok?"

I quickly tied my slashed top together in the front. My satin bra was showing above the knot, with my belly button left exposed below it. There was nothing I could do about either.

"Well." I sighed. "We'll pretend I'm the slutty type, then."

Suddenly, he shoved me behind him. Nerkan leaped from around a dumpster, gun in his hand.

I froze in horror at the sight of the weapon. Radax swung his fist at Nerkan's face, landing a blow. Something crunched—either his nose or his jaw. Or both. Blood sprayed Radax's forearm.

Nerkan dropped to the ground, his head a bloody mess.

More footsteps sounded from behind.

"We need to go." Radax's words snapped me back into action.

I'd think about all of this later, including the incredible strength this man possessed that allowed him to smash a person's face in with one blow.

"Right. This way." Grabbing my purse in one hand and Radax's hand in another, I ran to the taxi.

# Chapter Six

HEIKE

"You're too tall." I shoved on Radax's shoulder, making him sink lower into his seat in the taxi. That didn't really make him any smaller. I hoped the bouncers wouldn't spot him through the tinted windows.

At least we were inside the vehicle. Out on the street, he'd be towering over everyone, visible from any vantage point, like a lighthouse in the ocean.

Hiding my face behind the curtain of my long hair, I furtively glanced out of the back window to the exit from the alley.

Nerkan remained hidden from view, but two other bouncers ran out. They stopped on the sidewalk, scanning the street and the passing vehicles. When they turned our way, I ducked. Our taxi had moved too far for them to see me by then, even if the windows weren't tinted.

"Let's hope it worked," I breathed out quietly.

I made the taxi stop ten minutes later and switched the vehicles, making sure no one followed us. Only when I was certain no other vehicles pursued us, I told the new driver the actual address where we were going.

When we got out of the taxi, I quickly whirled off the main street and into a walkway between two tall buildings, dragging Radax along.

"Have you been to Singapore before?" I asked him.

He nodded, "A few times. Years ago."

"So, you know your way around then?"

"No."

I blinked, raising an eyebrow. "Not even a little bit?"

"I don't travel as a tourist," he explained. "I've been to many countries. But we always stay with Madame's menagerie, no matter where we are."

He'd traveled the world with Madame's show but had seen very little of it. That would make me hate her even more, if it were possible.

"Okay, well, just stay close then and..." I slid my gaze down his large body. Due to his size, he stood out like a tree in a desert. "Can you try to make yourself a little smaller?"

He gave me a confused look.

"Never mind." I waved my hand. "Let's go."

We circled the block, watching for any signs of Madame's bouncers. It was a good thing they were "exactly the same size" as Radax. They'd be easy to spot now if they had followed us after all.

It appeared they hadn't. At least, I couldn't see them around. Somewhat relieved, I headed for the entrance of the building where a friend of mine lived.

Radax stopped at the door. "Is that where you live?" He glanced over his shoulder, scanning the area around the building again.

"No. I live in New York, in the States. I'm just visiting in Singapore."

"Is this your hotel, then?" He tilted his head back, taking in the residential high-rise. "If so, it's not safe. It'll be too easy for the *bracks* to find out where you're staying. They probably already know that, anyway."

"You think they do?"

This wasn't my hotel. I'd figured it'd be safer not to go there tonight. But I hoped to stop by my room tomorrow, to pick up my stuff.

"They have your name. They know where you're from," Radax pointed out. "They'll find where you're staying easily enough."

I released a long, heavy breath.

"I'll have to figure out how to get my things from my room. Eventually." I rubbed my forehead, then took Radax's hand, tagging him along. "Come. This isn't a hotel. A friend of mine lives here. Madame's people won't find us here."

With another glance over his shoulder, he let me lead him through the lobby into the elevator, then up to the ninth floor where the studio apartment of my friend Xin was located.

"Xin is a DJ," I explained to Radax in a hushed voice while punching the code to unlock the apartment door. "She works in a night club and doesn't come home until morning."

Xin's studio was one open space, with a fold-out couch behind a silk screen, a separate bathroom, and a kitchenette in a niche. Painted in deep blue, the walls had tiny lights inserted in a pattern high under the ceiling. When I flicked the switch on, pink and purple constellations illuminated the room.

Radax clicked his tongue with appreciation. "That's pretty."

"Isn't it?" I smiled, closing and locking the door. "It looks so beautiful at night. Too bad Xin is rarely here when it's dark. She works nights and sleeps during the day."

"Will she mind us being here?"

"No." I shook my head. "I've stayed here before when I had no time to book a hotel. Xin has used my place in New York on quite a few occasions, too. We're fine."

That was how it worked between my friends and me. Most of us traveled a lot. Not all could afford a hotel for each trip. Having a worldwide network of friends made it easier.

Tossing my purse on the shoe rack by the entrance, I beelined to the computer on the desk by the only window in the apartment.

"Are you hungry?" I asked Radax, who remained by the door.

"No. Just thirsty."

"There's a jug of water in the fridge." I waved my hand toward the kitchenette. "Glasses are on the shelf over the sink. Help yourself."

My phone was now gone, crushed by Radax's giant foot in the cage. Logging in the guest account of Xin's computer, I made sure the video had been uploaded to my cloud account before the phone broke. The file was there, but I couldn't bring myself to watch it right now.

A glass of water in his hand, Radax lowered himself into the large beanbag in the middle of the room.

I glanced his way. So many questions roamed in my head. Would he answer any of them? If he did, I wanted to record all his answers.

Suddenly, the glass dropped from his hand. Water splashed over the lime-green, shaggy carpet on the floor.

"Radax?" I jumped from my seat.

He growled, bending over, and I rushed to him.

"What is it? Are you hurt? Is something wrong with the water?"

A young, healthy man suddenly doubling over in obvious pain was not normal. It meant something was wrong. Only I had no idea what.

I dropped to my knees next to the bean bag and grabbed his arm—the one with the tattoo. His skin felt unnaturally hot.

A zap of emotion hit me, knocking the air out of my chest. I sucked in a breath, jerking my hand away. It didn't hurt to touch him, not physically. But an arrow of intense hatred speared through me like an electric charge when I'd touched his heated skin.

"What is going on?" I muttered, shocked.

"Ghata..." he groaned. "Madame."

The dreadfully familiar sparks of red light flashed along the lines of his tattoo, reaping a strangled growl from him.

"Is she hurting you?" I hovered my hand over his arm, my fingers trembling. "But she isn't even here." I darted a glance toward the entrance, half-expecting to find Madame barging through the door in all her red-silk glory.

Propping his elbows on his knees, he panted, catching his breath. The pain appeared to let go a little.

"She wants me back." He rolled his shoulders, looking like he was bracing for another bout of pain.

"Back?" The former anger and indignation rose in me anew. "Back! So that she can stuff you in that cage again?"

"I belong to her—" His sentence was interrupted by a groan. He gritted his teeth as another surge of agony must be racking his body.

The entire length of his tattoo glowed bright red. I could feel the heat radiating from it, even from the distance.

"Can she tell where you are?" I asked. "Will she send the others to get you?" The last thing I wanted was putting Xin's apartment on Madame's criminal radar and possibly putting my friend in danger.

He shook his head.

"She doesn't need to know where I am. She can pull me back to her, from any place in this world or any other." He got up, untying the curtain cape we'd used to hide his back. He dropped the piece of fabric into the bean chair, revealing the crusty red scars on his back again.

My chest tightened at the thought of letting him go. Why would he go back to that horrible woman? How did he not have a choice?

It made no sense.

"Wait." I moved to the exit with him.

He roared in pain again, then slammed his back to the wall. His fingers rigid and curled, he hovered his hands over his crotch in the gesture I remembered back from the cage. The pants between his legs bulged, bringing more images from earlier to mind. I remembered Madame's words about "riding" him.

"Is that how she controls you? Through sex?"

That didn't surprise me as much as it should. Somehow, I expected that from someone like Madame, to control men through their base instincts.

Leaning against the wall, he panted, greedily gulping in air while the pain had let go, allowing him to breathe once again.

"You'll be okay here..." he managed between the rugged breaths. "Stay hidden for a few days. Don't go to your hotel. Wait until she leaves the country. I need to go. Only she can end this—" With another wild groan, he tossed his head back, grimacing in pain.

His tattoos pulsed with fire.

Anger slashed through me. Cursing under my breath, I dropped to my knees in front of him.

"How can she think it's okay to do this?" I raged, unbuckling his belt.

"What are you doing?" he croaked but made to move to stop me.

I glanced up, finding his eyes. Red and glowing, the sight of them made me pause. Could Madame turn him into the giant monster from far away?

Not if I could help it!

I unzipped his pants, then yanked them down his hips. "It worked before, didn't it?"

His erection sprang free, making me shrink back. Significantly smaller in this form, it still appeared monstrous. Engorged, thick and straining, it was almost purple, with thick veins bulging along his sizable length. His skin was so hot, it almost burned my hand when I touched it. Another hostile jolt of energy zapped me.

"You're not going to scare me," I said, as if Madame herself was here.

Reaching for my purse on top of the shoe rack nearby, I grabbed a tub of face cream from it. I'd gotten it as a part of a product package from a cosmetic company I'd helped with the launch of a new skin care line. People out there paid over a hundred US dollars for a tub of this face cream. And I slapped a generous amount of it on Radax's burning hot dick.

He hissed with a moan as I wrapped my hands around it.

"She wants you back, does she?" I gritted through my teeth, energetically smearing the cream along his length. "She can't fall asleep unless she sets someone on fire, can she? Well, she'll have to find herself another toy for tonight."

He hovered his hands over my shoulders, then jerked them away. Shoving his hands behind his back, he trapped them between the wall and his back, not touching me.

He was so hard, it took just a few pumps of my hand before he came with a strangled roar.

I scurried away from the spurts of his release, but it looked normal this time. Creamy-white, it harmlessly landed on the tiled floor by the front entrance, not causing any damage. No hissing. No corrosive steam, either.

"So, *that* comes in two forms, too?" I lifted an eyebrow at Radax.

His back to the wall, he slid down to the floor next to me. His face appeared flushed, but the tattoos looked back to normal and his eyes were of that rich, dark-chocolate color again.

Tension drained out of me. I leaned back against the wall, too, sitting on the floor with him.

"Thank you," he exhaled.

He didn't offer to return the favor, and I would've declined if he did. This wasn't about making each other feel good. It wasn't about attraction or even about sex. What I'd just done felt like an act of mercy, a desperate attempt to stop a cruel woman from exercising her power over a man.

"What is it between you and her?" I asked, rolling my head on the wall his way.

"She owns me," he said simply, as if that explained everything.

"Bullshit. No one *owns* anyone. Human trade is illegal, as I'm sure you know."

"*Human* trade..." He turned his head to face me, too. "But I'm not human. I'm not one of you."

I would laugh had I not witnessed too many things I couldn't explain tonight. Radax being something else might actually provide some explanations.

"What are you?" I asked, holding my breath in anticipation of his answer.

"I'm a *brack*, like the rest of us at the menagerie. Madame created me millennia ago. I belong to her now, hundreds of us do."

"What do you mean, she *created* you?"

He opened his mouth to reply, but I stopped him.

"You know what? How about you go take a quick shower." I gestured at the smears of the *bracks'* blood and gore on his hands and torso. "I'll order us some pizza. All this crazy shit is making me hungry. Then, we'll talk. Okay?"

If Radax was ready to tell me his story, I wanted to have it all captured on camera. I had no clear idea what I'd do with the footage, but if I really was on the verge of some incredible discoveries here, I needed solid video evidence.

Radax went to the bathroom to take a shower.

It turned out to be too late to order pizza. So instead, I raided Xin's fridge and found a few single serving frozen pizzas. I popped them into the microwave.

In Xin's dresser, I found a black t-shirt I'd given to her long ago, one with a logo from a cosmetic company I'd worked with. I changed into the t-shirt, tossing my ruined top in the garbage bin.

After that, I threw Radax's pants in the wash, wishing we'd taken Vuk's t-shirt with us, too. There was no chance I'd find anything remotely suitable for Radax in Xin's closet. She was a petite girl, almost a foot shorter than me. Even in his smaller form, Radax must be over six and a half feet in height. Each of his biceps would probably be thicker than Xin's waist.

I slid the silk screen aside, revealing the couch behind it. Then I turned the computer camera toward the couch, making sure it got in the frame of the video I was about to record.

The sound of water stopped in the shower. Radax came out with one of Xin's pink towels wrapped around his hips.

"Where are my pants?" he asked, looking around while I stupidly stared at him.

I'd seen him naked before. During the entire time I'd known him—as short as it'd been—Radax had been either completely or partially bare. Until now, however, I'd been too distracted to fully appreciate the sight of him.

Thanks to my dad's genes, my height was slightly above average for a woman, even back in the United States. I was used to sticking out of the crowd in many countries I'd traveled to.

Radax dwarfed me, however. Next to him, I felt tiny. He had to bend down to fit in the door frame on his way out of the bathroom. Thankfully, the ceilings in Xin's apartment were quite high.

Fresh out of the shower, his tanned skin appeared to glow with warmth, tempting me to run my hands over him. Every dip and valley of his body was well-defined and rippled with strength. In contrast, his beard seemed exceptionally soft and silky when freshly washed.

"Where did my pants go?" Radax asked again, since I just kept gaping at him silently, my hands fisted at my sides to stop myself from touching his smooth, damp skin or stroking his beard.

"Oh, yeah..." I blinked. "Pants. They're in the washing machine. I'll hang them out on the balcony right after. They'll be dry by morning." I slid my gaze down the hard ridges of his abdominal muscles. "How much do you have to work out to maintain all of...um, *that.*" I tipped my chin at his torso.

"Work out?" He cast a confused glance down his wide chest and flat belly.

"Yes. How much time do you spend in the gym?"

"None. I don't have time to go to the gym."

"Right." I huffed a laugh. "That's what I keep telling myself, too." I moved over to the kitchen table with the plate of pizzas. "Well, I hope it's your cheat day today, because we're having pizza."

"I like pizza." He nodded.

"Thin crust?" I handed him a napkin, then moved the plate closer to him, inviting him to take some.

"Any crust." He took one of the small pizzas.

"Hm." I watched him take a huge bite of it. "I thought you'd be living purely on raw steak and protein shakes."

I hopped up to sit on the table as Radax leaned with his hip against it. Xin's lone chair remained shoved under the table, unused.

"I like steak, too." Radax finished the entire pizza in a few large bites.

"Here." I shoved the plate even closer to him, and he grabbed another pizza. I wondered if I should've heated up more, even though he'd said he wasn't hungry just a little while ago.

"We don't get steak at the menagerie very often, though," he said between bites.

"What do you usually eat, then?" I asked, purely out of curiosity.

He shrugged. "Whatever is available. When on the road, it's the drive-through. When at a location, it's whatever food is served at the fair."

I lifted an eyebrow, directing a pointed look at his washboard abs. "Don't tell me you grew this big in all the right places while eating nothing but junk food and carnival fare."

Talking to Radax while eating pizza in a friend's kitchen felt so normal. It was almost too easy to forget how we met and why he was here in the first place.

Until he said, "I'm the way I am because Madame prefers this body shape for her slaves."

His words made the pizza stick in my throat. They were a somber reminder of all the horrors of that night and of what must be his life.

I swallowed hard, taking a big gulp from my glass of water.

"Will you tell me more about Madame, Radax?" I asked, putting the glass down.

"What do you want to know?" He finished the second pizza and took a drink from his glass, too.

"Anything you'd like to share, I'll listen."

He drew in a breath, as if to start, and I stopped him.

"Come to the couch over here," I suggested, leading him to where I had the camera set up. "It's more comfortable."

I briefly contemplated offering him a glass of wine or whatever alcohol he preferred to ease him into talking but decided against it. Making him inebriated reminded me too much of Madame's tactics. If he talked, I wanted it to be a fully conscious decision on his part.

"So." I plopped on the chair by the desk and turned to face him. "Who is Madame? Is her name really Tan?"

He gave me a long, penetrating look, and I couldn't hold it. Part of me wanted to tell him about the camera filming us right now. The right thing to do would be to get his permission to film first. If I asked and he declined it, though, I'd never get the answers to my burning questions.

But I needed the answers.

So, I calmed my conscience by promising myself not to make public any videos without his permission. Besides, there might be nothing valuable in what he was about to tell me, anyway.

Radax adjusted the pink towel around his hips, and I made a mental note to crop it out of the frame. Pink wasn't really his color.

"Madame is a goddess," he said, and I suddenly felt deflated.

A goddess?

So much for an amazing discovery. That just seemed like some serious brainwashing, a cult, nothing more.

"A goddess?" I repeated numbly, not sure where to go from there.

He nodded, leaning back. "A werewolf goddess from Nerifir, the world where we all come from."

"A werewolf..." I mumbled, feeling my eyebrows crawling up to my hairline.

"Her real name is Ghata. And there were times when she had great powers. People reveled and worshipped her. She held undivided control over the Moon magic. But she had misused her powers, making those who believed in her angry. Forty-four years ago, she escaped to this world to avoid being captured and prosecuted."

I tried to make sense of it all. The only thing clear so far was that the woman was a criminal.

"When she ran, she left us behind, in her temple in Nerifir. A few years after she'd come to this world, she managed to get a group of us here, too," Radax continued. "By then she had recuperated enough to use her magic to pull us across the dimensions."

"Okay." I decided to suspend my disbelief for the time being and hear him out. "Why are you with her?"

"I have no choice. None of us do." He rolled back his shoulders uneasily, as if Madame's presence weighted down on them even now. "At the beginning, Ghata lived in a hut in a forested area of the werewolves Plains of Sarnala. Out of gratitude for her patronage and protection, the people of Sarnala built her a grand temple. They have improved and expanded it many times over the centuries."

His words flowed easily, painting a picture that sounded more like a fable. I couldn't imagine anything of what he was saying happening in real life.

"At first, the goddess's relationship with the people was fair," Radax continued. "But gods get tempted and tested, too, just like mortals do. And Ghata had given in to the temptation of power. The more she had, the more she craved. Until she started demanding to be worshiped every minute of every day. She wanted revelers next to her permanently. And she wished to have unlimited power over them. She ordered each family to bring their first-born son to her the day he turned fourteen."

"Why just sons?" I was listening to his story with rapt attention. This apartment no longer existed as Radax's words transported me into a completely different world—Nerifir.

"Ghata is a feminine entity. She found a way to gain limitless control over her male followers," he said. "She turned the boys she took from their families into her monks to keep at her temple. People call us *bracks*, which means 'monks' in the werewolves' dialect. But Ghata often calls us her slaves because that's what we truly are."

I shook my head. "How so?"

"We're unable to deny her anything. Any of us would die for her, without having a second thought."

"But why?" I couldn't comprehend this utter lack of will of their own.

"She made the boys vow to serve her for life. She then used the Moon magic to bind their souls to her for eternity."

"Is that what she's done to you, too?"

His chest rose with a deep breath. He glanced at the computer at my right, then leaned closer, propping his forearms on his knees.

"What's your name?" he asked me, and I realized I'd never introduced myself to him.

"Heike," I said, licking my lips. The intensity of his stare fixed on me was both energizing and unnerving.

"I'll tell you everything, Heike. But I must warn you, you won't believe it all."

So far, I had a hard time believing anything at all. As fascinating as his story was, it sounded mostly like a fictional tale to me.

But I nodded, and he continued, holding my gaze firmly.

"The day I turned fourteen must have been a joyous day for my family. I became one of the Goddess's chosen. Though, I don't remember much of that day. In fact, I forgot almost everything about the first fourteen years of my life. My memories start when I came to Ghata's temple. She took me up into the tallest tower. There, in the very top room with no roof where she prayed to the Moon at night, she ordered me to strip naked. She chained me to the wall, locking my hands and feet into iron manacles. And as the Moon rose, she forced me to have sex with her as she recited the *brack's* vow to me, making me repeat it word for word. She wouldn't let me come until I said it all perfectly. Every single word."

I held my trembling hand to my throat. Horror chilled my spine as deep compassion reached out from my heart.

Radax rested his gaze on the computer. "By morning, I was her slave. In body and soul."

"You were only a child," I managed to say around the thick lump forming in my throat.

"Which made it easier for Ghata to break my resistance—mental and physical—and take over completely. She made me her *brack*. That's all I've ever been since."

Suddenly, his confession felt too poignant and intimate to even film. Radax was sharing with me the most sacred, defining part of his life. Having the camera rolling made me feel filthy. I was breaking his trust.

I reached over to the computer to turn the camera off.

"Don't." He stopped me.

I froze, caught red-handed. "You know?"

He nodded.

"And you don't mind?"

"Humans don't usually believe in anything that has to do with our world. Even if they accidentally discover something unusual, they tend to explain it away. You wanted to know, and I've decided to tell you because I think you've seen enough to understand that I'm telling the truth. If you need to record my words for any reason, so be it."

"But what if I share with others what you've just told me?" I asked carefully.

"Then, my story will be known."

"Is that what you want?"

"Yes." He rubbed the lines of the tattoo on his forearm. "Sooner or later, I will have to return to Madame. The moment I come back, I'll die." He raised his gaze to mine. "I want someone to know who I was. I wish for someone in this world to be aware of what Ghata is and what she's capable of. I want to warn you about the fate that awaits you all. And maybe humanity will prove itself stronger and smarter than my people were when they accepted Ghata and celebrated her as their deity."

I silently moved my hand away from the computer, letting the recording continue.

"Let me tell you what it's like to be Ghata's slave," Radax spoke directly into the camera. "It's not just about wordless obedience—that's a given. *Bracks* no longer have their own conscience or judgement. Their morals align with those of the goddess. What she deems right is their law. Her enemies become *bracks'* enemies. If she orders to kill, a *brack* won't hesitate to do so, even if it kills him in the process."

Yet *he* didn't kill me when she expected him to do so.

"Werewolves are acutely attuned to the Moon magic. It's in their veins. Their life cycle is closely connected with the cycles of the Moon. Ghata twisted that connection, diverting it to herself. She is the *bracks'* Moon, their everything. We no longer shift with the cycles of the Moon. Instead, the magic builds up in *bracks*, with urge and pain. Anger rises, and there's no natural way to release it. It festers and grows, racking our bodies with agony and rage, until Madame takes mercy on us."

"How?"

"Through sex."

*"I enjoy riding him..."* her words came to mind again. She'd turned them not just into her slaves, but her sex toys, too.

"We cannot touch ourselves," Radax continued. "She doesn't allow us to touch her when she uses us for sex. She is the only one who can take the pain away and soothe the rage."

I shook my head. It was so hard to believe something like that could be happening in this world. Yet I knew, I *felt* that every word coming out of his mouth was true.

"She made you addicted to her."

"*Dependent* on her, in every way," he corrected.

I drew in a breath, shaking my head. "How do you not hate her?"

"Hate?" He exhaled a humorless laugh. "We crave her. *Bracks* would fight, kill, and die for a night with Madame. Being with her is the ultimate purpose of our existence—the one bright light in life. A torture that heals."

I dreaded to think what kind of life he must lead if a night of abuse by a woman who wouldn't even let him touch her was "the one bright light."

Yet Radax didn't sound brain washed. He wasn't idolizing Madame. His story sounded like a somber but heartfelt and honest account. It wasn't the delirious ramblings of a misled mind.

"This part is important, Heike." He turned from the computer to me, leaning closer. "Ghata is powerful. The more people believe in her, the more her power grows. For millennia, she had ruled my world. And she is getting ready to rule yours. If she succeeds, she will start enslaving your people and taking your boys. There are already sects of her followers in this part of the world. Unlike some humans who claim to be the next messiah, Ghata actually can perform genuine miracles to take over people's imagination. She *can* demonstrate her powers in dramatic ways to prove her divinity. She now also has the means to *buy* what she can't gain by magic. And she will only grow stronger."

"How can I stop her?" I whispered, shaken to the core.

His eyes filled with regret and compassion.

"You can't. But if you know exactly what she is, you won't give her your trust or your faith. You will not make her stronger. You won't let her pollute your mind. And you'll know you have to stay away from her to be safe."

# Chapter Seven

HEIKE

We both sat in silence for a while. Radax appeared to be lost in thought, or maybe in his enormously long past.

And I... I simply tried to wrap my mind around everything he'd told me and connect it with what I'd seen.

Everything logical and pragmatic in me refused to accept the existence of another world where life ran parallel to ours, unknown to me. Where magic was a part of life, and where deities were as real and flawed as mortals.

Without accepting that, I struggled to explain what I'd witnessed at the show. How could a man grow many times his size? How could the gruesome wounds on his arm burst into flames, looking like he would never have the use of that arm again, then turn to harmless tattoo lines a little while later?

Was it all some sophisticated optical illusion? Smoke and mirrors?

I could get behind that explanation if I hadn't been in the cage with Radax myself, if I hadn't touched him.

The beeping sound of the washing machine's cycle ending brought me back to reality.

"Your pants are done." I jumped off my chair and got his pants out of the machine.

When I returned from the balcony after hanging the damp pants out in the fresh air, Radax stood by the desk. His hands propped on the back of the chair, he stared out through the large window into the brightly lit cityscape.

His mangled back was in plain view.

I quietly walked into the bathroom and raided the small medicine cabinet there. "Can I treat the wounds on your back, please?" I asked, coming back to the main room.

He turned slowly and looked suspiciously at the two little jars in my hands. "What are these?"

I raised my left hand with a spray bottle.

"An antiseptic to stop the infection—"

He jerked his head aside. "No need for that. They won't get infected. What's the other one?" He gestured at the jar in my right hand.

"Just Vaseline. To cover up the broken skin and stop it from drying."

He shrugged. "My back will heal on its own in a day or two. But if you wish..." He turned around and got down on his knees, right there on the floor, to make it easier for me to reach.

The cuts on his back looked clean now that he'd taken a shower. The smears of crusted blood were gone. The fact that they were there in the first place told me that no one bothered to clean the wounds before.

"How did you get them? What made these?" I asked, bracing myself for the answer.

"A whip," he said simply, matter-of-fact. As if whipping people was a normal thing, a regular, every-day occurrence.

But maybe in his life, it was?

My breathing hitched for a second. I bit my lip, dipping my fingers into the jar.

"Did...*she* do it?"

"No. Madame doesn't exert herself. She has *bracks* to do it for her."

So, they whipped each other, on her orders.

Gently, barely touching his broken skin to avoid causing him any more pain or discomfort, I spread Vaseline over the cuts.

"Why did she need to resort to that? Did you disobey her? You said the *bracks* would do anything she says."

"Most would. *All* of them would. Until recently, I was like the rest of them, ready to do anything she wished."

"What changed?"

His back moved as he inhaled deeply, and I jerked my hands away, afraid to hurt him.

"I'm not entirely sure." He scratched his beard. His voice sounded guarded now, different from the way he'd opened up to me before. "For years now, I've had my own thoughts and my own emotions, different from the rest."

"And being different gets you punished?"

"Yes."

It was so wrong.

I kept silent, applying a thin layer of Vaseline all over his wide back and diligently covering every inch of the cuts. Everything inside me protested fiercely against the very idea of letting him go back to that woman for more abuse. He'd said she'd kill him if he returned.

When I finished, I set the jar aside and touched his arm. "Don't go back to her. Ever."

He whipped around to face me. His eyes searched mine intently, then he blinked, glancing away.

"You just sounded like someone I know," he muttered under his breath.

Who?

Was there somebody else who wanted him out of Madame's clutches?

"Is there someone who wants you to stay away from Madame?" I asked.

He stared at my hand on top of his forearm. My knuckles were bruised, probably from bumping against the bars of the cage. A long scratch grazed my skin just under my thumb.

I should spray some antiseptic on it. It didn't hurt too much, but unlike Radax, I could develop infections.

He took my hand in his and brought it to his mouth, suddenly licking my scratch.

Startled, I jerked my hand away.

"It'll heal by morning, now," he explained.

"It will?" I examined the scratch.

It didn't look any different, but any trace of pain was gone immediately after he'd licked it.

"*Bracks* retain the werewolves' ability to heal," Radax said.

"You can heal others, but not yourself?"

"My healing is up to Ghata."

I groaned inside, and it turned into an audible growl. The atrocities of this woman made my blood boil.

"Stay away from her," I squeezed through my clenched teeth.

He shook his head. "I can't."

"That's what you say. Yet here you are." I pointed at his chest. "And Madame isn't here, is she?"

Sitting back on his haunches, he stared at me, as if what I'd said stunned him.

"See? You *are* staying away from her." I cocked my head. "How is that possible?"

He shook his head. "I have no idea."

"Well, maybe you just keep staying away. See how long you can make it."

He sat on the floor, staring straight ahead as if digesting this new concept—having a life separate from his "goddess."

"Listen," I said. "I was planning to leave here next week. I wanted to go back to New York. But I can certainly leave early now that they may be looking for me. Do you want to come with me?"

Radax had nothing on him other than the stolen pants and boots. I'd have to figure out how to get a passport for him on super short notice. There must be someone who sold fake passports either among my friends or their friends, or among those their friends knew. All I had to do was ask the right people.

Although I always strived to stay on the right side of the law, I felt the situation warranted me to cross the line in this case. Maybe I could get Radax far enough from Ghata that her reach would no longer bother him?

"Do you know someone in this world?" I asked. "Do you have a place where you can stay and be safe from her?"

"No." He shook his head. "There is no place like that for me in this world or any other."

"Then you will stay with me," I decided.

I still didn't know what to do about his story. Using the videos of him to generate revenue no longer felt right. However, I didn't think the videos would work for any other purpose.

His story was so incredible, most people would find it fake. If I posted it as is, it would possibly cause a splash. People would share it if only because of Radax's spectacular physique, but it would die out quickly. Despite my millions of followers, my sharing it wouldn't have the effect that Radax was hoping for. Few would take his warnings seriously.

Maybe I could get more evidence if I kept him around? Maybe I could find more witnesses to back up his story.

But mostly, I just wanted to get him away from the murderous woman who raped teenage boys, kept people in cages, and cruelly punished men for daring to have an independent way of thinking.

"Come to New York with me," I said. "It's a long way away. Maybe the distance will break whatever hold she's got on you here?"

His eyes twinkled with something I hadn't seen there before.

Excitement? Hope?

Sadly, it dulled quickly.

"Ghata pulls her *bracks* across dimensions to her. The distance wouldn't matter," he said, softly.

What was I to do with him?

The thought of Madame getting her cruel hands on him made me want to puke. The fact that he was immortal and could heal well if she allowed it only made it worse. It gave her endless opportunities for torture.

"How exactly does she *pull?*"

"She makes us want her, crave her to the brink of madness, until we have no choice but to go to her, wherever she is. The pull is so strong it defies physics and even death."

I thought back to him trying to leave here a short while back, and what I did to him in the hallway to make him stay.

"Well." I sat up straighter. "If she tries to *pull* you back to her again, we know what to do, right?" I gave him a playful smile. "I'll just jerk you off again."

He shook his head, but I caught a spark of amusement in his eyes.

"It's not that simple."

"Isn't it?" I wiggled my eyebrows. "What's so complicated about a hand job?"

His beard moved with a smile that for a moment took my breath away.

"Come on," I implored, touching his hand. "What do you have to lose? If you really think she'll kill you upon your return, why not try to stay away for as long as you can?"

# Chapter Eight

HEIKE

"Not bad," I admired Radax's picture on his brand-new passport. It cost me a pretty penny to make it happen this quickly, but the passport was definitely worth it. "How did you manage to turn out so well in a passport photo? Everyone looks ugly on those!"

He just smiled, rather shyly.

With the next flight to New York not leaving until that afternoon, we were sitting in the airport lounge. With so little time to plan, I'd only managed to get us economy class tickets.

On my way to Singapore, I had done a special coverage of the airline's luxurious sleeping suites and flown one of them. The experience had been amazing, of course, but not as relaxing as could've been expected. I'd had a cameraman follow me everywhere. He'd filmed everything, from me eating dinner to going to bed. I'd had to talk, smile, and wear a full makeup most of the twenty-hour flight.

Sitting in the airport lounge now, eating mini-burgers with Radax, both of us dressed in casual black t-shirts, felt more relaxing and comfortable than any luxurious suite could be. I was even looking forward to the flight, economy class or not.

Before leaving Xin's place, I'd checked Omkar's social media feed. Calling him didn't feel safe. With *bracks* on me heels, I didn't want to put Omkar at risk. He'd done enough for me already.

I was glad to see his new posts this morning. Omkar was alive and well. Completely oblivious to the danger he'd narrowly escaped last night, he gushed about "the most amazing show" on the social media.

Knowing he was safe and sound lifted a huge weight off me and made leaving Singapore possible.

"Here you go," I handed Radax his passport. "Keep it on you at all times."

He turned it in his hands with a frown. "You've been spending money on me."

"So?" I shrugged. Aside from paying for the passport, his ticket, and the food, I'd only bought him the shirt he was wearing—a plain black t-shirt was all he wanted. It stretched over his muscles in a visually appealing way. The view alone was worth every penny of the few dollars I'd spent on it. "Let's pretend I've hired you."

"To do what?"

I thought for a moment. "To be my bodyguard. With Madame's goons on my heels, I need someone to protect me, don't you think? In fact, I have to pay you a proper salary with benefits for your services."

I always tried to be mindful of my spending. I had to be when running a business. However, I rarely thought twice when spending money on my friends or family. People and relationships were the most precious assets in our lives. It made me happy to do things for them, including him.

Radax wouldn't really qualify as my friend—I'd known him for less than twenty-four hours. Learning his story, however, made me feel protective of him. I felt much closer to him than I normally would to someone I'd just met yesterday.

"I'll protect you, no matter what," he said. "You don't need to pay me for that."

"Why would you? Why would you do anything for me at all?"

He gave me a long look. "You've been kind to me."

I was flustered when met with his warm, umber eyes. My stomach fluttered in a way I hadn't experienced in a very long time.

"Kind?" I scoffed, unsure of what to do about my reaction to him. The admiration in his eyes disarmed me, and I scrambled to strengthen my defenses. "How? By jerking you off? It was a life-or-death situation. I didn't have a choice."

"The first time, maybe," he agreed. A slight shiver ran down my back at the thought that I could've died back in that cage with him. "Nothing forced you to do it the second time, though. I wouldn't have hurt you. I would've just left your friend's apartment, and you would've never seen me again."

"Yeah, and you would've gone back to that..." I let my voice trail off, unwilling to say her name or bring her up in any shape or form at all. I heaved a sigh instead. "I'm glad I could help."

He kept staring at me as if I were some kind of goddess myself. The wonder and admiration in his eyes unnerved me.

"Who are you?" he asked suddenly. The look in his eyes turned puzzled, like he was trying to figure me out.

"Me?" I squinted at him. "I'm Heike, remember?"

"That's your name, but where are you from?"

I blew out a breath. "Well, that's never an easy question. I was conceived right here, in Singapore. I grew up in Germany, near Munich in Bavaria, if you want the specifics. I live in New York now, but I travel a lot, so..." I spread my hands wide. "I'm from everywhere."

"But are you sure you are of this world?"

What was that supposed to mean?

"As far as I know. Yes!" I laughed. "That's the one thing I'm absolutely sure about, even if I never could quiet narrow down the country."

He kept staring at me intensely. I squirmed in my chair. It felt as if his gaze penetrated not only under my clothes, but deep into my heart, my very soul. I felt exposed, which made me extremely nervous.

I didn't have much to hide. My entire life had been laid open to public scrutiny since I was a kid, documented in every detail in promo shots, blog posts, videos, and Instagram pictures. Maybe that was why I guarded so rigorously the few parts of me I'd managed to keep private.

"You're a human," Radax finally said, releasing me from the trap of his gaze.

I exhaled in relief, masking my brief unease with a laugh. "Yes, I am. Never tried to conceal that fact or pretend otherwise."

"That makes no sense." He shook his head.

"How so?"

He took a long drink from his glass of water, looking like he was thinking hard.

"You went against Ghata's wishes," he finally said. "Twice. She called me to her, and you broke her pull. It takes magical powers to defy a goddess."

Magical powers? Did he really believe I was some kind of goddess, too?

Unease scratched harder inside me. I loved seeing that warm admiration in his eyes, but I didn't need his veneration. It implied a greater distance between us. I far preferred for him to see me as an equal.

I didn't want him to place me *above* himself. I wanted him to let me *in*.

I leaned over the table, closer to him.

"Radax, it was just a hand job," I said, keeping my tone casual. "Trust me, no magic powers are needed to do that. And Ghata might be a goddess, but she's a shitty person, if you ask me. If a little rub is all it takes to break free from her, then I personally will sponsor a massage parlor visit for each of her *bracks*."

He pressed his lips tight, hiding a smile in his beard, but it clearly reflected as a flicker of amusement in his eyes. It was gone way too quickly, like it always did, making me immediately miss it.

He shook his head. "Buying sex for a *brack* would be a waste of money. We don't physically react to a human or another fae. There's only Ghata for us."

She controlled everything, from his pain and healing to his arousal and release. Something pinched my heart. It wasn't just a compassion this time. It came with a hint of sadness and regret, and... envy.

It couldn't be jealousy, could it?

I wasn't vying for his attention over another woman. Yet the unpleasant feeling twitched inside me at the thought that nothing real could ever be possible between Radax and me. Because he literally "belonged" to someone else, against his will.

It felt like Ghata had won without her even trying.

Grabbing my glass of mango juice, I took a long drink. The familiar sweet taste helped push the unpleasant feelings away somewhat.

I dropped my gaze, and it landed on the arm Radax had placed on the table. The swirly lines of his tattoos formed a picture, I realized. Looking closely, I made out stylized figures of creatures with torsos of men and heads of beasts and landscape of vistas and trees. The long body of a serpent but with clawed paws and wings coiled all around his bicep.

"What do your tattoos mean?" I asked, trying to figure out the rest of the images. Many of them looked like symbols—intricate glyphs or possibly hieroglyphs of a language I didn't recognize.

He rolled his right shoulder back, glancing down at his arm.

"These are *voukalaks*, the animals that the werewolves came from." He pointed at the animal maws of the creatures with human bodies. "That's what they were called before they became sentient beings. That's the beginning of the werewolves, and therefore the origins of the *bracks*. The tattoo is a depiction of a *brack's* life and his dedication to the goddess—our vow to her in images and words."

Ghata not only forced them to recite the vow while she raped them, she made them wear it on their skin for as long as they lived.

I never hated anyone in my life as deeply as I hated her. The dark feeling threatened to suffocate me. I took another gulp of my juice, welcoming its thick, soft sweetness.

"How did she get away with all of it? Was no one ever appalled by what she was doing? Have the families of the boys never found out what was going on?"

"None of us were ever allowed to talk to our families. We forgot all connections to them the moment we entered Ghata's servitude. Eventually, however, her atrocities had spread beyond her temple, enraging the werewolves. She was overthrown and would've been held accountable for everything had she not fled Nerifir and come to this world."

"Great," I muttered under my breath. "Now we have to deal with her here."

A thought entered my mind.

"Listen, if Nerifir was able to get rid of her, there must be a way for us to fight her, too."

Doubt crossed his handsome face.

"My world is populated with fae who are much stronger and more resilient than humans. We have magic."

"And it took you… How long? Millennia? To figure out what kind of a person she really is."

"Exactly."

I bit my lip. If Ghata intended to do here the same things she did back in her world, she had to be stopped.

"But your kind didn't know Ghata's true nature when they embraced her," I said to Radax. "No one knew then what I know about her now."

Did it place an obligation on *me* to stop her then?

But how?

"You mentioned she'll get more powerful if a larger number of converts join her, right?"

He nodded. "A goddess's strength is in the faith of her followers. The more people believe in her, the more powerful she gets."

"Has she been actively recruiting new 'believers,' then?"

"That's going to be her main focus—her *only* focus—from now on."

"Is that why she ended her show?" I guessed. "To put all her energy in recruiting?"

He nodded again.

"The show was to raise the money she needed to gain the first followers. As her following grows, she'll be getting more in donations from them than she could ever make on her own."

I thought about what he'd said.

"If she's just starting to recruit in earnest, stopping her would be best done sooner rather than later, before she gets her full strength."

"I suppose." He looked closely at me again.

I finished my juice and clasped my hands on the table in front of me.

"Can she be killed?" I asked. "Like if someone were to stab her—"

He frowned, and for a moment, I thought he might be angry with me for daring to plot the demise of his idol.

"You're not going to do that," he said firmly.

"Well, I'm just brainstorming here—"

His eyes flashed red, sending a flock of cold shivers down my arms.

"You can't pull off an assassination of Ghata by yourself," he raised his voice. "You're a mere mortal human."

He said it as if being a "human" was like being some kind of primitive, one-cell life form, capable of nothing.

I snapped my back straight.

"First of all, I'm just trying to figure out what can be done at all, for now. It's not like I'm planning to rush her with a kitchen knife any time soon."

"A kitchen knife won't do anything to her. I don't think even the iron from Nerifir can harm her."

I squinted. "What's so special about that iron?"

"Weapons made from it are the only kind capable of killing a *brack* or a fae in this world."

"So, if even *they* don't kill her, does it make her invincible?"

How would one fight an immortal, indestructible goddess? Now, I actually felt like the weak, puny human Radax thought me to be.

His frown deepened. The way he shifted his stare away caught my attention.

"Are there ways to defeat her?" I asked quickly.

He worked his jaw, moving his beard.

"Radax?" I prompted, grabbing his hand. "If there are, I need to know."

He finally met my eyes. "You can't do it on your own, Heike."

"Why on my own? Wouldn't you help me?" I tilted my head, smiling at him sweetly.

My smile did nothing to lift the dark shadows gathering over his expression.

"I may not be around for much longer," he said.

His words crushed my heart. Just like everything else, his life and death were not his own. He couldn't promise me anything because he had nothing to give.

"Then tell me everything you know." I swallowed hard. "While you still can."

He stared at his empty glass, turning it on the table in front of him. The half-melted ice cubes clinked with each turn of his fingers, marking moments before he finally spoke.

"You can't do it alone," he said again.

I wasn't sure if I was going to do anything at all, to be honest. But I felt I had to do something. If Ghata really was what Radax told me she was, big things were coming. And if so, I wanted to be a part of that in some positive way.

Everyone I knew, every single person in my network, had always been searching for that one big event, a sensation that would blow up all over the world. No one knew exactly what that could be, just that it'd be something huge, amazing, incredible.

Extraordinary.

The more I spoke to Radax, the more I believed we might be on the verge of such an event. And there was no way in hell I was going to miss it. I needed to be a part of it.

"I don't have to be alone," I told him. "I could assemble an army."

If Ghata was recruiting followers, so could I. I might even have a head start already.

"No." Radax shook his head. "An army of humans wouldn't be effective against Ghata. You need fae on your side."

"Fae?" I stared at him, then it hit me. "Are you saying there're more beings who came from your world to ours? Holy shit..."

My breath hitched, and a tingle of anticipation along my back grew stronger.

An otherworldly goddess and her monks were an astounding discovery on its own. But an opportunity to meet a real-live fae...

"Are they werewolves? Where are they? We need to go meet them—"

Radax lifted his hand, cutting off my verbal stream of excitement. He rubbed his chin with the other hand, his fingers sinking into his beard.

He kept silent. Impatience drove me mad.

"If you don't want me to do anything stupid on my own," I urged him, "it would help if I could at least talk things through with someone who knows more than I do, don't you think?"

He heaved a breath, meeting my stare.

"Heike, you really don't need to do anything at all to stay safe."

I leaned back in my chair and crossed my arms over my chest.

"Of course, I can do absolutely nothing. You told me to stay out of her way and all would be fine for me. For how long, though, Radax?" I leaned forward again, peering into his eyes. "How long will my life be safe if I let Ghata wreak havoc in my world the way she did in yours? What if I have a son one day? Will he be safe from her? How about my grandson? How many human boys will she turn into her slaves before she gets to any of my friends and their families? You said you know what it's like to care for someone. You should understand, then."

He winced and shoved his glass aside.

"There're two fae in this world that I know of," he finally said. "But I have no idea if they'll be willing to help us or if they'll even listen to us."

Only two? I tried not to show my disappointment.

"As long as they don't shove us into a cage and ship us back to Ghata," I said.

"They won't," he replied confidently. "I know for a fact both of them have good reasons to dislike her, even more than you do."

"How?"

"Ghata had us kidnap them. She displayed them both, like how she displayed me for the past few months."

*Months.*

Last night might've been Madame's final show, but it wasn't the only one. My skin crawled when I thought about everything Radax had endured at the hands of his "goddess."

"What a bitch!" I cursed under my breath, unable to hold back. "Let's hope the fae you're talking about will be willing to help us. How do we find them?"

"Finding them is the easy part. I know exactly where they are."

"You do?" I blinked.

"I've known for months," he said. "But I've been covering up their tracks, so Ghata wouldn't find them again."

"Why?"

He shrugged. "I made a deal with one of them."

For someone who wasn't allowed to have any life of his own, Radax had found a way to defy the rules. I was glad that he had.

"You made a deal behind Ghata's back? What if she found out about that?"

"I'd be dead."

"Why did you do it then?" I tried to understand. "Do you care about them?"

He rolled his head to the side, stretching his neck in a gesture of unease. It appeared he wasn't entirely clear himself about his reasons to risk his life for the others in this case.

"I don't know them that well," he finally replied. "But if I helped Ghata find them before she closed her show, she would've tried to capture them again. Innocent people might've died."

"So, you risked your life for fae who were practically strangers to you?"

He rubbed the back of his neck.

"My life isn't worth much. And those two have something to live for."

"What is it?"

"Love."

My jaw dropped in surprise. This was not an answer I'd expected. "Love?" I repeated, dumbfounded. What would a *brack* know about that? It went against everything he'd told me about his kind.

"Both fae have women in their lives," he explained.

"And that makes their lives more valuable than yours? Makes life worth living?"

"What else if not that?" he asked sincerely. "My life had the most meaning when I had someone in it."

"You had someone? A woman you loved?" Questions burst from me as my curiosity spiked.

"There're many kinds of love," he said quietly, as if to himself.

The statement sounded cryptic in his case. Did he personally experience more than one kind of love? Or did he just hear about that from others? Was he simply quoting someone? Or did he speak from the heart?

He'd told me he remembered nothing before Ghata. And after she'd made him her *brack*, there hadn't been anyone but her. What kind of love was he talking about then?

"What do you mean? Where is that woman now?" I asked.

He blinked, his brows twitching into a frown.

"She's not here." He cleared his throat. "Anyway. You want to know where the fae I've mentioned are?"

"Yes, that too." I shifted closer, needing to hear more about the woman. "But also—"

"They're on an island, in the Bahamas." He cut off any questions I had about her. His expression hardened, letting me know he was done talking about the woman or his love for her. "About three months ago, Ghata figured out I'd been hiding their location from her. She used her power to force me to reveal it to her. Then she sent most of the *bracks* she'd just brought from Nerifir—over a hundred of them—to the Bahamas to kill the fae. None of the *bracks* came back."

"Did two fae kill the entire hundred?"

Each *brack* was the size and strength of Radax, impossible to kill unless one used some kind of special weapon he'd told me about or magic. And those two fae exterminated a hundred of his kind?

Apprehension tightened around my chest. There were some truly dangerous beings in our world.

"Yes," he replied. "I believe both fae are still on the island."

"What if they kill us too when we come to speak with them?" I was all for the adventure or the quest or whatever the heck this was I'd gotten myself into. But it would suck to die during the very first part of it.

Radax gave me a half smile. "We'll be coming to talk with them, not to fight them, right?" He patted my hand reassuringly.

"Right." I sure hoped so. "I guess we'll have to change our flight, then. Where about on the Bahamas are they?"

"You want to go there right away?"

"Well, I'm my own boss, free to do as I please." I smiled, getting my anxiety under control somewhat. "Like you said, Ghata is growing stronger every day. The sooner we figure out what to do about her, the better."

# Chapter Nine

HEIKE

The long flight felt endless, with two stops on the way. The only sleep I'd gotten was a catnap here and there, leaning against Radax's arm in the seat next to me.

Paid or not, Radax took his job as my protector very seriously.

A man bumped into me at the exit from the Miami airport, his shoulder crashing into mine.

"Fuck. Watch where you're going," he cursed, giving me a dirty look.

I drew in some air to say back something snappy. *He* bumped into me, after all, while he was looking at his phone. *He* should be the one watching where he was going.

Radax wedged his shoulder between us, shoving the man away without even using his hands.

"Hey! Easy there, fucking rhino!" the man yelled without looking up. He nearly choked on the last word as he slowly raised his eyes all the way up Radax's impressive height. His jaw dropped. Fear flashed across his face when he met Radax's glare. "I mean... You know..." he mumbled, trailing off.

"Apologize," Radax demanded. His voice was quiet, but it rumbled like approaching thunder, low and menacing.

"Sorry," the man squeaked, his eyes shifting between Radax and me.

"You better get off that thing." I tipped my chin at the phone in the dude's hand. "Or you'll risk getting crushed by *a rhino* next time."

Radax wrapped his arm around my back, drawing me closer to him as he maneuvered us through the crowd.

"Are you okay?" he asked me.

"Sure," I chirped.

Having traveled alone most of my life, I had no problems fighting my own battles. I never needed anyone to take care of me or protect me. But I never knew that it'd feel so...nice to have someone looking out for you.

Having Radax on my side made me feel invincible.

Once we climbed in the cab to take us to the hotel, I found his hand on the seat between us. Squeezing it tight, I held it all the way to the hotel.

"We'll get room service, if you don't mind," I told him. "I don't know about you, but I'm exhausted."

"I don't mind," he said simply. "Room service is fine."

I stumbled into the hotel lobby, hanging onto his arm. By that point, my shoes felt like torture devices. My intense love for high heels nearly cost me an ankle as I tripped over the threshold.

Radax caught me.

"You need some rest," he muttered under his breath, practically carrying me to the reception desk with his arm around my middle.

"Two double beds or one king size?" the lady behind the desk asked.

I furtively glanced at Radax, who was now scanning the street through the high windows of the lobby and seemingly paying little attention to my conversation with the woman. The memory of me pressing to him during my naps on the planes, in the cars, and the airports warmed my chest.

"King size, please," I said, quickly.

Radax had told me he didn't "react" to human women, anyway. What harm would there be if I stole some more of the comfort I'd felt when sleeping next to him? He wouldn't care either way, would he?

The moment we made it up to our room, I kicked off my heels.

"Aaah," I exhaled, walking barefoot on the soft carpet. "Honestly, the best part about wearing these shoes is taking them off."

"Why would you wear such uncomfortable shoes, then?" Radax walked the perimeter of the room and checked the window, watching for any signs of danger, I assumed. I was grateful for him doing what I was too tired to care about at the moment.

"Because they're pretty!" I smiled. "Just look at them." I pointed at my discarded colorful, crystal-studded, strappy heels.

He shrugged. "You don't need them for that. You're pretty just the way you are."

I'd been called beautiful by my followers, photographers, marketing campaign managers, my PR clients, by random guys who wanted to get in my pants. I couldn't recall the last time someone called me just pretty.

Somehow, Radax's simple compliment sounded more important than any of the praise I'd received from so many others.

My cheeks warmed, and I realized I also couldn't remember the last time a man had made me blush.

"Do you want to take a shower?" Radax asked, checking the bathroom.

"I want to eat first." My stomach seemed to be curling in on itself, it was so empty.

"Do you mind if I shower now, then?" He took his shirt off.

"Sure. What do you want me to order for dinner for you?"

"Whatever." He shrugged. "I'll eat what you'll eat."

Maybe because Radax had spent years living on fast food, he was the least picky eater I'd ever met.

"I'll get us steak?" I suggested, feeling like spoiling him with something nice.

"Thank you. I'd love that." He gave me an excited smile before going to the bathroom.

I ordered dinner, then took my clothes off, too. I'd left all my things in my hotel room in Singapore. We'd decided retrieving them wasn't worth the risk. When I'd really thought about it, all my belongings were replaceable, even my laptop. I'd bought a few necessities for Radax and me at the airports as we traveled. One of them was a thin terry-cloth bathrobe that I put on now.

Barefoot and in a bathrobe, all I needed now was some food, a shower, and a little bit of sleep to feel like myself again.

"Dinner is here!" I yelled toward the bathroom door when a hotel employee brought the tray with silver dome covered dishes. He deposited it on the bed as I'd asked.

Closing the door after him, I heard a loud thud from the bathroom.

"Radax?" I called, concerned. "Are you okay—"

A strangled groan cut me off, and I dashed for the bathroom door.

"Radax!" I knocked on the door.

He didn't answer. A dreadful premonition weighed heavily on my chest.

"I'm coming in," I warned, afraid to lose any more time.

He'd left the bathroom door unlocked, which made little difference —I would've broken the lock if I had to.

Radax lay in the tub, the shower water crushing down on him. Gritting his teeth, he arched his back with another groan of pain.

"What happened?" I ran to the tub, then shrank back as realization hit me. "It's *her* again, isn't it?"

His jaw clenched, he couldn't speak, but I already knew the answer.

His tattoos pulsed red. His body tensed, as if frozen. And his skin flushed, the veins on his neck and forehead bulging thick. I didn't need to look at his crotch, either. I knew Radax was hard as a rock.

I thought I'd taken him far enough from Madame's influence. But he was right. The distance made no difference to her.

"No fucking way," I gritted through my teeth, ripping off my bathrobe.

There was no one here to help him. He couldn't even go back to her soon enough—I'd taken him half the way across the world from her. It was just me here. I was all he had.

"Just give me a minute, babe." I climbed into the tub and under the shower stream with him. "It'll be fine," I promised, getting to work.

Grabbing the soap, I lathered my hands before taking him between my palms.

He hissed the moment I touched his straining hard length.

However, his muscle spasms must've let go, as he was finally able to sit up. His hands continued to grip the edges of the bathtub so hard his arms shook and his nails screeched against the hard surface.

"There you go," I murmured, as if my soothing voice was enough to banish the evil taking over his body.

He let go of the tub, reaching for me. His fingers flexed, trembling. Stopping short from touching my shoulder, however, he jerked his hands away and hid them behind his back.

The shower washed the soap off his erection. I moved to get more, but paused. His was probably the most beautiful dick I'd ever seen—perfectly proportioned, even if on the large side. I traced with my fingers the thick veins that ran along his erection, wondering what they would feel like under my tongue instead.

His moan sounded like an approval of my thoughts.

Leaning closer, I wrapped my lips around the tip. Hard and smooth like silk-covered rock, he smelled of the soap I'd just used. Flexing my lips, I slid my mouth up and down his shaft. Water sluiced down my head, plastering my long hair to the side of my face and over his thick, muscular thighs.

Sliding my mouth up, I glanced at his face.

He stared back at me. Unlike both times before when his awareness was obscured by pain and torture, the expression in his eyes was clear this time. The desperate need was still there, but he looked like he really *saw* me. And as if he wanted *me*.

Desire flashed in his red glowing gaze, brief like a spark of his tattoo. But it zapped through me with a flash of heat in response.

I pressed my thighs together, my hips rocked as if on their own. I worked him with my mouth, faster and faster. And when he came, with a tight strangled moan, I swallowed. He tasted fresh—a mild, pleasant fragrance with a hint of coconut from the hotel soap.

He released a long breath, mixed with a deep groan of relief. His hands slipped from behind his back, reaching for me again, but he yanked them away before touching my knees.

*"She doesn't like being touched,"* the memory of his words entered my mind unbidden.

I didn't want to think about Ghata, but I couldn't help it.

If being with her was the only experience he'd had, then his views of intimacy must be warped, too, like everything else that had to do with her.

I wondered if she'd gone down on him, too. She must have if she preferred to do all the touching herself. Maybe she'd even made him taste so good to please herself.

Thoughts of Madame churned my stomach. I hated thinking about her, not when I was in the bathtub with Radax, both of us naked. But her phantom presence seemed to hang over us like a storm cloud, invisible but menacing and ever-present.

I sat back on my haunches, searching his eyes.

The red had leached out of them, leaving their usual rich color of mocha behind. He dragged his gaze down my naked body. And this time, there wasn't just innocent curiosity in his expression. Heat pulsed in his gaze, warming my skin in its wake.

The muscles in his arms twitched. He raised his hands between us.

I drew in a shaky breath, unsure of what he'd do, unsure of what I wanted him to do.

He leaned in closer, still not touching me, his gaze the only connection between us. It had the effect of an embrace on me. I couldn't get away, even if I wanted to.

"Your eyes are black," he said with reverence. "The same color as hers."

His words were like a lash of a whip across my heart.

It was one thing to think about her, even to feel her presence with us. *Talking* about her made it all so much worse, stronger, and more real.

The fragile connection I'd just felt with Radax shattered into pieces.

I cleared my throat, brushing my wet hair away from my face.

"Well, glad you're feeling better."

"Heike, wait." He leaned after me, but I promptly climbed out of the tub and grabbed my discarded bathrobe off the floor.

"Dinner is getting cold." Wrapping the bathrobe tightly around myself, I left Radax to finish his shower on his own.

Back in the room, I stood by the dresser, staring at myself in the mirror.

I looked nothing like Madame, nothing at all. She was a redhead, I was a brunette. She had more curves than me. Her voluptuous breasts and curvy hips made me look almost willowy in comparison. Her skin appeared to glow with delicate light. Mine was plain. Human.

Her beauty was both luscious and ethereal. But her cruelty made her unattractive to me in every way.

Our eyes were a different shape, too. But their color... I had to agree with Radax, my eyes were as black as hers. The author of an article in a magazine I'd modeled for described them as "onyx." A photographer I'd worked with called them "mysterious."

When I stared into my own eyes right now, I could almost see Madame in them, and that made the bile come up in my throat.

"Heike?" Radax stood behind me, fully dressed, his beard still damp from the shower.

I swallowed quickly to get rid of the tightness in my throat. Yet my voice still came out with a croak when I said, "Um, ready for dinner?"

I lifted a random dome from one of the dishes. "It should still be warm."

We ate in silence. He at the desk, me on the bed, with the tray in my lap. As hungry as I was, the food proved hard to swallow.

"Something upsets you," Radax finally stated, obviously catching my changed mood.

I could just dismiss it, say all was fine. What would telling the truth bring, anyway? What were we, Radax and me? Why did it matter? But I blurted out, needing to know, "When you look at me, do you think of her?"

"Who?" he blinked at me, his fork with a piece of steak on it hovering in the air.

"Madame. Ghata, or whatever her name is. You said we have the same eyes."

He put the fork down and came to sit on the bed next to me.

I refused to meet his eyes, suddenly feeling childish for confronting him. I despised that woman so much, it hurt to think he found any similarities between us at all.

He leaned over my tray toward me.

"Heike, you're nothing like her. How could you even think that?

You're kind and compassionate. She's cruel. You're generous. She uses everything as a currency—every minute of her attention has a price. You care about others. All she thinks about is herself. Ghata has but one goal—she worships herself."

I finally ventured a glance at him, needing to see the confirmation of his words on his face. He met my eyes openly.

"I was created to serve her," he said. "I may crave her touch, but I despise everything about her. Her eyes... They are a window to the darkness in her soul. I never thought I could ever look into the eyes of the same color and love what I see in them."

"You... You like my eyes?" I mumbled, dumbfounded.

A smile parted his beard.

"So much it shocks me." He shifted as close as the tray in my lap allowed. "When I look at you, Heike, I see the opposite of her, and it thrills me."

It may be the jetlag that kept me up at night. It didn't seem to affect Radax. He snored softly next to me in our king-size bed while I watched the lights from the passing cars move across the ceiling of the room.

Every time I closed my eyes, I saw the cage again, the giant with torn skin on his arm and neck, flames bursting from his open wounds. I heard his desperate roars of pain.

I found Radax's arm under the covers and snuggled against it. His tattoos lay dormant. No light, no fire, no evil energy emitted from them, just the warmth of his body.

He had taken the job of protecting me on this journey. But his being here meant so much more to me.

Lying next to me, Radax chased the nightmares away while I slowly drifted to sleep.

# Chapter Ten

RADAX

The moment they got in a cab, Heike got hold of his hand again. Joy—pure, warm, and tingling with pleasure—spread from her fingers to his and up his arm. When the sensation reached his lips, he smiled.

Smiling was a rare thing in all his interactions outside of those with Amira. It felt almost foreign to him—an unnatural stretch of his lips. But next to Heike, he couldn't resist it.

There was something about this slender woman with eyes black like coal and hair as dark as rich mahogany. She was simply a human, weak and fragile, like the rest of her kind. But he sensed a power inside her, a strength of spirit that not many had.

Was it enough to stand up against a goddess, though?

Everything he'd learned in the millennia of his existence told him it was not. That Heike would lose. But she had the courage to try, and that was admirable.

It was also contagious. Her determination gave him hope. An emotion he had not experienced for ages.

Maybe there was a way to fight Ghata. And if there was, he wanted to be a part of the force against her, even if they were destined to fail.

He knew he was as good as dead already, a corpse walking the Earth on borrowed time. If Ghata didn't kill him when she inevitably got ahold of him again, she'd do something worse than death to him.

His life had no purpose. But maybe his death would? Heike—this fierce, beautiful, crazy in her determination to save him, woman—gave him the chance to try.

As if sensing his thoughts were about her, she glanced at him warmly and squeezed his hand.

Another burst of joy exploded in his heart, making it beat faster. She didn't just give him a purpose, she brought him back to life.

"We're here," she said as the vehicle pulled over in front of private docks on Miami waterfront. The closest one had a small float plane tied to it. With a middle-aged man inspecting it. "Just stay close and let me speak, okay?"

She slipped out of the cab—elegant and beautiful, and so painfully fragile, it made his heart ache.

Heike gave him hope and purpose, both priceless gifts. There was nothing he could give her to repay them. All he had to give was his life. And he vowed then and there that it belonged to her.

If she was his power in spirit, then he was her strength. He'd be with her every step of the way, and he'd protect her until his last breath.

*Heike*

"Are you going to the island of Blue Cay?" I asked the pilot hanging out next to the small float plane at a dock in Miami. I'd left Radax to wait in the shade behind the gate to the dock while I spoke to the pilot.

Radax had said plane would be the fastest way to get us to the island where the fae lived with their human mates. After some research and a few phone calls, I was told this plane was the only one allowed to land near Blue Cay.

However, convincing the pilot to take us there presented some difficulties.

"Um, Ma'am, it's a private dock. You shouldn't be here." The pilot frowned.

I had to find a way to turn that frown upside down. Some men were easier to deal with than others, and I hadn't figured out this one yet. I feared, however, that he might be a man of duty, the most difficult kind to convince to break the rules.

"Oh, I'm Heike Schneider." I offered him my hand with the brightest, friendliest smile I could muster.

He accepted it, albeit hesitantly.

"I'm here with a travel and tourism channel." Then I added the name of one of my own YouTube channels.

He'd probably never heard of it. I doubted he knew my name, either. But it didn't really matter. In my experience, it wasn't names or words that opened doors and obtained information, but confidence and attitude.

I kept my voice firm and my body poised.

"I need to get to Blue Cay, please."

His expression softened somewhat, but not much.

"Blue Cay is a private island. You need to be invited by the owner."

That I knew, but after having spent hours searching the internet on the brand-new phone I'd gotten that morning, I found absolutely nothing on the island's owner. No phone number or any other contact information. Not even a name.

The only reason I knew the two fae I needed to talk to were on that island was because Radax had told me he'd seen the owner board this very plane once, back when he'd needed to confirm the fae's location.

The pilot stepped my way.

"Ma'am, I'm sorry, but you'll have to leave."

Radax moved out of the shadows from under the covered entrance to the dock. The gate was closed but not locked. He placed his hand on the handle, his attention on the pilot.

At the sight of Radax, the man paused, running a hand through his dark wavy hair peppered with gray. Uncertainty crossed his deeply tanned face.

"It's private property," he insisted, but faltered under Radax's menacing glare.

"Jose?" a feminine voice suddenly called from behind the gate. "Is everything okay?"

I turned to find two young women standing behind Radax. With their appearance, Radax stepped back again, watching them from the shadows.

One had chestnut-brown, wavy hair pulled back into a bun. The other one had bright, ombre blue-and-pink waves that reached past her shoulders. Both women were dressed casually, holding several shopping bags in their hands.

"What's going on?" the dark-haired asked, her eyes flicking between the pilot and me. She placed her hand on the gate but remained on the other side of it. "How may I help you?" She focused on me, her expression polite but wary.

"She asked about Blue Cay," the pilot raised his voice behind me.

"Why?" The brunette's dark eyes remained on me.

Both women obviously knew the pilot and appeared to be on their way to board the plane. They must know the fae on the island, too. I suspected these were the mates of the fae Radax had told me about.

I gave them my best disarming smile. "We'd like to speak with the owner."

"We?" The brunette swung her head to Radax.

Her gaze landed on his tattooed arm, and her tanned face paled.

Dropping their shopping bags, both women recoiled from the gate as if it had suddenly turned into a snake. The dark-haired one placed her arm in front of the other woman, as if shielding her.

"Stay back, Ivy," she said softly, her guarded stare trained on Radax like a weapon.

Lifting my hands up, palms forward, I took a small step their way.

"He won't hurt you. I promise. We just want to talk."

My words had no calming effect on them, whatsoever. The woman with the pretty, multi-colored hair, the one the brunette called Ivy, looked around with a terrified expression.

Was she searching for more *bracks?*

"Ghata, or Madame, or whatever name you know her by, she's not here," I said slowly, in a calming, reassuring voice. "Neither are any of her *bracks*. Radax is the only one here with me, and he's not a threat."

I reached over the fence and placed my hand on his tattooed arm, not sure why. To demonstrate to the women that he didn't bite?

"Radax wants to help me," I said. "To help all of us."

"Who are you?" the brunette asked. The suspicion on her face didn't ease.

"My name is Heike. Heike Schneider." I decided not to offer my hand this time, lest I scare them more than they already were.

"What do you want?" Ivy demanded.

I glanced over my shoulder at Jose, the pilot. He was standing nearby, looking ready to physically kick me off the dock if he got the order.

I leaned closer to the women over the gate and lowered my voice, getting straight to the point. "I need to talk to the fae from Nerifir. The werewolf and the siren."

"Why?" the dark-haired woman asked. "What do you want with them?"

"Stella." Ivy's voice rang with warning.

By asking her question, Stella had basically acknowledged both the fact that the fae really existed and that she knew them. She realized that too, pinching her mouth tight.

Ivy squinted at me. "What did you say your name was?"

"Heike—"

"Oh!" Recognition spread across her lovely face. "Are you that girl from Instagram? The one with the fancy cars?"

I wasn't famous enough for paparazzi to chase me on the streets, but people often recognized me from some place or another. I did help launch a new sports car model last year, providing an extensive coverage across most of my social media accounts.

Personally, I would've expected Ivy to be familiar with my much more successful hair care product review series that I did this year. But if the fancy sports car had caught her attention, so be it.

"Not my cars." I smiled, shaking my head. "I don't own any of them, just helped promote them. But yes, the 'Speed and Style' campaign was me." I flicked my hair over my shoulder.

It was incredibly hot here today. Black might be my favorite color to wear, but it was so very wrong for Miami this time of year. Sweat started gathering on my back under the blanket of my long, dark hair.

"I know her." Ivy turned to Stella.

The other woman lifted a shoulder. "So she's on Instagram. That doesn't mean anything."

"Guys." I gripped the gate. "I swear, we don't mean any harm. I went to Madame's show in Singapore. That's where I met Radax." I tipped my head in his direction. "And, honestly, he's a victim here. Ghata has been abusing him for centuries."

Both women shifted their attention to Radax. He'd been staying quiet all this time, letting me handle this from behind the shield of his body.

He folded his arms across his chest, taking a wide stance—looking opposite of the victim I tried to portray him as.

"Can we come to Blue Cay with you?" I asked the women, imploringly. "To speak with your men?"

Ivy flicked her gaze back to Stella.

Stella shook her head resolutely. "He can't come anywhere near the island." She flipped her thumb at Radax.

"Will you take me if I came alone?" It wouldn't be ideal, but it'd be better than nothing.

"No," Radax broke his silence. "It's not safe."

I exhaled a sharp breath, throwing both hands in the air. "You know what, we're not going to get anywhere here without a little bit of trust from both sides."

"What do you want to talk to us about?" Ivy crushed the hem of her loose, canary-yellow top in her hands.

I opened the gate and came out to their side. "Radax shared some information with me about Ghata's plans. If she succeeds... Well, our world's not going to look like anything either you or I would want. No one on Earth knows what we're dealing with here. I need to talk to someone who is from Nerifir, who is aware of Ghata's true nature. And maybe together we can come up with a way to stop her."

"You want to stop a goddess?" Stella gave me a look filled with doubt, but not without some interest.

"And what's in it for you?" Ivy narrowed her eyes at me. "Do you want to get a viral video from it or something?"

I cocked a hip. "If I do get something worthwhile on camera, I'm not saying I wouldn't want to post and share it. But I promise not to make public any footage without your prior written permission. Would that work?"

Ivy chewed on her lip, and Stella kept eyeing Radax suspiciously.

I heaved a sigh, nudged by impatience. "Fine. I'll sign a contract if it helps. I'll put it all in writing."

"I don't care about contracts." Stella smoothed her hands down her pale-blue summer dress. Her eyes remained guarded. "I just don't want Lero and Zeph hurt."

I assumed Stella was talking about the fae. Radax hadn't mentioned their names.

"Stella," I turned to her. "Lero and Zeph have defeated hundreds of *bracks*. Just the two of them. Why would they be afraid of one Radax here? He has no intentions of harming them, at all."

I glanced at him, wishing he could make himself look smaller somehow, a little less threatening or imposing. Harmless. With his height, muscles, and glare, that was just wishful thinking, though.

"Do you know Radax has been protecting your whereabouts from Ghata for months?" I addressed both women. "She forced him to reveal it in the end, then brutally punished him for hiding it. I swear. He is not a threat."

Stella turned to Ivy, as if searching for her approval.

Ivy regarded Radax for a few moments.

"He saved my life once, against Ghata's orders," she said to her friend softly. "And he made a deal with Zeph to keep the rest of the *bracks* away from us."

Stella propped her hands on her hips.

"Fine. We'll take the two of you to Blue Cay, but we'll be watching you. And just to let you know," she said with added emphasis. "Zeph and Lero didn't defeat the *bracks* all on their own. Ivy and I were with them. There are four of us with special powers, not two.

And if you so much as think about hurting one of us, you'll be very sorry."

The island looked simply gorgeous from the air, like a green and gold jewel set in the lapis lazuli of the water.

Jose landed on the surface of the small lagoon, then beached the plane backward and tied it to a nearby tree.

A dark-haired man in a white shirt and light-colored pants jogged down the path from the house on top of the hill.

"Lero!" Stella climbed out of the plane and ran to him.

He caught her in his arms, kissing her thoroughly as if none of us were around.

Radax helped Ivy and me off the plane, then assisted the pilot with unloading of some crates and shopping bags.

Lero spotted him. "What is *he* doing here?" he barked gruffly, his tone hardly softened by his French accent. "Ivy, come here," he ordered, shielding Stella from Radax with his shoulder. "Stay away from him."

Grabbing some shopping bags, Ivy headed Lero's way.

"It's Radax," she said. "He's from Madame's freakshow."

"I know who he is." Lero kept glaring at Radax. A low, threatening sound rumbled in his chest. "How did he get here?"

Stella touched his arm.

"He came with us. Heike vouches for his behavior." She gestured at me. "They want to talk to you and Zeph."

"Where is Zeph?" Ivy glanced toward the large house sprawling on top of the hill.

"Fishing." Lero wasn't taking his silver-gray eyes off Radax.

Ivy kicked off her flat sandals and wandered into the waves that softly kissed the beach.

"Get back on the plane and leave if you value your life," Lero growled, moving to Radax.

Radax smirked at his words. "Not until you talk to Heike." He took his usual wide stance with arms crossed over his chest.

"Heike." Lero turned to me, schooling his expression from guarded hostility to neutral politeness. The purr of his accent now made his voice sound rather sultry when he addressed me with a slight tilt of his head, "We haven't met yet."

That was a courteous way to ask, *"Who the hell are you and what are you doing here, in my place?"*

"No, we haven't." I closed the distance between us, offering him my hand. "I'm Heike Schneider. It's very nice to meet you."

I gave him a friendly smile, which did little to soften the cold glimmer in his steel-colored eyes.

"How do you know him?" Lero jerked his head at Radax.

"We met when I came to Madame Tan's VIP show, and he was her main exhibit," I replied honestly.

"You?" Lero stared at Radax again. "Is that what Ghata has resorted to? Displaying her own *bracks?*"

"Are you surprised?" I replied as Radax remained silent. "Who or what would stop her from doing whatever she wants?"

The sea water bubbled and sprayed near the beach. Then an incredibly handsome man with silver-white hair emerged from the waves and rushed to Ivy.

"You're back!" He grabbed her into a hug and caught her mouth in a kiss, soaking her clothes in the sea water dripping from him.

"Zeph..." she murmured when he moved his kisses from her mouth to her neck.

A large fish in his hand jerked, slapping Ivy's thigh with its tail. She cried out in surprise, then burst out laughing.

"Dinner." He grinned, lifting the fish up by its gills.

Zeph spoke with a French accent, too. That I was not prepared for —French fae. Radax spoke American English, which was also bizarre, come to think of it. Somehow, I'd assumed someone from another dimension would speak some otherworldly language I'd never heard before and therefore have some out-of-this-world accent.

"How was the shopping?" Zeph placed another kiss on Ivy's cheek before finally paying attention to all of us on shore.

Zeph's handsome features distorted in an angry frown the moment his glare fell on Radax. The siren suddenly threw his arm forward. A thick stream of water blasted from the lagoon toward Radax. It hit him in the chest with so much power, it knocked him on his butt, both his black t-shirt and pants drenched.

"I said if I saw you again, I'd kill you and everyone who came with you!" Zeph roared.

He raised his arm again. The water around his ankles bubbled and rose—the magical power of a siren, no doubt.

Stunned, I dropped to my knees at Radax's side.

"We're not a threat!" I yelled in panic as Zeph flicked his wrist. The water leaped to his hand, like a well-trained dog ready to attack.

"Zeph, wait!" Ivy grabbed Zeph's arm, forcing it down. "They just want to talk."

The siren's chest heaved, his blue eyes sharp and cold like shards of glass. "How many of you are here?" he demanded from Radax.

Radax wiped the water out of his eyes with his arm. He shifted, placing his body between Zeph and me.

"Just me," he said. "I'm the only *brack* here, I swear. Heike is human. Please, don't hurt her."

Zeph swept the rest of us on the beach with his gaze. "How is he even here?" he asked Lero.

"Well," I spoke before Lero could answer. "It's a long story, and I'm not sure you need to know *all* the details, but we're on the run from Ghata."

"Is she after you?" Lero surveyed the horizon grimly as if expecting Ghata and her *bracks* to pop out from the water like Zeph had just done. "Will they follow you here?"

"No." Radax climbed to his feet. "She doesn't have many *bracks* left. You killed most of the ones she got from Nerifir last."

"Their fault." Zeph shrugged. "They'd still be alive if they didn't come here."

Water dripping from his beard and clothes, Radax helped me up from the sand. "I'm not here to discuss the past. Heike and I came here to talk about the future."

"Yeah, it won't be a nice future if we let Ghata do whatever she wants. She needs to be stopped." I brushed the sand off my black, tight-fitting pants. My clothes were also damp from the mist of Zeph's water blast, my high heels sinking deep into the wet sand of the beach.

"Are you planning to stop Ghata?" Lero gave me a measuring look. "You, a human woman?"

Stella nudged him with her elbow. "Lero, you of all people should stop underestimating human women."

He blinked, looking somewhat flustered by her remark.

"I've had the misfortune to glimpse what Ghata is capable of," I said somberly. "I don't want to go against her blindly and on my own. That's why I'm here. I need your help."

# Chapter Eleven

HEIKE

"Thirsty, anyone?" Ivy placed a large tray with drinks on the patio table.

All six of us were sitting outside by the enormous swimming pool at the back of the house.

"Oh, thank you so much." I grabbed the glass of apple juice mixed with sparkling water I'd asked for.

The sun had dipped to the west. The shadow of the house shielded us from its burning rays. Still, the heat remained unbearable.

"Let me check it first." Radax took the glass from me.

I licked my dry lips, looking longingly at the cold frosted glass as Radax inspected my drink closely, then took a sniff and finally a tiny sip.

The rest of them watched with interest.

"Are you afraid we'll poison you?" Stella tilted her head.

Ivy appeared less surprised by Radax's behavior.

"There's no *camyte* there," she said tersely. "I don't have *bracks* to supply me with the magical pink glitter that changes people's minds."

"*Camyte* is liquid." Radax calmly handed me my drink back. "The 'pink glitter' you're talking about is the pollen of *glacier saffron* that grows so high in the Mountains of Dakath that even gargoyles have a hard time finding it. The pollen has many uses. One of them is to facilitate obedience in humans."

"And in pigs, too, apparently," Ivy muttered under her breath.

For a human, Ivy seemed way too familiar with things from Nerifir that even the two fae, Lero and Zeph, kept silent about. I took a mental note to ask her a few questions later.

Radax studied the young woman intently.

"Did you feed your *glacier saffron* laced food to Yenric, the piglet from Madame's menagerie?" he asked her.

Zeph laughed suddenly. "Of course she did! The pig got the glitter." He gave Ivy an adoring smile, then pulled her from her chair and into his lap. "How else do you think she'd kept her presence of mind to help me escape?"

The siren had traded his swim trunks for shorts and a t-shirt before he'd come out to the patio. His hair was dry now. He nuzzled Ivy's shoulder, his hand sliding under the hem of her yellow top. She kissed his silver-blond head, wrapping an arm around his neck.

Lero's and Stella's chairs stood side by side, flush with each other. The werewolf and his woman held hands, their fingers intertwined.

Radax and I sat in the matching wicker chairs with almost two feet of space between us. A part of me wished he'd shift his chair close enough for me to hold his hand, too.

"How did *you* escape?" Lero asked Radax.

The stern expression on the werewolf's handsome face told me Lero might've believed Radax was not a threat, but that didn't mean he fully trusted him yet.

Radax slid his gaze my way. "I also had someone to help me. Heike got me out."

The warmth in his dark-brown eyes sparked a response inside me, rippling with pleasant tingles through my body.

"I left." Radax tore his attention away from me to address the rest. "But that doesn't mean I escaped Ghata." A dark cloud moved over his features. "A *brack* can never be free from her. I just want to use whatever time I have left to tell you everything I know and help you with whatever you decide to do next."

Lero narrowed his eyes to slits of steel-gray, sharp like blades. "What for?"

Ivy bit her lip before asking Radax quietly, "Do you think we really can do something about her?"

He leaned back in his chair, making it creak.

"It's for you to decide what you want to do with what I tell you."

Zeph shifted uneasily, both arms wrapped tightly around Ivy.

"Do you want to get even with Ghata? Is that it?" he asked. "And you hope we'll do your work for you?"

Ivy lowered her mouth to her man's ear. "There is no harm in hearing him out," she said softly.

"I'll settle my score with Ghata on my own," Radax bit out. "And I know I won't survive it. But *you* will live. You have a long life ahead of you. You must care about your future and what Ghata does to your world."

*"I won't survive it..."*

These four words kept ringing in my head, drowning out the rest. The need to hold his hand became unbearable. Instead, I took a long drink of my *apfelschorle* to force down the lump in my throat, then fisted my hands in my lap.

"How can a *brack* be angry with his 'goddess?'" Zeph asked sarcastically, a dark eyebrow arched gracefully.

"She took everything from him," I replied softly before Radax could.

Lero took a drink of his beer, looking perfectly composed. "Isn't that how one becomes a *brack* in the first place? That is the price of the immortality she trades—one has to give up *everything*."

He spoke about it as if Radax had made a fair deal with Ghata and now wished to back out of it.

"You obviously have no clue," I snapped at Lero. "A boy never gets to choose whether he wants to be a *brack*."

"Lero's not completely clueless, Heike. His brother was a *brack*," Stella explained softly.

Radax's brows twitched up. "Right. Dez was your brother, wasn't he?"

That was news to me.

Lero nodded somberly.

"Then you're lucky to be born *after* him." I refused to give him any slack, not when Radax was concerned. "Do you know how Ghata 'creates' her slaves, Lero?"

I turned to Radax briefly, silently asking his permission to tell. These people might be our hope, but they were practically strangers to us both. I needed to know he was okay with me speaking for him.

He nodded, and I whipped back to face the werewolf.

"Ghata rapes fourteen-year-old boys to make them hers. She breaks their will, robs them of their innocence and of any connection to their loved ones. She takes over their bodies and souls."

A muscle in Lero's jaw ticked and his throat bobbed with a swallow. Everyone stilled. Not a sound came as I continued.

"She's done it in your world. What and who will stop her from doing the same thing here, in ours?"

"Humans aren't werewolves. They don't have the magic that Ghata could use and corrupt," Zeph argued.

"She will use their faith," Radax stated. "She wants them to believe in her and worship her, and her alone."

Lero nodded slowly. "Their faith would serve as a direct connection with her, bypassing the Moon. It might give her an even stronger power over humans than she ever managed to get over werewolves."

"Is that really possible?" Zeph frowned.

Lero rested his chin on his hand, rubbing the dark shadow of stubble on his jaw with his fingers.

"We know now that humans can form bonds with fae, gaining access to the fae magic," he said. "They may not be born with it, but they can be its vessels. Strong emotions like love channel the magic. Human faith may carry that power, too."

"So, she will create faith in her human worshipers, then use it to further enslave them?" Zeph huffed with obvious disdain for Ghata.

"All the while feeding on it and growing stronger," Ivy added.

"Humans stand no chance." Lero shook his head.

Stella stared at him, then looked at all of us, one by one. "How do we stop her? Because we have to stop her."

That was the question that had been on my mind ever since Radax had made me realize the threat we were facing.

"How does one kill a goddess?" I asked slowly.

"Is it even possible? She's immortal, isn't she?" Doubt clearly reflected on Stella's face. "Maybe the best we could do is just neutralize her somehow?"

"Like locking her in a dungeon?" Ivy suggested.

Zeph exhaled a humorless laugh. "Even if that were possible, it'd be asking for major problems in the future—whenever someone releases her, accidentally or on purpose."

"Well, the werewolves managed to chase her out of Nerifir and into our world—" I started.

Ivy made a face. "Yeah, thanks a lot to them."

"Can we find a way to send her back?" I suggested.

Stella scratched her ear. "I don't think the werewolves would want her back."

"But they wanted to prosecute her, didn't they?" I glanced at Radax for confirmation. "What if we make her go back to Nerifir? Let them have her? They can prosecute her now. Hold her accountable for all her crimes in their world."

Radax shook his head. "One can't choose the time of arrival when traveling to Nerifir. She may arrive centuries into the future or several millennia back into the past when no one knew her. Then she'd start wreaking havoc there again."

Lero blew out a breath. "It's not like you can pack her up and ship away. She came to this world on her own. Werewolves didn't send her here."

"Because she was scared," Zeph added. "Maybe we could scare her again, enough to get her the fuck out of here?"

Lero looked skeptical. "Even if we manage to do it somehow, what will stop her from coming back?"

"Remember, unlike us, she is immortal," Stella inserted. "She can wait for a few centuries somewhere, until all of us are gone, then come back."

I had to agree with all of that.

"Banishing her would be a temporary solution." I released a sigh.

Worry pressed heavily on my chest.

"As long as she's alive, we'd spend the rest of our lives looking over our shoulder," Stella continued. "It'd be like sitting on a time bomb that may explode any day."

"Well," I moved my gaze around the table, stopping it briefly on each face. "The question remains, then. How do we kill a goddess?"

My gaze landed on Radax last.

"I have another question, too." Zeph leaned forward to better see Radax on the other side of me. "How often do *bracks* stray from their 'creator?'"

"Never." Radax held the siren's suspicious stare. "Unless she orders us to leave."

"Then how do we know you're not here on her orders?" Zeph arched an eyebrow in question.

Ivy raised her hand, silently asking for permission to speak. Radax's stare crossed with hers.

"Why are you not like the rest of them?" Her question was more on point.

Lero gave Radax a knowing look. "It's because of Amira, isn't it?"

I'd never heard that name before. Lero must know something about Radax that I didn't. I waited for his answer, barely realizing I was holding my breath.

Radax's eyes suddenly flashed red with understanding spreading on his face.

"You," he growled at Lero. "You told her how to cross the River of Mists, didn't you? Now she's gone!"

Lero squared his shoulders, gripping the armrests of his chair. Red flickered in his steel-gray eyes, too.

Goosebumps rushed down my arms. These creatures may look human, but they certainly weren't. I felt outnumbered. As if I've somehow landed in a different world, without ever leaving Earth.

A threatening rumble of warning vibrated deep in Lero's throat. "Amira made her own decision."

"Hold on." Stella placed a hand on the forearm of her werewolf. "What are the two of you growling about?"

For a human, she seemed awfully calm, unaffected by all this otherworldly energy crackling in the air around us. But being the "werewolf's woman" must have made her, if not a magical being herself, then obviously comfortable enough in this environment.

Her touch appeared to ground Lero. He closed his eyes, rubbing his forehead.

"Amira was a young woman who lived and worked in Madame's freakshow," he explained. "She helped me escape in exchange for the location of the portal to Nerifir. She made the decision to leave," he added with emphasis, staring straight at Radax. "She's had enough of Ghata's treatment. Unlike *bracks*, she was never bound to Ghata and could leave anytime. She saw her chance to be free, and she took it."

"Now I'll never know whether she's dead or alive." Radax's expression remained grim, though the red in his eyes dulled, rage replaced by sorrow.

I couldn't stand it and scooted closer with my chair, then grabbed his hand in mine. He immediately squeezed it so tight it nearly hurt, but I made no move to take it away.

"Give Amira some credit." Lero's voice softened. "I didn't know her well, but she seemed to have a good head on her shoulders and a plan. That's a good start to make it anywhere, even in Nerifir."

Radax inhaled deeply, then released a long breath, collecting himself.

"She was like a sister to me." He flexed his jaw.

"Your attachment to her must be what made you different from other *bracks*," Lero pointed out. "I've never seen one of them caring about anything or anyone other than Ghata and her wishes."

"Unlike other *bracks*, I have feelings of my own," Radax agreed. "I also have my own judgement, including that about Ghata's actions."

Ivy squinted at him. "Is that why you have a beard, while the rest of them don't have any hair at all?"

He rubbed his chin, raking his fingers through his beard.

"Hair loss happens right after one takes the *bracks'* vow. Ghata meant to distinguish us from werewolves whose bodies are completely covered in fur every full moon. It was supposed to be permanent, but I started growing a beard the year I found Amira."

"And Madame let you keep it?" Ivy asked.

He shrugged, with an icy glint in his eye. "It was that or forcing me to shave every day. Either way, it'd be a daily reminder to her that I'm different." He was clearly proud of both his beard and being different from the rest of the *bracks*.

"I bet Ghata hated to have the visual proof that her hold on you is weaker." Lero smirked.

"That must be the reason she stopped sending you to Nerifir," Ivy said. "It wasn't because *you* couldn't cross the River of Mists, but because *she* couldn't pull you through to her as easily anymore."

Radax appeared to think about that for a moment, then nodded in agreement. "That's entirely possible."

That could be why he'd been able to resist her pull now whenever she'd tried to force him to come back to her. He'd been fighting her hold on him. And as long as I could, I'd be helping him fight it.

"How long have you been with Ghata?" Zeph asked.

"I'm not sure. Longer than a millennium. Possibly two, two and a half? I don't remember."

Ivy's eyebrows shot up straight to her baby-blue hairline. "That's an awfully long time to be alive."

Stella whistled, her expression shocked. "Do you ever feel tired from living? Bored?"

"I felt resigned." Radax glanced at me, his beard parting with a smile. "But lately, I feel hopeful. Hopeful that all this long life may not be in vain after all."

He looked at me as if I gave his entire existence a new meaning. My chest felt suddenly too tight to draw a breath. I turned aside, blinking away the tears gathering in my eyes. His hold on my hand turned gentle, his thumb stroking across my knuckles.

Lero leaned forward. "You know Ghata better than anyone, then. What are her weaknesses?"

Radax huffed a humorous laugh. "I doubt she has any. Ghata has no attachments. She doesn't treasure anything, either a person or an object..." He paused, as if thinking of something. "Except for that book."

"What book?" Lero asked with interest.

"She has an ancient scripture. She keeps it in her shrine—"

"A shrine?" Ivy made a face.

Radax nodded.

"She had one in her temple in Nerifir, and she demands one built for her in every place where they worship her in this world, too. She has a small shrine she carries with her wherever she goes, either in a travel trailer or a hotel room. It includes hand-painted pictures of her in ceremonial clothing, magical moon crystals from Nerifir, candles, and that one book."

"What is in the book?" Lero insisted. "Have you ever had a chance to read it?"

"She stores the original in a gorgonian-made box. But a lot of people have read copies of it. The copies and pamphlets with excerpts of the text get distributed to all her followers to be shared. The text talks about her divine powers, about the wondrous things she's done, and the numerous blessings people who follow her will receive."

Of course. Every deity had a book—a written word to spread around to grow the faith.

"She copies and shares passages from it, but she always keeps the original locked and out of sight from humans. She once strangled a *brack* to death for leaving it out in the open."

Ivy gasped.

Stella lifted a finger for emphasis. "There must be something in the original text she doesn't want us to see."

Lero rubbed his chin in thought. "What do you think is in that book that she's guarding it so rigorously?"

"Her origin story, for one," Radax replied. "Ghata doesn't want this world to know that she's a lower goddess. Her original purpose was to serve as a connection between the werewolves and the Moon. Now, she wants to be known as the higher deity herself. Whatever is in that book, it contradicts her new ambition. She can't allow anyone to see that."

"If it has the story of her origin," Lero mused, "I wonder if it contains the path to her demise as well."

"*That* would make her want to keep it a secret," Stella agreed.

Zeph huffed a breath, leaning back. "Holy shit! That'd be like having an instruction manual on how to kill her."

"Why would she write how to kill her in her own book?" Ivy looked confused.

"A goddess doesn't write the scripture," Radax explained. "It comes with her."

"Just like an instruction manual comes with a toaster!" Zeph laughed.

Ivy frowned at his levity, but her stern expression didn't last long. Her lips twitched and her brow smoothed when faced with his disarming smile.

"How do we get a hold of the book?" Stella asked.

Lero turned to Radax again. "When is Ghata leaving Singapore?"

"The day after tomorrow."

"And where is she going?"

"To China first," Radax said. "Then, I don't know. Now that there're no more bookings for the show or ticket sales, she keeps her travel plans largely to herself."

"What is she going to do in China?" I asked.

"Visit her worshippers," he explained.

Stella cocked an eyebrow. "Does she already have many?"

"Thousands." Radax nodded slowly. "Hundreds of thousands. She's been working on that for years. Quietly, for now. She's been visiting communities, mostly disadvantaged so far—the less people have, the more she can promise them. But she's been gaining some footing in more affluent neighborhoods, too. One of the reasons she ended the show was because she's been getting enough donations. She no longer needs to run the exhibit."

Stella sighed heavily. "It's growing, then. Like a snowball."

"Right." Lero's expression turned more severe. "The longer we wait, the harder it will be to stop her."

"We need a plan." Any trace of amusement was gone from Zeph's face now. "We also need to know how to find her. We'll need to know how long she'll be staying in China and where she'll go after that."

"Finding Ghata won't be a problem," Radax said. The cold glimmer of determination in his eyes made me pause as everyone looked at him.

"Ever since I left," he explained. "I've been fighting her pull. All I have to do to find her is stop fighting it."

"Her pull?" Zeph asked.

"She wants me back."

# Chapter Twelve

HEIKE

Ivy placed a stack of clean towels on the foot of the queen-size poster bed in one of the guestrooms.

"Let me know if you need anything else."

She'd explained earlier that only she and Zeph lived in this house. Stella and Lero had another one on the opposite side of the island. I remembered seeing a second building from the air when we'd first arrived here. A narrow straight divided the island in two, with a small bridge connecting the two parts.

"Thank you. We're good," I replied as Radax placed our only piece of luggage—a generic carry-on suitcase I'd bought at the airport in Singapore—on a chair nearby.

Ivy paused on her way out, her attention on Radax. "What's your magic?" A spark of curiosity twinkled in her eye.

He looked at her with a slight frown of confusion. "I don't have any. I'm a *brack*. Ghata has control over my magic, now."

Ivy heaved a sigh, compassion crossing her face. "So, you no longer shift?"

Radax rubbed the side of his neck. “I do. Not into a werewolf anymore, but into something else. She calls us ‘rage shifters.’”

“Why *rage?*”

“Because it’s the build-up of rage that causes the shift in the first place.”

Ivy appeared to think for a moment. “I’ve never seen a *brack* shift.”

“Lucky you,” I mattered under my breath. An involuntary shudder shook my shoulders at the memory of giant, bloodied Radax in the cage, his wounds on fire.

Ivy slid her gaze to me. “How do his shifting abilities manifest in you?”

“Me?” I blinked. “Why? I’ve nothing to do with that.”

“But what can *you* do?” Ivy insisted.

I laughed. “Nothing. I’m just a human, remember?”

“Well, so am I, but...” She looked around, then grabbed a glass with my unfinished *apfelschorle* from the dresser by the bed. “May I? Or do you want to finish it?”

“No, go ahead.” I wondered what she needed it for.

“This is what I can do.” She dipped her finger in the liquid, swirling it around. The drink followed her movement, forming a funnel. When she lifted her hand, the liquid followed, rising in a glimmering spiral out of the glass.

“Wow!” I gasped, staring in awe. “How are you doing that?”

She grinned.

“When you love a fae, a bond forms between the two of you. I now have access to some of Zeph’s powers. Neat, isn’t it?”

She lifted her hand higher. The spiral stretched longer before disconnecting from her finger and splashing back into the glass.

Ivy licked the diluted juice off her finger. “Well, nothing too spectacular when I’m on my own. When I’m with Zeph, though, and there is a lot of water around, we can do a real show.”

I kept staring at the glass in her hand, struggling to believe what I’d just seen. It seemed so simple, like a stage trick that had to have an explanation.

“I’ve never heard of a magic bond between a fae and a human.” Radax looked outright shocked.

"Yeah, well, the bond is possible." Ivy shrugged with a smile. "We're a proof of it. Lero and Stella, too. She can make him shift any time, no full moon necessary."

Radax's eyes grew even bigger at that. "That's incredible."

Ivy nodded. "Lero's theory is that humans' strongest emotions are capable of performing miracles like real magic. Love is what created our bond. Heike." She turned to me. "You should be able to do something, too. Like Stella, I think you'd be able to make Radax shift. Have you tried?"

I cleared my throat, unsure of what to say to that. There was no love between Radax and me, no bond.

"I'm not a fae anymore," Radax pointed out.

"And, well... We're not a couple," I finally managed.

"Oh..." she suddenly looked flustered. "I'm so sorry. I put you in the same room, with one bed. You look so..." Her eyes shifted from Radax to me, then back. "I just assumed... Shoot. I didn't know. You each can have your own room, of course. There're plenty to choose from. Five."

"No," Radax protested quickly. "We'll sleep together."

I smiled, hearing that. Last night in the hotel, I'd made the decision to share the bed without asking him. Now, knowing that he also preferred to sleep with me made me feel all warm and fuzzy inside.

"We're good." I nodded without giving Ivy any explanation.

What could I say? I couldn't really explain the wonderful feeling I had when Radax lay in bed with me—light, comfort, serenity. I felt like next to him was the safest place in the world, and I didn't want to give up even a moment of that.

"Well, okay then." Ivy didn't argue. "Have a good night."

She left, and I turned to Radax.

"Would you like to go to the water for a little while?" It might still be the jetlag or maybe the events of the day, but I felt too anxious and unsettled to even think about going to bed yet.

"Sure." He opened the back glass doors for me. "Let's go to the beach."

The doors led onto a small private stone patio with a narrow path descending to a tiny strip of beach below.

I kicked off my high heels, leaving them on the patio. Radax took his boots off, too, then followed me down to the water barefoot.

"It's so beautiful here." I drew in a long breath of air rich with ocean scents.

The sun had almost set, now, with only a bright stripe of orange and red coloring the horizon. The heat of the day the sun had left behind lingered over the beach.

"Peaceful," Radax agreed.

It'd be too peaceful—too quiet—for me in the long run, but right now, it was exactly what I needed to free my mind from the gloomy feeling that had been hanging over me.

I walked to the water, my bare feet leaving clear prints in the firm, wet sand. "It'd be nice to have a place like this to come to relax once in a while, but I wouldn't be able to live here forever."

"Where would you like to live?" he asked.

"I'm not sure." I'd seen the world during my lifetime of travels and working internationally, but no particular part of it had attracted me to settle down yet. "The world is too big to settle in any one place, don't you think? There're still so many places I haven't seen."

He followed me into the water. The foam-laced waves lazily licked our feet.

"I think it's people not a place that make a home," he said thoughtfully—an unexpected insight from a man who had no home at all and didn't even remember what it was like to have one. "What other places would you like to see, Heike?"

I kicked at a wave, a spray of droplets glistening like jewels in the last rays of the dying sunset. "New Zealand, for one. I've been to Australia but haven't made it to New Zealand yet. Have you?"

His expression was serene—peaceful.

"No. I haven't been to New Zealand, either. The menagerie hasn't traveled that way yet."

Radax had traveled, but he hadn't really seen the places he'd visited. All his traveling had been done on someone else's schedule, with but one purpose—Ghata raising money for herself.

He had no idea how to enjoy a trip. Or how to live for himself.

Suddenly, I wished we could take a trip together one day, for no other purpose but to have fun.

I wanted to give him the world.

When I thought about the future, however, it was vague, like a heavy metal door slamming shut in my mind, not giving me a glimpse past tomorrow. What we had was only right now—this very moment—nothing more than that.

On the other hand, nothing stopped us from enjoying the little we had. Whatever tomorrow brought, tonight it was just Radax and me, and this warm, beautiful beach.

"Care to go for a swim?" I took off my black t-shirt with the picture of Singapore's skyline printed on it.

I only hesitated for a moment before taking off my bra next. It was the only bra I currently had, and I didn't want the sea water to ruin the satin. Besides, Radax had seen me naked before. Though, he was staring at me now as if seeing me for the first time.

"I don't have a bathing suit," I explained with a small shrug. "I should've bought one back in Miami."

Things had been happening so fast, there had hardly been any time for shopping.

"It'll be fine." I shimmied out of my tight black pants and lacy underwear. "No one will see us here."

The guest room was on the south side of the house, away from the other living areas like the main patio of the house on the east. The small beach nestled between two tiny peninsulas, each covered in tall, thick vegetation. Unless someone took a walk around the house, the beach was impossible to see.

It'd been too hot all day, and I'd been sweating in my black clothes for way too long. I was more than ready for a swim.

Walking deeper into the warm water, I heard the rustle of clothes as Radax disrobed behind me. I fought the urge to glance back, but lost.

Looking back over my shoulder, I stared with appreciation at his tall, muscular form as he strolled toward the water's edge. Strong and confident, he reminded me of a mountain that nothing would faze. The truth was far from that. Radax had not been his own person for an unfathomably long time. His mind, his heart, and his body weren't under his control…

A wave rolled above his knees, broken by his muscular thighs. Water sprayed his legs and hips. He splayed his hands open, catching the droplets on his fingers.

"So warm." He smiled, looking like he was genuinely enjoying it.

His body might not be fully under his control, I mentally corrected myself, but he had managed to wrestle some control over his mind lately. Neither did Ghata possess his heart, whether she wished for it or not.

Together, we walked a little farther, where the sea rose above my waist and where the waves concealed Radax's pelvic area from view. I raked my fingers through the swells rolling from the sea.

"Can you swim?" Radax asked, a note of concern slipping into his voice.

It felt oddly pleasant to have someone worry about me. I couldn't remember when anyone other than my parents did that. Radax's worry felt nice without being stifling.

"A little." I pushed off the sandy bottom, then swam for a few strokes. "Do you swim?"

Radax strolled next to me, the swells reaching up to his shoulders here. I threaded the water as it was too deep for me to reach the bottom.

"I don't swim, but I dive." Radax ducked under the water and out of sight.

"Radax?" I called with a smile. With the sun almost gone now, it was too dark for me to see him through the rolling swells.

My smile shrank and disappeared as the seconds went by without him coming up to the surface.

"Radax?" I called again, searching by touch around me. "Where are you?"

A moment before my worry would've leaped into panic, his bald head popped out of the water just a couple of feet away from me.

"You scared me." I exhaled in relief, swimming back to shore.

"How?" He followed me.

When the water was up to his waist, I reached down with my feet and touched the bottom. My heart was still racing, even though Radax was here with me, safe and sound.

"You were under for like...forever. How long can you hold your breath, anyway?"

Radax was not exactly a human. In this form, he looked so much like one that I kept forgetting he came from a different world.

"For as long as I want to," he said casually.

"You don't need oxygen to breathe?" I gaped at him.

"I do, but I can stop breathing for a very long time. Years, if I have to."

*Years?*

I stared at him in shock.

"So, you can't drown?"

"No." He cocked an eyebrow, a smile hiding in his beard. "It's not easy to kill a *brack*."

Another wave rolled around us, caressing my breasts. A fresh breeze puckered my wet skin with goosebumps, pebbling my nipples.

A chipped disk of the moon climbed from behind the horizon. It left a path of silver streaks across the surface of the ocean, the lights reflecting with silver glitter in Radax's eyes.

I dropped my gaze to the water churning between us.

"Good," I murmured. "I prefer you alive."

He came closer, his face right above me now. "I prefer to stay alive, too," he said, softly. "Now, more than ever."

"Radax..." I lifted my head, but forgot what I was about to say the moment my eyes met his.

His gaze trapped me. In the night settling over the island, his irises appeared like two pieces of the dark sky, sprinkled with a handful of silver stars—incredibly beautiful, almost ethereal, and rather out of place for the large, built-like-a-mountain Radax.

"Heike, I'm dying to touch you," he rasped, moving closer.

The little water that slipped between our bodies seemed to heat up. My skin warmed, tingling with anticipation. He'd never touched me before. Whatever intimacy we'd shared, he'd always kept his hands away from me.

"I'd love that, Radax," I breathed out. "I'd love to have your hands on me." I needed that more than I needed air at that moment.

He lifted his hand to my face. Sweeping away a strand of my wet hair, he traced the shell of my ear. Slowly, almost reverently, he caressed my jaw with the back of his knuckles.

A flock of tingles scattered along my skin in the wake of his touch, making me feel cold and warm at once. Had a man ever had this effect on me before? I couldn't remember. But this felt so new, so incredibly different from anything I'd ever experienced before with anyone else.

The sprinkles of stars in his eyes suddenly shifted. The sparks stretched into streaks, turning from silver to red.

Red! I began to hate this color.

Dread chilled me from inside, despite the warm sea.

"Radax," I whispered, worry spiking in me.

He gritted his teeth as the red streaks leaped from his eyes to his neck and right arm. The droplets of water on his shoulder sizzled and steamed.

"No..." I exhaled in horror. "Not again..."

I cupped his neck with both hands, as if I could stop the ominous red sparks just by blocking them from view. His skin burned under my palms. The muscles in his neck tensed. A grimace of pain crumbled his features.

The warm peaceful evening shattered, torn to shreds by the invisible, menacing force.

Ghata.

"Leave him alone," I hissed through my teeth, as if she could hear me.

I hated this. Hated to see him suffer. Hated what I had to do to stop it. That the intimacy between Radax and me had to happen out of necessity, not because I wanted to be with him. That I might never know whether he truly ever wanted to be with me or just accepted my help.

I hated that, for Radax, sex was impossible without pain.

Sliding my hands down his shoulders and arms, I kept whispering, "Leave him alone, let him be, stop hurting him. He is not yours."

My fervent wish expressed through words burned in my chest. I wanted her gone, vanished into the darkness she'd crawled out from. There was no place for her when Radax's hands were on me and our naked bodies were this close together. We needed no one else here with us, definitely not the evil of Ghata.

The intense hatred filtered from his tattoo, seeping into my hand, but I didn't recoil from it this time.

"Leave." I said firmly, packing a power of a punch in that one word.

Gripping his arms tighter, I pressed myself to him, the heat of his erection trapped between us.

"How has she been with you?" I kissed his chest, catching the salty droplets of seawater on my tongue. "Rough or gentle?"

He groaned, tossing his head back.

"Rough."

That didn't surprise me.

"Come to me, baby." I hooked one arm around his neck, bringing his face closer to mine. "I'll be gentle."

I'd be the opposite of her in every way. Nothing like her.

Taking his head between my hands, I touched his mouth with mine. A true kiss was impossible the way his lips were rigid and pulled back, baring his teeth in a grimace of pain. But I tried.

I slid my lips against his, flicking my tongue along them.

"Hold me, Radax," I begged against his mouth.

With a grunt, he circled my waist with his arm, lifting me up. I wrapped my legs around his middle, never stopping the caress of his mouth with mine.

Slowly, ever so slowly, his lips grew softer. I was able to gently suck the lower one into my mouth. With a tortured moan, he returned my kiss, curling his large body around mine.

I moved my hand to his back, pressing myself so close to him, there was no place either for air or water to pass between us. He took my breath away, leaving me panting when he finally broke the kiss.

My hand on his shoulder, I realized there was no more hostile power throbbing from his tattoo. When I slid my hand along his skin, a kaleidoscope of silver-white sparks fanned out along the black lines, instead.

*She* was no longer here.

Breathing got easier.

Radax's eyes, hooded and hot, stared at me, their irises like shards of starry sky. There was no pain in them now, just pure, undiluted hunger.

His erection hadn't subsided. Hard and hot, it poked me urgently from below.

"Are you feeling better?" I stroked his cheek.

"The pain is gone," he replied in a husky voice. "But I don't want to stop touching you."

He cupped my ass, holding me with one hand, my legs still tightly wrapped around his middle. With the other hand, he stroked my back.

Desire tingled and surged inside me. I squirmed in his arms.

A high swell rolled to shore. Radax braced against it, staying upright. I clung to him, like to a rock in a storm. The wave drenched us with foam and spray.

I giggled as Radax sputtered and shook his head, water dripping down his beard.

"I've no idea how sirens do it in the water," he grumped. "I'm taking you to bed."

# Chapter Thirteen

RADAX

For as long as he remembered, Ghata had been in his life. Even when he couldn't see her, he *sensed* her.

Her presence lived in him—unwelcome, feared, but necessary. He couldn't imagine existing without her. Stifling and suffocating, it allowed him to go on.

He always felt her displeasure. Lately, it had grown, churning in his mind and his chest like an inky-black monster, clawing and biting from the inside, urging the stray to return to his master.

Fighting her pull had grown harder as pain grew stronger, choking him, pressing him to run to the only place he knew he'd get a breath of air, even if the air was thick with poison—to Ghata.

Rage flared, overwhelming his senses. He needed to go to her, crushing anything and anyone who dared stand between him and his goddess.

Then, Heike touched him...

And his fight turned against himself. He couldn't hurt Heike.

Her hands glided along his skin—light and gentle. Her lips brushed his—warm, sweet, and fresh like summer rain. Every minute spent with her brought a new, rich experience. No one had ever touched him like that. No one had kissed him the way she did.

He couldn't sense her presence inside him, but he soaked up every sensation that being with her brought. His starved heart craved her attention, desperately, like a drink of water in a scorching desert. His very soul unfurled for her.

His reaction to her was visceral. And miraculously, his body responded to her, too.

Cool tingles pricked his neck and right arm, calming his pain and rage. The sea breeze chilled the feverish heat consuming his body.

Heike held his face between her hands, peppering his scowl with soft, tender kisses.

Something melted inside his heart, flooding his chest with gentle warmth. The sensation grew, spreading through his body and flushing his skin. Awareness of her naked body pressed to his rushed through him.

His cock rubbed against her lower belly. He was hard, and it had everything to do with the naked human woman kissing him—and with no one else. For the first time in many, many centuries, he drew in a full breath no longer tainted by the sickeningly sweet poison of Ghata.

"Hold me, Radax," Heike murmured, her soft voice chasing the last shadows away.

Fragile and delicate, she had the strength to challenge the goddess over him.

He held her in his arms, a true treasure that she was. Heat of her body seeped into his weary muscles, soothing the ache like a magical balm.

Gods, she was everything.

No matter how close he held her, he needed her closer. Every drop of sea water sneaking between them tried his patience. He needed to be in her. He craved to become one with her.

"I'm taking you to bed."

He needed to get her behind closed doors. Where he could have her all to himself.

She kept kissing his eyes, his mouth, the side of his neck. His tattoo sparkled and flashed with brilliant white, the lights rippling with iridescence.

"So beautiful," she whispered as he carried her up the path and into the guest room.

He held her tight, carrying her fast, like a thief stealing away with the most precious gem. The need for her grew, becoming a torture on its own. Sweet, achy torment that he couldn't get enough of.

Inside their room, he laid her on the bed. Her long, wet hair spread on the pillow like a splash of dark ink.

Her eyes shone in the night like a portal to a magical world he'd never even dared dreaming about. So beautiful. She was the most wonderful thing he'd ever seen in this world and any other.

His arms and legs on each side of her, he caged her in. Lowering his head, he kissed her lips. His hunger intensified, his cock straining harder. And with every glide of his lips against her soft, welcoming mouth, his confidence grew stronger.

He'd never made love to a woman before, but with Heike, he felt he could do it all. He could move mountains for her, cross the oceans and dimensions to get to her. And he could make love to her the way love was meant to be—pure and serene, passionate and pain-free.

She raised her bent knees, cradling his hips. His throbbing cock pressed against her core. A hot lightning of lust lanced through him. He wished to ravage her, right then and there. Instead, he broke the contact and shifted down her body.

Kissing her skin, he flicked his tongue out to taste her. Salt of the sea water mixed with her fragrance. He craved more. Moving lower, he dragged his tongue down her stomach, tickling her skin with his beard.

She squirmed under him, releasing a soft giggle. The sound sent another surge of lust to his cock, making it jerk.

Kissing her belly, he found her breasts with his hands and rolled her pebbled nipples between his fingers.

Her giggles turned to moans. Then she arched her back as he slid one thick finger between her legs.

At first, he drew on whatever limited knowledge he'd collected about female biology during his nights with Ghata. Now, he let his instincts guide him, carefully watching the way Heike's body responded to his touch.

He stroked between her warm, slick folds, then sunk his finger deep inside her. Tentatively, he brushed with his thumb over the hard, little bud above her opening.

Her hips jerked, meeting his touch. Her breathing hitched.

"Oh yes, Radax, yes…" she panted as he rubbed harder. "More…" she begged.

He'd give her more. He'd give her anything she asked for.

She fisted the sheets in her hands, her heels digging into the mattress, her toes curled.

He pressed his thumb harder, pumping his finger in and out of her.

Her eyes shut, her delicate featured distorted into a tortured expression. Her breathing stopped for a moment before rushing out in sweet, broken moans between her parted lips.

She was so incredibly beautiful.

Her skin flushed. Her wet hair tangled and mussed. Her legs trembled as she came hard on his hand.

She seemed especially vulnerable and fragile when exposed to pure pleasure like that. Protective feeling swelled in his chest. Whatever happened, he'd stay with her. As long as he lived, he'd shield her from any evil, even from the one that lived inside him.

"Oh God, yes," she moaned, fighting for breath.

She reached for him, her fingers skimming along his scalp, down past his ears, then sinking into his beard.

He shifted up her body, needing to be closer. She moved a leg, her thigh pressing against his rock-hard erection. He stifled a groan as lust surged through him like an electric shock.

"You said you don't 'react' either to human women or fae," she purred, drawing his face closer to hers.

The bottomless darkness of her eyes lured him, warm and exciting.

"You're not just *any* human woman," he drawled, unable to stop himself from rocking against her thigh. A swell of intense pleasure made his body shudder.

He'd do anything to get inside this woman, even if it killed him.

"You're so much more than any fae…" He kissed her chest, licking off the salt of the sea from her skin, then sucked on one of her breasts, nearly delirious from his need for her.

He wanted her. None of this blinding desire was for Ghata. The goddess wasn't here. Heike was the only one with all the power over him.

"I want you..." he moaned.

Letting her nipple slip from his mouth, he shifted higher, bringing his cock flush with her core.

"You're addictive, baby." She ground her hips against him. Her black eyes grew larger, the look in them heating up. "I can't get enough of you."

Pushing against his shoulder, she made him roll to his back.

"Radax, I want to make you feel things you've never felt before, no matter how long you've been alive," she said into his ear in a hot whisper.

He believed her—fully. Every single minute with her was like nothing he'd ever experienced before.

She climbed on top of him, straddling his hips.

He'd spent every night with Ghata in this position, bitten, clawed at, and ridden to exhaustion. The comparison momentarily blinded him with the memory of pain. His muscles locked up.

"What's wrong, honey?" Heike leaned over him, warm concern in her eyes.

She was nothing like Ghata. He hated himself for allowing the thoughts of the goddess to sneak up on him. He had to change it.

"I need to be on top," he gritted through his teeth.

Being with Heike was as close to heaven as he ever hoped to get. He couldn't let anything spoil it for them. He flipped her on her back, hauling himself over her.

Understanding flew across her beautiful face, and her features relaxed.

"Be on top." She lifted her hips, pressing herself to him.

He pinned her to the mattress, increasing the friction between them.

"I love you on me," she murmured, her eyes hooded and dark with desire.

He cupped her breast and plucked her nipple, still hot and hard from his attention earlier.

She stretched her arms over her head, submitting to him fully. Soft and pliable in his arms, she was at his mercy completely.

The need to take her overwhelmed him. He had to own her, to possess every inch of her body, every hidden corner of her mind, and every sacred part of her heart.

He had to make her his. Because regardless of who had the power over his life and death, she already owned the rest of him. Every bit of himself that he had wrestled from Ghata's control, he'd given to Heike. Gladly and willingly.

*"Mine,"* fluttered through his mind as he entered her slowly.

She whimpered softly, opening her legs wider. And he sank deeper into her slick, welcoming warmth. Bliss wrapped around him like a warm blanket. But she splayed her hand on his chest, stopping him from sinking any further.

"Just... give me a moment," she whispered breathlessly. "You're so big... You feel even bigger than you look."

"I don't want to hurt you." He flexed his jaw, straining his muscles to freeze over her.

He wanted her to experience the same euphoria he felt when inside her. It felt so right for him to be with her.

Did it feel wrong to her?

"It doesn't hurt." She lifted her hips, taking a little more of him. "I just don't think I've ever been stretched this wide before."

She hooked a leg around his middle, and he allowed himself to sink just a little lower.

"Oh God, this is so good," she moaned, arching her back under him. "You feel so, so good, Radax."

His pleasure flared at her words. Desire urged him to move. He withdrew a little, then plunged back inside her.

With a soft whimper, she lifted her hips again, meeting his thrust.

He never knew sex could be like this—full of sweet, intense, all-consuming pleasure, and without a hint of pain. Both people moving together in a dance of love, not a battle of dominance.

He tried to savor every glide inside her, but the desire quickly took over. It built up with every thrust. Needing to hear her breathless moans again, he reached between them and found the spot that had made her come undone the last time he'd rubbed it.

She exhaled sharply when he touched it again. Her legs clamped around him, trapping him into a most delightful snare.

"Come with me," he growled into her ear, holding back his own pleasure with everything he had.

Her long moan shattered into little gasps. Her hips jerked against him, her inner muscles tightening around him.

And his control snapped.

Release burst from him. Enticed and coaxed, not forced, his climax rocked through him so much harder than ever before.

"Gods, Heike!" he growled, burying his face in her hair.

It felt like he was exploding into tiny pieces while loving every moment of it. The world around him twisted and swirled. With only Heike's arms holding him together.

She held him tight, their bodies rocking against each other. Until the white fireworks of ecstasy finally stopped bursting behind his closed eyelids and some sense of reality filtered back.

"Wow..." She kissed his beard. "Where have you been all my life?"

He lifted his head, catching her gaze with his.

She stroked his cheek. "How are you feeling?"

How?

How could he possibly describe this?

Light without shadows.

Need without guilt or self-loathing.

Desire without dependence.

That was what being with her felt like. And so, so much more.

"Pure ecstasy," he told her, reverence radiating through his entire being. "Guilt-free pleasure, without hating myself."

She cupped his face, raking her slim fingers through his beard.

"My heart aches for your past, Radax. But I'll do everything to give you a better future. You deserve so much more than what you've been given."

She already gave him more than he'd ever had.

She'd brought him back to life and made him free.

# Chapter Fourteen

HEIKE

"Did it ever do this before?" I blew on Radax's bicep. Tiny sparks of white light scurried along the black tattoo lines in the wake of my breath.

He lay on his back, and I curled at his side with my elbow propped on the pillow.

Glancing at his arm, he lifted an eyebrow. "No."

"What do you think causes these lights?"

"You," he said, matter-of-fact.

"But how? Why?" My body felt exhausted after all the lovemaking we'd done. But my mind was still filled with questions.

"I have no idea." He shook his head with a lazy smile.

I blew another breath on his skin, trying to follow the curved body of the clawed serpent in his tattoo. Another series of tiny lights ran along the lines, shimmering like silver glitter.

"How does it feel?" I asked.

He wrinkled his nose in a new-to-me, playful expression.

"It tickles." He exhaled a laugh.

I giggled, and he grabbed my shoulders, rolling me to my back.

"And it makes me want to kiss you. Again." He caught my mouth in a kiss, swallowing my laughter.

I melted into his embrace. We'd synched so well together, our bodies moving as one. I'd never had this complete harmony with anyone before, not even with Otto...

"What is it about you that makes me feel like I'd known you all my life?" I murmured against his mouth, stroking his beard.

He trailed more kisses along the side of my face, then down my neck. "I wish you did. I wish I'd been there for you, every day of your life."

My heart pinched with a memory.

"I never thought I could feel this way again," I whispered.

"Again?" He lifted his head, catching my eye. "When did it happen before? Who was he?" he asked with an edge in his voice.

Was Radax jealous? Insecure? Curious?

Possibly all of those things in some combination.

I'd never told anyone about Otto. Mostly because I had reasons to be embarrassed about how it had ended between us. But also because my year with Otto—more specifically the feelings I used to have for him—belonged to that one secret place in my heart I preferred not to open to anyone. Before I'd met Radax.

"His name was Otto," I said. "He was a boy from my school. We started dating the year before I left Germany."

He released me from his arms, lying on his side next to me.

"Did you love him?"

"Um...love?" I tripped over what I was going to say, hit with his question straight on. "I think I did," I finally managed.

"You *think?* You're not sure?"

I shrugged almost apologetically.

"We were only seventeen, turning eighteen that year. So young. I still don't know how much of what we had was real, but it has been my one most memorable relationship."

*'Until you...'* I added in my mind but was too afraid to say it out loud yet.

"It was cute and unapologetically cheesy, with hearts, unicorns, and rainbows," I said instead. "It's been more than ten years now, and I still smile when I think about that year."

For that one entire year, Otto and I were inseparable. We became each other's world and purpose of living. Our feelings were everything —the first romance, the puppy love, the giddy infatuation, with hearts in the eyes and butterflies in the stomach.

"Why aren't you together anymore?" Radax asked.

It all had ended in the apt way too—with lots of drama and a real shit show.

The smile slipped off my face.

"He cheated on me." Such a cliché. "With my best friend."

The muscle in Radax's jaw ticked, twitching his beard.

The old shame stirred deep inside me, but I sensed I could tell him everything. Now that I'd started, I couldn't stop. "And I didn't come up with anything better in retaliation but to revenge-fuck a random guy from his *fussball* team," I blurted out, afraid to meet his eyes. "I believed it would ease my pain, or at least make Otto feel some of the hurt he'd caused me."

"Did it help?" he asked, his voice low.

"Of course not." I huffed a bitter laugh and rubbed my chest where the old hurt echoed from the year long gone. "Otto couldn't care less. He had Sabina, my supposedly best friend."

It'd been so stupid. So childish. Back then, I'd acted out of hurt, without thinking. My "revenge" didn't bring me any satisfaction and failed to make anything right. It just left me with a bunch of queasy memories of sex with someone I didn't care about.

"My parents were already divorced by then," I continued. "A month later, my dad got a job offer in the United States, and I left with him, happy to get away from the country and even the continent where Otto lived."

"You've never seen him again?"

"No," I said, without a hint of regret. "Years later, I heard through the grapevine of the social media that Otto had married Sabina. Apparently, they were truly in love and were expecting a baby. By then, I felt nothing for him anymore. I genuinely wish him and his family the best."

Every now and then, however, I still wondered if what we'd had would forever remain the most magical relationship for me. The year I'd spent with Otto remained one of the brightest in my life. He was my first, and once he'd taken my virginity, we couldn't keep our hands off each other. No matter how much time we had spent together, it was never enough.

After Otto, I couldn't even have a roommate. I couldn't tolerate anyone in my living space for longer than a few days. Yet with him, being together every minute of every day had felt as natural as breathing. After our messy break-up, I hadn't missed the man, but I'd wondered if I'd ever feel again the way he'd made me feel.

"As I got older," I said. "I've been trying to stick with men who make it easy to have a casual relationship. But sometimes..." I drew in a breath before confessing, "Sometimes, I wish to fall in love again, to experience that crazy feeling of being drunk on a person."

I ventured a glance at Radax. There was genuine interest in his expression. He listened without judgement, and I exhaled in relief. Lifting my hand, I traced the lines of his tattoo again, making the silver sparks light up the room.

"It's a fascinating thing, human love," Radax mused with a contemplative expression. "It can be as powerful as magic, but it can also disappear without a trace."

"Oh, it can be so many things," I agreed. "Love can break a person's heart, but it can also bring them back to life."

We lay in silence for a few minutes, my head on his chest. I enjoyed these moments of serenity, with the half-moon peeking through the large window, painting a silver path on the surface of the ocean.

"Tell me about Amira," I asked, drawing curvy lined on Radax's broad chest. "What is she like?"

"Was," he corrected. "You can speak of her in past tense, now."

"But she isn't dead, is she?" I lifted my head.

"I hope not. But she went to another world. And we will never see her in this one again." He sounded resigned.

"But can't she come back?"

"If she does, chances are she won't land in the same time again." His throat moved with a swallow, and he turned his head away, shifting his eyes from mine. "She is as good as dead."

I slid my hand up his chest and cupped his face.

"Why did she leave?" I asked softly.

"Because of me." He winced. His chest rose with a deep breath. "She believed Madame was unfairly punishing me for her."

"But wasn't she?" *Unfairly* was too mild a word for Ghata's actions.

He didn't reply, probably because there wasn't much to argue about.

I leaned over him, tracing the deep crease between his thick eyebrows, wishing I could smooth it out somehow.

"What was Amira like?" I asked. "Tell me."

His frown eased.

"Shy," he said. "Amira has always been painfully shy. Other than her name, she didn't say a word for years after I'd found her."

"What do you mean you *found* her?"

"That's exactly what happened. I saw a little girl crying on a street when Madame's menagerie traveled in the Middle East. The street was in ruins—well, the entire town was. The girl had no one alive with her. There were corpses..."

He winced, closing his eyes for a moment.

"So you took her?"

"She reminded me of my sister," he explained.

"You have a sister?"

"Had. I *had* a younger sister. She died shortly before I became a *brack*. I don't remember how she died, but I believe that grieving over her death helped me keep some of the person I used to be."

"How come Ghata allowed you to keep Amira? Madame isn't exactly a charitable type."

"No, she isn't," he scoffed. "She let Amira stay at the menagerie mostly because she was so quiet, it was easy to forget she was there at all. But Amira also turned out to be useful. She was smart and learned quickly. I taught her how to read, write, and count, and Madame put her in charge of ticket sales when she was still a kid. She was good with money and attracted much less attention than any of us when she ran errands outside of the menagerie. She learned how to drive, too."

His face lit up when he talked about Amira, who sounded like she was his friend and his family all these years.

"She gave my life a purpose," he said. "Once she was gone, my future became the endless abyss of faceless centuries again." He rolled his head on the pillow to face me. "Until you came along."

I placed a kiss on a corner of his mouth. I always had people I cared about in my life. Radax had quickly became someone I cared about the most. His words held a special meaning to me, too. Because of him, I too had a purpose, a mission to accomplish, now.

"It must've been hard for Amira to leave you."

"She planned it. She asked me about how to open a portal to Nerifir. I knew if she left, I'd never see her again. So I refused to tell her." He released a long breath. "In the end, she didn't need me. Lero told her everything she wanted to know."

The crease between his eyebrows grew deeper. I traced it with the tip of a finger again.

"You're worried about her."

He didn't deny it. "Nerifir can be a dangerous place, especially for someone unfamiliar with it. A gorgonian went with her. He was another fae Madame had kept captive in her menagerie. I didn't know him and have no idea if he could be trusted, but fae are good at tricking people. And gorgonians are better at that than most."

"Lero believes that she'll be fine, that she'll make it." I didn't know Amira, but I hoped she was well. Wherever she was now couldn't be any worse than being Ghata's servant, could it?

"Amira is a smart woman," he agreed. "She's quiet but observant. And she learns quickly. I have to trust her judgement and hope that she's well, wherever she is."

His beard parted with a smile. "She shot me, you know," he said suddenly.

"She did what?"

"A look at a gorgonian can kill," he explained. "It's involuntary for them. They have no control over it. Amira shot me before I had a chance to look at him. She saved my life."

This sounded too fantastical to absorb right away.

"She shot you to save your life?" I muttered, flabbergasted.

He nodded.

"As you know, it's not easy to kill a *brack* in this world. Only iron brought from Nerifir or magic can kill us. Human weapons can harm us barely enough to incapacitate. Amira shot me with a gun made by humans. It made me pass out for a day but didn't kill me. By shooting me, she also made Madame believe that I wasn't a part of her escape. Madame laughed, gloating that the girl I'd saved repaid me by shooting me in the head. Only I know that Amira did it to protect me." He paused. "Now she's gone."

I couldn't blame Amira for leaving. It was a miracle she had stayed for as long as she had, putting up with Madame all this time.

I splayed my hand on his shoulder. "She didn't leave because of you, Radax. Don't blame yourself. Amira left because of Ghata. She left in search of a better life, even if she had to cross dimensions to find it. I admire her for that, and I hope she found her happiness. She isn't dead. She lives in Nerifir. Let's hope it's a far better life than she had here."

Scooping me in his arms, he held me tight, burying his face in my hair.

"I don't care about the life Madame had taken from me. I'd long accepted my fate as a *brack*, but I will never forgive her for driving Amira out of this world."

# Chapter Fifteen

HEIKE

When I opened my eyes the next morning, Radax was there. My face pressed to his scarred back, I had one arm around his middle and a leg on top of his hip. I snuggled closer, closing my eyes again.

A warm feeling, fluffy like a baby kitten, curled inside me. It was so cozy and sweet, I wished I could purr in pleasure like a cat, too. A smile stretched my lips. Then it hit me...

I remembered when I had this feeling last, years ago, with Otto. It was even stronger this time, though. So intense, my heart ached.

Snuggling into him, I breathed in his warm, spicy scent, then kissed the scars on his back. Flat and pale, they were but ghosts of the gruesome injuries he had just two days ago. Away from Ghata, all his wounds were healing.

Radax stirred, turning in bed to face me.

"Morning," I whispered.

He reached for me, then stopped short of touching my face. Thousand-year-old habits were hard to break, I imagined. A touch was still so new to him.

I took his hand and brought it to my lips.

"You can touch me whenever you want, Radax. Any day, all day. I love your hands on me."

Spearing his fingers through my hair, he kissed my face. I smiled as his beard tickled my skin.

"Careful what you're allowing me to do," he murmured. "I'll keep touching you, then. Everywhere. And I won't stop."

And he did. Cupping my breasts with his hands. Playing with my nipples. Kissing my skin. And caressing between my thighs.

He trailed his kisses, accompanied by the caress of his magnificent beard, down my body. He dove between my legs and put his mouth on me.

I gasped, arching my back, my fingers scraping his head. The heat of his mouth and the prickle of his beard in my most intimate spot drove me wild with desire. The pleasure ebbed and swelled under his tongue. I moaned, breathless, when it crested with a white-hot orgasm.

Pulling himself up my body, he slid inside me, not letting me catch my breath. His thrusts were firm and powerful, but there was so much tenderness in his eyes, it wrecked me.

His release rocked through him, and I caught him in my arms when his body relaxed.

"I've never been as happy as when I'm with you," he whispered. "The past two days have been the best in my life."

That said a lot, considering he was talking about a lifetime that had spanned for millennia.

I snuggled into his chest as he held me tight.

"You set me free." He kissed my temple. "I didn't remember what freedom felt like. Now, I'd rather die than go back."

I froze at the thought of him ever returning to his old life.

"You're not going back, Radax," I vowed. "I won't let you. I'm not much of a fighter, but I'll fight for you. I swear, I'll fight a fucking goddess for you."

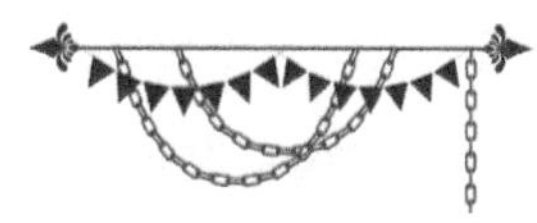

"Okay, here, look at this." I clicked on the blue link on a sloppily put together website with grainy graphics.

Radax leaned closer over my shoulder.

I sat in front of a desktop computer in the office Zeph and Ivy had in their house on Blue Cay. They had gone swimming this morning, and I'd asked to use their computer since it'd be easier than using my phone.

"That's her, isn't it?" I pointed at the image of a tall red-haired woman on the screen after the video had loaded.

"That does look like Ghata," Radax agreed, staring at the screen over my shoulder.

The information about Ghata and her whereabouts was scarce. I had to dive deeper into the web, bypassing the search engines, to find this video. But there she was, sauntering in front of a crowd of people, her voice and gestures as dramatic as ever.

"This looks like India." I examined the people in the crowd and the landscape around them. "What do you think?"

Radax studied the image.

"Could also be Bangladesh or Sri Lanka," he said. "Anywhere in South Asia."

"True," I agreed. "They're outside of a village. See those small buildings in the distance?"

The number of people with Ghata appeared larger than the population of a small village visible in the background of the video.

"The people from the surrounding areas must've come to hear her speak," Radax observed. "They didn't have space in the village to accommodate them all, so they gathered on the outskirts."

That was worrisome. People were willing to travel just to hear Ghata talk. I tried to listen to what she was saying but failed to understand a word.

"She's speaking their language," I noted.

Radax nodded. "Ghata speaks many Earth languages. It expands her reach."

"It must bring her closer to them, too," I said.

In the video, two villagers carried in a large metal brazier on a stand

and placed it in front of Ghata. She took a step back and lifted her arms. The wind caught the floor-long sleeves of her red outfit, making them billow behind her like sails. She flicked her wrists, and the wood in the brazier caught on fire, the flames shooting high into the air.

The crowd gasped, shrinking back. Then reverent noises rolled through it.

The next moment, people shuffled closer to her. They bowed. Some kissed the hem of her dress, her feet, catching and kissing the ends of her sleeves too.

"Fire wielding," I scoffed. "What a cliché of a miracle."

"But look how effective it is," Radax pointed out.

I had to agree with him on that. Spontaneously setting things on fire could be easily faked in many ways. Radax and I knew, however, Ghata had no need to fake anything. That part of her was absolutely real. And that was what made her dangerous.

Faced with a true miracle, people were more inclined to believe that the rest of her was genuine as well.

"Just look at her," I muttered, watching Ghata soak up the adoration of the villagers with a cocky grin on her face.

"She's feeding," Radax explained. "Their awe and reverence make her stronger."

His words sent a cold trickle of dread down my spine. Ghata no longer seemed like a woman, not even a deity, but some dark, soul-sucking vampire, feeding on people's love and adoration.

"Their faith and affection add another layer to her power," Radax continued.

"How about fear?" I asked. "Sooner or later, she will show her true colors. She will give them plenty of reasons to fear and hate her."

"Fear doesn't kill faith. Often, it enhances it, strengthening devotion and loyalty."

I rubbed my face. Ghata was obviously on a mission to charm more followers into her ranks. With every passing moment of her being out there, more and more people believed she was some kind of a messiah or even a deity herself. And with every passing moment, her powers grew.

"She started with the most vulnerable, the most desperate people who had little to lose," Radax explained. "I remember her visiting hospitals in the third-world countries, brothels, slums. She would go to places where people had nothing, and she would give them hope. Hope is a powerful weapon, Heike. Ghata is mobilizing her army."

"Is she moving up the social classes now?" The villagers in the video didn't appear to be rich or affluential, but they didn't look starved or desperate either.

"She's moving up," Radax confirmed. "Ghata needs donations to grow her empire to the level of splendor and grandeur she craves. She quit her show to dedicate more time to traveling and recruiting her army of followers. Donations will be her main source of income now. She can't take much from the poor, even if they give her their all. Either way, her ultimate goal is to conquer everyone on Earth. This entire world. Her ambitions are limitless."

I clicked on another link. It opened with a copy of a pamphlet with text in two languages, one of them English.

"The excerpt from Ghata's book." Radax leaned his hip against the computer desk.

*"The mother of the Moon, the daughter of the Sun,"* was written on the top.

"Is that what she calls herself?" I wondered out loud.

"It has a universal appeal," he commented. "From the ancient times, people all over Earth worshipped celestial bodies."

"Not anymore though."

"Isn't it natural for humans to long for the days long gone? In her message, Ghata appeals to that ingrained nostalgia."

Time had purified the ancient beliefs of the old. Worshiping the Daughter of the Sun had its appeal, I supposed.

I skimmed over the text of the pamphlet. As a feminine power, Ghata positioned herself as the mother of all people, loving and forgiving. With her, they could do no wrong, she claimed. She welcomed everyone, promising to fulfill their deepest desires.

I didn't need to see people hugging and kissing her feet in the video to understand Ghata's appeal to those in need.

Those who already had everything always wanted more. She promised them more—more power, more money, more recognition. All she asked in return was their faith and devotion, something even the poorest people could give her.

"She's a fucking menace to the world," I blurted out. The realization of what Ghata could do once she'd gained control of the masses terrified me. No one was safe. And the worst part was that no one but us knew the world was in danger. People welcomed their imminent demise with arms open wide.

"Ghata will ruin millions of lives if she isn't stopped," Radax agreed.

How to stop her remained the question, however.

"Where is Ghata now?" Lero asked as all six of us met up on the patio of the main house after dinner that night.

"She's moving to China." Radax leaned back in his wicker chair, making it groan and squeak.

"Where in China?" Stella asked.

"I'm not sure." Radax shrugged a shoulder.

I reached over both armrests and took his hand in mine, glad our chairs were close enough for me to do it this time.

"I believe we'll find out soon enough exactly where she is," I said. "If I've learned anything about gaining followers, one needs a solid presence on the web. Until now, Ghata has been converting people in person, focusing on the poorest layers of the world's population, with little to no access to the internet. As she moves up to more affluential layers, she will have to utilize the internet for a wider reach. I expect her presence on social media to grow as well."

"Would you fly to China to get the book?" Ivy asked.

"If I have to, I will." I nodded.

"I prefer we go when she is on a seashore somewhere," Zeph suggested. "Close to water."

"We?" I whipped my head his way. So far, the fae had been sympathetic and listening, but no one had promised me anything.

Zeph shrugged casually. "You can't do it alone, Heike."

"She won't be alone." Radax squeezed my hand. "I'll be with her."

Zeph and Lero cast a cautious glances his way. Sadly, as much as Radax meant to me, for the rest of them he remained a *brack* first and foremost. They'd had their share of dangerous encounters with *bracks*. Trusting Radax wasn't easy for either of them.

"You know Ghata can order you to fight against Heike. Will you be able to go against her direct orders?" Lero asked cautiously.

"I'll fight her orders," Radax replied grimly. "I've been fighting her ever since I left the menagerie. Even before I left, I defied her."

My faith in Radax was strong. But I didn't know enough about the hold Ghata had on her *bracks*—the power she'd had over them for centuries.

"A human woman, void of magic, and a rebellious *brack* going against a goddess who is quickly coming into her powers." Lero shook his head. "It's suicide."

"I'm not planning to go against her." I severely disliked Ghata and would give one of my kidneys to see her prosecuted for her crimes. But I was not looking forward to facing her again. "I would prefer to sneak in quietly, take what I need, and run."

"You'll still need help to get in and out," Stella insisted.

"And weapons. From Nerifir," Zeph added. "I shall get some from the bottom of the sea where I'd sent them last time."

"Do we even know *where* exactly we'll have to sneak in?" Ivy asked.

Zeph stirred uneasily. "I prefer you stayed here."

"Yeah, not a chance." She waved him off. "I'm not letting you go halfway around the world without me."

"Ivy. Baby..." He slid from his chair and crouched down in front of hers. "You can't face Ghata. She has way too many reasons to wish you dead."

"Zeph, darling." Ivy placed her hands on either side of his neck. "Neither Ghata nor the remaining *bracks* know about us sharing your powers. Those who attacked Blue Cay months ago never lived to tell the tale, you and Lero made sure of that. Do you know what that means? Together, you and I are a secret weapon. I need to be there."

Zeph looked doubtful, his lips pressed tightly together.

"I have to be with you," Ivy insisted. "I promise not to take any unnecessary risk. I'll be careful."

He dropped his gaze from hers but didn't argue.

"So, what's the plan?" Lero asked.

"You know I'm coming too, right?" Stella said softly.

Lero heaved a sigh. "I gathered you would."

"Good." She smiled. "I'm glad there's no argument."

"I know I'd lose if I started one." Lero gave her a look full of adoration. "No point in starting one."

"A wise man you are." She placed a peck on his cheek, then turned to me. "But I don't think Heike should join us."

I hadn't expected to be excluded. Having all of them coming with me had made me feel better about the whole thing. But they were supposed to be coming *with me*, not without.

"There is no need for you to endanger your life," Stella explained. "You don't have any special powers. You're more vulnerable than the rest of us. It would be safer if you stayed."

Dumbfounded, I moved my gaze from one face to another, finding the same sentiment in each expression.

"Oh no!" I protested, with a huff. "I'm coming."

"But why?" Ivy shook her head. "This isn't your fight."

"Isn't it? I have a beef with Madame, too." The memory of Ghata's fake, magical fairy laughter sent a chill down my arms. "I've met the bitch. I want her gone." My voice came out foreign and cold.

Would they understand? My burning need to stop that woman from hurting anyone else the way she'd been hurting Radax? The way she wanted to hurt me?

Just in case they wouldn't think it was enough of a reason, I decided to strengthen my argument.

"I'm not going to miss an opportunity like this," I added with conviction. "This may be my one chance to get a video of truly historical significance."

"Are you going to film this?" Lero asked, arching his black eyebrow.

"Please don't risk your life for a chance to go viral." Stella stared at me.

That wasn't why I was doing any of this. But if I had to convince them I was here just to do my job, then so it had to be.

"That's what I do for a living, among many other things," I replied. "I take videos others wouldn't or couldn't take, then share them with the world." I glanced Lero's way. "Don't worry. I've promised not to post anything without your permission. But it's always better to film it and never use it than to miss it and later regret never getting it on video at all."

# Chapter Sixteen

HEIKE

"Tired?" Radax asked as we entered our hotel room in Irkutsk, Russia after a long, long flight.

Ghata moved fast. In a few days, she had visited and already left China. According to the internet, her next gathering was supposed to happen in a camp on a mountain side by Angara River near Irkutsk.

"A little," I said, taking the room in.

It looked decent. Clean. I walked over to the desk and plugged my new laptop in.

Tossing our bags into the closet, Radax went to the bathroom.

I logged on. Tapping my finger on the corner of the screen, I waited for the laptop to connect to the hotel's wi-fi.

The noise of traffic from the street outside filtered through the large window. The brass light fixture on the desk looked scuffed somewhat but clean of dust. Brass. Why was it always brass? Hotels all over the world seemed especially fond of that particular finish.

Despite all the traveling I'd done in my life, I'd never been in Irkutsk before. I'd heard of Lake Baikal, of course, the largest fresh-water lake in the world that was situated about one-hour drive from Irkutsk. But I didn't remember hearing of this city before.

My mind was automatically logging things I could mention in my blog. I estimated the best angle to take pictures.

The room wasn't large. The bed was even smaller, not bigger than a double size by North American standards. Radax would take most of it, leaving hardly any space for me. Which meant I'd have no place to sleep but on his chest.

My heart made a thud, sending a wave of warmth through me. Radax's chest had quickly become my favorite sleeping place.

All my life, I'd never really belonged anywhere. I had my apartment in New York where I stored things I couldn't take on the road with me. But my real life happened on the go. I liked to think I belonged *everywhere*. A true citizen of the world. Comfortable, no matter where life would send me. Mostly, I spent my time between hotel rooms and my friends' places, all over the world.

So many places, so many new rooms, and different beds. So many more lay ahead of me, for as long as I wished to travel. Now, I also wanted Radax and his chest to sleep on wherever I went.

I couldn't see myself being attached to a place. But Radax made me believe I could grow attached to a person.

He made me want to belong. If not somewhere, then to someone.

To him.

The sound of running water in the bathroom sink snapped me out of my thoughts. The wi-fi connected. The browser window opened. I could start putting the notes for my blog together.

"Are you going to do some work?" Radax asked, coming out of the bathroom.

"I..." My mind wasn't on my work as he approached me from behind.

"You should get some rest." He placed his large hands on my shoulders, rubbing the weariness out of my muscles. "It was a long flight."

I wasn't a stranger to long flights. Besides, Lero's money and my status as an influencer had made the journey here rather comfortable for the six of us. We waited in stylish airport lounges during each layover and traveled in plush, comfy seats each leg of the trip. Still it was a long trip. And tomorrow...

Tomorrow could be a challenging day.

"I should take a shower first." I leaned into his touch, trying not to think about tomorrow yet.

He slid his hands closer to my neck, his thumbs gliding up my nape. His touch remained firm, but he slowed down, taking a more sensual rhythm. For a man who hadn't really touched a woman until he met me, he proved incredibly capable.

Ripples of pleasure slid down my arms to my fingertips. I closed my eyes, slowly stretching my neck side to side. A soft moan escaped my lips as the tension and weariness drained from my body.

With a low grunt, Radax spun me around to face him.

My eyes flew open.

Red streaks of light flashed in his irises, like spokes of a turning wheel, and...disappeared. Only the rich, dark brown remained—deep and mysterious, like a warm starless night.

He slid a hand up into my hair on the back of my head.

"I haven't touched you for way too long," he rasped, leaning closer.

"We held hands on the plane, remember?" I murmured.

Not just on the plane. He hadn't left my side during the entire trip. I slept on his shoulder, rested my feet in his lap, and kept his hand in mine for no other reason other than I liked it.

"That was nice." A corner of his mouth lifted, parting his beard with a grin. "But not nearly enough."

His fingers flexed on the back of my head, bringing me closer. He leaned down and took my mouth in a kiss.

I closed my eyes and parted my lips for him. I didn't hug him back. Made no attempt to even lift my arms. Barely aware of my own body, I lost myself in his kiss, soaking up everything that was Radax.

The smell of the airplane still clung to his clothes mixed with a trace of his cologne and the faint citrusy fragrance of the hotel's soap on his hands. But underneath it all was the familiar warm scent of his skin—male, salt, and spice.

With a soft moan, I melted into his kiss.

He hooked his arm around my waist, drawing me to him.

Slow and tender, the kiss was all Radax. There was none of the urgency and desperation of the hostile power. Letting go of my mouth, he kissed along my jaw, then down my neck. Unhurried, sensual kisses. As if we had all the time on Earth ahead of us, and every moment of it was worth savoring.

I lifted my hand, trailing the tips of my fingers up his arm. A soft, white glow followed in the wake of my fingers.

"So beautiful," I whispered, mesmerized.

"Hmm," he hummed against my skin below my collarbone. "Simply gorgeous."

I wasn't sure whether he was talking about his tattoo, about this moment, or about something else entirely. It didn't really matter, anyway.

His kisses reached the neckline of my blouse, and he popped the little buttons in the front open.

Starving for his touch, I wrapped my arms around his shoulders.

"How about a shower?" I murmured, kissing his chest through his t-shirt. "You and me? Together?"

"Sounds perfect."

He dragged my jeans down and helped me kick off my high-heeled pumps.

I was left standing only in a black bra and pink panties—not matching at all. Normally, I made an effort to wear a matching lingerie set, especially if there was a possibility of me getting naked in front of a man. Hopping between planes and airports, I'd failed to pay attention to that. And, frankly, I didn't even care.

The way Radax was looking at me, he didn't seem to care about what I was wearing, either. Standing on one knee in front of me after taking my pants off, he slid his gaze up my body.

"You are the most beautiful thing I've ever seen in this world or any other." His stare reached deep under my clothes and inside my very soul.

My heart seized with longing.

Rising to his feet, he scooped me into his arms and headed for the bathroom.

Here, he turned the tap on to fill in the tub. I pulled his t-shirt off over his head and unbuckled his belt.

He took off the holster he wore under his shirt. It contained a slim dagger with an elegant handle and a blade made from iron of Nerifir. Zeph had retrieved it from the bottom of the ocean where he'd buried the weapons that *bracks* had used in their attack on Blue Cay months ago. Radax brought it in his luggage and put it on first thing after landing here.

When we both were naked, he climbed in the tub and drew me into his lap between his legs.

"Not a shower," he said. "A bath is so much better."

He washed my hair for me, then rinsed it thoroughly.

"Do you shampoo your beard?" I asked, lathering it for him.

"I do," he chuckled at my efforts.

I rinsed the suds out of his beard with a shower head on a flexible hose. He closed his eyes and laughed as I showered his face.

"Payback time." He grabbed the hose out of my hands. Grabbing me around the middle, he fitted me between his legs again, my back to his front, then slid the shower head between my thighs.

I gasped as the streams of water grazed my folds, stroking my most sensitive spot.

Leaving the shower head positioned at just the right angle between my legs, Radax grabbed the bar of soap from the edge of the tub. He lathered it between his hands, then slid his palms down my shoulders and arms, washing the smell of airplane and the weariness of the trip off me.

I leaned back against his shoulder, letting him take care of me. Water rose in the tub, caressing my skin. The feeling of peace, comfort, and tenderness warmed me from the inside. I recognized this feeling. For years after Otto, I'd feared I would never experience anything like this again.

Only this was even stronger than my long-lost first love. What I felt for Radax was more solid, mature—a connection built on mutual understanding.

His hands caressed my breasts, paying special attention to the tips. I arched my back. The shower head shifted with my movement, and I didn't adjust it. I needed more than that.

I needed *him*.

"Radax," I pleaded, twisting in his arms to face him.

He groaned as one of my thighs rubbed against his hardened length.

I straddled his legs, rising on my knees over his erection. He positioned the tip of it at my entrance, then grabbed my hips and lowered me onto it.

Water sloshed around us. And when he bucked his hips up with a thrust, it splashed out.

"Fuck," he cursed under his breath.

One arm around me, he gripped the edge of the tab and got up. Throwing his long leg over the edge, he got out. He snatched a few towels from the rack nearby, tossed them on the tiled floor, then lowered me on them—all without breaking our connection.

"Radax..." I arched under him. Pleasure rolled through me in a swell.

Lifting my hips, I met his next thrust. I needed him more than my next breath.

His arms straight, he rose over me, holding me with his gaze as he pumped harder and faster.

"Yes, Radax..." I moaned wildly as my orgasm crested, hot and blinding. "God, yes..."

Ecstasy burst through me. I closed my eyes, surrendering to it. To him.

The complete and absolute power he had over me at that moment was frightening. And the only way I knew how to deal with fear was by trusting him fully.

He came hard inside me "Heike..." he exhaled, collapsing over me.

I caught him in my arms. He buried his face in the crook of my neck. His beard tickled my skin, making me smile.

"With you, every time is simply magical..." he panted. "Sweet and hot. Torture and bliss."

I stroked his head, his shoulders, and his back, wishing a place and a time existed where I could never let go of him. But the white lights spread along his tattoo under my fingers, reminding me how different he was. He was nothing like me. Not a human. And our future looked murkier than ever.

The dark presence of evil descended, no matter how hard I tried to fight it.

"Do you feel *her?*" I asked.

"Often." He knew whom I was talking about, without me even mentioning her name. "But not right now."

He shifted off me. I rolled to my side to face him.

"Does her pull get stronger as we get closer to where she is?"

"Distance doesn't matter to her. She could have me back any time if she cared to will it strong enough."

Maybe. But I didn't think it would be that easy for Ghata to get Radax back this time. She'd been trying. Yet he was still here with me, not with her. And I'd do anything to keep it that way.

He lifted a strand of wet hair from my face and placed it behind my ear. The tenderness in his eyes on me clashed with the hard force with which he'd spoken about her.

"You don't think she wants you back badly enough?" I asked.

*"My favorite creation,"* Ghata had called Radax.

Would she be missing him at all?

"Ghata doesn't get attached either to things or people," he replied. "When she finally does pull me back, she'll do it out of spite or simply to assert her dominance, nothing more."

He slid his gaze off me, staring over my shoulder. Tenderness slipped off his face. His features hardened.

"The only thing she enjoys, the only thing she lives for, is power. Control." His jaw muscles flexed, moving his beard. "I need you to make me a promise, Heike," he said with a grim expression.

"What is it, honey?" I cupped his cheek, sinking my fingers into his damp beard.

He reached over me to the holster with the dagger and pulled the blade out.

"I want you to promise me you won't let her take me."

Alarm cut through me, sharper than the blade he was holding—the only blade in this world that could kill a *brack*—him.

I sat up straight.

"What are you saying, Radax?"

Gently, he took my hand in his and wrapped my fingers around the bejeweled handle.

"My heart is with you, Heike," he said softly. "But Ghata has my will. I can never be truly free. Not while I'm alive."

"Radax...no," I whimpered, crushed by realization.

My hand on the dagger trembled, but he held on firmly.

"I can't go back to her, Heike. You gave me a taste of freedom, you're the one who can set me completely free. For good." Holding my hand in his around the handle, he lifted the blade to his neck. "Right here, sweetheart." The tenderness in his voice burned my eyes with tears. He placed the tip of the dagger below his beard, slightly to the side. "A stab and a slash, the iron will do the rest."

Horror shook me. I jerked my hand back, dropping the dagger as if it'd scorched me.

"No..." I clung to him, hugging his neck. "It won't happen. It doesn't need to happen. We'll fight."

"Oh, I will fight." He hugged me back so tight, I could barely breathe. "I'll fight with everything I've got, Heike. For you, for my freedom, for more moments like this." He kissed me. "But if I fail, I need to know you'll set me free. I need your promise."

"I... I can't." I cried openly now.

How could I? How could I do what he'd asked me for?

"I want you to live," I sobbed. "I need you with me. I don't want you to go there at all tomorrow."

I wished I could pull him inside me and lock him in my heart, far away from all evil. I wanted him safe.

"You know I'll have to come tomorrow, sweetheart," he murmured, soothingly stroking my back. "I'm the only one who knows the layout of Ghata's camp and her habits. The only one who can open the box where she keeps her book." He kissed my hair, rocking with me in his arms. "Would *you* stay here, in safety, if I told you to?" he asked.

"No." I shook my head. "I need to be there, too."

"Because you want to film it," he stated. "Is a video worth risking your life over?"

No. No video was worth it, but that wasn't the main reason I was coming with them tomorrow. I hated Ghata, with passion I'd never hated anyone and anything before. I wished to be a part of her demise.

"I want to end Ghata," I gritted through my teeth. "I want to see her crawl back into the hole she came from."

But there was more.

The main reason I wanted to come tomorrow was to be with Radax. Little by little, I believed I'd been helping him fight Ghata's influence all along. I'd kept him away from her for that long. If he were to face her tomorrow, I needed to be there with him. I believed my presence would help him.

We weren't planning to storm the goddess's camp. The plan was to sneak in quietly and steal the book, hopefully without raising alarm or being seen.

If worse came to worst, however, if Ghata decided she wanted her "favorite creation" back, if it came down to a fight, I hoped I could help Radax resist her.

But not by killing him...

I closed my eyes to avoid staring at the dagger, its dark blade glistening menacingly in the bathroom light.

"Promise me, Heike," Radax insisted. "Promise you won't let her have me. I can't be her slave anymore. I can't keep doing the things she forces me to do."

I cried into his shoulder softly, refusing to utter a word.

"If I fail, please don't let my loss be her win." Determination made his voice sound hard as granite.

It wasn't a human Radax was battling. He was going against a deity, a power larger than any human or fae, much larger than himself. He'd been a part of evil, an extension of it, for so long. Fighting it would be like going against his own nature.

He needed help to win. Even if the win could only come from a loss.

"Promise me," he implored. "Promise me you won't let her enslave me again."

I drew in a breath shuddered by tears.

"I promise..." I whispered, so softly I could barely hear the words myself. "I promise to set you free, Radax."

"Thank you." He kissed my hair as I sobbed into his shoulder.

"I won't let her have you," I vowed in a whisper.

# Chapter Seventeen

HEIKE

"Ghata normally eats dinner in her trailer," Radax was recapping the routine of Ghata's camp as we drove south along the road running east of Angara River.

The rented truck rattled and clanked on uneven pavement. Radax was sitting in the front with Lero while I was in the back seat with Ivy and Stella. Zeph was outside in the river, following us along the stream. The siren believed he was most useful in the water, and Ivy assured us he was most comfortable there, too.

"After dinner, she usually has sex with one of the *bracks*," Radax continued.

"Every night?" Ivy gasped softly.

"Almost every night."

"That's an energetic woman," Stella muttered under her breath.

"We make love almost every night, too," Lero pointed out.

Stella's cheeks colored with a soft blush. "Yeah, but that's just with you. Not a different guy each time."

"Thank the gods for that." Lero worked his jaw.

"Ghata doesn't *make love*," Radax said. "She uses sex to control the *bracks'* urge to turn."

"Right." Lero rolled back his shoulders. As a werewolf, he must know all about the urge to turn. Each full moon, he turned into a beast himself.

"Is it always just one, though?" I clarified. "One *brack* per night?" I didn't care about Ghata's sexual preferences, but we needed to know the number of people we might potentially encounter at her place, though it was still a few hours before the nightfall.

"Usually, one," Radax confirmed. "Could be two or three occasionally if the mood strikes her. But normally it's just one."

Lero turned off the road, taking the truck up the mountain along a barely there path. Once we made it far enough for the thick pine forest to conceal the truck from view, he stopped and turned off the engine.

"Ready?" He turned to us.

The three of us in the back seat nodded.

Despite it being the end of May, the afternoon air was rather chilly. I turned on the camera in my pocket, then pulled the sides of my denim jacket together, fighting the shivers that ran down my arms.

"Cold?" Radax wrapped one arm around my shoulders, drawing me into his large, warm body.

He wore a plain black hoodie over his t-shirt. The soft material of his clothes made his hug especially warm and cozy.

I fought the urge to snuggle against him. "I'm fine," I said, quickly breaking our embrace.

Anxiety vibrated inside me. Radax's hugs had the tendency to either relax or excite me—neither of which would help me stay focused and alert.

"Let's get this over with," I exhaled, stepping back.

Radax helped Lero take the small boat we'd brought with us from the truck. The men then carried the boat down the mountain while Ivy, Stella, and I followed. The soles of my running shoes slid in the loose dirt and brown pine needles as we hiked down the path.

We crossed the road, then descended to the river on the other side of it.

Ivy crouched by the water, dipping her hand in. "Zeph," she called softly.

I'd learned that a siren could sense people through water. Ivy used the river to let Zeph know she was here.

The water bubbled around her hand, then the silver-blond head of the siren broke through the surface.

"Are you okay?" she asked, cupping his face.

"Of course I am." He caught her hand, then placed a quick kiss inside her palm. "Slowpokes." Zeph smiled brightly at the rest of us. "I've been waiting here forever."

"Show-off," Lero muttered under his breath, his mouth twitching in a smile.

He and Radax lowered the boat into the water. Five of us got in. Zeph dove under the surface again, leaving a flurry of silver bubbles curling in his wake.

We brought no oars or paddles. Once everyone was seated, however, the boat gently eased into the stream, as if on its own, then moved across the river. It glided swiftly, with no impact of the current on its trajectory. Water was no longer in control here. The boat moved according to Zeph's will.

The river was wide, the opposite bank barely visible when we started moving across the stream. Never would I have ventured across it in this tiny boat had Zeph not been here. With him, however, the water around the boat remained calm—its surface as smooth as glass, no matter how strong the waves and the current might be anywhere else.

It didn't take us long to reach the other side. The bottom of the boat had barely scraped the rocky ground when the water rose in a gentle swell and set the boat, along with all of us on board, under the thick outcropping of pine trees on the riverbank.

Zeph emerged from the water and sauntered our way.

"How are you, my love?" He took Ivy's hands in his and kissed her lips. "I'd hug you, but I'm all wet." He grinned.

"Yeah, it's a bit too cold for a dripping wet hug." She smiled in reply, moving a few of his sodden strands away from his eyes.

"You know it'd take me only a few seconds to dry off," Zeph

murmured, leaning closer to her. Sliding his hand down his swim trunks, he sent the water in a rain of droplets out of their material.

"We need to get going," Lero urged, not at all impressed with Zeph's untimely flirting.

I was with Lero on this one. If we wanted to search Ghata's trailer without her there, we had to do it before she went in for dinner.

"The camp must be that way," Lero gestured up the mountain. "According to the map, there is a flat clearing behind the trees, slightly upstream."

"Let's go then." I headed that way, with Radax, and Stella by my side.

"Be careful," Ivy wished to us.

According to our plan, Ivy was staying by the river to serve as Zeph's link to the water.

"Hide. Don't let anyone see you. If you're in trouble, shoot me a stream." Burying his hands in her hair, Zeph gave her a kiss on the lips. When he let go of her, Ivy stepped into the shadows under the trees.

The five of us headed into the forest and away from the river.

Ghata's influence increased every day. Her believer base had been growing. She'd managed to convert an astounding number of people already. Some countries were erecting grand temples in her honor.

Others, however, still treated her as an outcast or a pariah. In some places, her "teachings" were called alternative religion, in others —heresy.

Local authorities had made it clear Ghata's gathering was not welcome in Irkutsk. She was forced to organize it outside of the city limits. However, the number of attendees was supposed to be high.

According to the quick research I'd done that morning, many people had traveled for days to get here today. Unlike a village or even a city, the mountains offered plenty of space for as many followers as Ghata could gather. Judging by the noise filtering between the trees, many had come to meet their new goddess and to worship her today.

Using the thick underbrush for cover, we crouched low, moving between the trees toward a small clearing. Here, several tents and trailers stood in a circle, with the largest one in the middle. An ornate red and yellow rug lay in front of the middle trailer.

Radax tipped his chin at it. "That one is Ghata's."

"Are you sure?" Lero asked, and Radax nodded confidently.

"She likes fine things." He gestured at the rug.

A door to another trailer opened, and a man jogged down the few stairs. We went silent, crouching under the trees. The man had a similar build as Radax. Dressed in a nearly identical black hoodie with black tendrils of a tattoo peeking above the neckline, he looked like Radax's twin, indistinguishable had it not been for Radax's beard.

*A brack.*

Radax kept his eyes on the man, watching him move around the camp. Radax's fingers stroked the grass that grew sparsely under the pine trees. He glanced at the small purple flowers in the grass, then plucked one. Turning to me, he threaded the stem of the flower through the buttonhole of my fitted denim jacket, next to the camera rolling in my pocket.

He wasn't looking at me. His attention was fixed on the flower in a purposefully deliberate way. When he finally raised his eyes to mine, I noted the slight apprehension there, his expression a little guarded, a little unsure.

I realized this must be the first time Radax had ever given a woman a flower—a normal, common thing for most people, an entirely new experience for him.

Mindful of making as little noise as possible, I hooked a hand around his neck and brought his face to mine. I paused, willing him to see in my eyes everything I couldn't say out loud—my full acceptance of him, in every way.

Then, I kissed the living hell out of him.

My kiss nearly cost him his balance. With a grunt, he strengthened his position in the crouch, then fisted his hand in my hair. He returned my kiss, his lips eagerly caressing mine, his tongue finding mine.

The world quickly fell away as he kissed me.

A slight tap on my shoulder had the effect of a punch in my stomach. I jerked, breaking the kiss.

"All clear." Lero touched Radax's arm, too, bringing us both back in the reality.

The camp seemed deserted, now. The *brack* was gone.

"Time to go." Radax's lips glistened from our kiss. Mine flushed hot.

"Be careful," I whispered.

A gaping hole formed in my chest when he left, heading toward Ghata's trailer. As if he took a part of my heart with him.

# Chapter Eighteen

RADAX

He walked across the clearing as noiselessly as possible but without hurrying or cowering. If anyone spotted him from a distance, he hoped they'd just take him for another *brack* doing Madame's bidding around the camp.

The noise of the crowd rolled from up the mountain. Chanting, singing praises. Humans turned out to be not much different from werewolves, after all—falling under Madame's charm with the same ease.

Not all of them were, though. Some, like Heike, saw Ghata for what she was.

His lips still warm from Heike's last kiss, he resisted the urge to touch them. He couldn't think about her or her kisses. He needed to keep calm. Focused.

He jogged up the stairs and yanked open the door to Madame's trailer. She never locked it. The only thing she'd ever treasured was in a cabinet under a lock no human would be able to open.

The luxurious silk floor rugs were rolled and moved aside. Vuk held a mop in his hands, washing the trailer's floor.

"Radax?" He squinted in disbelief the moment Radax opened the door. "What the fuck are you doing here?"

He could've asked Vuk the same question. Amira used to clean Madame's quarters daily after breakfast. With her gone, however, the schedule must've changed.

Aggression quickly displaced shock on Vuk's face.

"Traitor!" he yelled, launching at Radax.

The *brack* swung his mop over his head.

Radax snatched it from him, then slammed the long handle in Vuk's temple. The *brack* just grunted, barely affected by the blow.

"Madame will looove to see you!" Vuk punched Radax in the jaw.

The blow made his head snap back. His skull rung like a church bell.

"That's for knocking me out, asshole!" Vuk landed another punch under his ribs, cracking a few.

Roaring in pain, Radax grabbed Vuk's head with both hands and smashed the *brack's* face against his knee.

Bone and cartilage crunched. Blood sprayed, misting the fabric of his pants.

"I swear I'll end you!" Vuk bellowed, spitting blood and broken teeth.

"You didn't learn your lesson, did you?" Radax growled. "I'll have to teach it again, then." He twisted Vuk's head, snapping his neck with a crunch.

The *brack's* body sagged, and Radax let it drop to the floor.

Temporarily "killing" an immortal felt just as repulsive as any murder did. Radax rubbed his aching jaw. Vuk's punch would leave a bruise. His broken ribs hurt. They would take some time to heal, now. None of his injuries were serious enough to stop him, however. He'd lived through much worse, numerous times.

Ignoring the pain, he headed for the large ornate dresser opposite of the door.

The dresser was from Nerifir, like all the furniture in the trailer. Ghata detested anything from the world she was set to conquer. She demanded to be surrounded by things brought from the world that had exiled her.

All drawers were locked, but it was the top of the dresser that held the most meaningful items—evidence of Ghata's former grandeur. Images of her, artfully framed by the best artisans of Nerifir. Fragrant candles, precious crystals, and dried flowers that werewolves of Sarnala used to bring to her temple as a part of the offerings to their goddess. All these things were reminders of grand times now gone.

A metal cabinet, decorated with precious stones and filigree stood to the right of Ghata's shrine. A fine mesh of tiny gears covered the entire front of the cabinet. It was both decorative and functional—the lock masterfully constructed by gorgonians.

The fae race of gorgonians possessed the unique gift of combining art, mechanics, and magic in creations no one else could produce.

Radax had no idea how the lock was created, but he was one of the few who could open it. He'd had to open it before, to take Ghata's precious book out for copying the texts for her to use to recruit new followers.

Sliding his large fingers over the delicate gears, he unlocked the box. Inside, an even more ornately decorated book lay.

He took it out. Large and thick, the book had a hard, leather-bound cover and gold lettering that never faded despite the ancient age of the book. The bejeweled clasps held the pages closed.

He flicked the clasps open and lifted the top cover.

*"The power over both the beginning and the end lies with the creator,"* stated on the very first page.

This phrase had never been reproduced in pamphlets or copies of the book. More than all the gold, fine leather, and jewels on the cover, these words were the one true sign the book was the original one.

Shutting the book closed, he shoved it under his arm and stepped over the motionless body of Vuk on his way to the exit.

Outside, all seemed still deserted as he ran toward the trees.

"You got it?" Heike stepped out from behind the edge of the woods to meet him.

"Here." He handed her the book.

"Wow, that's impressive." She quickly opened the cover. "What does it say?" She traced with her finger the line of ancient text.

*"'The power over both the beginning and the end lies with the*

*creator,'"* he read. "This phrase is only in the original book. Ghata never allows it copied—"

"Radax!" the familiar female voice shrilled.

He jerked as if lashed at by a whip.

Ghata briskly walked across the clearing from the opposite side, where the noise of her worshippers hadn't dropped.

"You dare show your face here!" she yelled.

Nerkan was with her. Her hand fisted in the front of the *brack's* black hoodie, she dragged him along. From the pulsing red light in Nerkan's eyes and his wild, needy expression, Radax realized Nerkan was on the verge of turning, and Ghata must be taking him to her trailer for some relief.

Her eyes landed on the book in Heike's arms.

"Thief!" Ghata seethed.

Heike paled. "Come, Radax." She tugged his sleeve, retreating under the trees.

"Get her!" Ghata raised her hand.

The tattoo on Nerkan's neck flamed to life. His own neck and arm pulsed with heat, too.

"Radax!" Heike called, her voice high with worry.

"Go!" he yelled back.

The large shapes of *bracks* ran into the clearing from the woods, following the call of their mistress. Their tattoos ablaze. Their eyes glowing red.

"Get them! Now!" Ghata ordered.

"Go!" he shouted to Heike over his shoulder, positioning himself between her and the approaching *bracks.*

"What about you?" She frantically shifted her gaze between him and Ghata.

"I'll stop them." He turned to face the first *brack* who rushed him.

*"Zuso,"* he recognized.

Zuso slammed into Radax. His broken ribs sent an explosion of pain through his side. Bringing his fist back, he smashed it straight into the *brack's* ear.

Zuso blinked, momentarily disoriented by the blow. Radax used the moment to twist and break his neck.

"Traitor!" Ghata's sharp scream rose over the clearing. "You're nothing but a pathetic slave!"

His arm and neck caught on fire. Searing, paralyzing pain coursed through his veins like liquid lava. The goddess's power spread through his body like a disease.

*"I made you. You're mine,"* pounded through his brain. *"Mine to use. Mine to end."*

"Radax!" Heike's clear voice broke through the dark flaming cloud of torture.

H*eike*

Lero ran past me. His fist slammed into the ribs of one of the *bracks* rushing us.

The *brack* doubled over. I lifted the incredibly heavy book in my hands, then smashed him over the head with it.

The *brack* swayed on his feet. Lero sent him down to the ground with a kick.

From the corner of my eye I saw Zeph swiftly slash another *brack* with the iridescent fins that had opened on the back of the siren's forearms. Dark liquid dripped from the spikes of the fins and sizzled along the cuts on the *brack's* skin before he collapsed to the forest floor.

"Stella," Lero said quickly. "Take Heike back to the river. We have to get her out of here."

Stella gripped my arm.

"Radax!" I screamed over the noise of the worshipers and the fight.

My *brack* was almost in the middle of the clearing by now. The right sleeve of his hoody smoldered. The visible lines of the tattoo flamed red on his neck.

"Radax!" If I left for the river, he had to be with me.

Lero spun around, taking down another *brack* who'd made it close enough.

"Get the book, slave!" Ghata ordered.

She stood tall, her long red robes bellowing in the breeze. Her right hand raised, directing the mayhem around her.

"Radax, you thief. Bring back what you stole!" Her voice thundered.

With horror, I saw Radax halting his next blow and slowly turn around. His glowing red eyes locked with mine.

"Fight it, baby," I implored. "Please fight her."

A spark of recognition flickered in Ghata's expression.

"Isn't that the little German girl?" she scoffed, glowering at me. "The one who should've been long dead!" she shrieked, throwing her arm my way. "Get her, slave!"

Radax roared in pain, tossing his head back. The tattoo on his neck turned into a noose of fire. His sleeve burned away, the fabric falling to the ground in smoldering chunks. Moving heavily, he headed my way.

"No..." I whispered, watching the Radax I knew and cherished disappear before my eyes.

His familiar features distorted into a grimace of agony and rage. His neck muscles bulged, as if straining to shake the tattoo off his skin.

"Heike," Stella pulled at my arm.

I staggered backwards, following the momentum of her pull.

A *brack* slammed into us sideways, knocking Stella off her feet.

I reached into the holster strapped under my jacket and yanked out the dagger Radax had given to me. The book under one arm, I slashed at the *brack*, slicing through the hoodie on his shoulder. Red sparks flashed where the blade cut through the *brack's* skin.

With a feral growl, Lero attacked him.

"Get the book!" Ghata raged. "Then kill her already."

In a wide leap, Radax jumped in front of me.

"Radax, no." I searched for a glimpse of warm brown behind the red inferno in his eyes.

There was none.

"It's me, Heike," I pleaded, talking to this terrifying stranger. How could this be the same man who took my breath away with the gentlest of kisses. "Don't you remember me?"

There was nothing but madness and rage in his fiery eyes. He growled, prowling my way.

"Book, Radax!" The order came from Ghata like a crack of a whip.

He snatched the book from my arms, then shoved it to one of the *bracks* behind him. The *brack* ran back to Ghata with it.

"Lovely," she cooed in that sweet, seductive voice of her, receiving the book. "Now kill her, my pet."

She jerked her hand up, fingers spread.

The flames of Radax's tattoos rose higher, heating my face with a blast of hot air. He roared, reaching for me.

I retreated into the trees, backwards. My knees trembled, my legs refusing to run.

"Radax, Radax, Radax," I repeated his name like a mantra, desperate to break through the wall of fire that had engulfed his mind and took him away from me. "Stay with me. Please stay with me."

"Kill her!" The order thundered, reverberating in the mountains. The sound much more powerful than a mere woman could produce.

A dark shadow rose from behind Ghata. Its dark tendrils reached around her, stretching toward Radax.

He grabbed my shoulders, the way he'd never touched me before. Rough and punishing, his fingers dug into my muscles. With a deep, guttural snarl, he shifted his hands closer to my neck.

"Don't, please..." I begged.

I no longer asked him to fight the dark power that took over him. He'd fought, and he'd lost. I simply pleaded for my life.

The red in his eyes shrunk for a moment. The flash of brown zoomed in on me.

Breath caught in my throat.

"Radax? You're still there, aren't you?" I whispered, mesmerized by the fleeting transformation.

Hope stirred in me.

He grabbed my hand that held the dagger. A plea flashed in his eyes a moment before the red engulfed them again.

*"Don't make my loss be her win."*

His words rolled through my memory with paralyzing horror.

"No..." I exhaled.

He grabbed my throat. Another roar erupted from his chest, filled with rage and desperation. His body shook violently. Every muscle in his hand at my throat flexed, making his fingers stiff like rock. He could snap my neck like a twig, but he was still fighting. Fighting to give me one last chance.

"Please..." the word rolled in his roar, like a pebble in a raging torrent. "You promised..."

His hand over my fist with the dagger jerked up to his neck.

"No..." I sobbed loudly.

"Kill her, slave!" Ghata fumed.

*Slave...*

More than anything in the world, Radax wished to be free.

"You're not getting him," I gritted through my teeth.

I let Radax's hand guide me to his neck.

The lines of his tattoos split open. Exposed raw flesh pulsed in the tears of his scorched skin.

"End the pain," I whispered, sinking the dagger into his neck, right into the spot he'd shown me.

*Stab and slice.*

Just like he wanted. Like I had promised.

Hot blood splashed on my hand. The scorching flames fizzled and died. Red sparks burst from the blade and around his neck.

He staggered on his feet, then dropped to his knees.

The handle of the dagger slipped from my fingers. And he yanked the blade out of his neck. Blood rushed out in a stream.

"Radax..." I sank to my knees.

Blood pulsed out of his wound, draining the life from him. And with that, the wounds along his tattoo sealed closed. Red glow disappeared from his eyes.

"Free." He slid his hand from my neck to my face, cupping it. "Thank you..."

He slumped to the side, then crashed into the soft layer of old pine needles on the forest floor.

"Noooo!" I wailed, falling with him. "Radax!" I fisted my hands in his hoodie.

His eyes remained open, staring into the woods, unseeing. The stream of blood slowed to a trickle.

"Die! All of you!" Ghata bellowed, spreading her arms wide.

The shadow behind her formed into a living breathing shape. Dark and ominous, it flared with light and crackled with menace. Licks of fire ran across the clearing toward the river. Old needles on the ground burst into flames. The flames spread along the ground like tentacles of a monster.

Trees around us caught on fire, shooting the flames up into the sky. Heat squeezed the oxygen out of the air around us, making it hard to breathe.

The world stopped making sense.

I lay on his chest, the only place I really ever wanted to be. I heard his last heartbeat before his heart went silent. I felt the warmth seep out of his body. And I had no strength, no will to carry on.

Life seemed to hang suspended as the fire raged.

"Heike!" Stella's voice broke through the inferno.

A wall of water came from nowhere. It crashed into the fire in a sizzling, steaming battle.

Strong arms grabbed me, hauling me away.

"No!" I fought, clinging to Radax's hoodie.

"Shh," Lero soothed, pressing me to his chest. "He's gone."

"We need to get out of here," Zeph urged. "To the river."

Lero ran, taking me away from Radax and from what I had done.

# Chapter Nineteen

HEIKE

Some things I remembered vividly. The sensation of the dagger's handle in my hand. The way the blade cut through his skin, muscles, and life-carrying vessels. How his eyes filled with relief and regret when he looked at me that one last time. The very last beat of his heart pulsing against my cheek pressed to his chest.

Others, I could hardly recall at all. Somehow, we got back to the river. Somehow, we crossed it in a boat again and made it back to the hotel in Irkutsk. Then, I found myself sitting on the floor in my room...*our* room.

I knew I had to get ready. We were leaving Irkutsk. Ghata was abandoning her camp. *Bracks* could come for us any minute. But all of that was somewhere far behind a wall of thick, impenetrable fog.

*"Pack your things,"* Stella had said before leaving me here.

I didn't have much to pack. Most of my things were still in our bags.

*Our...*

I shut my eyes and squeezed my hands into fists so hard, it hurt. My nails dug into my palms. Feeling physical pain gave an odd relief to the agony inside me.

We were leaving this hotel, this city. Lero was booking flights for us right now. I had to hurry. I couldn't hold them up.

I scrambled to my feet and threw the few things I had unpacked back into my suitcase. The long habit of living in hotels sent me through the room, to make sure I didn't forget anything. Like anything was important enough to hold on to—nothing was.

In the bathroom, I turned around.

Radax's shirt was hanging on the hook on the door. The one I'd taken off him last night when we were making love... The one he'd picked up off the floor and hung up on the hook just that morning...

A sob tore from my throat. I grabbed the t-shirt off the hook and buried my face in it. It smelled like him.

The lid I had slammed on my emotions tore open. Pain erupted from me in a cry and a torrent of tears. My knees gave in, sending me to the floor. Curling into a ball, I bawled into Radax's shirt.

"I love you," I groaned, finally finding the name for what I felt for him.

I loved him.

And I'd killed the man I loved.

"We can't just leave here." Stella energetically mixed sugar in her coffee.

"We'll need to find a safe place and come up with another plan," Zeph replied.

Lero produced his cellphone from the inside pocket of his blazer.

"I'll have to confirm her whereabouts next," he said, casting a glance around the airport lounge in Moscow where all of us were waiting for our next flight.

Stella looked up at him with curiosity.

"How are you going to do that?"

"I have a few people watching her. It's getting easier as her following is growing and her travel itinerary gets shared. To my knowledge, she hasn't started creating *bracks* from humans yet. Which means she only has a few *bracks* at her disposal. She may not have many to spare to send after us yet."

"Right," Zeph exhaled a humorless laugh. "Ghata must be on a tight schedule. Taking over the world is a demanding and time-consuming business."

Their conversation echoed as if from a distance somewhere. It blended with the noise of other people in the lounge. I couldn't focus on what they were saying, even if I tried. So, I didn't try at all.

Instead, I stared at a small chip in the laminate of the table. This was an executive lounge that we got access to only because of a fancy credit card I happened to have. And there it was—a crack in the laminate. Normally, I would photograph it from all angles for my blog. People loved that—a fault in luxury, a blemish in perfection, a stain on beauty.

"But what can we do?" Ivy asked, her slim fingers nervously ripping apart the pastry on the small plate in front of her. "Without the book, we still don't know how to fight her or, you know...kill her."

"Did you see what she can do?" Stella shifted in her chair uneasily. "She started a huge forest fire out of nothing. And what the hell was that dark shadow around her?" She shuddered, hugging herself. "It looked like a demon-dragon from hell."

"Her powers are growing," Lero said softly, staring at the table in front of him. I wondered if he noticed the crack in the laminate, too.

"Should we try to get the book again?" Zeph sounded as if thinking out loud.

Lero jerked his head. "Too much risk."

Stella nodded. "Without Radax, we won't be able to open the cabinet where she keeps it."

His name cut through the fog in my mind, spearing my heart. I flexed my fingers on the mug of tea in front of me. Staring at the tendrils of steam rising over the tea, I concentrated on each curl and curve they made as swells of pain rolled through me.

"We don't even know for sure if the book has any answers," Ivy pointed out. "Who knows what it says, anyway."

*"'The power over both the beginning and the end lies with the creator,'"* I repeated out loud the words Radax had read to me. The

characters of the language I'd never seen before were engraved in my memory.

"Is that from the book?" Ivy turned to me. "Heike, did you see it?"

"What does it mean?" Stella wondered.

*"He's my first creation,"* Ghata had said about Radax long time ago.

"She called Ra…" I swallowed a painful lump in my throat, unable to utter his name out loud. "She called *bracks* her creations," I managed, keeping my eyes on the soothing tendrils of steam over my cup.

"Of course she did," Ivy muttered under her breath. "I bet she thinks herself a creator."

Zeph scoffed. "The one who has an absolute power over everything."

"Over the beginning and the end, too." Stella's voice sounded hollow.

Confronting Ghata had become even more challenging than before. She was more dangerous than ever, and her powers were growing every day. The silence that descended over the table made me wonder if that was what the rest of them were thinking about, too.

Lero left the table, punching something in his phone. He returned a few minutes later.

"According to my sources," he said, taking his place at the table again. "Ghata's next stop will be Kazakhstan. Then she plans to fly to Turkey and travel by sea to Syria."

"Why by sea?" Ivy asked.

"It looks like she's planning to visit several countries along the coast of the Mediterranean Sea," Lero replied. "Syria, Lebanon, Israel, then Egypt."

"I'd be staying away from big water if I were her," Ivy muttered, tilting her head. "She knows Zeph is after her."

Lero shrugged. "She doesn't care. She's growing more powerful and obviously cocky. Ultimately, the magic of a goddess is much stronger than that of an individual fae. She'll be stronger than Zeph."

"What if she's lying about her plans? Keeping her true intentions to herself?" Stella asked.

"She can't lie about that. Not anymore." Lero sounded convinced. "She needs as many followers as possible. The more people attend her gatherings, the better for her. She needs to let the world know where she is going to be next and give her followers enough time to get there."

*Followers.*

They were the main source of Ghata's power. Their faith in her was the way she grew her dominance over the world.

I cleared my throat and asked, still staring at my mug, "When do you want to confront her?"

"The sooner the better since every day her powers grow," Zeph replied.

Lero added, "She's hitting the Mediterranean in four days. That's when I think we should do it."

Four days. A lot could be achieved in that time.

"Give me four days." I nodded. "And I'll make Ghata weaker before we confront her."

A new purpose was born in me, bringing me back to life, too.

"You?" Ivy's eyebrows rose to her hairline.

"How?" Stella turned to me.

Finally, I was able to tear my stare away from my cup and meet their eyes.

"If there's anything I know well, it's followers and how fickle their loyalty can be."

# Chapter Twenty

HEIKE

The villa Lero rented for us was beautiful. Situated on the coast of Greece, it had gorgeous views of the sea. If only I could pay enough attention to appreciate the scenery.

Normally, I would enjoy, photograph, and share all these stunning views on every one of my social media accounts. I'd barely noticed them, now. My one and only requirement for the villa had been internet access.

The moment I settled in my room, I turned on my laptop.

Ever since we left Moscow, revenge was what had fueled me. It gave me strength to fight the agony of grief.

From the moment I'd met Ghata, I'd disliked her. Now, I let that dislike grow into pure, undiluted hatred. I hated everything about her—her presence in this world, her dark, twisted essence, and the very sound of her name.

I had a new purpose, now. I wasn't going to rest until I erased Ghata from existence, or until she erased me.

Even compared to the last time I'd checked the internet, her online presence had grown by leaps and bounds. It was no longer confined to the hidden corners of the dark web. Now, it was right there, in the open.

There were lots of pictures of her surrounded by her followers from every country she'd visited so far. With a flawlessly executed smile, Ghata posed with her arms wide open, as if in a welcoming hug.

Her playing the role of an all-forgiving mother-goddess, ready to embrace every hurt, unfortunate, rejected soul made me gag. I knew perfectly well she was the one happy to inflict the pain.

And I needed to let others know.

I carefully studied everything she'd put out there to create her public image. I took note of every vulnerability I could spot.

So far, Ghata had been accepted as a messiah in many places she'd visited and beyond. But I knew she wouldn't stop there. She didn't want to be taken as someone else's messenger. Her ultimate goal had always been to reign as the goddess that she was.

There were a few images and a handful of videos of her performing miracles. I sensed she would do more soon, to prove her divinity. I had to nip it at the bud. I had to sow doubt in hope that it'd take.

First, I contacted my network, letting them know I'd be needing their help in spreading a message.

*"It's going to be huge,"* I promised them. After all, it was in our power to make it so.

I hinted that it had everything to do with the new religion taking the world by storm.

*"Girl, it's already huge!"* one of my contacts replied.

*"You're too late,"* another one assured me. *"This stuff has been trending for days, now."*

*"I have something entirely new,"* I promised. *"A hoax exposé. With evidence."*

The replies came like raindrops during a downpour.

*"Are you saying she's a fake?"*

*"Well, there are lots of skeptics. Gods don't exist."*

*"Is she some kind of an illusionist? I knew it!"*

*"No way!"*

*"Can you prove it?"*

*"You have videos?"*

I did. I had videos. I just needed to figure out the most effective way to use them.

For that, I had to find the courage to watch them.

I downloaded them all, the video I took of Radax in the cage, the one of him telling his story, and the last one from the forest near Irkutsk.

No matter how hard I tried, I couldn't bring myself to watch that last one. It was late at night when I finally felt strong enough to press the play button on the video from Xin's studio apartment.

*"So, come over here to the couch..."* my own voice sounded from the screen.

Then Radax, naked save for the pink towel around his hips, came into frame.

I choked on a sob and slapped my hand over his image on the screen. The phantom sensation of the blade cutting through the skin and muscles of his neck vibrated through my right hand—the hand that killed him.

"Oh God, I can't..." I cried. "I can't... I'm so, so sorry."

Grief shrouded me. Thick, heavy, suffocating.

Pain twisted my insides.

"I killed you," I spoke to the image I kept hidden under my palm, unable to face even his shadow on the screen.

The videos were the only memories I had of him on tape. And I was about to butcher them into pieces, to destroy them the way I'd destroyed him.

What kind of a monster I must be to exploit the images of a man I'd murdered? The man I'd loved?

I closed my eyes, dropping my hand from the screen.

"I can't do this, baby..."

The video kept playing. His voice filling the room.

*"...I've made the decision to tell you."* He spoke softly, but with conviction that carried a weight.

*"But what if I share with the others what I've learned?"* the old me—a far cry from the emotional wreck I'd become now—prompted.

*"Then, my story will be known."*

*"Is that what you want?"*

*"Yes."*

He sounded sure.

I opened my eyes, needing to see him. I hit pause, then zoomed in on his face.

His beloved features filled in the screen. Radax's face. So familiar, yet unattainable. His eyes were hidden under his eyelashes, his attention directed down to the tattoo on his forearm.

I hit *play* again.

He lifted his gaze, shifting his focus to the right of the camera—where I was sitting that day. My memory of that moment overlapped with the image on the screen. I remembered Xin's place again. The way it smelled like flowery soap after Radax's shower. The way the scent lingered on his damp skin later when I...

I drew in a shaky breath, shutting off all memories past that point. I couldn't handle them without breaking down. And I couldn't afford to be broken right now.

*"Sooner or later, I will have to return to Madame."* Radax's voice sounded from the screen, haunting in its prophecy. *"The moment I come back, I'll die."*

He knew.

He always had known.

And he'd done the only thing he could think of to be free from her, once and for all. He'd asked me to kill him. He trusted me to set him free.

I drew in a long breath. My lungs filled with the warm, fresh sea breeze that gently invaded the room through the open balcony doors. My chest expanded fully, for the first time since I stabbed the dagger into his neck.

"You're free," I whispered. "Wherever you are, baby, you're now free."

I wiped the tears off my cheeks.

He wanted his story to be known, but not in the way I was going to present it. However, if it contributed to Ghata's demise, I knew I would have Radax's approval.

Still, I felt the overwhelming need to apologize.

"Forgive me for what I'm about to do," I said.

My hand splayed on the screen next to his face, I allowed myself to pull one tiny memory out of the treasure chest I kept tightly sealed inside me—the memory of the way his beard felt when I used to sink my fingers in it, kissing him with abandon. I could almost feel the tickling and the prickle of his thick beard between my fingers when I aligned my hand with his jawline on the screen.

"Please forgive me, my love. This is the only way I know how to avenge you."

A part of me died with those words. My heart hardened, and my memories sank to the very bottom of my soul.

Then, I got to work.

I butchered the video into sections. I selected the parts where Radax spoke of Ghata's crimes and omitted those where he said anything about her being a goddess.

Then, I spliced the clips with the videos I'd downloaded from the internet. The videos of Ghata in her temples, of those worshiping her at gatherings.

I went further than that. I deliberately inserted some unrelated clips, those of crimes and atrocities committed elsewhere by someone else. I took the videos of Ghata's miracles, including the one I made of her turning Radax into a monster, and inserted objects meant to be explained as props. I created explanation videos, tearing her miracles apart frame by frame and "finding evidence" of CGIs. I accused her of illegal drug use and medical experimentation.

The more shocking the accusations, the stronger was the chance of them finding their way into people's minds. If the most outrageous of my claims were rejected outright, the others would gain more plausibility in comparison.

I dumped my videos into the deepest bowels of the dark web, using fake accounts and anonymous profiles.

The fabricated videos would eventually be proven false by those who dug deeper in search of the truth, but that would take time. By then, my message would already have made its impact on those people who were content with superficial information, which would be most of us. Then the ripples would spread.

All I needed was for the videos to wreak havoc in people's minds for the next four days.

I was not exposing the truth. I was serving it with a hefty dose of lies.

My goal was to discredit Ghata as the deity, even as she truly was one. But I didn't have to go far to invent my accusations. I exposed her as a child abductor, rapist, pedophile, and slaver—all of which she also was.

Locking my feelings so deep inside even I couldn't find them, I zoomed in on Radax's eyes as he was telling his story. Even if everyone who watched this felt but a fraction of the emotions reflected in the deep darkness of his eyes, they would no longer be able to believe the lies Ghata was spewing. I added Radax's words as text, in a heavy, bold font, in every language I could think of.

No one could miss the essence of my expose: Ghata was a power-hungry monster—cruel, scheming, and corrupt—but she was just a mortal woman, nothing more.

Once posted, I started sharing all this content everywhere I could think of. I used every account I had. I created new accounts and used catchy hashtags. I directed the people in my network to all of it. Then, I called on every favor anyone had owned me, in my circles and beyond.

I made everyone share, like, and comment. Then, share some more.

Someone would bring me food through the day. It barely registered with me who—Ivy or Stella more often, sometimes one of the men. Exhausted, I would fall asleep with my face on the keyboard.

Then, the next morning, I'd do it all over again.

I spliced fresh videos. I made gifs of most poignant moments—low-definition, but graphic and easy to share. I scheduled re-runs and re-posting for the days to come.

Four days was enough time for the fire to catch, and I wanted it to keep burning. Four days was also not too long for it all to die down under Ghata's efforts to suppress my work.

On the fourth day, I watched a gif of Radax's face playing on a loop on my screen. The seal I had placed on my emotions cracked open once again, and I felt tears burn my eyes. I stroked the screen, wishing I could feel his skin, the tickle of his beard once again.

He wanted his story to be known, and by now, hundreds of millions of people had heard it, and the number was growing every day. It was impossible to track it all accurately once it had taken off.

I'd sown doubt about Ghata into people's minds, and I hoped it was taking root. I had millions of followers of my own. In my experience, there always were those hardcore believers that comprised the nucleus of any follower base, be it a celebrity or a cult. But the dedication and loyalty of most fell along a wide spectrum, and those I hoped to sway. If I succeeded to shake their faith in her, her power would diminish.

Finally, I used screenshots of Ghata to make memes. I used short, punchy lines, with a generous dose of humor and ridicule.

Fear might give birth to faith and reverence. But laughter killed them both.

By the time Ghata moved into Mediterranean, she'd no longer be a deity to many people, not even a messiah. Many of those who'd seen what I'd put out there would view her as nothing more than a fraud, a failed cult leader—laughable and despised.

# Chapter Twenty-One

HEIKE

It was a warm late-spring afternoon in the Mediterranean when we boarded another boat Lero had rented. Ivy nodded to me when I took a seat next to her. Her expression was grim, as mine must be too.

This time, we weren't planning to sneak around. We were going to put an end to it, one way or another.

And this time, no one questioned me coming along. I was a part of the team.

The sword in the sheath strapped to my back thudded against the bench as I sat down. I adjusted the strap across my chest.

Zeph had retrieved an entire arsenal of weapons from the bottom of the ocean where he'd buried them with the bodies of the *bracks* he'd killed when they had attacked Blue Cay. Now, we all were armed with weapons made of iron from Nerifir.

I had a blade hidden in each of my boots, one strapped to my thigh, and a sword behind my back. Dressed all in black, with weapons strapped all over my body, I looked like an assassin. Yet the only time I'd ever killed was...

Pain, as sharp as ever, sliced through my heart.

I sucked in a breath, closing my eyes.

I couldn't think about that...

*I couldn't...*

Ivy covered my hand with hers. My fingers were trembling. She said nothing, just held my hand while the boat glided smoothly across the sea. Swimming next to our boat, Zeph made it move ahead.

It wasn't long until Ghata's flotilla came into view. She had five boats—one of them a large luxury yacht.

"The bitch travels in style," Ivy muttered.

"She obviously has some money to spend, now," Stella echoed, sitting on the other side of Ivy.

"She made a whole chunk of it at the expense of Zeph and Lero." Ivy's grip on my hand tightened.

At the expense of Radax, too. Ghata had made him suffer, displaying his torture for money.

I removed my hand from Ivy's, lest I crushed her fingers by clenching my fists too tight.

Lero rose to his feet. Stella stood at his side.

The sea lifted Zeph higher, bringing him eye level with Lero standing at the stern.

With a flick of Zeph's wrist, a white-crested swell rolled across the sea, toward Ghata's entourage. About half-way, the swell split in five. Four of them lifted one of Ghata's smaller boats and neatly tipped them over.

It happened fast, with no mess or excessive noise. The sea smoothed out quickly. Now, only the yacht remained upright. The swell had crashed over its side, then slid back into the sea, without causing it any harm.

With a wave of his hand, Zeph sent a bigger swell out. It built up as it rolled across the choppy surface of the sea. Before hitting the yacht, it was met with a giant wave that came from the opposite direction.

The two waves collided and crashed. Sea foam flew in clumps like wet, torn clouds.

An eerie sound rose over the water. It sounded like the clinking of silver bells. Ghata's laugh.

Chill seeped through my skin and muscle, freezing to the bone.

Another swell rose in the sea, bigger than any before. This time, the giant wall of water rolled from Ghata's yacht to our boat.

"Oh, no!" I jumped to my feet, my heart pumping fast.

The swell rose higher and higher, like a wall of foamy blue water. It threatened to swallow the boat and all of us on it.

Ivy stood next to me. "Zeph will never let water harm us," she said with conviction, though her face turned as white as the seafoam.

Zeph's expression hardened. Spreading his arms wide, he made the sea lift him high above our boat. I had to tilt my head all the way back to see him up there.

The sea between us and Ghata's yacht bubbled. The surface bulged, swelling in the middle—more menacing in its nearly absolute silence.

With a gesture from Zeph, the giant mass of water rolled toward the incoming swell.

The huge waves collided with thundering sound. Two forces exploded in a blast of water and light.

The sea water rose into the sky but didn't crash down. Instead, the wall of it ran around both vessels, circling them. In a moment, both our boat and Ghata's yacht ended up enclosed by the circular wall of water, obscured from view of anyone at sea or on the shore.

The middle of the water funnel bubbled again. I glanced up at Zeph. It wasn't his doing, this time. He seemed to be just as confused as the rest of us.

"What is that?" Ivy grabbed the railing in a white-knuckled grip.

The water in the middle rushed away from the center. Hard ground rose higher, forming an island, with the yacht beached on it.

A door opened in the hull of the yacht and a ramp descended.

Ghata, in all her red-and-black silk glory, stepped out.

"How do you like my island, my little siren?" she cooed, tilting her head to the side. "I figured I'd rather meet you on even ground. The ground *I* created."

Zeph gritted his teeth, a murderous expression in his stormy-blue eyes. He cut through the air with both arms. The water ran from behind us, around us, and over the island.

"Not so fast!" Ghata lifted her arm, and the water rolled aside, joining the wall that circled us and the island.

"She has water power," Ivy gasped. "Even more than Zeph."

"Oh yes, I do, my useless little human," Ghata taunted.

Next, she flicked her wrist, and a steady flow of *bracks* poured from the yacht.

Lero drew his swords with a swishing sound. "Get me to the ground, Zeph," he requested, his expression hard as stone.

Stella released a soft gasp but didn't say a word of protest.

He flashed her a brief but tender smile.

"Turn me, my star."

Stella drew in a long, labored breath.

"Go, Lero," she said softly, even as I knew each word must be cutting through her heart with worry. "Be the beast you are."

Lero's clothes tore and fell away. He almost doubled in size. Black fur burst from his body. His face grew longer. His mouth turned into a maw full of long, needle sharp teeth.

I watched in horror and awe as the man turned into a werewolf right in front of my eyes.

"Neat," Ghata bit off, hurling daggers with her eyes at Stella.

Ghata had no use for Lero, but it irked her, it drove her mad that someone—a "useless little human"—had a power she didn't possess. No one, not a goddess, not even the Moon itself, could allow a werewolf to turn at will.

But Stella could.

Lero leaped into the wave Zeph had made rise for him. He roared as the water carried him to the island.

"Get him!" Ghata ordered to her minions.

*Bracks* jumped toward Lero. He slashed with his swords, cutting and slicing through their flesh.

"Me next." Stella put her foot on the railing, ready to jump, her stare firmly on Lero.

Things were happening so fast, I had no chance to process them. Her words finally snapped me into action. Ivy was next to us, her sword ready.

"We'll all go." I slid my sword out, too.

Zeph made a wave carry all of us from the boat, then gently set us down on the soggy ground of the island.

Ghata tapped her chin with her finger, looking amused.

"What a lovely bunch we have here. Isn't it nice when friends get to die together?" She made a sharp gesture, sending a group of *bracks* our way. "Fools," she hissed. "Weak, stupid females."

*Stupid?*

Blistering hot rage seared through me.

"Hey!" I yelled. "Where's your fire, Ghata?"

She shot me a glare, raising her hand. The tattoos on the *bracks'* arms lit up, pulsing bright.

"Time to end these humans, my pets," she said, not dignifying me with an answer to my question.

The *bracks* groaned as the tattoos burned into their skin. Sparks of light and licks of fire burst out. The *bracks'* skin split open. Their clothes tore to pieces as they grew into giants.

"What's happening?" Ivy leaped a step back.

Stella gripped tighter the knives in her hands. "What is she doing to them?"

"*Brack* transformation," I gritted through my teeth. "That's what she turns the boys she takes away from their families into. Monsters."

Ghata had ignored my question about her fire power. After that impressive display of her wielding it back in the woods outside of Irkutsk, it could be expected she'd use it here again. A wall of fire would've easily swept us all off this island.

Yet she hadn't lit a flicker.

A *brack*, grown in size and proportions to a monster, jumped my way.

I wielded my sword, trying to look like I knew what I was doing. In reality, the only lessons in killing people I ever got were one from Lero that morning and one from Radax in the hotel days ago...

*Stab and slice.*

Once again, I shoved that memory deep inside me. I couldn't let it destroy me. Because it would crush me if I just thought about that...

Luckily, fighting *bracks* when they were in their giant monster form didn't require much skill or finesse. One just had to be fast.

I sliced across the *brack's* ankle with my sword. He growled, tripping and falling to his knees. Sparks from the weapon's Nerifir iron blended with the fire blasting from his tattoo.

"Where's your fire power, Ghata?" I yelled again, jumping away from the fallen monster.

Did she lose it? Or was she planning something else? Something worse?

She glared at me.

"If it isn't the German girl who doesn't look German," she chuckled.

I didn't care about her insults. Her bitter expression told me enough. She couldn't use her fire power. The water battle with Zeph, the raising of the island, and now holding the sea back from flooding it depleted her magic. And there was not enough faith from her followers to replenish it.

"I guess people don't want to believe in you." I leaped aside, evading another attack from the injured *brack* who bumped into one of his kind in a clumsy effort to grab me.

Turning them into monsters might not have been a smart move on Ghata's part. There wasn't much space for them to turn around.

Very much like Radax's cage used to be...

Shit. Not again.

I forced that memory deep where it came from, too. The heavy lid I'd slammed on them to keep them down kept shifting.

"Everyone knows you're a fake!" I yelled. "A fraud!"

Ghata's glare grew dark and heavy with understanding.

"You!" she seethed.

"Me." I crossed my stare with hers, wishing that looks could kill. "I told the world exactly what you are."

"You've been spreading lies!"

"No. I've been exposing you where it matters. You're a greedy criminal and an evil monster. And that's the truth!"

Her expression melted into a fake smile that terrified me more than any of her scowls.

"I have something for you too, human." She gestured to the yacht behind her. "Come out, slave."

The island shook under the heavy steps of the monstrous *bracks*. Another set of footfalls added to the vibrations as one more *brack* exited the yacht.

His proportions and facial features were just as distorted as those of the rest of the *bracks*—flat forehead, long arms, impossibly thick neck. But his skin was much paler, with ashen gray tint. Even the flames from his tattoo appeared paler and cooler, too.

"Do you recognize your *boyfriend*, human?" Ghata gloated with glee. "I know you killed him, but that's what lovers do. Love kills. *I* bring back life!"

I stared at his monstrous shape as he approached us, so grotesque and strange, yet so painfully familiar.

"Radax..." Breath left me.

Life appeared to be leaving me with it.

# Chapter Twenty-Two

HEIKE

His eyes glowed with the same cool flames as his tattoos. The look in them unseeing.

"I knew you'd like my little surprise," Ghata chuckled, not hiding her delight at my shock and horror.

I glared at her.

"Don't you give me that look," she squinted at me. "I'm not his murderer. *You* are." She pointed an accusing finger at me. The long sleeve of her dress swayed, the end brushing along the wet ground. "*You* killed him, sweetie." She stroked Radax's thigh, which was as high as she could reach with him being this monstrous size. "But I couldn't let my most favorite creation die, could I? He is alive. Well, sort of," she added with another chuckle. "He can no longer change forms. But he's utterly and completely mine."

Radax stood at her side, not contradicting any of it. The dead look in his eyes twisted a knife in my heart.

I'd killed him, but she wouldn't let him die. She couldn't give him even that little mercy.

"Now, Radax, my pet," Ghata purred. "Kill that insolent girl. She dared defy your one true master. She needs to be punished."

Radax stirred at her words. He stomped heavily, moving on me like a mindless machine. A robot or a zombie.

"No..." I dropped my arm, still holding the sword in my hand.

I had set him free.

Even in the deepest pits of grief and despair, the thought of him being free from torture had brought me comfort. I'd thought he was far away from her reach, safe.

When all this time, he'd been suffering more than ever before.

"There is something poetic about dying at a lover's hand, isn't there?" Ghata kept mocking me. "Of course, dying from his dick would've been even more poetic, but we don't have time for that. You're not getting the pleasure of fucking him ever again. His life, his soul, and his cock are all mine, now."

She'd called him her favorite creation. But Ghata had no favorites. She didn't care about anything or anyone. She certainly was never attached to Radax, either. The only reason she did this to him was to prove that she could.

She tortured him in death as she did in life.

"Is there no limit to your cruelties?" I groaned.

"Cruelties?" she scoffed. "These are my powers! And they are limitless." Her voice turned cold and sharp. "Kill her, Radax, my slave. And this time make sure you do it right. Or I'll kill *you*, and then bring you back again and again. Repeatedly."

She sank her long, sharp nails into his thigh.

"I am a goddess!" Ghata's voice soared over the island and the sea. "Only a true deity can raise the dead. And I did it!"

Radax howled in pain, tossing his head back. Rivulets of red blood dripped down his skin from under her nails.

He bled.

He was alive.

Which meant he could be killed. Again.

I could still set him free—send him to another world and hide his body in a place where she wouldn't find him.

Radax launched for me, and instead of running away, I ran to him.

I would set him free as many times as it took, even if it killed me, too. Maybe if I died with him and there was no one left for Ghata to mock, then she would let him stay dead for good.

He roared, grasping for me. But I was faster. As he crouched, I jumped on his knee, then climbed on his bent arm up to his shoulder.

"Radax, it's me." I hooked both arms over his left shoulder, clutching my sword in my right hand. "Do you remember me, baby? Do you remember anything at all?"

I prayed to see any spark of reason in those dead, glowing eyes. Any light of awareness or recognition.

Did she really make a zombie out of him? Was he nothing more but an animated corpse, now?

Growling, he swatted at me with his right hand.

I pushed with my feet against his bicep and swung myself out of his grasp. My arms shook from the strain of holding my weight. I knew they wouldn't hold for long.

"I love you, Radax," I said hurriedly, panting for breath. I needed to say it whether he understood me or not. "I love you, and I miss you every minute of every day." I adjusted my grip on his shoulder, trying to stay away from the flames around his neck.

Finding a footing on his bent forearm, I lifted my sword, aiming at the same spot I'd stabbed him before. The flames would burn me this time, but I didn't care.

"I love you, and I want you free. You belong to no one."

*Stab and slice.*

Just like he wanted.

"Kill her," Ghata yelled. "Will you finally kill this human shit!"

He could, it dawned on me.

Right now, Radax could easily kill me. I was standing on his bent forearm, in the crook of his elbow. All he had to do was drop his arm down, and I would fall. But he didn't do it. He kept his arm bent, supporting me. Even as I had my sword aimed at his neck.

Whatever horrors Ghata had put him through, she could never erase the spark of defiance that had always burned in him.

"Radax, baby..." I breathed out.

My hand with the sword trembled, and I lowered it down on his shoulder.

I had to talk to him. I needed to try.

The words that had been churning inside me with nowhere to go spilled from me, now. Everything I'd wanted to tell him before but couldn't.

"I love you, Radax." I glided my hand over his gray, lifeless skin. "And I know you want to love me back. Love me, Radax, because you can. You can love with so much passion and devotion that no other man could ever rival. No one has ever touched me the way you have. No one can kiss the way you do. No man has ever cared about me as deeply as you have, with so much trust and affection."

Another *brack* took a swing at me from the side. I stuck my sword out, poking him in the hand. Radax yanked back his right elbow, jamming it in the ribs of the *brack*. The monster staggered and rolled to the ground.

"Radax!" Ghata wailed. "You treacherous beast. Brainless *voukalak!* I said kill her!" she ordered.

"Stay with me!" I gave him an order of my own, just as loudly. "Stay with me, Radax. Fight with me, not against me."

She'd called him *voukalak*—the animal all werewolves had come from. Ghata had twisted and distorted the nature of the beast inside them, but it must still be there in some form.

Like all *bracks*, Radax came from werewolves, too.

"I know you're still in there, Radax," I kept talking, afraid that if I stopped, whatever connection between us that kept him from hurting me would break. "Deep inside, you always have been your own person, my love. For centuries Ghata had you under her control, but she failed to destroy you. She didn't win. You did."

He turned his head my way, and I stroked along his jawline—beardless in this form.

The flames around his neck receded, the glow in his eyes did, too.

"Oh Radax," I groaned, my vision swimming with tears. "I'd die to have you back. Please, stay alive with me."

I heard a movement behind us. Radax jerked his head in that direction, but I gently guided his face back to me again.

"She doesn't own you, Radax. No one does. Your mind is your own. You've kept it against all odds for many centuries. And your heart is mine, not hers. I have it, and I'm not giving it up."

I leaned closer and kissed near the corner of his mouth.

He was a monster, his skin split, his body risen from the dead, but a tendril of the familiar scent still clung to him. I sobbed, catching it. Tears ran down my cheeks, dropping on his shoulder below.

"Fight with me, Radax," I pleaded. "Fight with me, and together we will win."

Certainty settled in my heart, stronger than anything I'd ever felt. As long as we were together, we could fight the world and any power in it. We could fight even death.

A blast of heat hit us from behind.

Radax lifted his hand to me. Instead of hitting me, he shielded me with it.

I glanced over his shoulder...and froze.

Spreading her arms out—her wide, long sleeves flying in the wind—Ghata grew. Her body stretched and widened. Her red dress melted into her skin and became scarlet scales. Her fiery red hair turned into a long plume, trailing behind her. And her arms shifted into a pair of black wings.

Radax turned slowly to face what his tormentor had become.

Ghata had always been a bigger monster than any of them. Now, she looked like it, too.

Her serpent-like body was covered in red, glossy scales. It undulated and coiled. Three pairs of legs with clawed feet dug into the wet sand. The black leathery wings flopped behind her back.

Radax carefully set me on the ground and gently pushed me behind him, placing himself between me and the abomination that Ghata's had turned into.

She lowered her large, elongated head and opened her mouth set with long curved teeth.

"Disloyal fool!" thundered from the throat of the nightmarish creature. "Burn in hell where you belong."

A hot air blasted from her mouth. It blew the fine hairs that strayed out of my ponytail back around my face and scorched my skin with heat. But the blast was otherwise harmless. It had not a lick of fire, just heat.

Ghata had lost a lot of her strength, and she couldn't replenish it with faith of followers who were no longer there for her. Thanks to me and my team.

"Running out of steam?" I taunted.

She whipped her head to me. Snapping her terrifying teeth, she lunged at me.

Radax jumped to cut her off. With his thick arms around her neck, he shoved her back.

"Don't you dare touch me, slave!" she roared.

With a lash of her long tail, she knocked him off his feet.

A thunderous growl sounded, right next to me. Lero had lost his swords somewhere. Unarmed, but in his terrifying werewolf form, he tore through the *bracks* with his claws and teeth. His saliva dripped on their bodies, hissing and steaming. The moment it touched them, they dropped to the ground and stayed there.

He whipped his head toward Ghata. His silver eyes narrowed to slits. He growled again and leaped.

Rising on four of her six feet, Ghata swiped with a front paw, blocking Lero's attack.

"Lero!" Zeph grunted, making his way to his friend.

Locked in a standstill with Ghata to maintain the funnel in the middle of the sea, Zeph couldn't use his water powers for anything else. With Ivy at his side, he fought using other means, instead. Weaving elegantly between the legs of the giant *bracks*, he sliced and stabbed with two long swords in his hands.

A brilliant, sail-like fin was also open on his back. Its spikes glistened, dripping poison. Like Lero's toxic bite, a scratch of Zeph's spikes sent *bracks* to the ground—dead.

A *brack* rushed by me to Ghata's aid, and I stabbed him in the foot with my sword.

He howled in pain, grabbing his foot.

Stella ran from behind him, slashing across his other ankle.

"Get him, Heike!" she yelled as the *brack* crashed to the ground. His head landed at my feet.

I raised my sword, searching for the spot on the *brack's* neck, the one that Radax had shown me.

Radax...

My heart beat with a loud thud.

In this form, the *brack* looked so much like the man I loved. They all were like identical twins. Flames burst between the lines of the tattoo that had split his skin. Just like Radax, the *brack* wasn't free. He was a slave, tortured and abused.

My arm with the sword grew weak, and I dropped it.

I couldn't stab him. I couldn't kill.

This man didn't just look like Radax. Each *brack's* history was the same. Like Radax, he used to be a boy long ago. Just like Radax, his family handed him over to Ghata to molest, rape, and abuse for an eternity.

I put away my weapon and stepped back.

Unlike Radax, this *brack* retained nothing of the boy he once was, though. He leaped to his feet, facing me.

I lifted my empty hands up, showing I wasn't going to fight him.

"You don't have to obey her," I told him. "Without you, she's nothing."

Meanwhile, Radax had staggered to his feet. And Zeph attacked Ghata in her monstrous form. He stabbed his sword in her neck, but the weapon bounced off her hard scales. He snapped a fin open on the back of his forearm and slashed at her with the poisonous spikes.

Nothing happened. The scales deflected the spikes, too.

"Silly little siren. Do you really think you can fight me?" Ghata hissed, raising a clawed foot to crush Zeph.

With a deafening roar, Lero leaped at her and sank his teeth into her leg.

She shook him off with a snarl, but his teeth left a mark. His bite had cracked the scales. Blood dripped from the puncture wounds left by his fangs.

Lero had harmed her. Was he the only one who could kill her?

The *brack* I'd spared lunged for me.

I leaped aside, but his hand brushed by my shoulder. The impact was strong enough to send me face down into the sand.

I flipped to my back, spitting out wet dirt and soggy pieces of seaweed.

"Wait!" I lifted my hands above me, as if I could stop this mountain of a monster from advancing. "You don't have to do this. You don't have to listen to her!" I yelled in desperation. "She feeds on your faith, fueled by your loyalty. Everything she is came from you. *You* created *her.*"

The realization hit me like a ray of light piercing through the darkness.

"You are the *creators,*" I whispered, overwhelmed by the clarity of it all. "Not her."

Ghata called herself a creator any chance she got, but she never created a thing. All she'd ever done was modify, warp, and transform the creations of others.

Werewolves of Nerifir were the ones who had brought her to life in the first place. She was an embodiment of the Moon they had wished to worship.

The line from the ancient book sounded in my mind again, filled with new meaning.

*"The power over both the beginning and the end lies with the creator."*

Werewolves of Nerifir created this abomination. They were the only ones who could rid the world from her, too.

That was what had happened in Nerifir. The werewolves rebelled against Ghata, rendering her weak and defenseless. They would've ended her then, but she ran.

The reason she never shared the phrase from the first page of her divine book was because she knew it was the warning meant to safeguard the people who created her. These words were indeed the instructions to her demise.

The *brack* pinned me to the ground with his hand.

"Heike!" Stella ran to us, her sword raised over her head.

I wrapped my hands around one of the the giant fingers that threatened to crush me.

"You are Ghata's creators!" I yelled to the *brack*. "The power of the beginning and the end lies with you. Your faith made her. Your wrath can end her."

The *brack* growled. Paying no attention to my words, he got a better grip on me.

Stella slammed into his arm, stabbing it with her sword. He yanked his hand away from my chest, and I gasped for air, hungrily filling my lungs with every breath.

I didn't know if any of the *bracks* had heard my words, but Stella had.

Her brow furrowed, understanding flashed on her face before she turned to the *brack* she'd just gotten off me. She placed her sword in front of her, holding it with both hands and pointing it at him.

"The werewolves are the ones who can destroy Ghata," she spoke as if to herself. "They're the only ones who can kill their goddess."

She tilted her head back searching for the *brack's* eyes high above us.

"Deep inside somewhere you're a werewolf, too, aren't you? Only you can end this. Only you can set yourselves free." Her voice was soft, just like it had been when she'd ordered Lero to shift into the beast, even when there was no full moon in the sky. Her bond with Lero allowed Stella to dip into the werewolves' magic.

"The Moon is the one true deity of werewolves," she said to the *brack*. "Ghata is nothing. She was made by you."

The *brack's* body tensed. He crouched low and tossed his head back. A long, blood-curdling howl tore from his throat as he faced the sky.

"She took everything from you!" Stella raised her voice, sending it ringing high above the island and the carnage of the battle. "Ghata took your freedom, your family, and your innocence. What did you get in return? Cruelty and an eternity of servitude." She turned around slowly, addressing all the *bracks* on the island. "She calls you her creations, but *you're* the ones who created *her*. Your loyalty, your trust, and your faith have been feeding her powers. She is nothing without you," she echoed my words.

A loud roar ripped through the air as Lero attacked Ghata again. His claws ripped deep gashes in the scales on her neck. But she closed her teeth over his shoulder and tossed him aside. He hit the ground with a groan of pain.

"Lero!" Stella ran across the island to him.

Ghata lunged after Lero.

Radax grabbed the tip of her tail and yanked her back, away from the werewolf. Her teeth snapped barely an inch from Lero's head.

Stella whipped around to face the *bracks* who stood nearby, no longer helping Ghata but not attacking her either.

"Are you just going to stand there?" Stella yelled, with tears in her eyes. "While that evil creature is slaying one of your own? Or are you going to help Lero fight her?"

She raised her hand, directing the *bracks* toward Ghata.

"Go, be the beasts you were born to be, not the slaves she made of you!"

One by one, the *bracks* fell to their knees. Their howls soared to the sky in a sorrowful choir. Stella wielded the power of the Moon. The same power that turned the tides of the oceans and turned men into beasts.

The hulking bodies of the *bracks* shrank. Black fur sprouted from their skin, scorched by the fire from their tattoos. The wounds on their arms and necks closed. The fire fizzled out and died.

For the first time in centuries—in millennia, for many of them—the *bracks* took the form they were meant to be in. They turned back into werewolves.

Stella raised her sword over her head.

"Take back your freedom!" she screamed at the top of her lungs.

Snarling, lethal saliva dripping from their teeth, the pack rushed their slaver.

"You fools!" Ghata roared. "Why are you listening to her? She is a pathetic human, a nobody. I. Am. A. Goddess!"

She flapped her wings, trying to rise into the air.

A werewolf leaped, snapping her wing with his teeth. His fangs tore long gashes through the leathery surface, the edges of the tear smoldering from his poison.

Ghata swayed off-kilter in the air, crashing back to the ground.

Another werewolf jumped, going for her throat. That one might've been Lero. But it was hard to tell for sure. With the *bracks* shifting to werewolves, he blended in with the pack.

Radax was the only one who retained his monstrous form.

Ghata rolled him on the ground with her clawed feet. He grabbed one of them with his hands. His face distorted into a grimace of rage. His biceps bulged as he bent the creature's leg, then broke it in half.

The otherworldly serpent bellowed in pain, stomping on him with another foot.

I drew my sword out again and rushed to his aid. Even if all I could do was to distract her by poking her in the tail, then that was what I was going to do.

Radax shoved her foot off him. Her claws sliced through his skin. The long gashes quickly filled with blood. It dripped to the ground, mixing with the sea water on the wet sand.

But it was Ghata who appeared to be weakened the most. Every attack by those who'd once blindly served her carried an impact beyond physical.

Every snap of the werewolves' teeth, each slash of their claws through her scales brought her lower to the ground.

Her wings drooped. The coils of her tail flattened against the island she'd made.

The werewolves swarmed her. A deadly pile of fur, claws, and poisonous fangs.

When they fell away, the demon-dragon was gone.

A beautiful young woman lay on the ground, instead.

The scratches and bite marks vanished, leaving her skin unmarred and glowing. Her eyes closed, her expression was peaceful and innocent.

The woman had Ghata's facial features. The same long, flaming red hair. The same pale skin. But without the goddess's expressions—either hateful or mocking—the woman was almost unrecognizable as her.

She was the physical entity meant to embody the Moon for the werewolves. But her own greed, cruelty, and unquenchable thirst for power ruined it all.

The woman's shape thinned, turning translucent. Her body appeared to glow from within.

No longer held back by Ghata, the sea water rushed the island. Zeph raised his hand. The wave washed over the ground, kissing our ankles, then retreated.

What remained of Ghata dissolved into the waves in a silver glow. I wondered if the Moon would simply gather the released magic back with the next tide.

“She’s gone,” Ivy whispered, standing next to me.

“Now that’s what I call poetic,” I said quietly. “Poetic justice.”

# Chapter Twenty-Three

HEIKE

"Where's the boat?" Ivy asked, looking around.

The wall of water still surrounded the island, held back by Zeph's power.

"We won't all fit on it, now." Zeph tipped his chin at Radax and the werewolves sitting on their haunches all over the island. "We're taking the yacht."

He gestured at the water, and a wave swept us all up, then deposited us onto Ghata's yacht. The wall of water dropped into the waves, flooding the small island that Ghata had forced to rise from the bottom of the sea. Now it, too, was gone.

The sea returned to normal.

"You'd better take him inside." Stella pointed at Radax who sat on the deck of the yacht with us.

Even when he was sitting on the floor, I could barely reach his shoulder.

Zeph nodded. "He's sticking out too much. Other ships might spot him if he stays out here."

I touched Radax's arm.

"Come, baby," I said softly, going to the glass double doors that looked like they led to a spacious lounge.

He followed me, crawling on his knees to fit through the doors. When he had settled down on the floor inside the lounge, his feet bent in front of him, he reached for me. He grabbed me around my waist, then placed me on his thigh.

"I missed you, too, honey." I smiled. Standing on his arm that he'd placed on his thigh, I was high enough to wrap my arms half-way around his thick neck.

His tattoo sparked white where my fingers brushed its lines. Ghata's magic was gone. But Radax was no mere human. The fae magic hadn't left him.

"He can't speak in this form, either?" Stella asked, coming into the lounge with us. "Just like Lero."

I stroked the side of his neck.

"I don't know if he can, but I haven't heard him speak when he is like this."

"You know you have to have sex with him," Ivy blurted out, entering from the deck.

A werewolf followed her in, then headed over to Stella. I recognized Lero's silver eyes glistening among the jet-black fur of his face.

Zeph was nowhere to be seen. He must've leaped overboard again, making the sea take us where he wanted the yacht to go.

"Why sex?" I asked Ivy.

"That's what Stella does to bring Lero back when there's no full moon."

"Really?" I shifted my gaze to Stella.

Blush colored her cheeks. "Thanks, Ivy." She made a face, glancing at her friend.

"What?" Ivy shrugged. "Heike needs to know how it works. Radax is kind of a werewolf, right? So, sex should do it."

I hoped sex was all it took. Ghata had claimed that Radax couldn't shift forms anymore, but it wouldn't be the only time she lied. Besides, Stella could do things that Ghata couldn't. Even if Ghata was unable to make Radax shift, it didn't mean it couldn't be done.

"Okay, but let's wait until we're back on Blue Cay before having sex," Stella quipped.

"Yes, please!" Ivy laughed. "Let's not do it here. Even though I really want to know how one would have sex with *that*." She cast a furtive glance at Radax's crotch.

I looked down, too.

He was naked in this form. Back in the heat of the battle, it wasn't as apparent somehow. Now, I cleared my throat, faced with his massive erection pointing straight up at me.

"Here." Ivy took a silk embroidered throw from one of the couches in the room and tossed it to me. "Hope it's large enough to cover that *thing*."

"I'll do my best." I shook out the throw, then draped it over Radax's giant member, concealing it the best I could. "That'll have to do." I smiled, lifting my face to his.

Need burned bright in his dark, tea-colored eyes. Deep and passionate, his desire now lacked the sickness of desperation it'd so often had before. Radax obviously wanted me, but not because he needed my touch to survive another day away from his tormentor.

He wanted me for me.

Curling my legs under me, I sat on top of his thigh. He rested his arms on his knees, and I leaned back against his hard abs.

Tension and stress of the past few days finally started to recede. Both my mind and my heart felt lighter. Even having Radax silent and frozen in this form for now didn't bother me much at the moment. We had defeated the evil goddess. I got the love of my life back from the dead. I would find a way to help him shift into his usual form. And if sex was needed for him to shift back, I'd be delighted to make it happen.

Looking completely exhausted, Lero crashed on one of the couches, drawing Stella in his lap.

"You don't look so good, darling," Stella fussed, hovering her fingers over his many wounds and blood smeared fur. "You should rest when we get home. Get better, first. I'll work on turning you back, later."

He growled in protest. Wrapping his arm around her waist, he drew her closer.

Ivy smiled, looking at them, then glanced at the deck through the glass doors. There on the back deck, the werewolves were shaking out water from their hides and licking their wounds.

Ghata used to have hundreds if not thousands of *bracks* in her power. She'd brought many of them to this world over the years. And she had gotten most of them killed.

Out of the several dozens of *bracks* who had been on the yacht with her, only nine remained.

"So," Ivy rubbed her jaw in thought. "Who is going to have sex with all of *them,* now?"

"You like me touching you, don't you, big boy?" I murmured against Radax's neck, my arms wrapped tightly around him. My hands didn't quite meet because his neck was so damn thick.

Even with Zeph's incredible powers, it still took us a while to make it back to Blue Cay. The moment Zeph had gotten the yacht as close as he could to the shore, he made a wave sweep us to the beach in front of the main house.

Radax grabbed me and carried me to the beach behind the room where we'd stayed before.

He remembered the place.

I snuggled closer to him. It was both amazing and unbelievable to have him back. I hoped I'd be able to help him shift into a man. I longed to hear his voice again. But at that very moment, I was just too happy to be able to touch him.

He stepped behind the rocks and trees. With his current height, it wasn't easy to hide him. He plopped onto the sand, concealed from view a little more. Though, I didn't think anyone would walk around the house right now. Stella and Lero had their own transformation issue to worry about. And Zeph would probably remain on the yacht with Ivy, staying as far away from the four of us as possible.

"Well, let's hope this works." I released Radax's neck and slid into his lap.

His hard, giant member bobbed eagerly, as if greeting me.

I sucked in a breath. "I keep forgetting how huge you are in this form."

Pressing both my hands to each side of his shaft, I slid them up to the thick bulbous tip.

A shudder ran down his massive body, making the ground shake.

"Just lay back and relax, babe," I said softly. "I'll do all the work."

But he didn't seem to be willing to leave it up to me. Curving a finger, he caught the bottom of my black t-shirt and yanked it up.

"You want me naked, too?"

The material barely held at the seams under his strength, and I quickly took the t-shirt off before he ripped it.

He tugged at the belt of my pants next.

"Fine, fine," I murmured, unbuckling the belt and kicking off my boots. "It's all coming off, big guy."

The sun was setting already, but the air was still scorching hot. It was a relief to get rid of my black, fitted clothes.

Impatient, he tugged at my bra, breaking the little hooks. My panties were torn next as he ripped them off me.

Completely naked, I stretched in the warm breeze from the sea, then hugged his giant cock. It was hard like a log. Hot blood pulsed under the silky skin that was stretched tight over the bulging veins.

Facing Radax, I scooted closer, holding him upright between my spread legs. As thick as my thigh and almost as long as my arm, there was no way he'd ever fit inside me. So, I didn't even bother to try. Instead, I kept sliding my hands up and down his incredible length.

Cupping my ass with one hand, he stroked my back with a finger of the other, then slid it along the side of my neck and down my chest.

"You remember..." I exhaled as he rubbed my nipple. "You remember the places I like to be touched."

The sensation of his touch in this form was very different. The tip of his finger nearly covered my entire breast. Regardless, my body met it with a thrill. My skin rippled with pleasure. It was a treat I'd never thought I'd have again, having his hands on me.

"Radax..." I moaned.

Shifting my hips closer, I rubbed myself against him. I wanted him inside me so badly. This had better work. I slid my hands up and down his shaft faster.

He groaned, tossing his head back. Arching his back, he fisted his hands in the sand. His hips jerked. I leaped aside, remembering the acid-like substance he'd released the last time he was in this form.

This time, it came with no red in it, though. Creamy spurts of his release shot out and harmlessly landed on the sand. The abundance of it was still astonishing, but there was no hissing or steaming.

Every trace of Ghata was gone from Radax. And with it, the pain had vanished. A wide, blissful smile spread on his face as he stretched in the sand. He scooped me off his thigh and placed me on his chest as he lay down.

I pressed my face against his skin and stretched my arms above my head to touch his neck. His body felt warmer, now. The gray color had disappeared, and his skin returned its former healthy appearance. His tattoos looked again like nothing more than body art. Spectacular but harmless.

A moment later, his massive body started to shrink under me, bringing his face closer to mine. My lower part dropped from him, my hip landing on the beach next to him. He flexed his arm around my shoulders, keeping our upper bodies connected.

"Radax," I whispered.

Tears sprung to my eyes when my fingers sank into his beard again.

He was back.

"Sweetheart," he moaned, hugging me tightly.

Then he just held me. He held me so tight, I knew he'd never let me go. And I never wanted to let go of him, either. His heart beat firm and steady—the best sound in the world.

Whatever evil magic had brought him back to me, it was now gone. Only he remained. And I reveled in the moment, simply being close to him once again.

"I thought I'd lost you," I murmured against his skin. A shudder ran through my body when I thought back to those dark days of mourning him.

"Heike, I couldn't leave. I couldn't go to a world where I knew you wouldn't be there."

I rose on my arm over him. My breath hitched when he gazed up at me with those warm-brown eyes. My eyes brimmed with tears, and I blinked them away, not letting anything obstruct the view of his beloved face.

"What are you talking about, my love?" I cupped his face, stroking his beard. "Ghata brought you back, didn't she?"

"I let her," he said simply. "When she tried to resurrect me, I didn't fight her, though I felt I could." He moved a hand to the back of my neck, then pulled me closer to him. "The moment my soul left my body, I knew no world would be enough for me if you weren't in it. I'd suffer anything for a chance to see your face again."

It wasn't Ghata and her divine powers that made Radax fight and win over death. It was his love for me. It made him transcend the worlds and time, life and death.

There was so much I wanted to say to him. So many feelings overflowed my heart, but no words seemed strong enough to express them.

Except for the three little words.

"I love you," I whispered.

"By gods, I love you too, Heike. And it is the most divine feeling of all." He lowered my face to his.

His kiss was everything. It filled me with life, light, and longing.

Holding me in his arms, he climbed to his feet, then headed for the patio of the room we'd shared before.

"I want to make love to you, Heike," he said, placing me on the bed in the guestroom. "Not because I'm in pain. Not because you need to help me turn. But only because I want to be with you. I want to enjoy you, and I want to have you enjoying me too."

I smiled, releasing a long breath. And with it, the worry, stress, and tension of the past days had completely left me, too.

Radax fitted his large body over mine, and I wrapped my arms around him, drawing him closer.

"I love you," I said again as he entered me.

Happiness glowed warm in me as he started to move.

That was the only reason we'd have sex from now on. Because we wanted to enjoy each other.

Because I loved him. And because he loved me.

# Chapter Twenty-Four

RADAX

The appetizing scent of freshly baked pastries filled his nostrils the moment he and Heike exited their bedroom the next morning.

"Oh, did Lero bake something?" Heike bounced with excitement. "I looove his scones."

*His.*

Hearing the word rubbed him the wrong way, and he wasn't even sure why.

"I'm starving," Heike declared. The urge to feed her flared in him, overshadowing his own hunger.

Lost in each other, the two of them hadn't even thought about dinner the day before. The night had been a blur of passion, relief. Life.

He didn't even mind the ravenous hunger this morning. It was just another sign of being alive. What he did mind was that *he* was not the reason of Heike's delight right now. Lero was.

"You love his scones?" he asked her, working his jaw.

Why did it upset him so?

"Can't get enough of them," she admitted, licking her lips in anticipation.

He frowned, adjusting the waistband of the thin lounge pants around his hips. The pants were Zeph's. They fit way too tight on him, but they were the only clothes he currently had.

"I wonder if Lero would share the recipe," he muttered to himself.

"You want to know how to bake scones?" Heike arched an eyebrow. "Why?"

That was a good question.

His irritation at Lero wasn't personal. He liked the werewolf well enough. But he had an unstoppable desire to be *everything* for Heike—the one and only reason for all her pleasures and delights. He owed her that much. He owed her more than that.

Unsure how best to explain that, he smirked, drawing her into a hug. "I'd rather you love *my* scones than his." He decided right then and there to learn how to bake the damn things.

Heike laughed as they entered the breakfast room off the kitchen. "Competing with Lero won't be easy, babe."

"Who's going to compete with me?" Lero asked, taking a cookie sheet of scones out of the oven. Dressed in a white, crisp shirt and light-colored slacks, he looked every bit the businessman on vacation...who happened to bake scones.

"Radax wants to learn how to bake." Heike smiled.

Stella entered from the large patio at the back where the table was already set with breakfast dishes. Zeph and Ivy were sitting in the wicker chairs at the table, each with a steaming cup in front of them.

"Do you want to compete with Lero in baking?" Stella laughed, shaking her head. "It's impossible. Lero is the best." Pride rang in her voice.

She grabbed a pot of coffee off the counter and handed Radax a large bowl with fruit salad.

"I'm willing to work hard and practice a lot," he assured her, matching her light tone.

"I'd love to be around while you practice," Heike said with a soft, girlish giggle. "Promise not to let the results of your labor go to waste. There is no such thing as a bad scone, is there?"

He had no idea. But he was looking forward to "practicing" with her. He was looking forward to doing...everything. To simply *live*. For the first time ever, a real future lay ahead of him. And Heike was in it.

She greeted Zeph and Ivy with a nod, then took a seat next to him at the table.

"No such thing as a bad scone, huh?" Stella huffed a laugh. "You haven't tried the results of *my* attempts at baking. Talk about terrible scones. Mine were inedible!"

Lero had arranged his scones on a checkered towel in a basket and brought them out to the patio.

"It wasn't that bad." He gave Stella a peck on a cheek, placing the basket on the table. "I had two."

"You ate them because you're a nice man and you love me." She smiled at him with adoration. "And you survived only because you're a fae—things from this world can't kill you, not even my scones."

Lero chuckled, sitting next to her.

Stella offered Radax the basket with pastries, and he took one. The werewolf really knew his stuff, he thought, taking a bite.

"Let's just leave baking to Lero and enjoy his wicked skills." With a grin, Stella bit into her scone, too.

Ivy put two cups of coffee in front of Heike and him.

"So happy to have you back, Radax," she said, giving him a friendly smile. "How are you feeling?"

Everyone turned to him. The sunny morning and an easy conversation hadn't made them forget he'd just come back from the dead.

He heaved a breath, rolling his shoulders back. How was he to describe this feeling? Elation? Soaring? Light?

It really felt like he was flying.

"Free," he said simply. "For the first time I can remember I feel absolutely free."

With a soft gasp, Heike blinked rapidly and turned away, brushing a tear off her eyelashes.

He reached out and took her hand in his. Gratitude flooded him, warm and vast like an ocean, but he had no idea how to express any of that in words. He simply squeezed her hand, hoping she'd understand.

"Freedom is something no *brack* would remember," he said.

Heike gripped his fingers, and he knew she understood. She truly *saw* him.

"Speaking of *bracks*." Zeph took a sip of his coffee and looked at Lero. "Have you decided what to do with them?" He tipped his chin at the beach behind the house.

There, in the shade of the trees to the right, the werewolves slept in a pile. They had to be really worn out by the battle and just like Radax, probably still overwhelmed by their newfound freedom. The power of rage that had fueled all of them for so long had receded.

They looked exhausted. Piled on the beach, their humanoid limbs tucked under their furry bodies, the former *bracks* looked very much like a pack of black wolves resting after a long hunt—strong and powerful but no longer violent.

"What are we going to do with them?" Ivy asked. "Wait for a full moon to turn them back?"

"No one knows if it will turn them back, though," Stella noted.

"What if it doesn't?" Ivy gazed at the werewolves with clear empathy. "What if it's just sex that can turn them back into men?"

Everyone suddenly stared at Stella.

"Don't you look at me." She laughed, shaking her head. "I'm not having sex with nine werewolves, no matter how much I sympathize with them."

"No one is having sex with you but me," Lero snapped, with a menacing growl vibrating in his chest.

Radax finished his scone in a few big bites and washed it down with a gulp of coffee. He felt he could eat the entire basket, and it wasn't just because Lero was really good at baking. Radax had a hard time remembering when he'd eaten last. In fact, the memories of everything from what had happened on the Angara River and up until they arrived at Blue Cay were fuzzy and blurry. He didn't miss them. Those were the memories he didn't care for, anyway.

"I don't think sex would work even if Stella did sleep with all of them," Heike said thoughtfully while munching on her scone. "Isn't a magic fae bond required to turn a werewolf into a man? Not just random sex?"

She was right. According to what he'd learned recently, the bond was possible with humans only through the power of love. The magic of love had turned out to be almost as powerful as any magic out there. It gave humans control over the elements, like water. It could trigger a werewolf's transformation at will. It could, apparently help bring people back from the dead.

"So, what are we going to do with them, then?" Ivy worried her bottom lip with her teeth. "We couldn't possibly let them stay like this forever. They have their full awareness but can only express themselves in roars and growls. It must feel awful."

Lero nodded, casting a glance at the pack. "The beast form has its purpose, but it's not pleasant to stay in it for too long."

"We need to send them back to Nerifir," Zeph concluded. "That's the only place with female werewolves. It'd give these guys a chance to meet one, form a bond, and trigger the transformation."

Lero rubbed his chin. "The next full moon may trigger a transformation, too. However, you're right. Their kind is in Nerifir. Werewolves there may know of other means to help them turn. And the chance of bonding with a female is much higher there than it is here."

"Now, how are we going to send them to Nerifir?" Zeph asked. "The only portal you know of is in Paris, isn't it? How will we transport a bunch of werewolves there?" He appeared to think for a moment. "I could possibly get them to the Seine River unseen, but then we'd have to travel by land."

Stella lifted a finger, requesting attention. "Does it have to be that particular portal, though? There're more of them, aren't there?"

"Right," Lero confirmed. "Portals to Nerifir are usually found over bodies of water."

"There must be one more accessible to Zeph than that in Paris, then," Ivy said. "We'll just need to find it."

"Searching may take a long time," Zeph replied, skeptically.

Since Ghata stopped sending Radax to Nerifir long ago, he'd forgotten the locations of the portals *bracks* had used. But there certainly were more than one in this world.

Lero got up. "*Bracks* traveled back and forth all the time. Let me go speak to them. In their beast form, they won't be able to tell me where the portals are, but maybe they can point them on a map or something."

Stella touched his arm, stopping him in his tracks.

"Let them sleep," she said softly. "Their minds and bodies have been abused for centuries. Give them some time to recuperate a little."

Lero sat back in his chair. "Right. We'll have lots of time later."

"Before you send them back." Radax scratched his beard, thinking of an idea. Sending the *bracks* back presented an opportunity he'd never hoped to have. "I want to talk to them about taking something to Nerifir for me."

Heike turned to him. Everyone else did, too.

Unable to hold their questioning stares all at once, he glanced out to sea.

"It's a long shot," he explained. "But I want to send something that may reach Amira one day."

Amira. The little girl he'd saved years ago. The one who'd become like a sister to him and helped him keep his humanity. Without her, he wouldn't be where he was now, he'd never know what true happiness was.

"Oh God, Radax..." Heike exhaled, grabbing his hand with both of hers. "Do you think that's possible?"

He heaved a long breath. Nothing was guaranteed of course.

"I have no idea," he admitted. "Traveling between the worlds is tricky. I haven't done it myself lately. But when one crosses the River, time and place get scrambled. It's impossible to predict where and when one would land on the other side. When the werewolves cross the River of Mists, they may come to Nerifir centuries before or maybe a millennium after they've left it last."

"Can they arrive in the time when Ghata was still in power?" Heike asked, anxiously flicking her gaze between the fae at the table.

He understood her anxiety. What would be the point of liberating the *bracks* if they sent them straight into her clutches again?

"That'd be entirely possible," Lero confirmed.

Radax shook his head. "Even if that happens, they're no longer her *bracks*. They're free werewolves, armed with knowledge of what Ghata can do. They won't fall under her charms, now. If they land in her times, they might actually help the others fight her."

"What if they land in the past and defeat her right there in Nerifir?

Would that change our present and future?" Heike asked, looking concerned.

Nipping Ghata's atrocities at the bud would prevent many horrors from ever happening. Heike must be worried that changing the past might mean he and she would never meet at all.

He stroked her hand with his thumb tenderly. "Worlds exist not just in a place but also in time, Heike. Our lives are taking place right here, right now. Our past has already been lived, and our experiences have been earned. If the past changes in Nerifir, it won't affect us here. We have our own timeline to keep living."

The matters of time and space were intertwined. There were so many worlds and dimensions out there, it was impossible to comprehend all of that in one lifetime.

"As long as I never lose you again." Heike gripped his hand tighter. "You've defied death to come back to me, and I'm keeping you, no matter what."

Her words spread with warmth through his chest.

"I'm all yours, Heike. For the rest of this life and beyond." He leaned closer, bringing her hand to his lips.

The fae bond with a human matched the lifespan of both. Since Ghata's power no longer maintained his immortality, Radax believed he'd live like all fae did, now, at least five hundred years. As his mate, Heike would have the same. And he was determined to make every year of each century magical for her.

"What are you thinking of doing next?" Ivy asked Heike and him.

"You're always welcome to stay here on Blue Cay, of course," Stella added. "We have plenty of space for you two."

Radax hadn't thought that far into the future yet. For now, he was happy to simply live in the moment. Having his own life to live and his own schedule to follow felt rather overwhelming. He made no plans.

"We can go anywhere in the world, honey," Heike said. "You can literally point at a place on the map, and I'll take you there."

Traveling could be a great way to get to know this world better.

He tilted his head. "Did you say you haven't been to New Zealand before?"

"You remember that?" She raised an eyebrow. "No, I haven't been to New Zealand. And yes, I always wanted to visit there."

"Well, then maybe that's what we should do? I'll be your bodyguard." He grinned.

"Oh, you'll be so much more than my bodyguard, baby." She leaned over to kiss his beard. "You'll be my everything. For as long as I shall live."

He'd been wrong about having no plans. He did have one. He planned to spend the rest of his life with this woman.

# Epilogue

## FIVE YEARS LATER

HEIKE

Radax shook sea water out of his short hair and full beard, then jogged to Ivy, Stella, and me as we reclined on lounge chairs on the beach behind the main house on Blue Cay.

I admired the view of his strong, tanned figure. His black swim trunks looked amazing on him. But then again, everything looked great on this man. He'd quickly won over all my followers and gotten me many more since I started posting pictures of the two of us on my social media.

After that one poignant video years ago, Radax had never gone in front of a video camera again. He refused to do interviews or any endorsements where he had to speak. Generally, save for the pictures with me, he preferred to stay out of the spotlight, content to be my bodyguard, my husband, my biggest friend and supporter, and the love of my life.

He was also soon to become the father of our child.

"I'm going back inside for a moment. Do you want anything?" He leaned to me, kissing me on the lips and dripping cold sea water on my sun-heated skin.

I squeaked and laughed, wiping the drops off my rounded, five-month pregnant belly. "Can you get me another glass of mango juice, please?"

"I will. Anything for you, ladies?" he asked Stella and Ivy.

"I'm good, thank you." Stella flipped a page in the book she was reading.

"Just some water, please, if you can." Ivy was watching the two toddlers running along the water's edge.

Jaze, Stella and Lero's son, was chasing Luna, Ivy and Zeph's daughter. The little girl was a year younger than Jaze. She giggled and laughed, running away from the boy. Her legs were so much shorter, though. Jaze was catching up quickly. Glancing over her shoulder, she must've realized she was about to get caught.

Suddenly, a wave rolled from under Luna's feet. It grew taller than her before shoving Jaze in his chest and knocking him down on his bum.

"Can't get me now!" Luna squealed in delight, running along the beach.

"Oh, my God," Ivy gasped. "Are you okay, Jaze?"

With a low growl, the boy jumped back to his feet and took off after Luna.

"He'll be fine." Stella glanced from her book at the kids. "A little water won't hurt him."

The blond head of Zeph showed up from the waves in the lagoon.

"Was it you?" Ivy waved at him. "Did you just knock Jaze on his bum?"

"Me? No." Zeph ran a hand through his wet hair, sending streams of water out of it as he came out on the beach. "It was all Luna." He grinned proudly.

"Wow!" Ivy gasped. "That was the biggest wave she's made yet."

Raising a human-fae child had its challenges. I splayed my hand on my belly. Our little boy had been kicking for at least a month now. With so much energy, I was sure he'd be keeping both Radax and me busy once he was born.

"Luna is going to be one powerful siren," Zeph said with delight, his eyes fixed on his daughter. He came up to Ivy and gave her a kiss "Care for a swim?"

"Um..." She glanced at the children. Somehow, Luna was now the one chasing Jaze, who howled with laughter, running away.

"Go." Stella put her book down. "I'll watch them."

"We'll be quick." Ivy jumped to her feet and followed Zeph toward the water, adjusting her bright pink bikini.

"Take your time," Stella waved her off. "They'll be fine."

"They'd make a great couple one day." I smiled, watching the kids play.

Stella shook her head. "Lero says a mating bond is not possible between a siren and a werewolf."

I'd been told that a child of a human and a fae would always be a fae.

"Don't you think our children are more than fae, though?"

"More?" She gave me a curious glance.

"They have human mothers. They must inherit the human power of love. You know the one that transcends all kinds of magic?"

Stella smiled with a shrug.

"Well, Lero had been proven wrong about the bond before..." She glanced back at the children. "If these two fall in love and decide to be together, we all will be delighted."

I followed her gaze to the children. "Is Jaze transforming on full moon nights already?"

She nodded. "He just started last year. He's the cutest little werewolf ever. So fluffy. You should see him."

"Oh, I'd love to!"

A werewolf's transformation was always fascinating. I could only imagine how adorable a baby werewolf would be.

"Well, you're here for two months," she said. "And the next full moon is in a couple of weeks. You'll get to see Jaze turn. He's been trying to howl at the moon, just like his dad. It's so cute. But he gets tired quickly and falls asleep way before midnight."

I wondered if our baby would be born a werewolf or if he'd be a rage shifter, like his dad. Unlike the rest of the *bracks*, Radax had never returned to being a werewolf. We suspected his journey to death and back must have something to do with that.

Full moon didn't affect him. When he got angry, however, his eyes would glow white. It didn't happen often as my man had admirable self-control. Only when there was a direct threat to me did he lose his composure.

I believed if pushed to the limit, he would shift into his giant monster form again to protect those he loved. I had never felt safer than when having him at my side.

Glancing back to the house over my shoulder, I saw Radax coming our way. A heavy, wrought-iron lounge chair under his arm, he carried my juice and Ivy's water in his hands, without spilling a drop.

The incredible strength of a *brack* had never left him, either.

"Here you go." He handed me the glass.

"Thank you."

"Ivy went for a swim with Zeph." Stella took the glass of water from Radax and set it on the small table between our loungers. "The two of them may be miles away from here, by now."

Moving through water was fast with Zeph around. Ivy also had become an amazing swimmer over the years. She was fearless. Together with Zeph, she had explored hidden lagoons and underwater caves never before seen by a human.

"Maybe they'll bring us some oysters." Stella licked her lips.

Radax set up his lounger next to mine.

"What a beautiful day." He stretched his large body on the cushioned surface.

I stroked his tattooed forearm, the fine hairs there tickling my fingers. Within a month after Ghata was gone from our lives for good, the hair on his head started to grow, followed shortly by the body hair. His tattoo remained only as a fierce but harmless body art. It lit up only when we were making love—beautiful white sparks wherever I touched it. It was our very own, private light show.

The three of us watched the kids play. Jaze's dark hair was ruffled and wet. Luna's wheat-blond pig tails were sticking out, stiff with salt water. Both his navy-blue shorts with baby-blue anchors and her ladybug-printed bathing suit were completely wet too, now. Happy smiles lit their tanned little faces.

Blue Cay was a great place to grow up.

"Where are you off to after here?" Stella asked.

"Not far, this time." Over the past few years, Radax and I had traveled around the globe a couple of times. We came to Blue Cay a few times a year to recharge and to catch up with everyone. With the baby on the way, however, it was time to slow down for a while.

"We're thinking about getting a place right here, in Miami," Radax said.

"Really?" Stella sat up, excitedly. "Oh, it'd be so good to have you close. Where are you looking?"

"We haven't started yet, but since we know a great real estate agent in the area, we're not worried." I wiggled my eyebrows at her.

Stella had been selling houses for years. We would never think about having anyone else but her to help us find a home for our family.

"Oh, I can show you some amazing places!" she exclaimed. "Just say when."

"Rather sooner than later, I'd say." I laughed, petting my belly.

"This will be so much fun!" Stella clapped her hands.

Lero headed to the beach from the house. He carried a tray in his hands and a metal box under his arm.

"Hungry?" He set the tray with hors d'oeuvres on the small table next to Ivy's water.

"These look so good, honey." Stella took a thin slice of toasted baguette with whipped cheese, capers, and other equally delicious things on it. "Is that what you've been busy with inside there?"

"That and this thing." He took the box from under his arm. "This was with the stuff we had in storage. It came from Ghata's menagerie."

Ghata had a whole pile of odd things that *bracks* had brought for her from Nerifir. After her demise, we'd gone through all the stuff she had on her yacht. Whatever animals she had left had been sent back to Nerifir with her former *bracks* who had transformed into werewolves. We also let them take anything they wished or whatever could be useful to them back in Nerifir.

It had taken several months, but eventually Radax, along with Lero and Zeph had been able to gain full access to Ghata's funds. It turned out to be a lot of money, and the fae used some of it to right the many wrongs she had done in this world.

The large chunk of the money had been earned by tormenting Lero and Zeph and displaying them to the public. They felt that Radax also deserved compensation for what Ghata had done to him.

None of them, however, wanted to keep any of Ghata's money for themselves. It had been decided to put it all in the fund to use later if required or simply leave it to our children one day.

Some of the old menagerie stuff had been put in storage.

"What is it?" I asked, eyeing the box Lero handed to Radax.

Luna and Jaze ran over, having spotted the tray of snacks. They each grabbed a piece of finger food, then ran to play again. Chewing on a cracker, Jaze started digging holes in the sand as Luna filled them with water.

A wave rolled onto the beach, bringing Ivy ashore. Laughing, she spread her arms wide to regain her balance as the water receded.

Zeph showed up in the wave behind her.

"Now me!" Luna jumped, clapping her hands. "Me, daddy!"

Zeph made a wave sweep his daughter off her feet. She giggled, tumbling in the water. Jaze jumped in with her, and Zeph made the water spin them both like a merry-go-around.

"They never get tired of that," Ivy laughed, coming to us.

"No oysters this time?" Stella asked, looking a bit disappointed.

"Sorry. We...um, got distracted." Ivy glanced back at her husband, soft blush coloring her cheeks.

Stella laughed, shaking her head. "I should've known."

Ivy spotted the glass of water on the table. "Oh, thank you, Radax." She took a drink. Her gaze slipped to the metal box in his hands. "I've seen this before," she said unexpectedly.

"You have?" He lifted an eyebrow. "Are you sure?"

She took it from him and examined closely from all sides.

"Yep. I dusted it so many times. It's from Ghata's menagerie. She had it displayed among the other unanimated objects at her freakshow. I used it to break the window when Zeph and I escaped." She scratched her chin in thought. "Ghata said it was from some wetlands. I forgot the name."

"The Lorsan Wetlands, the homeland of gorgonians," Lero explained. "It looks gorgonian-made."

"What's it for?" I asked, taking the box from Ivy.

It was made from dark green metal, like aged bronze, weathered and scratched. Intricate gear mechanisms that looked both functional and decorative were visible from the many openings on the surface. The design lines of the box were like nothing I'd ever seen before—fluid and smooth.

"This looks intriguing. But what's its purpose?" I handed the box to my husband.

"I'm not sure." Lero rubbed his jaw. "Do you know?" he asked Radax.

"Ghata said it was a communication device. She had it for over a decade, but I never saw her open it or use it in any way other than displaying it as a curiosity." He turned the box in his hands. "Gorgonians are incredible mechanics and craftspeople. They use magic to enhance their creations. These details here look like part of a lock." He slid his finger along the gears visible in the openings.

"Do you know how to open it?" Lero asked.

Zeph had joined us, too, now. Both children came closer as well, drawn by the object that commanded attention of the adults.

Radax continued to explore the box.

"Gorgonians often ward their locks with magic, so that only the people meant to open them can do so. Ghata stored her book in a gorgonian-made cabinet, too. Only she and us, her *bracks*, could open it. I never saw anyone ever unlocking this one—"

The gears suddenly turned under his fingers. With a musical whirring sound, the box split open into what appeared like a million parts. They shifted and turned, arranging themselves into a 3D picture of a majestic tree with a luscious canopy. The tree was surrounded by several others, all of them interconnected by bridges and archways, with platforms and constructions hidden between the branches.

"This is amazing!" Ivy gasped.

"So beautiful," I whispered, mesmerized.

It was incredibly life-like.

The small round leaves on the branches appeared to move with the breeze. Water streamed between the roots of the trees. I almost expected the miniature dwellers of this forest city to make their appearance any moment.

"What is this?" I asked.

"The castle of the Lorsan King," Radax replied, looking just as awe struck as the rest of us.

"King? Why would a king—" I didn't finish my question.

A beautiful music flowed from the tree castle in Radax's hands. Soft and lyrical, it carried a note of happiness. Jubilation.

*"Radax, my only family on Earth,"* a soft female voice drifted along with the music from the magical tree. The woman wasn't singing, but the cadence of her voice intertwined perfectly with the melody.

"Oh, my God..." Ivy gasped. "That's Amira, isn't it? It's her voice!"

I gripped Radax's arm. His expression shifted to intense focus.

*"For years, the pain of leaving you and the guilt of hurting you had been lodged in my heart like a knife. It was only relieved when I got a word from you today. You're well. You're in love. And Madame Tan is no more. For the first time since leaving Earth, I feel completely happy and free.*

*"I hope my message will find you. I hope that learning I'm also happy and in love will give you joy. It wasn't easy, but I have found my true home and my happiness here in Nerifir after all.*

*"I am Amira, the Queen of Lorsan. And I am forever your sister, no matter where we are. I will always love you."*

The voice trailed off, dissolving into the notes of the magical music that kept floating over the beach and the sea.

I released a breath, feeling lighter at heart. I knew the worry about Amira had been weighing heavily on Radax all these years. He didn't speak of it, but I didn't need him to speak to know how he felt. The deep connection between us allowed me to share his emotions.

Now, I felt that the mourning he'd carried for years was lifting.

He glanced out to sea. His throat bobbed with a swallow as he blinked a few times.

"She survived." His voice sounded raw.

I gripped his arm tighter. "She's more than survived, honey. She's happy."

"And she's a freaking queen!" Lero laughed, slapping his thigh. "Well done, Amira. I knew you had it in you."

"She deserves it all." Ivy's eyes glistened with tears. "After everything she's suffered here..." She shook her head, blinking her tears away.

"How did this box end up in Ghata's possession, in the first place?" Zeph asked.

Radax cleared his throat. "Through a *brack*, most likely. One that went to Nerifir to collect things for Ghata at some point. They all did that regularly. When one of them landed in Lorsan during Amira's lifetime, she knew he'd be coming back to Madame Tan's Menagerie, Ghata would pull him back to her. So, Amira gave the box to the *brack*, possibly as an exhibit for Ghata."

Time warped, looped, and twisted when one crossed to other worlds. The box that Amira had sent *after* receiving Radax's message had arrived back to Earth over a decade *before* he had sent his message.

"It's mind boggling," Ivy muttered softly. "And to think that all this time, it was collecting dust in the menagerie."

"Do you think Ghata knew exactly what it was?" Stella asked Radax.

"I don't think so." He shook his head. "She wouldn't have kept it if she knew. She might've done something bad to Amira, too, had she known."

Lero gently touched a delicate leaf on the majestic tree. "And you never tried opening it before?"

Radax stared at his magical gift.

"*Bracks* weren't allowed to touch the exhibits other than packing and unpacking them when the show changed locations. I never had the time to examine it closely or figure out the lock. Without an order from Ghata, I never had the desire to do that, either."

Ivy raked a hand through her wet, multi-colored hair. "To think that Amira had been dusting it for years, and she had no idea it was her own message from the future..."

"The Queen Amira knew when she sent the box that the Amira of the menagerie would be dusting it. She knew she'd have a full access to the lock. She could've made it possible to open by herself, but she didn't," Lero pointed out.

"She obviously didn't want to change a thing," Radax agreed. "Which means everything is exactly how it should be."

I leaned over and kissed him. "She came to terms with the past, baby. Now, you can, too. There's no place, no need for guilt anymore."

I knew Radax felt guilt for everything Amira had suffered from Ghata's hand. Amira had felt guilty for things Ghata had put Radax through on her behalf, too. There was no one to blame but Ghata for all of that. I was glad to hear that Amira had let go of the guilt. I was confident Radax would learn to let go of it too, now.

He gently set the magical tree castle on the table next to the food tray. The wonderful music continued to float through the air, lifting our spirits and soothing our souls.

Radax's chest rose and fell with a long, deep breath. Leaning back against his lounger, he smiled.

"It's a beautiful day," he murmured, taking my hand in his.

"It is, my love." I relaxed against my lounger, too.

Our baby boy stirred in my belly. The familiar flutter of his movement made me smile wider.

We had many beautiful days ahead of us. And if some of them turned ugly, we'd deal with those too. Together, there was nothing we couldn't overcome.

# Afterword

Thank you for coming with me on the journey into the world of Madame Tan's Freakshow. I hope you enjoyed reading the trilogy as much as I loved writing these books.

If you have fallen in love with this world and want to learn more, I have great news for you! I love this world, too. This has been my passion project, and I'm not ready to leave this world.

The trilogy is over. The fae and their mates have found their happily ever after in our world. But how about those who have left?

Next, I'm taking you to Nerifir with Amira. She has an exciting story to tell about the mysterious gorgonian man she's freed and the heartbreaking, dangerous journey she took before earning the crown of Lorsan.

Amira's story, Serpent's Touch, is now live, and I have many more books planned in this world.

To follow the updates on more books set in the many fantastic worlds of the River of Mists, please subscribe to my newsletter on www.marinasimcoe.com

# *Serpent's Touch*

## EXCERPT

*Amira*

I had almost finished sweeping the empty room inside a tent when Krin, one of Madame's *bracks*, carried in a huge wooden crate. A truck had delivered it earlier that morning and unloaded it in the yard while *bracks* were having breakfast.

"Get out of the way," Krin hissed at me.

I scurried closer to the striped canvas wall as he maneuvered a massive metal frame out of the crate.

A large creature was chained to the frame. It was upright, its arms and legs spread like a sea star, ankles and wrists locked into metal manacles.

Over the years, I'd seen many peculiar animals join Madame's menagerie. The *bracks* hunted and trapped them in Nerifir, the world where Madame and the *bracks* had come from to Earth. Madame could not return to Nerifir, Radax had told me. But her *bracks* traveled between dimensions, bringing marvelous things and magnificent beasts from the magical kingdom.

This one appeared disturbingly human-like, however. His distorted proportions made it look like the most grotesque version of a man.

It was most certainly a *he*—a huge penis dangled between his muscled thighs. The creature was partially covered in black fur. There was not enough of it to conceal his entire body, though. Patches of fur sprouted on his wide shoulders and narrow hips, some of his crotch area and thighs, leaving his gray skin bare in other places.

"Where does Madame want him?" Krin asked another *brack*, Dez, who followed him in.

I hadn't seen Dez for the past few months. He'd been away from the menagerie, but not in Nerifir. Madame had mentioned once that Dez was taking care of a beast in another location in the country for her. I wondered if this creature was the beast Dez had been guarding.

Dez shrugged. "Put him right here for now."

The beast snarled, snapping his needle-sharp teeth. Saliva dripped from his fangs. It sizzled and steamed when it hit the packed dirt of the tent floor.

"Easy, *voukalak*." Dez shoved a fist into the ribs of the animal. The beast snarled and clacked its teeth, narrowly missing Dez's arm. "Easy!" The *brack* jumped back, then noticed me as I tried to hide in the shadows by the wall. "Hey! What are you doing here?"

Madame had ordered me to sweep this room for the crate's arrival. She'd mentioned the creature would be her new VIP exhibit. I'd finished and was on my way out when Krin had blocked my escape route.

I lifted the broom in my hand, explaining my presence in the room to Dez without words.

Dez made a face as if he'd stepped into gum on a sidewalk, harmless but annoying. Except for Radax, the *bracks* didn't care much about me. For them, I was mostly a nuisance they had to share the space with. No matter how much I tried to keep out of their way, it wasn't always possible to avoid them in the small world of the menagerie.

"Get out of here," Dez dismissed me, jerking his head toward the exit.

Clutching the broom and dustpan in both hands, I hurried to the exit when Krin yelped in pain. Leaping away from the frame with the beast, Krin slammed into me. Blood dripped from the deep scratch on the pad of his thumb.

I staggered backwards, trying to regain my balance.

"What the fuck are you still doing here?" Krin shoved at my shoulder, knocking me to the ground.

The broom and dustpan tumbled out of my hands. I painfully slammed my tailbone against the hard ground but swallowed the groan of pain. There'd be no sympathy from the *bracks*. My cries would just irritate them further.

"Fucking *voukalak!*" Krin punched the chained creature in the head. The beast howled and thrashed in his restraints.

"What did he do?" Dex moved toward the animal, his fists at the ready.

"Scratched me with his claw." Krin sucked on the wound on his thumb.

Dez huffed a laugh and landed a blow in the animal's ribs, then turned to Krin. "Lucky for you, it was his claw. If it'd been his fangs, you'd be dead."

Gripping the broom handle, I collected the dustpan, then scurried behind the fabric partition into the narrow passage behind it. Only once I was out of the *bracks'* sight could I draw a full breath.

The morning was steadily running away from me. Many chores remained to be done, but I hurried to one of the storage rooms located in the bowels of the interconnected tents.

Despite being with the menagerie most of my life, I had no room of my own. Madame used a travel trailer or stayed at a hotel if she found one to her satisfaction. The *bracks* shared a few trailers between themselves. I usually remained in the tents.

I didn't need much space, and there was always a bundle of rags or a pile of bags for me to sleep on. Neither did I have enough clothes to require a closet. I wore what the *bracks* wore—black t-shirts and hooded sweatshirts. Their clothes were several sizes too big for me, but I didn't mind. They were warm and easy to hide in.

Besides that, I picked up lost things on the fairgrounds sometimes. That was how I'd gotten the gray scarf I now wore day and night. It was made from thin but soft material, wide and long. I loved how warm it felt coiled in thick folds around my neck and how I could bury my face in it by drawing my head into my shoulders. It made me feel safer somehow.

After putting the broom and the dustpan away, I found a dark place behind another large crate in one of the stuffy little storage rooms in the maze of the canvas walls. I wedged myself between the wooden side of the crate and the dusty canvas partition.

Cleaning Madame's trailer was next on my list of chores. But maybe she wouldn't notice if I took a moment?

Leaning with my back against the crate, I drew my head into my shoulders, buried my chin into my scarf, and hugged my knees, taking as little space as possible. Here, in this hiding place, I could pretend I was invisible.

The man at the ticket booth, one of Brad's friends, had called me a ghost. And sometimes I wished I were one—invisible, untouchable, ethereal. Impossible to hurt.

My tailbone ached, and I shifted into a slightly more comfortable position. I released a long breath. It came out shaky, but without tears. There was no point in crying. I learned long ago, tears never changed a thing.

A scratching noise came from the crate behind me. I jerked away, startled, then settled back down. Animals scared me far less than people.

This crate had been traveling with us for quite some time now. For whatever reason, Madame had been holding back from displaying the creature inside it to the public. Judging by the size of the crate, the beast must be big, maybe the size of a lion. But it was just another animal from Nerifir. Contained in the crate, it wouldn't harm me. I leaned back against the wood.

Of all the otherworldly beings in Madame's menagerie, I preferred the company of her animals. *Bracks* were heartless and often acted cruel.

Except for Radax. Had Radax been around when Krin pushed me to the ground, he would've certainly confronted Krin—punched him in retaliation, most likely. Then Madame might've ordered him whipped again.

All my life, Radax had been watching over me, but it came at a price. Madame detested the attachment between him and me. I believed that by punishing him, she tried to pry us apart. And in a way, it worked. I kept away from Radax whenever possible. I thanked the stars he had been busy elsewhere that morning. But there were so many other times...

"Where is it?" Madame's sharp voice sounded just outside of the room with the crate.

Panic rushed me, chased by icy fear.

Was she looking for me? How long had I been sitting here? Too long?

"Where did you put him this time?" Her voice sounded closer.

I stilled, halting my breath. Fear froze my insides, paralyzing my limbs—my usual reaction to Madame's presence.

"He's here, Madame," Krin's voice replied.

*"He"* not *"she."* Madame wasn't looking for me, for once. I allowed some tension to drain, relaxing my stiff shoulders.

"Put the mirror here," Madame ordered sharply, the sound of her footsteps stopping in front of the crate I hid behind.

Other footsteps joined hers—heavy stomping of *bracks'* boots. There were more *bracks* who came with her, not just Krin. I tried to make myself even smaller, hoping they wouldn't look behind the crate.

"Get me a chair, too," Madame demanded.

Too scared to be discovered, I didn't dare look out from behind the crate, keeping as quiet as possible.

"Open the crate," Madame commanded. "He's chained, isn't he?"

"Yes, Madame," Krin replied. The *bracks* complied with her orders, judging by the screeching sound of nails being wrenched out of the wood. "He has his hood on, too."

She huffed. "I don't trust their hoods. I'm not looking at a gorgonian directly. Neither should you if you treasure your life. Place the mirror so I can see him in it."

More shuffling and rustling sounded as the *bracks* complied. Then came the slamming of one side of the crate falling open.

"What a pathetic state to be in for a future High Lord," Madame murmured with a mocking note in her voice.

A rattling of chains came from inside the crate, as if the creature kept in there moved.

Madame chuckled. "Surely, working for me couldn't be any more demeaning than spending your days chained in a crate like an animal."

"I'd rather die as an animal than live as your slave." It was said in a low, cracked voice, barely audible. Yet the sound of it slammed over me like a hammer.

It wasn't an animal but a person in that crate! A person who could speak, think, feel...

How long had he been in there?

I'd never received the order to feed the occupant of this crate. Did someone else feed him?

"My slave?" Madame scoffed. "Like my *bracks?* No, honey. I'm not offering you the honor of becoming one of them. All I'm asking from you is a partnership, a business arrangement, if you will. You'll become my next VIP act. I want you to use your magic to wow my human audience, but without harming them. Dead can't pay, can they?" She chuckled. "Then I'll think about releasing you back to Nerifir one day. All I need is your promise to cooperate."

"You won't get it," the reply came. "I don't make deals with disgraced goddesses."

Quiet as the voice was, it carried the force of defiance and contempt. Madame's prisoner appeared to mock her. I marveled at how brave he was—stupid, but brave.

Stunned by his insolence, I almost missed the fact that he'd called her a goddess. Was *that* what Madame really was?

Madame's chair suddenly crashed to the ground with a slamming noise. She must've leaped to her feet.

Way too familiar with her temper, I drew my head into my shoulders, even though I knew she couldn't see me.

"Look at you!" she screamed. "You're pathetic! Shriveling and drying out from thirst. You haven't had a drop of water in months, and you're sure not getting any until you agree to work for me. Resist, and you'll die most pitifully. No one in Nerifir will ever know about your fate. You'll perish here, in this sad human world. Nameless!"

A soft, dry chuckle came from the crate. The person must be insane, laughing in her face. "I dare you to look at me directly, Goddess Ghata. Instead of hiding behind that old mirror like the coward you are—"

"Enough!" Madame's voice thundered, sending a bolt of terror through my chest. "Close the crate. Let him rot inside."

The *bracks* moved to obey her orders.

"His hood!" Madame suddenly yelled in warning. "Krin. No!" Genuine fear—an emotion I'd never encountered in Madame before—vibrated in her voice. "Zuso, Nerkan, close your eyes!"

The sound of a punch came.

Grunts of pain.

Then something hard and heavy crashed to the floor.

I covered my ears with my hands, trying to block the noises of whatever horrors were happening in front of that crate—things so terrifying, they scared *a goddess.*

The slamming of the crate being shut came, then the sound of the nails being hammered in.

"All done, Madame," Zuso, another *brack*, said.

"Clean this up," she ordered in a somewhat shaken voice. "And no water for the gorgonian. He made his choice. Let him die."

Afraid to breathe, I stayed behind the crate long after all sounds in the room ceased—the shuffling of the *bracks*, the sweeping of the broom, the footsteps of everyone leaving.

In the quiet that followed, I ventured to press my ear to the crate. The faint sound of the shallow, labored breathing came from inside.

A man?

A monster?

Fear surged through me with a shudder.

Trying to make as little noise as possible, I crawled from behind the crate on all fours. My hand landed on a piece of something hard on the floor. I picked it up.

Strings of white light hung high under the ceiling of the tent, aiding the sunlight filtering through the canvas in illuminating the space.

I examined the item in my hand. It was about an inch long, gray, and hard like a rock. It was shaped like the tip of a finger—a thumb—complete with the smooth, short nail on one end. When I turned it over, a long gash on the thumb's pad came into view, the scratch from the beast's claw.

Struck by horror, I tossed it away and ran from the room as fast as I could and as far from the crate as possible.

I had no idea what exactly happened in that room that morning. But I was fairly certain I'd never see Krin again.

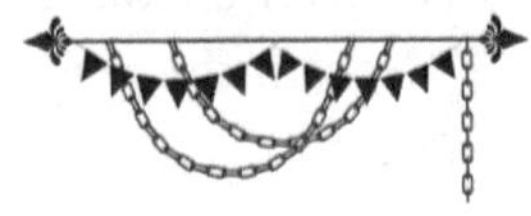

Serpent's Touch is available now.

# Acknowledgments

The Madame Tan's Freakshow trilogy is now complete, and I couldn't have done it without the help and support of so many wonderful people.

Thank you to the amazing writers who took the time from their busy schedules to read my very messy first drafts and steer me in the right direction. Bex McLynn, Mel Sterling, and Evangeline Rain, I'm forever in your debt.

To Amy from Cissel Ink for editing all three of these books.

To my fierce typo huntresses Janet, Kitty, and Avis. Thank you for cleaning up the final drafts from all those pesky, last-minute typos that often just seem invincible.

And of course, a huge thank you to all my readers. Without you, none of this would be possible.

# Also by Marina Simcoe

THE RIVER OF MISTS

*Fire in Stone (Elex, the "dragon-man" statue)*

Fire in Stone

Hearts on Fire

*Serpent's Touch (Amira's Story)*

Serpent's Touch

Serpent's Claim

*Madame Tan's Freakshow Trilogy*

Call of Water (Zeph's Story)

Madness of the Moon (Lero's Story)

Power of Rage (Radax's Story)

# Also by Marina Simcoe

PARANORMAL ROMANCE

*Demons (Complete)*

Demon Mine

The Forgotten

Grand Master

The Last Unforgiven - Cursed

The Last Unforgiven - Freed

*Stand Alone Novels*

The Real Thing

To Love A Monster

*Midnight Coven Author Group*

Wicked Warlock (Cursed Coven)

# *Also by Marina Simcoe*

SCIENCE-FICTION ROMANCE

*My Holiday Tails*

Married to Krampus

My Tiny Giant

My Birthday Getaway

New Year, New Planet

Mail Order Mom

My Pumpkin

*Dark Anomaly (Complete)*

Gravity

Power

Explosion

*Stand Alone Novels*

Experiment

Enduring (Valos Of Sonhadra)

# About the Author

Marina Simcoe likes to write love stories with human heroines and non-human heroes who just can't live without them. She firmly believes that our contemporary world could always use a little bit of the extraordinary.

She has lots of fun exploring how her out-of-this-world characters with their own beliefs, values, and aspirations fit into our every-day life.

She lives in Canada with her very own extraordinary hero, their three little offspring, and a cat who is definitely out of this world.

Readers' Group: Marina's Reading Cave on Facebook.

Newsletter sign-up is on www.marinasimcoe.com.

facebook.com/MarinaSimcoeAuthor
twitter.com/MarinaSimcoe
instagram.com/marinasimcoeauthor
amazon.com/author/marinasimcoe
bookbub.com/profile/marina-simcoe
goodreads.com/MarinaSimcoe
tiktok.com/@marina.simcoe

www.ingramcontent.com/pod-product-compliance
Lightning Source LLC
Chambersburg PA
CBHW030346310726
48979CB00001B/203
* 9 7 8 1 9 8 9 9 6 7 2 2 5 *